Falling For
Mr Wrong

Falling For Mr Wrong

Caroline Upcher

ORION

The characters in this book
are entirely fictitious.
Any resemblance to real persons,
living or dead, places or
organisations is coincidental.

First published in Great Britain in 1995 by
Orion
An imprint of Orion Books Ltd
Orion House, 5 Upper St Martin's Lane, London WC2H 9EA

A CIP catalogue record for this book is available
from the British Library

ISBN 0 75280 048 5 (cased)
ISBN 0 75280 060 4 (trade paperback)

Typeset by Deltatype Ltd, Ellesmere Port, Cheshire
Printed in Great Britain by
Clays Ltd, St Ives plc

For Hanan al-Shaykh, in whose house at Cap d'Antibes I began this book, and for Deborah Rogers, in whose house in Notting Hill I finished it.

And in memory of John Creightmore.

Thanks as always to Annabel Davis-Goff, and to Celestia Fox, Amanda and Steve Lay, Lewis Esson and Jane Wood.

All over the world women search
for Mr Right. If, and when, they
find him it never occurs to them
that he might, in fact, be Mr Wrong.

PART ONE

Johnny left her in the middle of the night.

For years afterwards, every time she heard Paul Simon singing 'Fifty Ways to Leave Your Lover' on the radio, she would be reminded of it. It was the line 'Just slip out the back, Jack' that got her every time. That's how he must have left. He couldn't have gone out the front door. It had been stuck fast for a month. It had been his idea to have the front door painted. There had been a week of discussion about it. Well, not really discussion. He rarely discussed. He had merely announced one night at dinner that it was time to have something done about the front door and he would be putting Rachel on to it.

Rachel was his long-suffering assistant at the office although it was hard to imagine when she had time to carry out such conventional duties as dealing with correspondence and answering the telephone since she was permanently distracted by a multitude of errands relating to her employer's personal life.

The front door presented something of a challenge – most people expected an all-in job including the back door and the windows – but eventually Rachel came up with Arnold Pinner. Arnold was an odd-job man who used to work as a chippy on film sets. He regarded the front door as being decidedly beneath him and after barely half a morning's work, he shouted 'That should do you, missus,' up the front stairs and took off, leaving the hapless front door ajar. Twenty minutes later the wind blew it shut and it jammed. It hadn't been opened since.

A man who decides to have his front door painted is not perhaps the most likely person to desert his wife but when he went, she wasn't really surprised. In fact she had been half expecting it.

She woke up about 8.45 and opened an eye. His side of the bed was empty. He'd gone. To the office, she assumed, until an hour later when he telephoned. This wasn't unusual. He often called throughout the day. He was a great checker-in.

'Just checking in to see what's happening about the Andersons coming to stay. You haven't forgotten? They're arriving in the morning. From Los Angeles. They'll be dog tired. Will their room be ready?'

'Just checking in. Did you take my jacket to the cleaner's because if not I can bring it in tomorrow and have Rachel take care of it . . .'

'Just checking in . . . are you OK? You were a bit quiet last night.'

This time there was silence on the other end of the line. She knew it was him since he'd had the faithful Rachel call first and put him through to her.

'What do you want for supper tonight? I thought I'd make a meatloaf and a salad. That all right with you?' She waited. He loved her meatloaf, loved the way she slipped in thick slices of chicken amongst the beef and flavoured it with sesame oil.

'Did you look in my cupboards?' he asked quietly.

'No, why? Do you want me to take something to the dry . . . ?'

'Did you look in the bathroom cabinets?'

'Are we out of mouthwash?'

'No. I've left you.'

'Oh.' She said it flatly, almost uninterested.

'I packed last night while you were out with your author. How was dinner, by the way? Did she like Cibo's? Did you have the fruit in zabaglione?'

'Yes,' she confirmed.

'I emptied all the cupboards in my dressing room and took all my things out of the bathroom cabinet and put them in a couple of bags. I put the bags in the broom cupboard under the stairs. You never noticed anything.'

'But . . .'

'No, you weren't meant to. I crept out around 4 a.m. You'd just taken my second pillow away from me in your sleep like you always do and pulled it over your head. You never heard a thing. I didn't want to discuss it. I just wanted to leave. I suppose I could have left a note. Hello? Hello, are you still there?'

'Only just. Jesus, Johnny, what do you want me to say? Should you have left a note? You make it sound like you were committing suicide. Much better to call, shows you're still alive at least.'

'You think so? That's what I felt.' He sounded pleased with himself. 'I didn't know how you'd take it. I wanted to hear your reaction.'

But you didn't want to see it. What was her reaction anyway? Shock, yes, but also a curious sense of relief. Should she tell him this?

'It's lucky I did it last night,' he continued chattily. 'As it happens, I'm having lunch with Luana today. I can explain it all to her.'

Luana was her stepdaughter. How about explaining it to your wife, she thought. Poor Luana. She would be more confused than ever. Although she never actually said as much, Luana went around sending out the message 'Please, please love me. My mother's a complete nutcase but that doesn't mean I am and even though my father still thinks I'm five years old, I'm actually a grown-up', as if it were emblazoned across her chest on a T-shirt. Of course she wasn't grown-up. Probably never would be, not with a mother like the demented Edith hovering in the background.

'What shall I tell her if she calls before you've seen her?'

'Tell her to phone the office. They'll know where I'll be.'

'What about tonight? Do you have a place to go?'

'Oh, I'll be fine. Don't worry.'

'Just one thing . . .'

'Yes? I've got a ten-o'clock. Is it a quickie?'

'I just wondered. Is this permanent?'

'Oh Lord! I can't get into discussing anything now. I just can't.

3

You do understand?' And he rang off.

That's my trouble, thought Polly, I always bloody understand.

So Johnny was gone. Coward! Polly thought as she lay in her bath. What a pathetic coward he was not to have had the guts to tell her to her face. Whoever heard of anyone creeping out of their own house in the middle of the night like a cat burglar? Typical childish Johnny behaviour. Of course she'd seen it coming. She could have done something about it but then she'd never taken it seriously. In many ways she'd never taken Johnny himself seriously. In any case, how long would he last out there on his own? He'd be back.

Polly finished dressing. No lunch today, mercifully, no meetings all day. Nothing to dress up for so she selected a pair of cotton leggings patterned with tiny black flowers and a sleeveless black top long enough to hide the bulging reminders of last night's sinning at Cibo's.

In the kitchen she opened the fridge and pressed two ice-cold oranges to her eyes for twenty-five seconds before cutting them in half and juicing them. She told herself it tightened the skin under her eyes and reduced the bags, and of course it was particularly soothing after she'd been crying. For after the bathtub accusations and the reassurances to herself that he would come running back by the end of the day had come the tears. She told herself it was the shock and maybe it was, but whichever way she looked at it, that

5

Johnny had gone so far as to actually move out of the house made her feel terribly sad.

She made herself a pot of coffee and took it through to the office on a tray, balancing it precariously with one hand as she stooped to pick up the mail in the hall. Her secretary did not arrive until eleven bringing the parcels delivered to Polly's PO Box with her. Polly liked an hour of relative peace at her desk, opening her mail, preparing the day's work.

She worked in a conservatory, what had once been an open red brick terrace on the end of the house. She had extended by adding another 14 feet of glass. Her visitors entered through a gate from the street half-way down the garden and came up a path to the glass end. Polly entered from the house through a door beside the kitchen. In summer the tiled floor rendered it cool and the long narrow blinds, pulled across the glass roof and down the window-panes to various lengths, kept out the sun on the rare occasions when it became too hot. In the winter heat emerged from a Norwegian stove jutting out of the kitchen wall and connected to it by a fat snaked pipe. Into this Polly threw bundles of wood, often opening the door and hurling them into the blaze when she felt a meeting was going on too long and she wanted to get rid of whoever it was. The sight of the roaring flames invariably made visitors extremely nervous as they sat on Polly's striped sofas arranged in a semicircle around the stove. Once, when faced with someone who was particularly entrenched, Polly began to toy with the edge of the wooden coffee table. 'I've never really liked this,' she said casually, 'do you think it would fit?' She eyed the stove. Five minutes later she was saying goodbye.

The glass door at the end of the conservatory opened straight out on to the garden and Polly had a rather disconcerting habit of suddenly rushing out in the middle of a boring telephone conversation to grab some chives for lunch, or check on her lettuces leaving Mrs Flowers, her secretary, to reach for the phone and explain that Polly would be right with whoever it was, could they just hang on a second, something had just come up on the other line.

Polly worked from two long refectory tables standing side by side

6

running the entire length of one side of the conservatory, beginning at the brick end and finishing at the glass end looking out over the garden. The tables were littered with cordless phones, calculators, staplers, overflowing wooden filing trays, long yellow legal pads and square transparent Perspex containers crammed with pens, pencils, paperclips, bulldog clips. Where the two tables met there was always a tall vase of beautifully arranged flowers. Several chairs were scattered along the tables, some of them on castors, on which Polly swivelled about, grabbing phones, dragging her keyboard with her as she went.

Down the other side of the conservatory was a line of bright red filing cabinets broken by a gap in the middle over which had been placed a block of wood. This was Mrs Flowers' desk and the gap was for her arthritic knees. Mrs Flowers did not swivel. She stayed – decidedly – put. She had her screen placed firmly in front of her and she knelt before it on a kind of designer prayer stool Polly had bought her from the Back Shop. There was support for her knees and she was tilted slightly forward all the time. 'Architects use them,' she told Polly's authors seriously, defying them to giggle or to point out that she was not an architect.

Mrs Flowers had been with her ever since Polly had left her job at an established firm and branched out to start her own literary agency. Mrs Flowers had been the temp she'd been sent around the time of her decision to break away.

'Oh, take me with you,' begged Mrs Flowers.

'Well, of course I'd love to but to begin with I simply couldn't afford to.'

'I'm sure you could. Lucy Richards will come with you and the others will soon follow.'

'That's rather wishful thinking.'

'Not at all. I'm certain of it.' Mrs Flowers nodded emphatically.

'Why, exactly?' Polly was curious.

'I was holding on in the middle of a telephone call to her while she took a call on her other line. She didn't quite cover the mouthpiece and I heard her say, "I'm on the phone to my agent's office." And the other person must have been someone in the know who mentioned something about you leaving and I heard Lucy

7

Richards say, "Yes, I know, I've heard the rumours about that too but I'll tell you one thing, if Polly goes anywhere, I'm going with her. If she'll have me, that is." '

'If she'll have me. Did she really say that?'

Lucy Richards' first novel had sold 15,000 copies in hardcover and there was a 200,000 first printing set for the paperback. Secretly Polly had thought the book to be in rather poor taste when she had first read it but she had been forced to admit that since she couldn't put it down, she was almost bound to be able to sell it. It was about the daughter of a prominent member of the cabinet and the artistocracy who, while on holiday in the South of France, falls in love with a St Tropez beach bum, becomes pregnant, has the baby and then discovers, rather late in the day, that the beach bum is gay, is HIV positive, and her baby has AIDS. When her father rather ill-advisedly washes his hands of her, she promptly sells her story to the tabloids finding true love (yet again) in the arms of the first journalist sent to interview her who stays with her while the baby withers and dies. LOVE STORY FOR THE NINETIES screamed the strapline on the paperback cover proof. A movie option had been sold to someone who had once worked for David Puttnam, and Madonna was said to be tempted.

'A likely story!' said Mrs Flowers, who knew a thing or two. 'Shouldn't think she's even read it. Be that Sinead O'Connor more likely. I mean, she'd be perfect as an English aristocrat's daughter.' Nevertheless the Madonna rumour had been circulating at exactly the right moment and it had secured an advance of $40,000 from the Americans and Lucy Richards – and several other lucrative authors – had indeed followed Polly when she left.

So did Mrs Flowers. At the time she had in fact been Miss Flowers but Polly couldn't help noticing that whenever her new secretary answered the telephone she always said: 'This is Mrs Flowers.'

'What does Mr Flowers do?' enquired Polly, feeling nosy one morning.

'My father is dead. He was a porter. At Liverpool Street,' she added after a beat lest Polly think he had worked at Billingsgate fish market or at an hotel.

Polly left it at that yet she had a feeling she did not know Mrs Flowers' whole story, that behind the bustling, efficient exterior with all the trappings of late middle age – the tightly permed hair, the old-fashioned Mrs Thatcher handbag, the silk scarf tied round the neck and the sensible flat brown shows – lurked a more sensitive, romantic soul, someone who still dared to hope . . .

Polly still had a little time before Mrs Flowers arrived. Should she telephone a dozen friends and tell them what had happened? She thought about it for a second. It would be so horribly predictable. To begin with they'd shriek. To them it was, after all, the ultimate disaster. They'd be embarrassed by what they would imagine would be her humiliation. Then, after about seven minutes, they'd start getting restless, anxious to get off the phone and call someone else with the gossip.

No, thought Polly, I won't call a soul. It's my marriage and it looks like it might be over. I'll just sit back and see how long it takes them to find out.

That did not include Joan.

Joan Brock had been a habit in Polly's life since they were thirteen and new girls at boarding school. Joan had been – and indeed still was – small and dark with a sleek black bob framing her pointed face while Polly had been large and cumbersome. Joan darted everywhere and Polly galumphed and Joan always made sure Polly felt like an awkward lump by comparison. Yet in the way that outsiders are often thrown together, Polly and Joan became Best Friends. Except that Polly wasn't really an outsider. She just felt sorry for 'the Jewish girl', as Joan was called behind her back. No one knew for sure if in fact Joan was Jewish but her father was apparently a refugee who had changed his name. He was also a self-made millionaire who doted on his sons and ignored his only daughter, a fact that made Joan strive constantly to seek his attention. Polly was by far the cleverer of the two but Joan was quick-witted and sharp and survived by getting away with the proverbial murder.

After school – neither went to university – they had arrived in London at more or less the same time when Joan had thrown herself at every available man while Polly watched shyly from the sidelines. Joan had succeeded in landing an eligible young Old Etonian antique dealer. They were married at Chelsea Register Office – all crushed velvet suits and floppy hats over flowers in the hair and absolutely no sign of Mummy and Daddy. Polly was a bridesmaid. In the wedding photos she stood predictably huge and galumphing, towering over the tiny bride.

The marriage lasted five years, by which time Joan had discovered she couldn't have children and the Old Etonian had decided he wanted an heir and divorced her. But by then Joan had wormed her way into a job on *Vogue* and was too busy clawing her way up the Condé Nast ladder and being smart and chic and fashionable to remember Polly's existence except for a frantic 'catch-up' lunch once or twice a year.

Then Joan was fired from Condé Nast, ousted from Vogue House and thrown out into the wilderness of freelance journalism. Since then she had telephoned Polly at least four times a week, generally first thing in the morning. Just as Polly had been there to support Joan the outsider at school, Joan had known Polly would also be there to pick up the pieces later on in life.

'Any sex? Any cheques?' Joan's life now revolved around getting work (her main aim was to get herself a column but it appeared to be the main aim of all newspaper and magazine editors to deny her one), and looking for a man. At one point she announced she was going to write THE NOVEL which, she told Polly, would outraunch Julie Burchill. She gave up after four paragraphs.

'Not exactly. Johnny's gone.'

'Well, that's great if he's going to be out of the way because I want to come over for lunch today instead of tomorrow. Something's come up.'

Joan rescheduled everything. She had no consideration whatsoever for anyone else's timetable. She was one of those people who found the thought of being left to her own devices for half a second so daunting that she crammed as much as she could into every day with the result that she frequently found herself overbooked. Polly was used to it. She knew better than to write a date with Joan in ink and kept a pencil with a rubber on the end inside her diary for the express purpose of rescheduling Joan. Her stepdaughter Luana disapproved strongly and called her Polly Pushover for being so obliging.

'No, Joan, listen for a second. He's gone. He's no longer living here. He's –'

'You mean *he's left you*? That's completely and utterly wonderful. The best news. Who is she?'

'What do you mean?'

'Who's he left you for?'

'No one as far as I know.'

'Oh, bound to be someone. Some little floozie in his office, much younger than you. When did you last have sex? Months ago, I bet. So can I come over for lunch today?'

'No, Joan, I don't think so. Not today. Do you mind?'

'But what am I going to do? I haven't got a lunch. I'll go mad. Anyway, I want to hear all about why he's left you. He was a mega-loser, called himself a bloody film producer but what's he ever produced? Polly, you're well rid of him. You do know that, don't you?'

Was this what everyone was going to tell her? That she was well rid of him? It wasn't, Polly realised, what she wanted to hear. Joan had never liked Johnny but that was no reason to go slagging him off at the first opportunity.

'Joan, I have to go. Mrs Flowers will be here at any minute.'

'I do not understand why you employ that menopausal old bat. It's bad for your image.'

'I rather think Mrs Flowers is well past the menopause. I, on the other hand, in the not too distant future . . .'

'Your husband leaves you and you immediately blame it on the menopause. You're too negative for words, darling. Call me when you've got a grip. Don't sit there feeling sorry for yourself. He's done you a favour. Now we'll find you someone sensational. After we've found me someone sensational. I must get off this phone and find someone to have lunch with. Bye.'

Polly finished her coffee, relieved at the welcome distraction of Mrs Flowers coming in through the garden door bearing parcels of manuscripts. Mrs Flowers flapped her *Daily Mail* at Polly.

'Nice piece about your Mr de Soto in Nigel Dempster's column.

Something about him and his "constant companion", that Lady Whyte, having a quiet dinner together to talk about the new film . . . and look, that Hector O'Neill's been in the news again. Broken up with his girlfriend right in the middle of shooting his new film. Says it's the last time he's going to play Conway so I suppose they'll have to replace him like they did Sean Connery in James Bond. It was never the same though, was it, Mrs de Soto? Look at Hector O'Neill! Irish, is he? Something like that. Dreamboat like that, make some girl a wonderful husband if only he'd settle down. Pity you've already found your Mr Right, Mrs de Soto.'

Polly realised she wasn't going to get away with it. She would have to tell Mrs Flowers about Johnny going. She would have to tell everyone. That night Luana called her and Polly was surprised at her stepdaughter's reaction: 'What a jerk my father is!'

Yes, Polly told herself firmly, what a jerk! Every morning she would wake up and shout *what a jerk*!

But she wouldn't really mean it.

Hector O'Neill raised his glass of champagne to toast the supermodel – he couldn't for the life of him remember her name – sitting in the seat beside him. He figured she must be a supermodel if she was flying First-Class. He wondered if he could be bothered to chat her up all the way to London in return for a quick fuck when they got there. Then he'd want to get rid of her and she probably wouldn't take the hint. They never did. He decided to give it a whirl and then feign sleep if she proved too stupid.

'Saw you on the cover of *Vogue* last month. What were you up to in LA?' What the fuck was her name? She couldn't be that super or he'd remember.

She giggled predictably. 'American *Vogue*? That wasn't me. That was Cindy Crawford. I look a bit like her. Everyone says so.'

'No, no, I meant British *Vogue*.'

'Well, I wouldn't be on that either. I'm not a model. Far from it. I'm an actress.'

No, you're not, darling, you're an MTA if you're anything at all. Model-turned-actress and a wannabe at that. Why was he wasting his time?

'Course you are. Been filming in LA?'

'Just seeing a few people. You know. You?'

13

'Meeings about my new Conway film. I start shooting next week.'

'Fully cast, is it?'

Oh, God, she'd never let him go. Then it hit him. Had he been set up? Had her agent fixed it so she'd be sitting next to him? Was she poised to make a play for him to try and get a part in the film? Stranger things had happened. He'd wait a little while so as not to offend her and then move seats.

'Not my department, darling, but I think it is, yes. It's the last Conway I'm doing, that's all I know. Yes, you do look a bit like Cindy. Talking about *Vogue*, they want me for a fashion shoot, model a few old rags with one of the girls.'

'Oh, that's nice.'

'Might be.'

'Will they do an interview too? What do they call it? In-depth. Get to the real you?' She giggled again. She was beginning to irritate him. Seriously.

'Not *Vogue*'s style, darling.'

Thank God!

No one in his new life was ever going to get him to do an in-depth interview. No one was ever going to find out the truth about his background. What a relief to be going home to England. Funny to think of it as home when he'd been born in America. How he hated going back to the States. It always reminded him of the past he wanted to forget.

The Kennedys had put the Irish on the map in America when Hector was growing up. He was only four when President Kennedy was assassinated but he was nine when Bobby was killed, old enough to recognise a hero when he saw one on television. That was when Hector decided he too would become an Irish hero – and here he was flying First-Class, an international movie star, the perfect Irish hero and, for all anybody knew, Boston born and bred just like the Kennedys.

Except that he wasn't. He was poor shanty Irish, born John Hector Maguire, in a small town near Pittsburgh, Pennsylvania, descended, if he chose to believe his grandfather's blarney, from

Celtic stock from Co. Mayo who had come to America in the 1870s to seek their fortune and wound up in the mines. He would probably fly right over the miserable dump he'd grown up in. His prevailing memory of the place was always of smoke rising into a grey sky peppered with jagged pylons and tall chimneys. The smoke came not only from the chimneys but also from the steam engines roaring through on the railroad raised high above the ground and from the trucks, the oil tanker rigs, the semis charging past belching smoke.

His father worked at the steel mill. He had another picture from his childhood: that of his father and his buddies coming home from work, a line of them appearing on the crest of a hill, lunchboxes and helmets tucked under their arms, silhouetted against the horizon, smoke rising behind them. They all dressed much the same: wool hats, fur hats, baseball caps; sleeveless quilted jackets over plaid shirts, hands plunged deep in jeans pockets, shoulders hunched against the cold. And they never made it home before midnight. Every day John Hector watched them stumble into the saloon with the red neon Budweiser sign winking at them in the window. Once, sent by his mother to find his father, he had gone into the bar and found his father lying fast asleep in the middle of the pool table, his white vest riding up over his belly, jeans loosened for comfort, boots sticking straight up in the air. All around him on the green baize were overturned beer cans.

Throughout his boyhood John Hector never saw his father hold a conversation with a woman. Jimmy Maguire was uncomfortable around women, a great brute of a man who only lost his shyness when drunk and he only drank with men, men who could be counted on to say little more to him than 'Hey buddy', 'Hey man', ask him how they were hangin?, tell him he was full of shit, let him tell them they were too.

John Hector didn't blame him for never coming home when home was a trailer without wheels. The boys who went to school with him, steelworkers' kids like himself, lived in rows of wooden houses originally painted white, now grey with the smoke, with front porches where people sat out at night, but the Maguires were too poor even for this humble accommodation. John Hector often looked at his mother and wondered how it felt to be so poor when she had been born rich. He was eight when his mother first took him to Philadelphia and showed him his grandparents' house on Henry Avenue. It was a four-storey mansion, standing in its own grounds. Fourteen rooms minimum, and he had to share a bed with his mother in the trailer.

'I went to stay with my Auntie Kitty in Pittsburgh and I met your father in a store,' Mary Maguire told him. 'I fell in love with him and I married him. Your grandfather hasn't spoken to me since. Your father wasn't the wreck of a man he is now. The drink did that to him. If I'd known I was going to wind up living in a broken-down mobile home with a steelworker who never came home for a husband, I'd have listened to my father, of course.'

'Does he know about me?'

'He does. I wrote him. Told him I'd named you for him. Those are your grandfather's names: John Hector. Only he's John Hector Kennedy.'

And that was when it had begun: his dreams of being related somehow to those other Kennedys. He'd seen where his mother was raised and it gave him a new-found sense of pride in himself to know that he came from good lace curtain Irish stock. He might be the son of a bum but he was also the child of a Philadelphia princess.

Only he wasn't.

He brooded over the Philadelphia mansion day after day. Why didn't his mother take him and run away, go back there, go back to her roots, where she belonged, where he belonged? Each time he saw his father jostling with his buddies, coming over the horizon and down the hill to the saloon to drink himself into oblivion, John Hector wanted to taunt him with the truth but Mary Maguire had made him swear never to tell his father what she'd shown him. So he hugged his secret to himself as a way of keeping out the cold and the smoke, and he dreamed.

He was nine when he wrote the first letter to his grandfather. Cheap paper, bad spelling, devoid of grammar – but the message was there. He was the old man's grandson. His mother was Mary Maguire. They lived in hell. Please would Mr Kennedy save them?

No reply.

He wrote again. Five times, before someone answered. It wasn't John Hector Kennedy. It was his wife. John Hector couldn't read his grandmother's spidery hand. He took the letter to the parish priest, Father Dominic. Father Dominic read the letter.

'Who is this lady, Nora Kennedy?'

'My grandmother,' said John Hector.

'No, son, I don't think so.'

The priest was kind. He broke the news gently. Nora Kennedy was confused about the boy who had been writing to her husband. They had no daughter called Mary Maguire. The only person she knew called Mary Maguire was the little daughter of a maid they had employed several years ago.

The truth was simple. John Hector's grandfather had not lived on Henry Avenue. He had been an out-of-work builder in the poor East Falls immigrant area of Philadelphia. His wife Annie had worked in the scullery at Henry Avenue to support her family. Little Mary Maguire had been one of eight children and as soon as she could had escaped to Pittsburgh where she had met Jimmy Maguire – and here was the only reality in her story – in a store. She was not even able to change her name when she married and the only reason her father never spoke to her again was because he was too blind East Falls drunk to notice she had gone.

But little Mary Maguire had witnessed something her father never had. She had seen the way the rich lived even if she had never lived that way herself, and in memory of that brief glimpse into another world she had named her son after a wealthy Henry Avenue socialite and concocted a childhood fantasy for him as a way of holding at bay the hell into which she had descended.

Once John Hector had discovered her deception, his mother gave up on him. She couldn't play the game with him any more, couldn't pretend it was all going to end some day when she would whisk him away to the life where they really belonged. She was just a poor Irish girl who'd married a poor Irish bum and between them they'd produced John Hector. Now she realised she was stuck in the smoke for ever, her child became a burden to her, holding her back. She could have taken to the bottle like her husband but she had

17

discovered something better. It was 1968, pretty late on in the decade, when Mary Maguire had began to smoke dope.

She was turned on to grass by a dropout student from Philadelphia who picked her up outside the supermarket and told her she looked like Joan Baez. Mary Maguire had barely heard of Joan Baez. Patsy Cline was more her style. Yet within weeks she was out every night with a crowd of hippies who gathered round a camp fire on the outskirts of town and sang half-hearted protest songs while someone strummed on a guitar and the joint was passed from hand to hand.

John Hector didn't mind. He had the trailer to himself. He lived off cans of cold beans and watched TV every night until he fell asleep in front of it. The irony was that when the draft call for Vietnam in January 1968 rose to 33,000, John Hector probably knew more about the growing futility and escalation of the war from all that he had seen on TV than either his father, drunk in the bar every night and about to be part of the draft, or his mother, stoned by the camp fire and playing at being an opponent of the war.

In the summer of 1969, with Jimmy Maguire safely out of the way in the Mekong Delta, Mary Maguire left John Hector with a neighbour and took off with her hippie gang to the music festival at Woodstock. When she returned she had a young Englishman in tow with blond hair down to his shoulders and an accent John Hector couldn't understand.

'John Hector,' she said casually, 'this is Tony. He's going to get us out of here. He's going to take us to England.'

'Coo-ee!' twinkled the model-turned-actress, wiggling her fingers at him, 'wakey-wakey. Shall we have something to drink and get to know each other better?'

Hector placed a hand on the inside of her bare thigh. *I didn't go to sleep, you silly cow, I just closed my eyes to make you think I had.* He squeezed the soft pink flesh a little.

'Listen, love, the Conway movie's cast. There's nothing I can do for you in that department. In fact I'll be totally straight, there's

18

nothing I can do for you in any department other than where my hand is right now. How about it?'

'I'm not like that,' she said, model-turned-actress-turned-prim-and-proper all of a sudden.

Like hell! 'Suit yourself. I'm going back to sleep.'

Polly met her husband at a party. She had just begun work as an assistant at the literary agents Patrick Fisher & Dunbar with the promise of promotion to baby agent status after an initial trial period. Before that she had been a secretary to an American film producer for whom she still read scripts and it was at his Christmas party, held in a cavernous film studio just off the Fulham Road used to shoot commercials, that she first encountered Johnny de Soto.

She still acted as a kind of scout for the producer, scouring publishers' lists for potential properties – books he might want to make into films. Once she had read the book she then had to 'cover' it which meant writing a five-line idiot's description of the plot (most of the money men in the film industry were barely capable of taking in even that much), followed by a longer, more detailed synopsis which could run from three pages to fifty-three. Each time a major character was introduced his or her name had to be typed in capital letters. Finally she had to write a short comment with helpful suggestions like 'suitable vehicle for Dustin Hoffman' or 'perfect for Greta Scacchi if the main character had surgery and the picture was reset in England.'

Polly was aware that the American never took the slightest bit of notice of anything she said yet she always took her coverages seriously. Long, multi-generational sagas were particularly demanding and it was because she had been tackling a synopsis of one of these that she was late for the party. She had become so absorbed in the task of chronicling every twist and turn of the baroque story that she had forgotten the time. When she arrived at 8.45 with her streaked hair still wet from the shower, the drinks were almost over.

The American's wife pounced on her the minute she stepped inside the door.

'Polly! There you are. Now, may I introduce Johnny de Soto?'

If you absolutely have to, thought Polly; what a seriously dreadful name. She eyed the rather grizzled-looking character being propelled towards her. He was on the stocky side, dark hair cut short, almost in a crew cut, and already greying at the temples. His face was square and smiling with rather a pugnacious nose and wide-apart dark brown eyes – the kind Polly described as 'melting' in her coverages. His mouth was twitchy, ready to break into a grin. He wore jeans, loafers, a beige crew-neck sweater underneath a black light wool jacket. He looked relaxed.

'It is, isn't it?' he said, taking her hand.

'What is?'

'A terrible name. It was written all over your face, as they say. Don't worry. I'm sure everyone has the same reaction. It's actually Gianni de Soto but I've sort of changed it to Johnny.'

'You're Italian?' He didn't sound it.

'Yes, but I was born here. My father came over from Naples and opened an ice-cream shop in Soho. It's still there. I'll take you there one day.'

Polly was startled. 'Will you? You don't even know my name.'

'Well?'

'Oh. I'm Polly Atwell.'

Someone slapped him on the back.

'Johnny, you old devil, how are you? Good to see you. This is . . .'

And he was gone, turning back to her with a rueful grin and a shrug before he was moved on.

21

To her intense irritation, Polly found herself thinking about him over Christmas with her parents in Norfolk. On her return to London in the New Year she rummaged through her cupboards till she found the Rolodex she had used when working for the film producer. She found his card under 'S'.

> Johnny de Soto
> 25 Roberts Gardens
> London SW7

Funny, she'd never noticed it before. Her predecessor had made a tiny note on the back:

> Wife's name: Edith
> Daughter: Luana

Wife's name: Edith. Damn! Forget it, Polly told herself firmly, just don't even think about it any more.

He turned up at Patrick Fisher & Dunbar four days later. He'd obviously done a bit of homework.

'Is he in?' He nodded towards Patrick Fisher's office.

'Do you have an appointment?' Wife's name: Edith. Be cold, Polly, be snotty.

'Don't give me that. I only want to ask him if I can take you out to lunch.'

'Well, why don't you ask me?' said Polly, falling straight into the trap.

He took her to Langan's and said 'Hello Michael' to Michael Caine as they passed his table. Michael Caine nodded vaguely. Polly wondered if he had the slightest idea who Johnny de Soto was.

She had the spinach soufflé with anchovy sauce because Johnny said she absolutely had to although she noticed he chose the *salade frisée aux lardons* for himself. He didn't say much as they ate their first course, just kept looking at her. Suddenly he said:

'You have the most perfect ears.'

'Have I?' said Polly, puzzled and a little thrown. 'How?'

'Flat against the side of your head, small, tiny lobes. Why don't you have them pierced?'

'I'm scared. I expect it hurts like hell.'

'Rubbish! Have them done.'

He lapsed into silence again until Polly's steak arrived. He made her have French fries with it although she pleaded that she was trying to lose weight. He ate a couple of mouthfuls of yet another salad, pushed it to one side of his plate and began to ply her with questions as she chewed her way through her steak.

'Tell me about yourself? How long have you been working in our business?'

It was worse than going to the dentist, thought Polly. They waited until they'd filled your mouth with the drill, clamps and cotton wool swabs and then they began making small talk. Besides, moonlighting as a part-time reader for a producer who didn't take her seriously hardly constituted working in the movies.

'Oh . . .' she shrugged as she dispatched the last mouthful, 'I'm in the book world now. What about you?'

'Me? Oh, I'm just getting going. I've got this property and –'

'You're a producer?'

'Yes, well, I am, I mean I want to be. No, skip that, I am a producer.'

'What films have you produced? Have I seen any of them?'

'Well, that's just it. I haven't actually made anything yet but I've got this property and I'm in the process of developing it. It's called *The End* and it's going to be *Jaws 2* and –'

'Didn't they make *Jaws 2*?'

'No, I mean it's as horrific as *Jaws*. It's about this couple who buy their dream house and they're set to retire there and live happily ever after and their grandkids come and stay – or maybe it's a young married couple starting out, we haven't really decided yet. Anyway they have acres and acres of land or a big garden or whatever and every day they get closer to exploring the perimeter. One day they're going to go down to the end of the garden and when they get there they're going to find the evil that lurks there.'

'What evil?'

'Haven't quite finalised the evil yet but, believe me, it'll be scarier than sharks.'

'Sharks at the end of the garden?'

'Oh, shut up. You're not taking me seriously. The whole point is that we, the audience, will know about the evil, the alien, or whatever it is because we'll see it intermittently throughout the movie. The suspense will be a killer.'

'But why do you want to make *Son of Jaws* when we've already had *Jaws*? Why not try and make something new and different?'

'You try telling the money men you want to make something completely different to something that's just been one of the biggest grossing pictures of all time. They'd laugh in your face. It will be different. I know that. But I have to pretend it's going to be something they're familiar with. So I've got this guy writing the script down in a basement in Chelsea somewhere . . .'

'And you're paying him peanuts . . '

'How'd you know?'

'I just did.'

'Well, it'll be his big break. He'll make his name with *The End* and I'll be the guy who made it all possible. He owes me.'

'So do you have a treatment to be going on with?'

He looked at her in admiration.

'It really does make a change to talk to someone in our business. I tell most girls I take out I've got a treatment and they think I'm talking about a course of penicillin. Yes, I've got a treatment and I'm talking to financiers, you know, venture capitalists and so on.'

'Yes, of course.' Polly nodded seriously. He was ridiculous but at the same time there was something enormously appealing about his enthusiasm, his optimism.

He glanced at his watch.

'Christ! Eh, do you want coffee?'

She did but since she would clearly be drinking it on her own, she declined.

'I'd run you back but I have to be in Wardour Street by three.'

'It's OK.'

They parted outside the restaurant. He didn't kiss her, didn't even take her hand, just jumped in a passing cab and waved goodbye through the rear window.

It was raining. Polly set off back to the office. What had been the point of that lunch? She should have asked him about his family. Wife's name: Edith. Daughter: Luana. Why did a man take a girl to lunch – and from the sound of it she wasn't the only one – when he had that written on the back of his address card?

He called a week later.

'Well, have you had them done?'

'What?'

'Your ears. Have you had them pierced like I said?'

'No.'

'So when are you going to get around to it?'

He booked her for dinner in a week's time on condition that she arrived at the restaurant with pierced ears.

She had them done at Harrods and treated herself to a new black skirt from Agnès B in the Fulham Road. It was a size 12 and normally she took a size 14 but she managed to squeeze into it. Polly was a big girl. Not fat, just big. Johnny de Soto was not a tall man. Nevertheless Polly put on a pair of three-inch heels when she went to meet him at La Poule au Pot in Ebury Street. She liked La Poule au Pot. They brought you huge bottles of wine and you only paid for what you drank. It had a warm, comforting French nursery atmosphere, the perfect restaurant for the misery of winter. She

25

already knew what she would have to eat: the gigot of lamb with lentils.

'Had them done?' He stood up to greet her, pulled back her chair and then brushed his hand through her hair, drawing it away from her ear. 'Good girl' he said when he saw the tiny gold studs and leaned forward to kiss her cheek.

'It really hurt,' said Polly, sitting down.

'Well, of course it did. What did you expect?'

'But you said –'

'Never mind what I said. Here's your reward.'

The little black box had the name Argenta written on it. Polly had seen Argenta, passed it many times. It was a jeweller's on the Fulham Road. She opened the box and parted the tissue paper.

To her horror her initial reaction was one of disappointment. But then what had she expected from someone on a second date, someone she barely knew, someone who had a wife named Edith? Diamonds? The earrings were tiny. Black dots circled with gold. Exquisitely tasteful.

'They'll look great when you've had your hair cut,' he told her.

Two weeks later, shaven and shorn at Molton Brown and wearing her new earrings, Polly allowed herself to be taken to bed by Johnny de Soto. At Johnny's insistence they watched a video of *The Boys from Brazil* and ate a Chinese takeaway.

'Trash!' complained Johnny, 'utter trash. How could Olivier allow himself to appear in such trash?'

'I thought he was brilliant. His character was based on that man, what's his name? The one who . . .'

'Simon Wiesenthal, the Nazi hunter. I'm not saying Olivier was bad. It's just the whole story was so unbelievable: Gregory Peck rushing round the world assassinating fathers and these identical boys all over the place. Ludicrous.'

Polly couldn't help wondering what exactly would make *The End* so credible when Johnny came to make it but she decided now was not the moment to ask him. Instead she said:

'He's a terrific storyteller, Ira Levin.'

'Who's Ira Levin, for heaven's sake? There was no one called Ira Levin in that movie.'

'He's the author of the book on which it was based,' said Polly patiently. 'He was only twenty-five when he wrote his first book, *A Kiss before Dying*. Now there's something you could have made a film of. It's full of suspense.'

'I know *A Kiss before Dying*. It's the one about the guy who goes after an heiress but he gets her pregnant which means she'll be disinherited so he stops and goes after her sister. They made it already, Robert Wagner and Joanne Woodward, I forget who directed . . .'

'Recently?'

'No, back in the Fifties. You're right. Great story.'

'Well, why don't you do a remake?'

'To tell you the truth I heard there's one in the pipeline. Anyway, where's the excitement in doing a remake?'

'Where's the excitement in doing another *Jaws*-type movie when it's already been done?'

'I told you. I'm going to make it different. Have you seen *Return to Peyton Place*?'

'Have I seen what?'

'I knew it. Greatest soap film ever made and it's on TV late tonight. We'll watch it in bed.'

His apartment was right at the top of the building and there was no lift. He hadn't turned on the light when they'd arrived but had taken her by the hand and led her up the staircase in the darkness to the fifth floor, pausing on the landings to draw her into his arms and nuzzle her neck.

She was surprised by the humble size of the flat: just one room under the eaves with a small kitchen leading off it, a box-like bedroom with only room for a king-size bed and built-in closets and a bathroom in which she could barely turn around. A bachelor apartment. No sign of the family.

As she had somehow expected he was an attentive lover, full of affection. First he ran her a bath and poured something sweet-smelling from a Floris bottle into it.

'Undress in the bedroom. Leave your things in there. No room in here, as you can see.'

He helped her into the bath and squatted down fully clothed beside her.

'Don't be shy. You have a sensational body.' He leaned back on his haunches to admire her. 'Now which soap shall I wash you with?'

He built up a lather in his hands and began to smooth it all over her, bringing the soapsuds to little points on her nipples. As she stepped out of the tub he wrapped her in a big towel and hugged her dry.

'Come on. Into bed now. Movie's about to start.'

He must have spent at least half an hour stroking her, kissing her, massaging her until she floated into a warm liquid sensation and heard herself begging him to make love to her.

As they watched the movie she nestled against him and he stroked her hair continuously. She could hear his heart hammering in his chest beneath her head and found she could barely concentrate on the film. Suddenly a line with the word 'wife' penetrated her drowsiness.

Wife's name: Edith.

'Johnny?'

'Hmmm?'

'Are you married?'

'No.'

'Divorced?'

'No.'

'What?' Polly sat up in bed. He tried to pull her back down but she resisted.

'What's this all about?'

'You've never been married?'

'Not exactly.'

'Well, who's Edith?'

'Ah, someone's told you about Edith.'

'No . . .'

'Then how –'

Polly explained about the Rolodex.

He laughed. 'Come here, you.' He clasped her to him and her head bumped up and down on his chest as he continued to laugh. He kissed her fiercely on the forehead several times. 'I like hearing you did that. You looked for my card because you were interested in me. I like that.'

'And Edith?'

'Edith was . . . is . . . the mother of my child.'

'Luana?'

'Hah! Her name was there too?'

She was silent. Waiting.

'All right. I'll tell you about Edith. She was my . . . we were together for four years. We had a child but we never married.'

'Why not?'

'She didn't want to. I confess I asked her several times but she wouldn't. Then, in the end, she left me.'

'Where is she now?'

'Battersea. South of the river.'

'And Luana?'

'Mostly with her. Sometimes with me in the house I have in Notting Hill Gate.'

'So what's this place?'

'This is just . . .'

'Where you bring scrubbers?'

'You said it . . .'

She punched him. He bit her – gently. She began to tickle him.

'What happened in the end?' she whispered after they had made love and were about to fall asleep.

'With me and Edith?'

'No, the movie . . .'

'Oh, she stays there in Peyton Place, she tells Jeff Chandler goodbye.'

'Like Edith told you . . .'

In the morning as they bumped into each other trying to make breakfast together in the tiny kitchenette, Johnny told her:

'We won't be coming back here. This place was Edith's old flat before we had a baby. We never got around to selling it. She probably doesn't even know I still have a key. So when are you going to meet Luana? You'd better make it soon if you're going to move in with me.'

As she walked up the aisle, Polly had time to catch her breath for the first time in two months.

'Polly and Johnny were lovers. . .' she sang in her mind to the tune of 'Frankie and Johnny'.

Would he do her wrong like the Johnny in the song? How could she tell? She'd barely had a chance to get to know him. Did all brides feel like this? A moment of sheer panic, the question 'what have I done?'better left unanswered.

'Where's the blighter got to?' muttered her father, fractionally tightening his hold on her elbow to restrain her. They were half-way up the aisle and Johnny, whose back view clad in morning suit had presented a disturbingly unfamiliar picture when she had first seen it on entering the chuch, had now disappeared.

Well, that's that, she concluded. It was never meant to happen. Then she saw him pacing nervously up and down to the right of the altar. He caught sight of her standing transfixed in the middle of the aisle glaring at him and gave her a broad wink. For one ghastly moment Polly thought he was going to vault over the pews and come running to her.

The rest of the service passed without a hitch. Johnny, a lapsed Catholic whose memories of the Catholic Church receded so far into his past he couldn't remember when he last went to confession, had agreeed to be confirmed into the Church of England so he could make Polly happy by marrying her in church. Polly knew her parents were sad that the little Norman flint church in their Norfolk village had been rejected in favour of a London wedding but she just couldn't see Johnny in Norfolk.

She sensed the electricity in the congregation behind her when the vicar said:

'Do you Gianni Mauro Ludovico de Soto take this woman . . . ?'

OK, so he was a wop and she was going to take him to be her lawful wedded husband whether they liked it or not.

'Engaging fellow, your Johnny,' chuckled her Uncle Matthew to her during the reception. That was the trouble, thought Polly. So engaging she had been unable to resist him.

Luana was not at the wedding. Polly had only met her once. She almost met her the day after she and Johnny had first spent the night together. Johnny had invited her to have dinner with him and his daughter at his house. Polly's friends didn't live in houses. They lived in flats and shared them if they couldn't afford the rental on their own. The only people she knew who lived in houses in London were friends of her parents.

As she climbed the stone steps to the front door she noticed it was open. She was about to knock when she heard a girl's voice from within.

'She's, like, moving in? Dad, are you crazy? How can she move in?'

'She's moving in because I'm going to marry her.'

This was news to Polly, who stood rooted to the doormat, trembling all over. Very slowly and very quietly she edged backwards down the steps till she reached the pavement whereupon she rushed into the street and flagged down a cab.

Every now and again Polly went into emotional shock. She protected her inner core with what appeared to be an efficient no-nonsense exterior but occasionally something shot straight through to the heart and dislodged her. Hearing that Johnny actually planned to marry her completely knocked her for six. For two days she simply could not function. She didn't go to the office and later she realised Patrick Fisher must have given Johnny her address since he turned up and rang her doorbell for eleven minutes until she answered.

'I've saved you your job. You can't do this sort of thing, you know. He was about to fire you by mail but I stopped him.'

Polly burst into tears.

'Oh, Polly, Polly, Polly! Come here.'

He held her, standing in the middle of the hall, patting her on the back as if she were a baby with wind. 'What's this all about? What's wrong? Don't tell me you were a virgin. You weren't, you know, even if you think you were. No use trying that one on. I've had 'em before. I can tell.'

'Not funny,' blubbed Polly into his shoulder, 'I'm far too old.'

'Yeah, well, getting on a bit, that's for sure. Feel like an old maid, do you?'

She hit him. And giggled.

'That's better. Now, I came to ask you to marry me. God knows why, your nose is all red but I want you. I really do. I want a Polly with a red nose and tiny pierced earlobes and great long legs to wrap around me when I'm cold and lonely. So what do you say? Will you marry me?'

He asked her every day for two weeks until she said yes. She wasn't especially confident with men and she hadn't had many lovers. She had no idea what Johnny de Soto saw in her but she knew she was not likely to encounter anyone like him again. If she turned him down she was destined to marry a nice young English gentleman who might inherit a bit of land somewhere (probably Norfolk, since most of the nice young men she knew came from there), where he would expect her to be chatelaine of his manor and raise a well-brought-up brood.

Johnny de Soto was totally different and she fell deeply in love with him without ever daring to ask if he was in love with her.

His mother, Carla de Soto, was five feet if she put on a pair of high heels.

'She's not a Catholic. She's taller than you are. Whatever would your father have said?' she gabbled in Italian when Johnny took Polly to the flat above his father's ice-cream shop in Soho where his mother still lived. Polly looked at Johnny helplessly and he translated.

'Do you mind?' Polly asked him.

'That you're not a Catholic? Are you kidding?'

'No – that I'm taller than – '

'I love it!' Johnny wrapped his arms around her and bent his knees, pretending his head only came as far as her navel.

'Gianni, *basta.*' Carla pushed him out of the way with surprising strength for one so small. She took Polly's hand and looked up at her seriously.

'You love my Gianni?'

Polly nodded.

'For ever and ever?'

Polly nodded again.

Then Carla wrapped her chubby little arms around her future daughter-in-law and her head only did come as high as Polly's breasts. 'So,' she said, 'I give him to you.'

'Mamma!' Johnny rolled his eyes.

'But first I want to tell you about him. Gianni, go away. Go to the store and fetch us some pastries for tea.'

To Polly's amazement he went without a word.

'Gianni is not like his father,' she explained in the privacy of her kitchen, 'my Mauro, for him, the shop, selling ice-cream, it was enough. All day he sell *gelati* then he come upstairs and I cook pasta for him and he is content. Gianni is different. I think I knew when he was in here – she patted her shapeless black dress in the region of her stomach – 'in my womb. Our life is not enough for him. He is Italian but he is also English. He wants the excitement of London. I knew he would marry English girl.'

'Was Edith English?'

'Edith is not important.'

Polly was shocked. 'But she's the mother of his child.'

'Now you will be the mother and you will have bambinos of your own.'

'But this daughter, your granddaughter, lives with Edith.'

Suddenly the tiny woman exploded. 'Edith! Edith. All I hear is Edith. She was wrong for my Gianni. She take too much from him.

She demand this, she demand that. Edith is no mother for his children. She's just a child herself. He need someone stronger. Someone like you. Edith couldn't keep up with him.' She clutched Polly's wrist. 'Don't let him get away. Don't hold him back like Edith did. Let him go fast and keep up with him.'

As she came down the aisle on Johnny's arm Carla's words haunted her. What did she mean – keep up with him? Maybe she should have listened to Joan Brock, who had been totally against the marriage.

'He hasn't a bean as far as I can make out. No one who's anyone has heard of him. He's not even particularly attractive. I just don't know what you see in him, darling. And why you have to get married two days before Paris fashion week starts, I just don't know. It's hugely inconvenient but I suppose I'll have to come otherwise you'll never speak to me again.'

Polly had refrained from pointing out that she never spoke to Joan anyway because Joan was far too busy playing at *Vogue* or wherever it was. She also omitted to mention that Johnny claimed to be allergic to Joan. 'She's a midget, she's got bad breath, she's a snob and she's seriously unintelligent. How you two ever became friends is a mystery.'

Why was all this going through her mind on her wedding day? Polly smiled in what she hoped was a suitably radiant fashion at the rows of guests and family on her side of the church – there was Joan Brock in the row behind her parents decked out in a little number she had undoubtedly swiped from the fashion cupboard at whatever magazine currently employed her – and the pathetic gathering of film people scattered abouts the pews on the other side. Surreptitiously Polly moved a little faster beside her husband. If only Luana had come then he would have had a family on his side of the church instead of just a little old lady standing there crossing herself.

Polly's one meeting with Luana had been a near disaster. At least as far as she was concerned; Johnny seemed to think everything had gone fine.

Polly had decided she wanted to meet her future stepdaughter on her own territory. Armed with Carla's recipes, she spent an entire day preparing a veritable Italian feast. Johnny ushered in Luana a little after 7.30, gave Polly a quick hug, thrust a bottle of Chianti into her arms and said proudly:

'Polly, this is my daughter.'

From then on he was utterly useless. He slumped in an armchair and turned on the television.

'Hello Luana. Come in.' Polly winced at how stilted she sounded in her embarrassment.

'Do you actually live here?' was Luana's opening gambit as she surveyed Polly's studio flat. Polly looked around in surprise. She'd given the place a thorough cleaning. Her futon was rolled up neatly. A vase of fresh flowers dominated the low Japanese table beside it. Impressive-looking books were stacked in piles. The floorboards were polished. The cushions were plumped on the sofa and on the two armchairs either side of it. All the usual debris on the trestle table she used as a desk had beeen cleared away. A fire was burning in her little Victorian grate and the octagonal Italian dining table was laid for three with the tomato and mozzarella salad already in place. Maybe it was a little too Habitat for some people's taste, but it was warm and welcoming.

Wasn't it?

'I certainly do. Why wouldn't I?'

Luana just shrugged. It was a nervous tic, Polly realised after a while, something Luana did when she didn't have an answer, couldn't care less. She was a skeletal creature, stick thin with olive skin, Italian-looking like her father but her face had a precociously elegant bone structure which made Polly think immediately that her mother must be something of a beauty. Bones like that didn't come from Johnny. She was nervy, forever fiddling with her fingers. In a few years' time those fingers would be occupied with cigarettes. Maybe they already were when her father wasn't around. How old was Luana? Polly realised Johnny had never said. She looked about twelve but she must be older.

'Are you hungry?' Polly asked her. Luana certainly needed fattening up. She shrugged predictably. Polly had a sudden panic that she might be anorexic.

'What's for dinner?' asked Johnny, barely looking up from the television.

'Tomato, basil and mozzarella salad and lasagne.'

'Where'd you get the mozzarella and the lasagne?' asked Johnny.

'Camisa,' said Polly, omitting to add that she had spent half her salary on the meal at Camisa as well as half the day in the kitchen.

'Of course. So, my little peachy girl, Polly went to Camisa for you. Maybe she even went across the street and got some of Grandpa's ice-cream too?'

Polly looked stricken. And she noticed Luana glared at the 'little peachy girl'.

'Well, if she did she can keep it because we bought some for her . . . Give her the ice-cream, Luana, there's a good girl.'

Luana handed Polly a plastic bag, scowling. Polly didn't blame her. Johnny treated her as if she was still about six.

'Come and sit down and have your salad, Luana. Are you still at school?'

Luana nodded.

'Exams this year?' Did they still have 'O' levels? Polly couldn't remember.

'Next.'

'Do you like school?'

Luana looked at her as if she was mad. Which I am, thought Polly, I used to hate it when people asked me these kinds of questions when I was a kid. But what kind of conversation should she make with Luana? She hadn't a clue. She tried a different tack.

'I'm an agent.'

Luana brightened visibly.

'Who do you look after?'

'Well, I'm just starting but we represent Lucy Richards.'

'What's she been in?'

'Nothing. She's a writer.'

'So you don't look after actors or rock stars or any famous people?'

'Nothing like that, no.'

Luana lapsed back into silence. She barely touched her lasagne.

Johnny watched *Match of the Day* with a plate on his knee, which Polly thought didn't set a very good example but she didn't say anything.

'Good food,' he said vaguely with his eyes fixed on the screen, 'no, no more, thanks. I'll have some of my ice-cream.'

Polly carried the lasagne into her tiny kitchen and felt the tears pricking. She'd worked so hard to make the food a success. She'd thrown away her first attempt and spent half the afternoon on the second. Johnny and Luana had only eaten a quarter of it between them. Polly herself had been too nervous to swallow a thing and now it looked like she'd be living off it for days.

'Polly's crying.' Luana was standing in the doorway watching her.

'Crying again!' Johnny came in and put his arm around her. 'How about some coffee?'

Johnny made desultory conversation while he drank his coffee. Luana sat looking miserable. At one point her eye fixed on Polly's nails which were an unfortunate bright pink, a disastrous experiment with a new varnish that Polly had forgotten to remove.

'My mum uses that colour,' Luana informed her.

'Does she?'

'I think it's really disgusting.'

'Tell you the truth, I do too,' confessed Polly.

Once again Luana looked at her as if she was mad. If she didn't like it, why was she wearing it?

Why indeed, thought Polly.

'Come on, little one,' Johnny stood up. 'Time to go home. Say thank you to Polly, there's a good girl.'

'Don't keep saying that to her,' Polly turned on him without thinking, 'she's not a little kid.'

Luana didn't say thank you but she did reward Polly with a look of real respect and the first smile of the evening. Her big brown eyes lit up like shiny buttons. She's beautiful, thought Polly suddenly, and resisted the urge to grab hold of the wiry black hair and plant a kiss on Luana's forehead.

'Come and see me again soon,' she called down the stairs after them, wondering if she dared ask Luana to be a bridesmaid.

38

Two days later Johnny called and said Edith had decided to go and live in Cornwall and take Luana with her.

For their honeymoon they went to Tuscany, to a farmhouse buried in the countryside outside Siena. It was built into the slope of a hill on several levels so that you could walk out of the bedroom on to the hillside and then down the slope and enter the kitchen or the living room below. It had belonged to Johnny's aunt, as had his London house.

'My father's little sister,' he explained, 'she married a rich man. A rich English businessman who wanted to spend his holidays in Tuscany so they bought this house. My father thought it was crazy. "You're from Napoli," he used to tell his sister, "why do you buy a house in the north?" He hated that she married an Englishman. He refused ever to go to her house – my house now – in Notting Hill. She couldn't have children so she left it to me. My father would've been furious to see me living there. Fortunately he died before she did.'

'And this house is yours too?' Polly envisaged family holidays in the future, imagined herself extending gracious invitations: 'What are your plans for the summer? Johnny and I will be in Tuscany as usual. How about coming down for a week or two? Bring the children . . .'

'No, it isn't mine,' said Johnny.

'Whose is it, then?'

'My aunt's rich English husband's.'

'But he's dead, isn't he?'

'Yeah.'

'So who did he leave it to?'

'Dunno.'

'What do you mean, you don't know? How did you get hold of it? How did we get in?'

'I've always had a key.'

'So we're here illegally? Someone – the rightful owner – might walk in at any moment?'

'Nobody knows we're here, if that's what you mean, except for

39

the old woman in the village who looks after it and she won't say anything. I hope.'

Polly felt a lurch in the pit of her stomach. There it was again, the question she kept asking herself: what had she done? Who was this man she'd married?

They stayed in bed for four days and when they got up to pee or to fetch food from the kitchen, he insisted she remain naked. It was as if there was a magnet floating between them at all times. Some part of their bodies was always touching. In the kitchen it took them an hour to make a salad as they constantly interrupted each other with their fondling and kissing. When she went outside to search, naked, for herbs he pressed himself to her until she sank to the earth and pulled him into her, squashing the basil plants beneath them. He would not let her bathe that night because she smelt of basil and he lay alongside her, sniffing her skin.

'There's some lavender bushes round the other side of the house . . .' Polly suggested.

'Tomorrow, maybe.'

On the fifth night he took her to dinner in Siena. They sat outside at one of the restaurants in the Piazza del Campo and Johnny told her about the violent horse race that was run in July called the Palio when the square was packed to capacity. Polly didn't much like the sound of it and she was pleased that they had come at a time when the square was relatively empty and she could gaze at the tall clock tower. But they couldn't finish their meal. Johnny's hands were stroking her shoulders, slipping down inside her top while she tried to eat her risotto.

'Come on, eat up, we'd better leave before I get arrested.'

She lay across the gear shift with her head in his lap as he drove home in the rented car. They left the car doors open in their urgent need to get to the bedroom.

'Lavender . . .' murmured Polly, 'we forgot.'

'Don't talk!' he silenced her and she smiled in the darkness. However much he might joke and tease her out of bed, for Johnny lovemaking was a serious business. It almost frightened her how much he seemed to immerse himself in the glorification of her body. If there was any talking it was his questions as to what she

40

liked – This? Here? Higher? Lower? Only at the very last moment did he allow himself to lose control and then again she found the intensity of his release terrifying as well as exhilarating.

Afterwards he liked to talk.

I'm going to call my production company Polly Productions. You're going to bring me luck, Pol, I know it. I'm going to finally get something off the ground. Lord knows, I've been trying for long enough but from now on it's going to be different.' Once he started there was no stopping him. By day seven of their honeymoon he was the saviour of the British film industry. Polly was content to lie beside him in the darkness and listen to his excitement. 'I'm going to make want-to-see pictures. Word-of-mouth pictures. The sort of pictures the press will latch on to early, create a buzz, and everyone will have to go and see them to find out what all the fuss is about. They'll be critical successes too but totally accessible. I'm going to develop scripts every major studio in Hollywood is going to want to make.'

'Where are you going to find them?' asked Polly, ever practical.

'Well, isn't it obvious?' He gathered her up in his arms and held her tight. 'That's where you come in. You'll quit that job you have and come and read scripts for me. You'll go out looking for properties, see the publishers, see the agents, working alongside me at Polly Productions.'

Polly couldn't help giggling.

'You can*not* call it Polly Productions. You just can't. It's silly.'

'Well, what do you suggest then?'

'You really want to call it after me?'

'I really do.' He gave her a squeeze.

'Well since I have to face up to the fact that I'm now Polly de Soto and no longer Polly Atwell, why don't you call it PDS Productions. It sounds more heavyweight somehow.'

'You know you're right. PDS. I like it. PDS. Looking forward to your new job as story editor at PDS?'

'Actually, no.'

She felt him tense.

'You don't want to work for me?' She couldn't make out the hurt little boy look in the darkness but she knew it was there.

41

'The thing is, Johnny – and I was going to discuss it with you, of course, but you have to admit we've sort of had other things on our minds – I've been offered a promotion at Patrick Fisher & Dunbar. They're willing to make me a kind of baby agent, a few minor clients of my own to look after, no one important but it's a start.'

'Baby agent. Oh, well if that's what you want.'

'Johnny, don't be like that. It's an opening for me. I'll learn about the agency business.'

He was silent for a while.

'Johnny?'

'OK, Pol. I think you should take it. They're big, you'll have access to a lot of material at an early stage. That could be very useful to me.'

'Of course, and I could always read stuff for you on the side,' said Polly, bending over backwards to please him as usual in her relief. Why did she always do this? She'd all but accepted the job before the wedding but somehow only Johnny's approval would make it a reality.

'I'm going to make it big, Pol, and I want you there with me. Don't you ever forget that. When I go up for my Oscar I want you by my side.'

'Johnny, what about Edith? Did she help you in your work?'

He didn't answer, just shifted over on to his side, away from her.

'Johnny?'

He rolled back and pinned her down.

'Just don't ask me about Edith, OK? There's only three things you need to know about her. One: I'm no longer with her, I'm married to you. She's the past, you're the present. Two: she's a very sad lady but it's nothing to do with you so stay out of it. Three: any mention of her name is always going to put me in a very bad mood, so don't say I didn't warn you.'

'But if we're going to see Luana won't I have to speak to her?'

'What have I just said? Drop it, Polly. If anyone has to speak to her about Luana, I will. I'm her father. End of story.'

He fell into a deep sleep after he had made love to her again but Polly lay awake. Although he was always saying what a wonderful father he was going to be, so far there had been no mention of children during their honeymoon, no mention of that side of their future and she was beginning to realise why. What was the point of contemplating children with Johnny when she was going to have her work cut out dealing with the fact that, despite his determination and his ambition, Johnny was in many ways still a kid himself.

To her immense surprise Polly found herself adapting to life as Mrs Johnny de Soto with ease once they arrived back in London. Having never had to cope with more than a studio apartment she was suddenly confronted with the running of a house. True, it was not exactly palatial but barely a week went by when Polly did not stop to give thanks to Johnny's childless aunt for leaving him a place to live. What they would have done otherwise she dreaded to think. Her salary at the literay agency was not exactly impressive and although Johnny appeared to have a little money of his own (which was just as well since he didn't seem to be earning any) Polly had never quite discovered where it came from. Her father had quizzed her on the subject before her wedding and while she had managed to fob him off with vague explanations, Polly was still a little uneasy. Meanwhile, another thing she was grateful for was the existence of a cleaner – Donnatella, an Italian who spoke no English supplied by Johnny's mother – since there were four bedrooms, two bathrooms, a living room and a dining room running the full length of the ground floor, connected by dividing doors, and a large kitchen. The vast master bedroom on the first floor ran from the front of the house to the back above the living room/dining room. A guest bedroom lay across the landing and Polly turned this into a little sitting room she and Johnny used in the evening for TV suppers.

Johnny, true to his word, started PDS Productions. What Polly hadn't bargained for was the fact that he would start it at their dining-room table. His first step was to kill the script for *The End*. Someone had apparently told him it sounded too like another film. Polly wondered sadly about the fate of the struggling scriptwriter in the Chelsea basement who presumably now wouldn't even get his peanuts.

She needn't have worried. In the ensuing months the young man, a willowy youth by the name of Lawrence Bedford, was forever in their dining room. Polly would arrive home from work to find the ground floor a hive of activity. PDS was up and running and Polly was beginning to see why. It wasn't only her Uncle Matthew who found Johnny 'an engaging fellow'. He clearly had no trouble getting people's attention. No end of young writers and directors appeared to want to work with him (despite the fact that he had not yet produced a film), often after what appeared to be their first meeting with him. Polly didn't know any of them but she was content to rush in and out of the kitchen with plates of sandwiches and beer and then sit quietly in a corner while Johnny and his team talked 'development'.

They tried having a few of the young men from Norfolk and Polly's unmarried girlfriends (excpet for Joan, whom Johnny had banned from his house) over for dinner but Johnny never opened his mouth so they didn't repeat the exercise. The place was filled with Johnny's movie crowd daily and Polly didn't get much of a chance to open her mouth but somehow she didn't mind. She felt needed even if no one spoke to her. It didn't seem to matter, since she had the progress she was making at Patrick Fisher & Dunbar to be proud of. Very soon now she would be starting to look out for some authors of her own to represent at the agency.

One night Polly went home around 6.30 to find the living room and the dining room deserted for the first time since she had moved in. She started upstairs to have a bath but stopped on the landing when she heard voices. Polly was angry. She had created what they called 'the little sitting room' for her and Johnny to use in the evenings, a private cosy retreat for just the two of them. She was outraged that Johnny should take someone in there. She was about to stride into the room but she stopped on the threshold when she heard Lawrence Bedford say:

'It's a natural, Johnny. Women are obsessed with finding Mr Right. Subconsciously they're looking for him everywhere in all areas of their lives. So here's this guy and he's a playboy, glamorous as hell, right? They all fall for him, rich women, poor women alike. But the reality is he's *Mr Wrong*! He's a serial killer. Not always women, but mostly. Then there's this detective. He knows Mr Wrong is his guy. At least, he suspects it but he can't prove it. So he sets a woman cop to trap him and this is a woman cop he loves, right? But there's this one big problem.'

'What's that?' asked Polly, coming into the room and seeing Lawrence by the fireplace. 'Hi Lawrence, haven't seen you in a while. How are you?'

'I'm fine, Polly. How about you? I've just had this great idea for a picture so of course I had to come right over and tell Johnny about it.' He spilled some of his drink and dabbed vaguely at himself. Polly smiled. Once he stopped pitching his idea Lawrence reverted to his usual awkward gangly self.

'Of course you did. Now, you've got Mr Wrong the serial killer and the detective who puts his girlfriend, the woman he loves, on the case to snare him. You were about to tell us the problem.'

'She's not his girlfriend. At least not yet,' corrected Lawrence. 'He wants her to be but he hasn't done anything about it yet.'

'Get on with it, Lawrence,' growled Johnny, who was slouched in front of the television with the sound turned down. 'What's the problem? It's clearly the hook.'

'She – the cop – falls for Mr Wrong too.'

'So what happens?' demanded Polly and Johnny almost in unison.

'Well, I suppose the detective saves her just in time and right at the last minute she realises that he is the man she really loves. He's Mr Right,' Lawrence finished lamely.

Johnny mimed playing a violin. 'Television!' was all he said.

'Johnny, it's not, it's wonderful. Think about it: romance,

murder, woman in jeopardy, cop hero . . .' Polly clapped her hands in excitement. She stared admiringly at Lawrence. He was absolutely correct about women looking for Mr Right. Her girlfriends – with the exception of Joan – never stopped telling her how lucky she was to have found Johnny. Sometimes she thought about what she would have done if he hadn't come along when he did. It bothered her that she always arrived at the same conclusion: she'd be on her own. Mr Right had never been part of her plan for her future. Dream heroes existed in books and movies just like the one Lawrence had just described. She might have married eventually, but Polly had grown up thinking that marriage was something that would happen to other women, not to her. How wrong she had been. She had found Mr Right right away, ha ha!

'What are you smirking at?' asked Johnny.

She looked at him sitting there with a morose look on his face.

'I'm not interested,' he snapped. 'TV cop movies, that's all it is. Sorry, Lawrence, nice try and all that. Look, let me fill your glass. There is something I want to talk to you about while you're here. Polly, what's for supper? Enough for Lawrence?'

'Always,' smiled Polly, feeling sorry for Lawrence, 'and you're wrong about his idea.'

'Wrong about Mr Wrong. Oh Yeah? Well, wait till you hear about my idea.' Johnny was up on his feet, slapping Lawrence on the back, kissing Polly on the nose. 'Wait till you hear about my idea, pretty Pol.'

Polly served the casserole into the big wide soup plates and handed them round the table. She gave Lawrence an extra large helping because she thought he looked like he needed building up. Johnny was now in fine form, shovelling his meal into his mouth and wagging his finger at them.

'Wait till you hear,' he kept saying, 'I'll tell you over dessert. You'll love it. Love it.'

Polly delved in the freezer for some ice-cream. She hadn't planned on pudding but since Johnny clearly wasn't about to divulge his great idea until she produced one, she had to come up with something.

'So here it is: werewolves and bikers.' Johnny waved his napkin in the air triumphantly. They stared at him with blank faces. 'Kid came to see me this afternoon with a proposal,' he continued. 'He wants to direct it and he's looking for someone to package it for him.'

'Werewolves and bikers,' repeated Lawrence dumbly.

'That's it. You write it. I develop it. The kid directs. Youth market. Up and coming.'

'Johnny, could you maybe tell us a little more?' Polly gave him another scoop of ice-cream to encourage him.

'Where'd you get this stuff, Pol?'

'Sainsbury's.'

'Don't touch it, Lawrence. It's poison. My old man makes ice-cream for thirty years and she has to go to Sainsbury's.'

'Johnny . . .' Polly warned.

'It's dead simple. There's this biker and he's part of a gang and he's trying to date a girl who is sort of dating a guy from another rival gang but he has this problem . . .'

'Him too . .'

'Every time his bike reaches a certain speed he turns into a werewolf so when he finally makes it with the chick and she's riding away with him, pursued by the other gang, he can only go so far –'

'Johnny, you can't be serious?' Polly's mouth had dropped open. She had never heard anything so stupid.

'I'm perfectly serious. It's *The Wild One* meets *West Side Story* crossed with Michael Jackson's *Thriller*. The kids'll love it.'

'It's pure popcorn,' argued Polly. 'Lawrence's idea had such a ring of truth to it. Women all over the world will identify with it. Have you any idea how many women fall for disastrous men? To have him be a serial killer makes it perfect. You have to see that.'

'Polly, you're over-reacting in a typically emotionally feminine way. You have to look ahead. "The Wild Wolf" – or maybe we should call it "The Wolf One", what do you think? – incorporates everything the kids go for these days. We'll add a strong rock soundtrack. It's a natural. The video sale will be huge. I tried it out on Luana, she thought it sounded great.'

'When did you see Luana? You never told me you'd seen her.' Polly was quite agitated. For some reason Johnny kept quiet about his meetings with his daughter. She only came to London sporadically and he never brought her to the house. Polly tortured herself with the thought that whenever he saw Luana, he also saw the mysterious Edith.

'I talked to her in Cornwall, for God's sake. On the phone, OK? I only heard about this project today. Now, Lawrence, how about it? Shall I give you the treatment, see what you think? I'd love you to write it.'

Neither of them noticed Lawrence quietly getting to his feet, pushing his chair into place and creeping out of the dining room. He paused at the entrance to the hall.

'If it's OK, I think I'll be on my way. Great meal, Polly. Thanks. See you.'

And he was gone.

Polly called him the next day.

'Lawrence, I don't know what to say. Johnny seems to have taken leave of his senses. There's only one suggestion I can make and it's the only area where I might be able to be of help. Have you ever thought of writing fiction? I can't get 'Mr Wrong' out of my mind. It's such a great story. Why don't you write it as a novel first?'

Polly was very aware that since the wedding they had seen very little of Carla de Soto, Johnny's mother. Johnny didn't seem to care.

'Don't worry about her Pol. She has a life, believe me. Loads of little ladies just like her, all dressed in black, all banging on about Italia, endless widows' get-togethers in tiny kitchens all over Soho. If she wanted to come over here we'd know about it. She's probably just waiting for you to produce bambinos and then we'll never see the back of her.'

'What about . . . ?'

'All in good time, all in good time. I can't think about having children while I'm in the middle of getting PDS Productions off the ground, now can I?'

And I'm not ready to have a baby until I've become a fully-fledged agent, thought Polly, but that wouldn't come into Johnny's equation.

'Actually I was going to say what about if I ask her if I can go over and see her in Soho?'

'You can ask. Why you'd want to is beyond me, but go ahead, ask, go and learn how to be a little old Italian widow. After all, you'll be one yourself one day.'

But Carla – when Polly went to see her – had other ideas. She welcomed Polly into her apartment on the top two floors of the house in Old Compton Street above the old De Soto ice-cream shop which had now been expanded into a delicatessen. Polly was fascinated by the evidence of real style in the choice of décor. Heavy old Tuscan farmhouse furniture blended in with lighter Conran pieces and here and there she spotted some beautiful antiques. Carla served lunch in the kitchen, and the round table was laid with crisp white linen and colourful hand-painted pottery. Carla produced a simple but delicious lunch of *prosciutto crudo* and thin slices of *soprassata* sausage followed by pasta with her own *sugo di pomodoro*, a tomato sauce the recipe for which she wrote down for Polly.

'I am so pleased you came to see me.' Polly noticed the old lady's English was much better when she was alone, without her son to ridicule her. She also noticed how elegant Carla was. She might be small and dumpy and dressed in black but when Polly looked closely she realised it wasn't just any old black dress but something with a solid Italian label and her white hair was soft and silky and gathered up in an expert chignon. She wore tiny pearl earrings and her make-up was immaculate. On a visit to the bathroom Polly saw the little white Clarins jars and realised her mother-in-law was a woman who took care of herself.

'I always knew Johnny would marry a proper English girl.'

'Were you secretly hoping he would marry a nice Italian Catholic girl?'

'His father, yes. Me, no. There was no point in hoping. Johnny was not Italian. I told you this when we first met. You are an English couple, an unusual English couple maybe, but you and he are not Italian. Johnny has Italian blood. He plays at being Italian when it suits him. You will see. But he is not like his father.'

'Tell me about his father. I'm sorry I never knew him.'

Carla uncrossed her tiny feet. Polly noticed a pair of smart shoes in soft Italian leather. Carla caught her glance and laughed.

'Yes, I buy nice things. I am a rich woman. My Mauro was very successful even if it was in a boring way. At least, I found it boring. Maybe you don't know De Soto ice-cream like you know Walls or Häagen-Dazs but you go into an Italian restaurant and they give you ice-cream and nine times out of ten it will be my Mauro's. Italians know it. Italian delicatessens, everywhere – here, Manchester, Glasgow. Johnny's cousin took over the business because Johnny was not interested. He only want to make films. But he is happy to live off his share in the company. But you asked about his father. He was successful in his own way but he was also very sad. In the beginning he thought he come to England for a very short time to help his older brother with the business. But his older brother die and we have to stay here.' Carla had begun to mix her tenses, a sign, Polly realised, that she was uncomfortable. That meant her own son must make this proud little woman uncomfortable. Carla continued. 'My husband always missed Italy. He always looked forward to the day he would go back. He was always waiting for Johnny to take over his business then he could leave London.'

Polly was horrified. 'You mean he waited in vain? Surely it must have been obvious that Johnny wanted to do something else. Why didn't his father go back?'

'There was no one to take over. Johnny's cousin was still in Italy, still too young. I knew how Johnny was but his father didn't understand. His father was a quiet man with no ambition beyond carrying out family business. Sadly he carried it out until he die. But Johnny is different. Johnny want more. Johnny want the world.' She smiled at Polly.

'Johnny is like me. I love my Mauro but in many ways for me he was too slow. Always sitting here wanting to go back to Italy. Never wanting to go forward, maybe to America. Everyone wonder why, now Mauro is dead, I don't go back but I love it here in London. I have lots of friends. Johnny thinks I just sit and have coffee with other Italian widows but he's wrong. I have other friends, but don't tell him. It's our secret – between women.' And the old lady actually winked. Can she be taking such good care of herself, Polly wondered, because she's on the lookout for Mr Right Number 2? 'Here, have some *biscotti*. I make espresso. So I tell you, Polly, Johnny is a bit crazy, I know, but he is not slow like his father, he is fast, he's ambitious and he always hope for the best.'

'He's an optimist.' Just as well, thought Polly wryly. He hasn't exactly got very far. He might as well have hope to keep him going, not to mention a little family money.

'Just like me,' Carla was becoming positively giggly now, 'I have one dream and I know it will come true. I want to stand up there beside Johnny when he receive his Oscar.'

'You and me both,' said Polly. 'Will there be room for me on his other side?'

'Only if you keep up with him.' The smile on Carla's face evaporated. 'It will take the two of you. Johnny cannot do it on his own. I told you, there is a little money for him from the business but soon he is going to have to provide for himself.'

'Does he realise this?'

'You know Johnny. I tell him but he only listens to what he wants to hear so I mean it, Polly, everything will be fine for you both but only if you look after him and keep up with him. Not like Edith.'

Polly pounced. 'Tell me about Edith. What is she like?'

But it was no good.

'Johnny call me when he know you are coming to see me. He ask me not to talk about Edith. She in his history now.'

Poor Carla looked very uncomfortable indeed.

I might have known, thought Polly, and wondered just how long it would be before Johnny's family income ran out. Would she find herself supporting them both all on her own?

Johnny went into action. He raised $50,000 development money for *The Wolf One*, split between ten people investing $5,000 each. The deal was that they would get 10 per cent of the net profits of the film split between them.

He was never off the phone. At night while Polly was trying to get to sleep beside him he would talk to potential investors way into the small hours. If this was how he went about getting the relatively small development money, Polly dreaded to think what it would be like when he set about raising the production money.

He found another writer and commissioned a first-draft screenplay. When it was finished he showed it to Cruise, the lead singer with Cruise Missile. Cruise's real name was Billy Powers. He was a degenerate Liverpool heavy metal star with a notorious cocaine habit. Cruise had his girlfriend, Belle – who was really Lady Annabel Creightmore, educated at St Paul's with a first in English from Girton, and Cruise's supplier – read the script to him and then explained it to him scene by scene. When he had finally grasped the plot he called his manager and conveyed his desire to star in it. No one had ever approached him to be in a film before for the simple reason that it was widely believed that he had little brain power left, assuming he had had a brain in the first place. To play the Wolf One, he didn't need one, just the ability to ride a motorbike – preferably a

Harley Davidson Fat Boy, something for which, luckily, he had a remarkable gift.

After a few well-placed phone calls by Johnny, the press went to work.

CRUISE TO STAR IN MAJOR MOTION PICTURE

Heavy Metal idol Cruise of Cruise Missile says he won't need stunt man for his role as the Wolf One. The 22-year-old Liverpool star says he will perform his own stunts for the picture. 'I'm going to give them music, I'm going to give them action,' promises Cruise.

Polly sat at her desk at Patrick Fisher & Dunbar and waded through the tabloids, telling herself that if this was what Johnny wanted then it was what she wanted too. But then the phone rang and the switchboard informed her that a very disturbed Rebecca Price was on the line and Polly knew the tabloid stories were only just the beginning of what looked like turning out to be one of those days.

Patrick Dunbar was away in America. Rebecca Price was one of his biggest clients. Up to now she had written megasellers, long detailed historical sagas set in Cornwall. They had each sold well over half a million copies in paperback. The problem, if it could be viewed as such, was that Rebecca Price had tired of writing this kind of book and was demanding to be taken more seriously. Polly felt she had every right. Although she had been categorised as a historical writer, Rebecca Price's prose was definitely a cut above that of other writers in the same genre. Her publishers, however, were decidedly nervous. Change terrified them as it did many large publishing houses led by their marketing departments. Marketing and sales directors thought retrospectively. The idea of a bestselling author delivering something new and different was enough to send them into instant panic. When they told the world that their flagship title on the Spring list would be 'the new Rebecca Price' what they really meant was, 'Here's more of the same, everyone knows what they're getting. Go out and flog it like you did the last one. Piece of cake!' The notion that they might have to use their non-existent creative powers and market Rebecca as a new kind of author altogether was just not on.

'The old bag's going through the menopause, must be,' Rebecca's publisher had told Patrick before he left for New York. 'Maybe we'll just have to bite the bullet and accept we won't have a new Rebecca Price next year and wait until her wretched hormones calm down.'

Polly was outraged. Rebecca Price was forty-nine years old and it was possible that she was in the throes of the menopause but to make it an excuse for her perfectly rational decision to write a different type of novel was ludicrous.

Still, it wouldn't do to upset either Rebecca or her publisher and with five hours to go before she could call Patrick in New York for guidance, Polly took Rebecca's call with apprehension.

'Rebecca?'

'Polly hello how are you is Patrick there?' Despite her proficiency with the written word, Rebecca Price invariably ran all her spoken sentences into one.

'No, I'm sorry, he's not. He left for New York yesterday. He won't be back for two or three weeks.'

'Of course I'd forgotten, Aahhh . . .' Rebecca's sigh blew down the line in desperation, 'have we had a reaction yet do you know Polly?'

Polly knew she ought to let it wait until Patrick came back, that he should be the one to break the news to Rebecca that her publishers were holding out for 'more of the same', yet she knew that Patrick would never tell Rebecca the whole story and Polly felt that Rebecca deserved to hear it. And then, as she was trying to think how to phrase it, Rebecca beat her to it.

'They want another *Dark Shores of Tregarra* or another *Penhaligon*, don't they?' she said, referring to two of her earlier successes. 'Don't they understand that I want to break out of that type of thing? I want people to realise that I have something to say about the world we live in now rather than Cornwall in the last century. I want to be reviewed.'

'It might mean less money,' Polly warned.

'I'm rolling in it. It wouldn't matter a damn.'

'And it might mean changing publishers.'

'Well for goodness sake of course it will if all they want is more of

56

the same. I'll have to find someone who's prepared to gamble with the new. Do you think it will be hard Polly?'

'Not in the slightest. Rebecca, have you any idea how many requests a year we receive from publishers asking if there's a chance you'll move? Now, I shall have to give them one last chance to change their minds about their attitude to your new plans and if they still say no I think you should come up to London for lunch with Patrick so we can draw up a list of publishers to whom we can submit the new outline.'

'Well you must be there for lunch too Polly.'

'Yes, well, maybe.' Polly was suddenly beginning to wonder what Patrick would make of her suggestion. Maybe he would have been able to talk Rebecca into yet another Cornish saga and a hefty advance to go with it. But once again Rebecca Price second-guessed her.

'I shall want you to be at the lunch Polly because I trust you and I want you to handle me from now on. I'll let you into a secret. I know Patrick would have tried to make me write another saga and I'll tell you something – if he had I'd have left Fisher & Dunbar in spite of all they've done for me. You say there are publishers after me. Well has it ever occurred to dear Patrick bless his balding head that there are plenty of other agents after me too? But I'll stay put Polly on one condition. You take care of me from now on.'

'But I'm only just starting to take on clients of my own. I've been Patrick's assistant up till very recently,' blurted Polly.

'Rubbish. He ought to be yours. Bye dear.'

Polly sailed home that night on the top of a 31 bus, desperate to tell Johnny her news. Rebecca Price was hers. She'd saved the day for Patrick Fisher & Dunbar. She was about to become a fully-fledged agent. She walked up Westbourne Park Road, swinging her book bag in her excitement, but when she finally arrived home and turned the key in the front door she was greeted by a heavy silence in the hall. There wasn't even a light on downstairs. She found a note propped up against the toaster in the kitchen.

Darling Pol,
Tried to call you this morning but you were on a long call to Rebecca someone and they said you couldn't be disturbed, not

even for me! Have had to go to Los Angeles. V. last minute. Chance of raising money for Wolf One. Staying at Chateau Marmont on Sunset. Will call on arrival. Don't be lonesome.

All my love. J.

Polly climbed into bed at nine o'clock and tried to watch television. Extraordinary though it seemed to her this was the first time in their marriage that she had been separated from Johnny and the worst thing was that she had had no time to prepare herself for it. She was amazed at how quickly her euphoria over Rebecca Price evaporated when there was no Johnny waiting for her to share it with. She could imagine the conversation. He would be lying in the bath, she would be crouched on the floor beside him, reaching out to pass him his whisky, the soap, the ashtray, whatever he wanted.

'So who is this Rebecca Price woman?'

'Johnny, you must have heard of her. She's been a number one bestseller for years. Don't you remember *Penhaligon*?'

'The LWT series? A thirteen parter, three or four years back? It was huge.'

'Yes, they did make a TV series of it. Rebecca hated it.'

'You should get her to do something contemporary. No call for costume drama. Too expensive. No one could afford the budget. I'd never get it set up.'

'Johnny, you haven't been listening. That's exactly what she's going to do and I'm going to be her agent . . .'

'Will you get the commission? Personally?'

'Well, no . . .'

'Make sure they give you a whopping great rise and show me an outline as soon as you've got a first draft.'

No 'Well done, Pol' or 'I'm so pleased for you, Pol!' but even so she missed him. She could almost hear her mother's voice: 'We mustn't boast about our achievements, Polly. We must let other people congratulate us and even then we must pretend it's nothing.' The trouble was, Polly had always thought to herself, if you didn't tell people what you'd achieved, how on earth could they congratulate you? And in the end no one ever seemed to congratulate her anyway. Looking back, the only thing her friends had ever congratulated her on was Johnny.

She wished he was with her now and arranged his pillows down the middle of the bed, hugging them to her as a poor substitute. He might view everything she did in terms of how it affected him but at least he was interested, at least he encouraged her. Keep up with him, his mother had said. Well, she would but in her own way. He'd be a successful producer and she'd be an equally successful literary agent right along with him.

It was only when she woke up the next morning that she realised Johnny hadn't rung her on arrival in LA as he'd promised.

Johnny was away for nearly a month during which time Polly received two or three telephone calls a week and in each one his mood was more euphoric than the last. To begin with, Polly was mystified.

'He says they've put him in a bungalow at the Chateau,' she told Patrick at the office, 'he sounds deliriously happy about it. A bungalow in a castle. What on earth is he on about?'

'He means exactly what he says, Polly. They're self-contained bungalows away from the hotel itself – which is called the Chateau Marmont – and they're right by the pool. Of course, he really ought to be at the Beverly Hills Hotel or the Beverly Wilshire if he wants them to take him seriously.' Patrick was rather proud of his knowledge of America, not that he'd ever been further than New York. Another part of the agency took care of the film deals.

'Why aren't you staying at the Beverly Wilshire or the Beverly Hills Hotel?' Polly couldn't resist asking after getting an earful of Johnny's lunch at the MGM commissary with Jane Fonda.

'Much cooler at the Chateau, more of a funky crowd around here, more into *The Wolf One*, saw Leonard Cohen at the pool yesterday . . .'

'I had no idea he was still with us.'

'Oh he is, Pol, he certainly is. He thinks Cruise is really amazing.'

'Was she wearing a leotard?'

'Who? Oh, Jane. Don't be silly, Pol, it was lunchtime but it is incredible, she looks as young as you.'

'Thanks,' said Polly drily.

By the second week he was into the lifestyle.

'It's all so outdoors, I can't believe it. Everyone's got two cars, at least four bedrooms, a garden, a maid, a pool – '

'And a psychiatrist, so I've heard,' said Polly.

'They call them analysts. They kind of become your friend. Everyone's so friendly and hospitable. I'm going to people's houses all the time, Pol. When does that happen to us in London?'

'Well, never, because you're always inviting them to ours.'

'Imagine it, Pol, when I'm really off and running. We'll move out here and have this great lifestyle.'

'It sounds like a great place for kids.'

'You're right. You're absolutely right! Luana would love it.'

'No, I meant our kids.'

'Yeah. 'Course. They'd love it too. Not trying to tell me you're pregnant, by any chance, Pol?'

'No.'

'Phew! Would have been very bad timing. I've thought it all out. We ought to do a movie then a baby, a movie then a baby. Soon as *The Wolf One*'s in the can we'll start a family. What do you say?'

What could she say?'

While Johnny was safely out of the way in California, Polly rang Joan and invited her to lunch one weekend.

'I'll cook us something sinful and delicious and we can kick off our shoes and have a good old gossip.'

But Joan would have none of it.

'Darling, you know I can't bear home cooking. Much too fattening. Let's doll ourselves up to the nines and go out and be seen. Tell you what, I'll do you a huge favour and come up to Notting Hill Gate then we can go 192 and you won't have to move an inch.

Polly understood the subtext. 192 Kensington Park Road was a fashionable media restaurant and Joan could bounce up and down from the table and go hopping all over the room, networking frantically. As usual Polly gave in.

Polly ordered a starter followed by risotto. Joan ordered a salad. Polly was wearing a long T-shirt and jeans. Joan was wearing a Sonia Rykiel jacket and a pair of baggy linen Italian trousers. Joan had a tan even though she hadn't been anywhere as far as Polly knew.

'Sunbeds! Polly, don't you use them? What do you do about looking pale in the winter months?'

'Nothing.'

'Doesn't Johnny complain?'

'He hasn't yet.'

'Does he ever see you starkers?'

'He's my husband. Of course he – '

'Oh, never mind. What's he doing in California anyway?'

'I'm not really sure. Seeing people about getting money for his film, I think.'

'Typical, Polly. You're so unclued up. And why aren't you out there with him, swanning around LA, getting a bit of sun while he's in meetings, doing the producer's wife number?'

'Well, he never asked me to go with him.'

'That's exactly what I mean, Polly. You're such a pushover. Why didn't you ask? In fact what you should have done was just announce you were going with him, got his secretary to book your flight and everything.'

'But he doesn't have a secretary. He works from home, from our dining-room table.'

'Talk about Mickey Mouse productions!'

'But in a way it's just as well I didn't go because I would have missed Rebecca Price.'

'Miss who?'

'Rebecca Price. She's a wonderful saga writer who wants to move up a notch . . .'

'Is she good looking? Who's she married to? Do they live in a beautiful home? Does she collect art? Whose clothes does she wear?'

'Oh, Rebecca's beautiful. She must be over fifty but she's still got this wonderful rosy skin. She's married to a retired vet and they live in this rambling old place on the Welsh coast with dogs and cats and sheep and ponies wandering all over the place. She collects brass rubbings, I think and she once confided to Patrick Fisher that she wears her husband's old clothes because they're the only ones she can get into these days.'

'Polly, what on earth made you think this woman might be the subject of a *Vogue* feature?'

'Oh, she'd be quite wrong for *Vogue*. She'd hate it. She's terribly shy in many ways.'

'Then why are we talking about her?'

'Because I'm going to be her agent. It's a wonderful break for me.'

'Rubbish! How do you think it's going to sound, Polly? People ask you what you do. You say I'm a literary agent. They ask who are your clients and you come out with this old bat who collects brass rubbings and lives in the back of beyond with a lot of smelly animals and wears her husband's clothes. Why can't you represent the new Martin Amis?'

'I'd have to find him first. It takes time but now I'm starting to take on my own clients I'll be on the lookout everywhere. I'm going to write to – '

'Darling, of course you are. I'll alert the media, as they say. Oh, there's Duncan. I must just go and say hello. Now he's a real agent. He looks after Hector O'Neill and we're doing a feature on him in the autumn.'

By the time Joan came back – rather quickly Polly noticed, Duncan-the-real-agent didn't seem to have much time to spare for her – Polly had been joined by a publishing editor who had been lunching at the next table. He stood up to let Joan sit down.

'Forgive the interruption but I couldn't help eavesdropping. When I heard that Polly here is to represent Rebecca Price I had to try and persuade her to give me first look at the new book. It's a real coup for you, Polly. Congratulations! Sorry, you are . . . ?'

'Oh, this is my friend Joan Brock. She works on *Vogue*. She's the features . . .'

'I'm features assistant,' said Joan quickly. Polly never read *Vogue* so she'd always spun her a line, told her she was features editor. But this bloke looked like he might check her out.

'But I expect she'll be features editor very soon,' said Polly cheerfully, totally unaware that for once she'd actually managed to put Joan down.

Johnny came back on a major high and walked through the door on a particularly hot July morning before Polly had left for work.

'We gotta get AC,' he said, dumping his bags in the hall, shrugging off his jacket and loosening his tie. He had stripped off his shirt before Polly had rushed downstairs and into his arms.

'What's that?' Polly had only ever heard of AC/DC, an expression she believed was used to describe someone who swung both ways sexually. What had Johnny got into while he had been away?

'Air conditioning,' he murmured into her ear before he bit it, 'everyone's got it in LA.'

'Did you really have lunch with Jane Fonda?' she asked as he started upstairs, unzipping his trousers as he went.

'You bet! Well, she was at the next table.' He sat down at the top of the stairs and grinned at her, holding out his hand. 'Come on, Pol, time for a quick one. Just to show you how much I've missed you.'

It was a very quick one. He came almost as soon as he entered her but Polly didn't mind. His excitement was infectious and she understood it because she was excited about something herself. Today was the day she was to have lunch with Patrick and Rebecca Price to talk about which publishers should be shown Rebecca's new book. Much to Polly's relief, Patrick had been wholly supportive of the way she had handled Rebecca.

'The most important thing is that she stays with the agency and from where I'm sitting it looks as if that's all down to you. You deserve her, Polly. She'll be your first proper client.' Polly knew she had really lucked out. Her first submission of a Polly de Soto book would be by a megaselling author.

Johnny had launched into a long monologue from the shower:

'So I took it to Tri-Star, I took it to Paramount, I took it to Orion. I was talking about a budget of $8–9 million. I told them I could get half of that in foreign pre-sales. Cruise has got a European tour coming up, should be a sell-out. His American tour last year was dynamite. Dy-na-mite!

Anyway, Orion really went for it. They love Cruise. They love Jason, that's the kid who'll direct. Of course they only know his commercials but they love the idea of him . . . so anyway, it looks like it's a go, pending one small thing.'

'What's that?' asked Polly, trying to sound interested.

'We still have to cast the female lead. Cruise's love interest. She's got to be American and she's got to be bankable. As soon as the rewrites are done the script is going out to Demi Moore, Rosanna Arquette, Susan Sarandon (she can age down), Alley Sheedy, Debra Winger, Carrie Fisher, Kathleen Turner . . .'

'To play the teenage girlfriend of a werewolf?' asked Polly incredulously, 'but then, what do I know?'

They all said no. Johnny threatened suicide.

'Why don't you get Cherry Fox to play her?' suggested Luana who was staying with them for a couple of days. She was having braces fitted on her teeth by the London dentist she had always gone to. Apparently she refused to go to a Cornish dentist.

'Who on earth is Cherry Fox?' asked Polly.

'Oh *Polly!*' Luana and Johnny accused her in unison.

'Well, sorry, I know I'm just a fuddy-duddy old books person but you're just going to have to tell me.'

'She's a model. Only about nineteen years old but a smash hit both here and in New York. The kids are crazy about her. Luana,

65

you're a genius. You ought to go and work with Annie Martin. She doesn't appear to have an original idea in her head.'

'Who's she?' asked Luana.

'Oh *Luana*! Don't you know who Annie Martin is?' teased Polly.

'She's the casting director on *The Wolf One*,' Johnny explained.

'Casting director,' repeated Luana thoughtfully. 'If you get Cherry Fox can I come up again and meet her?'

'Johnny, get a move on,' Polly told him. 'They called from the production office. You were due there an hour ago.'

Johnny had finally vacated the dining room now *The Wolf One* was in pre-production and had rented offices in Soho. He had also hired himself an assistant called Rachel who had appeared the previous day to escort Luana to the dentist.

'Hardly the sort of work she was expecting,' commented Polly. 'Treat her like a skivvy and you'll lose her.'

'No I won't,' Johnny assured her. 'I laid it on the line when I hired her. She gets to take care of all my personal shit – dry cleaning, appointments to get my hair cut, getting the car serviced, stuff like that. You should be pleased, means I won't ask you to do it although in fact I do need her today so if you wouldn't mind taking Luana back to the dentist. . . She's so terrified of having her teeth done if she doesn't have a minder she'll never get there.'

What if I'd had an important meeting, thought Polly, who would take care of Luana then? As it happened she'd deliberately taken the day off in order to be able to spend time with Luana. She had not exactly got off to a good start with her stepdaughter at their only meeting before the wedding and she hadn't even spoken to Luana on the phone since. This visit to London was a golden opportunity for her to establish a bond for the future.

The visit to the dentist was pretty hair-raising and Polly felt unbearably sorry for Luana. No girl should still have to wear braces when she was bound to have started thinking about boys. Besides, Luana appeared to be using the braces as an excuse to maintain an uncomfortable silence no matter how hard Polly tried to draw her out of it. Then, as they were going down the Haymarket, she suddenly came to life.

'McDonalds!' she breathed with more respect than Polly had seen her show for anything, 'please, Polly?'

'Those braces you've just had put in, will they be able to stand the strain of a Big Mac?'

Luana nodded. Polly relented. 'Here,' she handed Luana her purse, 'you can get me some chips while you're at it but don't tell your father.'

'And you won't tell Mum either, will you?'

Polly refrained from pointing out that she never spoke to Luana's mum. 'Edith? Tell her what?'

'That I've had a Big Mac.'

'Doesn't she approve?'

'She'd die!'

'Well, in that case . . .'

'Polly, I adore you . . .'

Polly was amazed at the endearment. She's so scrawny, she thought, watching Luana running up to the counter.

'Want another?' she asked when Luana had demolished her burger in seconds like a dog wolfing its dinner and was rewarded with a look of utter devotion in Luana's eyes.

'Why doesn't Edith let you have them?'

'She says they're poison. They're not organic.'

'No, I don't suppose they are,' mused Polly. 'Tell me, darling, what does Edith do with herself all day in Cornwall?'

If neither Johnny nor Carla would tell her about Edith, Polly was forced to turn to Luana.

'She cries.'

'She what?'

'She cries,' said Luana beginning to look rather uncomfortable.

'Why? What about? Does she miss your father?'

'Oh, probably. But she was miserable long before that. She can always find something to make her unhappy. She's always telling us that if we eat the right food, you know, organic stuff, it'll bring us inner peace but I think if she'd only have a Big Mac every once in a while she'd feel a whole lot better. Any chance of a strawberry milkshake?'

And that was as far as it went. No more information about Edith was forthcoming. No matter how hard Polly tried to engineer the conversation back to the subject of Edith, either Luana wasn't about to be drawn or she simply wasn't interested.

'I don't suppose we could go to a movie?' She eyed Polly hopefully: 'one with lots of actors. I have this competition with Susie at school. We write down all the actors in all the films we see on telly or in the cinema during the holidays and when term starts again we see who has the most. And actors in cinema films count double, d'you see?'

Polly took her to see *Working Girl* even though she'd already seen it herself. She was touched by the sight of Luana tearing down the aisle in her duffel coat, the hood flapping behind her, to sit in the front row and furiously scribble down the cast list by the light of the screen.

'Who's your favourite film star?' Polly asked her on the way home.

'Daniel Day-Lewis.' The reply was instant.

'I don't think I know him.'

'Oh, you will, you will. You can see him soon in *My Left Foot.* I tore his picture out of *Spotlight* and put it up on my wall. He's special.'

'I see,' said Polly, 'and how come you have a copy of *Spotlight?*'

'Mum's got a set.'

'Oh really? Is she an actress?'

'She says she was once. Probably a hundred years ago before I was born. I heard her fighting with Dad about it. She said it was because of me she never made it. He said how could she have made it when she never even went to drama school and was never offered any parts? Then she started crying again . . .'

The next day, as she put Luana on the train back to Cornwall, Polly kissed Luana for the first time and even though Luana didn't really return the embrace, Polly felt she was beginning to make a little headway.

'Bad luck always comes in threes.' Polly recalled her superstitious grandmother's dark warning, repeated at every opportunity, and towards the end of the following year Polly began to see what Granny Atwell had been on about. Later she would look back and realise that the three deaths, which seemed to happen one after the other with frightening symmetry, marked the turning point of her marriage.

Johnny was hardly ever there. *The Wolf One* was almost a month into shooting, mostly on location. He left the house at 5.30 every morning and arrived home dead on his feet every evening rarely before ten. Polly was well aware that the producer didn't actually need to be on the set the whole time but she appreciated that as it was his first film he wanted to make sure everything was running smoothly.

In fact everything was swimming along for both of them. Cherry Fox had indeed been cast as the love interest and the publicity this had generated had been phenomenal.

Whatever the quality of the outcome, Johnny's first film was already fixed firmly in the public's mind. Polly too was deriving enormous satisfaction from her work. She had negotiated a successful two-book deal for Rebecca Price with a shrewd and sympathetic young publishing director to whom Rebecca was already devoted, and other authors were beginning to come her way. Even though they barely spent any conscious time together except on the occasional Sunday, Polly and Johnny were each making exhausting but happy progress and the news they brought each other from the front was always cheerful.

Until one evening Polly came home from work and for several seconds was transported back to the days when Johnny had run PDS Productions from their dining-room table. The place was in chaos. Empty beer bottles and overflowing ashtrays covered every available surface. Grimy leather jackets had been thrown on the floor. Polly's seventeeth-century French mirror (a present from her superstitious grandmother: 'my dear child, whatever you do, don't break it, you'll have seven years' bad luck'), had been removed from the wall and placed on the dining-room table. Razor blades and jagged lines of cocaine lay on the glass.

Assorted members of Cruise Missile lay sprawled about the room while Cruise crouched in a corner, his head in his hands, his whole body heaving as he emitted loud, disgusting sobs. To Polly he looked like a caveman with his shoulder-length mane, freed from its habitual pony tail, springing matted and wild from his head.

'Johnny?' she appealed.

Johnny was standing over Cruise, ineffectually patting him on the back. He looked up, put a finger to his lips and gestured to Polly to go upstairs. He joined her a few minutes later.

'It's Belle. She's OD'd. Someone found her in the bath at lunchtime. Looks like it was an accident. She was on smack. I mean, I didn't know, thought they both did coke and that was it. I closed down the set and brought Cruise straight home. He can't handle it. As you see.'

They kept Cruise with them for two days – Polly insisted the rest of the band went home – and then his mother came down from Liverpool to fetch him.

'Come on, Billy lad, come home to me and yer dad. Look at the state of you! We'll get him sorted in no time,' she assured Johnny, 'always was a bad influence on him, that woman.'

Polly watched in fascination as the huge leather-jacketed oaf allowed himself to be helped into a taxi by his tiny white-haired mother and marvelled that Mrs Powers could still have such control over her son. Lady Annabel's family closed ranks and barred Cruise from the funeral. Johnny frantically rearranged the film's schedule to shoot around Cruise but if he was away for longer than a week they would be in trouble. But little Mrs Powers delivered him back on the set three days later. There was only one problem. She'd cut off all his hair and the continuity girl nearly had a heart attack until Hair and Make-up came up with a wild and matted wig within hours and filming resumed the next day.

The second death occurred on a balmy September afternoon. Patrick Fisher had just taken delivery of a manuscript he had been awaiting with unusual anticipation. He was rather proud of the fact that he represented a handful of eminent politicians and the fact that one of these had decided to write his surprisingly scurrilous memoirs pleased Patrick enormously.

'Don't disturb me, Jennifer, there's a dear,' he told his secretary. 'I'm going to spend the afternoon reading Sir Godfrey. Bring me some tea around 4.30, otherwise no calls please.'

It seemed Patrick had taken advantage of the clement weather to lift a chair through the french windows on to his balcony. There he had placed the manuscript on the parapet, where it lay precariously poised, and settled down to read, reaching out for handfuls of pages as he went. A witness saw it all. A sudden gust of wind had swept a hundred pages into the air and Patrick had instinctively leapt after them. The parapet was low, Patrick large and clumsy. He had lost his balance and plunged head first from the fourth floor to the pavement below, narrowly missing the basement railings on which he might have been impaled.

The ambulance men said there was nothing they could do.

Patrick's partnership with Jules Dunbar had been a jocular and affectionate one. Patrick had always referred to Jules as the Old Codger. Polly looked at Jules now as she sat across the table from him in the window of Hilaire in the Old Brompton Road, Patrick's favourite watering hole, resplendent in his red braces and habitual

71

bow tie. Later they would go back to the office and spend the afternoon planning Patrick's memorial service at St Martin-in-the-Fields.

'Come on, old girl, you must have a drink. What's your poison?' Polly nearly giggled. She hadn't realised people actually said things like 'What's your poison?' but if anyone did it was bound to be Jules. 'Well, I'm going to have a Martini. Join me?'

Polly nodded. She'd never had a Martini before but Jules was a notorious drunk and Polly had long since resigned herself to the fact that this lunch was going to be a question of if you can't beat 'em, join 'em.

'It's awful to think of such a thing when it's barely a fortnight since the funeral but will you be looking around for a new partner, Jules?' Polly reckoned she'd better get down to basics before Jules became too pissed.

'He was only fifty-two,' remarked Jules, neatly evading the question. 'I remember when my father took him on as an office boy. He was only just down from Balliol . . .'

'Trinity, Cambridge,' corrected Polly.

'Well, who was at Balliol?'

'No idea, Jules. Maybe you were?'

'No, don't think so. Anyway Patrick was only a kid and keen as mustard. Made me feel quite exhausted just to look at him. Just as well, since I've never had the energy to bring in the blasted authors. I think the old man knew it, that's why he took on Patrick. He's devastated, by the by, never thought Patrick would pop off before he did. Talking of the blasted authors, what are we going to do about them, Polly? Patrick's, I mean.'

'Well, I brought along a list –' Polly proffered a sheet of paper.

'Good girl. Any on here you fancy?'

'Jules, are you serious?'

'Never more so. I don't want to look after anyone under thirty-five. How many of these scribblers are under thirty-five?'

Polly leaned over and glanced down the list.

'Only four I think.'

'Oh Christ, Patrick always did go in for pompous farts. Boring politicians, diplomats, lady horticulturists, no, worse, botanists.

Who was that fearful old bat who produced that lengthy tome on fleas, Hortensia someone? Before your time, probably. I suppose I shall have to look after them all for the time being. Do you know what that prize fart, Godfrey Moore, said on the telephone the day after Patrick's accident? I rang to tell him what had happened and the first thing he said was, 'Did anyone retrieve my manuscript?'

Polly groaned. Johnny's reaction had been almost as bad when she'd told him about Patrick: 'Well, look on the bright side, Pol. It's bound to mean a step up for you. They'll probably give you all his clients.'

'Rebecca Price. She's yours now, isn't she? And you've got a few more of your own. Sure you feel up to handling Patrick's leftovers as well?' asked Jules. 'I'll have the gigot and bring me the wine list, would you please? Oh, it's here. So it is.'

Polly knew that once Jules' attention switched from the client list to the wine list, she would lose him.

'Yes, Rebecca's mine,' she said hastily. 'So, I'll take over these four, shall I? Oh, and what about Lucy Richards? Have you read what there is of her manuscript? I don't think it's quite your thing, Jules. Better leave it to me. I'll write to them all this afternoon and you'll deal with the rest. Would you like me to write a preliminary letter to them all for you, Jules, explain the situation, say you'll be in touch in due course?'

Jules looked at her through his bifocals. 'Would you, my dear? Most kind. Do me a little memo thing about who's due to deliver what and when and perhaps you'd have to go at getting Sir Godfrey to deliver us another copy of his manuscript now he's calmed down a bit. S'pose I'd better read the bloody thing. In the meantime perhaps you could hold the fart . . .'

'Jules!'

'Oh, you know what I mean.'

Polly did know exactly what he meant. Poor old Jules, he really was a bit of disgrace. She felt rather sorry for his clients, inherited from his father who had founded the agency and none of them under sixty, but somehow, she had observed, they and Jules seemed to rub along. It was a style of gentlemanly, rather lazy agenting that was rapidly going out of style. She doubted if Jules had ever auctioned a book. He merely relied on the relevant editor being in the same place when an author had a new book to be sold. The book was delivered to the editor, who duly read it, lunch was then consumed and at the appropriate moment the subject of money was hurriedly discussed, after which Jules forgot all about the book until he was invited to the publication party. He's going to be lost for a while without Patrick, thought Polly. Patrick had always shielded Jules from the more cut-throat side of their business while quietly bringing it further and further into the latter part of the twentieth century. The least she could do was hold the fort until he had recovered enough to administer to Patrick's clients, although quite what Jules would administer Polly was at a loss to say. All she knew was that she intended to be a very different kind of agent – she would really care for her authors, for their work and their well-being. Like Patrick – indeed, in his memory– she would be, what had Jules called it, keen as mustard?

Cruise came off his Fat Boy at 180 m.p.h. He had never made any pretence of recovering from Lady Annabel's death and it was as if with each new stunt he performed in the film he was entertaining some kind of personal death wish.

'My friends were always putting him down, down down,' sang Polly under her breath, wondering why she had this particular song on the brain, 'they said he came from the wrong side of town. . .'

'Why did he have to go and be the bloody Leader of the Pack?' sighed Johnny on his return from the hospital, giving her her answer. 'He's getting worse every day.'

There it is, thought Polly, bad luck always comes in threes. This is the third death.

But she was wrong.

CRUISE LIVES screamed the headlines, omitting to mention that he might never walk again.

'I'm ruined,' moaned Johnny, choosing to ignore that it was entirely his own fault. First, Cruise was on Pay or Play which meant that even though he would never return to the film, he would be paid for it. Second, Johnny had been foolish enough to overlook the necessity of a completion guarantee in the budget. Like an insurance premium, a guarantor is paid a fee in exchange for which he agrees to pay all costs above the agreed budget in order to guarantee completion and delivery of the picture. The fact that Cruise had insisted on doing his own stunts had resulted in his insurance being so ludicrously high it was out of the question, but Johnny should have put in a completion guarantee. Now with no Cruise and no money with which to hire a replacement star to finish the film, even if he had wanted to at such a late stage, Johnny had no choice but to announce that *The Wolf One* had 'bitten the dust'.

His film has died, thought Polly. That's the third death.

Again she was wrong.

Prudence Atwell telephoned at eight o'clock on a Friday evening in late October.

'Polly darling, your father's gone into the Norfolk and Norwich. The thing is – ' there was a catch in Polly's mother's voice – 'this time I don't think he's going to come out.'

'Why on earth haven't you told me? Christ, Mummy, cancer!' Polly's agitation made her uncharacteristically aggressive with her mother when Prudence picked her up at Norwich station the next morning.

'Don't get in. Wait!' Prudence threw a rug over the passenger seat before Polly's black Agnès B jacket and trousers became covered in dog hairs. 'There. I didn't tell you for the simple reason that your father asked me not to. He didn't want you to know he was dying.'

'I see,' said Polly abruptly. Until that moment she had not in fact acknowledged that her father was dying. They drove in silence to the hospital and Prudence drew to a halt in the car park.

Polly shuddered. 'Horrible place. Why's he in here, Mummy?'

'And not in some private nursing home, you mean? Oh, you know your father, Polly. He's always supported the National Health. Never one to spend when he could save,' she added drily. It was an old family joke that Polly's father had installed central heating in their home in only those rooms open to the public, leaving the family to freeze over antiquated electric fires in the rest of the house.

75

They'd put him in a room on his own instead of in a ward, which told Polly they didn't hold out much hope at the hospital. He was in a coma. Her mother hadn't told her that either. It put paid to the heart-to-heart with her father Polly had rehearsed in her mind on the train journey up from London. She was horrified by his breathing: the long silences followed by an agonising rasp. It seemed to Polly, as she sat in the sparse hospital room at her father's bedside, that the gaps grew longer and longer between rasps. The suspense, waiting to hear if he would breathe again, was almost more than she could bear. She waited for her mother to leave the room then clasped his hand and spoke to him.

'I'm all right, Daddy. I know you thought I wouldn't be but I am. I love Johnny. We have had an odd life together. I don't imagine you've been able to make much sense of it. Not exactly what you expected for me but we both have to work very hard otherwise it wouldn't work, the marriage I mean. I'm sorry we didn't have grandchildren for you, sorry we haven't yet anyway. I want them, Dad, but there's time. I like my work. I know I'm going to be a good agent. I only wish I knew Johnny was going to be a good producer.'

A nurse came into the room and caught the last sentence. 'No use talking to him, love, he can't hear you. All right, is he?'

'Fine,' said Polly. He's just dying, and how do you know he can't hear me?

She was rather shaken by what she had just told her father. She had, she realised, been talking to herself whether or not her father could hear her, using him as an excuse to face up to a few things she had been trying to keep buried inside her. Did she really think Johnny wouldn't make it?

'I may be totally wrong, Daddy. He'll probably come marching home one day with Oscars under both arms. Doesn't matter whether he does or not, I still love him. He knows who I am, Daddy, like you did. Like you do,' she corrected herself quickly, glancing up at him. 'Mummy hasn't a clue who I am. I've given up expecting her to see the light. She sees me as she wants me to be, a nice country girl, grown up and married, living in London and waiting to have her grandchildren. I think she prefers to think I don't go out

76

to work. . .' She stopped guiltily as the door opened again, expecting Prudence, but it was only another nurse.

'That's it, dear. You talk to him. I'm sure it helps. Looks like he can't hear you but how do we know for sure? Most likely he can. You his daughter, then?'

Polly nodded gratefully. She could have sworn her father's hand, clasped in hers, gave an almost inperceptible squeeze.

The next morning as they walked through the swing doors of the ward next to his room, three nurses came flying round the corner to head them off at the pass. Cups of tea materialised out of nowhere. Polly's father had died twenty minutes before they arrived.

'Can't we see him?' begged Polly.

'Best not, dear,' said the nurse who had thought he could hear her. 'They're not a pleasant sight when they've gone like he did. He was in pain at the end but he's at peace now. You had a nice chat yesterday, said your goodbyes then though you probably didn't realise it. He wouldn't want you to see him. Here, drink your tea.'

Bet she says that to all the girls, thought Polly miserably and put her arm round her mother who had begun to cry quietly.

To Polly's amazement, Johnny drove up for the funeral.

It was four days after her father had died and she had gone for a long walk towards the end of the afternoon having spent most of the day on the telephone, telling people all over the country of the funeral arrangements, speaking to the vicar and the undertaker, putting announcements in the newspapers, while Prudence entertained a stream of visitors to what she called 'condolence tea'. She's loving it, thought Polly, she hasn't had so much attention in years.

Polly put on her wellingtons, picked her way across a cattle grid and stomped off across the field. As a girl she had imagined herself walking across these same fields one day in her wedding dress to be married in the little flint church that stood on the edge of their land. She had always planned a harvest wedding so she and her bridesmaids could form a procession between the bales of hay. As it had turned out, she had married in London and the only procession here in Norfolk would be that of the pallbearers carrying her father's coffin through the mud in two days' time.

She squelched through the slimy red earth and suddenly broke away to walk towards the woods. The gloom of the narrow brambled paths, cut off from the weak sunlight by overhanging branches, was somehow comforting. She was really getting into her stride, approaching a clearing where she intened to lean against the vast trunk of an oak and rest, when she heard rustling from the thicket to her left. A deer, probably. She stopped and kept absolutely still. If it leapt out and saw her it would be very startled. The rustling grew nearer, twigs snapping underfoot. Then a dog crashed through the path, dripping wet.

'Ashby!' The retriever shook itself, sending a shower of muddy water all over her and padded up to her, wagging its tail. Ashby was her mother's dog. 'Ashby, clever dog. How did you find me?'

As if in answer a figure appeared in the clearing at the end of the path and began running towards her. He held out his arms and beckoned to her to come and meet him. She ran with outstretched arms feeling as if she was in the final frame of a weepie movie. Then, just as she was about to rush into Johnny's embrace, he stepped to the left and she missed him, continuing on down the path, arms still flapping.

'Oh, Johnny!' She couldn't help laughing. He clowned around for a while, pretending to look for her, and when she reached him she punched him on the arm. 'You idiot! What are you doing here?'

'I arrived in time for what I hoped would be a terrific tea, buns and things, only to find you'd gone out. Your mother gave that – what's it called? – retriever a pair of your knickers and told it to find you. I followed. Here we are.'

'My knickers? Oh, no, he's probably dropped them somewhere in the woods for everyone to see.'

'No, wait, here he comes, he's got something in his mouth. Bit grey, Pol.'

'Ashby, come here. Good dog! Now, drop! Go on, drop.'

Ashby dropped a dead squirrel at Polly's feet. She screamed hysterically and then she lost control. She hadn't let go since her father died, hadn't cried, had been proud of her composure. Johnny wrapped his arms around her and began to lead her slowly back to the house.

'Blubbing again, Pol, what are we going to do about you? There, there, go on, spit it out. I never knew you could look so disgusting.'

She hit him again half-heartedly.

'You know, my father died once,' he said conversationally.

'Anything I can do you can do better,' grumbled Polly into his chest.

'What's that? Accusing me of being competitive, are you? Typical! Poor old Poppa. He would have liked to go back to Italy to die but he never made it. Oh no, don't go blubbing again just when we've dried you out. Your mother will think I've been beating you up. Shall we have a practice funeral here in the woods? Ashby's got something over there he wants us to bury so he can dig it up again on his next walk.'

'Oh, shut up, Johnny. Were you close to your father, did you love him?'

'No. Yes. I loved him, he was my poppa, he was warm and Italian and I recognised myself in him, but I didn't respect him.'

'Why not?'

'He never made anything of himself. Not in a way that impressed me in any way. He was just an ice-cream maker all his life. OK, so he made money but. . .'

'So? Did he enjoy being an ice-cream maker?'

'Dunno. 'Spect so.'

'Well, what's wrong with that?'

'Oh, Pol, you just don't understand.'

'No, I don't. Do you think Luana respects you?'

'Oh, she sends her love, even wrote you a letter. Here, I've got it somewhere . . .'

Edith, thought Polly immediately, he's seen Luana so maybe he's seen her.

Why couldn't they just bury Edith?

'Have you seen *Beverly Hills Cop*?' Johnny asked Great-Aunt Molly over dinner. 'D'you know, it was originally conceived as a vehicle for Sylvester Stallone. Great idea having a black cop, great moment when Eddie Murphy arrives in LA and his girlfriend from Detroit calls his car "a crappy blue Chevy Nova", real put-down.'

Great-Aunt Molly beamed happily at him. She was almost completely deaf but stubbornly refused to wear her hearing-aid.

Polly toyed with her food. Johnny was busy doing what he called 'making an effort' with her relatives and in return they all thought he was a lunatic. At lunch the next day he excelled himself. The dining room was at the front of the house with a clear view of the flat countryside dotted with gnarled trees bent into slanting positions by the Norfolk wind like arthritic old women. Conversation had already totally dried up and everyone was trying hard not to slurp their soup in the ensuing silence. Suddenly a group of ramblers sauntered past, the adults looking studiously ahead while the children stared blatantly through the windows at them.

'Want me to see 'em off?' asked Johnny, getting to his feet, 'trespassing etc.'

'That won't be necessary. They're not trespassing,' Prudence said calmly, tipping her soup plate away from her and dipping her spoon to catch the last drop, 'it's a public footpath. They're perfectly entitled to walk past the house.'

'But they're on your land.'

'It really doesn't matter, my dear Johnny, do sit down. We're quite used to them.'

'But that's a bit frigging much!' Johnny wasn't about to sit down. He rushed over to the window and watched as the last of the walkers climbed over the five-bar gate at the edge of the fields. 'What's the point of living in a posh place like this' – Prudence winced at the 'posh' – 'if you've got people traipsing past while you're eating your lunch, going Coo-ee. . .'

'Johnny!' warned Polly.

'I mean it's hilarious . . .' Before she could stop him he had run outside and was walking past the window like Charlie Chaplin, pretending to swing his walking stick and grinning in at them.

'Coo-ee, coo-ee!' he called. Great-Aunt Molly waved back. Everyone else ignored him for the rest of the day.

Polly had to admit to herself that she couldn't have done without him at the funeral. Although she had grown up amongst these excruciatingly polite relations who surrounded her now, she still felt they patronised her, that she was an oddball amongst her numerous cousins in their uniform Alice bands, pearls and pie-frill collars, braying at their husbands-who-did-something (probably nothing)-in-the-City. Johnny held her hand as they walked across the fields to the church and continued to clasp it throughout the service, stage-whispering 'No blubbing, Pol, good girl, keep it up' at intervals.

At the drinks afterwards she saw him deep in conversation with her Uncle Matthew. Uncle Matthew had always been something of an embarrassment to the family and if it wasn't for the fact that he was loaded (and enormously generous, a reliable soft touch in times of need) he would have been dropped from family gatherings years ago. He had once had a reputation as a bit of a bounder. This wouldn't have been too bad in itself except that Uncle Matthew himself was extremely proud of his reputation and bored every-body who came near him to death with much-embellished stories of his flings with 'poppets' and 'floozies' in the past.

As Polly wandered by, Uncle Matthew hailed her:

'Fellow works in the films. You never told me, Polly. I've been telling him all about my little adventures in the film business.'

'With Rank starlets, Uncle Matthew?'

'Those were the days. We've been having a good laugh. He's been telling me about his misfortune with this wolf business. Terrible shame. I've offered to help but he won't hear of it. I've told him any time, any time. I'd like to get back to the films, meet a few popsies.'

'He's eighty-two,' Polly whispered in Johnny's ear, 'it'll be pop-off time before he meets a few popsies.'

Prudence appeared at Polly's side.

'Polly, I'm a little worried about Joan. So sweet of her to make the effort to come and so well turned out as always. That's a Chanel suit, I'm sure of it.' Prudence looked rather disdainfully at Polly's eternal Agnès B.

'What's the matter with her?'

'How can you ask such a thing? She's desperately upset about your poor father. I found her in absolute floods in the pantry and sent her up to my bedroom. Do pop up and see if she's all right.'

Polly found Joan crumpled in a heap – having first removed the jacket of her Chanel suit which was hanging over a chair – in the middle of her mother's bed.

'Polly, it's the cruellest cruellest thing that ever happened. I don't know how I'm going to show my face in London again. I've been fired by Condé Nast!'

'What's your mother going to do with that great pile?' asked Johnny on the drive back to London, 'Sell it? Carve it up into flats? Old man leave you quite a bit, did he?'

Polly had known for some time that her father had left her £25,000 with a good deal more to come to her on her mother's death. She hadn't told Johnny and she wasn't going to just yet. She didn't know why. She had never kept anything from him before. It was her money and at the back of her mind she was beginning to plan what she could do with it.

'Is that why you came up for the funeral, Johnny? Lured by the smell of filthy lucre?' She had no idea what made her say such a thing and when she saw the hurt look on his face, she wished she hadn't, especially when he began to steer the car with one hand so as to be able to reach out with the other to push her hair away from her face and stroke the back of her head with infinite tenderness. And she felt even worse when he said: 'Poor old Pol, you really loved your dad, didn't you? I never reckoned you'd be so upset when he popped his clogs. But you have got me, you know. Pretty crappy substitute but I do love you and I will take care of you. You're lumbered with me, Pol, an embarrassing Italian who worships you even when you've got a red nose and piggy little eyes from blubbing all the time. Here, I'll even lend you my best silk handkerchief. . .'

She laughed as she always did when he said that and then handed her a filthy screwed-up bit of Kleenex. He was so corny but he always touched her and she loved him.

Yet she still didn't tell him about the £25,000.

Now that she was out of work and at a loose end, Joan was never off the phone to Polly, demanding that she be free to lunch at least three times a week. Joan always behaved as if Polly's job was nothing more than that of a glorified secretary. She would ring Polly every morning around eleven.

'Hi, darling, it's me. Can you talk or are you taking dictation or something?'

If Polly said she had an author on the other line, Joan would merely come back with: 'OK, I'll hold on till you've put him through to whoever it is.'

'Joan, they're ringing *me*.'

'Are they? Why? Oh, never mind. Call me back.'

One of her first questions was always: 'Where shall we go?'

'Go?' Polly was invariably distracted, wishing Joan would get off the line but sensitive to how she must be feeling, banned from the centre of her universe, Vogue House.

'To lunch. Where shall we go today?'

'Joan, I told you, I have a lunch today with a client.'

'Oh, well, we'll have to natter on the phone then.'

Polly would try to get on with her work with the phone crooked to her ear while Joan prattled away.

'There's a perfectly wonderful picture of Hector O'Neill in

Dempster today. Have you seen it, Polly? He's finished shooting the last Conway film. Did I ever tell you how sweet he was to me when we did that shoot with him for *Vogue* last year? He's so utterly classy. Boston Irish, you know, like the Kennedys.'

'He's American? I never realised. The Kennedys were hardly classy. Old Joe Kennedy came from the East Boston slums, he was a bootlegger.'

'Oh Polly, you're such a pedant. So what if he was a bootlegger originally? Rather romantic. He became Ambassador to the Court of St James later on. That's what matters.'

'And Hector O'Neill grew up with the family?'

'Something like that. One didn't like to pry too closely. Dempster says he's here in London for a while. I wonder where he's staying. Maybe he has a house here. Someone will know. Now listen, Polly darling, I can't sit on the phone gossiping with you all morning. I've got to rustle up some freelance work. Can you do lunch tomorrow?'

Polly couldn't but she said yes just to get Joan off the phone. She felt very guilty. It wasn't as if she could even invite her round in the evening, because Johnny still wouldn't have her in the house. In any case since *The Wolf One* had collapsed he needed Polly's undivided attention at night which was a bit of a problem given the amount of manuscripts she had to read.

And there was one in particular which just couldn't wait.

In the summer of 1989 Lawrence delivered the final draft of *Mr Wrong*. When Polly read it she knew without a doubt that she had a star author on her hands. Lawrence might look like a prize wimp, all goofy and gangling with stringy black hair and glasses so thick you could hardly see his eyes, but his books showed that he certainly had a better understanding of women than most men. Polly was entranced. She sat up in bed reading into the night while Johnny grumbled away under the duvet beside her.

'What the bloody hell's that? For God's sake, Pol, turn the light out, let's get some sleep.'

'Nothing that would interest you,' she told him tartly.

After all, Johnny had sent poor Lawrence away with a flea in his ear. Why should he care what had happened to *Mr Wrong*?

Polly couldn't wait to sell *Mr Wrong* but she forced herself to take everything one step at a time. First she had to get a buzz going. Then, when she had enough people begging to see it, she would auction it to the highest bidder. She duly lunched several prospective editors and hyped *Mr Wrong* as much as she dared.

Polly picked her restaurants carefully. It would never do to take one particular young power editor in her thirties to a place where she wouldn't be seen and be able to wave at people. Ally Keppel was an editor without talent but who had been given a fair amount of financial clout at a hungry house with a large chequebook. She'd expect nothing less than the Groucho or Le Caprice or else she'd assume Polly – and worse, Lawrence – weren't worth her attention.

Similarly, Rosemary Perkins, an enormously experienced, rather dowdy lady editor in her late fifties whose unerring judgement and care with authors had earned her an excellent reputation, hated noisy fashionable restaurants and liked to sit quietly in the corner of a run-down Greek taverna and talk about gardening. Yet Polly knew her endorsement of a book often encouraged her employers to dig deep into their coffers.

As it turned out, the *Mr Wrong* auction was not without its complications. By the second day there were only three bidders left in the auction out of the nine to whom the book had been submitted. In the first round, one of them, Pat Walsh of the Lambert Group, had come in with a staggering £50,000 opening bid.

'That should see off the competition, babe,' Pat boomed down the phone to Polly. 'Barely worth you going any further, I shouldn't think.'

Polly couldn't abide Pat Walsh's bossy, jolly hockey sticks manner and her curious predilection for calling absolutely everyone 'babe'.

She was also rather worried when four people promptly dropped out. She listened to the standard excuses:

'Too rich for my blood, I'm afraid, Polly. Wonderful book but in the current climate, fifty thou for a first novel, a bit steep . . .' Scaredy cat!

'I'd like to offer more, Polly, but I'm being sat on by my editorial board . . .'

Wimp!

'If I thought it'd stay at 50K I'd hang in there, Polly, you know I would, but you've got a high roller there or you don't know what you're doing . . .' Oh, thanks!

In round three Pat Walsh was at £95,000, Rosemary Perkins was at £97,000 (her endorsement the best news so far: that meant everyone would know the book was good when it came to post-mortems), and the third contender, Arthur Allen-Jones, had pushed it over the £100,000 mark to £105,000. Arthur and his high offer was the complication. Eighteen months ago Arthur had been Pat Walsh's assistant (secretary, to be precise) but his general pushiness and obsessive ambition had secured him, at twenty-seven, the job of editorial director at the brand new publishers Hollywood House (so called because of their offices in Hollywood Road off the Fulham Road rather than any affiliation with the film industry). Arthur, who insisted on being called Art, or Artie, was fiercely competitive and desperate for books to fill his first list. But Pat Walsh had absolutely no intention of losing out to her erstwhile minion. She would be the laughing stock of the industry. She was overheard slagging off Arthur in the Groucho: 'I tell you, babe, he never read more than fifty pages of a manuscript. He just went by the reader's report depending on which reader he was sleeping with.'

Arthur retaliated from 2 Brydges Place, a smaller, more exclusive club in a tiny alleyway next to the Coliseum.

'Talk about paranoid!' he told a table of rising young Turks from *GQ*, *The Face* and Channel 4. 'She even arranged for the conception of her children so that the births should not coincide with the ABA or Frankfurt.' Annual jaunts to the American Booksellers' Association and the Frankfurt Book Fair were standard fixtures on publishers' calendars.

In the end Polly decided to go for a sudden death. Let them all make their final bids and whoever came in the highest would acquire the book.

They all bid £124,000 (the previous bid had been £120,000 from Pat). There were slight variations in the frills over and above the basic offer. Pat offered a £5,000 escalator if the book stayed in the top ten on the *Sunday Times* bestseller list for a minimum of six weeks. Top ten wasn't good enough, thought Polly, it had to be top five. Rosemary Perkins guaranteed a £25,000 promotional spend (not excessive but a smart gesture), and Artie Allen-Jones remained true to Hollywood by throwing in a movie escalator of an extra £7,500 if a 'major motion picture' of *Mr Wrong* was released in the UK.

Polly was about to go back to each of them and ask them all for their final package, with everyone including promotion budgets plus film and bestseller escalators, when Lawrence threw a spanner in the works by revealing, rather late in the day, his dependency on astrology.

'Polly, when is Pat Walsh's birthday?'

'Lawrence, I have no idea. It's not an event I celebrate. Besides, she hasn't actually won the auction yet so you don't have to start thinking about her birthday.'

'Oh, but I do. I must know what sign my editor is before I sign with them, and the other thing is I've had the book's chart done by a mundane astrologer. *Mr Wrong* is a Scorpio and he has to be published on either November 28th or the following April 2nd. I want it written into the contract.'

Polly silently counted to ten very slowly. This was the most important step of her career so far. She must not lose her cool.

'Lawrence, I have £124,000 sitting on the table. I simply cannot go back to people and ask them when their birthday is.'

'I knew the book should never had been submitted when Mercury was in retrograde. I meant to tell you that. Call me when you get their sun signs and try and go for their moon and their ascendent as well. You'll need to know the exact time they were born.'

Polly allotted each of the bidders a star sign without even asking them, waited twenty-four hours and then called Lawrence back.

Lawrence said he was personally allergic to Geminis (Pat Walsh) but that Artie Allen-Jones' sun in Pisces and moon in Cancer were perfect with his own Cancer star sign and *Mr Wrong*'s Scorpio.

'So we're all set then?' Polly was weak with relief. 'The book goes to Hollywood House for £124,000 with a £35,000 guaranteed promotion spend plus a further £10,000 movie bonus and an extra £5,000 if it stays in the *Sunday Times* bestseller list for longer than six weeks.'

'One more thing.'

Polly couldn't trust herself to speak.

'What sign are you, Polly?'

'I'm Cancer, Lawrence, just like you but I am beginning to think that is the only thing we have in common. I'm going to hang up now, Lawrence, before you ask me what sign this telephone is.'

When Polly proudly showed Johnny the report of her *Mr Wrong* auction in the publishing trade magazine the *Bookseller*, he was more interested in hearing about the rivalry between Pat Walsh and Artie Allen-Jones.

'I like it, I like it. Very *All about Eve*. There might be something in doing a remake with a new twist, a Bette Davis character and an ambitious young boy instead of a girl. Call him Eddie instead of Eve. All about Eddie. Great! Thanks, Pol.'

'Don't mention it.' All About Eddie! Polly shuddered. 'So you aren't impressed then?'

'By what? Your little sale? I suppose it's OK for this pathetic country but you've got to understand that the agents I'm around, the agents in my business, I mean, we're talking millions.'

'In your business.'

'Yeah.'

'Johnny, what exactly is your business right now?'

Polly knew it was below the belt but she was smarting from his condescending attitude to what was for her a tremendous achievement.

'That just about sums it up,' he snarled at her. 'Your're so uninterested in what I do, so wrapped up in your own life, that you actually have to ask me what I do.'

'I didn't ask you what you do. I asked you what you were doing right now. It's almost a year since *The Wolf One* fell apart.'

'Go on, rub it in. How am I supposed to option anything without any bloody money?'

'Banks?'

'There's a better way, something where we could work together.'

'Johnny, I am not giving you my father's money.'

'It's not his money. It's yours to do with as you want.'

'Precisely.'

Conversations along these lines had become a regular occurrence between them ever since Polly's mother had told Johnny about the £25,000. Prudence hadn't known she was revealing a secret. In fact she'd assumed Johnny knew about it. She was, she told Johnny, merely enquiring as to what he planned to do with it. Presumably he looked after Polly's investments, didn't he?

No, he didn't, but not for want of trying.

'I simply can't understand it,' said Prudence. 'Her father always looked after my money.'

One night, when he was especially low, Johnny even accused Polly of having fallen out of love with him.

'You mean I can't love you because I won't give you my money. Johnny, my money and my love are not one and the same. You can't expect to receive one and think the other goes with it automatically.'

'But do you, I mean are you still in love with me?'

'Much much more than I was when we were married.'

That shook him.

'Really, Pol? He sat up in bed, reached for the remote and jabbed it in the direction of the television. 'Well, that is a turn-up. Much much more, you said. How much much more? Come on, show me.' He was reaching for her under the bedclothes.

'Turn that bloody thing off. I've got to make an early start.'

'You're such a boring old woman these days. No late nights. Always sitting there with your glasses on, reading through those blasted boxes of paper. How do you ever expect to get pregnant if you sit up reading all night?'

'Pregnant?'

'Right. Pregnant. My movie went down the tube and I can't even console myself with being a father.'

'Johnny, we're going to start a family but there's something I've been planning and I feel I ought to discuss it with you first. I feel

89

nearly ready to break away from Patrick Fisher & Dunbar. I want to start my own agency and I want to do it here, in this house.'

'Fine by me. Perfect timing. You'll be right here at home to look after the baby.'

Polly had never liked his approach to motherhood. As his mother had warned Polly, Johnny played the all-Italian male only when it suited him, and it suited him now to turn her big career step into an excuse for motherhood.

'That's just it. If I decide to go ahead with my own agency I shall need to devote all my time to it. I'd want to wait and have a baby once the agency's up and running.'

'You're not getting any younger, Pol. Thirty-six? Thirty-seven?'

'I saw my gynaecologist a couple of weeks ago and she says I'm in tip-top condition. No problem waiting a year or two.'

'Well, I'm not going to wait a year or two to do another movie. Whereabouts in the house are you planning to have this agency anyway? Going to do deals in the kitchen or what?'

'Well, that's precisely what I wanted to talk to you about. I want to use my father's money to build a conservatory.'

'You what?'

'On the back of the house. It'd be beautiful and it could be heated and I could have my office out there. People could come and go through the garden gate.'

'Got it all worked out, haven't you? Just as well I already have a child. Doesn't look like I'm going to have much chance of fatherhood while you're pottering around in the conservatory, talking to your bloody plants.'

Polly sighed. 'Johnny, why did you marry me?'

'You thought I wanted to marry you to have children? Just for that? I married you because you were so warm and loving and natural and bright and I knew if I had you with me I'd be all right. I know it sounds corny but I wanted you to share my dreams.'

'Didn't it ever occur to you that I might have dreams of my own and I'd want you to share them with me as well?' asked Polly.

She had him there. Johnny was generous by nature but he didn't exactly lie awake at night worrying about anybody else but himself.

'I thought you were, you know, just a kid. I thought I'd teach you everything and you'd sort of be here beside me . . . not like Edith . . . she was so. . .'

'What?' Polly grabbed his arm. 'Edith was so what?'

'It doesn't matter.'

'No go on, Johnny. Tell me about Edith.'

'Well, it was just that she was so terrified of life itself I couldn't tell her anything in case it set her off on one of her . . .'

'One of her what?'

'Nothing. Leave it alone, Pol. All in the past. Anyway, she left me and I found you. Except now you're trying to run the world and don't have time for me.'

Johnny was looking very sorry for himself, sitting hunched up on the pillows in his pyjamas, his arms around his knees.

His hair, very pepper and salt by now, was dishevelled and the stubble on his chin made him look decidedly swarthy.

But Polly loved him like this. He was so far removed from the type of man she had been programmed to love. He was vulnerable. And any second now he would probably make her collapse with laughter in a way that no one else could, and no matter how badly he behaved he always managed to make up for it in some way.

She crawled into the space between his knees and slipped her arms around his neck. She pretended to bite his stubble, taking nips here and there. She licked the inside of his ear. Then very slowly let her tongue slide down over his cheek and into his mouth. They kissed for five minutes, ten minutes, on and on and all the time Polly thought: this is what it's all about. He's got no work. We've got no children. But this is all I want. The fusion of their bodies never failed to reassure her. She loved this man and one reason for this, amongst many many others, was that she hadn't a shred of doubt in her mind that he loved her too.

When she was here at home in bed with him, she never needed to ask him if he loved her. She *felt* it.

In the morning she retrieved the *Bookseller* from under his side of the bed. He looked up at her sheepishly.

'Well done, Pol. That *Mr Wrong* thing, don't know much about your business but it looks like you did good.'

But as she was going out of the front door he called down the stairs:

'It'd make a crappy movie though. Poor old Lawrence. He hasn't got a clue.'

A week later she had made up her mind once and for all, told Jules Dunbar what she was going to do and there was no going back. That night, lying in bed next to Johnny, she knew she had to try one more time to make him understand.

Johnny was watching *Sweet Smell of Success*, one of his favourite films, occasionally reaching out to pat her and murmur mechanically: 'You all right, Pol? Bit quiet tonight.' He was watching the bit where Sidney Falco, the opportunistic publicist played by Tony Curtis, pretends to call J.J. Hunsecker, a powerful columnist played by Burt Lancaster, and get him to place an item about a comedian in his column. The comedian is standing right beside Tony Curtis, hears every word and is suitably impressed without realising that in fact it is only Curtis' bewildered secretary on the other end of the line.

Johnny knew the film so well he picked up the telephone in the bedroom almost on cue and began to mouth the lines:

'J.J, Hi, how are you sweetheart, I know it's late but is it too late to add something to the column?'

Polly watched him. She had to admit he did look rather like Tony Curtis and it was weird seeing him sitting there talking into the phone and then looking at the screen and seeing Tony Curtis saying the same words.

Johnny went on and on playing Sidney Falco so when Polly said in a small voice, 'Johnny, I told you about my plan to use Daddy's money to build myself an office at home. Well, I'm definitely going to do it. Is it OK with you? It is your house, after all. What do you think?' he never heard a word.

That year Polly and Johnny spent a quiet Christmas at home. It wasn't a good one and later Polly dubbed it the 'Love you too' Christmas.

Prudence rang up on the dot of 3.16 for her annual post-mortem of the Queen's speech on television.

'I do wish there wasn't so much of her going blah, blah, blah. I do so like it when they have those jolly films of them on holiday and having picnics and things with all those little cartoon doggies trotting around her.'

'I think they're called corgis, Mummy. Well, anyway, Happy Christmas. Thank you for my apron and my set of tea towels and Johnny was thrilled with his trowel. Here, he wants to say Happy Christmas . . .what?' Johnny was signalling frantically. 'Oh, you loved your bedjacket? Well, we know how draughty it gets at home.'

'Has he done anything about your money?' hissed Prudence.

'No, Mummy, not a thing.'

'Why not, for heaven's sake?'

'Because (a) I won't let him and (b) I'm planning on doing something with it myself. Very soon, actually.'

As soon as she had put the phone down, it rang again. Luana for Johnny. Polly chattered happily to Luana who appeared to be ecstatic about her present, a VCR machine. Who wouldn't be, thought Polly. It was a ludicrously precocious present for a sixteen-year-old but Johnny had insisted.

'I've taped four movies already,' she told Polly proudly.

'Well, in that case you cheated and opened it early. Come and see me again soon. Here's your father.'

'Hi, my little sweetie-pie, taping away are you? No, Luana, we discussed this already. You are too young to see *My Beautiful Laundrette* and you have to understand that Daniel Day-Lewis will still be there when you're old enough to see it. That's a promise.'

It was only some time later that Polly realised that Johnny was no longer talking to Luana. She tried to pretend she wasn't listening. She had never actually been in the same room before when he spoke to Edith. He had lowered his voice but Polly could still make out the odd sentence.

'I thought you didn't let it get to you any more. You've got to put it all behind you. You're doing fine now. You've got to believe in yourself. Come on now, promise me you won't fret.'

That's what he says to me, thought Polly. That's his way of comforting me when I go over the top about something. How dare he say it to her. Yet, of course, she reasoned, he had probably said it to Edith long before he'd ever said it to her. Did he still see Edith? Did she come up to London? Did they meet? He sounded incredibly close to her still. Polly strained to hear his next words . . . and wished she hadn't.

'Yeah, yeah, all right. I know. Sure, sure. Look, I've got to go now. Yeah. Love you too.'

Love you too!

Love *you* too.

Love you *too*.

Whichever way she played it back in her mind, Polly knew that Edith had said the words 'I love you' to Johnny and Johnny had responded with 'Love you too.' But Edith was supposed to have left him. She wasn't supposed to love him any more.

That night as Johnny snuggled up to her and suggested that he engage her in some energetic festive sex, she went through the motions until the tip of his penis was about to penetrate her and

then the words 'Love you too' began to scream silently in her head. For the first time ever her vagina clenched as he entered her and the pain made her cry out. Johnny withdrew immediately.

'What's up? Why did I hurt you?'

Polly rolled over on her side and began to heave noiselessly.

'Pol?' said Johnny a little nervously. 'Tired?'

Polly nodded her head up and down on the pillow.

'Well, you'd better get some sleep. Go on. Good girl. You go to sleep,' he told her and turned on the television full blast so that Polly wondered if anyone anywhere in Notting Hill Gate would get any sleep that Christmas.

When *Mr Wrong* was published it went straight to Number 7 on the bestseller list. On Wednesday of the next week they heard it would be Number 1 in the *Sunday Times* the following Sunday and Lawrence decided to throw a party. Johnny refused to go and Polly arrived making excuses, saying he had a stomach upset and fooling no one.

Polly was amused to see the transformation in Lawrence. Among his other guests he had invited all the top literary editors and their partners, various columnists and a number of influential actors' agents she was quite sure he did not count among his closest friends. Lawrence was going to make it big but he wasn't about to leave it to chance.

On the way home, Polly decided there could not be a more auspicious time to make the break from Patrick Fisher & Dunbar, always assuming the likes of Lawrence, Lucy Richards and Rebecca Price would follow her. She rushed into the house anxious to tell Johnny but it turned out he had made an important decision of his own while she'd been gone.

He was watching Crufts on television, perched on the edge of his seat, yelling at the judge.

'Pick the Irish setter, you bloody wally, the Irish setter, can't you hear me? Best in Show, Pol,' he explained, seeing her come in, 'if she doesn't pick the Irish setter, she should be shot.'

'Incredibly stupid dogs, most of them. Very highly strung.'

'Who asked you? Go on, you stupid woman, get it over with.'

The judge walked past the Irish setter and picked another dog. Johnny slumped back in his armchair, totally dejected.

'Nobody bloody listens to me any more,' he said gloomily, 'that's why I'm going to get one. It'll listen to me. It'll have to.'

'What will?'

'A dog. Polly, I am going to get myself a dog. Why do you think I've been watching Crufts? I wanted to get a look at all the different breeds before I decided.'

He only ever said Polly instead of Pol when he was in seriously bad shape. Polly delayed yet another conversation about starting the agency to give him her full attention.

Together they studied the *Observer Book of Dogs* and together they finally decided on a springer spaniel on the grounds that it wouldn't be too 'poncy' (Johnny's words) but neither would it be too big to keep in London (Polly's stipulation).

The next day Johnny went out and came back with what looked to Polly like an overgrown chihuahua.

'What,' she demanded 'is that?'

'A Papillon. Don't look like that, Pol. It's a very special breed. When its ears stand up they look like butterfly wings. *Papillon* is French for butterfly.'

'I know that, Johnny. What happened to the springer spaniel?'

'They didn't have any.'

'Who didn't have any?'

'Harrods.'

'Well, why didn't you try the springer spaniel club of Great Britain and find a breeder, why didn't you ring the Kennel Club?'

'Because Zutty looked so sad when I walked away.'

'That's the oldest trick in the book. It looks pretty miserable now. What did you call it?'

'Zutty. His real name is Zut Alors! which means Damn and Blast in French but I suppose you know that. But we'll call him Zutty for short after the drummer, you know, Zutty Singleton, on my Fats Waller records.'

Zutty dined with them. He watched television with them. He tried to shower with them and he came to bed with them. Polly marvelled at the irony of Zutty's arrival. He was the baby they had never had yet instead of her maternal instinct being showered upon him, Zutty was basking in non-stop attention from an ever-anxious Johnny.

'Zutty slept through the night for the first time,' he told Polly as she was preparing to leave for work.

'Wonderful,' said Polly, 'he'll be on solids next. Better add dog food to the weekly Sainsbury's list.'

Yet she was happy that Johnny had something to occupy his time. If he didn't get a picture soon she didn't know what they were going to do. She had already called around for advice about builders for her new office on the back of the house but she didn't want Johnny hanging around doing nothing when she started working in it.

In the event the construction of the conservatory over the next few months didn't bother Johnny in the slightest. By then he had a new interest in his life in the form of Lady Whyte.

Every morning Johnny lay in the bath and belted out 'Sixteen Tons', a hit record from his childhood, while Polly fished her tights out from under the bed and applied what she called 'whirlwind make-up', protesting: 'Oh, Johnny, please!' in between gulps of coffee.

'It's all right, Pol,' he said one morning, 'one day I'll be another Gordy Whyte and you'll be Lady de Soto. Sounds good. What d'you think?'

Sir Gordon Whyte had been knighted for his services to the British film industry. After producing a string of highly successful romantic comedies dubbed the Ealing Valentines, he went on to mount lavish costume dramas followed by an action adventure film series featuring a daredevil Special Branch operative called Conway. The violence was extreme, the sex explicit, but Conway's dialogue in the scripts was that of a sophisticated stand-up comic and the character made a star out of Hector O'Neill, who had now played the role at least half a dozen times. But the future of the Conway films was in abeyance following the sudden death of Gordy Whyte from a coronary.

'Maybe I should offer my services to produce Conway,' suggested Johnny, surveying his naked body in the mirror while he rubbed his back with his bath towel.

'Christ!' said Polly suddenly, 'that reminds me. Jules gave me tickets for his charity thing.'

'Whose charity thing? Gordy Whyte's? Jesus, Pol, nothing like keeping a secret from your old man.'

'His widow – what's her name? – Juanita's running it now. Whyte Knight it's called. In aid of MS. Jules is on the committee, God knows why, the only thing he can raise is a glass. But he can't go to the charity première of the latest Conway film and he gave me the tickets.

'When is it? Whoopee, Pol. This might be my big break.'

'Johnny, you do not go prancing up to people touting for jobs at charity premières.' Polly was scrabbling in her handbag: 'here they are. Oh, it's tonight. Black tie. That means a trip to the same-day cleaner's for my old Valentino. I suppose you want me to take your monkey suit while I'm at it . . . ?'

Johnny insisted on hiring a limousine to drop them at the Odeon Leicester Square and was furious when they were deposited round the corner in Charing Cross Road and had to walk conspicuously through the cordoned-off area to the cinema entrance. He brightened up when they took their £100 seats in the front circle upstairs.

'This is more like it. Where's Princess Diana?'

'It's Princess Michael.'

'She'll do. This is great, Pol.' He leaned over the balcony. 'Blimey! Place is stiff with clapper loaders and gaffers. Hey, Steve, up here, hey!'

'Johnny, shut up. Anybody'd think you'd never been to a royal première before.'

'There she is, there's Juanita.'

'Lady Whyte to you, Johnny. You don't know her.' Polly shifted in her seat, curious to see Gordy Whyte's exotic widow, reputed to be Nicaraguan.

'Goggles!' she said loudly and clearly and completely involuntarily. Juanita Whyte stiffened and sat down without looking at Polly, although everyone else did.

'I was at school with her. I can't believe it. Goggles Grant. She had specs thicker than Lawrence's, poor thing. Couple of years ahead of me. What on earth has she done to herself? Who would have thought . . . Goggles Grant becoming a society beauty. But I'll tell you one thing, Johnny, her name was never, ever Juanita. It was something like Sandra. Sandra Grant. I know it's her. Nicaraguan, my foot! Bournemouth, more like.'

At the party afterwards Johnny insisted on Polly introducing him to 'your old school chum'.

'She's not my old school chum. I was a little squirt to her. She won't remember me.'

But Johnny wasn't about to pass up a golden opportunity.

'Lady Whyte – ' he planted himself squarely in front of her – 'you may remember my wife, Polly. She says you were at school together.'

Juanita Whyte took in Polly's five-year-old sale-bought Valentino, her insignificant single strand of pearls, her hastily Carmen-rollered bob, her 'whirlwind' make-up and her rather down-at-heel Charles Jourdain pumps with their clip-on grosgrain bows. She patted her own immaculately highlighted hair, obviously cut and coiffed that very afternoon, fingered her stark jet choker and stood triumphantly in her hot-off-the-collection Karl Lagerfeld.

'Polly?' she looked blank.

'Polly Atwell,' murmured Polly.

'Of course!' Juanita extended her arms, moved forward and without actually ever touching Polly, kissed the air beside her left cheek.

As she felt the cool hiss of air Polly looked over Juanita's shoulder straight into the eyes of the most gorgeous man she had ever seen. Tall, dark and handsome – TDH, as they'd called them at school – and then some. This creature was the prefect specimen, the dreamy Celt with the melting blue eyes, good strong nose and cruel, sardonic mouth. She'd never seen Hector O'Neill in the flesh before and having him standing so close right after she'd drooled over him as Conway in the film for the past two hours somewhat unnerved her. As Juanita turned to Johnny, Hector slipped past her, ducked and whispered quickly in her ear:

'If I ever kissed you I'd make sure I didn't miss.'

'So good of you to come,' Juanita was telling Johnny. 'Gordy would have been so pleased to see you.'

Artificial bitch, thought Polly, watching as Juanita allowed her hand to be clasped in Johnny's. She hasn't a clue who I am but one look at my clothes tells her she doesn't want to know.

A week later she dragged Johnny, moaning all the way, to dinner at Jules Dunbar's.

'I know it would have been good for your career, Pol, dinner with the boss and all that, if you still worked for him but you don't any more and besides, what's in it for me? Can't I stay home with Zutty and watch the fight on the box?'

'No,' Polly insisted, and in so doing unwittingly signed the death sentence on her marriage.

Juanita Whyte was the guest of honour and Jules placed her next to Johnny.

'You can talk shop until the fish,' he told them genially.

'Can we really?' Juanita leaned towards Johnny. 'What is it that you do exactly?'

Johnny told her. And he didn't stop at the fish. Polly caught the fatal words 'in our business' over and over again but as far as she could see, Juanita Whyte was riveted.

Eventually Jules had to prise Johnny away with the offer of an Armagnac.

It's like he used to be, thought Polly, watching him. He's his old self, engaging as hell. She's loaded. He knows it. She hasn't got a prayer.

Indeed, Polly decided Juanita was the best thing that could have happened to them when she agreed to provide the funding for whatever property Johnny wanted to option – if not buy outright.

'And she's not even after my body,' Johnny winked at Polly.

'Well at least she learned something at that dreadful school we went to. Do me a favour, Johnny, get her to rent you an office and hire Rachel for you if you can find her. I don't want you cluttering up the dining room all over again.'

Polly couldn't wait to tell Joan about 'Goggles' Grant.

'You must remember her, Joan,' she said when, true to form, Joan telephoned at eleven the next morning, 'she wore specs as thick as pebbles. She was seriously stupid.'

'Sandra Grant. Yes, I remember her. Well, good for her. She's really come up in the world if she's become Lady Whyte. Why are you being so down on her, Polly? Bit jealous, are you? She's done really well for herself.'

'She's married someone successful, that's all,' protested Polly, 'it's not as if she's done anything herself.'

That was Joan all over. It was who you were married to, where you stood on the social ladder, that's what counted with Joan. When Polly had told her about *Mr Wrong* going to Number 1 on the bestseller lists and that she was now breaking away from Patrick Fisher & Dunbar to start her own agency, Joan had gone strangely quiet and just stared at her for a while before going 'Hmm, well I suppose you know what you're doing.' She hadn't seemed pleased for Polly, hadn't congratulated her.

'Anyway she's taken a real shine to Johnny and she's going to back his next production.'

'What do you mean, his next production? He hasn't made a film unless you mean that Wolf fiasco. You're right, Polly, she must be a bit stupid if she's taking up with a loser like Johnny. Sorry to be so brutal about your precious husband but I've never made any secret of the fact that I think he's hopeless. You'd better keep an eye on him, Polly, hadn't you?'

'Why? He'll be fine now.'

'She's after him. You don't seriously imagine she wants him professionally, do you? Polly, why are you always so naive? What's that wonderful nickname Luana has for you?'

'What nickname?' said Polly. But she knew perfectly well.

Polly Pushover.

Johnny moved out to his new office the week the builders finished Polly's conservatory. Polly was delighted to be rid of him. When he was at home it was non-stop 'Juanita this' or 'Juanita that' so that Polly became so sick of the sound of Juanita's name that she stopped asking about how he was progressing in his search for a film property. As far as she could make out, Juanita had found him some offices in Shawfield Street in Chelsea and he had installed himself and Rachel, who had been discovered earning a small fortune as an advertising copywriter. One lunch with Johnny and she chucked it all in for what Polly knew was a ludicrously hollow promise that she would be associate producer on whatever film Johnny eventually made.

Polly had the number at Johnny office's should she wish to call him but she found, rather to her surprise, that as the weeks – and then the months – went by, she didn't particularly wish to do so.

As for Johnny, he rarely bothered to look outside the back door and see how her new office was coming along.

'Beats me why you want to work in the bloody garden,' was his only comment. 'I would have thought the way your career was taking off you would jump up and down a bit till you got snapped up by ICM or the Morris office, became a real player. Now, Pol, I've been thinking, why don't you call Juanita? You girls could have lunch at San Lorenzo one of these days. Old school chums' reunion. Be nice, wouldn't it?'

Polly registered from this first snippet of dialogue Johnny had thrown her way in some time that he obviously wasn't up to any hanky-panky with Juanita, not that she'd ever really suspected it. The way he still snuggled up to her every night and murmured idiotic things, almost in his sleep, reassured her that however much he might be trying to toughen up his image in the outside world, affection was still his middle name.

Polly wasn't a lady who lunched – unless it was for work – and told him so. Nor would she trot round London every night to whatever chic soirées were being hosted by the ladies who did. She went to book launches – for her authors only – and when she came home she was usually so tired she put her feet up and watched television while eating her supper before invariably returning to her desk in the upstairs sitting room for an hour or so.

Polly and her new assistant, Mrs Flowers, moved into the conservatory. To stop herself from going mad while she waited for the builders to finish her new office, Polly had begun to garden furiously and now, able to view the fruits of her labours from her desk, she thought she had never been so happy. Her new cordless phone enabled her to wander outside and weed while she negotiated. She wondered what the ambitious Pat Walsh would say if she knew she had just offered an advance of £43,000 to someone whose knees were buried in moist soil instead of sitting in a corner office at a black desk with a hi-tech Italian lamp.

Polly threw a party to launch the new office. She called it the Atwell Agency since Johnny already had PDS – Polly de Soto Productions. *Le tout* publishing turned up and as they wandered happily around her garden, champagne glasses clinking and Mrs Flowers' home-made bite-size vol-au-vents and sausage rolls disappearing rapidly, Polly knew she'd made it. There were people here who wouldn't even take her calls two years ago. She hadn't asked them but the news of her hit authors – Lawrence, Lucy Richards, Rebecca Price *et al.* – had made them curious and they'd come along and crashed her party. A sure sign of success.

There was one person who didn't enjoy the party at all: Joan.

The problem was that she was out of work so when Polly introduced her and people asked her where she was working, she didn't have an answer. No one was interested in her, Polly was the centre of attention for once and Joan wasn't used to it. She left after an hour pleading an entirely phoney dinner date.

Polly could see Johnny was proud of her. He didn't know who any of the people were either but unlike Joan he didn't let it bother him and he was enjoying his role as the successful agent's other half. Before long his notebook was being extracted from inside his jacket and he was busily scribbling numbers and, Polly realised, plots of books from various gushing editors who would declare at their editorial meeting that 'the film rights have just been sold in this book or that . . .', such was the naivety of the publishing world that a producer had only so much as to say they were interested and the editor thought the film was as good as made.

A hard core of twenty or so were still scoffing vol-au-vents and sausage rolls at ten o'clock. Polly heard the doorbell in the distance, and groaned.

'I'll go,' said Johnny. When he didn't return Polly extricated herself from one of her more inebriated authors and went looking for him. As she started down the long passage to the hall, she heard Luana's voice.

'But I had to come, Poppa. Where else could I go?'

'You shouldn't have gone anywhere. Edith will be worried stiff,' Polly heard Johnny reply.

'She won't, Dad. That's the whole point. I just can't take it any more. She's crazy. She keeps threatening to –'

Polly stepped forward and Luana ran to her.

'Polly, I'm sorry to arrive without any warning. Please let me stay.'

'Of course you can stay. Your room's always waiting for you but why didn't you let us know you were coming?'

'She's done a runner.'

'She's what?'

'Run away from home.'

'Why?'

Luana looked at Johnny. Johnny slipped his arm around Luana's shoulders and took her upstairs.

'Bed for you, sweet peach. We'll decide what to do with you in the morning. Polly's got a party to take care of, haven't you, Pol?'

Johnny wouldn't even discuss it. Amidst the remains of the party he poured himself a whisky and refused to be drawn. He had gone very calm and still as he always did just before he lost his temper. Acidly polite. Answering all Polly's questions – what had happened? Had Edith gone away? What couldn't Luana take any more? Why had she run away from home?' – but never giving her a proper answer.

Finally he stood up.

'Polly.' Polly. Not Pol. A danger signal. 'I've said this before and I'll say it again. Please don't ask me questions about Edith and I don't want you quizzing Luana either. Edith is my past life. You are my present. That should be enough for you.'

'Why should it be enough for me? Why is there this mystery surrounding Edith?'

'There's this mystery because she wants to be left in peace and I respect that. I do not want her disturbed. Is that understood?'

He was livid now. He had gone perfectly still. Polly could feel his anger charged towards her. She left the room and went back to her party.

'Po-leee!' called Luana from her bedroom window, 'are you still down there? Come and tell me what Hector O'Neill was like? You must have met him at the Conway première. He's so scrummy! Polly . . .'

Luana had obviously been briefed. She became nervous whenever Polly mentioned Edith.

'I promised Dad. Mum's ill. No, actually, she's better now but you just have to be careful. Please let's not talk about her, Polly, please?'

And Luana was so appealing – like Johnny in a way – that Polly could never refuse her anything. She was growing to love her stepdaughter. Luana was sent back to Cornwall two days after

Polly's party, but two weeks after that she was back. For good. No explanation. No message from Edith. Nothing.

Nor was Luana forthcoming.

'It's what I've always wanted to do, you know that, Polly. Dad's been trying to persuade Mum for yonks. Every time he comes down he talks about it. Now he's finally got her to agree.'

Every time he comes down.

Polly couldn't believe it. Going down to Cornwall from London took a good five or six hours. He must have been lying to her when he said he was going to Paris or wherever it was he went. But she knew better than to raise it with him.

Mr Wrong went to the top of the American bestseller list and Juanita Whyte read it because *Vanity Fair* told her to. In actual fact she was reading one of the interminable serial killer profiles in *Vanity Fair* which mentioned *Mr Wrong* en passant.

Juanita told Johnny that they absolutely had to make the film. Johnny told Juanita to talk to his wife.

Suddenly it was 'Polly, darling, we simply must see more of each other. What about lunch next week at the Caprice?'

Fuck the Caprice, thought Polly with the phone cradled to her ear; if she wants to negotiate for the film rights in *Mr Wrong* what's wrong with here and now? Sitting in a wicker chair beside the Norwegian stove in her conservatory and marvelling at the stark beauty of her snow-covered garden, Polly played her tough agent role to the hilt and took Juanita to the cleaner's. If only you could have heard that, Joan, she thought. Johnny didn't speak to her for a week.

'All that sodding money to that scrawny little bastard!' she heard him mutter in his sleep.

Still, now he was back at work for real. He had to find a writer. Polly knew better than to suggest Lawrence immediately. She bided her time and sure enough Johnny shelled out Juanita's money for one dud script after another until Juanita came on the phone again.

'That boy you represent, darling. Johnny seems to think he couldn't possibly write his own screenplay. What do you think?'

106

'Of course he could – for the right price . . .' said Polly and promptly took Juanita back to the cleaner's.

'You'll take her money but you won't be friends with her!' complained Johnny.

'Oh, and what do you think you've been doing? Taking her money and supping with her. That makes your behaviour OK, does it?'

'I just wish you could be around a bit more for me, give dinner parties, that sort of thing.'

'I thought Juanita gave her little dinners for you. You spend enough time at them.'

'Well, why won't you come?'

'Because they bore me. It's like reading *Harpers & Queen* out loud all night. I've got better things to do. I'm sorry, Johnny.'

'But Pol, people are beginning to ask about you. I mean I was at Sophie Warner's party last week – Juanita took me so we could network –'

'I hate that word – network! There you are, Johnny, that's the difference between us. You go out and network and I stay in and tune in to the networks in the comfort of my own living room.'

Johnny wouldn't give up.

'People know who you are, you know. They say to me: "You're married to Polly Atwell, aren't you?" By the way, when did you change your name back, Pol? Anyway, they want you there, they want to see who you are.'

'Oh, I'm somebody now, am I?'

'Yeah, that's it. We could become a real London couple. I want everyone to know about you. We'll be invited everywhere.'

'That's just it, Johnny. I don't want to be invited everywhere just for the sake of being seen. I want to get on with my work, take care of my authors and Luana and see people who really mean something to me.'

'Mean something to you? Where do I fit in?'

'Wherever you want, Johnny. What you have to understand is that I don't fit in out there with all that crowd and I never will.'

'But I need you, Polly.'

'In what way, exactly?'

107

'I need someone to share everything with. I don't understand you. Here we are on the brink of making it all happen and you want to stay in every night.'

'Not every night.'

'Well, most nights. You go off and sit on your own and I never know what you're doing.'

'I'm reading manuscripts, I'm working. You know I have to read in the evenings. And as for not knowing what I'm doing, are you always where you say you are?'

'What's that supposed to mean?'

'Made any more trips to Cornwall lately?'

He acted as if she had never said it, just moved right on.

'I don't know how else to explain, Polly. I'm no good on my own. Some people just aren't. I want you out with me, that's all, by my side.'

'Johnny, I don't think it really matters who it is by your side. You just need someone. Anyone. What's wrong with Juanita? She seems to be prepared to hang on your every word. Why doesn't it ever occur to you that I need someone here at home with me in the evenings every now and again? Oh, God, now where are you going, Johnny? Come back. Don't rush off like that. Hold on . . .' As the front door slammed behind him she suddenly remembered his mother's words: 'Keep up with him, Polly. Don't let him get away. Don't hold him back. Let him go fast and keep up with him.'

As she lay in bed, surrounded by manuscripts she could no longer concentrate on, Polly found herself looking at the telephone, waiting for it to ring, waiting to hear Johnny's voice with the noise of a restaurant in the background begging her to join him.

Had he gone too far ahead of her and she'd been left behind? Or was it – could it be that it was the other way round? Had she gone too far ahead and he didn't like it?

She had her answer soon enough. The very next week he left her in the middle of the night.

PART TWO

Hector O'Neill was scared. He kidded himself he was excited at the prospect of looking for a new role to play now Conway had come to an end but in fact he was terrified. The world knew him as Conway. The world loved him as Conway. Worst of all, there was now a chance the world would discover that he couldn't act. Playing Conway he hadn't had to. He just had to look good and leave the rest to the special effects. Now his agent was proposing that he do something completely different. He picked up the script that had just arrived by messenger. That was another thing. He didn't really know how to read a script. For Conway he had just read the pages given him by the script girl every night, learned his lines for the following day's shooting, and then delivered them in the Irish brogue familiar to audiences all over the world. That had been enough. Lucky for him he had a good memory. His only preparation for his roles had been daily workouts in the gym and nightly workouts with available women.

That was something he had developed to a fine art: the art of seduction. Before the sex he wined and dined the women and over the years he had honed his patter to perfection. He had learned that what women liked most of all was a man who listened to them.

He opened the script and saw the title.

Mr Wrong.

'All over the world women search for Mr Right. If, and when, they find him it never occurs to them that he might, in fact, be Mr Wrong.'

Too true! Take his mother, for example. She had picked Mr Wrong twice – his father and then Tony. If anyone had turned out to be Mr Wrong it was Tony.

He could have been Mr Right if it hadn't been for his parents. The universal hippie uniform worn by everyone attending Woodstock – jeans, T-shirts, waistcoats over bare chests, beads, flowers, long flowing dresses and shawls, sometimes nothing at all – had done away with any kind of class distinction. Somewhere in the back of her mind Mary Maguire must have known Tony had some kind of money, otherwise how could he afford to whisk her and her son away to a new life, organising their passports, and then their air tickets with the flash of a credit card. It was the first time John Hector had ever seen a credit card and he thought Tony must be some kind of magician to be able to wave a piece of plastic in the air instead of money and acquire things immediately.

Mary Maguire was so ecstatic at the thought of leaving behind her miserable existence in the shadow of the steelworks that she never stopped to wonder what kind of life awaited her in England. When the taxi made its way up a drive bordered by tall pines and drew up outside a Tudor mansion, Mary thought they had arrived at a castle. It would be some time before she understood the reality of her situation. It was a mock-Tudor house in Surrey and Tony's father was an ex-army stockbroker. After a stifling suburban childhood Tony had escaped to London where he had embraced all aspects of Sixties permissiveness, culminating, after the obligatory trips to India and Morocco, in the journey to Woodstock.

Nothing could have prepared Tony's parents for the arrival on their doorstep of an almost illiterate American steelworker's wife and her ten-year-old son. When he had told them he had met 'someone special' in America, his mother had implored him to forget whatever differences they might have had in the past and bring her home to meet them. Tony, who had not taken into account that his Chelsea pad would be too small to house his new family, welcomed it as an invitation to move Mary and John Hector into the Surrey mansion.

Tony's mother was appalled. After a week under her roof Mary Maguire traded her flower-power glad rags for polyester and cheap perfume. She left dirty coffee cups in every room. She roamed around the house in her underwear, rarely dressing before dark. She played loud music in Tony's room and she let her child stay up until all hours of the night.

'How long do they plan on staying, Tony? Do they have nowhere to go?'

'They're here for ever. They're with me,' Tony told his mother.

'Well, where is the child's father?'

'Killed in Vietnam.'

This was a myth that had been created by Mary. She hadn't exactly lied to Tony and told him her husband had been killed. She just hadn't bothered to correct him in his assumption that that was what had happened. John Hector was left in a similar hazy state as to the whereabouts of his father.

'Tony, they can't stay here. I can't have people to the house while they're here. It's embarrassing. You'll have to take them to London.'

By this time Tony had realised what he'd done. In a drug-crazed field in upstate New York with Ten Years After blasting out 'I'm Going Home', from the stage, Mary Maguire, her skin damp and glowing, clawing at his body and telling him he was blowing her mind, had seemed exactly what he wanted. So what if she had a kid. They could start a commune. But nobody started communes in Surrey, not even in Chelsea for that matter. Suddenly Mary and her kid had become a liability, a bore. Tony wanted out so he did what he always did when things became too heavy. He left.

His mother would have thrown Mary and John Hector out after him if it hadn't been for the intervention of Tony's father. He was, after all, a military man and the fact that the child's father had served his country in Vietnam and died for it made him a hero and they couldn't turn a hero's family out into the streets. As usual he would clean up after his son's mess.

But how?

Mary Maguire flatly refused to go back to Pennsylvania. She had been in Surrey for nearly two months and she liked it.

'John Hector has to go to school,' Tony's mother told her. 'You will have to find a job. It is our responsibility to support you until you have found one.'

Unfortunately Mary was unskilled and virtually unemployable. In the end it was the cleaner at the Surrey mansion who came to her rescue. She had been making good use of Mary's idle hands and had shown her the delights of domestic work. To everyone's amazement, given the slut she had been when she arrived, Mary proved to be a natural cleaner and she asked Tony's mother for a job. This was acceptable. Providing the girl knew her place she could stay in the house. A live-in cleaner was an unheard-of luxury. She could be described as 'my new maid'. In the end Mary Maguire had come full circle from below stairs at Henry Avenue, Philadelphia to the kitchen wing of a mock-Tudor mansion in the stockbroker green belt of Surrey. She had always told John Hector that one day she would return to the life from whence she came and now, as she piled laundry into the washing machine and vacuumed the bedrooms, she felt she had fulfilled her promise.

On arrival in England John Hector retreated into himself as a kind of self-defence. He didn't understand where they were, he barely had time to get to know Tony before Tony upped and left, and he couldn't make out whether they were there to stay. With a child's simplistic intuition he could sense that he and his mother were not welcome in Surrey and he lived in constant fear that they would depart as suddenly as they had arrived and return to the Pennsylvania mobile home. Yet at the same time he became accustomed to the new-found luxury surrounding him. He slept in Tony's boyhood bedroom and played with Tony's abandoned toys. So when suddenly Mary moved him downstairs to a bleak little room behind the kitchen he didn't like it. He observed that they no longer had their meals with Tony's parents and he was relieved that he no longer had to listen to the old man's endless stories about the war – what war? – and the constant reminders that he must be so proud to have a father who had died for his country.

114

John Hector didn't have a photograph of his father. The only picture he had he carried in his mind: that of Jimmy Maguire coming up over the horizon in the haze of smoke and mist with the steelworks behind him, joshing with his buddies and disappearing into the saloon. Yet when he went to school, he found that Jimmy Maguire's alleged heroic death in Vietnam was one of the ways to put an end to the merciless teasing of his new English schoolmates in the playground. That and his American accent. These kids, he realised, had never met a real live American before. To them he was the nearest thing to the movies they'd ever seen. When they all sneaked in to see *Kelly's Heroes* one afternoon, suddenly John Hector sounded just like Clint Eastwood to them. They invited themselves to tea just so they could sit at the kitchen table and stare up at Mary Maguire, imagining she was a star from Hollywood.

Mary Maguire barely noticed them. She had her own problems. There was a man she'd met down the bingo who wanted to marry her but how could she marry him when as far as she knew she already had a husband? She didn't know how to find out what had happened to Jimmy Maguire without revealing her whereabouts to those she had deserted back in Pennsylvania. She was beginning to tire of being a cleaner. It was demoralising when Tony came home for the odd weekend with his parents and found she'd become the maid. But what could she do? For the second time in her life she felt trapped.

As for John Hector, it was one thing having the boys forever getting him to do his Clint Eastwood impersonation. It was quite another to discover the effect his American roots had on the girls. He hadn't been aware that he was good looking. When he had arrived at the school he had been too young for the girls to notice him but when his voice changed and his legs grew longer and longer, he found himself surrounded. And confused. He had begun to lose his accent. There were traces of it here and there – he always said 'plenny' instead of plenty – but he was actually making a determined effort to become English in every way. Then the girls began to feature in his life and they wanted him American again. Yet while he could *sound* American, he now felt English. England

115

was his home. So he had to pretend to be American. He had to act American.

He didn't have to act horny. He wanted all the girls he could get his hands on but just as he was poised to fall in love for the first time something happened to shake his faith in the female sex. From that point on, without even being fully aware of it, he distrusted women.

Mary Maguire left him.

She ran off for the second time – with the man from the bingo – only this time she left her son behind. OK, so he wasn't a small boy any more but he was an impressionable sixteen-year-old.

John Hector crumbled. By way of consolation he demanded sex of every girl who presented herself to him, ignoring them if they refused, dumping them the next day even if they consented. He smoked dope, he started drinking and Tony's father threw him out.

'You're a disgrace to your dead father's name,' he told him. 'Go and find your mother.'

It wasn't as if Mary Maguire had made a secret of her whereabouts. She had just made it clear that her new man did not want John Hector around, so the last thing John Hector was going to do was go looking for his mother.

He went to London and for two years he eked out a living as a labourer, an Irish brickie, whistling at the girls from the scaffolding and developing the powerful muscles that were to become part of the devastating overall Hector O'Neill package. Gracie Delaney's first sight of him was a pair of long jean-clad legs and a rippling bare torso. She responded to his 'I'd give you one any time, darling' not because she wanted him but because she was scouting for a male hunk to feature in a television commercial.

The product, predictably, was aftershave. John Hector, once persuaded down from the scaffolding, attended a casting and landed the part. He had to shave, naked from the waist up, looking at himself in the mirror and stroking his chin. Footsteps could be heard approaching throughout the commercial. As they reached John Hector he had to whip round and point what the audience assumed would be a gun at the intruder but which was of course the product, a product which was totally upstaged by John Hector's brilliant blue eyes.

John Hector received a sad little note from Tony's parents, who traced him through the advertising agency, informing him that his mother had died suddenly. When he called them for further details it became clear that she had been pregnant – at forty-four – with the bingo man's child and had tried to abort it dangerously late. They told him where she had been buried but John Hector was surprised to find that he had no desire to visit her grave. Thinking about her depressed him. Mary Ellen Maguire, dead at forty-four. What a pathetic, useless life. Thank God it was over. Now he could get on with his own.

He was living off the repeats from the commercial, waiting for something else to happen and trying to get into Gracie Delaney's knickers without success when he had the call for the Conway role.

Gracie was not a beauty. She was large and plain with a big nose but she had glossy chestnut hair and the most beautiful white skin John Hector had ever seen. He longed to touch it, to see more of it, but Gracie evaded any attempts he made to steer the conversation towards sex and went right on talking about his work.

'You'll go for the audition, of course?' Gracie was making him lunch at her flat. She was Irish American just like him and – the beauty of it – she was also from Pennsylvania. But she was a good Catholic girl and she wouldn't sleep with him just like that.

'But why not, Gracie? Where's the harm? You like me, don't you?'

If he only knew it, Gracie was dangerously close to falling in love with him but her time in London was up. She was due to return to Philadelphia the following month and she didn't want to complicate her life.

'I like you fine but I've a sweetheart waiting for me back home and I can't let you distract me, now can I?'

'Why not?' said John Hector, grinning at her and maddening her and thoroughly enjoying it. 'Tell me about him. How long have you known him?'

'Four years.'

'But you've been in London for two years. He's waited for you all this time? Is he good looking?'

'Not especially.'

'So what's so wonderful about him? Is he gentle with you? Does he understand you? You're an unusual person, Gracie.'

'Am I? How so?'

'You're sensitive. You need someone who can see beyond that stupid tough-girl "I can take care of meself" image you're always promoting. I bet you cry a lot when you're on your own, at music, at sentimental movies with happy endings. Am I right?'

'How does a brickie know what makes me tick? But yes, you're not far wrong. Frank is the "what-you-see-is-what-you-get" type. It'd never occur to him there's anything more to me than good old reliable Gracie Delaney, always there when you want her. My parents like him. He's from the neighbourhood. He's Catholic. They know where he's coming from. His brother's a priest. Frank's a teacher. Don't look like that, John Hector. Some of us want stability in our lives. Anyway, what about your parents? I bet they want you to marry a nice Catholic girl too. Oh, God, why does it always come down to what my parents want? Why can't I grow up and break away from them? I thought coming to London and landing a job in the glamorous world of casting would place me beyond their reach. But here I am going right back to them.'

'And to Frank.'

'Damn Frank! I don't want Frank. He's so . . .'

'Boring?'

'Unadventurous. He wouldn't come to England with me. He's not interested in anything that happens outside of his precious little world. How can he teach anybody anything when he hasn't even got an enquiring mind? Oh, why am I telling you all this?'

'Because I'm listening.' John Hector said it without thinking but he also realised that because he had remained silent without distracting her, she had let it all spill out. Now, typically, she felt guilty. 'And because there's a part of you that is terrified at the thought of settling down in Pennsylvania for the rest of your life. Believe me, I'd be pretty confused if I were you. But you'll be OK once you're back there.'

'All this talking about myself when it's you we should be thinking of. And you never answered my question. What about your own parents? Are they not after you to bring home a nice Catholic girl?'

'They're dead. I think.'

'They're not? How altogether terrible. What do you mean, you think? Don't you know?'

She was the first – and only – person John Hector told about his background, probably because of the coincidence that she too came from Pennsylvania. As he talked about his father and the fact that he didn't know whether he was dead or alive, he choked on his words. Gracie put her arms around him. She held him close and kissed his temple, stroked his hair and soothed him. Within minutes she was letting him make love to her and afterwards John Hector reflected on how he had learned another valuable lesson. Open up to a woman, tell her a sob story, make yourself vulnerable, engage her sympathy and the chances are you'll hit a home run.

Gracie was angry with herself. She should have seen that coming. To hide her embarrassment she became super-practical.

'I've been thinking about this Conway audition. You need to have something to make them remember you. A whole new image. How Irish can you be?'

'As Irish as you want.'

'Then we'll work on the accent. Use the American angle. OK, so you don't want to say you were raised in a mobile home and you're a steelworker's kid but you can still be Irish. Why don't we change your name? With a new name you can psych yourself into a whole new persona. How about O'Neill? The O'Neills from Beacon Hill, Boston. You grew up on Newbury Street. Your mother shopped at Bonwit Teller, no Filene's bargain basement for the O'Neills. And you should lose the John. Just Hector from now on. Hector O'Neill.'

It was a game they played until she left, a diversion to distract her from what had happened, to stop her thinking about life with Frank as a schoolteacher's wife. On her last morning she approached him shyly and told him she had an idea.

'Why don't I go back to your home town and find out what happened to your father? I could make the trip, easy, and you have to know one day. I'll be discreet, find out all I can, then I'll write you.'

He knew it was in part a way for her to keep in touch with him

119

but he agreed. Again he was surprised that while he had been ready to bury his mother for good, he remained curious about his father. The picture of him coming over the hill with his lunchbox was as vivid as it had always been.

Her letter arrived the day his newly acquired agent confirmed that he had been cast as Conway. The press were on their way to interview him. It was a great story: young Irish American heart-throb catapulted from nowhere to instant stardom. They had the brand name all ready: Kennedy/Conway.

Hector read the letter as his agent's voice rose in excitement on the other end of the phone.

Dear John Hector,

I am going to give you the truth because that's what I promised you I would do.

Your father, Jimmy Maguire, is alive. He came back from the war and found you and mother gone and apparently it hit him very hard. He started drinking heavily and he hasn't stopped. He's on welfare. I had someone point him out to me and I'm sorry, John Hector, but I had to go and speak to him. He is a mess. He has only one set of clothes and they stink. He sleeps rough most nights. He was wounded in 'Nam and he has difficulty walking. John Hector, you have to do something. I can't pretend your father is a hero. He's a vile smelling drunken bum but he needs your help. Send him money care of me as soon as you can. I'll see he gets it.

The letter went on for two more pages. She was going to marry Frank, she missed John Hector, she prayed for his success, but always she returned to the subject of his father.

In a flash Hector saw how it would look to the press. With a washed-up Vietnam vet for a father, his story would take a very different turn. It'd have to be dirt poor Pennsylvania instead of Boston. Everything would have to come out. He was on the brink of entering the kind of world his wretched mother had fantasised about in vain. What was the point in jeopardising such a chance?

He threw away Gracie Delaney's letter without answering it.

Yet he never forgot her. She had discovered him. She had changed his name for him, she had reinvented him. As he read *Mr Wrong*, he found himself wondering what she would have made of it. When he finished it he knew he had to do it. His agent had been right. It was a logical step to take. Suave playboy murderer seducing women in every frame. He dialled his agent.

'It says Whyte/De Soto Productions. Who the hell's De Soto?'

'Some wop Juanita's got into bed with, metaphorically speaking I hope,' said his agent.

'You mean it was Juanita Whyte who thought of me for this role? She's got more brains that I've given her credit for.'

'No, Hec, it was the other guy, Johnny de Soto. Matter of fact it wasn't even him. It was his daughter. Kid called Luana. Works in a casting agency.'

Just like Gracie Delaney, mused Hector. He wondered what she was like, this Luana de Soto.

Luana had never met the man placed beside her at dinner. She hadn't even been introduced to him before they sat down and so far he had spent the entire meal deep in conversation with the girl on his left.

So it was all the more exciting when she felt his hand move under her skirt, his fingers firmly kneading the flesh on the inside of her thigh beneath her stockings. She almost choked on her apricot soufflé as he unpopped a suspender.

She moved her chair further under the table to enable him to continue his exploration unwitnessed by their fellow diners, but to her intense disappointment he removed his hand. She was about to turn and silently implore him to go on when the man on her right began to talk to her again. She tried to concentrate on the earnest young publisher's description of the biography he was bringing out next month, was about to ask him if he knew her stepmother, the literary agent Polly de Soto – or did she call herself Polly Atwell since Johnny took off, Luana never could remember, probably not, it wasn't as if they were divorced – when she felt the hand return. Higher this time. To her horror she sensed the button at the side of her waist being undone, the zip of her skirt sliding down and the hand reaching in, moving across her stomach, skin on skin, and

122

down to her cunt. It squeezed. An index finger probed, found her clitoris, stroked.

Luana plunged a spoonful of apricot soufflé into her mouth and sucked on her spoon.

The hand withdrew.

Luana discreetly did up her skirt and murmured to the publisher: 'I'm so sorry, I have to go to the loo. Would you excuse me?'

'Of course.' He half rose to his feet as she escaped. Outside the dining room she realised she didn't know where it was. She went into the hall and sat on an ottoman at the bottom of the stairs, wishing she could masturbate, staring at the black and white tiles on the floor, wondering how long she would have to wait.

She had noticed him the minute she'd arrived with Frederick, the young actor who had brought her. Frederick had introduced her to her host and hostess, friends of his parents, and the stranger had watched her from across the room, never looking at her face, staring at first one part of her body and then another till she obliged him by deliberately dropping her bag on the floor and bending over to pick it up so that he could see right down the front of her low-cut dress to her tits, and probably as far as her navel.

He came into the hall and grabbed her by the hand, pulling her up the stairs. Half-way up, before the stairs doubled back to the first floor, there was a door. He drew her into the bathroom behind it, closed the door and pushed her up against it. A pair of towelling robes fell to the floor. Without even taking off his jacket, he undid his flies and took out his erect penis, thick, uncircumcised with a large smooth cap. He fished a condom out of his pocket.

'Want to suck first?'

Luana opened her mouth automatically. She did want to suck but she didn't have time. She flicked her tongue in and out of her mouth at him and he sucked on that a few times, squeezed her breasts through her dress and turned away to ease the condom on to himself. Luana took hold of him and guided him back to her, hoisting her dress up with the other hand. In one quick movement he was right inside her. He began to move fast, taking her by the shoulders. Behind him she could see them reflected in the mirror above the basin, his trousers down to his ankles and just below his

123

jacket his bare buttocks thrusting into her, banging against the door making a hard rhythmic sound that increased in momentum. She wouldn't climax. She never did. Her mind began to wander. She recalled what their position reminded her of: the scene in *The Godfather* where James Caan screws a guest in an upstairs room at his sister's wedding.

Her moans increased as she pretended to come and he clasped a hand over her mouth although the sound of her body being hurled against the door had been just as loud. She was trembling all over as he withdrew from her. He pulled up his trousers, tucked himself away and left without looking at her once.

When she went back down they had left the dining room and were having coffee next door. He was sitting on the arm of a chair, stroking the blonde hair of the woman sitting in it. He was the hostess's brother, she learned, the blonde woman his wife. She would never see him again. How did they always manage to pick her out, she wondered. How did they always know about her?

Frederick drove her home, or rather back to his flat in Earls Court. It never occurred to Luana that she had already fucked one man that night. She let an eager Frederick undress her and attempt clumsy foreplay before entering her. It took him over a quarter of an hour to come. His skinny penis inside her rendered a pleasurable tickle but there was no way he was going to satisfy her. No one could, especially not Frederick. She licked his face absentmindedly and as she began to feel sleepy, she began to tweak his nipples to hurry him up a bit. It usually worked.

Poor Frederick.

As soon as she arrived at the Hendersons', Polly saw that they'd asked Edward Holland again. Christ, Grania Henderson was persistent. Polly's only Mills & Boon author, Grania clearly thought that her career as a romantic novelist gave her an automatic licence to be the perfect matchmaker. Ever since the news about Johnny's leaving had begun to travel, Grania had been on the telephone once a month with unfailing regularity, issuing invitations. Polly had managed to be busy for all except two and on each occasion Edward Holland had been there. Now here he was for the third time. Polly had not really said more than a few words to him at the drinks party and the buffet supper to which they'd both been invited before but this was a sit-down dinner and, feeling somewhat trapped, Polly realised she was being placed beside him.

'Did you get a chance to chat to Edward Holland?' Grania had asked after the buffet supper, trying to sound innocent. 'You know, you met him once before at our Christmas drinks, remember? No? What a shame. He's been divorced for just two years. She was a complete cow. I hated her. Dear Edward, we do so love him . . . never mind. I'll make sure you meet again.'

And here they were. He was attractive enough, Polly conceded. Fiftyish. Not much hair on top but what there was of it was surprisingly thick without much grey. Nice grey eyes. Rather florid cheeks. Not very tall. Square frame. Expressive hands with carefully manicured fingernails. Polly hastily took her elbows off the table and placed her unvarnished nails in her lap out of sight.

'We've met before, haven't we?' He offered her the bread basket. 'I'm Edward Holland. I'm in advertising. You're Polly, aren't you?'

'Well remembered. Polly Atwell.'

'Remind me what it is you do.'

'I'm a literary agent.'

'Of course. You're Grania's agent. How's business?'

'Pretty good. How's advertising?'

'Better than ever. I worked with Peter Mayle, you know?'

'Really?'

'Oh yes, me and Peter. Like that, we were.'

'Heavens.'

'Long time ago, of course.'

'Of course.'

'I wonder if I've got a bestseller in me?'

'I don't know. Have you?'

'Well, I am an ad man. Like Peter.'

'I'm not sure it follows. Can you write? Have you spent a year anywhere? Like Provence?'

'Eh, no, not really. Been stuck in Camberwell for years. Ever since my wife left.'

Polly ignored it.

125

'So did you enjoy your old friend Peter's book?'

'*A Year in Provence*? Truth is, I never read it.'

'Truth is,' said Polly laughing, 'nor have I – at least not that one. But I did read – or rather look at – *Wicked Willie*.'

'So what on earth is that?'

'Huge hit. Cartoon book about a talking dick.'

Edward Holland went bright pink. Oh God, I've embarrassed him, thought Polly, he really is rather sweet.

At the end of the evening she asked Grania for the number of the local minicab firm and Edward leapt to his feet.

'I won't hear of it. I'll drop you home.'

'Edward, we're in Clapham. You live in Camberwell. Polly's in completely the opposite direction. She lives in Notting Hill Gate.' Even Grania was amazed. 'The Simpsons are going right past her door.'

'I insist,' said Edward gravely and Polly tried hard not to giggle.

'That *Wicked Willie* book,' he said as he drew up outside the house, 'sounds fun. I shall buy a copy.'

'Then you can get your friend to sign it for you.'

'Well, he's not really my friend,' Edward confessed. 'I was just showing off a bit.'

'Well, thank you so much for the lift. I fear I've taken you terribly out of your way. May I offer you one for the road by way of compensation?' Polly was half out of the car, assuming he'd say no.

He leapt out with her.

'That'd be wonderful.'

As they walked up the steps a ferocious yapping broke out from inside. Polly tentatively unlocked the front door and was assaulted by Zutty, flying up at her, feathery tail uncurling and wagging. She picked up a note from Johnny on the hall table.

Dear Pol, where are you? I rang and rang but just got the answering machine. No answer when I came round so I let myself in. Hope you don't mind but I've left Zutty. Got to go to Paris till day after tomorrow. His food is in box under hall table. Ditto his new basket. I'm trying to train him not to sleep on my bed. Bit late now but still. Say BARKEY! to him, point at the basket and he's supposed to jump in it and go to sleep. I'll pick him up in 48 hours. He eats once a day in the evening. I've fed him tonight so don't give him anything whatever fuss he makes.

J.

Zutty didn't like Edward Holland and went for his shoelaces, growling.

'Barkey!' said Polly firmly. Edward looked very startled. 'Not you, Edward. That. *Barkey*!' Polly picked up Zutty by the scruff of the neck and shoved him in his basket. 'Now, stay! Bloody dog. What'll you drink, Edward?'

'Whisky please. With water. Right up to the top.'

'So how long have you known the Hendersons?' she asked him.

'Oh, years. My wife was at school with Grania. Grania adores her. She was devastated when we broke up.'

Polly heard Grania's voice saying distinctly: 'She was an absolute cow!'

'You're divorced too, aren't you?' said Edward, edging crab-like along the sofa towards her.

Zutty saved her by going berserk, charging out of his basket and sniffing the bottom of the front door, tail going wag, wag, wag.

'Zutty! Barkey! This minute!' began Polly then there was the sound of the key in the lock and Johnny came in wearing a baseball cap and a long black coat over jeans and sneakers.

'Hi, Pol.'

'What happened to Paris?'

'Missed the bloody plane. Pile-up on the M4. Cab couldn't get round it. How's my *Baby*?' Zutty had flown into his arms.

What an utterly ridiculous sight, thought Polly fondly.

'Johnny, this is Edward Holland.'

Johnny came forward, still carrying Zutty.

'Edward, this is Johnny de Soto.'

'Your husband?' Edward looked utterly bewildered.

'Yes, and the film producer,' said Polly. 'Edward's in advertising. He was a friend of Peter Mayle's.'

'How is Peter?' Polly raised her eyes to heaven. She knew perfectly well Johnny had never met Peter Mayle in his life. 'Pol, did I tell you I was going to Paris to get the final go-ahead for *Mr Wrong*? Any day now. After all this time.'

Johnny had set up *Mr Wrong* as a French co-production on the understanding that half the picture was relocated in France.

'I'd better be getting back to Camberwell.' Edward put down his drink.

'Couldn't drop me and Zutty off on the way, could you? Roland Gardens.' Polly turned away. Johnny sometimes used Edith's old flat where he had first seduced Polly and the reminder of it still made her nostalgic. As she showed Johnny out, Edward whispered nervously: 'May I call you? Could you give me your number?'

'I'll give it to you in the car,' yelled Johnny over his shoulder. 'Night, Pol.'

Polly kicked the door shut behind them.

She opened it again a few seconds later.

'Johnny,' she yelled into the night, 'you forgot Barkey!'

And she flung it after him.

Polly went out early the next morning before Mrs Flowers arrived. She wanted to shop for food in Portobello Road. Luana was coming to supper that night and Polly had been looking forward to it all week. Her stepdaughter had moved out of the house to share a flat with a friend and Polly missed her. Worse, she worried about her. Luana was so thin. Polly was convinced she never ate anything unless someone else fed her so she insisted Luana come to eat with her at least once a month when Polly would cook a veritable feast and always ensure that Luana left clutching the leftovers in little silver foil takeaway containers.

Polly bought a couple of sirloin steaks from Lidgates, some new potatoes, some tomatoes to grill and some mangetouts. She had left a bowl of chick peas to soak and planned to cook them and mix them in a salad as a starter with lemon, walnut oil, garlic, salt and pepper, and fresh coriander and flat leaf parsley. For pudding there was tiramisu for which she had made a special trip to soho the day before. Luana adored tiramisu and Polly had bought enough for the takeaway containers as well. There would be some of the chick pea salad left over but it would be hard to eat cold leftover steak the next day. Polly returned to the butcher's and exchanged the steak for a fillet of beef to roast. They could have it hot and then Luana could take away a pile of cold slices to pick at from her refrigerator.

As she walked back down Ladbroke Grove to the house, Polly thought about Johnny's surprise appearance the night before. Not that it was a rare occurrence. In the time since he had left she realised she still saw him every couple of weeks. The problem was that wherever he lived there was never enough space for all his clothes. The basic plan was that he took his summer wardrobe and left his winter one and then returned to exchange it when it grew colder. But being Johnny, he never seemed to have the right things. There was always something he needed just as he was going away on a trip.

Then there was Zutty to be looked after. In the beginning Polly tried to explain in vain about the existence of kennels but Johnny wasn't having any.

'Zutty doesn't like kennels.'

'How do you know? You've never sent him to one.'

'We discuss it. He tells me. I say, Zutty, old fruit, want to go to kennels or Polly? He says Polly every time. He loves being with you, Pol. You should be flattered. He doesn't like everybody.'

It wasn't just when he went away. Johnny arrived on the doorstep at seven o'clock one morning holding his dog at arm's length.

'Zutty's got fleas!' he told Polly accusingly as if it were her fault, and nipped into the hall before she could shut them out.

'Well, what do you expect me to do about it?'

'You know about dogs, Pol.'

'I don't know how to deal with fleas. Take him to the vet. Get some powder or something.'

'I don't know a vet.'

'Yellow Pages.'

'I haven't got a Yellow Pages.'

'Is Rachel still on this planet?'

'Rachel hates dogs.'

'She didn't until you got one. Does she hate Yellow Pages too?' But he looked so genuinely crestfallen that as usual she relented and dealt with Zutty's fleas. In her mind she heard Luana's voice: 'Polly, you shouldn't be such a pushover with Dad. You spoil him rotten!'

But now that Luana had left and Johnny no longer picked her up from the house, Zutty, Polly realised with a lurch, was their only bond. Yet she loved her freedom – manuscripts spread out all over the bed and no need to clear them up to make way for him. She could eat whenever she wanted. No more hours wasted in the kitchen preparing his meals according to his 'just checking what's for dinner' requests issued down the telephone only to receive a further call at nine o'clock to say he was at Le Caprice, the Ivy or wherever.

No more videos blaring in the bedroom till three in the morning. Now she could bank up her favourite soaps and watch them in peace. But the most infuriating thing about Johnny had been his constant need to know exactly what she was doing every second they were in the house together – and even when they weren't.

'What are you doing, Pol?'

'I'm on the loo.'

'What are you doing, Pol?'

'I'm dicing carrots for the casserole.'

Five minutes later. 'What are you doing now?'

'I'm putting them in the pan.'

Or: 'Johnny, where are you?'

'I'm in a phone booth at Charles de Gaulle. What are you doing?'

'I'm standing here answering the phone.'

'But what were you doing?'

'I just walked through the door.'

'Well, what are you going to do now?'

It was always the trivial everyday things that interested him, never her big deals or her excitement when she read a wonderful manuscript by a new author but where she had been for lunch that day, what she had eaten, who with, what had they said?

Grand dramas left him cold. 'There was a security alert on the Underground. They found a bomb. They defused it but think, Johnny, if I'd been there five minutes earlier I'd have been killed' was greeted with 'Why didn't you take a bus? I like buses. Did you buy me my toothpaste?'

131

Well, he was gone now. She no longer thought about him every day.

Now she only thought about him every other day.

M rs Flowers was in the midst of opening parcels when Polly arrived back with the meat.

'Mrs Brock called. She wanted to know if you were free for lunch.'

'Call her back and say yes, fine. Ask her to meet me in First Floor at 1.15.'

Polly disappeared into the kitchen to put away the meat. She could hear Mrs Flowers on the phone in the conservatory.

'Well, she did say First Floor. Just a minute, I'll ask her. Mrs de Soto, Mrs Brock was wondering if you would meet her at a new Lebanese restaurant she's discovered in Knightsbridge?'

'No!' shouted Polly, 'I've got far too much to do. If I have to go all the way to Knightsbridge I won't be back here till three. She's not working, ask her if she'll . . .'

'She's rung off, Mrs de Soto.' Mrs Flowers always insisted on absolute formality. 'Just as well I wrote down the name of the restaurant.'

It was an old trick of Joan's. If Polly rang her back she would already have left – or at least she wouldn't pick up the phone so it would look as if she had. That way Polly was forced to go to wherever Joan had chosen.

'Cup of coffee, Mrs Flowers?'

'Decaf?' Mrs Flowers was on a health kick. She brought in a container of lentil soup every day which she proceeded to heat up for her lunch.

'Decaf beans, no less,' called Polly. 'I went to the Monmouth Coffee House yesterday.'

Mrs Flowers took her cup and looked at Polly gravely.

'Don't think I don't appreciate what you do for me, Mrs de Soto.'

'It's just a cup of coffee . . .'

'Maybe, but if I was working at Patrick Fisher & Dunbar or any of those other big offices nobody would be making me a cup of coffee, it'd be the other way round. And after all you've been through . . .'

Polly began to look through her mail. The words 'And after all you've been through' always heralded a recitation of the ills Mrs Flowers imagined Polly had suffered as an abandoned wife. Mrs Flowers had taken Johnny's leaving far worse than Polly had and there were times when Polly wondered whether the mythical Mr Flowers had indeed existed and done a similar bunk.

Polly found she had been sent four special book proofs – early promotional paperbacks of hardcover books printed to garner publicity and support for the book from the trade. She looked at the covers. Each one had a dashing young man in uniform clasping a beautiful fragile heroine in his arms. 'An epic story of a love that triumphed,' said one. 'An epic tale of a love that triumphed,' said another. Story, tale, what was the difference? thought Polly. 'They braved everything for each other in World War I,' said the third, and 'Their love conquered all in World War II,' said the fourth. Turning them over she was informed in more or less the same words that the books would all paint a passionate picture of love and loss, sweep the reader along on a tide of emotion, depict a cast of unforgettable characters, brilliantly capture the intensity of the period, and last but not least, they were all 'Fiction on a Grand Scale'.

The nationwide promotion for each one would include: HUGE MEDIA COVERAGE, SPECTACULAR WINDOW DISPLAY MATERIAL, 12 COPY DUMPBIN AND HEADER, FULL COLOUR POSTER, TRADE

MAGAZINE INSERT, COLOUR ADVERTISING IN `COSMOPOLITAN´, `SHE´, `GOOD HOUSEKEEPING´ AND `WOMAN´S JOURNAL´. They were all being published in the same month, two in the same week.

Polly stared at them. If she hadn't been able to see the authors' names she knew she would not have been able to tell them apart. Yet as they were all written by her clients she knew they were all very different books. It looked as if the same book was being published by four different publishers. How would the public know which story of tumultuous passion to choose? If Polly had a problem recognising their books how would the authors themselves feel? She knew she ought to be jumping up and down because her authors' books were getting such a big push from their publishers but there was one book that caused her particular concern: the new Rebecca Price.

There had been a takeover by one of the big conglomerates of the publishing house to which Polly had sold Rebecca's novel when she had changed direction prior to Patrick Fisher's death. Rebecca's editor was still there but hanging on to her job for dear life. She no longer had any clout whatsoever. The marketing department ruled and had decreed that Rebecca Price should get a new look. This, it would appear, was it. No matter that Rebecca had in fact written a sensitive and delicate exploration of the feelings of a young novice in love with a reckless Fenian, a piece of writing worthy of entry for a literary prize. Here it was, tarted up like a Mills & Boon (why was there a man in a British soldier's uniform on the cover and why did the woman look like Vivien Leigh in *Gone With The Wind* when even Audrey Hepburn in *The Nun's Story* would have been a step in the right direction?), with the words 'They braved everything for each other in WWI'. World War I hadn't even started by the end of the book – and what had happened to the marvellous quote from William Trevor?

'Mrs de Soto, there's someone called Zoë Nichols on line two. Shall I ask her what it's in connection with?'

Polly shoved the book proofs aside and reached for the phone in relief. She knew she would have to wade in and sort out the marketing of Rebecca's book but she just couldn't face it right now.

'Presumably it's in connection with me,' said Polly who hated it when Mrs Flowers asked her that question. She knew Mrs Flowers was only trying to protect her but she thought it sounded so offputting, as if Polly Atwell was just too grand to talk to most people. That simply wasn't the case. Polly needed access to any potential client who might come her way. The name Zoë Nichols rang a bell somewhere but she couldn't quite place it. 'Put her through.'

'Hi, my name's Zoë Nichols. You probably won't have heard of me. I've written a couple of Mills & Boons and the odd piece of journalism. The reason I'm ringing you is that I've been meaning to get myself an agent for some time as I'm in the middle of writing a novel. Now something a little more pressing has come up and I feel I need some advice. I've been approached to ghost a novel for a supermodel.'

'Well done, you. Which one?' Polly remembered now. She'd read a piece on casting directors Zoë Nichols had written for one of the colour magazines. It was warm and funny and Polly had enjoyed it.

'Aroma Ross.'

'Good Lord!' Aroma Ross was trouble, or so the tabloids would have everyone believe. On Sunday afternoons, Polly sometimes took a break from the pile of manuscripts to watch *The Clothes Show* and they featured her as much as they could because, despite her exotic heritage, Aroma Ross was a British citizen and alongside Naomi Campbell and Kate Moss, one of the few British supermodels. Polly was fascinated by her. She was half Italian/half Thai and the mix resulted in a smouldering Latin look with long black hair, a strong jaw, a beautiful long straight nose, high cheekbones and a slightly slanting Oriental cast to her huge doe eyes. 'Why does she want to write a novel? She can't be more than twenty.'

'I'm not even sure she does. I've just been approached by the publishers. It's probably their idea, or her agent's.'

'Well, look, I can't talk now. I'm due somewhere for lunch. To tell you the truth I'm more interested in the fact that you, Zoë Nichols, are writing a novel than I am in you writing Aroma Ross's great work. How are you fixed tomorrow?'

Polly jumped in a cab feeling rather excited as she always did at the prospect of a new client. When she arrived at the restaurant Joan was sitting there fuming, literally, puffing furiously at a cigarette. Patience had never been one of her virtues.

'Darling!' she blew smoke into each of Polly's ears by way of greeting, 'any sex, any cheques?' she asked as usual. 'Any men ring you this week? Waiter, ashtray, waiter!' The word 'please' was not part of Joan's restaurant vocabulary.

'No,' said Polly truthfully. 'You?'

'Only Victor.' Victor was a crime reporter from Nottingham who had a face like a bloodhound and had been in love with Joan for twenty years. Or so Joan claimed. Polly knew the entire lunch would focus on the subject of men or rather the lack of them. If Polly ever said something like 'I went to see *The Commitments* last night', Joan's first question was always 'Who with?', never 'What was it like?'

'So how was it at the Hendersons'?'

'How did you know about the Hendersons?'

'You told me you were going ages ago. Who was there?'

Polly realised she couldn't remember anybody besides Grania, her husband and Edward Holland.

'Oh, there were about eight of us.'

'Yes, but who? Who did you sit next to?'

'Edward Holland.'

'Who's he?'

'Friend of the Hendersons.'

'Well, obviously. Now, Polly, what are you going to have to eat? I don't suppose you know anything about Lebanese food. I'll order for you. We'll have some *kibbeh*, some *tabbouleh*, some *fattoush*, some *falafel*, some . . .'

Polly tried to convey that she adored Lebanese food and knew exactly what she wanted but Joan rattled on.

'Polly, see that bloke sitting behind us, big, thickset, heavy man having lunch on his own. Don't look at him for heaven's sake. Well, he's a bodyguard. Bound to be. Those two women sitting in the corner with the veils and whatsits, one's a Saudi princess and this man sitting here is her bodyguard. She sent him out to get her something while I was waiting for you. So what was he like?'

'What was who like?' Polly looked round again at the body-guard.

'Edward thing. The man you met at the Hendersons'. What was he like?'

'What do you mean?'

'Is he married?'

'Oh. No. Divorced.'

A rare species. Joan's eyes widened with interest. 'Really? So what happened?'

'We had coffee in the drawing room after dinner and – '

'Poll-ee, did you sleep with him for heaven's sake?'

Polly sighed. All over London, she assumed, available women went out to dinner and leapt straight into bed with the man they sat next to. Everyone, it seemed, except her.

'No.'

'Why not? Why didn't you go home with him?'

'I did. Or rather he came home with me.'

'So what went wrong?'

'Johnny came in.' Polly felt rather pleased with herself. It had never entered her head that Edward Holland wanted to sleep with her but now she could pretend to Joan that he wanted to and Johnny had ruined it.

'So did you sleep with Johnny?'

'I didn't sleep with anybody. I read twenty pages of a manuscript and fell asleep.'

'Have you slept with Johnny since he left you?'

'You know I haven't. Have you?' she added wickedly. Just for a second Joan looked quite taken aback.

'He's your husband. You know I wouldn't. In fact I find him quite repellent as you very well know and you're well rid of him but we won't go into all that again. Just to put your mind at rest, he's never even asked me out. Fact is, no one has for over two months.'

'What happened to that guy on *Newsweek*?'

'He went back to Washington. It was a week of bliss, just enough to really whet my appetite then nothing, not even a phone call.'

'Maybe he'll be back.'

'Maybe he will but meanwhile I need someone now. I gatecrash drinks parties every single night but it just doesn't seem to work like it used to. These days they all seem to have dinners arranged before they arrive. They're all work parties. No one comes to drinks parties any more looking for a dinner date, especially not someone with lines all over her face and varicose veins all over her legs. May God be eternally thanked for opaque tights but what will happen if I ever get as far as the bedroom again? Do I clamber 'tween the sheets in my opaques in case he catches a glimpse of my unsightly calves? So, Edward Holland. Attractive?'

'I suppose so.'

'Rich?'

'Advertising.'

'Any money of his own? Oh, don't look so horrified, Polly. I'm sure you didn't ask him outright but there are ways of finding out these things. Where does he live?'

'Camberwell.'

'Camberwell? Oh, dear.' Joan made it sound like the Outer Hebrides. 'Well, maybe he's got a house in one of those nice Georgian squares one hears about. So when are you seeing him again?'

'I'm not as far as I know.'

'You mean you let a divorced man disappear into the night without getting a date out of him?'

Polly nodded glumly. Here she was, becoming a highly successful literary agent, yet Joan always managed to make her feel as if she wasn't trying hard enough.

The truth was that since Johnny had left, Polly's life had settled into an ordered calm that was really rather comforting. To exist without a man in her life brought a certain serenity she had never before experienced. Not having to pander to Johnny's whims and whirlwind tours in and out of the house meant Polly could give far more attention to the areas in her own life that were important to her. Her work flourished; she felt less tired at the end of the day and the abundance of early nights she was getting was doing wonders for her skin. Trying not to feel smug, she observed the wide fan of lines etched out over Joan's cheeks away from her eyes.

'Well, Polly, there's just no hope for you. I must tell you though, I do have a treat in store later this week. You know I've been doing some freelance work. Well, I've hit the jackpot. I've been commissioned to do a profile of Hector O'Neill.'

'Conway!'

'Exactly, except he says this is the last Conway he's going to do.'

'Bet they all say that. I met him once.'

'Polly, you dark horse! Did you sleep with him?'

Polly frowned in exasperation. Why couldn't anyone mention a man without Joan wanting to know if you'd been to bed with him?

'I met him for twenty seconds at a première I went to with Johnny. We weren't even introduced. He just whispered something in my ear.'

Joan looked incredulous. 'Was it filthy?'

'I honestly can't remember. How many words do they want on him?'

'Three and a half thousand.'

'Long. Actually, I've got a treat tonight too.'

Joan looked up from her onion soup.

'Luana's coming to supper.'

Joan raised her eyes to heaven.

'Your stepdaughter? Why do you still see her? Trying to keep tabs on Johnny?'

'Not at all. I adore Luana. You know that.'

'I suppose I do although I just don't get it. There's something creepy about that girl. What does she look like now that she's grown up?'

'Frighteningly thin. She darts everywhere. Never still for a second. She sort of flashes at you like a streak of lightning . . .'

'How exhausting.' Joan yawned.

'No, she's beautiful. Honestly!'

'Polly, you're too kind for your own good.' Joan rested her chin in her hand and smiled at Polly. 'That kid always did take advantage of you.'

'Nonsense. I genuinely adore her. I'm so looking forward to seeing her.'

'What about her mother?'

'No idea. Luana never mentions her. She lives in Cornwall.

'Yes, of course she does. Did I tell you that I was lunching at Kensington Place last week and Johnny was at the next table. Come to think of it, he said he'd just come back from Cornwall. Is he making a film there?'

'Not as far as I know.' Did Joan do it on purpose? Surely not.

The waiter appeared at their table.

'The two gentlemen sitting over there would like to buy you lunch.'

'Oh no,' said Polly, 'we couldn't possibly – '

'Thank them very much.' Joan looked in their direction and flashed a phoney smile.

'Joan, we can't. They'll come and sit with us.'

'No, they won't. They're Arabs, for heaven's sake. In their world they don't like to see two women eating on their own. The man should pay. If they were half-way decent looking I'd invite them over, if only to do my bit for your predicament.'

'My predicament?'

'Husband left you. No man. Got to find you another one because you obviously aren't trying hard enough yourself.'

Polly decided it was time she got Joan off the subject of men.

'Did you ever come across Aroma Ross when you worked on *Vogue*?'

'Of course. She was darling. She was always asking me over, wanted me to be one of the girls.'

'Weren't you a bit old?'

'Ooh, bitchy Polly. Thank you very much!'

'Sorry. What I meant was, if you were a friend of hers, tell me, what was she like?'

'I told you. Darling.'

'So you wouldn't mind if a client of mine came to talk to you about her?'

'Who's that?'

'Zoë Nichols.'

'Two-bit writer who does the odd piece for the colour mags? Why would I want to talk to her?'

'So you've heard of her. She's been approached to ghost Aroma Ross's novel.'

'Oh, I don't think I could help her there. In fact I don't think I'd have anything to do with her if I was you, Polly.'

'Zoë Nichols or Aroma?'

'Zoë Nichols. Bit of a loser, frankly.'

'We'll see,' said Polly, feeling suddenly disheartened. She'd rather liked the sound of Zoë Nichols on the phone. 'You will keep quiet about this, won't you, Joan?'

'Who on earth would be interested? Anyway I didn't know Aroma that well.'

You mean you probably didn't know her at all, thought Polly. By now she was becoming wise to Joan's desperate need to be known to be on first-name terms with celebrities. Once she'd interviewed Hector O'Neill, it would be Hector this and Hector that for months.

It was as if Joan had read her mind.

'It's probably about time for a biography on Hector, wouldn't you say, Polly? Who do you think you could sell it to?'

'Who said I had a biography of Hector O'Neill to sell?'

'Well, I'm just speculating here but if the interview goes well, I could cultivate my association with him, develop it into a book, you know . . .'

And she automatically assumes I'll be her agent just like that. For some reason she couldn't quite fathom, the idea made Polly furious. When it suited her Joan was perfectly capable of remembering Polly was not just a secretary. Polly called for the bill, ignored Joan's frantic flutterings about the two Arabs who wanted to pay for them, slapped down her Access card and didn't say a word till they were out on the pavement.

Polly didn't go back to the office. She was rather surprised at the extent to which the news about Johnny having been in Cornwall had shaken her. She didn't even know if he had been anywhere near Edith. It was ridiculous to give it a moment's thought. She decided to take the afternoon off. She rang Mrs Flowers from a call box and was instantly reassured.

'Very quiet it is. Very quiet indeed. You go off for a couple of hours. Do you good. After all you've been through . . .'

'Yes, thank you, Mrs Flowers. See you later.'

142

Polly went to the gym and worked off her rage at Joan, at Edith, at Johnny, and most of all at herself, on the stairmaster for half an hour. Dripping with sweat, she showered and flopped naked on a towel in the sauna.

Conversations between other naked women and girls of varying shapes and sizes were going on all around her. As Polly lay and listened, willing the toxins to ooze out of her, she realised they were all variations of the same theme.

'Has he called you yet?'

'Have you heard from him yet?'

'So he finally called last Saturday and I told him . . .'

'So when are you seeing him again?'

It was the way the world worked, thought Polly. You were nobody unless you had a man to talk about. Why was it that she didn't want to be one of these silly chitter-chattering women, why didn't she have Joan's desperate longing for a man, any man? What was wrong with her?

She picked up a lemon tart for Luana's supper and only remembered afterwards that she'd already bought tiramisu. Never mind. She'd slip the tart into Luana's takeaway bag. The phone was ringing as she walked into the hall. She had no idea what made her pick it up and say 'Johnny?'

'No,' said a puzzled voice. 'Edward.'

'Edward.' repeated Polly in a flat tone of voice.

'Edward Holland. You remember? Last night . . . ?'

'Oh yes, of course, how are you?' asked Polly as if she hadn't seen him for months.

'Fine. You?' He didn't wait for her to answer. He sounded nervous. 'Polly, I was wondering if you would be free to have dinner with me tonight?'

'Oh, I can't possibly,' said Polly trying to keep the relief out of her voice. 'I've got my stepdaughter coming to supper.' She could almost hear Joan's groan: 'Don't tell him it's your stepdaughter. Pretend it's another admirer. Honestly, Polly!'

'Ah, well, another time.' Edward Holland seemed disappointed but determined. 'What about tomorrow. Bit short notice I know but . . . ?'

'Oh, no, you see – ' began Polly automatically then stopped. She knew that she was in fact utterly, blissfully free for night after night as far as she could see. She recalled Joan's face drenched in misery because there was no man on the horizon. She thought of the endless happy hours of speculating enjoyed by the girls in the sauna. Edward Holland was giving her a chance to join in. 'Has he called you yet?' Yes, he has and I shouldn't be churlish about it, thought Polly.

'Actually, Edward, that would be very nice. Tomorrow night.'

'I'll pick you up about eight.'

'Make it 7.30 and come and have a drink first,' Polly heard herself say before they hung up.

She went into the kitchen to begin preparing Luana's supper. She turned on Jazz FM and sang along to the radio, far happier at the thought that she had half an hour's pottering about the kitchen ahead of her than at the notion of a date the following night. She'd better get a move on. Luana was due in less than forty-five minutes.

Polly hoped she would be hungry.

Luana was starving – but not for food. She wanted sex – with Chris Perrick.

She'd had a nightmare day and Chris Perrick, a twenty-year-old James Dean lookalike, had been the only good thing about it.

Luana worked as assistant to Colvis Redmond, a casting director. Luana's obsession with films and actors had not gone away and eventually Johnny had decided there was no point in keeping her at college if all she wanted to do was learn about casting. She might as well learn on the job.

Clovis was larger than life, literally. She weighed in at fourteen stone. Her dress sense was non-existent. She tended to act upon advice from others, often disastrously, and then leave the suggested style change in place for the next twenty years. Thus a purple-black punk haircut from the Seventies, an Armani jacket (actually a man's but Clovis had never noticed) from the Eighties and a pair of eternal Gap tracksuit trousers became her standard daily wardrobe. She hailed originally from Dublin and had never lost her accent.

'We'll not be wanting him,' she had a habit of yelling down the phone at actors' agents, 'he's much too young.' She pronounced it Jung and behind her back actors cheerfully told each other, 'You're much too Freud for that part, darling.'

Clovis was tactlessness itself when it came to actors. She would walk in and interrupt a reading she'd set up between an actor and a director and shout over the poor actor's head to the director: 'Wrap it up right now, if I were you. Wastin' yer time. The pairfect pairson's just become available.'

Yet Clovis Redmond was the undisputed queen of London casting. She had an eye for talent that was unparalleled. The minute a young *ingénue* walked on stage in rep Clovis filed him away in her mind. She knew all five volumes of *Spotlight* backwards and rarely even referred to them, and while she was curiously insensitive with actors, she was beloved by producers and directors alike for her ability to deliver the perfect cast well within the budget. Other casting directors, jealous of her success – she was said to earn £250,000 a year – were overheard muttering about how she took kickbacks from the producer whenever she brought in the casting under budget. But the real secret of Clovis' success was simple: she was a complete whore. She didn't care who she cast for. Unlike other casting directors who would only cast feature films for a big-name director and the occasional prestigious theatre production, Clovis would cast commercials, training films, Europuddings, short films, TV series, feature films, anything as long as she was paid top whack. And she was.

All week she had been casting an American mini-series. The story was ludicrous. Someone had had the bright idea of taking the basic theme of the musical *Seven Brides for Seven Brothers* and updating it to the Nineties with seven American Rhodes scholars seeking seven brides at Oxford. The leads were now in place but there was one outstanding part that was proving extremely difficult to cast.

One of the English brides in the script had a brother who categorically refused to let her go off and marry an American and who further complicated matters by falling in love himself with another of the seven brides and trying to stop her going off too. The role called for a handsome, headstrong, truculent-looking young

145

actor and the part was that of support lead and a vital element in the overall casting.

It didn't bother Clovis in the slightest that the loud American director wanted to see the actors every five minutes. Keep 'em coming, was his attitude, let's get it over with as quickly as possible, never mind whether they can act or not. But then it was all right for Clovis; she was closeted with the director in the drawing room of his suite at the Dorchester. Outside, in the little entrance hall, Luana was trying her best to inject some sort of order into the proceedings. If only the director could have had a casting session at Clovis' office, Luana could have made the actors cups of tea to keep them happy. It had taken her a day and a half to call virtually every agent in town and check the availability of the actors on the list Clovis had drawn up and then fix a time for them to attend the casting. Ordinarily Luana would make sure actors up for the same part never bumped into each other at a casting. Now they were arriving in quick succession, Clovis was calling 'Next!' through the door with embarrassing speed, the actors were backing up and running into each other and there was nothing Luana could do except hand out pages of the script for them to read and apologise again and again for the discomfort.

They were not exactly a silent bunch.

'Can I ring my girlfriend?'

'Who's he then, ducky?'

'How much longer?'

'Can I call my agent?'

'Give us a read through, Luana, there's a love.'

'So who did old Clovis cast in that part I was up for last week?'

'Don't know why I'm here. American telly? Me? Not on your life.'

'Why can't we use the phone?'

'Darling, you were wonderful in that thing on Sunday night. They wanted me but I turned it down, you know?'

'Cheer up.'

Luana jumped. The man was talking to her. It was Chris Perrick. She hadn't realised he'd been watching her.

'It's such a nightmare and Clovis just doesn't care,' she told him, feeling guilty at her disloyalty.

'Well, it's nice that you do.'

'Not much I can do about it except open the door to let them in and out. I can't even give you a place to sit down.'

'No problem.' He slouched against the wall in his white T-shirt, jeans and loafers. Was he coming on to her?

'*Next!*' shrieked Clovis.

Chris Perrick winked at Luana and slipped through the door.

On the way home on the bus to the tiny flat she rented in Shepherd's Bush Luana wondered if he'd get the part. If he did it meant there was a chance she'd see him again. He fancied himself but then, didn't they all?

Her phone rang twenty minutes after she got home.

'It's Chris.'

'How'd you get my number?'

'Simple. I asked Clovis.'

'And she gave it to you? Just like that?'

'Just like that. Actually, she's called me back for another read-through with that girl they've cast as the second sister but in the meantime I thought I'd get a little practice in with you. Here's my address. Can you make it in, say, an hour? And don't forget the script.'

He opended the door to his flat naked and took her straight to bed. He's not fucking me to get the part, Luana told herself as she did every time she screwed an actor from a casting session, it's Clovis he'd have to fuck for that.

Still, she'd put in a good word for him the next day. If Clovis asked.

And even if she didn't.

Polly sat quietly at the kitchen table laid for two until ten o'clock. Then she slowly put away the unused plates, the knives, the forks, the spoons and the glasses. She scooped a small amount of the carefully prepared chick pea salad into a soup bowl and stood at the kitchen window silently spooning it into her mouth. She had called, of course, but there had been no answer from Luana's number.

She must have forgotten, thought Polly.

It wasn't the first time.

'Deirdre, love are yer there? If y'are please pick up, there's a good girl. Hello? OK, so yer not there. Now listen, soon as you get this give me a call. They want you for a Screen 2, y'know, those high falutin' fillums that go out Sunday nights. They're talkin' to Alan Bates so they say. The script's in the mail. So give us a call. Bye.'

Clovis turned to Luana.

'If they give her the part they're mad. She's an old slag, so she is, and her looks went years ago. Don't know why I called her at all. Oh, sweet Jesus, have I done it again?'

She grinned as Luana leaned over and settled the receiver back on its hook. Clovis had a disturbing habit of not replacing her receiver properly and when she had been speaking into an answering machine this could be dangerous. Everything she'd just said both to – and about – Deirdre McShane had been recorded for Deirdre to listen to on her return.

The phone rang again immediately.

'Oh my God, she was there all the time and listening to me. I'm not in. Tell her I had to rush out. Emergency.'

Clovis disappeared into the kitchen.

'Any casting?' The usual bleat Luana heard twenty times a day from desperate agents touting for non-existent work for their clients.

'Sorry. Nothing at the moment.' Luana's stock reply.

'Want some, then?' The voice at the other end of the line had dropped several octaves.

'Dad! How are you?'

'I'm fine. Couldn't be better and there's a reason. I've finally got the go-ahead on *Mr Wrong*. The script's approved and the Frogs and the Americans have come up with $16 million between them. Now I've got a star interested I'll start pre-sales and get even more cash.'

'Who do you have in mind to play Mr Wrong?' asked Luana, who had read the script.

'Oh, it's gone to all the usual suspects. Pacino, De Niro . . . but it was your idea to send it to Hector O'Neill. His agent's called and says he really loves it. Of course he's not in the same league as De Niro etc. but I'm going to go with him. So thanks, little peachy one, you've done me a big favour.'

'And he's available. But Dad, there's something you have to promise me. Don't tell Clovis I thought of Hector O'Neill otherwise my life won't be worth living. We have to make her think the idea came from her, you know what she's like.'

'Whatever you say. I'll get Juanita on to it right away. She's good at planting suggestions in people's heads and then letting them think they suggested it in the first place. But I did tell O'Neill's agent you were the one who thought of him. Credit where credit's due, and I was so proud of you. So, seen Polly lately? You two were due to have dinner this week, weren't you?'

Polly! She'd forgotten all about Polly. She hadn't even rung her. She'd spent a long and sweaty night in Chris Perrick's bed without paying Polly a moment's thought.

Furthermore, it had all been in vain. Clovis had come in that morning announcing that she had spoken to the director last thing the night before and he had gone and changed his mind and decided Chris Perrick's legs were too short or his neck was too thick. Whatever his deficiency – and as usual it had nothing whatsoever to do with his acting skills – he wasn't going to be offered the part. Luana knew this meant she might well not see him again. She had not delivered and while it was not in any way her fault, she was under no illusion that Chris Perrick would invite her into his bed until he was up for another plum part in something Clovis was casting. Pity. He had shown the potential to become the first man to give her an orgasm.

'Luana? You still there?'

'Sorry, Dad. I was miles away. No, I didn't see Polly after all.'

'Well, I saw her the other night. She had a man there.'

'Probably an author.'

'At nearly midnight?'

'Dad! You were the one who left, remember?'

'OK, OK. No prying. It's just that Zutty didn't like him. He told

149

me. So, is herself there? I'd better get on and see if she'll condescend to do my picture.'

'Hello, Johnny, how are yer?' Clovis was all charm. 'What can I do fer you? What? 'Course I am. Fer you I'm always free. Who's the director? Well, who's he when he's at home? A friggin' Froggy? Does he speak English? No, I don't speak bloody French, Johnny, don't be daft. Can't you give him English lessons? I don't care if you've got Japanese money, you're not telling me you'd get a Japanese director if you had. All right, all right, send over the script. I'll have a read. Have you anyone in place? You're thinkin' of Hector? Well don't be tellin' me he speaks French. What? You simply can't ask the likes of Hector O'Neill to read for a friggin' Froggy. He's too big a star already, that's why. I'll tell you what. I'll take a look at the script and if I like it I'll meet with your Froggy. Meet, I said! Don't be committing me just yet. I don't know. Your father . . .' she said, turning to Luana, 'if this fillum goes it'll be me summer holiday out the window. Script's coming over this afternoon. *Mr Wrong*. Sounds like he's got Mr Wrong Director for a kick-off.'

But Luana wasn't listening. She rang Polly and listened while Mrs Flowers told her her stepmother was in a meeting, was there any message? No messge. Luana hung up and the phone rang again instantly.

'Sorry, nothing at the moment,' she said automatically. 'No, wait, call back in a couple of days. There might be something then.'

'Come on *Mr Wrong*,' she said to herself, 'make my day!'

Polly wasn't in a meeting. She was riding the elevators in Harvey Nichols staring at the name Thyssen on each step. She reached the first floor in a daze and wandered through the halls, stopping occasionally to rifle through some dresses. The trouble was she had no idea what she was looking for. All she knew was that for some idiotic reason she had woken up that morning strangely excited at the thought of her impending date with Edward Holland.

The anticipation of it had sustained her through a particularly trying morning. A young and pretty author with considerable potential had proved to be totally irresponsible by calling to say she was going off on someone's yacht and wanted to extend the delivery date of her manuscript by a further six months. Since Polly had sweated blood to get her the commission in the first place, she was not about to let her get away with it and for the first time in her career as an agent she heard herself say, 'If you go ahead and do that then I no longer wish to represent you.'

Then an irate, self-important editor had rung demanding to know why he had not been included in Polly's recent multiple submission of a book. Polly refrained from telling him that it had been because she thought he was utterly hopeless at his job and there was no way she would allow an author of hers to be published by him. Instead she told him tactfully: 'I'm sure when you come to read it, Peter, you'll find it just wouldn't have been for you.'

'I'd have liked to have seen for myself,' he had whined. 'Everyone's talking about it.'

Then the photocopier went on the blink and a fax had come through from one of Polly's more controversial authors saying a politician was suing him for libel and what should he do? Four New York agents had faxed asking when she was going to decide who would sell her clients' books in America and Mrs Flowers had brought in something for her lunch that was so foul smelling in its health-giving properties that it stank throughout the conservatory. At this point Polly had simply upped and walked away from it all to wallow in her dreams of Edward Holland.

It was ludicrous. The night before last he had just been a friend of the Hendersons who had given her a lift home. Lunch with Joan and being stood up by Luana had made her vulnerable. Edward Holland wanted her, he was a man, growing more eligible and attractive in her mind by the minute. Where would he take her for dinner? More important, where would he take her *after* dinner? Would she even recognise a pass, it had been so long since she'd been out with anyone?

In the end she didn't buy herself anything new. She knew from experience that it was fatal to go out and look for something for a special occasion on the day. She always wound up buying something far too expensive and regretted it for ever more. On top of which she never wore it.

Her futile shopping expedition made her run late. She had only half an hour to wash her hair. She was kneeling on the floor with her head over the bath, rinsing out the shampoo, when she heard footsteps coming up the stairs.

Johnny had come into the bathroom and moved up behind her. This had been one of their marital rituals. Whenever she washed her hair Johnny would always rinse and towel it dry. He had what she called 'magic hands', like a really good masseur's. When he massaged her head she had invariably wanted to have sex, so sensuous was his touch, and as she felt his fingertips on her scalp now an involuntary shudder went through her. At least, with a T-shirt over her bra and pants, she wasn't naked.

'There. Now I'll dry it for you.' He pulled open a drawer. 'Where's the drier? You've moved the drier!' he said accusingly as if he had only been gone a day.

'Doesn't it ever occur to you that things just might have changed a fraction since you left?' snapped Polly, using irritation to cover her surge of desire for him. 'I mean you walk in here without so much as a quick ring first to see if you might be disturbing me . . .'

She'd sworn she'd never act like this, never give him the injured party number, never show any sign of bitterness. She need not have worried. Johnny, true to form, was barely dented by her tirade.

'All right, keep your hair on, especially when I'm about to dry it for you. What's up? The old PMT strikes again? Juanita swears by B6. Ever tried it, Pol? Juanita says . . .'

'Johnny,' warned Polly, 'shut up about Juanita. I don't want to know what Juanita uses. I don't want to know what you use. I know it's still your house but I just think you might use your key with more discretion.'

She sat at her dressing table in the bedroom where she now kept the hairdrier and proceeded to blow-dry her hair herself, waving Johnny away when he tried to do it for her. He sat gloomily on the edge of the bed they had once shared and watched her reflection in the mirror. Finally, above the noise of the drier, he mouthed the words:

'I came to talk to you about something.'

She pointed to the drier and mouthed back: 'Nearly finished.'

As she put in the Carmen rollers, wincing and knowing they were too hot and would ruin her hair, Johnny came and sat beside her on the long stool in front of the dressing table, something he had always done when he wanted to be sure of her full attention.

Polly found herself holding her breath. Just when he'd given her a sexual jolt, just when she was about to go out on her first proper date since he'd left – was he going to ask if he could come back?

'It's Luana,' he began, and Polly didn't know whether to be relieved or disappointed.

'Tell me about it!' she said with feeling. 'What is the matter with that girl? I waited three hours for her to turn up and have supper with me last night. Three hours! I'm going out tonight and all the food I've cooked is going to go to waste.'

'What did you make?' Johnny looked hopeful.

Polly glared at him although she had to admit she'd rather he took it than throw it in the bin.

'As long as you don't give it to Zutty. So what's your problem with Luana?'

'Word's got back to me. She's beginning to get herself something of a reputation.'

'In what way?'

'A nympho.'

'A what?'

'A nymphomaniac.'

'Oh, don't be ridiculous. You don't even know the meaning of the word, Johnny.'

'Is that a slur on my wop heritage? No, I'm serious. It's common knowledge apparently. You go for a part in a casting session with Clovis Redmond and you have a pretty fair chance of getting laid by her assistant, if you're a bloke that is. I've heard actors talking about it. They obviously don't know she's my daughter.'

'Does Clovis know? Have you spoken to her?'

'Of course not. And yes, I expect she does and turns a blind eye. There used to be plenty of stories about Clovis asking actors to come and pick up the script at eleven o'clock at night at her home.'

'Well, I don't know, maybe that's what happens. The casting couch, maybe it still exists.'

153

'Not with my daughter, it doesn't. Not if I have anything to do with it.'

Polly looked at him in the mirror. She could see he was agitated.

'It's probably nothing,' she tried to reassure him, 'it's probably all talk. Actors bragging to each other. Maybe they do try it on with her. Who wouldn't? She's such an attractive girl. But why rush to believe everything you hear? Have you talked to her?'

'Oh, Pol please! How would I begin? I'm her father, for Christ's sake. It needs a woman. I did ring her today to sort of try and sound her out but I chickened out and started telling her about getting the go-ahead for *Mr Wrong* instead. Hey, Polly, did I tell you? I've had this brainwave about who should play the lead. Hector O'Neill.'

'Oh, Johnny, that's a brilliant idea. How clever of you.'

Johnny kept quiet about whose brilliant idea it actually was.

'Well, I always wanted Clovis to cast it so I would have been ringing there in any case but this other matter I know I just haven't got the bottle. That's why I came over and barged in like this. I was wondering, Polly, would you talk to her for me? Find out what's going on?'

'Johnny, I'm not her mother.'

'Jesus, Pol. Edith's the last person I'd want to let loose on Luana, not in the state she's in now . . .'

'What state?'

The doorbell rang very loudly.

Edward Holland.

Polly extracted the hot rollers from her hair and dived back into her jeans. She'd give him a drink then make her excuses and come back up to change. Somehow she had to get rid of Johnny. How on earth was it going to look to Edward when they walked downstairs together?

As it happened Johnny's untimely arrival had saved Polly considerable embarrassment. Edward Holland was dressed very casually in jeans and a sweater.

'I thought we'd go somewhere informal and relax,' he told her on the doorstep. 'I don't know about you but I've had a hell of a week. Oh, hello.' He had been leaning forward and Polly assumed he'd been about to give her a peck on the cheek until he saw Johnny coming down the stairs behind her.

'Just leaving, just leaving. Eh, Pol, what about that food that's going to . . .?'

Polly stood firm, holding the door wide open until he slipped out and down the steps, turning to point at Edward and make a face behind Edward's back and a thumbs-down sign, grinning at Polly. Polly slammed the front door.

Bugger Johnny! Although if he hadn't arrived when he had she'd have had time to put on a chic little black dress and high heels and be looking a right overdressed tart beside Edward in his jeans.

Edward took her to Lou Pescadou in the Old Brompton Road where you couldn't book and had to stand outside ringing the bell until you were let in. Luckily they had a table and Polly followed Edward past the long bar to the more secluded raised area in the back. She liked this restaurnat. It was a downmarket version of La Croisette or Le Suquet, fancy fish restaurants Johnny used to take her to because he'd seen Mick Jagger in one of them once and always hoped he would again. At Lou Pescadou you could have oysters when in season, *fruits de mer*, pizzas, pasta or an omelette, wash it down with a pichet of *rosé* and, if you got sufficiently drunk, pretend you were on the Côte d'Azur.

Edward got around to talking about his marriage rather sooner than Polly had anticipated. She had hoped they would steer clear of their respective ex's as a topic of conversation but Edward clearly saw it as the most important thing they had in common. Which it probably was.

'The thing is, Barbara was never really my type. I like tall girls like you, Polly, and she was only five-foot four.'

Polly looked away. So he liked the way she looked and he wasn't afraid to tell her before she'd even finished her *soupe de poissons*.

'So what attracted you to her?'

'She wanted me. It was as simple as that. She was a very pretty little thing – still is, I suppose – and she gravitated towards me at a party and sort of latched on. Before I knew it everyone was saying what a wonderful couple we made and everything just seemed to follow on from there.'

'Are you saying you didn't actually love her?' Polly was rather appalled by her question but she was curious. He seemed to want to talk about it and besides, these sort of details would be lapped up by the insatiable Joan.

'Quite the contrary. I fell head over heels in love with her. I'm a romantic, Polly, like you.' (Bloody nerve, thought Polly, how would he know if I'm a romantic or not?)

'She was exactly the kind of pretty girl a chap fell in love with.'

'But?'

'I didn't really fancy her. I mean in the beginning I thought I did but after a couple of years I found I just wasn't interested in her in that way any more. She used to wear these little girly gingham nighties and she put her hair in bunches when she went to bed. Bunches! She looked about twelve years old. I know that's a real turn-on for some men but I'm not one of them.'

The waiter was hovering to take away the first course.

He grinned at Polly. Could he understand? Polly had always thought Lou Pescadou waiters were so super-French they didn't even understand a word of English. They always spoke French – 'Et pour Madame? Voulez-vous des legumes? Et comme dessert?' – and if you asked a question in English they immediately summoned *le patron* in panic. Perhaps it was just an act.

Polly didn't really want to hear any more. It looked as if Edward might start revealing what had happened, or rather hadn't happened, when he unbunched Barbara's hair and pulled up her girly nighties. She hoped to God Johnny wasn't running around London regaling people with stories of her bedroom eccentricities although once she thought about it she was hard put to recall a time in the last year of their marriage when Johnny had taken his eyes off the television long enough to notice her in the bedroom.

Edward was talking again. 'The children took her mind off it for a while once they came along. When they were babies she was too tired for anything anyway. But then she got her energy back and started coming out of the bathroom in her birthday suit, drenched in Joy. She'd come marching round to my side of the bed and I'm afraid somehow her stretch marks were always at eye level.'

156

Polly winced at the 'stretch marks'. Barbara sounded a bit of a nightmare but Polly couldn't help feeling sorry for her.

'Didn't you . . . couldn't you talk to each other? I can't believe she walked out because of sex alone. There must be thousands of couples who've stopped making love but they don't automatically get up and go.'

'Yes, we did talk,' said Edward, 'but the trouble was, all we talked about was our sex problem. She went on and on until she got me to admit it. She got me to look her in the eye and say, "I don't fancy you." What she kept saying was, "If we're completely honest with each other, completely honest, Edward, then it'll be all right." Well, the minute I was completely honest with her, then it was all over bar the shouting. She walked out a week later. Bloody hell, Polly. I've never told this to anyone. I don't know why I'm wittering on to you like this.'

I don't know why you are either, thought Polly. But she said: 'It's good that you are. Do you miss her?'

'Do you know, I'm not sure that I miss her but I miss being part of a family. I miss the kids. I'm rattling around in Camberwell on my own while she and the kids are crammed into a tiny flat but she would insist on being the one to move out. Now I can't sell Camberwell. Ah, what a mess, and the worst thing is there's loads of miserable blokes just like me.'

'Really?' said Polly, 'I thought it was the other way round, that there were loads of lonely divorced women all desperate to find a man and there weren't enough of you to go around.'

'Well, that doesn't make sense. For every divorced woman there's got to be a divorced man out there looking for an available woman. Women never look at it like that.'

'I have to admit you've got a point.' Polly smiled at him. 'You make it sound like it ought to be one big musical chairs.'

'Well, it would be except you women are much more picky the second time around. You found Mr Right and he didn't work out so now you're all so paranoid you go around with this ideal man in your heads which, of course, you're never going to find. It's not enough for us to be kind and courteous and gentlemanly. I'm not sure even rich works any more. You take a woman out and before

157

you know it she's quizzing you like you're there for a job interview which, as far as she's concerned, you are: as her potential significant other. Running through her mind is not, "Should I let him take me to bed? Does he make me laugh?" but, "There's no way it would work out because he wears a cravat but then of course he does have a house in the country which would be nice for the children (hers, not mine), he's a Leo and I'm a Capricorn but he does have moon in Gemini same as me, he contributes nothing to the conversation when he's with my work friends because he's not in television, he lives in Camberwell and I couldn't possibly move south of the river, he's away so much on business trips he wouldn't be able to come to dinner parties with me but on the other hand he does go to some rather dishy places and could take me with him . . ." Meanwhile, us poor bastards are pretty bloody hopeless on our own, lonely and desperate for someone to look after us, but we haven't got a prayer unless we become a New Man overnight. What is a New Man, that's what I want to know? Maybe you can enlighten me, Polly?'

Polly was warming to Edward Holland by the minute. It had never occurred to her that on her first real date since Johnny's departure she would be given such an insight into the male point of view even if Edward's was rather woolly.

'So you've had lots of affairs since Barbara left?' How could she be asking such questions when she barely knew the man yet he seemed to be inviting them, and beside it was much more fun than talking about what they'd read in the paper or watched on television.

'I wish! Women are so blatant now. Whatever happened to good old-fashioned subtley? Unless they're in the cradle-snatching category which, frankly, isn't my scene at all, they make it crystal clear from the outset that what they're looking for is a relationship. Capital R. Some even mention the M word. Jesus! Every breath you take they're assessing whether or not you're husband material. I mean, as I've said, I'm lonely, I want someone but I rather fancy a bit of a courtship before I take the plunge. To tell you the truth, that's what I liked about you, Polly. I meet you three times and you barely even notice me. And marriage is out for you because of course, you are still married, aren't you?'

Polly looked at him, speechless. He was absolutely right. She was still married. There had been no talk of divorce between her and Johnny. Edward had seen him at the house twice. Poor Edward. He must think he had found himself in a highly awkward situation. Did he think she was planning to commit adultery? But then he'd given Johnny a lift home the other night so he knew he wasn't living with Polly and surely Grania Henderson must have been forthcoming with the details at some point.

'He left you, I understand, your husband?' prompted Edward on cue. 'Turned out to be Mr Wrong?'

'Oh, no, not a bit of it.'

'So he's come back? Listen, Polly, are you married or aren't you? I wouldn't have asked you out except that . . .'

'We're separated.'

'But he comes back from time to time?'

'Not in that way.' She wasn't gong to elaborate. She was damned if she was going to give Edward the same details about Johnny as he had imparted about Barbara.

'Was he Mr Wrong in every department?'

'He wasn't Mr Wrong in any department,' said Polly, aware that she was being over-defensive but Edward was overstepping the mark. 'He was funny, he was affectionate, he was terrific in bed . . .' And I loved him! She didn't say it out loud.

'So why?'

'Why did he leave me? He left, you know. Of course, you know. Everyone knows. I'm not like Barbara. I didn't up and leave. I waited until I was left. And you want to know why I was left? Well, I'll tell you. It's quite simple. I wasn't keeping up. His mother did warn me. She knew her boy. She knew he would always be running, like some scalded chicken. Johnny never stops. He marks time at a hundred miles an hour. If anybody nailed him down he'd probably peck himself to death. Well, I'm not like that. I wanted to progress more slowly, to grow gradually into who I was and where I wanted to go. He was moving farther and farther away from me until eventually he just moved out of the house. The funny thing is, I see him and speak to him now about as much as I did during the

159

last year of our marriage. So am I still married to him? Yes, I suppose in a way I am.'

Their main course had grown cold in front of them. She might not have gone into the same kind of detail, Polly realised, but in her own way she had opened up to Edward Holland as much, if not more, than he had to her.

'The tortoise and the hare,' said Edward quietly, taking her hand across the table. Polly let it rest there. 'But you'll get there just the same.'

'Get where?' asked Polly, 'that's what I don't understand.'

'Terminé?' The waiter appeared and looked disapprovingly at their untouched plates. Edward let go of her hand abruptly.

'Let's pig out on puddings instead,' he suggested, 'and then I'll take you home. If I may?'

'I've got a better idea.' Polly looked him straight in the eye. She'd made up her mind about Edward Holland.

Johnny was the only man she'd slept with since her wedding day. It was time for the tortoise to progress to the next stage: sex after Johnny.

'You may take me home but why don't we have pudding there?'

She laid out Luana's tiramisu, the lemon tart and a giant tub of De Soto ice-cream on the coffee table. Furtive glances through the kitchen door showed her that Edward had kicked off his shoes, piled his plate high and made himself comfortable on the sofa. The only trouble was that he was stretched out full length and there was no room for her unless she lay alongside him. Was this a deliberate move on Edward's part? But there were two empty armchairs staring at her. Polly's nerve failed her and she sat down in one of them.

He finished his pudding. She poured coffee. They drank in silence. Polly didn't know what to do next and Edward kept glancing at her as if he expected her to make the next move. But that wasn't her style. Not that she'd exactly had much style lately. She had forgotten how to be seduced. It was years since Johnny had led her up the staircase to what had turned out to be Edith's flat and taken her into his arms in the darkness. She'd known exactly what was going to happen then. Right now she hadn't a clue. Did Edward fancy her? Was he sitting there wondering if she fancied him? Were they going to sit like this all night?

Polly got up to pour herself another cup of coffee and it was while she was bending over the tray on the coffee table that she felt Edward's hand on her leg. It took her by surprise to the extent that she sat down rather abruptly and found herself in Edward's lap. Her instinctive reaction was to say, 'Oh, how clumsy of me, I'm so sorry', and begin to get up again before Edward put both arms around her waist and held her down.

'Where do you think you're going?'

Her face was now inches from his. Several things immediately popped into her head.

Was she still wafting the garlic from the *soupe de poissons*?

Was her forty-something-year-old body up to being scrutinised by a first-time lover, even if it didn't have any stretch marks?

Then she nearly blacked out with the shock of Edward's unfamiliar lips meeting hers. They were so different from Johnny's. Johnny had been a long, slow kisser. Edward proved to be a quick aggressive stabber, his tongue prising her mouth open with sharp piercing movements.

He moved fast, too fast for Polly who began to panic as she felt his hand on her knee, moving up along her thigh to pull down her tights. She felt awkward and clumsy lying across him. She realised she ought to be participating in some way so she fumbled with the buttons on his shirt. To her amazement they opened to reveal a hairless freckled chest – quite a shock after Johnny's swarthy growth which, even though she hadn't seen it for a year, she recalled instantly – but there, right in the middle, Edward had a mole which looked exactly like a third nipple. Polly laid her head on top of it to suppress a giggle. Edward promptly began to stroke the top of her head, moving his fingers through her hair. At the same time his other hand had reached inside her panties to touch her there.

There was something familiar about him and after a while she realised it was the smell of his aftershave: the same as Johnny's. Polly closed her eyes and it was as if Johnny was still there, washing

161

her hair. She began to move dreamily against Edward and it was only when she felt him grow hard through his jeans that she remembered.

This wasn't Johnny, someone she'd slept with for years. This was Edward, someone about whom she knew very little other than what he had told her at dinner. If he hadn't fancied his wife then presumably he'd had other women, however much he might pretend he hadn't. So wasn't there something they should discuss before going any further? Polly simply did not know at what point you brought it up. Pre-Johnny, before her marriage, the subject had never arisen. Nobody had even heard of it then.

Now she had been off the open market for so long, she had never had a chance to learn the language.

She sat up abruptly and moved away to the armchair, leaving Edward lying in an ungainly heap on the sofa.

'AIDS,' said Polly helplessly, 'I forgot. Aren't we supposed to . . . ?'

'Polly, what *are* you talking about?'

'Shouldn't you be wearing something? Safe sex?'

Edward stared at her and shook his head in apparent amazement.

'A johnny? Is that what you mean? We're lying here necking on the sofa and you want me to wear a johnny? Christ almighty, Polly, I think I've had enough. I haven't got a johnny, as it happens. You're the one who has if you bother to think about it. He was here the other night, he was here when I arrived and to all intents and purposes he's still here in this room with us and you're still bloody married to him. You want a johnny, Polly?' By this time he was almost dressed.

'Go whistle for your husband and stop wasting my time. Goodnight, Polly.'

Casting on *Mr Wrong* began a month later.

'I'm only doing it because he's your father,' Clovis told Luana twenty times a day. 'Fuckin' Froggy director! He may have won the Director's Festival prize at Cannes but, shite, it was only for some crappy little film with subtitles and the only people who saw it in the Yoo-Nited States were two men and a dog which isn't going to make my life any easier.'

Clovis had agreed to cast the film because (a) she cast anything if the money was half-way right, and (b) Johnny had promised her she would deal only with him and not have to spend time with Froggy. Because Luana's father was the producer and because, as Clovis had inevitably discovered, she had been the one to come up with the idea of Hector O'Neill, it was agreed at the outset that Luana would be very much involved in the casting.

'Fine by me,' said Clovis cheerfully. 'Your father's coming in this afternoon so we can talk through what we want. You'd better sit in.'

Johnny climbed the narrow stairs to Clovis' Soho office an hour later than he had said he would, which did not exactly put Clovis in a good mood. He was followed by Zutty who flew into the room and jumped straight into Clovis' lap, wagging his tail in her face. Clovis had such a shock her fag fell out of her mouth.

'You've set fire to my dog,' Johnny accused her, grabbing Zutty.

'I've done no such thing. Now, what'll youse all have to drink?'

'Bit quiet, angel one,' Johnny bent over and kissed Luana. 'Too many late nights? Boyfriend keeping you at it?'

'What a thing to say to your own daughter.' Clovis poured three glasses of whisky.

'I haven't got a boyfriend.'

'Is that true, Clovis?'

'You're askin' me?'

'Don't any of these hunks who come and audition take any notice of you?'

Luana pretended she hadn't heard him and picked up Zutty for a cuddle. Why was her father being so beady? He couldn't know about Chris Perrick (not that there was anything more to know) – or any of the others before him – could he?

Clovis saved her further interrogation. Whisky in hand, she was ready for action.

'So, you've got Hector O'Neill. He signed yesterday. As Conway I suppose you can say he's an international star but only just. So you've got to find the detective and the detective's girlfriend. Now, you badly need an American because of this Froggy director. You want to hook a US distributor for this fuckin' fillum, you'll need an up and coming US name for the girlfriend, the lady cop, the one who falls for Hector.'

'Why up and coming?' Johnny wished there was a bit more 'we need' instead of 'you' to Clovis' approach. She was making it clear he was more or less on his own on this one on account of the Froggy director. Really rubbing it in, she was, but what else was he supposed to do when half the money was coming from France?

'Look, Johnny, this is *Mr Wrong* we're casting, not Indiana fuckin' Jones. We're not talkin' major first-grade stars like Julia Roberts or Michelle Pfeiffer.'

'They weren't in *Indiana Jones*,' Johnny pointed out, 'so who are we talking then?' He had descended into a dejected slump, still in his overcoat and baseball cap.

'Well, Winona's too jung, Geena Davis is too hot and too busy. Could she be black, d'you think?'

'What? Could who be black?'

'The fuckin' part we're trying to cast, that's who.'

'But the script –'

'Oh, she's not black in the script. What I'm askin' is could you rewrite her black? Then we'd be talkin' Whitney Houston, Robin Givens . . .'

'Lisa Bonnet?'

'She hasn't really cracked it in movies. People think *The Cosby Show*. She's much more a TV name. Think, Johnny!'

'Sorry.'

'What age are we talkin' here? Hector's thirty-three or thereabouts. This girl's presumably younger? Twenty-seven, eight?'

'What about Naomi Campbell?' said Johnny, suddenly brightening, 'I could do for her what I did for Cruise in *The Wolf One*.'

'Break every bone in her body, you mean. What else did you do for Cruise in whatever it was? What happened to it anyway? Oh, this is too hard. Let's go back to white.'

'Demi Moore?' said Johnny hopefully.

'CAA would give youse such a hard time it's not even worth thinking about her. There's Ellen Barkin but she's already played a cop. Besides, her husband's Gabriel Byrne, he'd be pissed off altogether that you'd cast his Irish rival, Hector, as the lead. Jodie's a possibility, I suppose, but is she glamorous enough? Now what about Andie MacDowell?'

'And what about the detective?' asked Johnny.

'I suppose he'll have to be French to get you quota money, one of those bilingual American actors who has a French passport and works under the quota . . .'

'Christopher Lambert,' suggested Luana. Hardly worth saying, he was such an obvious candidate. She wondered what he would be like in bed. There she went again. Movie stars, gas station attendants, politicians on TV, it didn't make any difference who they were. Of course some she discounted straight away. She had never fancied redheads, so Mick Hucknall was quite safe. Simply yucky as far as she was concerned. All those freckles and that pale skin.

Luana's friends teased her and called her 'a slave to sex' and she reckoned they were probably right but she just couldn't help herself. She'd never had what other people called a 'relationship'. In fact when she stopped to think about it there were precious few men she had slept with twice. So she tried not to think about it. She was nineteen years old and having fun. Who needed to get emotional? Tina Turner had got it right – What's love got to do with it? She'd always been wild about Tina. All that bump and grind. Luana wouldn't dream of mentioning Tina to Mum, though. She hated noise of any kind.

Ever since she had been a very small child Luana had been aware that her mother was different. She was never the same from day to day. Luana knew that whatever else happened, she must not upset her. She learned to tiptoe around Edith and not disturb her in any way. Where other mothers bashed and clanged around in their kitchens, preparing their family's meals, Edith cooked her organic messes while everyone was out and left them in the fridge to be eaten – or thrown away in Luana and Johnny's case. The rest of the time she spent alone in a room with the door closed and Luana knew an enquiring knock would not be welcomed.

When Edith left Johnny and moved them to a sprawling, dark mansion flat across the river in Battersea, Luana had missed her father. 'He was too fidgety. I need peace and serenity,' was Edith's only explanation. Luana had cried herself to sleep every night, silently of course. She missed the way her father took the mickey out of Edith, creeping round the room with his finger to his lips in exaggerated compliance with Edith's rule of silence, winking at Luana while Edith said grace then leaping up when she'd finished and running out of the room calling back, 'I forgot to wash Mr de Soto's grubbby paws!' But at least Luana still saw Johnny fairly frequently and when Edith suddenly went round the world to find herself, Luana spent months with her father in Notting Hill. Johnny sent out for pizza virtually every night, ignoring Edith's nutritional instructions, and he clasped Luana to him and asked her a dozen times a week: 'Who's my beautiful peachy girl?' And when her father introduced her to Polly, his new girlfriend, who seemed to be genuinely interested in her, Luana thought she was in heaven although she made sure she didn't let on for quite a while.

Heaven collapsed when Edith swooped down like a maniacal Mother Goose and took her off to live in Cornwall. She tried to pretend it had nothing to do with Polly's arrival on the scene but Luana knew that the unthinkable had happened. Edith's fragile world had been disrupted and she was taking flight.

Edith sold the Battersea flat and retreated to a desolate Cornish farmhouse, square and gloomy with a stone façade covered in ivy and standing behind a wall encrusted with lichen. At the end of a narrow dirt road, the house stood in an exposed position at the top of the cliff and in winter the rooms were literally freezing, with the exception of the kitchen which had been unimaginatively modernised at some point in the Fifties. Later, when she came to read Daphne du Maurier's novels, Luana dubbed the place Formica Inn on account of the kitchen's incongruous plastic feel.

In Cornwall Edith promptly took to the bottle. Luana had watched her mother's gradual disintegration through precocious child's eyes, hitting the vodka, disguising it in tumblers of juice squeezed from organic oranges.

From the moment they moved to Cornwall Luana had started to feel she no longer existed as far as Edith was concerned. Edith barely left her room for the first six months. Trips to London to visit her father and Polly became the high points in Luana's life. Eventually everything Luana did was calculated to get Edith's attention even if it meant destroying the precious silence and playing Van Morrison and Them blasting 'G-L-O-R-I-A! GLO-RIA!' Still nothing. She wore her Flip baseball cap twenty-four hours a day. Edith never noticed. Luana turned it back to front, went to school in ripped jeans and DMs instead of her school uniform and told Edith she wanted to be a rock guitarist and play with Springsteen or Prince. Edith responded by saying she was starting to write a book and would Luana please not disturb her for six months. The only time she vaguely took an interest was during the Summer of Love revival when she started talking about becoming a New Age traveller. She wanted Luana to accompany her to love-ins and sit around cross-legged in damp fields waiting for the dawn. Luana went along with it in the hope that her mother might want her. Luana could not make anybody understand that she had so much to give: to her mother, to her father, to anybody, but nobody, it seemed, wanted her.

Until she met Roger Mainwaring. It was the summer of 1988. She had just turned fifteen and she had spent so much time outside, roaming the cliffs, away from the misery of Formica Inn, away from her mother, that her skin was nut brown and she looked like a wild Sicilian bandit with the bandanna tied around her black hair. She lived in a pair of tight black Lycra pedal-pushers and a big floppy white T-shirt which she knotted on her hip. She never bothered to exchange them for a swimsuit when she went swimming in the sea with the result that the drenched cotton clung to her sharp little triangular breasts, leaving nothing to the imagination when she climbed the narrow cliff path, cautiously edging her bare legs past the brambles, and bumped into Roger.

He was on holiday with his mother. They lived in Hemel Hempstead. He worked in a bank. He accompanied her up the cliff path and asked if she swam there every day at that time? They arranged to meet the next day. Luana was in a state of bliss about the fact that at last someone seemed to enjoy her company and she never noticed that he did all the talking and never asked her anything about herself. On the third day when he mentioned how pretty she was she received such a mammoth jolt of adrenalin, it was better than any rock'n'roll high. He kissed her mouth on the fourth day, her breasts on the fifth and her pussy on the sixth. And on the seventh day he didn't allow her a moment's rest. He went home a week later but he was followed by plenty of other summer Rogers. Suddenly she wasn't lonely any more. In exchange for her body men were prepared, it seemed, to take an interest in her and having been ignored for the first fifteen years of her life that was all Luana required of anybody. Interest was interest and sexual interest was as good as any other.

Two years later, she couldn't take Edith any longer and ran away to live with Johnny and Polly and it was then that Johnny sat her down and told her the truth about her mother, the reason why she had left him, the explanation for her erratic behaviour and why they must all take special care not to upset her.

'Oh Dad, for goodness' sake, I've known about Mum all along.'

168

'Well, whatever you do, don't tell Polly.'

When her father left Polly, Luana went into a state of panic that she would be sent back to Cornwall. She never rang her mother unless prompted to do so by her father or Polly. Polly, she noticed, always hovered in the background obviously hoping to pick up some clues but Luana was careful to keep her conversations with Edith on an even keel. If her mother embarked upon one of her hysterical fits, Luana would hang up. Once she tried to whisper, 'He won't come back to you, Mum. Just because he's left Polly it doesn't mean he's coming back to you. You left him, remember?'

Polly could not control her curiosity.

'Is she sitting down there in Cornwall waiting for him to come back now he's left me?' she asked Luana.

'Well, are you sitting here in Notting Hill waiting for him to come back?' Luana fired back, more brutally than she had intended. 'Polly, you know I promised Dad I wouldn't discuss Mum with you. It's Dad's problem. Don't get involved. Believe me, you're better off this way. If I had my way I'd tell you all about Mum. Don't you think I want to talk about her to someone? I feel like I'm piggy in the middle, caught between the two of you. When I was down in Cornwall she wanted to know about you. Now you want to know about her. Why can't we just drop it. Please, Polly!'

Apart from the ghost of Edith hovering between them, Polly and Luana muddled along very well together. For the first few months Luana had worked hard at acquiring an Attitude. Polly, it transpired, was a complete pushover, seemingly happy to produce a key to the front door and mouthwatering meals on tap. Polly had never heard of raves or Acid House. She did not know of the existence of Steve Strange, as Luana discovered when she tried to establish some kind of common ground with Polly by asking her if she used to go to Blitz. It was when Polly confessed to being an Old Romantic rather than a New one that Luana abandoned all hope. Still, the fact that her stepmother never asked what she did outside college hours endeared her to Luana and in return she consented to accompany Polly to the movies every once in a while although vast concessions on both sides had to be made when it came to the choice of film. Luana wanted action, the more violent the better.

169

Polly sat through *Lethal Weapon 2*, *Rambo III* and *Black Rain* with her hands over her eyes. On those occasions she allowed Polly to drag her to *Accidental Tourist*, Merchant Ivory's *Maurice* or one of those slow, soft-focus sloppy French films her stepmother liked to cry her way through, Polly couldn't help noticing that Luana spent rather a lot of time in the Ladies and prayed she wasn't doing drugs. Then Luana chucked in college to go and work for Clovis and, tired of sex in a different bed every night, she moved out to a rented flat.

Luana observed her father as he flicked through his script and held up a protesting hand to halt Clovis, who by now was thoroughly carried away with the idea of casting *Mr Wrong*. Luana tried to imagine Polly in bed with Johnny. As far as she could make out Polly had embraced celibacy with open arms ever since Johnny had left. This was completely beyond Luana's understanding and she kept a lookout for signs that her stepmother was about to shrivel up and wither before her eyes as a result of such deprivation. Poor old Polly. Luana knew she really ought to call and apologise for not showing up the other night.

'Call your mother, don't forget,' said Johnny.

'I will. I promise. I just clean forgot, I swear, Dad. I'll take her to see one of those slushy French movies she likes, the ones that make her blub.'

'Everything makes Polly blub,' said Johnny, smiling rather wistfully. 'No, I meant call your mother. Call Edith.'

When Luana saw Hector O'Neill for the first time she was on the telephone to the girlfriend who was her current favourite. Luana had a mild problem with her friends – she tended to drop those who told her things about herself she didn't want to hear.

'You really shouldn't drink so much. You're a nightmare when you're drunk.'

'Luana, are you one hundred per cent sure you're in love with him? Last week you were in love with Harry. You can't fall in love with every man you meet.'

'Why don't you wait at least for the second date until you go to bed with them? How do you expect them to respect you if you don't respect yourself?'

'Jesus, Luana, you can't afford that jacket. Why do you have to shop at Joseph? You still haven't paid off your overdraft. Why make it worse?'

In other words, anybody who criticised her or challenged her about her lifestyle was out. Luana got out of bed every morning, pushed everything under the carpet and started a brand new day. It was only a matter of time before a prince would come along and carry her off.

Ironically, the only thing her friends were wrong about was the reason she was working for Clovis. They thought she worked in casting in order to have a constant supply of men to screw in her role as a 'slave to sex'. Nobody realised that she had been fascinated by the world of casting since she was a child. Except perhaps Polly. To Polly, who could remember the girl in the duffel coat running down to the front of the cinema at the end of *Working Girl* and frantically scribbling down the cast, Luana's chosen career made perfect sense. For to Luana it was a career. Working for Clovis was just the beginning. Eventually she would move on and start up on her own, just like Polly had done.

The man who walked through the door was drop-dead gorgeous. Six foot two inches tall. Black hair with a lock falling over his forehead. Huge wraparound sunglasses. Long arrogant nose. High cheekbones. A wide slash of a mouth, very mobile. Broad shoulders and chest, incredible muscles on the arms. White Gap T-shirt with a pack of Marlboro Lites in the breast pocket. Jeans. Very long legs. Loafers.

Luana had stood up without realising it and now found herself peering right over the desk. She ran her eyes quickly back up to his face. He'd taken off his shades to reveal dark blue eyes.

'You're . . . you're . . .'

'Yes. Got it in one. I'm Hector O'Neill. Got any twenties?'

'Any what?'

'20p's? For the meter? I've only got half an hour's worth.'

'Oh, sure, wait a sec.' Luana emptied Clovis' meter piggy bank on to the desk and gave him the contents. He pocketed them, winked and left.

Five minutes later the phone rang. It was him.

'Luana, do me a favour. Tell Clovis and Johnny I'm at the Groucho, upstairs in the Soho Room, waiting for them, would you?'

'Yes, of course.'

'And is it OK if I pay you back another day?'

'Oh, no, please, be my guest.'

'Beautiful and generous.' He laughed and was gone.

Half-way through lunch at the Pizza Express with the man she

172

had draped herself over the night before, Luana suddenly wondered how Hector O'Neill had known her name.

To Luana's immense relief he came back four days later. She had washed her long black hair every morning and dragged herself out of bed half an hour earlier than usual in order to put together several different looks before finally setting off for the office satisfied that she was as alluring as possible in case he dropped in.

She had nearly been fired when Clovis had come flying in after a long lunch in a panic because the wardens were lurking only to find her meter money piggy bank was empty. She was furious. There was a lot of sniping along the lines of 'if yer sainted father weren't the producer of this shite and onions film I'd . . .'

'Yer supposed to keep that full at all times, yer dozy mare,' she told Luana. 'Turn out yer purse! Give us all yer 20p's.'

'Can I be a knight in dirty basketball boots?' said a voice behind Clovis and Hector O'Neill walked in dangling a polythene bag full of 20p's. 'It's not her fault, Clovis. Don't give her a hard time. I made her raid the little piggy for me earlier in the week.'

'Well, she should have said,' grumbled Clovis, only slightly mollified, and marched out.

'So, Luana, how's things?'

'Fine.' Luana smiled at him to cover the fact that she suddenly felt very gauche and awkward.

'My agent tells me that it was your idea to approach me for the lead in *Mr Wrong*.'

Luana nodded.

'What made you think of me for the role?'

'Oh, you know . . .'

'No, seriously, I'd like to hear. It's a fantastic part and it's come up just at the right time. It's got me out of doing another Conway. I have a lot to thank you for. In fact, why don't I buy you lunch? Are you free tomorrow?'

'Yes, of course.' Shit! thought Luana. I was too quick, too available.

Clovis came huffing-stuffing-puffing back upstairs.

'Fuckin' clampers'll not be getting me. Come on in, Hector.'

Luana, if you can make a cup of daycent coffee in under an hour you've got a taker.'

Hector winked at Luana and followed Clovis into her office.

'Will I be sitting in on this meeting?' called Luana.

'You will not,' Clovis called back.

Well, shite and onions to you too, whispered Luana under her breath, I'll have him to myself tomorrow.

'You still haven't told me why you cast me.' Hector squinted at the menu on the blackboard at Joe Allen's. 'What are you going to have to eat?'

He was oblivious to the surreptitious glances he was receiving from half the restaurant, or at least he was pretending to be, whereas Luana had been positively basking in the attention ever since they walked in together.

'I'll have a caesar salad and I didn't cast you. Clovis does the actual casting. I'm her assistant. I just suggested you to my dad.'

'Yes, but why me?'

'Dad had French co-production money. I thought he'd be more popular if he produced an actor who could pass for Latin if necessary but was still an international star. I mean, part of the film is going to be set in France. Your role in the script looks flexible to me. You could be a French womanising serial killer if necessary. And besides, you'd come cheaper than the big American names that immediately spring to mind.'

She'd said it without thinking. She felt herself going red. How could she have said that?

'But then, of course you're younger than most of them and better looking and . . .' she floundered.

'The quality of my acting was never part of the equation, I suppose?'

'Well, you never really had to act as Conway. All you ever had to do was look good and . . .'

She'd done it again!

'You're absolutely right. That's exactly why I was looking around for something else. Why are you looking so miserable?

174

You've only spoken the truth, which is more than an actor hears from most people who work in casting.'

'Have you taken a big cut financially?'

'Up front, yes. But I've got points. So, OK, you didn't think of me because of my acting but your reasons were good ones, shrewd ones, and I'll repay your faith in me. I'll surprise you. Do you want to be a producer like your father? You seem to have the right instincts.'

'Producer?' Luana was genuinely baffled. 'I haven't even cast a film on my own yet and I won't for years. I haven't thought any further than that.'

'Don't worry, you will and probably sooner than you think. Those are beautiful earrings you're wearing. And that's a great jacket. You've got sensational taste.'

Luana blushed again. What was wrong with her? Normally she'd be acting cool and laid back but for some reason today she seemed to have totally abandoned her act. The insecure bundle of nerves beneath the flirt was coming out and taking over. She reached for her cigarettes.

'You don't need those.' Hector had his lighter out instantly.

'Well you do.'

'True.' He laughed and turned his head sideways as he exhaled so the smoke wouldn't blow in her face, looking back at her with half-closed eyes. 'So tell me about yourself.'

'What do you want to know?'

'Don't be so defensive. I just want to get to know you.'

'Why?'

'Why are you so suspicious? Relax. Have another glass of wine and tell me – I don't know – whether you have any brothers or sisters?'

She shook her head.

'You're the only one and the apple of your father's eye.'

'I don't know what my dad thinks and I don't care. I'm just his little peachy girl.'

'Well, what's wrong with that?'

'Nothing. Ten years ago. But I'm grown up now. He ought to take me more seriously. I mean, who thought of you for *Mr Wrong*?'

'So, boyfriends?'

'Why do you want to know? Oh, sorry, mustn't be defensive. My stepmother once said I rebuild the Berlin Wall the minute someone asks me a personal question.'

'I don't know your stepmother.'

'Don't know Polly?'

'Well, at last here's someone who brings a smile to your face.'

'She's so funny. I mean, like, she's sweet. I love Polly. I really do. She's always been terrific to me but she's so sort of, you know, out of it. Of course, she's middle-aged . . .'

'How old is she?'

'Forty-something, I think.'

'Ancient!'

'She's not bad looking when she remembers to get her hair highlighted. She's got great legs but her breasts are sort of wobbly and her tummy comes and goes. It's just so sad. Ever since Dad left her she never goes out. She works flat out all day then makes herself this huge supper on a tray and takes it up to bed to eat it watching telly. She says it's what she wants.'

'Then maybe it is.'

'It can't be. I think she's chicken. It's easier for her not to face the world so she hides from it. She hides from the truth. She hides from men in case they reject her. She spends too much time putting herself out for other people. I call her Polly Pushover. She's a literary agent. She's good at that, but she lets Dad walk all over her.'

'And do you walk all over her too?'

Luana looked up in surprise. 'Yes, I suppose I do but she asks for it.'

'Luana, what is it that makes you so angry with Polly?'

'How do you know I'm angry with her? All right, I admit I am but it's because she's so bloody happy. No, that's going a bit far. She's contented. She seems to actually enjoy a life without men. She has no problems being on her own.'

'And you resent that? You don't like people who are comfortable with their lot because you're miserable yourself.'

'Who said I was miserable?'

'No one. I'm asking, that's all. Are you?'

'What's Clovis been saying? What did my dad tell you?'

'Nothing. Nothing at all. Clovis said you were great at your job.'

'Did she? Did she really?'

'And your dad said you were his little peachy girl.'

Luana frowned automatically then saw he was laughing at her.

'You've got to lighten up,' he told her, 'you're so pretty but there's an air of "Hey, what about me?" about you as if you think people don't care about you. You've got to give them a chance. You've got to learn to trust people when they take an interest in you. Now, I'm going to take these cigarettes away for the time being and order you some pecan pie with whipped cream. You're too thin.'

'I'm not anorexic.'

'I never said you were. There you go again, assuming I'm thinking the worst of you. You're too thin and nervy but you're still very pretty. You're dark like your father but you don't have his pugnacious bone structure, thank God. You must take after your mother.'

Luana said nothing.

'Well, do you? What about your mother? She's the one person you haven't mentioned.'

'Nothing to tell.'

'Please yourself,' said Hector with a shrug.

For the rest of the meal they discussed the film and who was up for the other roles, yet discussion was hardly the right word since afterwards Luana realised all he had done was coax out her suggestions as to who should play what role. He offered no opinion of his own nor, she reflected, had he said one word about his own family or indeed about himself. He'd provoked her into talking about herself for almost the entire meal. It was a first. No one had ever bothered to listen to her before, not properly. Sure, men had taken an interest in her but it had always been in her outer casing, never in what went on inside her head.

He walked her back to the office and there was something odd about it. It was only as they turned into Old Compton Street that she realised what it was: each time they crossed a street or turned a

177

corner and he wound up on the inside, he quickly ran around her so that he was walking on the outside between her and the street.

Working in a casting director's office Luana had come across plenty of well-known actors before, but Hector O'Neill was her first exposure to a gentleman.

Hector would have laughed out loud if he had known Luana thought of him as a gentleman. He was anything but. He found he couldn't stop thinking about her throughout the afternoon and comparing her youthfulness with the brittle sophistication of the journalist who had come to interview him.

Inviting Luana to lunch had been a spur of the moment thing although if he thought about it, it made sense to charm his producer's daughter. Yet if anything it had been the other way round. Hector had been surprised at how captivated he had been by Luana, how her vulnerability had touched a nerve in him making him want to draw her out and protect her. He knew what she was going through, he'd been there.

At least she made a refreshing change to the kind of hard-nosed middle aged bitch sitting here with him in his hotel suite, crossing and uncrossing her scrawny little legs, flashing her panties at him whenever she got the chance. The trouble was, he knew once the interview was over he'd probably find himself giving her exactly what she wanted, more out of habit than anything else.

'Luana, will you come down out of the clouds, for goodness' sake, and photocopy the scene in the script where Hector kisses the lady cop for the first time right after he's taken her to dinner.'

'Hector . . . kissed . . . who?' Luana tried to keep the misery out of her voice. It had been a week since her lunch with Hector and the one time he'd called, all he'd said was 'Hello darlin', that was a wonderful lunch the other day. Is herself there?' and she'd had to put him straight through to Clovis. Now here was Clovis talking about him kissing someone else.

'Will you just listen. For all I care he can kiss the blarney stone for a publicity photo opportunity and be done with it but what we're trying to do here is cast the fuckin' fillum. In case you've forgotten, perhaps I can remind you that there's a cracking good part for a woman. The cop's girlfriend. Well, sweetheart, we've got all these tarts they call actresses coming in tomorrow to read with himself. You made all the appointments with their agents but I suppose you've forgotten that too. Now, I reckon they should read the scene where they get to kiss Hector for the first time so we can see which one clicks best with the old ham since they're going to have to act the ro-mantic couple. No point casting a girl he's allergic to. Or vice versa, come to think of it.'

179

'How could anyone be allergic to Hector?'

'Oh, you'd be surprised. To my way of thinking there's something not quite right about him. They say he's Irish American from Boston but he hasn't got a Boston accent. No trace of it. Then he's supposed to be Irish but he never talks about Ireland to me. Never even asked me where I'm from. OK, since you've come back to life you can photocopy the scene. We've got eleven girls coming in. They can do the dialogue from the end of dinner right up to the kiss.'

Luana knew she had to come to terms with the fact that she was going to have to watch Hector kissing eleven girls. He arrived the next day with the director. Luana had had no warning that the director was coming to the casting. Nor, apparently, had Clovis, who went into a major snit. Hector introduced him to Luana.

'Luana, this is Henri La Plante, our director. Henri, this is Luana de Soto, Johnny's daughter. It was her idea to cast me.'

'Bravo!' Henri was a good ten years younger than Luana had imagined. He didn't look much more than thirty. He had a tousled mop of curly brown hair, eyes crinkled from smiling and a warm, friendly manner. Not at all the pseudo-smooth charming Frenchman.

'Clovis darling,' called Hector, 'you don't mind Henri being here, do you? I thought he ought to see me with the girls.'

'I'd have brought him in for the short list,' muttered Clovis. 'How do, Henry, we've met before. Luana, get yer father on the line and ask him why he's not here.'

'Because we never asked him,' explained Luana.

'Well, we never fuckin' asked the Froggy but he's turned up so we might as well have Johnny in on the act as well,' hissed Clovis so loudly Luana was convinced Henri must be able to hear.

The first girl arrived and Luana sent her straight in, handing her the pages. The other girls began to arrive at intervals and Luana kept herself busy in the outer office, unable to resist glancing through the half-open door every now and then. She need not have worried. Henri was in the process of putting Clovis' nose severely out of joint. Two hours went by. Hector still hadn't kissed anyone. Henri never let it go that far. He clearly knew exactly what he was looking for and as the actresses came and went, he wasn't finding it. He let them read with Hector for a few minutes then he politely interrupted, chatted with them in halting English before sending them on their way.

'So what was wrong with her if it's not too much to ask?' By the eighth girl Clovis was seething. 'I'll have you know I've hand-picked those girls. They're pairfect – at least three of them anyway – pairfect!' Clovis had broken her golden rule of never arguing with the director. 'One thing you have to learn in this business,' she was fond of telling Luana, 'is you always have to let the director think it's his idea, not yours. Even if you find someone who turns out to be the new Emma Thompson or the new Julia Roberts, it's the director's discovery, not yours.'

Henri wasn't thrown. 'Is no good,' he explained, crinkling his eyes at her, 'is too preety-preety. I need woman who is strong but who also cry.'

'He only wants the shite and the bleeding onions!' Clovis told Hector, smiling sweetly at Henri all the while.

'He wants vulnerability. I can understand that. Frankly, I'm getting a bit frustrated myself at not being able to play the whole scene. What time's the next girl due, Luana?'

'She'll be here in fifteen – twenty minutes.'

'Fine. We've got time. Come in here and read the scene with me all the way through.'

'I can do that – ' began Clovis.

'No. Is good. Luana young. Is better,' said Henri.

'Well thank you very much!' Henri had made an enemy for life.

Although she was quaking inside, Luana calmly read through the scene with Hector, feeding him his lines, already aware that there was no trace of Conway left in him. Henri was watching him with a bemused look on his face.

'You are killer, 'Ector. Never forget you are killer' – he pronounced it 'keeler' – 'even when you make love,' he murmured as they neared the end of the scene. 'Now you are walking down the street, you stop, she say "Bonsoir" and you kiss her . . .'

Luana felt Hector's arms go around her and draw her to him. She felt him grasp the back of her head and propel her face towards

181

his. She felt his mouth on hers forcing open her lips. She felt his tongue dart quickly into her mouth before he pulled away abruptly.

'Henri, should I kiss her as she's actually saying good night or let her turn away and then grab hold of her?'

Luana's eyes were pricking. Here she was about to swoon, literally, yet to Hector it was all part of the job. In the background she could hear Henri asking them to run through it again and yes, this time could Luana please turn away so Hector could grab her. Fighting back her tears, Luana stumbled through her lines wondering if she would be able to contain herself when Hector kissed her again.

On cue she turned away, felt Hector reach out and roughly pull her to him, felt her heart hammering. Any moment now . . .

'Excuse me. Sorry to interrupt. Am I in the right place? There was no one outside.'

Hector released Luana a fraction of a second before his lips met hers. They all turned to see an unbelievably attractive woman standing in the doorway. She was tall, five foot nine at least, with a small head on a long neck. Her dark red hair was cropped in a gamine feathery cut but her face had an undeniable strength: wide apart green eyes, a long straight nose and a big mouth with a full lower lip. Her skin was white with freckles and even though she was wearing a beat-up denim jacket, pale grey T-shirt and frayed jeans, she exuded elegance.

'Hello, Julianne, good to see you.' Clovis seized her opportunity to regain command of the proceedings while Luana retreated, both literally and metaphorically, into the background.

Julianne Reynard, twenty-nine years old, daughter of a French father and an American mother, born in France, educated in America, bilingual, dual nationality, able to work both in Europe and America and already known in both countries following her hit film, *Violette*, in which she played a young French woman who becomes engaged to an American living in New York in order to obtain her Green Card only to discover he's a murderer. If she turns him in will she jeopardise her chances of US nationality?

Luana watched as Henri, who obviously knew Julianne, kissed her warmly on both cheeks and introduced her to Hector, who was watching her with blatant appreciation. Luana wanted to run, to get as far away from Clovis' office as she could, but some masochistic force compelled her to watch Hector and Julianne read through the scene. She even leaned closer to get a better view as Hector's mouth fastened on Julianne's. Was it Luana's imagination or did the kiss seem to go on for twice as long as hers had?

A noise in the outer office alerted Luana to the fact that the next girl had arrived. Aware that Hector and Julianne were preparing to run through the scene again, Luana fled. Eventually Julianne emerged with Hector's arm around her shoulders. They went out on to the landing together and Luana could hear a quick muted exchange. On his way back Hector barely acknowledged Luana. The last three girls were called in and out with indecent haste and by the end of the afternoon it was clear Julianne would be offered the part.

'Shouldn't someone call my father?' asked Luana. 'She's not going to come cheap, not after *Violette*.'

'It's his fault for not bothering to show up for the casting in the first place,' said Clovis.

'Besides, he's in Paris,' volunteered Hector. 'I spoke to him earlier in the day. That's why I brought Henri along in his absence.'

'But he can't be,' protested Luana, 'we were supposed to be having dinner tonight.'

'In that case I shall have to stand in for him *ce soir* as Henri did this afternoon,' announced Hector.

'That's fuckin' gallant, O'Neill.' Clovis looked at him sharply. 'I don't ever recall you askin' meself to dinner.'

'Well would you like to join us?' asked Hector as Luana held her breath.

'I would not. But I do not want you keeping her out half the night, Hector. We've got a load of little Froggy boys dragging their non-existent bollocks in here tomorrow for the next casting and I want herself fresh as a daisy to cope with them. She'll have to read with them and all unless we can sign young Julianne overnight.'

'I'll just have one course,' said Luana, studying the menu as she sat with Hector at the corner table by the stairs in the Ivy. She'd been to the Ivy once before and she'd seen Al Pacino sitting at this very table. In fact she was sitting where Al had sat and a flush of warmth ran through her at the thought.

'Now why is that? Aren't you hungry after all that work today?'

'Oh, yes, I'm starving, I could eat a . . .'

'Then why?'

'Well, I know you only asked me out because Dad stood me up. You're probably dying to get home and rest or something.'

'Luana, I rarely have to do anything I don't want to any more. I enjoyed our talk at lunch the other day. I really wanted to spend some time with you again.'

'Why?'

'Why not? You're a very pretty girl – I mean woman – and you're very bright. Apart from the fact that you have a warped and deeply suspicious mind, I enjoy your company and if you ask why again I shall get up and leave you here.'

Luana wanted to ask him if he had enjoyed kissing her that afternoon. She wanted to know how she had compared with Julianne Reynard. But instead she sat quietly as several luminaries passed their table and greeted Hector.

'This is Luana,' he told them each time and she smiled, pleased by the fact that he didn't explain her connection with him via work so they assumed she was his date.

Well, she *was* his date. Relax, she told herself, for God's sake relax.

'So what's Dad up to in Paris?'

'Haven't a clue. I called him about something, said I'd look forward to seeing him at the casting and he said he had to go to Paris at the last minute. Maybe he's got a lover over there.'

'Dad?!'

'Well, it's been a while since he left – Polly, is it? Surely he must have seen a few other women since then even if he is your ancient father.'

'I suppose you're right. It's just what with Polly appearing to have taken some vow of celibacy, I sort of lumped Dad in there with her. Of course, there is Juanita.'

'Juanita Whyte? Think there's something happening there?'

'Not if there really is a God.'

'Bad as that, is she? What about your mother? Might they ever get back together?'

'No way. Can I have the smoked salmon and scrambled eggs?'

She looked straight at Hector for a second and her gaze said: I do not talk about my mother.

'Tell me, do you like Clovis?'

This was so out of left field it threw her, as it was meant to do.

'She's a very good casting director.'

'That's not what I asked.'

'It's my way of answering what you asked. I want to learn the business. She's good. I'm learning. It's not important whether or not I like her.'

'Ambitious little thing, aren't you? But you don't like her.'

'No,' replied Luana without looking up at him. 'Do you like her?'

'Not much. She's so brash.' And they both laughed.

'Do you live on your own?' he asked, another unexpected question.

'Yes.'

'Like it?'

'Yes.'

'Don't get lonely?'

'Sometimes.'

'What do you think about marriage?'

'Well I don't think about it. I'm too young.'

'But you're not against it?'

'Why on earth should I be?'

'Child of divorced parents.'

'No I'm not. Dad and Mum were never married. Dad's married to Polly even though they're separated.'

'So who do you think of as your mother?'

'Well I call Mum, Mum and Polly, Polly so I suppose . . .'

'But you don't like her: your real mother, I mean . . .'

'My biological mother is what they say now, isn't it?'

'Why don't you like her?'

'Maybe I do. She doesn't like me.'

'How do you know?'

185

Luana realised suddenly that he'd done it again, slipped in underneath her guard and started her talking about herself – and not only about herself but about her mother. But, dammit, she wanted to tell someone about Edith. She'd always longed to talk to Polly about her mother but her father had made it quite clear that was out of the question. Now she was nineteen, an adult, able to make decisions about her own life. Hector seemed genuinely interested in her, which was more than she could say about anyone else.

'Mum ignored me. She was always wrapped up in her own world, shut away from us. She'd always been sick, I knew that, but I never realised just how bad she was until Dad and I talked about it recently. Poor Dad. When he met her she was only seventeen and he can't have been much older. From what I can make out he was heavily into his Italian father role, wanted to start a family. He gets like that sometimes and it's completely stupid. He's a perfectly ordinary English bloke but sometimes he comes on like he's the original Italian Catholic poppa, all hugs and kisses and don't you dare let a boy so much as look at you. Anyway, Mum was young and very pretty and she got pregnant with me so he must have done more than just look at her! He wanted to marry her, so he told me, but she wouldn't let him. He should have suspected something then but he's dead thick sometimes. He's a born optimist. He just kept hoping she'd say yes if he kept asking her enough times. Then I was born and apparently it was after she'd had me that she really began to go crazy. Post-natal depression or whatever it's called. They reckon she must have always been pretty fragile. Then one day I came home from school and found her unconscious. I was too young to understand but I remember there was a hell of a fuss, people running and carrying her off.'

Hector leaned forward. 'You mean she took an overdose?'

'I suppose. After that, well I suppose she needed Dad too much and he just couldn't take it. He's pretty needy himself.'

'So he left her?'

'No. She left him. That's what did his head in. She said she knew what she was doing to him and she knew she couldn't be the woman he wanted, so she left. You can just imagine it, all his Catholic guilt came rushing to the surface. That's why he won't let any of us upset her. He's terrified she'll do herself in and he'll be to blame. Poor old Polly, she can't understand why there's this mystery surrounding Mum. I've tried to drop as many hints as I can but Dad has forbidden me to discuss Mum with Polly. Polly's pretty smart though. She must have sussed out Dad's guilt complex by now.'

'Is your mother still having any kind of treatment?'

'That's just it. While she was still in London she was going to this shrink of hers once or twice a week but once she moved to Cornwall she never found anyone down there. Hence Dad's paranoia. He holds himself responsible. You see, the thing is, if he hadn't met Polly and married her he might have gone back to Mum out of sheer guilt.'

'Do you really believe that?'

'Sometimes I do, sometimes I don't, but I'm sure it's what Mum thinks.'

'But she left him.'

'I know. Ironic, isn't it?'

'Would you have wanted them to get back together?'

'Well, that's where my lapsed Catholic guilt comes in. The answer is no. I respect Polly. She's good for Dad. Oh, here's my scrambled eggs.' Suddenly Luana felt uncomfortable. Had she said too much?

Hector was rather quiet for the rest of the meal. This made Luana even more nervous and she chattered frantically to make up for it. Now and then he took her hand and smiled and once he leaned over and kissed her on the cheek.

By the end of the meal Luana was in a state of elation. She wondered if he could possibly understand the relief she felt at having been able to talk to someone about her mother. He had come into her life at exactly the right moment and he was meant to be the one she talked to. It was destiny, she told herself dramatically. She felt closer to Hector O'Neill than to any other person she had ever encountered.

As they walked to the car, Hector slipped his arm around her as if it was the most natural thing in the world. She was oblivious to the fact that she had drunk so much that if he had not supported her she would have fallen in the gutter.

That night she fell in love for the first time. She realised that everything that had come before had been infatuation. This was the real thing and the reason she knew was that she climaxed for the first time.

It didn't happen until nearly dawn. They made love as soon as they were in Hector's suite but unlike the other men Luana had slept with, he knew she hadn't come. He asked her in the darkness, holding her close to him:

'Why did you fake it?'

Luana made no effort to pretend.

'I always do.'

'But why?'

'I always want to please . . . the man.'

'And it doesn't matter if you're not satisfied?'

'I'm always afraid he won't want me any more if I don't pretend that it was great for me too.'

'So have you always pretended you're happy – with your mother, for example? Does she have any idea of the effect her illness has had on you?'

He rocked Luana to sleep as she cried into his chest. Later he woke her and began gently to arouse her, stroking her all over, forbidding her to touch him, forcing her to submit to his caresses. He did this for a long time, and when he finally entered her he was quite rough, deliberately, and it worked. It excited her. She came noisily, surprising herself with her first ever genuine cries of pleasure.

He left her to sleep again and went to the window, stretching. He wandered into the sitting room where he had had an answering machine installed and listened to his messages. Joan Brock had called four times. He plucked a piece of hotel writing paper from the folder on the desk and scrawled a note.

Dear Joan,
Can we call it a day? I'm off to France
to begin filming in a month or so. It

was fun but it was really only a fling.
Let's be adults and put it behind us as a
terrific memory.

Hector

He'd get the hotel to fax it in the morning as soon as he'd sent little Luana on her way.

Polly was furious with Joan. It had been weeks since they'd lunched and Joan hadn't returned a single one of her calls despite the many messages she'd left on Joan's answering machine.

Joan might be an aggressive, competitive friend who often made Polly feel inadequate but she was also a good listener and Polly wanted to tell her about her night out with Edward Holland. She wanted to inform Joan that she, Polly, was now through with men for ever. She was even looking forward to Joan's look of horror and the subsequent lecture on how she'd better get a grip on herself and stop uttering such crap, they were neither of them getting any younger.

In the end she decided to drive over to Joan's house off the Fulham Road and bang on the door late at night. Joan would be livid if she had miraculously managed to lure somebody into her bed but Polly didn't care.

There was no answer.

Joan hadn't managed to lure anybody into her bed but she had managed to worm her way into someone else's. The previous week she had interviewed Hector O'Neill for the profile she was writing, after which she had enjoyed three successive nights of carnal lust with him in his suite at the Berkeley. Only now she had received his fax and was indulging in some very un-Joan like behaviour: crying

190

her eyes out. When her doorbell went she rushed to the window in relief only to glimpse Polly standing at her front door. Joan returned to bed and pulled the pillow over her head. Polly was the last person she wanted to see.

In the end Polly asked Zoë Nichols to come for a drink at the end of the day. It would be easier to talk without Mrs Flowers fussing around. It turned out to be a particularly frantic day and when Zoë arrived, Polly was in the midst of some delicate negotiating on the phone.

'Take her into the drawing room and give her a drink, would you, Mrs Flowers?' Polly mouthed. 'Stay and chat with her if you have the time until I get there.'

When Polly finally went through she could hear Mrs Flowers in full flow but she couldn't make out what she was saying and then when Polly arrived in the room Mrs Flowers suddenly stopped as if she had been talking about Polly herself.

Zoë Nichols was attractive with expressive brown eyes set very wide apart and a mass of curly blonde hair. She was small with big breasts and a curvaceous figure. She reminded Polly of an upmarket Dolly Parton. She was older than Polly had expected. Polly realised they must be about the same age.

'Goodnight, Mrs Flowers. Thank you so much,' said Polly, knowing she ought to invite Mrs Flowers to join them for a quick drink.

'Yes, goodnight, it's been fun to talk to you. Good luck,' added Zoë and Mrs Flowers reluctantly took the hint and left.

Good luck with what, wondered Polly. With me? Am I that bad a boss? Has she been having a moan?

'What a character!' said Zoë. 'What's it like having an author for a secretary?'

'I don't,' said Polly. 'What will you have to drink?'

'You mean you don't know?'

'Know what?'

'Your secretary is Mabel Lucy Flowers.'

'Are those her names? I had no idea. How clever of you to worm them out of her. She's always insisted on being just Mrs Flowers to me.'

'I'll have a whisky if I may. Mabel Lucy Flowers. She's a Mills & Boon author. Haven't you seen her books at the supermarket? I think she's one of the successful ones.'

'I don't believe it.' Polly had stopped pouring whisky in amazement. 'You come in and get more out of her in twenty minutes than I have in all the time she's been working for me. Why is she working for me, as a matter of mild interest, if she's so successful in her own right?'

'Oh, she's got it all worked out.' Zoë was obviously highly amused. 'She's given up writing Mills & Boons and she's working on something much bigger. She went to work as a temp at, where was it, Patrick Fisher & Dunbar in order to learn more about the requirements in the marketplace for that kind of novel and that's where she met you.'

'But she never breathed a word to me about the fact that she wrote herself. She sits here all day working for me and – '

'Then she goes home and works on her own blockbuster at her kitchen table. It's coming along rather well, so she says. It's going to have a very happy ending, a real weepie. She's very keen on happy endings, thinks we all need to be uplifted more. She nearly had a fit when your husband left because I gather the timing coincided with her hero behaving rather badly, had a bit on the side and all that and was thinking of leaving her heroine.'

Damn Mrs Flowers. How dare she be so indiscreet about Polly's private life with a total stranger.

'And did he?'

'Yes, but as she keeps saying, her book will have a happy ending although personally, from the sound of her characters, I think it'd probably be happiest all round if her hero and her heroine walked off into two different sunsets and stayed there.'

'Did she indicate what she was planning to do with this masterpiece once she's finished it?'

'I'll give you three guesses. You happened to walk in just as I was asking exactly the same question.'

'I wondered why she went so quiet. You're not married then, Zoë?'

'I'm not, actually. Never have been. I'm thirty-eight and somehow it just hasn't happened and I can't say I'm in any way unhappy about it. I'm more worried about what I'll do if I ever meet anyone who wants me to move in with him. I've got so used to being on my own and doing exactly what I want when I want, I don't think I could accommodate anyone else very easily. Do you have children to keep you company since your husband left?'

'I had his daughter but now she's got a flat of her own and I'm all on my own but the terrible thing is, I'm getting to be just like you. Johnny used to watch TV till the middle of the night. He couldn't be on his own for a second, spent the whole time following me about asking me what I was doing. He didn't like me doing anything that didn't include him: as a result I wound up doing very little of what I actually wanted to do and rather a lot of what he wanted. Now I'm making up for a great deal of lost time, and it's bliss.'

Zoë laughed. 'Don't you miss him just a bit?'

'Sometimes I miss him desperately, sometimes not at all.'

'Do you want him to do a Mabel Lucy Flowers and come back to you? Oh, I'm sorry, that's a pretty personal question.'

Polly put down her drink. 'No, it's OK. It's a perfectly reasonable question and one I happened to have avoided asking myself so I can't give you an answer right this minute.'

'I'll stop being so nosy. Forgive me, it goes with the job. Listen, it's very good of you to see me. I've done a bit of homework and your client list is really amazing, considering how short a time you've been going. I absolutely loved *Mr Wrong*, lapped it up and begged for more. Is he writing another? I gather it was your idea to get him to write the book in the first place. And Rebecca Price, now her books are a real treat. That's who Mrs Flowers ought to be looking to for guidance. A superior writer in her genre, as they say. The reviewers are so snobby about her. It seems the more successful a writer is financially the worse the reviews, and even if they are good, they're always so removed. I mean, you never get someone writing something as straightforward as, "If, like me, you like Jackie Collins, Sidney Sheldon and Barbara Taylor Bradford you'll absolutely love this new novel by X." It's always, "The writing is execrable, the grammer non-existent, the characters half-dimensional but no doubt fans of the genre will be fooled yet again" sort of thing. Obviously written by some former Booker prize judge who collapses if he has to read anything that hasn't recently been translated from the Latin or Greek or even Serbo-Croat. Of course, if it has a good story it's damned for ever.'

'How enormously refreshing to hear a member of the so-called Mass Market speak out. I wish you'd do it in print. Irwin Shaw said when he was reviewing one of Mario Puzo's books, I forget which one, "For some literary critics, writing a book that is popular and commercially successful rates very high on the list of white collar crime." I agree with you, Zoë. It's hard enough for anyone to write anything without people being put off at the first fence by mean-spirited critics. It never seems to work both ways. The elitist reviewers can dump on popular fiction but the plebs who enjoy a good story, bless 'em, are never allowed to review William Gaddis and say they don't understand a word, now are they? So, what's happened with Aroma Ross?'

'Well, I was right. It was her agent's idea, her model agent. Seize the moment and all that, supermodels are the world's new icons, they've replaced film stars in the eyes of the young, more teenagers in the United States can name a supermodel than their own president and so on and so forth. I've had a giggly girly meeting with her and a couple of the bookers at her London agency. She kept me waiting for an hour but what the hell, she's not the first and I've waited worse places than Claridge's lobby. She's rather sweet and quite shrewd in a childlike way. No one's got any idea what the book should be about, least of all the publishers. All they'll say is that it should be "like Ivana Trump's book". How *passé* can you get? At least Aroma knows exactly what she doesn't want the book to be about: her. Nothing about her boyfriends or her private life. She's pretty paranoid about that, but fair enough. We discussed the market and she figures it's kids, twelve to twenty. I felt a bit mean: in order to get her OK on doing the book I let her think it was going to be some kind of Sweet Valley High romance but in fact it'll have to be more than that to justify the publisher's advance, which is £100,000 by the way. She says she's going to dictate stuff into a tape recorder but to be honest I suspect I'm going to have to conceive and write the whole thing from start to finish and frankly, it's easier that way. I can just get on with it.'

'But you don't have a deal with her yet?'

'I won't have a deal with her at all. She and I will have separate contracts with the publishers and never the twain shall meet.'

'So you'd like me to negotiate your deal for you?'

'If you think it's worth your while.'

'It could sell very well. We'll have to get you a royalty, not one of those flat fee deals. Who's the publisher?'

'Artie Allen-Jones at Hollywood House. Do you know him?'

'I know Artie. Younger than springtime but keen with it. It'd fit his profile perfectly doing a supermodel's novel. Leave it to me. Now, another whisky? Where are you from, Zoë? London?'

'Born and raised, but my mother's French. Poor woman met my father during the war and came over and married him. He's south London working class, a costermonger. I was bilingual thanks to my mum. I started writing for the music press when I left school, just bulldozed my way in and took it from there. I wasn't proud. I wrote for anyone who'd let me – the *Mirror*, the *Sun*, *Woman's Own*, and now it's the *Guardian* and the *Sunday Times* and *Tatler*. Get that – a costermonger's daughter writing for *Tatler*. But it's not a patch on what you've done, Polly, starting up your own agency and everything.'

'My father left me £25,000,' Polly confessed. 'I used it to build the conservatory, my office through there, and since then I've just been lucky.'

'Money isn't everything. You've been shrewd and smart and you've clearly got excellent judgement. Don't run yourself down. You're a budding success story. Be proud of it. I would.'

After she'd gone Polly made herself a snack and watched television but she didn't really take anything in because her mind kept on going back to Zoë Nichols and how good she'd felt at the end of their meeting. She kept on comparing Zoë with Joan and wondered why. They were both journalists but they could not be more different: Zoë with her get-out-and-do-it attitude and Joan with her elitist Vogue House airs and graces. Well, it was not hard to see who was going to go further in the end. But the more she thought about it the more Polly realised that it was not their work that made her lump Joan and Zoë together. It was their approach to her. Joan was competitive and always succeeded in putting Polly down whereas Zoë had made her feel wonderful with her generous praise, and Polly was sure it had been genuine, that she wasn't just saying it to make Polly feel more inclined to get her a better deal. Polly went to bed having decided that she wanted to see more of Zoë Nichols whether she became her agent or not. While she'd been talking to Zoë, Joan had left a message on Polly's machine, the first in over two weeks. It sounded suspiciously like Joan was in tears.

To her own surprise, Polly didn't ring Joan back that evening or the following morning. She rang Zoë Nichols instead and suggested they go and see a movie.

'My goodness, you look smashing,' commented Mrs Flowers, looking at Polly admiringly as she came back into the conservatory having been upstairs to have a quick bath and change before going out. 'Must be someone really special. Someone new?' she asked coyly.

Polly had rung her Mills & Boon author Grania Henderson and asked her about Mabel Lucy Flowers. Grania was riddled with guilt.

'Of course I've known who she was and I knew you'd find out sooner or later but she made me swear not to talk about it. I think she thought she was quite safe. I'm your only Mills & Boon author, after all, and although you pretend to be a champion of popular fiction, you never come to any of the Romantic Novelists' Association lunches. If you had you would have seen Mrs Flowers hiding in a corner.'

'Well, she always says she'll go as my representative. Now I know why. She's there as an author. Oh, Grania, what a mess. Why do you think she blurted it all out to Zoë Nichols? She must have known Zoë would mention it. Do you think I should tackle her about it?'

'Polly, I'm going to be fearfully indiscreet here and don't jump down my throat when you hear what I've got to say. Mrs Flowers has shown me this saga thing she's writing and it's simply awful. She hasn't got a clue. Don't be upset that she hasn't shown you. She's terrified of what your reaction will be. I've headed her off at the pass and suggested some more work she might do on it before she shows it to you. I don't think you need say anything for the time being. You don't want to lose a good secretary, do you?'

Mrs Flowers might well ask if she was on her way to meet someone special. Polly knew she looked good in her grey silk top, long silk-knit black cardigan, which clung seductively to her hips while hiding their bulges and her black Italian trousers with the little slit just above the ankle. The two-inch heels on her mules showed off her legs to perfection. The overall effect was chic but casual. But why was she all dolled up like this? She was only going to have supper with Johnny in his new flat. Was it pride? She wanted Johnny to see she looked good with or without him. Or did she really want Johnny to take notice of her again?

As she drove to Mayfair, she wondered why Johnny wanted to see her. The words 'happy ending' flashed into her mind but she banished them immediately, cursing Mrs Flowers. Johnny had called at the beginning of the week.

'Pol? How are you? Fancy a bite at my new place? Love you to see it. I'll cook. You will be astounded.'

Polly arrived to find he had an antiseptic flat on the first floor above a shop in Mount Street. Johnny didn't belong in Mayfair. However much he might think he had acquired a sophisticated veneer, he was wrong, and in Mayfair his rough-and-readiness stood out even more. The flat was like a hotel suite. It was as if Johnny had rented it for the night, not for the next three years or whatever it was. Polly found herself looking at the ashtrays to see if there were matchbooks with his name on them. She pressed the brand new wood panelling to see if it would open to reveal a minibar. It had never occurred to her that someone was actually commissioned to paint the usually dreadful paintings hanging on the walls in hotel rooms until she read Dirk Bogarde's novel *Jericho* where a character did just that. Looking at the motley collection on Johnny's walls, she deduced it must be a job lot from a defunct hotel.

She had been met by the most extraordinary sight when she walked through the front door. Johnny was arranging flowers, hopping about in his jeans and sneakers, trying to tuck stray stems into a tall rectangular glass vase standing on the hall table. The result looked decidedly unprofessional. Broken lilies and squashed foliage lay on the floor in a puddle of water. Polly gently pushed him aside and began again. She was oddly touched by the sight of him attempting such a task.

'I've got a Mrs Thing,' he explained, 'and she orders these flowers for me once a week to cheer the bloody place up and then she leaves them for me to deal with.'

'Well, I'm glad you've got someone to look after you.'

'Yeah. Me too. Ivana.'

'Ivana?'

'It's not her real name. That's something quite unpronounce-able. She's Czech so I call her Ivana.'

'Does she mind?'

'Never asked her. She makes me dinner too and leaves it in the fridge. Come and look, Pol. Same thing every day. Two pork chops and boiled potatoes. I never touch it.' He opened the fridge in the tiled and chrome kitchen and pointed to a row of Pyrex ovenproof dishes, 'See: Monday, Tuesday, Wednesday . . .'

'Is this what we're having for dinner?'

'Of course not. I'm cooking, I told you,' he said proudly.

'But it's such a waste! Can't you tell her not to do it?'

'Oh, it all goes to good use, you'll see. Besides, I like the notion that someone cares about me.'

Polly refrained from pointing out that he hadn't even kissed her hello or said how nice she looked and if he wanted someone to feel sorry for him he was going the wrong way about it. Yet strangely that's exactly what she felt. She yearned to go home and return with fridge-loads of nourishing home-made food for him. But she couldn't resist commenting on the décor.

'What's wrong with it?' Johnny was immediately defensive. 'Don't blame me. Juanita handled everything. Found the place, did it up, hired Ivana, and Bob was my uncle. All I had to do was move in – and here I am. Now, food! Go and sit down and relax with your drink while I rustle up a little something in the kitchen.'

'A little something' turned out to be Marks and Spencer's Chicken Kiev followed by De Soto ice-cream.

'Do you know about M&S, Pol? Amazing place for food.'

Polly smiled. Trust Johnny to go for megabucks microwave cooking. It really was rather sweet – the thought of him pottering round Marks & Sparks and tottering back to nuke his salmon *en croute* or his fish pie every night before he curled up in front of the telly with endless tubs of the family *gelati*. She wondered what his mother would say if she knew he was living off frozen meals.

She poured herself a glass of wine and started idly flicking through *Hello!* She stopped at a massive spread on Juanita Whyte and goggled. It was just as well Johnny hadn't actually fed her yet otherwise she might have thrown up.

'FIVE YEARS AFTER HIS TRAGIC DEATH, SIR GORDON WHYTE'S BEAUTIFUL WIDOW INVITES US INTO HER LOVELY HOME . . . and tells us how she is gradually beginning to enjoy life again.'

Polly studied the pastel décor of Juanita's Chelsea mansion and saw immediately how her bland taste had extended to Johnny's flat. The last few pages showed Juanita in Paris posing under the Arc de Triomphe, outside Chanel, in the rue de Rivoli, on the banks of the Seine and, to Polly's horror, having dinner with Johnny who was described as 'a new companion who has brought a sparkle back to Lady Whyte's eyes'. Hardly a new companion, thought Polly, and besides it was more likely to be a new facelift that had brought about that sparkle.

'Johnny de Soto, co-producer with Lady Whyte of the forthcoming film *Mr Wrong* starring Hector "Conway" O'Neill,' read the caption. 'Mr de Soto has been a firm fixture in Lady Whyte's calendar ever since he offered his kind and sympathetic support at the time of her husband's death.'

'My arse,' said Polly.

'What's that, Pol? Now, I've just got to feed Zutty then we'll have ours. *Zutty!* Where are you hiding? Din-dins!'

There was a frantic scrabbling underneath one of the sofas and Zutty shot out, a tornado of red and white fur, skedaddling across the parquet floors, paws splayed in all directions in his desperate haste to get to his food. Polly hadn't even realised he was there.

'Say hello to Pol,' said Johnny firmly, holding the plastic dog bowl high in the air. 'After all, you're going to have to be very nice to her, aren't you?'

'Just why is he going to have to be very nice to me? Johnny, give him his dinner, for Christ's sake. He'll do himself an injury.'

Zutty was prancing about on his hind legs, pirouetting, leaping in the air, losing his balance on landing and falling over.

'Here you are then. See, Pol, Zutty gets Ivana's pork chops and spuds. They don't go to waste. Now, you do like Zutty, don't you?'

'I suppose so, yes.'

'Well, that's terrific because he really likes you.'

'Well how come he didn't utter a sound when I arrived?' Polly was beginning to smell a very large rat.

'You're looking great tonight, Pol.'

'Johnny!' warned Polly. If only he'd said that when she walked in.

'OK, OK. I'll come to the point. We start filming in France in about three weeks.'

'I know.'

'Well, I can't take Zutty.'

'Oh, Christ, Johnny!'

'He does adore you.'

'Bullshit! He adores anyone who feeds him, just like any other dog. How long will you be away?'

'About a month, maybe six weeks.'

'Why can't Luana look after him?'

'Luana? Luana doesn't know how to look after a dog.'

'What on earth makes you say that? She takes care of actors, doesn't she?'

'Oh, I get it. What's the difference? Ha, ha! Have you seen her lately, by the way? She's looking terrific.'

'Well, tell her that and she'll probably agree to look after Zutty.'

'Oh, shut up, Pol. Seriously. I popped into the office and there she was, my little peachy girl again.'

201

'Well, for heaven's sake don't let her hear you calling her that. She hates it. So that other problem has blown over?'

'What other problem?'

'The constant nymph of Central London.'

'Haven't heard any more about it.'

'Because, you know, I think she does have a man.'

'Really? Who?'

'I don't know but she keeps hinting she's seeing someone. Johnny, what's this?'

'Salad. I thought you liked it. You lived off the stuff when we were living together.'

'You're meant to take it out of the packet. In fact, you're not meant to buy it in a packet in the first place. You're supposed to buy lettuces and rocket and endive and wash them and chop them up and serve them with a good dressing.'

'No shit? Well, I'll chop open the packet if you make the dressing. So what's she said about this bloke?'

'Nothing specific. In fact she seems to be quite secretive about him but I saw her the other day and she showed me this present she'd bought him. Johnny, it was a gold propelling pencil. It wasn't exactly cheap. She'd obviously gone to a lot of trouble choosing it and she wanted my approval. My guess is the man has to be considerably older, otherwise why would she ask what I thought and why would she get a gold pencil as opposed to the latest R.E.M. CD? The other thing that intrigued me was when I asked her if it was his birthday, she said, oh, no, it was just that he'd lost his old one and she wanted to replace it.'

'Sounds serious. Do you suppose we'll get to meet him soon?'

Polly warmed to the 'we'. It made it sound as if they were still a couple. Zutty's nose pressed its way into her lap.

'See, he adores you.'

'Johnny, he wants the rest of my Chicken Kiev.'

'Oh, you're so cynical. I want you to have him, Pol, because you're there all day. He's used to coming with me to the office and being with me all the time. I dread to think what Clovis would say if Luana turned up with him there and he'd go mad if Luana left him in her poky little flat all day. Probably chew his tail off or something.'

Polly knew she was going to have to give in.

'Mrs Flowers likes dogs,' she began by way of capitulation.

'Does she? That's perfect. She can look after him when you're away.'

'Now what do you mean? I'm not planning on going away.'

'No. I'm planning on you going away. Thought you might like a little holiday, Pol. We're shooting down in the South of France. Cap d'Antibes. That bit where Mr Wrong is seducing all those rich women at the Hôtel du Cap and bumping them off. The opening sequence of the film. The cop hasn't even sussed him yet. Why don't you come down for a few days, long weekend, something like that? Do you good. My way of saying thank you for finding *Mr Wrong*. After all, if you hadn't made Lawrence do the book I'd never have had my movie. I don't mind admitting that now.'

Dear Johnny. She felt a strange rush of affection for him but then she remembered *Hello!* and fought to control it.

'I suppose I could get away for a few days in July,' she said as casually as she could.

'So, yes to Zutty? Yes to a little holiday? Yes to some De Soto ice-cream?'

What could it hurt? thought Polly as she drove home. It wasn't as if he'd asked: 'Can I come back to you, Pol?' He'd just invited her to spend a holiday with him.

And she was surprised to find how much she was looking forward to it.

By now Luana was seeing Hector three times a week. He no longer picked her up at the office; instead he called and told her where to meet him. He had explained that he thought they ought to keep it quiet that they were seeing each other, that it was more professional if they kept it a secret for the time being.

He left for France and he would be gone for six weeks. Luana did not know how she was going to be able to bear it. She was devastated that he had not invited her to visit him in France but she supposed it had something to do with his insistence on secrecy. If only Clovis hadn't gone and said the day before he left: 'So long as Hector O'Neill doesn't go and fuck everything up by jumping on Julianne Reynard too early in the proceedin's, this fillum's got a pretty good chance of being a hit.'

Carla de Soto nodded at Mrs Flowers who was off to lunch, disappearing out of the conservatory and through the side gate.

'Polly, what is that woman's name? I always forget.'

'You've only met her once. Why should you remember? It's Flowers. Mrs Flowers.'

'Fiore. La Signora Fiore. Of course.'

'That might not be a bad name for her. Drop the Mabel Lucy rubbish. Lucia Fiore. Not bad at all.'

'Polly, what are you talking about?'

'Oh, take no notice. Come into the kitchen while I make lunch. I'm giving you pasta. Don't know how I dare. Talk about coals to Newcastle but this rocket and blue cheese sauce is just divine. You just whizz it up in the blender.'

Carla, who hovered over sauces that simmered for hours on her hob, and didn't go in for whizzing, tactfully changed the subject.

'So Gianni has invited you out there?'

'You didn't put him up to it?'

'Polly, don't be so negative. I know my son well enough to let him make his own decisions.'

'What do you think it means?'

'It could be he's just offering you a holiday like he say. Or it could be that he wants to test the water with you and he think it's good to do it in the South of France where it's warm and romantic.'

'Where he can soften me up?'

'Do you need him to soften you up, Polly? Are you so hard? I don't think so. I think you are too soft with Johnny. I warned you. I said "keep up with him", didn't I? But he got away.'

'You think I'm running after him? You don't think I should go?'

'Of course you should go. Let him pay for a nice holiday, why not? But don't be too soft with him. You must get tough, Polly. Not too tough. *Al dente*, like this pasta. It's delicious. Maybe I shall begin to whizz.'

'Has Johnny ever said anything to you . . . about me . . . about us?'

'Of course he has.'

'But you're not going to tell me what he said.'

'Of course I'm not,' said Carla, thoroughly enjoying being maddening. 'All I can tell you is I think it is worth you going down there. Beyond that, who knows? Can I have some more please with some chopped rocket leaves on the top. That's what it needs.'

What I need, thought Polly as she studied her mother-in-law sitting there in her simple elegant linen dress and her expensive shoes, is to be more like you, to decide what I want and ask for it.

A small Gentle Ghost removal van was parked outside a house in Roland Gardens where a slender brunette was supervising two men as they struggled with boxes and small pieces of furniture.

'It's the top floor,' she told them.

'It would be,' they muttered.

It took them nearly an hour to carry everything up, commenting on everything as they did so.

'You don't see many of these any more.'

'Bit poky, this place, if you don't mind my saying so. Hope you didn't pay too much for it. Why'd you ever want to sell that nice place by the sea?'

The woman ignored them. When they had gone she unpacked a few boxes then ran herself a bath and soaked for an hour. Wrapping herself in an old dressing gown she flung herself across the bed and picked up the phone.

'Surprise surprise. It's me. Edith. I decided it was time I moved back to London.'

PART THREE

As the day approached for her to leave for the South of France, Polly's anxiety level rose higher and higher on her personal Richter scale. It started when she went to Harvey Nichols to buy a new swimsuit. Despite Joan's persistent badgering, she had had the intelligence not to appear in a bikini since she was in her mid-thirties.

'For God's sake, Polly, it's not as it you've even had any children. Your stomach ought to be as flat as the proverbial pancake. Why are you so pathetic about showing it off?'

Joan, of course, had never had any children either but then she was a size 8 who occasionally resorted to shopping in children's stores in order to find something to fit her.

Polly had once been on holiday with her to Ibiza and she had been highly embarrassed, much to Joan's amusement, when Joan had promptly stripped off in front of everyone and sunbathed naked, her virtually non-existent breasts hardening to minuscule chocolate pyramids. Polly had ignored Joan's derision and refused to expose her breasts to the sun. She couldn't bear the thought of all that soft precious tissue being burned to blobs of hard leather by the time she was forty. If there had been one thing about which Johnny had always gone berserk, it was her soft skin.

Polly stood in the narrow cubicle, struggling to ease herself into a

209

black Calvin Klein one-piece that had looked so simple and elegant when it was hanging on the rails without her 140-pound body inside it. She thought about Joan, feeling guilty that she still hadn't called her, wondering what had upset her. Whatever it was, Joan would be over it by now. Life was very simple for Joan. She woke up every day with the expectation of cheques and sex in no particular order and never understanding Polly's priorities which were food, affection, work probably in exactly that order.

Polly squeezed into the swimsuit and tried to hoist it up over her generous breasts. Nothing doing. She turned to inspect her back view and shuddered. Were those faint strips of orange peel *cellulite* running across her thighs, or was it her imagination as usual? What was the point of having good legs, long and shapely, if she always got in a panic when she saw them naked? Joan's version of the old maxim 'A man should always look at a woman's mother before marrying her' was 'A man should always look at a woman in a swimsuit before taking her to bed', and she had had a point. If a man looked at her in a skirt and high heels, Polly had more than a chance, but one look at her naked thighs – forget it! And the mirrors in Harvey Nichols were supposed to be flattering. Still, everyone was always telling her she had a perfectly good figure. Maybe it was time she started believing them.

But then there was her passport photo. Just in time, Polly had noticed that her passport was due to run out. In her panic to acquire a new one in the forty-eight hours she had left, she had rushed out and used one of the booths. Joan would have had a fit, she told herself, trying not to blink as the flash popped in her eyes. Joan had once needed a new passport before going to New York on an assignment to profile a well-known lesbian author who had made a pass at her five minutes into the interview. Polly's comment that, as she understood it, Joan was usually rather chuffed when someone made a pass at her, had not gone down well. But Joan had set up a special photographic session for her new passport photo. Hair and make-up had taken nearly two-hours. The result had made her look like a twelve-year-old Natalie Wood. Polly had not understood what all the fuss was about. Surely Joan was not planning to look good for an immigration official at JFK? Who else saw your passport photo? Only you.

But when she received her new passport complete with the photo taken ten years after the photo in her old one, Polly understood. It was the very fact that you did see it and were faced with the evidence of the extent to which your face had changed, no matter how much you might have ignored it. Polly sat looking at the two passports lying open on her desk in front of her. It wasn't as if she had any wrinkles but her whole face had dropped ten years. In the old passport a puppetmaster appeared to be holding up her face with invisible strings and in the new one, he'd let go.

This was the face she was going to present to Johnny in the South of France.

Predictably, as Polly was in the midst of her last-minute packing on the morning of her flight, Mrs Flowers called up the stairs to ask if she might 'have a word'.

'I'm afraid you'll have to come up here, Mrs Flowers,' Polly called down, trying to mask her mounting hysteria. 'I'm running late. I haven't finished packing and the cab'll be here in twenty minutes. Put the answering machine on in the office and come on up.'

'Shall I bring you a cup of coffee?'

'No! I haven't got time.' Blast the woman. Polly knew she was sounding unnecessarily harsh but Mrs Flowers had a knack of always picking the wrong moment. Yet in so many ways she was invaluable, to the extent that Polly had absolutely no qualms about leaving her in charge of the office for ten days.

Mrs Flowers shuffled into Polly's bedroom clutching a carrier bag and immediately began trying to help her pack, picking up piles of clothes and depositing them neatly into Polly's suitcase. Polly promptly removed them. She had her own system for packing dating back to the days when Matron had instructed her how to pack her trunk at boarding-school. Hard things like shoes, books, handbags at the bottom with socks and underwear stuffed into the holes. Then a layer of lightweight garments like nightdresses, T-shirts, shorts in piles and finally, spread out on top so they wouldn't crease, skirts, jackets, trousers, dresses. Polly's problem ever since had been that her suitcases were about a quarter of the size of her cavernous school trunk and she always ran out of space.

'Sit down, Mrs Flowers, over there if you will,' she said firmly. 'Now, what's the matter?'

'Well, it's a bit hard to know where to start and I know I should have mentioned it before but what with one thing and another . . .'

'You're writing a book, is that it?' Polly didn't have time to wait for her to get to the point.

'You do know all about it? I've always wondered.'

'As it happens, I've only recently found out. To be honest, I did sort of feel rather put out. I think you should have mentioned you were a writer when you first came to work for me. It's nothing to be ashamed of, after all,' said Polly, stuffing Marmite and Johnson's Baby Oil, and all the other items she feared being deprived of by the French, into the gaps between her shoes.

'I'm dreadfully sorry. I meant to tell you right at the beginning then I kept putting it off. I thought you might ask me to leave and I do so love working for you.'

Stop gushing and let me get on with my packing. Polly was getting frantic. 'I don't mind a bit but why are you telling me now?'

'Well, I've been working on this longer book. Very different. I was hoping, I was wondering . . .'

Too late Polly remembered Grania's warning: 'It's simply awful. She hasn't got a clue.' She turned round to see Mrs Flowers produce a large and cumbersome manuscript from a carrier bag.

'Is that your book?' asked Polly stupidly, feeling well and truly trapped.

'It's just I thought you might have some time to read it while you were down there, well some of it anyway. I'd just love to know what you think of it.'

Polly could not believe it. The nerve of the woman. She was going away for a rest, to have a break from work. Why on earth would she want to lug some great manuscript with her? Yet time was running out and it was a question of reasoning with Mrs Flowers and missing the plane or taking the book from her.

212

'Give it to me, Mrs Flowers. I'll see what I can do. Now seriously, I must get on. Perhaps you could get back to the office?'

Mrs Flowers stayed until she had witnessed Polly putting the precious script in her suitcase then she left, apologising profusely for the inconvenience she had caused.

As soon as she heard the conservatory door bang Polly whipped the manuscript out of her case and shoved it under her bed. Enough was enough.

As her Air France flight to Nice took off Polly read the papers and saw a piece about Aroma Ross's novel which mentioned that the supermodel would be 'helped' by journalist Zoë Nichols. Polly had negotiated as good a deal as she could for Zoë, making sure she got a piece of the publisher's income on everything except film rights, which the publishers didn't control. Zoë had begun work so they could have something to show at the Frankfurt Book Fair in October. She and Polly had spent a couple of rather drunken evenings together when Zoë had attempted to brush up Polly's French conversation in readiness for her trip to the Côte d'Azur. At the end of the second evening Polly had confided to Zoë how much she was looking forward to spending time with Johnny, and Zoë had hugged her and said she hoped everything would turn out well but whatever happened Polly should be sure and have a proper holiday. Polly couldn't help thinking of the tirade she would have received from Joan about accepting Johnny's invitation.

Polly picked at her tray of airline food – a piece of rolled-up ham, a cornichon, a triangle of Camembert, a plastic glass of Evian and a little bottle of chilled red wine – and looked out of the window at the clouds puffing by. She began to daydream. Johnny would be brown. He always went black if he so much as looked at the sun and now his close-cropped hair was almost totally white, a tan gave him a particularly roguish look like that of a sea captain. She'd missed his nervous energy. She'd even missed his endless questions: 'What are you doing, Pol?' every five minutes. At least it meant he cared what she was doing, was interested. If only he'd been a little more interested in her agency and a little less obsessed with his pretentious social life. Still, he had asked her down for a holiday. It was a gesture and she was prepared to accept it. Could it mean that he wanted to come back to her? Did she want him back?

Suddenly she could hardly contain her excitement at the thought of seeing him again. She handed her half-empty tray to a passing stewardess and rummaged in her bag for her Walkman. Listening to a tape would distract her for the rest of the flight.

The captain announced they would be landing at Nice in ten minutes. Almost before she knew it Polly was on the ground and lugging her baggage off the carousel. She wheeled her trolley into Arrivals in a daze and when a swarthy-looking bare-chested man with skin the colour of bitter chocolate and a back to front baseball cap over his crew cut tried to wrest it from her, she screamed out loud.

'God's sake, Pol, get a grip!'

'Johnny! Why are you here?'

'Polly, I'll speak very slowly. Read my lips. You've arrived at Nice. You're at the airport. I've come to meet you. Is that all right?'

'Johnny, it's wonderful. I just didn't expect you.'

'But I said I'd come and meet you.'

'Yes, I know, but I thought you'd send a minion, not come yourself.'

'So how is he?'

'Who?'

'Zutty. How is he? Does he miss me?'

No 'How are you, Pol? Have you missed me, Pol? I've been looking forward to seeing you, Pol. You're looking great, Pol.'

'Zutty's fine. He misses you dreadfully and I have a very smelly bone buried somewhere in my luggage that he insisted I bring out to you.'

'Very funny. Polly, just give me that trolley and follow me out to the car. Perhaps you'd better sit in the trolley too if you're feeling so feeble and I'll push you along with the bags.'

She followed him, watching his arse move in his tight jeans, the taut muscles in his suntanned back, his broad shoulders. She wanted to run after him and hug him to her from behind but she didn't dare. It was ridiculous. She didn't know how she stood with him. It was almost as if she was dating her own husband for the first time.

Johnny had hired a battered Renault and he drove like a maniac on the wrong side of the road while Polly closed her eyes and sent up silent prayers.

'See, Pol, sensational weather, blue skies, da da da *da*, nothing but blue skies from now on. Perfect place to film. The light's great. We're on schedule. Maybe even a day under. Henri's a terrific director, knows exactly what he wants. We didn't really get going until the second week. The crew needed time to get to know each other and of course Henri's never worked with any of them before. Nor have I, come to think of it. We've got a sensational first assistant. We're using all these Froggy extras to save costs and Spider, that's the first, he can speak fluent Frog. You should see him shift them from place to place, get them in position, get them fed, don't know how he does it. He's more aggressive than the Frogs themselves. Hector's terrific. Came out the week before last. We're shooting all his stuff in one go, of course. He costs a bloody fortune. Budget would go through the roof if we had him here all the time. He's here for another three weeks. The first week he was here we shot the sequence where Julianne – who's playing the girl cop – has her first date with him. You remember the script, Pol?'

'I remember the book, Johnny.'

'Yeah, 'course. It's when Caspar sends the girl – '

'There's no one called Caspar in the book,' protested Polly.

'No, no, Pol, Caspar Cartier is the guy who plays Frank, the cop. He's shit hot. French Canadian. The Froggy money men love him. This is his first international picture. It's going to make him a huge star. So, we've got Caspar – so he's playing the cop who suspects the womaniser, Mr Wrong, played by Hector, might be the serial killer he's looking for and he follows him to the South of France and puts

Julianne – who's playing a woman cop Frank/Caspar's falling in love with but he hasn't told her yet – he sets Julianne to seduce Mr Wrong and bait him, OK? With me so far? So we shot this fabulous sequence where Hector takes Julianne out on a date and Caspar follows them and you see him really doing his nut when at the end of the evening Hector kisses Julianne and she really enjoys it – because of course she falls for him too – and Caspar's sitting in his car across the street and he can't do a damn thing about it. But the best bit, Pol, are you listening? The best bit is that we filmed all the car sequences where Hector's driving Julianne to dinner in the same places they used with Cary Grant and Grace Kelly in *To Catch a Thief* . . .'

'Wasn't that back projection?' Polly tried not to think about Princess Grace going over the cliff in her car as Johnny veered over to the wrong side of the road again.

'Well, you know what I mean. We've got Hector taking out all these rich American women and seducing them . . .'

'Real ones?' Polly was horrified.

'No, Pol, for Christ's sake, this is a movie, remember? Actresses playing rich American women, the ones he seduces and then kills.'

Polly leaned forward in anticipation for they had arrived at the Hôtel du Cap.

'Great hotel, Pol. Bill Cosby's staying here. This is the boulevard JFK and he stayed here with Jackie. Great place to stay for the Cannes Film Festival, much more chic than the Carlton. They've had no end of names here: Hemingway, George Bernard Shaw, Somerset Maugham, Chaplin, Dougie Fairbanks, Rita Hayworth, Orson – in the old days, of course. Scott Fitzgerald based that book of his here . . .'

'*Tender is the Night*,' murmured Polly.

'That's it. Then you get people like De Niro, Madonna, Stallone, Schwarzenegger, Tom Cruise. All been here. Place to be, Pol.'

He glanced at her to see if she was impressed. Polly smiled. Same old Johnny. Knocked out by the famous names attached to the place and completely oblivious to the magic surrounding the elegant cream-painted marble mansion with its pale blue shutters,

217

built nearly a hundred and fifty years ago and set in acres of beautiful gardens overlooking the Golfe Juan.

As Polly walked up the sweeping stone steps, nervously trying to straighten the crumpled linen blazer and trousers she had travelled in, she couldn't help feeling a bit like a movie star herself. The cool of the marble lobby – with its floor of black diamonds on white and the staircase curving up round the little wooden elevator – was bliss. Polly sank into one of the large white sofas and looked out at the palm trees and the wide avenue that led from the hotel to the sea and the famous Eden Roc restaurant and beach club.

'Come one, Pol. Check in before we go out.'

'Go out?' Polly had been looking forward to going up to the room and taking a shower and changing.

'Yeah, I'm taking you to a little place in Juan les Pins for dinner.'

'But what about my luggage? Can't I at least . . . ?'

'Oh, don't fret, Pol. I'll have them send it up to the room.'

Polly made the snap decision that it was better to go along with Johnny to begin with. The fact that he had even thought about dinner with her, let alone planned it, was a good sign. As she checked in, she asked wistfully: 'Perhaps we could have a drink on the terrace before going out?'

'Are you crazy, Pol? They charge about fifteen quid for a fucking Campari and soda out there.'

'Well, why are you staying in this place if you can't afford it?'

'Because I'm not paying for it, am I? The Frogs who are putting up half the finance, they're coughing up for me, Henri, Julianne and Caspar to stay here.'

'What about Hector?'

Johnny scowled for the first time.

'Hector insisted on hiring a bloody villa all to himself. It's up the road on the boulevard du Cap. Fucking stars! Got me by the short and curlies. Can't live with them, can't live without them. I got this picture set up because of Hector being attached to it so I have to live with the consequences. But I ask you, what's wrong with the Hôtel du Cap? Hector, old son, I said, if it's good enough for Tom Cruise, surely it's good enough for you. You should have seen the look he

218

gave me. Anyway, the bastard's got two days off so he's out of my hair for the time being.'

As they drove to Juan, Polly wondered if he was going to talk about the film business for the entire evening but, as she was soon to be reminded, one of the things that had made her fall in love with Johnny in the first place was his ability to constantly surprise her.

He took her to the kind of place she adored: an unpredictable little bistro in a narrow street on the waterfront where they could sit outside on the cobbled street with a gingham tablecloth and a candle between them. Polly was no stranger to the South of France. Prudence Atwell had insisted that Polly's father allow them to escape from the Norfolk winds for at least a month every year and they had invariably come to the Côte d'Azur. They had rented villas, usually those owned by friends, and in the evenings they had often eaten out at places like this.

Johnny ordered a kir for Polly and a Scotch for himself.

'Pol, I really am pleased you came out. Oh, now, look, you've gone and started blubbing. God, yours must be the world's most overworked tear ducts. Probably start charging you overtime. Oh, don't mind me, I'm thinking like a bloody producer all the time. Here, give me your paw . . .'

He reached for her hand across the table and held it in his, patting it consolingly. Polly giggled and her tears turned into splutters. He'd always called them her paws. He'd always treated her rather like a dog. Sometimes she wondered if she was interchangeable with Zutty in his mind but she couldn't deny that she liked it. Men, she reflected, were often more affectionate with dogs than with women.

'Spit it out,' Johnny ordered, 'tell me all about it: are you tired and emotional or is there something actually wrong? Are you OK? Agency doing all right?'

Polly was astounded. Had Johnny been going to night classes to learn how to be a New Man?

'Pretty good,' she replied. 'All the regulars are performing well and I've got two or three new writers who look rather promising.'

'Lawrence got any further with his new book?'

219

'Oh God, I completely forgot to call him before I left. Don't know what's the matter with me. I never called Joan either.'

'Well, that's understandable. Hard-bitten old bag, don't know why you have anything to do with her. You can literally see her claws sharpening in anticipation when she claps eyes on a potential fuck. She's a disaster area, Pol, you'll see. She rang me, you know, nearly blasted my head off.'

'When?'

'After I left you. Called me all kinds of names. Said I'd never been worthy of you anyway. Is that what you thought, Pol?'

'No, of course not.'

'But you were pretty angry too, I expect. We've never really talked about it.'

He had his head turned away from her. He was pretending to look down the street to the waterfront but she knew he was watching for her reaction out of the corner of his eye. It was a fairly electric moment. Your husband walks out on you and casually remarks many months later over dinner, 'We've never really talked about it.'

'I wasn't particularly angry. Sorry to disappoint you, Johnny. I suppose I'd seen it coming. You and Juanita.'

'Me and Juanita? What about me and Juanita?'

'She had such a hold over you.'

'Oh, I thought you meant we were having an affair.'

'Well, were you?'

'Oh, don't be ridiculous. She was my business partner. We needed to spend a lot of time together. Anyway if you weren't even angry when I left, what the fuck does it matter what we were doing together?'

'I said I wasn't particularly angry, or surprised. That doesn't mean I wasn't upset. I remember asking myself if in fact you had ever really loved me. You clearly had one route mapped out for your life from the very beginning. God knows, your mother even warned me about it. "Keep up with him," she told me; "don't let him go too fast or he'll get away from you." What I don't understand is why you thought I was the one who would be the right person to be by your side.'

'Look,' said Johnny, glaring at her across the gingham, 'I was always straight with you. On our honeymoon, if you recall, I said I wanted to produce movies and I wanted you right there beside me. I didn't know you had these crazy plans to go and start your own agency.'

'I didn't have any plans at the time. It just happened and there was nothing crazy about it. My agency is now one of the best in London and – '

'Yeah, I know that, Pol. You've got a pretty good rep. You did what you wanted to do and you succeeded. It's not as if I tried to stop you. Stop making me out to be the bad guy.'

'Johnny, did it ever occur to you that while you wanted me beside you while you were struggling to get your movie off the ground, I might have also wanted you beside me while I was struggling to get my agency off the ground? Being supportive works both ways, you know.'

'Well, what the hell was I supposed to do? Rush to my office, rush to Paris for money meetings and then rush home to sit beside you while you sold some little magical realism first novel to Jonathan fucking Cape? You wanted me to be in ninety-two places at once?'

'No, Johnny. I just wanted you home more in the evening so we could have kept up with each other, talked about what we were both doing.'

'But I kept calling you and asking you to join me for dinner, I kept asking you to come and meet all my friends, the people I was working with. I wanted us to be more of a couple, I wanted people to meet you and invite us to places together. You were the one who always wanted to stay at home.'

'That's just it. I stayed at home because it was always so one-sided. I had to go out and meet your friends. It was never a question of you coming out to meet my authors or my friends.'

'Like sweet and charming Joan Brock? OK, OK, strike that, Pol, it was below the belt.'

'I wanted us to be together, Johnny. Not the whole time, but just occasionally. Together, on our own, and the only time that happened was much too late at night, when you were too tired to do anything, if we're going to talk about below the belt. But it wasn't even as if I minded that, Johnny. If you'd just come home and got into bed with me and talked like you used to do, about us, or even just about you and your problems, I'd have listened. But when you moved out, you took away any chance of that ever happening again, however much I was prepared to try. You negated all the affection and shared experiences we had had in the past. That's when I began to question if you had ever really loved me. It's understandable. Can't you see that?'

She expected an instant defensive tirade from Johnny. It was the longest time she'd voiced her thoughts on their relationship. Usually he interrupted her, forcing his blinkered view on her, but once again he surprised her.

'You're right, Pol,' he said quietly, 'I destroyed it all. You probably won't believe me but I do think about it sometimes. I do remember what we had. But you're wrong when you say I never really loved you. I loved you. The real you. But I never took it into account that you might not want the same life as me. I needed you in those early days when I was getting started. I needed you more than you needed me. I need support. I can't function on my own. I suppose I'm not strong enough. You might have wanted my support but you didn't really need it. There's a difference. You were quite capable of doing it all on your own. If you really want to know, I think I took off because I needed you as a prop, you weren't prepared to prop me up twenty-four hours a day and I knew you never would be, so I left. My mother was right. I was moving too fast. I always have. I never wait for other people. I never thought about you as someone I could come back and lean on at home. I just always noticed that you were the party pooper who stayed at home.'

'And that isn't what you want?'

Johnny looked at her and Polly was devastated by the sadness in his brown eyes.

'The truth is, Pol, I have no idea what I want any more. I remember the Polly I married. I loved her and if you're still her, then I still love you. But it would be too much to expect you to still love me.'

Another electric moment. She could sense the tension in him as he waited for her reply.

'Johnny, there is so much about you that I do love that it is never going to be overshadowed by changes in you. We've turned out to be two very different people who pretended they didn't know the meaning of the word compromise. Maybe we were meant to split up but there's a part of you that I'll always love, no matter what. You know that.'

'Yes,' he said, getting up and coming round to stand behind her and stroke the back of her neck. 'Come on, let's go back to the hotel. You must be pretty tired.'

Somehow they had ordered their food and eaten it. At some point Johnny had ordered a bottle of *rosé* and they had drunk that too. He settled the bill, holding her against him with one arm as he did so as if he were afraid she might run away from him, and once they were in the car he drew her head down to rest in his lap as he had done when they drove back from Siena on their honeymoon. As they turned off the boulevard JFK and through the hotel gates, Johnny tugged at her hair.

'Better sit up. It's not exactly the kind of hotel where the guests arrive in the middle of a blow job.'

Polly sat up smartly and blushed as the doorman opened the car door for her. Johnny grabbed her hand and they ran up the steps into the marble hall and up the curving staircase. He didn't turn the lights on in the room or check his messages, just threw her across the bed.

'Stay!' he ordered.

'Where's my bone?' laughed Polly, burrowing into the bed. She watched as he took off his clothes and found she couldn't help clambering off the bed to pat his little bare arse, stark white against his tan. She reached around his body from behind and fondled his erection. He turned and pressed it into her linen pants, reaching down to unzip her, stroke her and slide his fingers inside her. They stood together in the moonlight, bringing each other off, tongues probing in each other's mouths, her hand around his penis moving up and down, increasing the pressure until he groaned while she squirmed and rode on his finger stroking her clitoris.

They came almost together but not quite, Johnny first, Polly a second or two later, and he pulled her back on to the bed where they lay side by side, panting softly.

It was a minute or two before she realised he was asleep. She had left her jacket in the car. Now she wriggled silently out of her linen pants, opened the buttons of her blouse and reached round to undo her bra. Tenderly she lifted Johnny's sleeping head on to her bare breasts and cradled him in her arms before she too fell asleep.

Her first thought on waking was: we're back together.

But Johnny had managed to disentangle himself without waking her, and had left for the set. A note on the pillow said simply: See you tonight.

Polly stumbled off the bed and into the bathroom to splash water on her face, blearily recognising Johnny's things scattered around the basin. She looked around the room and saw no sign of her luggage. She rang down to the front desk and asked for it to be brought up.

'Where are you, madame?' asked the hall porter, as if he didn't know. Did she detect a hint of a sneer in his voice?

'Room 502. Mr de Soto's room.'

'Ah, well, you see, madame, Mr de Soto instructed us to take the bags to Miss Atwell's room: 602 on the floor above.'

Mr de Soto and Miss Atwell. Two separate rooms.

'I'll be down to collect the key,' snapped Polly and forced herself not to bang down the receiver.

The view out over the bay from her corner room was stunning. Directly above Johnny's, the room appeared to be identical except that it didn't have a terrace and instead of striped, swathed curtains and plain white covers on the armchairs, she had pink and green chintz which she could have done without. A flower arrangement sitting in the middle of the coffee table turned out to be from the management. For one split second she had wondered if it was from Johnny.

By the time Polly had unpacked she had persuaded herself that Johnny had booked her a separate room because he had been as unsure about her reaction to him as she had been about his to her. That night she'd probably find herself repacking everything and carting it down to Johnny's room.

She went for a walk amongst the pine trees, past the tennis courts. Little white Go-Karts with EDEN ROC painted on them sped past her. Entry to Eden Roc was included in the price of the room – so it should be at 4,000 francs a night, thought Polly – and she decided to spend the day there by the pool and the terrace built into the rocks overlooking the sea. She cheerfully ordered herself a Negroni, hoping it cost at least £20, and charged it to Johnny's room. Then she settled down to get a tan. Polly was lucky. She had the kind of skin that turned brown within hours of being exposed to the sun.

She returned to her room around 5.30 and called the office. Mrs Flowers reported no problems. Luckily she didn't mention her novel. Polly soaked in a Floris bath and wondered where Johnny would take her for dinner. She dressed to kill in a black silk shift which had strategically placed pleats over the stomach. Scrabbling around in her jewellery box, she found the little black earrings he had given her on their second date, when he had made her get her ears pierced. Would he remember them? Then she swept her hair back into a loose knot in the nape of her neck and held the sides in place with tortoiseshell combs. Her face was already beginning to tan and the whites of her hazel eyes stood out, making them look larger. She applied a light coating of brown eye shadow and ran a narrow line of kohl around her eyelids to make them look smudgy. She finished with two applications of mascara, a light dusting of loose powder on her nose and a touch of Lancôme's Rose Nocturne on her lips, heavily blotted. The end result was the healthy, natural look she knew Johnny had always liked.

Finally she took her Christian Dior Dune atomiser and sprayed herself liberally. She was ready. Now what was she supposed to do? She rang Johnny's room. No reply. Well, it was only 7.30. They might not have even finished filming. She really should have waited until she had heard from him before getting ready but she wanted to be waiting for him, looking her best.

At 8.30 she was still sitting there, coming to the end of her *Vanity*

Fair which usually lay around the house for a month before she had time to read it. She rang his room again. No reply. She rang the front desk and asked would they have him call her when he got in and was told he'd already come back, gone up to his room and come down again.

Of course, thought Polly, he's waiting for me downstairs at the bar. She almost ran down the stairs like a girl, imagining him waiting for her in the lobby, leaning on the banisters, looking up at her and saying something like: 'So, Pol, what took you so long?'

He was nowhere to be seen. She couldn't bring herself to go back up to her room and she didn't want to sit alone in the bar so she wandered outside down the avenue to Eden Roc.

I'll go inside and have another Negroni and charge it to his room, she thought, feeling wicked. That'll teach him to be late.

He was sitting at a table on the terrace. He had his back to her and his arm was around the person he was drinking with. No, it was more than a drink. Plates of food were on the table in front of them. Johnny was in the middle of dinner and as Polly drew closer she saw he was dining with Juanita Whyte.

Polly had been about to call out, but his name stuck in her throat. Anger, disappointment and deep, deep hurt came together in a hard lump in her throat and she felt the tears well up in her carefully made-up eyes. The kohl and the mascara began to trickle down her face. As she turned and ran out into the grounds, she heard Johnny's voice in her head as she had heard it so many times before: 'Blubbing again, Pol' and then two outstretched arms stopped her and she let herself collapse against a broad chest in a white T-shirt.

Johnny had seen her, Johnny had come after her. She waited for him to stroke her hair as he always did when he was comforting her, and when he didn't she looked up at . . .

'*Hector!*'

His face was cruel, sardonic and devastatingly handsome.

'That's right. Have we met? I stopped you because you seemed to be distressed but don't I know you from somewhere?'

Yes, only then I didn't have make-up pouring down my face, thought Polly. What a sight I must look. She remembered his soft

226

voice whispering in her ear: 'If I ever kissed you I'd make sure I didn't miss.'

'Yes, it was at the last Conway première.'

'Oh yes,' he said although he clearly still couldn't quite place her.

'I was there with my husband, Johnny, your producer. Johnny de Soto. I'm Polly de Soto. Polly Atwell.' Oh God, why was she gabbling on like this.

'Of course. I heard you were coming out. Now, are you all right? Are you ill?'

'No, I mean, not really. I've just had a bit of a shock. I felt a little strange suddenly.'

'It's the heat. It can affect you that way. Perhaps you should come and sit down in Eden Roc for a second.'

'No!'

Hector smiled. Despite her confusion Polly was aware that he was amused by her discomfort and that he knew what was causing it.

'Well, can I escort you back to the hotel? You are staying at the hotel, aren't you?' She nodded. 'Are you and Johnny dining there tonight?'

'No. Johnny has a dinner engagement with Juanita Whyte.'

'Ah, yes. Juanita flew out today to see how her little investment was doing.'

'Her little investment?'

'Our film. *Mr Wrong*. She's put quite a lot of Gordy Whyte's money into it, you know. Johnny was pretty smart to latch on to her.'

And if he knew she was coming out why did he ask me at the same time? Polly wondered.

'Listen,' said Hector, releasing her and placing a hand lightly in the small of her back to guide her up the avenue towards the hotel, 'why don't I run you up the road to my villa and my cook can prepare us a little something?'

'Oh, no, I couldn't possibly.' Her response was instinctive, typically English, reserved. The exact opposite of what she really wanted, and he knew it.

'Yes, you could, possibly. Now would you like to go up to your room before we leave? My car's right outside.'

And do something about that mess on your face? Polly slipped up to her room and rushed into the bathroom. It would take at least twenty minutes to re-do her make-up properly. She couldn't keep him waiting that long. She removed her make-up, splashed her tanned face with cold water and left it at that.

He was waiting for her at the bottom of the staircase just where she had been hoping to find Johnny earlier in the evening.

'You look beautiful without make-up,' he said, taking her hand; 'you don't need it, you know, and your hair is lovely. So healthy, so glossy' – and with one quick movement he had removed the combs from her hair and undone the knot, releasing it to her shoulders. 'That's better. I love hair,' he bent to sniff hers quickly. 'I love the smell of freshly washed hair. Come on, let's go.'

He had rented a Mercedes convertible and sitting beside him as he drove slowly up the boulevard du Cap towards Antibes, Polly wondered if she would ever feel so glamorous again, riding in an open car with a movie star through the sweet pine-scented night air of the Côte d'Azur.

Hector turned off into a side road and stopped in front of a pair of tall black and gold painted iron gates which he opened by remote control, easing the Mercedes through as they slid to one side. He ushered her inside before she had a chance to look around. The front door was opened for them and a tall servant in a turban and floor-length white tunic bowed as they entered.

'Hussein, we'd like a little supper out by the pool. *Tabbouleh*, salad, some of that cold chicken, a bottle of Puligny-Montrachet and some fruit. That all right for you, Polly?' But he barely waited for her reply.

Her first impression was that she was in some kind of Egyptian palace. Cool, high-ceilinged rooms with marble floors and tall archways instead of doors. Straight in front of her was a sheet of plate-glass window and through it she could see a rectangular floodlit pool with palm trees strategically placed at each corner. Hector pressed a button in the wall and the window began to rise, silently moving upwards until they were able to step out into the night.

This isn't real, thought Polly, as she sat at a glass table at the far end of the pool and looked at the pale pink villa lit up like a fairytale palace. Overhead, as if they wanted to bring her gently down to earth, planes silently lowered themselves across the navy sky on their way to land at Nice airport, their tail lights blinking on and off in the night.

'This is quite beautiful,' said Polly, 'who . . .?'

'Arabs. Lebanese. And they threw in Hussein. He's from the Sudan by way of Tunis. He looks after me very well.'

I wonder if Johnny knows about Hussein. I wonder if he's going to create a few more budget problems. Well, thought Polly bitterly, he's got Juanita to solve them for him. She picked up a chicken leg in her fingers and bit off a sizeable chunk of flesh.

'That's right,' murmured Hector, watching her, 'get it out of your system.'

'Get what out of my system?'

'Whatever it was that made you so upset. I don't want to know what it was. I just want to distract you a little, take your mind off it so you can enjoy your holiday.'

He knows, thought Polly, he knows exactly what my problem is. Well, to hell with it.

'Is the film going well? Johnny's told me about the scenes you've been doing with the women and with Julianne. He seems very pleased.'

'Don't feel you have to make conversation,' he said almost tersely, 'just relax. Hussein will bring us some mint tea to help your digestion and then I'll run you back.'

To her surprise she found she was disappointed that he did not require anything of her. It was almost too good to be true. He had a soothing effect. She felt safe with him, temporarily protected from Johnny's unreliable behaviour. And she didn't even have to sing for her supper.

In the car he said: 'Tomorrow I'll take you out in the boat I've hired. We'll go along the coast, have lunch at St Tropez; come back and swim. You'd like that, wouldn't you?'

She nodded, smiling in the darkness. She didn't even need to think about it. He was going to take care of everything.

'I'll pick you up at 10 a.m. Bring sunscreen. You can really burn out there in the wind.' And then he was gone.

She was just falling asleep when her phone rang and Johnny said:

'Pol? How've you been? I rang your room but they said you'd gone out. Sorry I was so late. I got tied up, business meeting, so . . .'

Business meeting! With Juanita! Same old Johnny.

'I was asleep . . .'

'Oh, Pol, I'm sorry. I'll let you sleep. Call you in the morning.'

'Not before 10.30,' she heard herself say. 'I want to sleep in.'

At 10.30 the following morning Hector was holding her hand as she stepped aboard his boat in the marina at Juan les Pins. The boat was a 40-foot cruiser with a cabin under the prow and a seating area behind the steering wheel. Hector steered the boat himself, going about 30 knots all the way to St Tropez. To begin with Polly stood beside him and they shouted to each other over the whap whap whap of the boat hitting the water and the spray flying up on either side. Then Polly stretched out and lay supine, looking up at the pure blue sky above her. She hadn't been to St Tropez since she was a child and she was looking forward to it. When they pulled into the little walled harbour, Hector gave the harbour master 500 francs to give them a place to dock while they lunched.

'Only thing to do,' he explained to Polly. 'Expensive business, running a boat in high season. It's another £300 to fill her up with gas.'

Polly gulped. Was this all going on Johnny's budget? It seemed a lavish expense when all they wound up eating for lunch was a slice of pizza as they wandered around. Hector didn't seem to want to engage her in much conversation and for this Polly was somewhat grateful. She was beginning to unwind after the shock of her intense conversation with Johnny, the brief moment of intimacy, and the subsequent disappointment of finding him with Juanita.

On the trip back Hector continued his strong silent act, his hawk-like face a mask hidden by his dark glasses as he stood behind the wheel. Polly found herself casting surreptitious glances at his tanned thighs below his white shorts and the concentrated patch of black hair in the middle of his chest.

When they were almost back in Juan he swung the boat to the left and dropped anchor.

'Baie des Millionaires,' he told her, 'we're going to swim in Millionaires' Bay.'

Polly laughed. She looked around her and glimpsed the roofs of elegant houses between the pines, saw a bank of wide stone steps leading up to one house, several tunnels up through the rocks, and here and there people could be seen on terraces being served with drinks. Hector unhinged a ladder from the end of the boat.

'Swim to that raft over there,' he pointed to a raft bobbing in the middle of the exclusive bay with the word PRIVATE clearly painted on the side. There was no one else around although other boats were docked in the bay and Polly could see people on deck. 'Climb on to it and wait for me. I'll be with you soon.'

Polly had heard stories about how polluted the Mediterranean was supposed to be but as far as she was concerned the water in Millionaires' Bay was a dream. She felt a sudden rush of undiluted happiness. Apart from the fact that swimming in the sea was so much more refreshing than in a pool, her holiday was developing into a bit of an adventure. Swimming in Millionaires' Bay! What would Mrs Flowers say if she could see her now? Polly giggled and climbed up on to the private millionaire's raft. She slicked back her wet hair and imagined she looked like Ursula Andress coming out of the water in *Dr No*. She looked round and saw Hector swimming towards her. He reached the raft and as he climbed up out of the sea, Polly saw that he was completely naked.

He stretched out beside her on his back and she saw his long prick hanging across his thigh. He'd obviously been sunbathing in the nude since the skin around his crotch was as dark as it was everywhere else.

Polly was wearing a strapless one-piece and it took Hector about twenty seconds to peel it slowly from her. Then he leaned over and fastened his mouth on her left nipple. He sucked gently until it became hard and moved across her to begin work on the other one, easing her legs apart as he did so. Polly's body was warm from the sun and totally relaxed. She could feel his penis stiffening slowly as it lay between her legs. He eased himself totally on top of her and she raised her knees. He lifted his head and looked down at her, putting a finger to her lips to silence her as she opened her mouth to speak

232

to him. She sucked on his finger and he grinned suddenly, lowered his head and plunged his tongue into her mouth. Soon he was biting her, brusing her lips with his. She felt herself go completely wet and he sensed it and manoeuvred his erection to the tip of her vagina. She brought her arms around him and pulled his weight down on her, clasping his naked buttocks and bringing him inside her. He began to fuck her very hard, almost violently, but she responded, bucking her pelvis up to him.

As he came he let out a yell that echoed round the bay and as he lay on top of her they felt the raft rocking furiously beneath them.

'You do know the entire bay was watching us from their terraces,' he whispered in her ear.

'I don't care,' said Polly and she meant it.

They swam back to the boat naked, pulling their swimming things behind them. At one point they came together, treading water, and kissed and pressed against each other. She climbed up the ladder in front of him and he came up behind her, pushed her on to her front and lay on top of her.

'Have you ever been fucked in the arse?' he whispered.

'No.'

'Do you want to be?'

'No.'

'Then I won't go any further.' He covered her with a towel. 'You realise we're a lot further in than the raft. They really can see us quite clearly now – if they're looking, that is.'

He pulled on his swimming trunks and hauled up the anchor. She stood beside him at the wheel and he put his arm around her, steering with one hand. She laid her head on his shoulder and thought that as the boat slipped into the marina under the setting sun, they must look like a corny commercial or an MTV video, standing there with their arms around each other. But she didn't care. She felt about twenty-two years old.

When they got into his car she knew he was going to take her to his house on the boulevard du Cap rather than back to the hotel. I'm putty in his hands, she thought, but to hell with it. Fuck Johnny!

As they drove up the hill, he started speaking softly to her: 'This morning, while you were still asleep, I got up very early and went to

233

the market in old Antibes. I'm so used to getting up for my call that I wake early anyway. It's Hussein's day off. I walked down to the market. It takes about half an hour, maybe a bit less, and I bought fruit and vegetables and flowers and brought them all back for our supper tonight.'

'We're going to eat flowers?'

'No, of course not, but I've put them all over the house to greet you everywhere you go. Irises. Those huge sunflowers. You'll see. We'll eat a light supper – tomato salad with olives, some shrimps with lemon juice, some asparagus maybe. A little cheese. Nothing too heavy. We want to feel comfortable. We're going to have sex all night.'

The flowers were sensational. Polly couldn't help thinking of Johnny's clumsy efforts at his Mount Street flat. Hector prepared supper and brought it up to the bedroom on a tray. They ate sitting cross-legged on the bed, naked, with the tray between them, feeding each other. He fondled her breasts as he munched on a piece of bread and cheese until Polly couldn't stand it another minute and pushed the tray aside. Was this really the behaviour of a literary lady in her forties? Apparently yes, since she wanted him at regular intervals throughout the night.

He talked only about her: her body, her face, her hands, her legs, what she wanted, how he could please her.

In the morning he slipped away to the set without waking her and she slept until noon. She found a towelling robe in the bathroom and crept barefoot down the marble staircase to find the kitchen. As she was tiptoeing – why, she didn't know – across the hall a shadow moved in the dark passage in front of her and she screamed out loud.

It was Hussein.

'Madame wants breakfast? Tea? Coffee?' He didn't seem remotely surprised to see her.

'Yes please,' said Polly, drawing the towelling robe a little more tightly around her.

He served her croissants and hot rolls and honey and piping hot coffee on a little folding table on the terrace. Propped up against a stem vase containing a single red rose was a square white vellum envelope with her name on it.

His handwriting was large and jagged:

Can't wait to be with you again.
When you're ready, Hussein will call you a taxi to take you back to the hotel. I'm filming and may be back late otherwise I'd suggest you spend the day at my house. I'll call.

H.

P.S. Take a bath and use the oil in the glass flagon. It's rose scented, rose and honeysuckle.

Polly had a tremendous urge to snoop in his drawers, his wardrobe, his desk. How many other women had been to this house before her even though he had only been in it for a few weeks?

Hussein appeared.

'I have drawn your bath, madame.'

How did he know? Had he read the letter? She nodded, yes, she was ready.

Lying in her bath she wondered how old Hector was. Younger than she was, but by how much? Then she felt a pang of guilt and sadness as she thought how thrilled Joan would be with her.

Back at the hotel she asked for her key, feeling rather sheepish, wondering if everybody knew her bed hadn't been slept in, if the *valets d'étage* were, even as she spoke, gossiping about her with the chambermaids in the laundry room.

Two days later Hector still hadn't called her and Polly went into a full-scale panic. Johnny called and left maniacal messages for her downstairs, which she ignored. Let him sweat!

Fools rush in, she told herself. How could I have been such a fool? The sun goes straight to my head and I think I'm as desirable as Cindy Crawford. I must have been out of my skull. A bored actor feels like a quick lay and I walk straight into his arms, literally. I lie on a raft stark naked and assume he never notices the way my breasts flop to the side instead of sticking straight up. He probably cricked his neck sucking my tits.

By the second day she'd remembered something more sinister. He'd hadn't used anything. How many other women had he had over the years? She thought of the ludicrous end to her evening with Edward Holland. Why had she thought about AIDS with poor Edward when it had never entered her head to say anything to Hector – although what could she have done? Told him to swim back to the boat and get his condoms like a good dog?

She ached for him and by the third day she knew it was no good. Only four more days of her holiday left and she had to see him. She rang LSR (Long Suffering Rachel as Johnny called her, who had been promoted to production secretary on the picture) at the production office in the little hotel in Juan where the crew were

236

packed in like sardines. Rachel was sweating it out with her laptop in 97 degrees heat with a phone that was almost permanently on the blink and a groaning fan in the absence of any air conditioning.

'Bet it's not like this in Hollywood,' she moaned to Polly, becoming less long-suffering by the minute. 'I have to use the hotel fax and they don't like it one bit. It's down in the office behind reception and they won't let me in without a fight and they never bother to let me know if I've received one. If it wasn't for the fact that I'm screwing one of the sparks and he's the best fuck I've ever had, I think I'd go mad.'

Polly was a little scandalised by Rachel's explicit revelations. She hadn't remembered her as being such a trollop but then who was she to talk?

'Poor old you,' she sympathised. 'Rachel, I was wondering, do you think it'd be all right if I went and watched some filming? Would they mind if I went on the set?'

'No, I don't expect so.' Rachel's tone implied they probably wouldn't even notice.

'Is there anything interesting coming up in the next day or so?'

'Well, tomorrow morning they're shooting down at the old market in Antibes. It's very pretty. Fruit and veg and people haggling. A real old street market. It's the scene where Julianne goes shopping there.'

'Is . . . is Hector in it?' Polly fought to hide the excitement in her voice.

'Oh, yes, sure, he follows her. It's the scene when we first know he might be thinking of doing something horrible to her, like he's done to all the other women, because he doesn't let her know he's there even though they've slept together a few times. It should be pretty spooky. Always assuming Hector shows up.'

'What do you mean?'

'Your sainted husband – sorry, Polly, but Johnny really is a bit of a wanker sometimes – has gone and taken it into his head that there's a publicity angle for the film in these robberies that have been happening down here. Millionaire Americans wandering around with loads of cash – probably because the Hôtel du Cap doesn't take credit cards – and then wondering why they get hit on the head and robbed. Johnny's on at the unit publicist to get Hector to do interviews about the similarity between *Mr Wrong* bumping off the women in the movie and the pattern of true crimes happening here. Needless to say Hector's not frightfully keen and Johnny's furious and the atmosphere on the set is a bit fraught.'

'Should I leave it, then?' asked Polly anxiously.

'Oh, Lord, no, go ahead. I'll tell Spider to expect you. The call's at eight so as to get the light but the gaffers and the grips'll be there before then so go whenever you like. They'll be there all morning.'

Polly thought it would look too obvious to ask what time Hector would be there. That night she had room service for the third night running despite a note from Johnny pushed under door inviting her to dinner. What was the point? She felt sorry for herself. This was no way to be spending a holiday, sitting in a hotel room by the phone waiting for Mr Wrong to call.

At nine the next morning she took a cab to Antibes. She soon found the crew. A group of short fat gossiping Frenchwomen, dressed in black and with toothless smiles, gave the game away. Spider was trying to get them to move back out of the way and at the same time collaring stray kids who were trying to fiddle with the camera. The grips had laid down camera tracking the length of one of the aisles of the market and the director of photography was riding the camera up and down, rehearsing. The focus puller was busy colouring in a calendar of squares on a chart taped to the side of the camera. To try and make herself part of the proceedings, Polly introduced herself to Spider and asked him what the chart meant. To her surprise Spider, a strapping lad of twenty-five wearing a sleeveless T-shirt announcing he was BORN TO BOOGIE and whose arm muscles indicated he worked out regularly, blushed.

'It doesn't include you, Mrs de Soto,' he said. 'Honest!'

'What doesn't?' Polly was mystified and somewhat thrown by the Mrs de Soto. She hadn't been called that in quite some time.

'The camera chart. It's a game they play every film they work together.'

'Who do?'

'Bill, the focus puller and Ken the clapper-loader. The colours of

238

the chart show the colour of the script girl's knickers on that particular day. They get to see right up her skirt when they do low-angle shots and lie on the ground.'

'Ah, I see.' Polly tried hard to enter into the spirit of things. 'And where it's blank it means she was wearing white knickers?'

' 'Fraid not. She doesn't go in for white knickers, this one. It means she wasn't wearing any!' Great big Spider blushed again.

'*Araignée! Viens là, s'il vous plaît.*'

'That's Henri, the director. He will have his little joke. *Araignée* means spider. I wouldn't mind only it's a female word in French. Better go. The first set-up's ready and I should go and call the actors. Tell you what, Mrs de Soto, if you wouldn't mind, perhaps you'd like to be in this shot? Wander up and down the market, pretend to buy a few things, you know?'

'Oh,' said Polly, pleased, 'like a native?'

'Oh, no, you'd be an English tourist. Plenty of them. Quite authentic.'

'Thanks,' muttered Polly and wandered off among the stalls.

She saw a caravan parked at the far end and beside it a TV camera. Maybe Hector was doing an interview after all. But as she grew closer she heard Johnny's voice:

'Personally, eh *franchement*, I have to say the crimes may be copycat crimes based on our movie. The filming's stirring up a lot of excitement down here and . . .'

'There's been no indication that the criminals are playboys, Mr de Soto, unless, of course, you have inside information?'

'Me? No. Oh, no. I'm just saying that it sounds like *Mr Wrong*. Maybe they heard about our movie and it gave them the idea.'

Polly about-turned. Sometimes Johnny did sound just like Rachel had described him: a wanker. A girl clutching a clipboard collided with her.

'Whoops! Really sorry. Overslept. This bloody heat. Henri's going to be mad as hell,' the script girl said. Polly couldn't help wondering if she'd had time to put her knickers on.

'Everybody very quiet now please!' yelled Spider. 'And that goes for *vous* too,' he added to the chattering housewives, who giggled and waved at him.

'Scene 34, take 1,' called the clapper-loader and then Polly saw him, moving silently out of the shadow of an alleyway. It was exciting, almost as if she were in the movie herself, which in fact she was. She saw Spider mouthing frantically at her: don't look at Hector, look at the stalls, look at the fruit and veg, pretend to be buying something.

But Hector was walking straight towards her, looking her in the eye, happy to see her, making kissing movements with his lips. Surely they didn't want all this on film. Then she realised he had his back to the camera and they were tracking him as he moved through the crowded market. In the next set-up Julianne would look up from buying some fruit, turn to face the camera and Hector would duck out of sight. In the meantime it was just him but the audience would know exactly who he was after – and it wasn't her, Polly. She'd better get out of shot. Yet if she turned and ran it would look as if she was running away from Hector. All she could do was to keep moving forward until she crossed paths with him, and as she did so he slipped a piece of paper into her hand.

Was it on film? Polly looked about her frantically to see if anyone had noticed and the director yelled '*Cut!*'

'Who's that bloody woman who's just ruined the last take? There's nothing in the script about anyone wobbling their head all over the place like they're in a Punch and Judy show when Hector goes by.' The continuity girl was almost spitting in irritation.

'Shhh. That's the producer's wife.'

'Ex-wife. He dumped her.'

'Who for?'

'Some say Persil.'

'Who's Persil?'

'Where have you been? It's what we call Lady Whyte. Persil washes whiter. Juanita-than-Whyte. Geddit?'

'Get away. She's a tart. Even dear old Johnny wouldn't be that stupid. This one looks quite a sweet old bat.'

Don't they realise I can hear them? Polly was flabbergasted. It wasn't enough that she was mortified for having ruined a shot, now she had to listen to this. She unwrapped Hector's note.

'Dinner? Tonight? Nine o'clock? Eden Roc? Nod if you can make it.'

She might be a sweet old bat in the eyes of the crew but it didn't stop an international movie star inviting her to dinner. She looked up at Hector who was walking back towards her for the next take and nodded like mad.

'Blimey. See what you mean. Mrs de Soto can't keep her head still. I'd better get her out of here,' she heard Spider say before she turned and ran.

As she was fighting her way through the crowd of onlookers blocking the aisles in the market she ran straight into Johnny.

'There you are, Pol. I've been leaving messages for you day and night. Where the hell have you been?'

'Enjoying my holiday. Isn't that what you expected me to do?' Polly, caught off guard, was unnecessarily curt.

'Look, what the fuck have I done? I've got a film to produce here. I can't be looking after you every second of the day. Be reasonable, Pol. You knew I'd be tied up. There's no need to get into a snit. Anyway, here's what I'll do. I'll take you out to dinner tonight. Little place up the coast. Away from these cretins on the film, driving me nuts, they are. Meet you in the lobby at 8.30? We'll have a drink down at Eden Roc, bugger the cost, and then push off. Try and be in a better mood by then. See you.'

'*Johnny!*' She yelled but he was off, waving goodbye to her without looking back. Now what was she going to do? Spin a coin?

Hector solved the problem for her by having Hussein deliver what looked like an entire rose bush with a note attached saying: 'Don't forget. Nine o'clock. Hector.'

Polly felt sufficiently confident to wear what Johnny had always called her summertime *pièce de résistance*. It was dead simple, had cost, according to Johnny who had bought it for her in a rare display of fashion sense, an arm and a leg and a hip, and it exposed most of these into the bargain. Polly had been thirty-five when he had bought it. Could she still wear a strapless bit of exorbitant nothing and get away with it? Where was it written that she couldn't? Polly asked herself and banished the two words that kept popping up in her mind like a jack-in-the-box: skin tone. She was tanned, she was smooth and she had freckles not liver spots. It was her body so she knew what was what about it. All those articles in beauty magazines were wrong.

Of course Johnny was waiting for her in the lobby.

'My God, the *pièce de résistance.* I thought you'd put it away for good. They didn't have a table any later than nine so we'd better move off sharpish. No time for a drink here first. Sorry.'

But Polly was on her way out the door and down the wide avenue to Eden Roc.

'Oh, all right, Pol. Wait for me. But we'll have to be quick.'

Hector was early. He was already at the bar and came towards her, holding his arms wide ready to embrace her.

'You look truly delicious.' His arms were around her, 'Oh, hello Johnny. Join us for a drink?'

'Other way round, but yes, why not. We can't be long though. You going anywhere interesting tonight, Hector?'

'Dinner here with the beautiful Polly. About as interesting as you can get.'

Johnny looked at her and suddenly Polly couldn't bear the expression of disappointed misery on his face. She wanted to be rid of him as soon as possible.

'I'm sorry, Johnny. I tried to call out to you in the market but you just wouldn't listen. It's your own fault. You never listen.' She was getting too personal in front of Hector.

'No drink. Thanks. Changed my mind. Gotta be somewhere.' Johnny was babbling, still staring at her.

'Hector, could we go straight in to dinner? I'm starving.'

'Nothing easier. Bye, Johnny. See you tomorrow.'

Polly didn't look at him again, didn't look at anybody until the *maître d'* had seated them at a window table overlooking the sea. She watched a raft with the words Eden Roc – Cap d'Antibes bobbing up and down, looking very lonely now it had been deserted by the sunbathers. Poor Johnny. He would be very lonely too with nothing to do all evening but it served him right. Then she glanced at Hector quickly.

'I'm sorry. He thought we were having dinner. I never said I would.'

Hector ordered her a champagne cocktail.

'You two still married?'

She nodded.

'None of my business, of course, but why haven't you divorced?'

'I don't know,' said Polly, 'I simply don't know.'

'Do you still love him?'

If I did why would I be here with you? 'Of course not.'

'Otherwise what would you be doing with me?' It was uncanny how he could read her mind. Or maybe it wasn't. 'Maybe you're trying to make him jealous. Revive his interest a little? It wouldn't be the first time I've been used this way.'

'I am not using you!'

'Calm down, Polly.'

'Sorry. What did you mean, it wouldn't be the first time?'

'I look good on a girl's arm. They feel special. I go along with it. Sometimes they don't even realise I care about them. As soon as the boyfriend or the husband starts taking an interest again, back they go.'

'But I'm not like that. I really care . . .'

'Do you, Polly? Bless you. Was it a good marriage?'

'Yes.'

'In what way?'

'He was my friend. He was so different from the type of man I'd envisaged winding up with, I couldn't believe it. Being with him made me feel interesting.'

'You are interesting.'

'Now, maybe, but I grew up thinking I was an ordinary English girl, a pudding from the country, nothing exotic about me that would attract someone like Johnny. And he made me laugh. Best of all, I made him laugh. I never knew I could make someone laugh before I met Johnny.'

'So what went wrong?'

'I don't know. Or maybe I do. In many ways Johnny was a little boy. Still is, probably. His enthusiasm was one of the things I loved most about him, but when it came to his work his enthusiasm became obsessive.'

'Criminal.'

'Not really. It's very common. I was very tied up in my own work and I know I wanted him to take an interest in that too. It just didn't seem to work both ways. Hector, this is ridiculous. I'm talking about myself too much. What about you? Have you been married?'

It was as if Hector hadn't heard her.

'What about children?' he asked her.

'It wasn't really discussed. Johnny didn't actually say he didn't want any but we never got around to planning one. So I stayed on the pill. Besides, he had Luana.'

'Have you ever met her mother?'

'Never. Something terrible happened there and it's a big secret. Nobody knows. Johnny won't talk about it.'

Hector leaned forward in his seat and took her hand. 'You poor girl. You mean nobody's told you?'

Polly shook her head, stunned.

'Would you like me to?'

'Do you know?'

'As a matter of fact I do. But it's a depressing story. I don't want to put you off your food. I'll tell you over coffee. Come on, eat up.'

Polly gobbled shamelessly, not because she was particularly hungry but because she couldn't wait to get to the coffee stage and hear about Edith.

'Well?' she said when they had been served with their second cup of coffee.

'Well what? Would you like an Armagnac or something? Sorry, I should have asked before.'

'No. Oh, yes, all right. Whatever. Tell me about Edith, Hector. I can't bear to wait a minute longer.'

'Oh her. Suicidal nutcase. Severe case of post-natal depression after Luana was born. She took an overdose a few years later and Luana came home from school and found her unconscious. Poor old Johnny never realised what he'd let himself in for. Apparently she's a real looker. She and Johnny got together when she was just a kid and he thought he was in heaven, wanted to start a family, couldn't understand it when she wouldn't marry him, desperate for her. Then it turns out she's a triple-A depressive, anything could trigger off another attack. It's like living with a time bomb. Are you

244

going to come home from a hard day's work and find your woman with her head in the oven? Then she hit him with the ultimate deadly weapon.'

'What?' Polly was devastated.

'She left him.'

'I know.'

'Well, think about it. She walks out saying I can never be good enough for you, I don't want to be a millstone round your neck, I'll go and be miserable on my own and you can be riddled with guilt about me for the rest of your life. Charming! Then you come along and make it even worse.'

'What on earth do you mean?'

'Well, of course she was sitting there in Battersea or wherever it was praying he'd call and beg her to come back to him but what does he do? He meets you and marries you. Now you've split up with him she's probably waiting for him to summon her. But what I can't understand is why Johnny's never told you. Too guilt-ridden, I expect.'

'Me too. It's extraordinary.' Polly was seething. It was so typical of Johnny to keep something as important as this a secret. Typical! 'How did you hear about it?' she asked Hector.

'Oh, Lord, I can't remember. It was just something everyone knew.'

She was about to ask for more details when the bill came. Hector produced his American Express gold card. The waiter looked embarrassed.

'I am sorry, monsieur. Eden Roc does not accept credit cards. House rule. If monsieur has cash or maybe . . .'

Hector exploded. 'This bill is for nearly £200. This is the Riviera. A guest from this hotel was robbed the other day. You've got masked gunmen holding up cars and ripping off jewels. What kind of idiot is going to go around with wads of cash in his wallet?'

'Monsieur.' The waiter didn't say sorry, nor did he offer any kind of quintessential Gallic shrug. He just waited for his money.

'I'll tell you what. You can put it on Mr de Soto's bill. He's staying here at the Hôtel du Cap.'

'Without Mr de Soto's permission, monsieur . . .'

'I'm staying here at the hotel,' said Polly hurriedly. She hated scenes in restaurants. 'If you could perhaps accept my I.O.U until tomorrow I'll come down here with some cash. Let me sign the bill. I'm Mrs de Soto.'

The waiter disappeared to confer with his superior and came back nodding. He managed not to look in Hector's direction as Polly signed the bill.

Johnny was still in the bar as they left the restaurant. He was very drunk. He lurched up to Polly.

'He let you pay for dinner, didn't he? He's been doing that approximately once a week since he arrived. Conveniently forgets they don't take credit cards. That poor old trout who was robbed a couple of weeks ago had dinner here with Hector and had to pay up. I think he's taking his role a bit too seriously.'

Polly ignored him. All she could think about was the fact that he hadn't told her about Edith.

'Look Pol, he's waiting. Better go running after him. Don't expect the earth to move, though. If you ask me he bats for both sides and never makes a run for either of them.'

'Well, I didn't ask you so shut up.'

She about-turned and ran straight into Hector.

'Like to come for a midnight swim? I heard what Johnny said. What did I tell you about my taking a woman out getting her man all jealous. Seems to have worked with your ex.'

She expected him to take her back to his villa but to her surprise he drove to the marina and led her aboard his boat. Millionaires' Bay was even more beautiful at night with the candlelight flickering through the pines as people dined on their terraces.

He stripped off all his clothes and dived in naked.

'See you on the raft.'

It was dark in the middle of the bay. If the people on the terraces could see her it would only be a silhouette. They would not be able to make out she was naked. Still, Polly undressed nervously.

The water was much colder than it had been in the afternoon they were last here. Polly swam slowly, tentatively. And suddenly Hector dived in again and sliced through the murky water towards her.

'Coming to get you . . .'

She screamed, only half in jest.

He reached her and gripped her hard, pulling her with him back to the raft. Gone was the tender lover and in his place a mean, almost brutal force was carrying her through the darkness, lifting her out of the water and throwing her down on the raft.

'Hector, please, you're hurting me . . .'

He took no notice. He fell on top of her and pinioned her to the deck, forcing her legs apart so she could feel his penis hardening against her pelvic bone. His hands came up and circled her neck.

Squeezed.

Hector O'Neill was dangerous. Polly thought she had never felt so vibrant. All the way home on the plane she virtually shook with excitement at the thought of their last night together. In the morning he had just upped and left. No undying declaration of love. No promises to call. Nothing. He could be the attentive, caring listener, leaving red roses on her breakfast tray. Or he could make savage, passionate love to her and walk out on her the next morning without a word, leaving the bruises on her neck and thighs as a souvenir. But whatever he was he had brought her back to life, and made her want more of him.

There was a message from Johnny on the answering machine as she walked into the house.

'Pol. It's me. Thanks to you I've got a bloody awful hangover. I waited for you at the hotel last night. Fuck knows where you went. I must have run up the national debt at the bar. You might at least have had the decency to come and thank me for your holiday before you left. No doubt you'll inform me as to why you avoided me like the plague for most of it when it suits you. If you really want to know I'm calling to check whether you've arrived home safely. Don't know why I bother.' There was a pause. He cleared his throat. 'But I do.'

She waited to see if there was a message from Hector but there wasn't.

Upstairs she unpacked and soaked for half an hour in the tub, reliving her morning bath on the boulevard du Cap. Back in the bedroom she groped underneath the bed for her slippers and found Mrs Flowers' manuscript instead. It was Sunday night. Mrs Flowers would be in the next morning expecting her to have read at least part of it in France. There was nothing else for Polly to do but begin it that night.

She finished it at 2.30 in the morning in a towering rage. Not with Mrs Flowers, not with herself, but with Grania Henderson.

Grania Henderson had lied to her. Mrs Flowers' book was not a saga, nor was it 'simply awful'. In fact it was very much the reverse. Polly lay and wondered why she had not seen through Grania Henderson before. Grania had made a big thing about being Polly's only Mills & Boon writer, saying she felt Polly was ashamed of her. Yet it had always been understood that Grania would earn her living from writing Mills & Boons while she worked away at her blockbuster, her massive multi-generational saga that would make her a fortune. Suddenly Polly saw what had happened. Mrs Flowers, herself a Mills & Boon writer, had come along and pipped Grania at the post. Worse, she had not written a blockbusting saga for, as Grania had probably realised too late, this kind of book was no longer fashionable. The core market would always be there for the regional sagas, the downmarket 'clogs and shawls' romances as they were known in the trade, but the elephantine epics covering family dynasties over a hundred years were rarely seen at the top of the bestseller list any more unless there was a literary quality to the writing.

Mrs Flowers had written something incredibly commercial in that it was a page turner about obsessive love, murder and betrayal which could be summed up in one line: *Rebecca* from the man's point of view. The nameless narrator of the book was a young man, a quiet unassuming writer, who marries a beautiful socially prominent television personality whose first husband, Christopher, was a bestselling novelist and Rhett Butler lookalike. The first marriage was a tempestuous one of Taylor/Burton proportions, rarely out of the tabloids. All around the narrator, as he tries to write his own delicate first novel, are Christopher's books and evidence of their success. As executor of Christopher's estate, the wife is constantly embroiled in meetings with film and television companies wanting to dramatise the books or make sycophantic documentaries about their author. She does not take her new husband's work seriously, yet after the turmoil of her first marriage she craves the narrator's shy, adoring puppy-love. At the same time she expects him to hold his own in her hard sophisticated media world, to be scintillating and glamorous and entertain every night. And always hovering in the background, the constant voyeur, is Christopher's gay literary agent who was clearly in love with him and resents the narrator as a usurper to the throne. When the narrator discovers that Christopher was murdered, he knows his own days must be numbered.

Grania Henderson was obviously downright jealous of Mrs Flowers and had blatantly undermined the older woman's confidence by advising her not to show her manuscript to Polly. She had lied to Polly in order to sabotage Mrs Flowers' chances of success. While Grania prattled away at her stupid dinner parties Mrs Flowers had been working an eight-hour day, often longer, for Polly and then going home and allowing her imagination free rein. Mrs Flowers was a real writer. Grania Henderson was an unimaginative hack.

Mrs Flowers cried when Polly asked her if she would do Polly the honour of letting her be her agent.

'And it will be an honour, Mrs Flowers. *Christopher* will be the most exciting book I've had to sell since *Mr Wrong*.'

Polly now saw Mrs Flowers in a completely different light. Gone was the old frump and in her place was a talent to be admired and a potential moneyspinner to boot. The blue-rinsed hair and the sensible shoes were still there but Polly decided she would let whichever publisher was lucky enough to secure the book decide whether or not they wanted to revamp Mrs Flowers' image.

She realised she had barely given Hector a moment's thought until she glanced at the phone – which she had switched off the night before – and saw there had been four calls already that morning.

They weren't from Hector. They were all from Joan, the first one beginning 'You said you'd be back today so I had to call and . . ' and the last one ending in tears. What on earth was wrong with Joan?

'Mrs Flowers, could you call Mrs Brock in about an hour and ask her to meet me for lunch at Clarke's. If she wants to go somewhere else say I'm out and you can't reach me so she'll have to go there. I mean, that is . . . if you're still prepared to go on being my . . . ?'

'We haven't sold my book yet, Mrs de Soto. One step at a time.'

As soon as Polly entered Clarke's she remembered it was a restaurant Joan absolutely hated. At lunch there was a set menu. No choice and Joan didn't like that at all. In addition, because of booking rather late, Polly's table was downstairs tucked away in a corner.

'Why do you always manage to get a table in Siberia?' grumbled Joan. 'If I move my chair a fraction of an inch I'll have one leg in the kitchen.'

'I don't think so, Joan. The kitchen's open plan in full view at the bottom of the stairs over there.'

Polly waited for Joan to tell her she looked great – tanned, glowing from sex with Hector. Surely Joan would be able to tell right away what had happened. But Joan just glared straight ahead. She didn't get up to kiss Polly hello, she didn't even ask the usual 'Any sex, any cheques' question to which Polly had her answer all ready. Polly was exasperated. Why did Joan have to be so negative? She was always complaining about something, always had a grouse to be aired, some new hate against someone.

Polly decided to ignore Joan's mood and launch straight in.

'Let's have some champagne. I have something to celebrate.'

'Bit chi-chi,' sniffed Joan.

'Who cares? I've met a man. I've begun an affair at long last. I couldn't wait to tell you.'

'Where on earth did you meet him? You've only just come back from France. Did you meet him on the plane or what?'

'Joan, you and I didn't talk to each other for weeks before I left.

You never returned my phone calls. I could have met him before I went to France for all you know but as it happens, I met him in France.'

'He was working on the film?'

'He certainly was.'

'Polly, you didn't go and screw one of the technicians? The sun went straight to your head and you jumped into bed with the third assistant director who has now gone back to his little wifey in East Sheen?'

Polly laughed. 'Nothing like that. I'm the cat that got the cream. Can't you tell? I was seduced by none other than Hector O'Neill.'

Joan didn't say a word. Polly was a little thrown. She had expected to hear a loud whoop and to be pestered for details.

'Well, don't you want to hear all about it?'

Joan still didn't answer.

'Oh, for God's sake, Joan. You've been on at me to get myself a man, have some sex, and now I have and I've done it in style. I bumped into him outside Eden Roc and he whisked me off to this villa he was renting on the boulevard du Cap and it just sort of took off from there.' Polly was aware that she hadn't mentioned her disappointment at finding Johnny with Juanita but she didn't want to give Joan the impression that Hector had taken her up because he felt sorry for her. That simply hadn't been the case.

Had it?

'And he took me out in his boat, all the way to St Tropez for lunch and I watched the filming, in fact I was actually in one scene with him. You'll see it when the film comes out. I've never had such a wonderful time. You were absolutely right about the sex. I should have done something about that ages ago. Did me the power of good. He's a wonderful lover. Joan, what's the matter?'

Joan had stood up.

'I've just looked at this ridiculous set menu, Polly. There's not a thing on it I feel like eating.'

'Well, we'll go somewhere else. Across the road to Kensington Place. You love it there. It's so vast, they're bound to have a table.'

'Polly, would you mind awfully if we did this another day? I just don't feel like it. Mrs Flowers didn't give me a chance to say so on the phone. Just told me you'd booked a table here and rang off. Bit inconsiderate if you don't mind my saying so.'

'Look, Joan, you were the one who left messages on my answering machine suggesting lunch . . .'

'It wasn't your idea. Is that what you're trying to say? Well, if it's such a chore . . .'

'For God's sake, don't be so bloody defensive. What on earth's the matter with you? Why were you crying when you left a message? Joan!'

But Joan had fled.

Polly felt cheated. She had been looking forward to holding her own for once in a conversation with Joan about men. She simply could not understand why Joan just wasn't interested. Something was up.

Walking slowly back home, Polly remembered Zoë Nichols. There was someone who could be excited to hear about her holiday. But Zoë's answering machine informed callers that Zoë was away in New York researching a book – Aroma Ross's novel, no doubt – and wouldn't be back until the following week. Polly left a message and wondered when Hector would be back in town. She realised she didn't even know. Should she call him in France – or wait for him to call her? Of course he would be filming all day and probably so exhausted every night he fell asleep without so much as eating whatever Hussein had prepared for him. So he almost certainly wouldn't have time to call her, she told herself, by way of prior consolation in case she didn't hear from him. Why had Joan gone off in such a grump? She needed Joan to remind her that men were bastards, no understanding of how women needed things like phone calls and constant communication. For despite her caustic, bitchy surface Joan was normally a good listener and she knew when to be comforting. Polly chastised herself for having let her relationship with her other close women friends slide once the agency had begun to demand more and more of her time. There was no one she could call and gossip with about Hector, no one she could trust anyway.

In the end she called Luana out of sheer loneliness.

'Polly, you're back? How's Dad?'

Oh, God, now Luana would want to go on about Johnny.

'Driving everyone crazy. You know your father. Come to supper. I'll tell you all about it.'

'When?'

'Tomorrow night? I'd say come right over but there's absolutely nothing in the house.'

'Actually, Polly, how would you like to come here?'

'Where?'

'Here. My flat. I'll cook you something.'

'Christ, that'll be a first.'

'What do you mean?'

'Well, half the time you don't even bother to show up when I ask you over here. Have you any idea how many perfectly good meals I've thrown away because you've forgotten all about me?'

'Polly, what's the matter?'

'Nothing. Why should there be? What do you mean?'

'I've never heard you sound like this.'

'Like what?'

'Sorry for yourself. Listen, you come over here and I'll cook you a delicious meal and cheer you up about whatever it is.'

Shall I tell her, wondered Polly. What were the rules about discussing your love life with your stepdaughter?

'The thing is,' Luana giggled, 'I've got a surprise for you. I want to tell you my secret. I can't bear to keep it to myself any longer.'

Join the club, thought Polly. Aloud she said:

'Take no notice of me. Too much boring work, such an anti-climax after all that sun, sea and se— sleep in the South of France. So what have you got to tell me? Going to spill the beans about that boyfriend of yours?'

'How did you know I had a boyfriend?'

'Oh, your father and I aren't exactly blind. You dropped hints all over the place. We just didn't know who it was. You were being really cagey.'

'Well, by the end of tomorrow night you will, only I'd rather you didn't tell Dad. By the way, did you and he . . . ?'

'See you tomorrow, Luana. I'll be there about eight.'

'Could you make it 7.30? The film starts at eight.'

'We're going to the movies?'

'No, there's something on the box I want to see.'

Charming, thought Polly. Invites me to supper then spends the whole night watching television.

The minute she stepped through the door of Luana's poky little flat in Shepherd's Bush, Polly regretted having come. There was a smell of fish hanging in the air. A rickety card table had been placed in front of the television and two places laid with chipped, mismatched china. Luana opened a bottle of rather dubious-looking plonk and Polly kicked herself for not having brought some decent wine. Yet in spite of herself she was intrigued by the identity of Luana's boyfriend, especially if it was someone Johnny shouldn't know about.

'You look sensational, Polly. I've never seen you looking so good. So brown! You must have been really attractive when you were younger.'

Polly had to laugh. Luana meant well. She had no idea of the implications of what she thought was a compliment.

'And your hair's grown too,' Luana went on. 'It really suits you longer. Makes you look younger.'

'Your father always liked it short. He was kinky about my ears, wanted to be able to see them.'

'Really?' Luana looked mildly horrified yet fascinated at the same time. 'Dad kinky? What else was he kinky about? Is he still kinky?'

'I wouldn't know,' said Polly. 'Make mine a spritzer, will you?'

It was just as Luana was struggling to lift a soggy-looking fish pie out of the oven that Polly remembered what Hector had told her about Edith.

'Why didn't you tell me your mother was a depressive?'

Luana dropped the pie. The dish cracked instantly and the runny cheesy sauce spread all over Luana's rather dirty kitchen tiles and she burst into tears.

'Why did you have to bring her into this? Who told you, anyway?'

'I understood everyone knew. I was the only one who wasn't

255

allowed to be let in on the secret. Here, give me a cloth. I'll help you wipe this up then I'll go out and get us some hamburgers to eat in front of the box. It'll be like old times when you used to come and visit us from Cornwall. We can have them with that nice salad you've made.'

The lettuce leaves were tired and wilting and the avocado had turned grey but Luana looked pathetically grateful and flung herself into Polly's arms.

When Polly returned, Luana was curled up in one corner of the sofa, kness tucked up under her chin, chewing her knuckles – an old childhood habit. The remains of the fish pie was still splattered all over the floor and Polly cleaned it up as best she could. Luana didn't move.

'Darling Polly, you are an angel but do get a move on. The film's really good and you'll miss him. Did you get the burgers?'

No 'Thanks, Polly' or 'Leave that, I'll do it later.' Like father, like daughter.

'Here's your burger. Who will I miss? Is your boyfriend in the film?'

Luana nodded happily, her old self again.

So what Johnny suspected was true, thought Polly. Luana was sleeping with the actors.

'It's one of his old films,' Luana told her, 'I couldn't believe it when I saw it in the *Radio Times*. Look, it's beginning. Isn't he just divine? Who would have thought he would take the slightest bit of interest in me? So, how was he in France, Polly? Did you see him at all? Did he . . . did he mention me . . . did he ask about me at all?'

Polly sat, rigid, tense, forcing herself not to react. It was an old Conway film and she found herself staring at a younger Hector as he moved through the opening credits. He looked stunningly handsome. If she watched another second of this Polly knew she would begin to cry.

'Hector O'Neill.'

'Doesn't he look a scream? Much better now I think.'

'You met him during the casting of *Mr Wrong*?'

'Yeah. Then he asked me out. He was so understanding about Mum.'

'You told him about Edith?'

Luana nodded.

'And yet you never told me.'

'You know that Dad told me not to.'

'But he said it was all right to tell Hector?'

'He doesn't know about me and Hector. You won't tell him, Polly. Promise me you won't tell him. He wouldn't get it. You know what he's like. He'd say Hector was too old for me. He'd say he was wrong for me.'

'And he'd be right?'

'What? Oh no, Polly, you can't say that. I thought you'd understand. You've always understood. I've always thought we were so close. Polly, what are you doing? Don't turn it off. I want to watch him. I think I'm in love with him.'

Polly hated what she was about to do but she couldn't stop herself.

'Luana, there's something I have to tell you. You won't like it but you're going to have to listen. Better you find out now than when it's too late and you've been hurt.'

Luana had buried her head under a cushion.

'I'm not a kid any more, Polly. I can be with whoever I like.'

'Of course you can. And you can still see Hector after you hear what I'm going to say – if you want to. You know you said earlier about how you were frightened that he might not want you any more, about how he might have met someone else out there. By that I realise you mean France. On the film. Well, Luana, that's exactly what happened. I was there. I saw him. He was with someone. He had this villa and he took her back there at night. She . . . she slept there . . . with him.'

'*It's not true!* Was it someone on the film?'

'No.'

'Then how do you know? I don't believe it.'

'I just know. I saw it. You can believe what you want but someone like that . . . he will always have a woman . . . somewhere.'

As she spoke Polly realised she was explaining Hector to herself as much as to Luana.

'But he's sent me postcards . . . look – '

Luana leapt up and scrabbled in a drawer, hurling a pile of postcards at Polly.

'Luana, maybe he will call when he gets back and you can go on seeing him but he doesn't love you and you're not the only person in his life. Just so long as you understand that.'

'You're jealous. That's what it is. Dad's dumped you and you'd like someone like Hector O'Neill yourself, wouldn't you, Polly? But you're too old. He wants someone young and firm like me. You can play the kind old stepmother looking out for me all you want but I won't believe a word of it because you know what, it's sour grapes. Jesus, Polly, you're getting on. You've got to give it a rest. OK, we had some good times when I was a kid but I'm a woman now. The last person I need to give me advice about my sex life is dear old Polly Pushover. Did you know we used to call you that? Hey, Polly, where are you going? Let's watch the end of the movie. So Hector has other women. Big deal. He's just like all the rest. I'll learn to live with it.'

But I won't, cried Polly, all the way down the stairs to the street.

258

If things don't change, a wag once told Polly, they'll stay as they are. This was meant to be reassuring but it didn't take into account the fact that things often changed for the worse. What Polly could never have foreseen was that they could get worse in a sauna.

She found it was the only place where she could lose herself in her agony and relax at the same time. She could not remember a time when she had felt so utterly humiliated. It wasn't that she cared what other people thought about her making a fool of herself over Hector. It wasn't as if other people even knew, unless Hussein was running round the flower market in old Antibes spreading the word that there was a situation vacant for a new sucker on the boulevard du Cap. But she, Polly, knew. She had betrayed Luana, she had betrayed Johnny even though neither of them knew it, but worst of all she had betrayed herself. She might get enraged by Joan's refusal to take the success of her literary agency seriously but what was the point of that success when she was making such a disaster of her emotional life. How could she be shrewd and clear thinking in her professional life and so completely gullible in her private one?

Why had she let her imagination race ahead of reality? Why had she started thinking of all the nights she was going to spend with Hector, all the places they would go, all the people they would meet – together? Why had she rushed blindly into the non-existent role (for her at any rate) of celebrity's girlfriend? Were all women like this? Receive a crumb and imagine they could be president of the bakery chain the next day?

One thought kept her going. Three times a week she made it to the gym at lunchtime and rewarded her vigorous efforts on the treadmill and the stairmaster with half an hour in the sauna. As she lay soaking up the heat, she found herself appealing silently to Johnny: take me back, ignore what I did, take me back. Not once did she remind herself that in fact it was Johnny who had left and she who had the option of taking him back. She would call him and beg for his forgiveness. It was all that mattered. It had become like a mantra: take me back, Johnny, take me back.

The door opened and a woman stood there, letting in the cold air, waiting for someone to follow her. Polly hated people who did that. It was so inconsiderate. They were invariably strangers with a guest pass to the club, women who didn't know the ropes. She peeked at the naked woman. She was almost skeletal with an angular body, olive skin, tiny pointed breasts like Joan's and an utterly beautiful gaunt face with huge expressive brown eyes. The body was in perfect condition, rock hard without an ounce of flab. Only the neck gave her away, and her mottled hands. The woman was probably around the same age as Polly. She was impatient, nervy. Polly could sense it. She had long dark hair and she flicked it over her shoulder constantly with an uncomfortable jerk of the neck. The kind of person who would remain wired no matter how long they tried to chill out in the sauna.

The woman was joined by her friend, a different animal altogether. Slow moving, placid, pink and white skin already blotched red by the heat, heavy thighs, pendulous breasts, thick ankles, flat feet below a tiny head, a pretty face with a turned-up nose and a mop of short platinum curly hair. The dark woman almost catapulted herself on to the top shelf and her plump friend clambered up after her. Polly was on the bottom shelf so they had to climb over her. They barely glanced at her and once they were above her she could no longer see them. But she could hear them.

They talked in that low tone just above a whisper which people imagine cannot be heard by anyone else in the room but which remains infuriatingly audible, so that Polly found herself straining to listen and gave up all attempts to relax. From what Polly could gather the two women had not seen each other in quite a while. Dark and Nervy was the out-of-town guest invited by Plump and Blondie. They spent several minutes trying to pinpoint how many years it had been since they had last seen each other – as if it mattered, thought Polly irritably – and then Plump and Blondie suddenly asked:

'So tell me, how is your depression? It's a good sign that you've decided to brave living in London again.'

'I'm never going to feel completely better,' Dark and Nervy spoke very quickly in rather a smoky voice, 'but I'm certainly on the mend. I feel so much more positive. The truth is. I had this little fling down in Cornwall last year. Just some guy who picked me up in the village, offered to carry my shopping, walked me home. He was staying at the pub, doing research on local churches or something. He told me I was beautiful – like a gypsy, he said. Turned out we'd done all the same things in the Sixties and Seventies. One thing led to another. It gave me back my confidence.'

Like me, thought Polly, with Hector. The bastard.

'The reason I was excited was because I was able to take it for what it was, just a bit of fun.'

Not like me, thought Polly, sweating below.

'And it made me realise what I really wanted. Or rather who I wanted.'

'Johnny,' said Plump and Blondie.

Yes, just like me. Polly turned over.

'Exactly. I've never stopped loving him.'

'Are you quite sure about that, Edith?'

Polly's heart lurched.

'What do you mean?' snapped Edith.

'Well, I always wondered if you really did love him or if you were just in love with the idea of being in love with him. Why did you leave him?'

'Because I loved him so much, I had to let him go. It's like that American general said about that massacre in Vietnam: it was

261

necessary to destroy the village in order to save it, or words to that effect. That's how I felt about our marriage. It was better to leave it than destroy it. In many ways it was the perfect marriage until I became really ill after Luana was born.'

'But you weren't even married. There you go again. I only hope you haven't passed on your daft idealism to your daughter. Is she pleased to have you back in London?'

'I haven't seen her yet. She's coming over at the weekend. I mean, I haven't even called her yet but that's what I've planned.'

'Doesn't it occur to you that she just might have a life of her own?'

'Oh, she does. She's a casting director. She cast Johnny's film.'

'And I suppose you assume Johnny's going to be there for you just like that. You have to face the truth, Edith. Besides, didn't he get married?'

'Yes, and he left her.'

Polly couldn't ignore the note of triumph in Edith's voice.

'He's free as a bird and I've already rung him. He's definitely coming round at the weekend. I'll get Luana over and it'll be just as if I've never left London. Come on, I can't stand it in here a second longer.'

Polly pulled a towel over her face as they climbed over her and walked out of the sauna. She left what she hoped would be enough time for them to get dressed and leave the club before she slipped out to the locker room.

She had arranged for Zoë Nichols to meet her downstairs in the restaurant for lunch. As she made her way to the reception area, trembling all over, she saw they were still there. Edith was in the process of joining the club. Seeing her fully dressed, Polly wondered how on earth she could ever have imagined that Edith was this shy, fragile mouselike creature shivering down in Cornwall. Before her stood a horribly familiar beast: a man's woman, a predator, brittle but lethal and 100 per cent worldly wise. And her clothes! She must have been on a shopping spree since she arrived in London. Surely you couldn't get what looked like Issey Miyake – a designer Polly wouldn't have a clue how to wear and only recognised thanks to

Joan's merciless education – in Cornwall. Where did Edith get the money? Was Johnny paying her extra-marital alimony?

'No smoking in the club, please, madam.'

'Oh fuck you!' But Edith was laughing as she blew smoke in the girl's face. She was unpredictable and exciting and suddenly Polly wondered what Johnny had ever seen in the woman he had actually married.

Zoë, coming in, stood aside to let Edith past.

'Who's that?' Zoë was very impressed. 'She could give Aroma Ross a run for her money. Or Lauren Hutton at any rate.'

'Don't ask,' said Polly miserably and dragged Zoë in to lunch.

They ordered vegetable lasagne and salad and Polly couldn't help remembering the one time she had brought Joan here. Joan had taken one look at the menu and gone across the road to pick up a hamburger, returning to eat it at the health club. Thank God Joan hadn't seen Edith. Polly could just imagine Joan being utterly fascinated by her and the instant lecture that would inevitably follow on how if only Polly could be like that, Johnny would never have left. It was a relief to have Zoë to turn to for comfort and reassurance but as it turned out Zoë had another agenda.

For a start she was high on New York and wanted to talk about Aroma Ross now she was getting further into the book.

'I met with this black model agent and I asked her if she thought anyone would ever give Aroma one of those lucrative cosmetic contracts and she said, "No way! Aroma's scandal, always will be. They want Family Hour." And as I watched her, Polly, I'm telling you that agent was dead right. Aroma's supposed to be engaged but if a man takes her fancy they'd better watch out. She whispers in someone's ear and she expects them to set it up with whichever guy she's got her eye on. And she's so capricious. One night her manager was taking her out to dinner with a party of ten and she couldn't decide which restaurant she wanted to go to so she made him book these huge tables at half a dozen restaurants. Then when she walked in she just sort of looked around and decided she didn't want to eat there and moved on to the next, leaving a wake of bewildered *maître d's*. She's crazy but she can be absolutely enchanting at the same time.'

Zoë continued in this vein right through to coffee, pausing only to chomp on her lasagne, before she noticed she did not have Polly's attention.

'Polly, what's the matter? Oh my Lord, you've been in France and I haven't asked you how it went and you think I'm a self-obsessed bitch. Well, you're wrong. Now I want to hear what *you* think of my adventures with Aroma Ross.'

Polly didn't smile.

'Joke, Polly. What is it? What's happened?'

Polly told her about France and the dinner with Johnny and the nights with Hector and coming back and discovering he had been involved with Luana. She told her about her rage and humiliation and the comfort she had derived from knowing that maybe she still had a chance of getting back together with Johnny. And then she explained that the wildly exotic creature Zoë had admired on her way into the club had in fact been Luana's mother, newly arrived back in London to reclaim both Luana and Johnny.

'Which leaves you where exactly?' asked Zoë.

'I just don't know. I didn't return Johnny's calls in France. I was there at his invitation. He left a pretty shitty message on my machine when I got home, I haven't dared ring him since. For all I know he can't wait to see Edith at the weekend. I can't even call Luana since we had that bust-up over Hector.'

'You didn't tell her . . .'

'No, but I told her Hector had been seeing another woman in France. I just didn't say it was me. I couldn't let him go on deceiving her as well. She was so upset she threw a complete wobbly, started telling me I was over the hill, that I didn't understand, that I was jealous because I was too old and Hector would never have an affair with me. It was pretty hurtful but I don't hold it against her. Still, I can't just carry on with her as if nothing's happened. I don't trust myself, what I might say to her without thinking.'

Zoë ordered two glasses of wine.

'We'll need these if we're going to talk this through. Just suppose you do manage to get Johnny back, what would be the point? You're on a roll with your career. The agency's doing fine. From what you've always said he's competitive rather than supportive as far as your careers are concerned . . .'

'Well, yes, he was,' said Polly, 'but I think that's changed now. He's had to face the fact that I've made it work and if I hadn't commissioned Lawrence to write *Mr Wrong* as a book, Johnny would never have had his film.'

'But why would you want to give up your hard-won independence? Why not retain control of your life now you've finally got it? Men are such control freaks they always want to interfere. I was watching that kid of an editor who's in charge of my book, Artie Allen-Jones. I was sitting in his office and a call came through from a literary agent. Even though I only heard Artie's side of the conversation, I've become pretty good at deciphering what goes on. He said, "Thanks for returning my call", and then he launched into how one of his female colleagues had just come back from New York and was jumping up and down about this potential bestseller she'd heard about over there, and when the time came to submit it to Hollywood House could the agent please be sure to send it to Artie, not the woman editor. I mean, of all the cheek! Those little boys always want all the kudos for everything and it never stops, I'm telling you, Polly. It's all show. If you ask me, you should just lie low and let Edith try and creep back into his life because if he wants a trophy female like that then he's welcome to her and he's not what you want. Just ride it out and see what happens, although personally I think you'd be better off staying on your own. At least you know where you are and you can have a bit of peace and quiet.'

She's bitter, thought Polly. I never realised it before. She's had these bad experiences with men, she's told me about them, and she's opted out of the race. But is that what I want too? On the one hand I have Joan urging me to jump into bed with every available man and now here's Zoë telling me life's better without a partner.

It came to Polly gradually over the next few days that she was not going to give up on Johnny. As she moved through the house and came upon his things still stashed away in cupboards and drawers, she refused to accept that it was over, Edith or no Edith.

What irked her about Zoë's suggestion that she opt for a solo existence was that just as Joan dismissed Polly's career in favour of her love life, so Zoë dismissed Polly's emotional needs in favour of her work. OK, so she was Zoë's agent but Polly was sure that wasn't what was behind Zoë's push for independence at all costs.

What they don't realise, Polly thought crossly, as she drew up a list of editors to whom she would send Mrs Flowers' book, what they don't seem to understand is that having made a success out of my career, I want to make a success out of my marriage. They see me as a woman on my own like them. But I'm not. I'm still married to Johnny and to be his wife in name only is to be a failure. It's as if my time on my own has been a little fling I've had on the side, my version of an extra-marital affair. Now it's time I settled down to the business of fighting for my marriage and making a profit out of it. All I have to do is corner the market and see off the competition.

That night she removed her make-up sitting at her dressing table with its hand-painted triptych mirror. Three different reflections looked back. In the right-hand panel Joan's disgruntled face glared at her. In the left-hand panel Zoë gave her an encouraging smile.

In the middle panel the New Polly returned her confident gaze.

Then the reflections changed and suddenly there in the right-hand panel Polly saw Juanita's immaculately made-up face and in the left-hand panel there was Edith, cigarette dangling out of the side of her mouth.

In the middle Polly Pushover was back, trapped between them.

PART FOUR

He was a bit young to be having a mid-life crisis but as the pre-launch publicity for *Mr Wrong* mounted and Hector O'Neill was confronted daily with pictures of his handsome face in all the tabloids, he found himself suffering a severe and hitherto unexperienced crisis of confidence. This wasn't about not being able to act beyond the role of Conway. Hector knew his performance in *Mr Wrong* was very good, and that with the help of Henri, the director, his character had emerged as a complex one, a charming and sophisticated psychopath who beguiled the audience one minute and petrified them the next so that they remained in a state of constant ambivalence.

The trouble was, so did Hector. But this was not about Hector the actor. This was about Hector the man.

Throughout the Conway years, when it came to relationships with women, Hector had been Conway both on and off screen. He had never questioned why women were attracted to him. He took it for granted that it was a combination of his lethal looks and his fame as Conway. Nothing more was required.

Now, having acted a more complex character, he had been forced to admit that that was what he had been doing: acting with women all his life. He, Hector O'Neill, was a million miles removed from the fascinating creature up there on the screen in *Mr Wrong*.

Not that he wanted to go around murdering women. Far from it. But the experience had dislodged him somehow, made him more introspective, something up till then he had avoided. He took to spending less time going out at night and more time staying in, wandering round his newly acquired penthouse apartment in Bishop's Park with its stupendous view of the Thames. He was even trying to learn to cook, although this was a bit of a throwback to the old Hector since he had an ulterior motive. He had heard someone say that men who cooked for women were irresistible to them. He had received a vicious little note through the mail from Joan Brock – how had she discovered his new address? – informing him that she had wangled a lucrative commission from a publisher she didn't name to write a biography of him. Since she didn't anticipate his cooperation in this project he could expect the dirt to be dug up and dished. When he diced spring onions that evening and tossed them into his wok, he imagined he was chopping up the spindly bones in Joan's pin-like legs.

Without being fully aware of what he was doing or why he was doing it, he set in motion a process of reinventing himself. It wasn't the first time. Hector O'Neill was an invention. The lonely boy who grew up in a trailer and watched his drunk of a father return from the steelworks was still there somewhere, buried underneath layers of surburban Surrey and superficial cinematic hype, but it would take Hector a long time to find him if he ever bothered to look. Now he was propelled towards a course of self-education which would take him even further away from the stench of the steelworks.

Over the years he had kept a series of little notebooks in which he recorded the tastes and likes of his various conquests. These records served as useful seduction aids when it came to buying presents or selecting restaurants that would impress. Now he found himself immersed in the names of books, clothes labels, artists, wines, delicacies, perfumes which had in the past meant precious little to him beyond an instruction to a sales assistant or a secretary in the Conway production office.

'I'd like a copy of something called *The Innocent* by Ian McEwan.'

'Send a box of marrons glacés to Marie Christiansen at this address.'

'I want a CD of an opera called *Tosca*. Gift wrapped, please.'

The notes were copious. Sarah dresses at Joseph, size 12. Lucy likes Maud Frizon shoes, size 6. Angela likes Jazz. Someone called Ben Webster. Also Coleman Hawkins. Judy likes plants, followed by a string of unpronounceable Latin names.

Once back in London, using his notebook as a guide, Hector worked his way through the items, going out and buying the books, the wine, the food, the music – everything but the clothes and the perfume – for himself. It was no longer enough for him just to know the names. He had begun to feel he was missing out on something. There was a wealth of experience he wasn't getting first hand.

It didn't work. He didn't understand or enjoy half the books. He thought the opera sounded like caterwauling. He had only come half-way to building profiles of his conquests and he was still light years away from nailing down his own.

It wasn't until he came to his notes on Polly de Soto that the penny began to drop. It wasn't so much what he had written – 'likes flowers, especially roses; baths, essential oils (lavender, geranium, melissa from Neals Yard), food, is the agent for authors called Lucy Richards, Rebecca Price' – it was more the fact that Polly was somehow different to the usual women who were attracted to him. For a start she was older, more mature, had her own business. But there was something else. She reminded him of someone. She was big and tall, attractive rather than glamorous. She was warm, she was genuine, she had seemed grateful for his attention rather than taking it for granted, she had listened to him and she had seemed comforted by him and – here was the surprise – *he* had found *her* presence oddly comforting.

He missed her.

There was only one other person who had had that effect on him, someone he had never forgotten, someone he still missed: Gracie Delaney.

Hector had called Polly upon his return from France and she had not called him back. Time and again he had come up against her formidable assistant, Mrs Flowers. Mrs Flowers, he could tell, was enormously excited to be talking to the great Hector O'Neill himself but when it came to putting him through to Polly she turned into the most stubborn mule he had ever encountered, launching into a never-ending stream of excuses and fabrications as to why Mrs de Soto was not available.

Hector wanted to see Polly. He wanted to impress her. To this end, although he did not really admit it, he was trying to reinvent himself as someone she might want to know off screen and out of bed. What he couldn't really decide was whether he wanted to see Polly for herself or because she was the first woman who wouldn't take his calls.

Polly could have set him straight in one short, sharp sentence. She was not about to waste any more time on someone who two-timed her with her own stepdaughter, someone who obviously thought he was a real clever dick leading both of them up the garden path.

Polly had been relieved when the phone had rung rather late at night and she had answered it with some trepidation, hoping it would be Johnny, dreading it would be Hector and rejoicing to find it was Luana nervously asking to be forgiven.

'I don't know what came over me, Polly. All those things I said. I didn't mean a word, I swear. I think you're stunning for your age. I think I've been a complete idiot about Hector O'Neill. He just wanted a quick fuck and I gave it to him thinking he wanted me for myself, that we were beginning a real relationship. In my dreams!'

Tell me about it! thought Polly wryly. She longed to console Luana by telling her that she too had fallen for the same blarney but in the end she opted to retain what little dignity she had left.

'Make what you can out of it,' she advised Luana, 'amaze your friends, tell them you had an affair with a movie star, tell them you finished it but it was great while it lasted, accept it for what it was.'

'What it was was the latest in a long line of romantic disasters.' Polly could tell Luana was close to tears. 'Why does every single man I meet treat me like shit, Polly?'

Because you've been treated like shit by your mother and now you treat yourself like shit without realising it, thought Polly, knowing that while she was dredging up oversimplified platitudes there was an element of truth there somewhere.

'Just try to be patient. Better these lousy men treat you like shit at

272

the outset before you get too involved. Look on the bright side. It's almost as if you're always drawn to the type of man who'll turn out to be wrong for you in the end. You'll know when the right man comes along. You'll recognise him. Seen your father lately?'

She slipped it in innocently at the end, but she was unprepared for the shock of Luana's reply.

'Sure. Dad and I are getting together quite a lot these days because of Mum. That's one of the reasons I called you, Polly. Has Dad told you about Mum coming back to London?'

No, of course he hasn't. Your father has barely spoken to me since I virtually ignored him in the South of France. Once again Polly edited what she said out loud to Luana.

'He hasn't, actually. How do you feel about that, Luana? Do you see a lot of her?'

'I'm gobsmacked, Polly, I really am. If you'd said to me even six months ago that my mother was coming back to London I'd have freaked but now that she's here I'm thrilled. I can't get over how much she's changed. She's so positive, so determined. She looks great. We go shopping together, we go to the movies, all the things you and I used to do. She doesn't treat me like a kid anymore. It's like she's my older sister. I'm trying to get her and Dad together as much as possible. It's so great when it's just the three of us. I can pretend I have a family.'

What about me? wailed Polly silently. I made a family for you in my home with your father. Doesn't that count for anything?

At least it took her mind off Hector. For the next few days Polly raged with jealousy. Her conversations with Johnny since their return from France had been abrupt and to the point – 'I need to come by the house and pick up a raincoat I know I've left in the downstairs closet, I won't disturb you'; 'Lawrence Bedford is due a final payment when *Mr Wrong* opens, anything you can do to speed up the cheque, Johnny, I'd appreciate it' – with any further conversation floundering as if they were two people who had once been friends, who hadn't seen each other for a long time, who had nothing left in common and who no longer knew what to say to each other. It was terrifying. She and Johnny had become near strangers to each other just when she wanted to bridge the gap between them. Now Edith was back in the frame Polly suddenly lost her nerve. She remembered what Zoë had said: sit tight and let it all work its course. Let Johnny discover for himself that he was through with Edith once and for all.

But what if he discovered just the opposite?

In any case Zoë was in a bit of an irrational state herself. She was having a difficult time with Hollywood House, who had suddenly decided that she should not do any publicity whatsoever for Aroma Ross's novel. Since it was a ghost-written project, this would have been perfectly acceptable except that when the project had first been announced the press release sent out by Hollywood House had stated quite categorically that Aroma Ross would be 'helped' in the writing of the book by Zoë Nichols. At the request of the Hollywood House publicity director, Zoë had even given an interview to one of the tabloids about how she would be writing the book with Aroma. Now suddenly she was not allowed to talk to them. Zoë had no problem with her name not appearing on the dust jacket or the title page. What she did want was to be credited with having conceived the characters and the plot of the book. This she felt was only fair. Aroma had been positively paranoid that the book should not be remotely autobiographical, which meant that Zoë had had to come up with a totally fictitious story. Where Aroma had proved enormously helpful was in opening as many doors as she could to enable Zoë to research the world of modelling. Zoë had interviewed model agents, other models, photographers, fashion editors, attended fashion shoots, been given front-row seats at the Paris collections – all of which helped to authenticate the background to her story. But it remained *her* story.

It was during one of her telephonic tirades against Artie Allen-Jones that Zoë dropped a piece of information into her lap that really shook Polly.

'And another thing. I've been meaning to talk to you about an idea I had about doing a biography of Hector O'Neill. From what you've been saying he's about to move into a whole different league once *Mr Wrong* comes out. The word is he's going to be dynamite. Well, I began mumbling about it to that little prick Artie Allen-Jones when I last had lunch with him and do you know what? He's only gone and taken my idea and commissioned a biography from Joan Brock. Joan Brock! That old slag! I'm so furious, I could . . .'

Polly let her ramble on. She was so shaken that Joan had gone ahead and got herself a commission without asking Polly to represent her that she forgot to tell Zoë that in fact Joan had had the same idea about a book on Hector before filming had even begun. She also conveniently erased how angry she had been that Joan had automatically assumed Polly would be her agent.

So who had Joan asked to be her agent? What had Joan been up to? Polly hadn't heard a word from her since that abortive lunch at Clarke's. For some reason which Polly simply could not understand, Joan had not returned a single one of Polly's calls.

Throughout everything Polly was grateful for the calming influence of Mrs Flowers, who went about her work in such an unassuming way that Polly sometimes had difficulty remembering that here was the person who would become her next bestselling client. Sometimes she watched Mrs Flowers out of the corner of her eye, marvelling at her energy. She wondered how old Mrs Flowers really was and what kind of passion she had experienced in the past that had enabled her to write the steamier scenes in *Christopher*. Maybe that was the answer, wondered Polly, indulge in unbridled lust until a certain age and then give it all up and plunge your energy into something else. It would certainly make for a calmer life. But hadn't that been exactly the life she'd adopted pre-Hector, the life for which Joan had had nothing but contempt but which Zoë had advocated? Why do I seem to be the only person without a view? Polly asked herself.

'Mrs Flowers, do you have any thoughts as to where you'd like *Christopher* to go? You must have built up certain impressions about the various editors I deal with. Any preferences?'

'Oh, Mrs de Soto, I leave that entirely to you. You're the expert.'

Polly hated it when people said, 'You're the expert.' It usually meant they thought they knew better but didn't want to get involved, but if you made a mess of it they'd be the first to criticise you. She had forgotten this rather priggish side of Mrs Flowers.

'Well, do you want them to know who you are? Should I say this is a wonderful novel by my assistant who has been writing Mills & Boons up to now?'

Mrs Flowers looked aghast. 'Do you have to say I'm your assistant? Not that I'm ashamed or anything, it's just . . .'

'That's what I mean. You have to get involved in some way. Of course, I won't say you're my assistant but are we going to use your real name? Mabel Lucy Flowers? Everyone knows you as Mrs Flowers. They might guess. It's not such a terrible thing. People think you're wonderful, Mrs Flowers, they really do. And are we going to send a photograph?'

'I just want it to be published by someone who really loves the book,' was all Mrs Flowers would say.

In the end *Christopher* went to just three carefully chosen editors and Polly made sure one of them was Sally Mackenzie, the young female editor whom worked alongside Artie Allen-Jones at Hollywood House who Zoë said was being upstaged by Artie. Mrs Flowers brightened visibly when Polly mentioned her name. It transpired they had talked often on the telephone when Sally had rung up to request Polly's books.

'But why didn't you tell me?'

'I did in the beginning but nine times out of ten when it comes to Hollywood House you always seem to have a note that Mr Allen-Jones has asked for it. It's as if no one else exists there.'

She's right, thought Polly, I'm as much to blame as anyone. I should make more of an effort to get to know the up and coming editors. I'm getting lazy in my old age.

The *Christopher* sale worked like clockwork. Sally Mackenzie loved the book from page one, bid more than the other two editors, and, most important, got on famously with Mrs Flowers when they met for lunch.

Then it all fell apart.

Sally Mackenzie called Polly early on a Monday morning before Mrs Flowers had arrived.

'She's not here yet,' Polly told her. 'Shall I get her to call you?'

'No, it's you I want to talk to. I don't know how to tell you this and if I don't know how to tell you, you can imagine the difficulty I'm going to have in telling Mabel Lucy.'

Polly stifled a giggle. It was going to be very hard to get used to hearing Mrs Flowers referred to as Mabel Lucy.

'Telling Mabel Lucy what?'

'I'm leaving Hollywood House. I've been offered the job of editoral director at Odeon Books. It'd be my chance to shape my own list . . .'

'And get away from Artie,' Polly finished for her. Odeon had only been going about five years but already they had made a good reputation for themselves as publishers of upmarket and middle-brow fiction and non-fiction. They were about to launch their own paperback line.

'Mabel Lucy Flowers would be so perfect for Odeon. I just don't know how I'm going to leave *Christopher* behind but I do have to take this job. I may not be offered such a great opportunity for ages if I wait.'

'You know Odeon were the underbidder on *Christopher*.'

'What are you saying, Polly?'

'I'm saying that I can always ask Mrs Flowers, I mean Mabel Lucy, what she wants to do. It could just be that she'd like to move publishers with you if you can persuade Odeon to up their offer to match Hollywood's.'

Mrs Flowers didn't bat an eye.

'Of course I want to go with Sally if she'll have me. No question.'

Artie Allen-Jones, who by this time had read the book, had other ideas. He persuaded Hollywood to up the advance payment by £5,000 to £40,000. He began calling Mrs Flowers three times a day, flattering her, cajoling her, telling her she was a star. He faxed Polly a revised marketing plan with a budget of £50,000. He biked over stunning visuals for a very commercial cover design. Polly began to realise that with so much money thrown at it the book was destined to go straight to Number 1. She owed it to her client to recommend she stay with Hollywood. There was no way Odeon could begin to compete in these stakes. But as she soon discovered, Polly did not know her client.

'Now I've got this far I'm going to go on writing for a long time,' said Mrs Flowers, maddeningly calm as ever. 'I've only just begun. The trouble with this Allen-Jones chappie is that he can't really tell the difference between me and that supermodel Aroma Ross. To him we're all authors whose books will sell and he can take all the credit. We're not individuals. We're just names he can chalk up in his spring catalogue. I want to go with Sally and be treated properly. I don't care if it is for less money. That young man needs to be taught a lesson.'

That young man promptly announced he was going to sue for breach of contract, but once again Mrs Flowers had the last word.

'I think he might have a bit of a problem.'

'I hope you're right.' Polly was beginning to feel a little nervous.

'You see I haven't been very efficient this week, Mrs de Soto. I've been so distracted with all this business, all the contracts we've had from the publishers for the authors' signatures, I've forgotten to do anything about them. They're all just sitting here in a heap.'

'Don't worry about that now. I never even noticed, Mrs Flowers.'

'You don't get it, do you, Mrs de Soto? One of those contracts is mine with Hollywood House. I haven't even signed it. Young Mr Allen-Jones hasn't got a leg to stand on! Perhaps you could give Sally a ring and ask her to get a contract round here as soon as she gets her feet under her desk at Odeon. By that time I'll have put a little ink in my pen.'

It was a problem solved but at the same time Polly felt even more dejected. It seemed not only was she doomed to the life of a single woman whether she wanted it or not but her professional abilities were also deserting her.

Still, life went on. If there was one person who was in the same boat as Polly it was Luana so, fighting her apprehension about hearing more glowing stories about Edith, Polly invited her stepdaughter to accompany her to the opening of a new restaurant in Chelsea.

'Why have they asked you?' asked Luana, tactful as ever.

'One of my authors, a foodie writer, has put some money into it. He's asked me. He's a bit pompous, sports a bow tie now and then, but it's not as if we'll be stuck with him and at least we'll get some food and drink.'

'Sounds wild. OK, you've twisted my arm.'

Polly picked Luana up the following evening. Luana obviously thought she was in for a very boring time since she had dressed very conservatively in a simple short-sleeved beige dress. The hem was at least six inches above the knee but it didn't alter the classic image. Polly thought she looked beautiful. On the way she filled Luana in on her client, Winthrop Hamilton.

'He's half American, I think. His mother's from one of those old Eastern seaboard New England families, he summers in the Hamptons and all that. He's not short of a bob or two is our Winthrop. Known as Win, by the way. Owns a town house in St Leonard's Terrace and a country manor in Wiltshire. He's only about thirty-five but he seems much older somehow. He's doing rather well as a food and wine writer. There's a new gourmet magazine starting up and they've offered him a column.'

Polly knew she was prattling on so that Luana couldn't get a word in edgeways about Edith and Johnny but as they turned into the King's Road Luana began to talk about Edith.

'She made me wear this dress when I told her where I was going. You never know who you might meet, she kept saying. You won't get riff-raff at an event like this. I couldn't believe it was Mum talking. You'd never think she was once this batty hippie with an alternative lifestyle. She's got this new thing where she refers to everything in decades – 'That's so Seventies,' she'll say. This from someone who still listens to her Neil Young albums. Her fashion sense is weird. She's discovered deconstruction with a vengeance but if you think about it that's a bit Seventies. Yet she wants me to be so uncool with my clothes.'

'Did you tell her you were coming out with me this evening?'

'I didn't, actually.' Luana looked shifty.

'Does she ask about me?' Polly couldn't resist it.

'She thinks she knows all about you. Dismisses you as the archetypal career woman. So Eighties!'

They arrived at the restaurant which was crammed with hoorays and their dates stuffing themselves, most of them already rather red in the face. Polly hadn't met any of Win's friends before, hadn't expected this kind of braying crowd. But it was too late. They were here now.

Win was standing by himself in a corner and the minute Polly saw him she knew this wasn't his scene either. If she'd only stopped to think about it she might have guessed he'd be embarrassed by this kind of crowd. He wasn't exactly shy but he was quite reserved, quite private. Polly realised she knew absolutely nothing about his life beyond the sketched profile she'd given Luana.

'Who is that dreamboat?' asked Luana beside her.

Polly followed her gaze and saw she was staring straight at Win. And suddenly Polly noticed Win's looks for the first time. He wasn't Polly's type – for some reason blond men did nothing for her – but she had to admit he was a bit of an Adonis. Well over six feet, with almost silvery fair hair, a straight nose and a strong jaw, he looked rather like a blond preppy Elvis.

Polly couldn't believe it. She introduced Luana and didn't see her again for over an hour. When she wanted to leave and went to find her, Luana was still talking to Win. Polly stood beside her, not wanting to interrupt. When Luana finally noticed her, she grasped Polly's arm.

'Are you off? Don't worry about me. Win's taking me out to dinner away from all this racket.'

'Will you j-j-join us, Pp-polly?' Win asked politely. Polly had forgotten to tell Luana about the stammer. She caught the look of panic on Luana's face and took the hint.

'I have to get back. Thanks, Win. It looks as if this place is going to be a big hit.'

Luana kissed her on the cheek and handed her an envelope.

'Dad asked me to give this to you. I nearly forgot. Thank you for bringing me tonight, Polly. Thank you, thank you, thank you.' She leaned closer to Polly's ear. 'You knew, didn't you,' Luana whispered, 'you knew he'd be perfect for me and you never said a word.'

Polly had known nothing of the sort. She had always assumed Win was gay, which proved how wrong she could be. As Joan was always pointing out: 'You are such a goose, Polly. You always think the ones who aren't gay are, and the ones who are aren't.'

In the car she opened the envelope Luana had given her. Inside was an invitation to the première of *Mr Wrong* and on it Johnny had scrawled: 'You will come, won't you, Pol? See you then.'

Polly nearly blasted the horn in exultation. Johnny wanted her by his side on his big night.

It was one of the worst evenings of Polly's life.

The day before, Zoë came round and took her in hand.

'What are you going to wear?'

'Oh, I expect I'll get out my . . .'

'You'll get out something you've worn a million times before, something you feel comfortable in, as you always put it, you'll give it a bit of a dust down and say it'll have to do. No, Polly, that's not good enough. You want to make a sensational impression on Johnny, on everybody who's going to be there. What we're going to do is we're going to make an appointment for you to go to the hairdresser's tomorrow afternoon. Meanwhile you're going to take the rest of the day off and we're going to hit the shops. One of the perks of writing Aroma's novel is that my profile has been heightened about an inch or two in the fashion world and before they realised how insignificant I really was some of those pushy designer PR women heard Aroma's name and promptly offered me a discount at one or two stores. Now's the time for me to make use of it.'

As she rang for a minicab the next evening Polly decided she had never felt so glamorous. Her hair was up for the first time in her life, piled on top of her head in an exotic chignon all the better for Johnny to be reminded of her ears with their tiny lobes that he had always admired so much. Her midnight blue silk trouser suit was from Armani and its brilliant cut was flattering and emphasised the fact that she was tall and striking with long legs.

She strode confidently into the Odeon Leicester Square imagining she must know how it felt to be a model on a catwalk. The press were milling around outside with cameras at the ready. Polly's euphoria was slightly dented when they gave her a quick look and moved right on past her. She consoled herself with the thought that at least her appearance had been sufficiently stunning for them to look and see if she might be a somebody even if she was instantly dismissed as a nobody.

The foyer was buzzing. A hand clasped her elbow and she looked round to find Spider, the first assistant on *Mr Wrong*, looking quite ridiculous in what was clearly a borrowed dinner jacket much too small for him, a bright blue shirt with ruffles all down the front and a blue velvet bow tie.

'Nice to see you Mrs de Soto. How've you been keeping?'

'I've been keeping absolutely fine, thank you, Spider.' How much did Spider know about me and Hector? was Polly's first thought. 'How about you?'

'Getting married, as it goes. You remember Pauline?'

Polly found herself face to face with the script girl on *Mr Wrong*, the one whose knickers had kept everyone guessing.

'She's wearing 'em,' Spider whispered with a broad wink. 'They're blue tonight to match my shirt.'

'And your eyes,' said Polly and had the satisfaction of seeing great big Spider blush. 'Now congratulations, you two. Speaking of marriage, I'd better find my old man.'

She noticed Spider and Pauline hesitate for a second. They might call her Mrs de Soto but they couldn't quite reconcile themselves to the fact that she was still Johnny's wife.

'His big night tonight,' said Spider; 'he's over there.'

Johnny was more nervous than she'd ever seen him. He was also being very Johnny. He was still wearing his long black overcoat over his dinner jacket and his baseball cap. Not only that – and Polly had to look twice to make sure her eyes weren't deceiving her – he had Zutty on a lead.

Johnny was working the foyer, pumping hands like a politician, going 'Hi, how are you, great you could make it' to absolutely everyone. He got as far as 'Hi, how are you?' before he realised it was Polly.

'Pol, great, isn't this terrific? Like my new monkey suit? Bought it specially for the occasion. Dead snazzy, what do you think?'

No 'You're looking great, Pol.' Nothing changed.

'Look, here's Pol, Zutty.' Zutty was completely ignoring her. 'He's really pleased to see you. He insisted on coming. I told him you were going to be here. I thought maybe you could sort of look after him for me. He really adores you, you know that. Perhaps you could go on ahead, take him upstairs. I've got a special seat for you, Pol. Front row of the balcony.'

This is Johnny, Polly told herself. This is the man I married. He's never going to change. If I want him back I'm going to have to live with this. She continued with this positive, rational line of thought as she tried to make her way as elegantly as possible up the staircase with Zutty frantically yapping at her ankles.

When she arrived at the entrance to the circle, Zutty pulled furiously on his lead so she was forced to run down the steps to the front row. The centre section had place names on the seats reserved for Johnny's party.

'Good evening, Polly. You're here.'

Polly could not believe it. Sitting right there bang in the middle of the front row with a place between them were Juanita and Edith. It was Juanita who had spoken to her.

Edith was looking wild and mysterious wrapped up in a velvet opera cloak with a hood.

'No, stop, you're there. One away from me,' Juanita said. Looking down, Polly saw her name on her seat. The place next to her had been reserved for Henri the director. She looked for the place name on her other side and found that Juanita had managed to knock it on to the floor. It had to be Johnny. Obviously, he would have to have Juanita as his co-producer on his other side.

Wrong.

Johnny came bounding down the steps a few minutes later

followed by Carla, Luana and Win. He picked up Zutty and handed him to Polly.

'You'll have to hold him up otherwise he won't be able to see.'

Polly found herself sitting in all her finery with Zutty on her lap while Johnny brushed past her and threw himself into the seat between Juanita and Edith. But if Polly was filled with disappointment at this arrangement, Carla was outraged.

'Johnny, I sit next to you.'

'No, Mamma, I've put you between Edith and Luana so you can – '

'Johnny. I sit here.'

Carla stood in front of Edith until Edith shrugged and moved to the next seat. Luana and Win took the seats next to Edith. In spite of her fury at being upstaged Polly couldn't help smiling at the way Luana was literally bubbling over with happiness. Win waved to Polly. Luana gave her a secret thumbs-up sign and made an 'I'm in heaven' look. And then Carla stood up and moved past Johnny to kiss Polly on both cheeks.

'I didn't see you. I'm so sorry. How are you? Why haven't you been to see me? Come to lunch next week.'

Carla's small act of warmth defused Polly's rising anger. She thought she saw Johnny sneak a guilty look at her, or was it her imagination? Nobody, she noticed, introduced her to Edith. She prayed it was impossible that Edith would recognise her as the naked woman lying below her in the sauna.

As the lights went down Polly made to move into the empty seat next to Juanita, offloading Zutty in the process, but Juanita pressed her back.

'Here he comes.'

There was a rustle of anticipation throughout the entire cinema. Downstairs the audience had risen and were looking up at the balcony. How *could* she have forgotten? He was only the star of the film.

Hector was born to wear black tie. His sleek frame looked as at home in it as Johnny's stocky build seem ill at ease. Hector's evening clothes fitted him perfectly: made to measure, obviously. He was tanned and his black hair was short and swept back away from his temples with just one stray lock falling over his forehead. Old-fashioned words like suave and debonair lodged themselves in Polly's brain. He sauntered down the steps of the balcony, waving to the crowd, and slipped into the empty seat beside Polly. He rose to kiss Juanita, shake Johnny's hand and slap him on the back. As he turned back to Polly the film started.

It was an experience for which she could not possibly have prepared herself, no matter how hard she might have tried – to sit there and watch the man on the screen looking so breathtakingly handsome, to know that every woman in the audience was secretly (and in some cases not so secretly) wanting to sleep with him, to know that she had slept with him and that he was sitting so close that if she moved a fraction of an inch she would touch him. Her composure lasted until the scene in the old market at Antibes and suddenly she saw herself on screen and Hector moving towards her. They passed and she remembered the note he had given her and it all came flooding back. Her throat constricted, her shoulders heaved and try as she might, her eyes filled with tears.

She felt a hand take hers and squeeze. In her head she heard Johnny say: 'Blubbing, Pol. Brilliant! Film must be really good. But why are you crying at this bit? It's the beginning of all the excitement. Suppose I'd better lend you my best silk handkerchief – come on, give me your paw.'

She waited for the wad of filthy screwed-up Kleenex and when it didn't appear she remembered. She wasn't sitting next to Johnny. She was sitting next to Hector. It was his hand she was holding.

She snatched her hand away and felt Hector flinch beside her.

From the first few frames it had been clear the film was going to be good but by the time the final credits rolled, what was also clear was that it would be a huge success. It was suspenseful, and entertaining. Hector and Julianne were dynamite together as were, to an appropriately lesser extent, Julianne and Caspar who played the cop boyfriend who arrested Hector in the end and claimed Julianne as his own. Johnny had a hit on his hands and Polly was proud of him. She was also surprised at how cool he had been about it up to now. There must have been screenings. He must have known what he had.

Downstairs in the foyer it was bedlam. The press were descending in droves on Hector, Julianne, Caspar and Henri. Polly heard a loud Irish voice proclaiming: 'So Froggy had it in him after all. Didn't think he could direct his way out of a tub of cottage cheese.'

'Clovis, leave it alone,' Polly heard Luana's embarrassed voice. 'Hello stranger.'

Lawrence Bedford was beside her and Polly felt riddled with guilt. In her excitement – pointless, as it turned out – at the thought of accompanying Johnny to the première, she had forgotten to find out what would be happening with Lawrence. He should have been sitting up there with everyone in the front row of the circle. In fact he had far more right to be there than she did. How could she have been such a neglectful agent?

'Come on, Polly, don't look so horrified to see me. Take my arm. I'll escort you to the post-première party. I thought the film was absolutely brilliant even if I did write it myself. What about you?'

'I agree. Just think what it's going to do for sales of the book. I shouldn't be surprised if you don't sell another quarter of a million copies. Now tell me, how's the new book coming along?'

She barely listened to Lawrence as they made their way through Soho to dell'Ugo where Johnny had booked two floors for dinner and dancing. It was typical! She had set out for the evening as the glamorous wife of the successful movie producer and wound up back where she started: playing the sympathetic agent supporting her client.

Yet if she were honest she was using Lawrence just as much as he was using her. Without him she would have been lost. She needed an escort. At the party she introduced him to Luana and Win.

'Winthrop's a food writer,' she explained quickly. Clients often became jealous of each other, vying for her attention: 'very successful.' It was Lawrence's night but she didn't want Win to feel put down. Hector, who had been swallowed up by the press, made his entrance and Luana moved closer to Win. She wouldn't look at Hector. Polly wondered what Win must be making of her performance. But at least Luana had Win. Polly knew that clinging to Lawrence wasn't going to fool anyone.

She survived the dinner thanks to Carla, who needed a certain amount of attention – or pretended she did. Johnny flitted about the room, wallowing in all the adulation. Polly was pleased. Edith had rushed to sit next to him but now she found herself neglected. When the dancing began she crossed the room and manoeuvred her way into Johnny's arms. Carla clucked disapprovingly.

Suddenly she turned to Polly.

'In France? What happen? I never ask but I want to know.'

'I was foolish. He gave me a chance but I made a mess of it. Please don't ask me for the details.' Polly knew it was pointless to be anything but straight with Carla.

'I told you to keep up with him. Look at you, here you are. There he is. And look who he's with. You know who that is, don't you? Now, if Johnny gives you another chance, take it and hold on to it. Wait here, Polly.'

Carla got up. Polly watched in fascination as the tiny woman, a good head shorter than anyone else on the floor even in her little high-heeled shoes, made her way over to Johnny and Edith. She took Johnny's arm, pulled him gently away from Edith and made a big show of being apologetic, was Edith quite sure she didn't mind? Then she waltzed off with her son, leaving Edith standing there.

Carla monopolised Johnny for four whole dances and suddenly Polly saw what she was doing. She was engineering her son closer and closer to the table until finally they were almost on top of Polly, at which point Carla literally handed Johnny to Polly.

Polly had forgotten what an utterly hopeless dancer Johnny was. He didn't dance, he walked, and not necessarily in time to the music. Keep up with him, Carla had said. Well, Polly was trying in more senses than one.

'Great party, Johnny.'

'Great party, great movie, great evening. Everything's great.'

'Including you.'

'You said it, Pol.'

'Your mother's having a wonderful time.'

'With Mamma it's a question of so far so good. She won't be truly happy till I've won an Oscar.'

'I never realised she was so ambitious for you. She's quite an impressive woman. In different circumstances she'd probably have been a pretty successful career woman herself.'

Johnny stopped dead in the middle of the dance floor.

'Mamma's not a career woman.'

'I didn't say she was. I said she could have been.'

'No she couldn't.'

'Why not?'

'She's my mamma.'

'Meaning you don't like women having successful careers.'

'Of course I do. Look at Juanita.'

What about me? screamed Polly inside but kept smiling.

'You must be pleased Edith's here.'

'How do you know Edith's here?'

'You might well ask since no one's bothered to introduce us.'

Johnny looked very nervous.

'Anyway she looks very well, Johnny.'

'Why wouldn't she look well?'

'I heard she'd been ill.'

'Who told you that?' He was very defensive now.

'Luana. Tell me, how do you like Win?' Polly longed to quiz him more about Edith but if it was going to alienate him, there wasn't much point.

'I don't. Looks a bit of a wally to me. You introduced them, didn't you?'

'Is it something specific or just the fact that he's screwing your little peachy girl?'

'He isn't. That's what's bothering me.'

'What do you mean?'

'He isn't going to bed with her. Says he respects her. Sounds like an old-fashioned matinée hero who's only allowed one knee on the bed. Forget about respecting her. I've never heard such crap. He just doesn't fancy her.'

'Well, would you like him if he did – and I'm sure he does.'

'No.'

Polly gave up. She should never have mentioned Edith. Then, unpredictably as ever, Johnny suddenly pulled her closer.

'I left a message on your machine for you when you got home from France. You never rang me back.'

'We've spoken plenty of times since then.'

'Yes, but only about Luana or work. Did you have a good holiday?'

'Of course I did. I should have thanked you. I know I should.'

'What made it so good?'

'The hotel. Being able to relax.'

'What else? You didn't seem to have much time for me after that first evening. I'll lay it on the line, Pol. I was a bit pissed off with you for not wanting to see much of me. It felt a bit like you were using me, tell you the truth.'

'You were busy. You had a film to produce. I didn't want to get in the way.'

'That's all it was? No hidden agenda?'

'No hidden agenda.'

'I'm quite pleased to hear that, you know, Pol.' He was holding her very close now. 'I'm going to have to network a bit. It's my party and all that, but we could sort of have a dance later on and . . .'

'Mind if I step in and take this opportunity to renew an old friendship?'

Hector was looming over Johnny's shoulder, gently but firmly moving him aside and drawing Polly to him. Polly couldn't bear to look directly at Johnny. She could sense him, standing there, fists clenched, smaller than Hector, stocky, pugnacious, angry. Tell him no, Johnny. Say you want me to yourself. Send him packing. Fight for me. Do something.

'How can I refuse my star anything? I'm surprised he didn't write you into his contract, Pol. Take her away, Hector. Good to see you, Pol. Thanks for looking after Zutty.'

'I have my uses,' said Polly bitterly, and was rewarded with one of Johnny's blackest looks.

'I shouldn't have done that, should I?' said Hector. 'Do you want to go after him?'

'I'd rather run after his flaming dog.'

'You're looking so beautiful tonight.'

Right words. Wrong man.

'Polly, I've never had to do this before but I want an explanation from you.'

She looked up at him as he moved her expertly round the dance floor. He was an effortless dancer and after Johnny's clodhopping she relaxed in spite of herself. He was so undeniably handsome. People were watching them. She knew he was making her look good.

'What kind of explanation?'

'Why didn't you return my calls after I returned from France?'

'Why didn't you tell me about Luana?'

She had nothing to lose and it made her bold. Hector tensed. He didn't answer her for several minutes.

'I can see I'm the one who owes you an explanation. I'd like to give it to you but I can't do it while we're shuffling round a dance floor surrounded by all these people. Can I see you some other time?'

Polly was about to say thanks but no thanks when she saw Johnny looking at her. He was dancing with Edith. Without taking his eyes off Polly, he buried his lips in Edith's neck. Polly didn't stop to think. Before he looked away she moved her hands up to stroke the back of Hector's neck.

'Of course you can. Call me tomorrow and we'll make a date.'

Luana sat at her desk and tried not to think about the kind of mood Clovis would be in when she arrived for work. Clovis had taken the week off after the première and during that week as *Mr Wrong* opened to sensational business, Hector had given several interviews to the press. Luana's personal view of Hector was that he was a piece of dog turd but she couldn't ignore the fact that he had stated several times in print that she, and she alone, was responsible for the idea of casting him as Mr Wrong.

Clovis was going to be furious. Hadn't she always said that one of the most important things Luana had to remember about a casting director's job was that it was always, repeat always, the director's idea. Of course Clovis was the first to accept compliments about the casting. Now Hector had blown her whistle. She was going to go ballistic.

As if that were not enough, Luana had, in the week Clovis had been away, already been offered three jobs, two to work for rival casting directors with the promise of much more responsibility and a third to cast a film on her own. Ordinarily she would have been flattered and excited, but this week all she could think about was how soon would Win propose? They had spent the weekend in the country. Not at his place in Wiltshire, he still hadn't taken her there despite her constant begging. Apparently some kind of renovations were being carried out, the place was filled with dust, it just wasn't a good idea. He had taken her to some friends who had a weekend place in Suffolk. They were a couple in their forties, childless, old friends of Win's. The wife, Peggy, had confided in Luana during the washing up in the kitchen.

'Perhaps I shouldn't tell you this but we're both quite excited about you and Win. It's the first time he's brought a girl to stay and he's been coming here for years. The truth is, he's always been incredibly secretive about his private life. George and I decided he was probably once very badly hurt and has decided to be very careful.'

Luana had started hearing wedding bells before they'd even finished loading the dishwasher. And she too, she realised, had been careful. She hadn't introduced Win to all her friends as she usually did, rushing him round to meet everyone as the new man in her life. That would come. She sensed that he wanted to take things one step at a time. She banished the irritating voice that kept saying: if you introduce him to your girlfriends the first thing they're going to ask is what's he like in bed? And you're going to have to say you don't know. They wouldn't understand about him respecting her.

So how could she think about going for a new job when this time next month she might be planning her wedding?

Clovis arrived in a real grump but it didn't have anything to do with Hector's interviews. The minute she entered Reception she delved into her bag and brought out a bottle of syrup of figs. Clovis suffered from chronic constipation and did not see the need to keep quiet about it. Luana was kept constantly informed as to the state of Clovis' bowels. Clovis downed half the bottle.

'I seem to have run out of the stuff at home. Now, what've I got on today? Give me me call book, I'd better get on the phone.'

'Did you have a nice holiday, Clovis?'

'Oh, don't be makin' small talk while me stomach's like the Rock of Gibraltar. What's this? Lunch with Joan Brock. Who the fock's Joan Brock?'

'Well, I can help you there,' said Luana, 'she's an old friend of Polly's. I met her quite a few times when I was living with Polly and

Dad. She always came to the house when Dad was away because he couldn't stand her.'

'And why was that?'

'I never really discovered. Dad always said her breath smelt.'

Clovis laughed. 'Sounds like yer father. Poor bitch probably suffered from constipation like meself. Why am I having lunch with her?'

'She's writing this biography of Hector and she wants to interview you about him.'

'Maybe she'll want to talk to you too.' It was a throwaway remark as Clovis disappeared into her office but Luana didn't miss the implication.

'You're due to meet her at Chez Gerard in Charlotte Street at one o'clock,' Luana called as Clovis slammed the door.

'Why me?' asked Clovis rather ungraciously as Joan Brock took her place opposite Clovis in the banquette. 'I'll have a Dubonnet and lemonade. Don't look like that, Miss Brock. We don't drink Guinness all the time.'

Joan had been unable to stop herself wincing at the request for Dubonnet and lemonade. How naff could this woman get?

'Do call me Joan. I'll have a Kir Royale.'

'Ooh, very chi-chi, Joan.' Clovis emphasised the Joan. 'Polly's an old friend of yours, I hear.'

'We were at school together. Juanita was there too, under another name.'

'You mean she was incognito?'

'No, no, no. She was called Sandra something. She's changed her name since then.'

'She's not the only one.'

'What do you mean?'

'Oh, we'll get to that. So what was Polly like at school?'

'Much like she is now.'

'And how's that?'

'Oh, you know, sweet, of course. I adore Polly. But she's a bit of an innocent when it comes to men, sex, that sort of thing. Can't really hold her own.'

'Really?' Clovis knocked back her Dubonnet and lemonade. 'Didn't look that way to me at the post-première party the other night. She was dancing with Johnny and then Hector came along and cut in and waltzed off with her. She had her pick of the two of them. Hector was with her for the rest of the evening.'

Clovis had the satisfaction of seeing she had taken the wind right out of Joan's sails.

'Now, Hector. Why you?' Joan was back on course. 'You cast *Mr Wrong*. You must know him pretty well. Did you cast the Conway films?'

'I did not, as you'd have known if you'd done your homework. If you really want to know I first met Hector before he was even cast as Conway.'

'How was that? Who did cast him as Conway?'

'I forget but you can easily check. When I met him I was working as a casting director for an advertising agency. I had a young assistant, sort of like the job Luana has now but with more responsibility. This kid actually went out looking for people, scouting in the streets. She was pretty good. We were looking for a hunk for this commercial. She found him. Hector. John Hector Maguire I think he was called then. He was up a ladder.'

'He was where?'

'Up a ladder. He was a brickie. She made him come down and brought him in and the client went for him just like that. It was after the commercial came out that someone thought of him for Conway.'

'And this girl who discovered him, has she become some top flight casting director with her own business? Where is she now?'

'She was American. I hired her because she had a good Irish name. Gracie Delaney. Red hair. She went back to Philadelphia to get married. Poor kid, she was sweet on Hector.'

'They had a thing together?'

'I don't really know. All I remember is that she came in really cut up one morning because he'd spent the night blurting out all his deep dark secrets to her, confided in her like, and she said she'd felt so sorry for him she'd wound up spending the night with him. But she wasn't stupid. She knew he was trouble. She knew he'd probably done it on purpose to get her to succumb. She didn't allow it to stop her going back and getting married.'

'What were his deep dark secrets?'

'She never said. I didn't ask.'

'Are you still in touch with her, Clovis?'

Clovis looked at the little rat-like woman on the other side of the table, positively salivating at the thought of getting at those 'deep dark secrets'.

'I am. I get a Christmas card from her every year.'

'Does it give her address?'

'It does. I'll give you a bell with it tomorrow. Now, let's order ourselves a real drink and I'll tell you all about the scumbags in the British film industry.'

Polly wasn't entirely sure about Hector's suggestion that he try out his new cooking skills on her but in the end she couldn't resist a peek at his new apartment. She was disappointed by it.

He had obviously done what so many people do. He had gone out to expensive stores and chosen large cold masculine pieces of furniture with no apparent thought as to how or where they would fit into his home. Someone had obviously told him grey was *the* colour. A vast grey leather sofa stood plonked in front of the plate-glass window. A 10-foot slate-coloured table monopolised the dining room, making it look like an operating theatre. The chairs dotted along it were much too small and spindly by comparison. His kitchen was cavernous and steely. He took pride in the fact that he hadn't hired a decorator and had put the place together himself but as far as Polly could see, if anyone needed a decorator it was Hector. He had absolutely no taste. With his wardrobe it was a different story. He was a natural clothes horse and designers flocked to have him wear their suits, sportswear, whatever. He just had to put it on in the right size and forget about it. He had clearly imagined he could apply the same approach to his home.

On top of everything he was a lousy cook. Polly couldn't help thinking that she'd had a better meal when Johnny had cut open cellophane wrapping and upended the contents into bowls. Hector attempted a cheese soufflé which failed to rise, before which he served some seriously poisonous pâté. Polly suspected it was meant to be chicken liver but it tasted – and certainly looked – more like putty. Finally he produced one of the stodgiest chocolate cakes Polly had ever encountered. Hector was looking utterly crestfallen.

'Leave it. It's hopeless. I'm hopeless. I do everything the cookbook tells me to and this is what happens.'

'Don't be so hard on yourself,' said Polly. 'Very few people are natural cooks and I've never been able to make an acceptable soufflé. Why do you bother cooking anyway? You love restaurants, don't you?'

'I read somewhere that women like men who cook for them.'

Polly choked to stop herself from laughing out loud.

'Anybody likes someone who cooks well for them. I don't think your cooking is going to get you anywhere.'

'I know that,' he snapped.

'To be a good cook you need to love food. Food, not restaurants. And I think you have to be caring about other people, to want to please them.'

'I want to please women.'

'Tell me about it, but you must want to please men as well. So did you cook for Luana?'

'Polly, I met Luana and took her out a few times long before I met you in Antibes.'

'But you never even mentioned her.'

'There was nothing much to mention.'

'She doesn't see it like that. She was pretty upset when you didn't call when you came back from France.'

'I didn't even call *from* France. I just sent a few postcards. It was no big deal.'

'Hector, I just can't believe this. You seem to have no consideration for other people's feelings. Is there anybody you actually care enough about to try and avoid hurting them? What about your mother?'

'She's dead.'

'I'm sorry. Were you close to her?'

He didn't answer.

'Hector?'

'What's the score between you and Johnny?'

'Score? There's no score.'

'You're not back with him?'

'Why do you ask?'

'I'm curious, that's all. I could never figure out your marriage. I've been thinking about it. I can't understand why you jumped into bed with me in France.'

'You were there.'

'Oh great. I was conveniently to hand. Don't you remember what I told you about women who go out with me because they like to be seen with me? Because I'm famous. So they can make their man jealous. You hear about trophy wives. I'm the trophy date. Is that what I was for you?'

Polly didn't know what to say. She had used him. There was no denying it. She had seen Johnny with Juanita, jumped to an instant stupid conclusion and rushed straight into Hector's arms.

'Not exactly. I mean, I didn't go out and flaunt you, Hector. We had one dinner in public. Apart from that we were on our own. But yes, if you really want to know, when I first saw you outside Eden Roc I had just seen Johnny engaged in what I thought was amorous contact with Juanita and it destroyed me. I confess I had built up in my mind the notion that Johnny had asked me down to the South of France as the beginning of a reconciliation. In fact we'd even had a wonderful dinner together. Seeing him with Juanita threw me right off track. You caught me on the rebound. You were fantastic in bed. You made me feel wonderful. You listened to me. Johnny never listens.'

'Yet you fell in love with him.'

'Yes, I did. I fell desperately in love with him. What we always forget is that you don't fall in love on paper. If a woman is asked what is her type of man, she's going to say something like "Tall, dark, he must have a sense of humour, he must be kind and considerate, he must listen to me, he must be a New Man" – whatever that is – "someone who lives close by and has a regular income and is reliable", and then they go and fall in love with a short man who treats them like shit and is probably a visiting

American, to boot. A woman knows who her Mr Right is on paper but when she meets him she's usually bored to tears. It's Mr Wrong she falls in love with. Don't you always fall for Miss Wrong?'

'No.'

'Well, of course you're Superman. I forgot. I suppose you only fall in love with Superwoman.'

'No, I mean I don't think I've ever fallen in love.'

'Not ever?'

Hector shook his head. He looked miserable.

'Hector, that's so sad. Why is it, do you think?'

'I've never thought about it. Maybe it's because I do all the listening and no one ever listens to me.'

'Now you're really feeling sorry for yourself.' Polly got up and went and sat beside him on the dreadful hulk of a sofa. 'Maybe you just don't open up to them enough. You have to let people in, let them get close to you.'

'I listen to women because I know they like it and it makes it easier to get them into bed.'

Polly flinched.

'Charming! At least you're honest and God knows, it worked with me.'

'But look where it's got me. I've been out with all these women, I've been to bed with them but I've never had a proper relationship. I wouldn't know where to begin.'

Polly was feeling rather confused. She had drunk enough for Hector's undeniable physical charms to have begun to have an effect on her. She had meant it when she told him he was fantastic in bed. He was the last man she had had sex with. She could recall what it was like with him more vividly than she could remember sex with Johnny. Poor Hector. He was so magnetically attractive that it really was a question of if he was there to be had, any woman would take him. Polly understood why he felt used. His effect on women made them behave like men, made them think only of sex without bothering to get to know him first – or indeed afterwards. His sudden vulnerability was also very attractive.

His hand was lying on the sofa between them. She took it and stroked the palm with her thumb.

'You'll find someone. I just don't think you've been looking.'

He keeled over to rest his head in her lap and she cradled him in her arms, bending down over him to bury her face in his hair. Then he had turned his face to hers and they were kissing. He moved so that he was kneeling on the sofa above her, clasping her head in his hands and she could see the shape of his erection through his jeans. She unzipped him, fondled him, let him push her down into the depths of the sofa. He pushed her skirt up to her waist and stabbed at her stomach with his penis. She raised her buttocks and eased her way swiftly out of her underwear, then shifted herself so that he could enter her.

He came almost as soon as he was inside her and she rocked him on top of her until his breathing subsided. To her surprise instead of climbing off her he began to kiss her, sucking gently on her mouth, stroking her tongue with his own, over and over until she was melting. He was still inside her. She felt him grow hard again and moved her pelvis slightly, up and down, up and down, until he matched her rhythm then overtook her. This time they came together and he shouted out loud.

Polly smiled into his shoulder. It had been fantastic in France but this was different. He had let himself go. He had surrendered to her.

Still sprawled on the sofa, he watched her as she stood up and straightened her skirt. She held out her hand and when he took it she pulled him to his feet.

'I'm going to go home. We might spoil it if I stay. Do you understand?'

He walked her out to the lift, rode down with her, holding her tight against him and looking into her eyes. When they hit the ground floor he let her go so suddenly that she nearly fell over. He stayed in the corner of the lift as she left and pressed the button to ascend before she had even reached the front door. She turned to see his long legs disappearing upwards.

It was just like it had been with Gracie Delaney, thought Hector. In France he had listened to Polly and she had succumbed to him. Tonight he had used his other trick. He had poured out his heart to her and once again she had surrendered.

Yet he hadn't meant to. He hadn't been aware of what he was

doing. He had reached out to her naturally, instinctively and, he realised, he wanted to again. You'll find someone, she had told him, and she had been right.

'What is so amazing is that you just don't need sex when you're really in love,' Luana informed Polly and Carla.

It was a glorious May day, the type of day when everyone assumes summer has arrived early and throws off their clothes to bask in the sunshine only to come down with a cold a few days later.

Carla had invited Polly and Luana to lunch on what she called her terrace. In fact it was a tiny square of paved roof leading off her kitchen, big enough for several tubs filled with the herbs Carla grew for her cooking, a little round wrought-iron table and two chairs. Luana had to perch on an upturned orange box.

She was a very different Luana these days, Polly observed. Gone were the skimpy black dresses, the bandage-like skirts that had barely reached her crotch, the black leather jacket, the giant crucifix, the DMs, the stilettos, the leggings, the tank tops that exposed her navel. In their place Luana now wore crisp white cotton shirts buttoned up to the neck and dress-for-success grey or taupe classic straight-leg trouser suits. Her long black tangled hair was harnessed in a sleek pony tail hanging down her back. She was even wearing a rope of pearls.

On top of everything she had been pontificating about love ever since she arrived. Normally Polly would have felt inclined to hit her but the warm weather made Polly feel so relaxed that she let Luana witter on uninterrupted. Carla, refusing all offers of help, was in the kitchen chopping and dicing and stirring sauces, and, Polly hoped, had the good fortune to be out of earshot.

'I just don't understand why none of you told me what it was like to be in love like this. Win and I are coming together on a spiritual plane every time we meet.'

'How often do you see him?' asked Polly, bored out of her skull, 'on this spiritual plane, I mean.'

'Three or four times a week.'

'Does he snore?'

'Polly, you know we don't do it. I don't spend the night with him. That's why our love is so special. It's not cheapened in any way.'

'You mean you don't have to worry if he snores or not?'

'You're just not trying to understand. He's the first man in my life who has respected me. I have discussed all my previous affairs with him, I haven't kept anything from him. He believes we should be able to communicate on a purely platonic level before we even think about sex. He says there is so much more to me than my body. He thinks I have a really creative mind and that I haven't even begun to use it.'

'Oh, by the way,' Polly interrupted, 'those jobs you were offered, how did you get on?'

'Win thought I shouldn't rush into anything just yet.'

'I thought you were supposed to have this creative mind. Does Win think you're fulfilling your creativity by taking phone messages for Clovis?'

'Polly, why can't you just listen? I'm being creative in other ways – for Win.'

'How?'

'I'm writing his new book with him.'

'He never told me that. He's writing a book on medieval Italian food from the first century AD. It's full of recipes from Cuminatum in Ostrea et Concilla and Lus in Dentice Asso Olus Molle or, if you prefer, oysters and mixed shellfish in cumin sauce and roasted sea bream with celery purée. I gave some of them to your grand-mother. God forbid, she's probably knocking them up in the kitchen as we speak. How has he got you involved?'

'Yes, I know, Polly, I'm typing it for him.'

'I see. Now that's what I call being very creative. I thought his manuscript was becoming easier to read. No wonder he doesn't want you running off to cast movies of your own.'

Carla emerged from the kitchen and climbed the four steps up to the roof terrace, struggling with a large tray over which she could barely see. She had made a mushroom risotto accompanied by a spinach salad, and she had heard every word Luana said.

'When I marry my Mauro I am supposed to be a virgin. I am a good Catholic girl. But on my wedding day I am not a virgin. I make love with my Mauro many many times before. We go into the countryside on a hot day like this and we make love on the ground, on the earth.' Carla raised her face to the sun and basked for a few moments, her eyes closed. Polly guessed she was remembering those days of early passion. The heat made Polly think of sex on the raft with Hector in the Baie des Millionaires. Carla continued: 'When we fucked – what's the matter, Luana? You think your generation invented fucking? – when we fucked before we were married, I thought my Mauro was the most exciting man in the world. I thought my life with him would be an adventure. But I was wrong. He was just a boy when we made love like that. When he became my husband and he grew into a man he became boring. Successful, yes, but boring. His sense of adventure left him. You know what happened? I think he passed it to Johnny. So what I am saying is who cares if you make love before or after you marry. You just have to make sure your man is not going to change when he does marry, that he keep his sense of adventure. Does Win have this sense of adventure?'

No, he's a pompous stuffed shirt, thought Polly, even if he is one of my clients.

'He's my hero in my adventure,' said Luana, and Polly thought she was going to throw up. To think Johnny had once worried about his little peachy girl having a reputation as a nymphomaniac.

'Polly doesn't have to worry.' Carla ladled risotto into large wide bowls, 'Johnny will always have adventures. He is too much. You need to have a rest from him sometimes.'

Polly had to admire the old lady. It was a diplomatic way of referring to the fact that her son had left Polly, not the other way around. She knew what Carla was getting at. When were Polly and Johnny going to get back together? But Polly was not going to be drawn into that discussion.

Carla leaned back in her chair.

'It's good to have you both with me. Here we are, three generations exchanging views about our men. I am feeling very modern, very Nineties as they say.'

Luana spoiled it as Polly had known she would.

'That's not quite right, Nanna. Polly's not my mother.'

It was very telling, Polly thought, that Carla had asked her and not Edith to the lunch.

'So how is your mother? Edith, who never calls me, never comes to see me like Polly does.'

'Well, you never liked her and she knows that,' protested Luana. 'Why didn't you like her?'

'It's hard to like someone when they don't know who they are. She did not know how lucky she was with Johnny, with you,' said Carla, 'but I wish her well. She is your mother. That's why I ask: how is she?'

'Oh, you don't need to worry about her. She's having a ball. She's out every day, she's going on spending sprees. She's buying all these things.'

'What things?' Polly and Carla demanded, almost in the same voice.

'Clothes. Then there's this new house Dad's bought for her, she's buying lots of furniture for that.'

'Who told you Johnny's bought her a new house?'

'She did. And he's paying for all those clothes. He has these charge accounts for her at Harvey Nichols and everywhere and that little apartment in Roland Gardens is getting chock-a-block with shopping bags. Don't worry about Mum, she's in heaven.'

Polly looked Carla straight in the eye. So much for your plans for me and Johnny getting back together, she thought. It's just as well I've got Hector to keep me warm.

As if to crown it all, Luana announced:

306

'Win thinks she's a truly elegant woman. He's crazy about her and she thinks he's 100 per cent right for me.'

'Then of course he must be,' said Carla; 'no question. Now, eat your risotto before it gets cold.'

'Don't eat too much,' said Polly drily, 'or else you won't be able to get into your virginal white wedding dress.'

'Oh, I've got tons of time,' said Luana, totally missing the irony. 'He hasn't even asked me to marry him yet.'

Polly had begun to read scripts for Hector. He was inundated with them following the success of *Mr Wrong* and Polly noticed he never looked at them but left them lying around his apartment. He was rather shamefaced when she tackled him about it.

'I just can't stand reading the bloody things. I never got the hang of it. I just leave it to my agent to recommend something but lately there have been so many he's just been sending them on. I'd better have a word with him.'

It wasn't until a script arrived heralded by a frantic message from Hector's agent on the answering machine that Polly began to understand the problem.

'Hec, are you there? OK, you're not. Listen, I'm sending over a script this afternoon and I've fixed a meeting tomorrow with the director. Hec, this man is a major player in Hollywood. We're bypassing casting directors on this one. This is your big chance. You're up for the part of the brother. Call me when you've read it.'

'What does he mean, this is my big chance? That's what he always says. Doesn't he realise I've made it?'

Polly said nothing. The director was a huge name. Surely Hector would take the part seriously.

Polly took the script from him and read it in just over an hour. Then she talked him through the part as well as the overall story.

She read a few scenes with him. He met with the director. He didn't get the part but as he and Polly had agreed before the meeting, he wasn't right for it. His agent had been blinded by the thought of his client working with such a big name.

From then on Polly read Hector's scripts for him and gave him advice. She was still lying in his bed on Saturday morning finishing a script when he went out to get the papers.

'Bring me a *Telegraph* and an *Independent*,' she yelled after him. She heard his front door bang and settled down to finish the script. After a while she grew restless. She looked around at the austere sleek lines of Hector's bedroom, the ubiquitous grey, the wall-to-wall cupboards, the total absence of Hector's possessions negating the stamp of an individual personality. How could she possibly work here even if it was just reading a script in bed? It was a beautiful summer's morning and she could have gone out on to the terrace overlooking the Thames but Hector's apartment was on the ninth floor and Polly was neurotic about heights. She thought with affection of the perpetual chaos spread across her trestle tables in her conservatory, leading safely out to the garden. Everyone always asked her how on earth she knew where anything was. The answer to that was simple. She knew exactly where everything was because she could see it all laid out before her.

While she put everything on display Hector hid it all away, and not just his possessions either. Their affair was a private one. Once when she took him to a signing session for one of her authors in a bookshop, Polly witnessed the effect he had on the public. His sudden appearance had rendered them first self-conscious, trying not to look at him, then, when someone had approached him, the rest had followed in a wild stampede to gather round him. Polly had found herself shut out to the extent that no one even realised she was with Hector. They had been seeing each other for nearly two months now but from that day she had avoided going out with him in public, which was just as well for it meant that neither Johnny nor Luana knew about their relationship.

At home alone with him it was hard to reconcile the insecure man who was becoming increasingly dependent on her with the public Hector idolised by his adoring fans. He may be lithe, he may move with animal grace, thought Polly, his bearing may be aristocratic even, but it's all part of his outer casing. The Hector I am beginning to know is little more than a clockwork toy who's been wound up and pointed in the right direction for fifteen years and now his mechanism is getting cranky and he doesn't know what to do.

Hector threw the newspaper at her from the bedroom door and it landed on her stomach. She heard the bathroom door slam and the sound of the shower running. Hector never showered until after they had made love and he always made love to her in the morning when they spent the night together. Something must be wrong.

She unfolded the paper and cursed him. He'd brought her the *Mail*. Then she saw why. Down in the right-hand corner of the front page was a grainy picture of an old man, dishevelled with a long beard, slumped against a wall and clutching a bottle in a brown bag. Even though the picture was blurred it was possible to see the abject misery on the man's face. But it wasn't the picture that caught Polly's eye. It was the headline above it:

CONWAY'S FATHER A DOWN AND OUT DRUNK

Shaking, she read the text below.

Movie idol Hector O'Neill's father is a down and out drunk who does not even know where his son is. A tramp who haunts the slum areas of the Pennsylvania town where O'Neill allegedly grew up (although he claims to have hailed from Boston) has been identified by journalist Joan Brock, biographer of Hector O'Neill, as Jimmy Maguire, O'Neill's father.

Arthur Allen-Jones, Publishing Director at Hollywood House who are bringing out the biography of O'Neill, said Joan Brock had confirmed she had tracked down O'Neill's father.

'She was very excited about her discovery,' said Allen-Jones. 'She had a lead which took her to a small defunct mining town in Pennsylvania where she met this man called Jimmy Maguire whom a woman friend of Hector O'Neill's from his early days in London identified as being his father. Maguire didn't recognise his son when shown a photograph of the actor. He told Joan

Brock he had gone to fight in Vietnam and when he returned he found his wife and son had fled. He never saw them again.

'The cheap bitch!' shouted Hector. He had a towel wrapped around his waist.

'Who?'

'Joan bloody Brock! Where did she get hold of this stuff? No one knows my father is called Jimmy Maguire. Nobody back home knows I've changed my name. I was a kid when I came over here. My mother's dead. Tony's parents are dead. No one knows who I am or where I came from.'

'Someone must have known,' Polly chatted on while trying to come to terms with the fact that from what Hector was saying, this miserable creature in the picture really was his father. 'They mention a woman from your early days in London who identified your father.'

'Gracie. Has to be. But Gracie could never be a bitch. It was that other prune mouth, that shitty little bundle of bones Joan Brock who turned on me. She must have wormed it out of Gracie somehow.'

'This man really is your father?'

'Everyone has one, Polly. Yours was a lord of the manor and mine's a drunken bum. You want to make something of it?'

'You know I didn't mean it like that. It's just you've never spoken about your father. You said your mother was dead and I suppose I assumed your father was too.'

'For all I knew he was.'

'How did you lose touch with him like that?'

'Read the piece. He went off to Vietnam.'

'But he came back. Where were you?'

'My mother ran off with someone else while he was away. An Englishman. That's how I wound up in England.'

'But didn't your father contact you when he got back from Vietnam?'

'He didn't know where we were. My mother never let him know. She even let me believe he'd been killed over there.'

'And this is the first time you've found out that he might still be alive?'

311

'More or less.'

'More or less. What does that mean?'

'It means I don't want to talk about it. It means I was born in a place I wanted to forget about. I loved my father, Polly. I know that now. I still have this one picture of him in my mind. He's coming home from the steelworks, he's coming over the hill with his buddies and he's got his lunchbox under his arm and he's laughing and bullshitting with them and he's happy. It was the only world he knew before Vietnam. My mother was the bitch. She left him and then she left me. But she was right. She had to survive. My father was a loser. Underneath I guess I'm still my father's son. But my mother made sure I became as much like her as possible. Keep an eye out for the main chance and grab hold of it.'

'But deep down you think you're probably like your father. Do you remember anything about him at all, apart from this picture you have of him?'

'He never spoke to women. He was scared of women.'

'But he liked them?'

'I never asked.'

Scared of women. Scared of getting close to them. That sounded like the Hector she was beginning to get to know.

He had picked up the phone and was dialling, punching the numbers angrily.

'Joan? You're a fucking bitch, you know that? Yeah, of course I've seen it, why else do you think I'm calling you? What? I don't care who told them. So what if it was Artie whatsisface. It was a shitty thing for him to do, I agree. Shitty for me not for you. He knows what he's doing. By planting this in the press way ahead of publication, he knows damn well it's going to make your book sell like crazy.'

When did he get to know Joan? thought Polly listening. When she interviewed him for that profile, of course, but why had Joan never talked about that?

'Yes, excuse me, you are a bitch. You know why? Because you had to go and put all that crap about my father in your book in the first place. How else would Artie have found out? That was a real petty way to get back at me, not that you had any reason. What did

312

I ever do to you? What? It was over, Joan. Three days! Christ! It was never anything serious. Like I said, we're both adults. It wasn't a question of me not wanting to be with you any more. A few nights together isn't being together. Wise up. Get a life.'

He put down the phone and Polly understood why Joan hadn't been returning her calls. Before Polly there had been Luana. And before Luana – or maybe even since – there had been Joan. Well, for once she seemed to have got the better of Joan in the man department. And why not, for heaven's sake? Suddenly Polly was seething. All these years Joan had been putting her down for not trying hard enough, making her feel she was badly groomed and too big when in fact she'd done just fine for herself. What's more she'd worn far better than Joan as the years had gone by. Johnny had always maintained Joan was jealous of her and for the first time Polly was inclined to believe him.

'By the way, this script's crap.' Polly threw it across the bed and got up to get dressed. 'You tell Joan to get a life, Hector. Don't think it's about time you got one of your own?'

For some time Polly had been feeling guilty about the fact that since her affair with Hector had blossomed she had been neglecting her authors. She had taken to reading film scripts rather than books in the evening and Mrs Flowers had begun to make rather a show of placing a pile of manuscripts in front of her each morning and asking:

'You haven't forgotten about these, have you, Mrs de Soto?'

When she first started her own agency Polly had fully intended only to take on those authors she liked, but she soon realised this was being naive. Yet she was constantly amazed at the way her least favourite authors managed to know exactly when she was below par and chose that time to call her *en masse*. There was one particular first-time woman author of a middlebrow novel which, of course, she thought of as literary, who whined daily down the line into Polly's ear.

'Poll-eee, I just don't think my readers will like this cover. It's too downmarket. It's not what they're expecting. They'll be disappointed.'

Polly was mystified as to how anyone who had not yet been published could actually have any readers.

Another arrogant young male writer seduced his publicist in a hotel room in Manchester in the middle of his author tour but by

314

the time they'd reached Edinburgh he'd gone off her. The publicist, having already telephoned her fiancé in London to break off her engagement, was now left high and dry and in floods of tears and refused to continue the tour. The publishers insisted that Polly sort her author out.

'What exactly do you want me to do?' Polly asked the hysterical editor in London. 'Go up there and tuck them both up in bed?'

'He should never have slept with our publicist in the first place. So unprofessional.'

'It's a bit late to say that now,' countered Polly reasonably. 'Besides, haven't you got it the wrong way round? What was she doing jumping into bed with him if she had a fiancé waiting for her in London?'

'But she won't work with him any more and we might lose him to another house,' wailed the editor.

'Then lose your publicist and keep your author.'

Zoë Nichols was a breath of fresh air, calling as she did with updates of her sightings of Aroma Ross.

'I was sitting there the other day in her hotel suite and she suddenly whips up her tank top and shoves her stomach in my face and she goes: "D'you like it?" Polly, I swear, I didn't know what to do. She's got the world's flattest most beautiful stomach. Why did she need my approval? Then I noticed this little diamond tucked in her tummy button and all I could think of was, "Ow, that must have hurt!" '

From time to time Polly had asked herself whether it was a good idea to have become so friendly with one of her clients. Then she would see Zoë for lunch or supper and have such a good time, and come away feeling so uplifted by Zoë's constant praise for her efforts, that she always banished her qualms. The only area where they skirted around each other, never actually coming to blows but never really saying what they felt in order to avoid just that, was the subject of men and relationships. Polly had confided in Zoë about Hector and waited for Zoë's endorsement of the affair. After all, Zoë had not been very encouraging about Polly's chances of getting back with Johnny. But Zoë seemed to see danger in any relationship with a man. She intimated that she had been blown up in too many emotional minefields and that now she valued her serenity at any cost, even if it meant a life devoid of excitement. However much Polly tried to persuade her that that was exactly how she, Polly, had felt after Johnny had left, and that things changed in time, Zoë would not be moved.

One client whose personal relationship did become a little too close for comfort was Winthrop Hamilton. Because he was so important in Luana's life Polly treated him with kid gloves and dreaded the day when any trouble might arise. Inevitably it did.

Winthrop had had a disastrous time with his last publishers. The work in question, a cookbook divided into four seasonal sections, had had a highly inexperienced copy-editor who had managed to place spring menus in the winter section and summer menus in the spring section throughout the book. Worse, she had mislaid several captions for the photographer and had been too terrified to own up to Winthrop and ask him to replace them. Instead she had looked at each photograph and taken a wild, sometimes highly imaginative guess at what it might be. Thus Winthrop's famous chocolate mousse found itself described as a pheasant terrine. Polly thought she had solved the problem by moving him to another publisher for his new book on medieval Italian food.

She hadn't. But through no fault of the publisher.

His editor rang in a panic.

'Polly, he's delivered the book. It's truly divine as far as it goes but we can't find the basic recipe section anywhere.'

'The what?'

'In each recipe Winthrop instructs us to "use the basic fresh pasta dough as described on page whatever in the section at the end of the book" or the basic dressing on page this or the basic bread recipe on page that. He keeps referring to them all the way through but he's gone and left them out. The book doesn't have a centre. Without this missing section it simply doesn't work.'

'And I suppose it was due at the printer yesterday. Have you tried asking Win for it?' Polly tried to be patient.

'Of course we have. It's not as simple as that. He's gone away to stay with some friends in Suffolk and they don't have a phone.'

'Well do you have an address?'

'Yes but by the time we write to him . . . we need the text today.'

'Give me the address. I'll drive there this afternoon and doorstep him till he hands it to me or comes back to London to find it.'

It was a sun-drenched August day. Perfect for a drive to the country. Polly called Luana.

'Suffolk? I thought he'd gone to Wiltshire. Oh I know, he's gone to see that sweet couple we went to stay with.'

'Without you?' Polly was guarded but curious.

'I'm frantic. I couldn't get away. Anyway he never takes me to Wiltshire. It's his bolthole. I'm assuming I'll get to see it when we're . . . anyway. I suppose he changed his mind at the last minute. He only went today. I expect he'll ring me tonight and tell me where he is.'

'I can't wait that long,' said Polly and explained why. 'Can you let me into his Chelsea house so I can have a peek there before driving all the way to Suffolk.'

'Oh, I couldn't. He'd hate anyone going through his things. He's very particular like that. I'm not allowed to touch anything. Besides, I don't have a key.'

Polly thought it very odd that Winthrop seemed to shut Luana out of so much of his life but since Luana didn't seem particularly worried, Polly didn't comment.

The drive to East Anglia gave her time to think. What to do about Hector? Her anger about his affair with Joan had enabled her to view him in a more detached light. As she drove – much too fast – through the flat countryside towards Newmarket she embarked upon a mental checklist for and against him. He was breathtakingly handsome and sophisticated on the outside but, as she was discovering, a rather childlike character underneath. He had no real taste. It had dawned on Polly rather belatedly that the beautiful house that had so impressed her on the boulevard du Cap had not been Hector's. He had rented it and the stunning interior decoration that came with it. As a companion he had no real depth, his conversation was becoming rather one note and there were times, increasingly, when he bored her. For example, he never made her laugh. True, he was terrific in bed but he had never heard of the concept of fidelity. He had been an attentive listener in the

317

past and that had indeed been flattering but, as she had become aware, that was part of his overall seduction plan. Now he was opening up to her, the tables had turned and she listened to him but the more she listened the less interested she became. Poor Hector. It seemed the one thing he had been intelligent enough to understand was that he was the perfect trophy lover. He looked good but it was best to leave it at that.

Yet somehow he was good for her. He had given her confidence to the extent that she was the one now pulling the strings in the relationship. She could walk away from it at any time, and as she realised that she also realised that she was not remotely in love with him.

On arriving at the village where Win was staying Polly checked the address. It was nowhere near where Luana said they had gone for the weekend. The house turned out to be a rose-washed timber cottage set at right angles to the road. Polly parked up a lane beside it next to a barn and walked around the house to the little porch.

The man who answered the door was in his early twenties and very neatly dressed in a pale green Lacoste shirt and white jeans. He was medium height and of very slender build with thin arms and legs. His hair was short at the back and parted in the middle with two curled locks caressing his temples. His skin was smooth like a baby's and lightly pink from the sun. He peeped – rather than peered – at Polly through round granny spectacles.

'Can I help you?'

He was American.

'Gracious,' said Polly, a little thrown, 'have I come to the right place? I'm looking for someone called Winthrop Hamilton.'

The young man's face lit up.

'Right place. You missed him. He left about an hour ago. He had a bit of a crisis on. He delivered his book to his publishers and he suddenly remembered he hadn't given them some of the text. He's gone back to London for the night to sort it out.'

'Great. I've come all the way to Suffolk to ask him to do just that. Well, at least it'll all be sorted out. Could I just use your phone to call his publishers and put their mind at rest? I'm Polly de Soto, his agent, by the way. Oh, of course, you don't have a phone here, do you?'

The preppy young man looked surprised.

'Sure. There's a phone. Why wouldn't there be? I'm Jed Wharton. Good to meet you. Win's talked about you. Come on through and make your call.'

It was a typical ultra-English country cottage with an inglenook fireplace and beams. The ceilings were too low in places for Jed to stand up. Large floral chintzes covered the sofas either side of the fireplace and the long velvet curtains were gathered up by tassled cord tiebacks. The roses in a circular glass bowl were beautifully arranged.

'Sit here, and there's the phone. Coffee? A drink? I've just made some lemonade.'

Polly nodded 'yes please' while she dialled. As she spoke to Win's editor she studied the photographs in silver frames either side of the rose bowl. They were both of Win with Jed on a beach. In one Win had his arm slung round Jed's shoulders.

'Win apparently left word that you weren't on the phone,' Polly told Jed when he returned with a pitcher of lemonade.

'Can't imagine why he would do that unless it was just to work-related people so he wouldn't be bothered.'

Polly was about to say that he hadn't even told his girlfriend but something stopped her.

'Are you and Win related?' She picked up one of the photographs. 'His mother's American, isn't she?'

'We met in America,' said Jed, 'but we're not related.'

'This is a sweet little cottage. Do you own it or have you rented it for the summer?'

Jed was like a bewildered marionette, raising his arms and letting them fall and shaking his head at the same time.

'I don't get it. Where did you get the idea that this is my place? It's Win's. He's rented it.'

'What on earth for?' Polly was so surprised she forgot to be polite. 'He has a house in London and a place in the country in Wiltshire.'

'So we can be together.'

'Are you working with him on a new project? Something I should know about? Maybe I could help.'

'The only thing you should know, and I'm sorry to drop it in your lap like this since I guess it might come as a shock, is that Win and I are lovers.'

When Polly didn't say anything he went on.

'It's so typical of Win to keep me a secret. As I'm sure you know, he's one of these people who keep their life totally compartmentalised. Lots of people do, but if you're part of that life it can be pretty hurtful. I've known him since I was at Yale. We met in the Hamptons when he was summering with his mom. I was there with my parents. We went off to Fire Island together and after that we met in New York. Frequently. I know nothing about his life in England but from your shocked reaction it looks as if he hasn't even come out. When I told him I was going to come to England for the summer he straight away rented this cottage and installed me here. I don't even get to come to London.'

'He's seeing my stepdaughter in London.'

'How cute. He dates girls, especially when his mother's around. He has these fantasies about getting married but he never goes through with it. How do you think it makes me feel?'

Polly had had enough. She wanted to get out of this snug little hidey-hole and away from Win's secret life and this polite young man who looked as if he might burst into tears at any second.

'I can imagine how it makes you feel and I'm sorry. If Win hadn't forgotten to include those pages in his book we would probably never have met. Maybe it was meant to happen. Will you say something to him about my coming here?'

'You know I think I will. I've had enough of being shunted into the background.'

'You do that, Jed, because I'm going to tell my stepdaughter. I have to. Who knows, maybe you'll have Win all to yourself from now on in a totally decompartmentalised world.'

'Yes, but will I like it?'

Polly laughed. She rather liked this young man. He'd obviously had to put up with a lot and he still had a glimmer of a sense of humour, which was more than she could say about Win.

But how was she going to tell Luana?

Luana took it very badly indeed and only rallied slightly when Johnny offered to take her to Paris for the French première of *Mr Wrong* to cheer her up. Polly thought fondly how kind Johnny could be sometimes. She imagined him in Paris embarrassing Luana by insisting on speaking his execrable French. Johnny had to be the only Italian who spoke French with the worst possible English accent. He began every sentence with the word 'Alors' on which he never failed to sound the 's'.

But it wasn't his French that let him down. Luana called Polly as soon as she got back.

'I had the worst time,' she wailed down the line, 'the worst! Dad was just awful.'

'But why?'

'First off he was in a foul mood because Hector pulled out of the trip and the French were really pissed at him and took it out on Dad.'

Polly opened her mouth to spring to Hector's defence and explain that the news about his father had sent him into a terrible depression and remembered just in time that Luana didn't know she was seeing Hector.

'Yes, I can imagine that must have been a bit awkward. Then what happened?'

'Well, it wasn't so much what happened, it was more that this little jaunt was supposed to be about cheering me up and Dad did nothing but talk about himself. I tried to talk about how I was feeling but he just doesn't listen. It's like he took me over there so he could tell me about his problems.'

'What are his problems?' Poor Luana. At least Hector listened, if for all the wrong reasons.

'The Big Question is what's he going to do next. How is he going to follow *Mr Wrong*? Apparently Juanita doesn't have a clue about scripts and keeps getting excited about these real pieces of shit. Dad's words. And she won't agree to hiring a script editor so he's having to plough through all this stuff himself. Do you know what,

Polly? I don't think Dad knows a good script when he sees one either. Do you remember *The Wolf One*?'

'He told me you were crazy about that idea.'

'Oh, please! No, the truth is Dad needs someone like you. He kept going on and on about you, asking me how often I saw you, how did I think you were, did I know if you were seeing anyone? I mean I adore you, Polly, but I did get a bit sick of listening to him go on about you. It was weird. Maybe he wants you back.'

'As a wife or a script reader?' laughed Polly. Because if it was the latter she already had a job.

Polly was secretly relieved when Hector announced he was making a trip to Pennsylvania to see his father. Familiarity was breeding far too much contempt. Sex with Hector gave her an extraordinary energy and sense of well-being but beyond that he was beginning to drive her insane.

Yet she was touched by his excitement at being reunited with his father.

'There was always something missing from my success all the way down the line and that was that I didn't have anyone to share it with. I didn't have my mother and father to be proud of what I'd done. Now I have you but you can understand, can't you, what it's going to be like to sit down with my dad and tell him everything. I can barely remember that place. I'm prepared for it to be a real dump even though they closed the steelworks, but I'm going to do right by my dad now I know he's alive.'

'Have you let anyone know you're coming? It's going to be something of a shock for him to see you after all these years.'

'I've called Gracie. Gracie Delaney, you know, my friend who went back to Philadelphia. She's been looking out for him, going over there whenever she can.'

'But why?' Polly didn't get it.

'Search me. Guess some people are like that.' But Hector wouldn't look her in the eye. 'All I need to know, Polly, is that you'll be waiting for me when I get back.'

'Where else am I going to be? Zoë's book's about to be published. And Mrs Flowers'. I'm not going anywhere.'

'You just don't get it, do you? Are you doing it deliberately? I'm trying to tell you that I love you and I want you to be here for me when I get back. I know you're really busy at the moment otherwise I'd ask you to come with me. I'm scared shitless at the thought of going back, don't you see? I ought to be going home like a conquering hero, the hometown boy who made good. Instead all anyone's going to be thinking is how come he never looked after his dad? I don't even sound American any more. It's as if I never existed there.'

He looked terrible. Polly knew he had been agonising over his father ever since Artie Allen-Jones' leak to the press of the contents of Joan's book but he had refused to talk to her about it. Now he was telling her – probably the first time he had told anyone – that he loved her. He needed her. Maybe that was what it was all about: mutual needing. Filling a gap in the other person's life. Maybe she was expecting too much of him. Maybe it was her fault, not his, that she had been growing bored with him. He was younger than she was. She always forgot that. Perhaps now she knew how insecure he was inside she could work at building his confidence. Maybe it was her fault that he seemed one-dimensional. She just hadn't been trying hard enough with him. She had met him as a glamorous movie star, reacted to him on the rebound as a sensational lover, been disappointed that his glamour was only skin deep and now, at a traumatic time in his life when he was trying to show her the man underneath, her response was to be irritated. She was being unfair. It wasn't even as if there was anyone else offering her a better deal.

She drove him out to the airport, stood proudly to one side as he signed a mass of autographs and then clung to him in the First-Class lounge.

'Of course I'll be here when you get back. Call me as soon as you can and let me know what's happening.'

He went through the gate and turned back to wave at her but all she could see was the figure audiences all over the world saw on screen. Someone so handsome it was hard to imagine he could be real.

He didn't call.

For the first few days Polly didn't worry. She hadn't even asked him for a number, so sure had she been that he would call her. When a week had gone by and she still had no word she called his agent, who was the only person who knew of their relationship.

'Yeah, I spoke to him. He's fine. Worked out exactly as we planned.'

'What do you mean?' asked Polly.

'When this whole thing broke about his father, I got him together with his publicist and we said Hec, you have to go out there, be reunited with the man. He didn't want to at all, said "What's the point? My father doesn't even know me" and all that crap, but when I explained to him what a good publicity story it would make, how we'd get the press there and turn the whole thing to his advantage, get his father all cleaned up, show Hec with his arm around him, buying him a new house, all that stuff, he loved it. Hec's no fool. He knows that Brock woman's raking up all kinds of dirt about him and if he can show her stories to be crap before the book's even come out then he's ahead of her game. She can say anything about him and he'll be right there proving her wrong. That Allen-Jones character played right into our hands.'

Polly read the stories in the papers the following week. It was exactly as the publicist had predicted. There was Hector with his arm round his father who had indeed been shaved and fitted out with suitable clothing. The older man looked bewildered, Polly noted, as well he might. There was even a snapshot of father and son taken when Hector was barely five years old with the steelworks looming in the background.

Hector talked of his shame in lying about his background by pretending that he came from Boston. He expounded on his theory that everyone had to face up to who they really were at some time in their life and his time had come. Columns of syrupy prose turned Polly's stomach as she remembered that she had actually felt sorry for Hector.

What most astounded Polly was the revelation that he had been reunited not only with his father but also with his childhood sweetheart, Gracie Delaney. Gracie, now a lonely divorcee, had apparently been overjoyed when Hector had come home and had welcomed him with open arms. The couple were said to be talking seriously about their future.

Another publicity stunt, wondered Polly, or should someone warn this woman to stay away from Hector? No, let her learn from experience. We all need a Mr Wrong – if only to show us who is Mr Right.

Polly was dreaming about tape recorders when she was awakened at two in the morning by the sound of her front doorbell blasting persistently through the house.

She had been at Zoë's publication party, or rather Aroma Ross's. Zoë had needed her support. She was having a hard time controlling her temper with the book's publishers, who had released some cock and bull story to the press about Aroma having dictated the novel on to tapes which had then been transcribed by Zoë into the book.

'Yes, Aroma had a little tape recorder. Yes, she did say she would be recording stuff for me on transatlantic flights and who knows, maybe she did, but I have never received a single tape from her. Aroma's so out of it half the time she probably believes she really has done it all herself via tapes. What irritates me is that the publishers can't keep their story straight. One minute they announce I'm writing it with Aroma, the next minute there's no mention of me whatsoever, I feel really tempted to start stirring it up by . . .'

Polly had calmed her down and led her away from the party. She had seen this coming. Zoë wouldn't regret it in the long run once the royalties started rolling in. The publishers had, after all, done a great job marketing the book. She had had enormous fun doing the research and writing it. She bore no grudge against Aroma and her agent, whom she had liked. It was the publishers' lack of attention to the ghostly details that had understandably enraged her. Either she was a ghost or she wasn't. The pre-publication press had been snide and nasty and it looked like poor Zoë was in for plenty of flak without any credit.

Besides, Polly felt bound by guilt to be especially mindful of Zoë's needs. Hadn't Zoë warned her that men were not worth the trouble they caused? And hadn't she been proved right by Hector's defection? From now on Polly resolved to listen to Zoë and take all men with a fistful of salt.

A rain of pebbles clattered against her window.

Johnny was standing in the street with his long black coat over his pyjamas, his baseball cap on his head back to front as usual, and Zutty in his arms. Half asleep, Polly opened the window and instantly regretted it.

'Polly, let me in. Please.'

'Fuck it, Johnny. I am not having Zutty at this hour. Go home and call me in the morning.'

She slammed the window shut. No sooner was she back under the covers than the pebbles started again. Then the doorbell. Then more pebbles. She could hear Johnny through the closed window, shouting away in the street.

'Christ's sake, Polly. It's an emergency. You have to let me in. It's Joan. She's had an accident.'

She gave him a stiff whisky and tried to prise Zutty from his arms without success.

'Johnny, you can't drink and hold Zutty. Hand him over and I'll give him something to eat.'

'He's all I've got,' she heard him mumble. Who left whom? went through her mind but she kept it to herself.

'So what's happened to Joan? You wake me up in the middle of the night. It'd better be good.'

'She's dead, Pol. She was on the motorway driving back from doing an interview somewhere and they think she must have run out of petrol. They found her car with an empty tank by the side of the road. Silly cow must have been trying to flag down a passing car

327

in the middle of the road by the looks of things. She got hit. Strawberry jam all over the M6.'

'Johnny!' Polly was horrified.

'Sorry, Pol. I wasn't her number one fan but I shouldn't be so flippant. Was she still your best friend?'

'I don't really know,' said Polly, too shocked for tears.

'You haven't even asked how I know. The police couldn't find a next of kin. She didn't have an address book on her, just one of those personal organisers and they didn't know how to work it so they came up with the idea of calling some chap called Artie Allen-Jones because they'd seen his name in the papers quoting her about Hector's father. So anyway he goes and tells them no, you don't want to talk to me, you want to talk to the agent, Polly de Soto. So they get your office number and there's just a machine and then they check out Enquiries and would you believe there's only one other De Soto in the book besides me and his initial is E so they call the poor bugger first and wake him up, then they try me, "J", and I say yes, I'm Polly de Soto's husband – well, I am, Pol, don't look at me like that – and they ask me if I knew a Miss Joan Brock and I suss what's happened right away by the "knew" and ask if I can be the one to break the news to you. I didn't think you'd like the police turning up on your doorstep.'

'Thank you, Johnny.'

'There's a bit more to it than you think.'

'Bit more to what?'

'Someone has to identify the body.'

'*No*! I couldn't, not if she's all, like you said . . .'

'Would you like me to do it?'

'Johnny, could you? Would they let you?'

'I think they would.'

'Could you bear it? It's probably a gruesome task.'

'It is.'

'You mean you've had to do it before?'

'In a way.'

'Who with?'

'Edith.'

328

'Edith's *dead*! Christ, Johnny, why didn't you ever tell me? Why didn't Luana tell me?'

'Take it easy. She's not dead. It was all a mistake that happened years ago. The police in Cornwall rang me. Don't bloody know why. I'm not her husband but she had me down as her next of kin. They said she'd taken an overdose but, typical Edith, apparently she'd got herself all dolled up in one of her long white nighties and taken herself out to die some kind of idiotic pagan ritual death lying on the grass on the top of the cliffs. So, of course someone saw her and she was taken to hospital. They thought she was going to pop her clogs and called me. I hurtled all the way down there and it was like something out of *Casualty*. They come running straight at me as soon as I walk through the door, tell me my wife has died, how they did all they could for her, etc. etc. and would I please identify her for them. I'm marched into this cordoned-off cubicle and there's this total stranger lying on a gurney all mangled to pieces. But her face is intact and it's not Edith's. They made a right cock-up.'

'But Edith did take an overdose?'

'She did.'

'Was she depressed?'

'How should I know?'

'Don't be so defensive, Johnny. What I mean was, did she have a history of depression?'

Now was his chance to tell her about Edith.

'Polly, Edith was stark raving bonkers. I never told you before because, frankly, I didn't think it was any of your business. I thought I ought to be the one to deal with her, I could take care of everything. I was playing what Luana calls my all-embracing Italian father role to the hilt, trying to be a father to Edith as well as to her. I didn't want anyone else getting in on the act. Besides, I thought you'd think I was heartless for leaving her. Except I didn't leave her. That was the whole problem. *She* left and somehow I just couldn't bring myself to go and get her back. I knew someone ought to look after her. I thought I could handle it by flitting down there every now and again and, yes, lying to you about it. But I was wrong, I realise that now. I knew Luana shouldn't spend too much time with her, that it was wrong for her to see Edith how she was.

That's why I let her come and live with us. And then you had to go and be successful and I kept thinking that's made it even worse for Edith. She never could do anything, couldn't keep a job down. Poor Edith! Out on the cliffs in her nightie. You were always a T-shirt-to-bed girl. Still are, I see. Edith wore these long diaphanous things with bits of lace all over the shop. She put flowers in her hair to go to bed, for Christ's sake, said she could commune with nature while she slept. Fine for her but I was always waking up with a bloody dandelion in my ear or a cornflower in my mouth.'

Polly let him ramble on. It all came pouring out and she pretended she was hearing it for the first time.

'She looked pretty glamorous to me at the première. Have you been seeing a lot of her since she moved back to London?'

'As little as possible. Now it looks as if I'm going to have to do something serious about her.'

'What do you mean?'

'She's gone completely over the edge. It's all the more frightening because when you see her she appears perfectly normal but she's not. She's going – there's no other word for it – insane. She's got these crazy delusions. She thinks she's very rich, fabulously rich. She's under the illusion that I'm giving her money, loads of it. She goes into shops and buys clothes that cost a fortune. We're talking thousands of pounds' worth. She tells people I've bought her a new house and she's running round London shopping for that. Her cheques are bouncing all over the place and because she keeps on citing my name, I've had a visit from the police. She's going to be declared bankrupt. That's a given. I'm not responsible for her financially but what can I do? I can't let her starve. Her parents are dead. She won't go and see a doctor, any kind of doctor. The awful thing is that she thinks she's totally cured and she's not. She's dangerously ill. Several people have told me she's going to have to be committed but if she is, who's going to commit her?'

He looked so forlorn sitting there on the sofa in his pyjamas. He was so untogether, so un-looked-after. Yet here he was taking responsibility for identifying Joan and coping with the demented Edith. He might never listen but no one could accuse Johnny of being unkind. She felt a rush of affection for him and sat down

330

beside him, wrapping her arm around his shoulder, trying to give him a comforting hug. To her amazement, he turned his face into her chest and began to sob.

'Blubbing again, Johnny?' she whispered softly.

'I'm not blubbing,' he insisted, sniffing and snorting into her neck.

'No, of course you're not,' she smiled into the darkness above his head.

'I came round here to comfort you about Joan and here you are mopping me up.' He raised his head and looked up at her. Their lips were almost touching. She lowered her head. He opened his mouth.

She had never forgotten Johnny's kisses. Long melting kisses that went on for ever until everything else was obliterated from her mind.

'I have to go,' he murmured. 'Wish I didn't.'

She risked the question she'd always wanted to ask.

'Did you love Edith, Johnny?'

He put his baseball cap back on his head, buttoned up his overcoat, told Zutty to 'Stay here and look after Pol', then he laid his head briefly on Polly's shoulder.

'Not like I love you, Pol, but yes, once, I must have done.'

He was out of the door before it hit her.

He'd said, 'Not like I love you.'

Very present tense.

Polly had witnessed authors come unstuck when their book was published. The sheer anti-climax of it all was often enough to pitch them into the depths of gloom. For weeks there would be the publishers' hype and anticipation of sales, the publicity, the celebration party and then suddenly the book was out there in the shops and after all the fuss the author had to go home and begin the agonising wait to see what happened to it. And these were the authors who were fêted by their publishers and the press. Some authors just sat at home.

Mrs Flowers' publication went to her head. Literally. She rushed out to the hairdresser's on the day of her publication dinner and returned with a disgusting blue rinse which looked like a cotton wool special effects halo on top of her head.

The dinner given by Odeon Books at Christopher's restaurant in Covent Garden for the publication of *Christopher* the novel was a rather grand affair with several rival, self-important literary editors showing off to each other and being rather patronising to the author. As a result Mrs Flowers grew nervous and drank so much that Polly had to slip her away before the end of the dinner.

In addition the press opted to focus on the story of a staid older woman writing about sex.

But *Christopher* sold out of its first printing in less than a week, and kept going. Mrs Flowers booked herself a cruise.

At any other time Polly would have been overjoyed but everything was clouded by Joan's death. To Polly's amazement she learned that Joan had left her her house. When she went there for the first time since Joan's death and sat on her high brass bed – Joan had had to use library steps to climb into it – and stared at her walk-in closet, Polly wept. The doors were open and Joan's immaculate size 8 suits and dresses hung in a row like toy soldiers. Underneath stood a line of tiny high-heeled shoes with toes pointing inwards almost as if Joan were still standing in them.

Overflowing ashtrays covered every surface, severely out of kilter with the stultifying neatness everywhere else. Polly could smell the smoke, could hear Joan's husky voice demanding fiercely: 'Well? Any sex? Any cheques?'

On Joan's desk beside her Apple Mac, downstairs in her office, Polly found a typescript. A fax was attached to it.

> Dear Joan,
> Can we call it a day? I'm off to France
> to begin filming in a month or so. It
> was fun but it was really only a fling.
> Let's be adults and put it behind us as a
> terrific memory.
>
> > Hector

Not even 'love, Hector.'

The book – as far as it went – was vicious. Polly had assumed it would be a hatchet job but she was not prepared for the sheer vitriol that had dripped from Joan's long red nails as she tapped away at the keys of her computer.

The real revelation was from Gracie Delaney, the alleged childhood sweetheart, whom Hector had not met until he was grown up and living in London. The most damaging section was where Gracie recalled how she had been asked by Hector to go and find his father, how she had written to Hector begging him to do something about the washed-up Vietnam vet, and how Hector had ignored her pleas.

Polly wondered what the real story was about the reunion between Hector and Gracie. There was one scenario in her head that would not go away. Hector, knowing that Gracie must have told Joan everything, had gone all out to charm his way back into her life so that they could present a united front to the world when the book came out and deny everything Joan had written.

The book was unfinished. Even if it were completed by someone else and published it could only hurt poor Gracie Delaney, whoever she was. And try as she might, Polly found she didn't really want to hurt Hector with it either. She was an adult. She had walked into her affair with Hector with her eyes wide open and she could not deny that she had derived a fair amount of enjoyment from it.

Polly took the typescript down to the end of Joan's tiny patch of garden and made a little bonfire out of it. On top of everything else, she was more than happy to cause problems for Artie Allen-Jones, who would now find himself with a big hole in his spring publishing programme.

Joan's funeral was a nightmare.

No one turned up except Polly and the faithful Victor, the crime reporter from Nottingham who had been in love with Joan for twenty years. Not a single editor for whom Joan had written countless pieces had shown his or her face; her parents were long since dead and she had been both an only child and childless. Not even her ex-husband had made the effort to come. Somehow, standing in the gloomy chapel, Polly became convinced that Joan knew no one had turned up to say goodbye to her. Polly simply could not bear the pathos of it. Poor Joan. She had never given up, waking up every day with the expectation of cheques and sex in no particular order and never understanding Polly's priorities which were food, affection, work probably in exactly that order.

As Joan's coffin was lowered into her grave there was a sudden scrabbling in the earth and a ball of red and white fur charged towards the hole.

'Zutty! Come here, for God's sake.'

Johnny had arrived. Late, but at least he'd come and his baseball cap was the right way round for once as a mark of respect.

Not that he'd ever had much respect for Joan, as he hastened to point out.

'It's you I've come for, Pol. Thought you might need a bit of support. Couldn't stand the woman myself but I know she meant something to you. Lord knows why.'

'Johnny, get Zutty out of there before they go and bury him too. You do realise it's all over, don't you? Bit pointless to come at all.'

Polly knew she was sounding shrewish. She couldn't help it. Joan was gone. There would be no more competitive lunches. There would be no one to keep her up to the mark, no one to chivvy her into finding a man and smartening up her act.

'Take it easy, Pol.' Johnny put his arm around her shoulders.

'I'm sorry, Johnny. I'm going to miss her so much. I know you think she was a cow and in many ways you were right but for some reason I needed her approval. She mattered to me. She was spiky and difficult and I suppose she wasn't as smart as she thought she was but she had what they call edge. I don't care if she was a bitch. Give me a bitch any day rather than some mousy little twit who's going to bore me to tears.'

Johnny was looking at her with interest.

'That's a bit strong for you, Pol. I thought you were the caring, sharing type.'

'Well, I've wised up. It's good to trust people in your life but you shouldn't rely on them. The only person you can rely on is yourself. Yet in a way I could always rely on Joan. One thing about her, she was constant. She never changed.'

'How did you get here?'

'In that great big black car. Joan left money for her funeral. The awful thing was that she left enough money to cater for at least fifty people coming to it and look how many turned up.'

'Who's that funny-looking bloke walking away?'

'That's Victor. Joan claimed he loved her and I never believed her but I do now. I've never seen a man cry like that.'

'I'll give you a lift back home. You can't sit all by yourself in that Bentley or would you like Zutty to keep you company? He really . . .'

335

'Yes, I know, he really adores me even though he ignores me half the time. No, you can drive me home, Johnny.'

'What's happened about Edith?' Polly asked tentatively as they approached the Shepherd's Bush roundabout.

'She's in hospital, you know, a clinic. The police called me in the middle of the night at the end of last week. First Joan, then Edith.'

'Edith had an accident too?'

'Not exactly. They found her wandering up the Old Brompton Road at two in the morning in her nightdress. She was so out of it we were able to get her straight into hospital and then I got a doctor to see her and get her admitted to this place. I don't know what'll happen from here. No, it's Luana I'm worried about now.'

'Still pining for Win?'

'Not in the slightest. She's met someone new.'

'And?'

'She's madly, passionately, totally in love with him.'

'Of course she is. Why should anything change? Have you met him?'

'No, but I know all about him. He's in advertising. He's extremely successful. He's a good-looking guy even by my standards as to who's good enough for my little peachy girl.'

'But?'

'He's married. Very married, whatever she thinks. It has to end in tears.'

'With Luana it always has to end in tears. I'm sorry to say this, Johnny, but I think that's what she gets off on.'

'What does she get off on?'

'Being a victim. I don't think she's ever had a married man before. It had to happen.'

'Well, Jesus Christ, what will she move on to next?'

'Axe murderers.'

'Now I think you're going to have to ask me in for a drink to help me get over the shock.'

Polly couldn't get the front door open. Johnny took her keys from her and tried again but he couldn't get it to budge.

'Fucking hell!' he said suddenly. His fingers were covered in wet paint. 'Polly, you might have told me you'd had the door painted.

It's blown shut with wet paint on it. No wonder it's stuck. Don't tell me, it's . . .'

'Arnold Pinner!' they shouted together.

'Got your back-door key, Pol?'

She shook her head.

'Don't worry, I have.'

'I thought I took your keys off you.'

'The front door keys, yes.'

Without thinking she took him up to the little sitting room on the first floor. He wandered about while she poured him a drink, making irritating comments about what she'd done to the room. Finally he sat down.

'So were you a bit cut up when Hector went off to Pennsylvania?'

'Why would I be cut up?'

'Because you had a thing with him.'

Polly sat down too. Rather suddenly.

'How did you know?'

'I know you. I know what happens to your skin and your eyes when you've had good sex. It started in France, didn't it?'

Polly nodded, not looking at him. 'Didn't you mind?'

'It was none of my business who you slept with. I was the one who left in the first place. I couldn't very well dictate who you had sex with after that.' He thumped the cushions between them. 'But why on earth would you choose Hector O'Neill? The man is such a total bore.'

'I know.'

'You know? Well, what made you have anything to do with him?'

'You didn't want me. He was there.'

'Just like that? And who says I didn't want you? Don't you realise I've regretted leaving you since the day I left? Or rather the night I left. Didn't it occur to you that I might have made a terrible mistake?'

This was typical Johnny. Trying to make her feel guilty for his mistakes.

'So there was never anything between you and Juanita?'

'There was – and still is – a great deal between me and Juanita.

It's called a business partnership. Although I'm considering walking out on her in the middle of the night too, she's so useless when it comes to recognising a good script.'

'And you, of course, are an expert.' Polly couldn't resist it.

'No, but you probably are. Why don't you come in with us, Pol? Make it a sideline to your agency, scout for properties for us, read scripts. After all, that's what you were doing when I first met you.'

'I've moved on a little since then.' Was that all he wanted from her? Someone to read scripts for him?

'I know that, Pol. You've moved on a lot. In fact, I don't know where you get the energy, frankly. The thought of producing another movie fills me with dread. I'm an old man now, Pol. I need someone to look after me.'

'Do you?'

'I do. I absolutely do. Why are you sitting so far away from me? Come on, give us a kiss.'

Zutty interrupted them, demanding to be fed.

'I suppose you want something too?' Polly asked Johnny. He sat up and begged, imitating Zutty, and she hit him on the head with a cushion. He bobbed about behind her in the kitchen as she cooked, driving her mad.

'What's that? Don't put too much salt in. Got to think of my sodium intake. Can I have some of this pâté? Are you going to make a salad? What's for dessert?'

He gobbled, had seconds and eyed her until she gave him what was left of it.

'That was great, Pol. Now I'm going to watch the news.' She loaded the dishwasher and went upstairs to find him in her bed with the TV blaring. She picked up a manuscript and climbed in beside him. It was as if he'd never left.

Until she found the manuscript taken out of her hands and placed on the floor beside the bed.

'I've missed you so much, Pol,' he told her as he made love to her. 'You were meant to beg me to come back the day after I left except you became such a hard-bitten old career woman I suppose you never gave me another thought. Don't you realise that I've been waiting for some kind of signal from you.'

'What kind of signal?' Polly's voice was muffled as Johnny pressed her face into his chest.

'The kind of signal you're giving me now.' He released her for a second and then clasped her face in both hands and kissed her endlessly until she wriggled out of her underwear and jerked the remote at the television to turn it off. Since he seemed reluctant to let go of her even for an instant, Polly unzipped Johnny's jeans for him and pushed them down over his buttocks. She could feel the moist tip of his erect penis protruding from his Y fronts. His tongue was still stroking the inside of her mouth, building up a steady rhythm with her own. They lay locked together. Every now and then Polly would begin to open her legs but he held her at bay, tantalising her until she could stand it no longer and in one urgent movement she flung a leg over him and drew him into her.

Afterwards he fell asleep beside her, Zutty curled up in a ball between them, his bushy tail covering his nose like a fox, and she lay awake in a state of panic. Johnny had come almost immediately, which meant that unlike her he probably hadn't had sex with anyone for a long time, but even so he had given her a taste of the Johnny she used to know.

Trust Johnny to place the onus on her to ask him to come back. He might have left in the first place but of course it was still up to her to climb down. He might joke about having made a mistake in leaving her but he'd rather die than admit it for real. Well, she could play that game too. She'd make sure she was up in the morning before him and hard at work, incommunicado in the conservatory, if he came looking for her. Let him sweat for a while.

Besides, did she really want him back? He would be as infuriating as ever, probably even more so. If she agreed to read scripts for him and help him in any professional capacity whatsoever she knew perfectly well he would take unspeakable advantage of her. Her life would no longer be her own until he had another project to produce. Even if he wasn't around during the day he would be calling her all the time to find out what she was doing, demanding this, suggesting that. If she didn't love the conservatory so much, she would offer to give Johnny back his house and go and live in Joan's. But she knew it would destroy her to live in Joan's house with all its memories of her. She supposed she could offer it to Johnny. No, she couldn't. But what about Luana? She needed a decent place to live. And if Johnny did come back he wouldn't need it anyway. But if he came back it would be with all the baggage that went with him. Was it worth it?

She got her answer when she awoke and found he had crept out of bed in the middle of the night and slipped away once more while she slept so he wouldn't have to discuss it.

She was devastated.

Arnold Pinner rang the front doorbell at eight o'clock the next morning while Polly was sipping coffee in the kitchen and pressing ice-cold oranges from the fridge to her eyes to reduce the puffiness from two hours' crying.

She went to the door and then remembered it wouldn't open. As she bent down to speak to Arnold through the letterbox, there was a crunching sound and the door was winched open. Arnold stood there looking very pleased with himself.

'Mr de Soto asked me to come and sort you out. That should do you, missus.'

Behind him stood Johnny surrounded by a mass of luggage. He had Zutty in his arms. He handed him to Polly.

'Zutty insisted that he couldn't live without you. He's been on at me for ages about it. I finally couldn't take it any longer so here we are. Oh, Christ, Pol, not blubbing again!'

Essential Revision Notes for the Cardiology KBA

EDITED BY

Ali Khavandi
Consultant Interventional Cardiologist,
Written while at Bristol Heart Institute

OXFORD
UNIVERSITY PRESS

UNIVERSITY PRESS

Great Clarendon Street, Oxford, OX2 6DP,
United Kingdom

Oxford University Press is a department of the University of Oxford.
It furthers the University's objective of excellence in research, scholarship,
and education by publishing worldwide. Oxford is a registered trade mark of
Oxford University Press in the UK and in certain other countries

British Library Cataloguing in Publication Data

Published in the United States of America by Oxford University Press
198 Madison Avenue, New York, NY 10016, United States of America

Data available

Library of Congress Control Number: 2013946135

ISBN 978-0-19-965490-1

Printed in Great Britain by
Clays Ltd, St Ives plc

Preface

I conceived the idea for this book (and the accompanying MCQ book) in 2009 as a Specialist Registrar at the Bristol Royal Infirmary. After some initial speculative emails to prospective contributors, conversations with colleagues, and concept development, the project was formally established in 2010.

Reflecting on my own needs at the time as a cardiology trainee there appeared to be an obvious gap. I was part of the first cohort to sit the Knowledge Based Assessment (KBA) but as well as a revision text I wanted a single accessible core textbook to form the knowledge foundation throughout my specialist training and everyday clinical practice.

It became clear that such a book did not exist. At one end of the spectrum there were well established, large volume, highly detailed reference textbooks with chapters authored by international experts, and at the other end concise specialist pocket handbooks, but nothing current in between. At MRCP level we had all become familiar with certain well recognized and trusted revision books which had formed our foundation for core knowledge. Why didn't something similar exist for cardiology?

The vision was to produce an easily accessible, concise yet comprehensive cardiology textbook based on the curriculum, which would become a core knowledge foundation for cardiology trainees. This could then be supplemented with the latest evolving guidelines, research information, and expert opinion.

A further observation had been that books written by experts can sometimes end up being inaccessible or intimidating as their outlook on the subject is very different from someone starting out. This concept is fundamental to this book, which is written by senior trainees or new consultants with empathy for training cardiologists, but with validation and refinement from senior experts. This can be seen in the author structure for each chapter, and the structure of the book is an exact mirror of the national cardiology curriculum (which also has very close parallels to the European curriculum).

The two biggest challenges have been to coordinate a large number of authors and to keep pace with a fast moving cardiology landscape and international guidelines. After a 4 year journey it is exciting to see the original vision come true with a textbook that can develop and evolve with cardiologists and the exciting world of cardiology. I am grateful for the hard work and enthusiasm of all the authors and contributors involved.

Ali Khavandi

Contents

Contributors

Aruna Arujuna
Clinical Research Fellow, Guy's and St Thomas'
Hospital NHS Foundation Trust, London
Chapter 9—Atrial fibrillation

Daniel Augustine
Cardiology Specialty Trainee Bristol Heart Institute
and Cardiovascular Research Fellow, Division of
Cardiovascular Medicine, University of Oxford
Chapter 5—Valvular heart disease

Stephen G. Ball
BHF Professor of Cardiology, University of Leeds
Chapter 12—Hypertension

Palash Barman
Speciality Trainee, Derriford Hospital, South West
Cardiothoracic Centre, Plymouth
Chapter 7—Supraventricular tachycardia

Andreas Baumbach
Consultant Cardiologist, Bristol Heart Institute
Chapter 32—Invasive and interventional cardiology

Nigel S. Beckett
Consultant Physician, Guy's & St Thomas' Hospitals,
Honorary Senior Lecturer, Imperial College London
*Chapter 11—Primary and secondary prevention of
cardiovascular disease*

N.G. Bellenger
Consultant Interventional Cardiologist, Director of
Cardiology, Clinical Lead for CMR, Royal Devon and
Exeter Hospital NHS Foundation Trust, Senior
Lecturer Exeter Medical School
Chapter 29—Magnetic resonance imaging

Andrew Bishop
Consultant Cardiologist and Medical Director,
Hampshire Hospitals NHS Foundation Trust,
Basingstoke
*Chapter 19—Assessment of patients with
cardiovascular disease prior to non-cardiac surgery*

Edward Blair
Consultant Clinical Geneticist, Department of
Clinical Genetics, Oxford Radcliffe Hospitals NHS
Trust
Chapter 27—Clinical genetics

Richard Bond
BHF Clinical Research Training Fellow, University of
Bristol
Chapter 30—Heart rhythm

William M. Bradlow
Specialist Registrar, John Radcliffe Hospital, Oxford
Chapter 26—Pulmonary hypertension

Alan J. Bryan
Cardiac Surgeon, Bristol Heart Institute, Bristol
Royal Infirmary, Bristol
*Chapter 16—Diseases of the aorta, and trauma to the
aorta and heart*

Amy Burchell
Clinical Research Fellow and Specialist Registrar in
Cardiology, Bristol Heart Institute
Chapter 18—Cardiac rehabilitation
Chapter 25—Community cardiology

Lorna Burrows
Specialist Registrar in Anaesthesia and Intensive Care,
University Hospitals Bristol NHS Foundation Trust
*Chapter 21—Management of critically ill patients with
haemodynamic disturbances*

Zhong Chen
Cardiology Research Fellow and Specialist Registrar,
Guy's and St Thomas' Hospital, London
Chapter 6—Presyncope and syncope

Luisa Chicote-Hughes
Cardiology Specialist Registrar, Bristol Heart
Institute, Bristol Royal Infirmary, Bristol
Chapter 15—Infective endocarditis

Timothy R. Cripps

Consultant Cardiologist and Electrophysiologist, Clinical Lead, Bristol Heart Institute
Chapter 7—Supraventricular tachycardia

Stephanie Curtis

Consultant Cardiologist, Adult Congenital Heart Disease, Bristol Heart Institute
Chapter 23—Pregnancy and heart disease

Nick Curzen

Consultant Cardiologist/Professor of Interventional Cardiology, University Hospital Southampton NHS Foundation Trust, Southampton
Chapter 2—Acute coronary syndromes and myocardial infarction

Edward J. Davies

Speciality Trainee, Derriford Hospital, South West Cardiothoracic Centre, Plymouth
Chapter 17—Cardiac tumours

Patrick J. Doherty

Professor of Rehabilitation, Department of Health Sciences, University of York
Chapter 18—Cardiac rehabilitation

Timothy A. Fairbairn

Cardiovascular Research Fellow and Cardiology Registrar, University of Leeds
Chapter 12—Hypertension

Farzin Fath-Ordoubadi

Consultant Interventional Cardiologist, Manchester Heart Centre, Central Manchester University Hospitals NHS Foundation Trust
Chapter 24—Radiation use and safety

Adam Paul Fitzpatrick

Consultant Cardiologist and Electrophysiologist, Central Manchester University Hospitals
Chapter 6—Presyncope and syncope

Paul Foley

Consultant Cardiologist, Wiltshire Cardiac Centre and Oxford Heart Centre
Chapter 31—Heart rhythm

David J. Fox

Consultant Cardiologist and Electrophysiologist, North West Heart Centre, South Manchester University Hospitals
Chapter 8—Ventricular tachycardia and sudden cardiac death

Ben Gibbison

Fellow in Cardiac Anaesthesia and Intensive Care, Bristol Heart Institute, University Hospitals Bristol NHS Foundation Trust
Chapter 22—Care of the patient following cardiac surgery

J. Simon R. Gibbs

Consultant Cardiologist, Pulmonary Hypertension Service, Hammersmith Hospital, London
Chapter 26—Pulmonary hypertension

Hanney Gonna

Cardiology Specialist Registrar, St. George's Hospital, London
Chapter 13—Lipids

Oliver E. Gosling

Consultant Cardiologist, Musgrove Park Hospital, Taunton & Somerset NHS Foundation Trust, Formally Gawthorn Trust Cardiac Fellow
Chapter 29—Magnetic resonance imaging;
Chapter 30—Cardiac computed tomography

Lee N. Graham

Consultant Cardiologist and Electrophysiologist, Leeds Teaching Hospitals NHS Trust
Chapter 7—Supraventricular tachycardia

James Harrison

BHF Clinical Research Fellow and Cardiology Specialist Registrar, St Thomas' Hospital, London
Chapter 15—Infective endocarditis

Rob Hastings

BHF Clinical Research Fellow, Department of Cardiovascular Medicine, University of Oxford
Chapter 27—Clinical genetics

Andrew Hogarth

Consultant Cardiologist and Electrophysiologist, Leeds Teaching Hospitals NHS Trust
Chapter 7—Supraventricular tachyarrhythmia

Yasmin Ismail

Specialist Registrar in Cardiology, Bristol Heart Institute
Chapter 23—Pregnancy and heart disease

Paramjit Jeetley

Consultant Cardiologist, Royal Free Hospital, London
Chapter 4—Cardiomyopathy

Nick Jenkins

Cardiology Specialist Registrar, Bristol Heart Institute
Chapter 2—Acute coronary syndromes and myocardial infarction

Thomas W. Johnson

Consultant Cardiologist, Bristol Heart Institute
Chapter 1—Chest pain and stable angina

Ali Khavandi

Consultant Interventional Cardiologist, written while at Bristol Heart Institute
Chapter 14—Adult congenital heart disease; Editor

Kaivan Khavandi

NIHR Academic Clinical Fellow and BHF Clinical Research Fellow, Guy's & St Thomas' Hospitals, King's College London
Chapter 11—Primary and secondary prevention of cardiovascular disease

Nitin Kumar

Cardiology Speciality Trainee, Bristol Heart Institute
Chapter 1—Chest pain and stable angina

Paul Leeson

Professor of Cardiovascular Medicine and Consultant Cardiologist, University of Oxford
Chapter 5—Valvular heart disease

Steven Livesey

Consultant Cardiac Surgeon, Southampton General Hospital
Chapter 20—Assessment of patients prior to cardiac surgery

Margaret Loudon

Cardiology Specialist Registrar, Oxford University NHS Trust
Chapter 28—Nuclear cardiology

Navroz Masani

Consultant Cardiologist and President of British Society of Echocardiography, University Hospitals Wales
Chapter 10—Pericardial disease

Elisa McAlindon

Cardiology Clinical Research Fellow and Speciality Registrar, NIHR Bristol Cardiovascular Biomedical Research Unit, Bristol Heart Institute, Bristol
Chapter 3—Heart failure

Gareth Morgan-Hughes

Consultant Cardiologist, South West Cardiothoracic Centre, Plymouth NHS Trust, Derriford
Chapter 30—Cardiac computed tomography

Angus Nightingale

Consultant Cardiologist, Bristol Heart Institute
Chapter 3—Heart failure

Michael Norton

Consultant in Community Cardiology, South Tyneside NHS Foundation Trust
Chapter 25—Community cardiology

Bernard Prendergast

Consultant Cardiologist, Oxford Heart Centre
Chapter 15—Infective endocarditis

Kausik Ray

Professor of Cardiovascular Disease Prevention, St George's University of London
Chapter 13—Lipids

C. Aldo Rinaldi

Consultant Cardiologist (Electrophysiology and Devices), Guy's and St Thomas' Hospital NHS Foundation Trust, London
Chapter 9—Atrial fibrillation

Rani Robson

Specialist Cardiology Registrar, Bristol Heart Institute
Chapter 10—Pericardial disease

James Rosengarten

Specialist Registrar in Cardiology, Southampton General Hospital
Chapter 19—Assessment of patients with cardiovascular disease prior to non-cardiac surgery; Chapter 20—Assessment of patients prior to cardiac surgery

Ian G. Ryder

Consultant in Cardiac Anaesthesia and Intensive Care, Bristol Heart Institute, University Hospitals Bristol NHS Foundation Trust
*Chapter 21—Management of critically ill patients with haemodynamic disturbances
Chapter 22—Care of the patient following cardiac surgery*

Nik Sabharwal

Consultant Cardiologist, Oxford University NHS Trust
Chapter 28—Nuclear cardiology

Rajiv Sankaranarayanan

Cardiology Specialty Registrar in Electrophysiology and British Heart Foundation Clinical Research Fellow, Manchester Heart Centre and University of Manchester
Chapter 24—Radiation use and safety

Leonard M. Shapiro

Consultant Cardiologist, Papworth Hospital
Foundation Trust
Chapter 17—Cardiac tumours

Anoop K. Shetty

Clinical Research Fellow, Guy's and St Thomas'
Hospital NHS Foundation Trust, London
Chapter 9—Atrial fibrillation

David Smith

Consultant Cardiologist, Worcestershire Royal
Hospital
*Chapter 32—Invasive and interventional
cardiology*

Graham Stuart

Consultant Cardiologist (Paediatric and Adult
Congenital Heart Disease), Bristol Heart
Institute and Bristol Royal Hospital for Children,
Bristol
Chapter 14—Adult congenital heart disease

Ian P. Temple

Cardiology and Electrophysiology Specialist
Registrar, BHF Clinical Fellow, The University of
Manchester
*Chapter 8—Ventricular tachycardia and sudden
cardiac death*

Bryan Walker

Clinical Lead Radiographer, Cardiac Catheter Labs,
Manchester Heart Centre, Central Manchester
University Hospitals NHS Foundation Trust
Chapter 24—Radiation use and safety

David Wilson

Cardiology Registrar, Bristol Heart Institute
*Chapter 16—Diseases of the aorta and trauma to
the aorta and heart*

Abbreviations

AAA	abdominal aortic aneurysm	**CEA**	carotid endartectomy
AADs	anti-arrythmic drugs	**CGH**	comparative genomic hybridization
ABC	airway, breathing, circulation		
ABPM	ambulatory blood pressure monitoring	**CHB**	complete heart block
		CHD	coronary heart disease
ACE	angiotensin-converting enzyme	**CIN**	contrast-induced nephropathy
ACM	arrythmogenic cardiomyopathy	**CKD**	chronic kidney disease
ACS	acute coronary syndrome	**CMR**	cardiac MRI
ACT	activated clotting time	**COPD**	chronic obstructive pulmonary disease
AF	atrial fibrillation		
AFL	atrial flutter	**CPVT**	catecholaminergic polymorphic ventricular tachycardia
AHA	American Heart Association		
ALS	advanced life support	**CRP**	C-reactive protein
AMI	acute myocardial infarction	**CRT**	cardiac resynchronization therapy
AP	accessory pathway		
ARB	angiotensin receptor blocker	**CTI**	cavo-tricuspid-isthmus
ARDS	adult respiratory distress syndrome	**CVD**	cardiovascular disease
		CVE	cardiovascular events
ARVC	arrhythmogenic right ventricular cardiomyopathy	**CVP**	central venous pressure
		DA	ductus arteriosus
AS	aortic stenosis	**DAPT**	dual antiplatelets
ASD	atrial septal defect	**DCCV**	direct current cardioversion
AT	atrial tachycardia	**DCM**	dilated cardiomyopathy
ATP	antitachycardia pacing	**DES**	drug-eluting stent
AV	atrioventricular	**DFT**	defibrillation threshold
AVNRT	atrioventricular nodal re-entrant tachycardia	**DSCMR**	dobutamine stress imaging
		DSM	defibrillation safety margin
AVRT	atrioventricular re-entrant tachycardia	**EAM**	electro-anatomic mapping
		EDMD	Emery-Dreifuss muscular dystrophy
BAV	bicuspid aortic valve		
BB	beta blocker	**EDS**	Ehlers-Danlos syndrome
BMI	body mass index	**EF**	ejection fraction
BNP	brain natriuretic peptide	**ERNV**	equilibrium radionuclide ventriculography
BNP	B-type natriuretic peptide		
BrS	Brugada syndrome	**ERO**	effective regurgitant orifice
BSE	British Society of Echocardiography	**ETT**	exercise treadmill testing
		FFR	fractional flow reserve
CABG	coronary artery bypass grafting	**FH**	familial hypercholesterolaemia
CAD	coronary artery disease	**FISH**	fluorescent in-situ hybridization
CCBs	calcium channel blockers	**FO**	foramen ovale

FTAAD	familial thoracic aortic aneurysm and dissection syndrome	**MPS**	myocardial perfusion scintigraphy
HBPM	home blood pressure monitoring	**MR**	mitral regurgitation
		MRA	mineralocorticoid/aldosterone antagonists
HCM	hypertrophic cardiomyopathy		
HDL	high-density lipoprotein	**MRCA**	magnetic resonance imaging coronary angiography
HDL-C	high-density cholesterol		
HF	heart failure	**MS**	mitral stenosis
HFPEF	HF with preserved ejection function	**MUGA**	multi-gated acquisition
HIT	heparin-induced thrombocytopenia	**MVA**	mitral valve area
		MVD	multivessel disease
HUT	head up tilt-table testing	**MVO**	microvascular obstruction
H-V	His-ventricular	**NCEP ATP**	National Cholesterol Education Panel Adult Treatment Panel
IABP	intra-aortic balloon pump		
ICDs	implantable cardiac defibrillators	**NDHPs**	non-dihydropyridines
IE	infective endocarditis	**NNH**	numbers needed to harm
IHD	ischaemic heart disease	**NNT**	numbers needed to treat
INR	international normalized ratio	**NPV**	negative predictive values
ISR	in-stent restenosis	**NS**	Noonan syndrome
IST	inappropriate sinus tachycardia	**NSTEMI**	non-ST elevation MI
IVUS	intravascular ultrasound	**NSVT**	non-sustained ventricular tachycardia
JBS	Joint British Societies		
JT	junctional tachycardia	**NYHA**	New York Heart Association
JVP	jugular venous pressure	**OCT**	optical coherence tomography
LA	left atrium	**OH**	orthostatic hypotension
LAA	left atrial appendage	**oxLDL**	oxidized LDL
LBBB	left bundle branch block	**PACs**	premature atrial complexes
LDL	low-density lipoprotein	**PAH**	pulmonary arterial hypertension
LDS	Loeys-Dietz syndrome	**PAOP**	pulmonary artery occlusion pressure
LGE	late gadolinium enhancement		
LiDCO	lithium dilution continuous cardiac output	**PASP**	systolic PA pressure
		PCI	percutaneous coronary intervention
LMWH	low molecular weight heparin		
LQTS	long QT syndrome	**PCWP**	pulmonary capillary wedge pressure
LV	left ventricular		
LVEDP	left ventricular end diastolic pressure	**PE**	pulmonary embolus
		PEEP	positive end expiratory pressure
LVEF	left ventricular ejection fraction	**PET**	positron emission tomography
LVH	left ventricular hypertrophy	**PFG**	plasma fasting glucose
LVNC	left ventricular non-compaction	**PFO**	patent foramen ovale
LVOTO	left ventricular outflow tract obstruction	**PHT**	pulmonary hypertension
		PICCO	pulse-induced contour cardiac output
MACE	major adverse cardiovascular events		
		PJRT	persistent junctional reciprocating tachycardia
MDCT	multi-detector computed tomography		
		PMC	percutaneous mitral commisurotomy
MetS	metabolic syndrome		
MI	myocardial infarction	**PVARP**	post-ventricular atrial refractory period
MIC	mean inhibitory concentration		
MMP	matrix metalloproteinases	**POTS**	postural orthostatic tachycardia syndrome
MODS	multiple organ dysfunction syndrome		
		PPV	positive predictive value
MPA	main pulmonary artery	**PVD**	peripheral vascular disease
mPAP	mean pulmonary artery pressure	**PVR**	pulmonary vascular resistance

QOL	quality of life	**TAA**	thoracic aortic aneurysms
RA	right atrium	**TAPSE**	tricuspid annular plane systolic
RBBB	right bundle branch block		excursion
RCM	restrictive cardiomyopathy	**TC**	total cholesterol
RNV	radionuclide ventriculography	**TCFA**	thin-capped fibro-atheromas
ROS	reactive oxygen species	**TCPC**	the total cavopulmonary
RP	refractory period		connection
RR	relative risk	**TFT**	thyroid function tests
RRR	relative risk reduction	**TIA**	transient ischaemic attack
RRT	renal replacement therapy	**TLC**	therapeutic lifestyle change
SCD	sudden cardiac death	**T-LOC**	transient loss of consciousness
SCORE	systematic coronary risk	**TNF α**	tumour necrosis factor α
	evaluation	**TOD**	target organ damage
SIRS	systemic inflammatory response	**TOE**	transoesophageal
	syndrome		echocardiography
SNRT	sinus node recovery time	**tPa**	tissue plasminogen activator
SPECT	single photon emission	**TPG**	transpulmonary gradient
	computed tomography	**TR**	tricuspid regurgitation
SQTS	short QT syndrome	**TS**	tricuspid stenosis
SR	sarcoplasmic reticulum	**TS**	tuberous sclerosis
SSFP	steady state free-precession	**TTE**	transthoracic echocardiography
ST	stent thrombosis	**TTR**	transthyretin
STE-ACS	ST elevation ACS	**UCM**	unclassified cardiomyopathy
STEMI	ST segment elevation myocardial	**USS**	ultrasound
	infarction	**VAD**	ventricular assist device
STS	Society of Thoracic Surgeons	**VKA**	vitamin K antagonist
	Score	**VSMCs**	vascular smooth muscle cells
SV	stroke volume	**VT**	ventricular tachycardia
SVC	superior vena cava	**VUS**	variant of unknown significance
SVR	systemic vascular resistance	**WHO**	World Health Organization
SVT	supraventricular tachycardia	**WPW**	Wolff–Parkinson–White

Chest pain and stable angina

1.1 Chest pain

- One of the most common acute/emergency presenting symptoms
- Acute coronary syndrome (ACS) accounts for only 15–25% of patients presenting with acute chest pain
- More than 75% of patients present with a non-ischaemic aetiology.

The causes of chest pain

- Differential diagnostic list for acute chest pain is extensive (Table 1.1)
- Appropriate diagnosis requires effective history taking, examination, and investigation
- Investigation should augment not replace physician–patient communication.

Cardiac

Angina pectoris:

- Typical anginal chest pain:
  - Is constricting discomfort in the front of the chest, or in the neck, shoulders, jaw, or arms
  - Is precipitated by physical exertion
  - Is relieved by rest or GTN within about 5 min
  - Characteristically involves build up of pain—crescendo in nature
  - 'Shooting' or 'stabbing' pain that reaches maximum intensity fast is more likely musculoskeletal or neural in origin
- Location:
  - Classically retrosternal or just left of midline with radiation bilaterally (left arm > right arm) and into neck and lower jaw
  - In the arms the pain passes down the ulnar and volar surfaces to the wrist and then into the fingers. Note Levine's sign, which is one or two clenched fists held over the sternum
- Exacerbators of anginal chest pain include:
  - Exercise
  - Mental stress

Table 1.1 Common causes of acute chest pain

System	Diagnosis
Cardiac	
Ischaemic origin	Angina pectoris
	Aortic stenosis
	Hypertrophic cardiomyopathy
	Aortic regurgitation
	Severe systemic hypertension
	Severe pulmonary hypertension
Non-ischaemic origin	Aortic dissection
	Pericarditis/myopericarditis
	Mitral valve prolapse
Respiratory	Pneumonia
	Pneumothorax
	Pulmonary embolism
	Pleurisy
Gastrointestinal	Oesphageal reflux
	Oesophageal rupture
	Oesophageal spasm
	Peptic ulcer disease
	Gallbladder disease
	Pancreatitis
Neuromusculoskeletal	Degenerative joint disease of cervical/thoracic spine
	Costochondritis (Tietze's syndrome)
	Thoracic outlet syndrome
	Trauma/musculoskeletal injury
Psychogenic	Anxiety (Da Costa's syndrome)
	Depression
Infectious	Herpes zoster

- Anxiety
- Anger
- Lying down—angina decubitus
- After meals—post-prandial angina
- Extreme heat/cold
- Anaemia
- Thyrotoxicosis
- Hypoxia

- Response to GTN cannot always be used as a marker of cardiac chest pain as it induces widespread smooth muscle relaxation
- GTN may relieve pain secondary to oesophageal spasm or biliary colic.

Aortic dissection
- Uncommon but potentially catastrophic
- Severe sudden onset pain (often at maximum intensity compared to crescendo in ischaemia)—often described as 'tearing' inter-scapular pain and resulting in collapse
- Location of pain can mirror site of dissection with radiation of pain into abdomen and legs if dissection propagates

- Associated signs include altered/absent peripheral pulses, neurological disturbance, and acute congestive cardiac failure
- Acute congestive cardiac failure suggests dissection extending into the aortic root, with consequent severe aortic regurgitation
- Commonly associated with background history of hypertension, pregnancy, connective tissue disease (Marfan's/Ehler's, Danlos etc.), or atherosclerosis
- Definitive diagnosis is commonly made with either transoesophageal echocardiography or contrast-enhanced computed tomography
- Transthoracic echocardiography can reveal features of life-threatening type A dissection at the bedside. It has a sensitivity and specificity of 59–85% and 63–96%, respectively, and therefore should not be used as a rule-out modality.

Pericarditis
- Sharp and penetrating quality of pain
- Relief with sitting/leaning forward
- Worsened with movement/respiration
- Viral prodrome or antecedent history of fever are common
- Examination may reveal a pericardial rub
- 12-lead ECG classically demonstrates diffuse 'saddled' ST segment elevation. PR depression can also occur. ECG changes may evolve with T wave inversion and resolution can take weeks (see Figure 1.1)

(a)

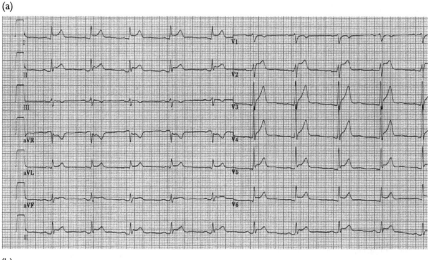

(b)

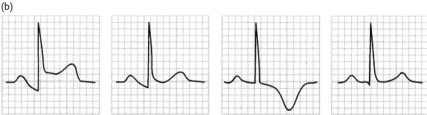

Figure 1.1 (a) ECG changes in pericarditis (with permission from ECGpedia.org). (b) Several stages of pericarditis (with permission from ECGpedia.org).

- Troponin/creatinine kinase may be elevated, indicating associated myocarditis
- It is important to consider a late-presenting 'silent' myocardial infarction (MI) as the cause for pericarditis.

Mitral valve prolapse
- Chest discomfort may mimic angina but is usually atypical without obvious relationship to exercise
- A sharp pain at the apex may represent abnormal tension within the papillary/chordae structure of the mitral valve.

Respiratory
- Commonly sharp and localized, with exacerbation through inspiration or coughing (often described as pleuritic)
- Pain in the shoulder tip suggests irritation of the diaphragmatic pleura
- History, including assessment of risk factors for venous thrombo-embolism, associated symptoms (cough, sputum), and signs on examination required for assessment of aetiology.

Gastrointestinal
- 'Heartburn' secondary to gastrointestinal irritation sometimes difficult to distinguish from cardiac chest pain
- Classically symptoms may associate with meals or a recumbent position
- Burning quality with associated belching is common, and symptoms often can be relieved with use of antacids.

Neuro-musculoskeletal
- Often difficult to distinguish from cardiac chest pain
- Reliant upon thorough history taking, with particular emphasis on precipitating factors, the duration of symptoms, and localization
- Thorough patient examination will aid differentiation of neurological causes for pain
- Antecedent history of trauma/injury, prolonged duration of pain, exacerbation of symptoms with movement or respiration, reproduction of pain on palpation, and pinpoint localization of discomfort all increase the likelihood of a musculoskeletal aetiology
- Chest pain relating to nerve impingement is likely to be confined to specific dermatomes and may involve associated paraesthesia.

Psychogenic
- Many terms exist to describe psychogenic chest pain, including: Da Costa's syndrome, soldier's heart, effort syndrome, and cardiac neurosis
- All listed as 'somatoform autonomic dysfunction' by the World Health Organization in the ICD-10 classification
- Physical manifestation of anxiety disorder—classically symptoms include:
  - Sharp or stabbing left submammary chest pain
  - Palpitations
  - Breathlessness/hyperventilation.

1.2 Stable angina

The pathogenesis of atheroma and the importance of risk factors are shown in Figure 1.2.

- Atherosclerosis is a chronic and multifocal immuno-inflammatory, fibroproliferative disease of medium- and large-sized arteries, mainly driven by lipid accumulation

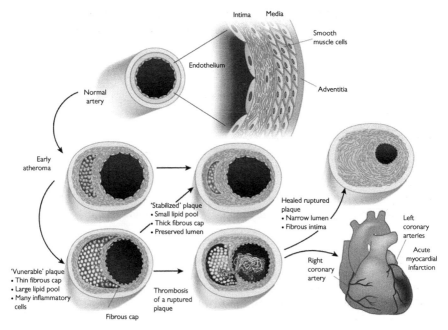

Figure 1.2 Graphical representation of the development of atherosclerosis from infancy to adulthood.

Reprinted by permission from Macmillan Publishers Ltd: Nature, P Libby, *Nature* **420**, 868–874, copyright 2002.

- Develops over many decades, first evident in the second decade of life
- Basic knowledge of the normal arterial structure is required in order to understand the process of underlying atherogenesis (see Figure 1.3)
- Progression of atherosclerosis is unpredictable and is impacted by well-characterized risk factors
- Coronary plaque progression is complex and heterogeneous
- Initial lipid deposition is triggered by activation of endothelial cells and recruitment of inflammatory leucocytes such as monocytes and T lymphocytes, via chemo-attractant and adhesion molecules
- Monocytes within the plaque transform into macrophages and scavenge modified lipoproteins, becoming lipid-laden foam cells
- Foam cells play an important role in the dynamics of the plaque through release of cytokines including tissue factor, tumour necrosis factor α (TNF α), interleukins, and metalloproteinases
- Further recruitment of leucocytes is driven by release of inflammatory cytokines and growth factors, with additional effects on smooth muscle cell migration and proliferation
- Ultimately plaques consist of fibrous, calcific, lipidic, and necrotic components—vulnerability is discussed in Chapter 2
- Arterial remodelling is bidirectional—initially the vessel compensates for the accumulation of plaque through outward expansion (positive remodelling) and ultimately plaque accumulation overtakes vessel expansion and luminal narrowing develops.

Risk factors for atherosclerosis

Risk factors for athersclerosis are shown in Table 1.2.

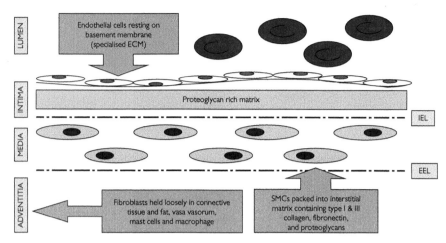

Figure 1.3 An illustration of the normal composition of the arterial wall. ECM, extracellular matrix; IEL, internal elastic lamina—a further layer of ECM composed primarily of elastin fibres which acts as a barrier to the transport of high molecular weight molecules between intima and medial[2]; SMC, smooth muscle cells—packed between the internal and external elastic laminae, predominantly orientated in a circumferential pattern; EEL, external elastic lamina

Table 1.2 Risk factors

Conventional	Novel
Smoking	hs-CRP
Hypertension	Homocysteine
Hyperlipidaemia	Fibrinogen/fibrin
Diabetes	Lipoprotein (a)

Smoking
- Smoking accelerates atherosclerosis through:
  - Increase in blood pressure and sympathetic tone
  - Reduction in myocardial oxygen supply
  - Oxidation of low density lipoprotein (LDL)
  - Impairment of endothelial function through disruption of nitric oxide synthesis
  - Spontaneous platelet aggregation
- Smoking cessation offers the greatest impact in preventative cardiology, with a reduction in cardiac mortality of 30–40%.

Hypertension
- Prevalence of hypertension increasing
- Systolic and diastolic pressure are important determinants of risk.

NICE recommends drug therapy for:
- Patients with persistent high blood pressure of 160/100
- Patients with 10-year cardiovascular disease (CVD) of more than or equal to 20% or existing CVD or target organ damage with blood pressure of more than 140/90
- Additional risk factors, particularly diabetes, should trigger aggressive blood pressure control to less than 140/80mm of Hg.

Hyperlipidaemia

- Raised total cholesterol and LDL levels are positively associated with ischaemic heart disease (IHD) mortality
- Inverse relationship between high density lipoprotein (HDL) level and vascular risk—attributed to 'reverse cholesterol transport'
- Elevated triglyceride levels are associated with increased CVD risk
- Low HDL and high triglycerides level are components of the metabolic syndrome
- Joint British Society guidelines on prevention of CVD in clinical practice (JBS2) suggest achieving a total cholesterol level of less than 4 mmol/l and LDL level less than 2 mmol/l.

Diabetes and metabolic syndrome

- Diabetes is a potent risk factor for coronary artery disease (CAD) and is associated with a high burden of atherosclerosis
- Hyperglycaemia is associated with microvascular dysfunction and insulin resistance appears to promote atherosclerosis
- Presence of the metabolic syndrome elevates risk of CAD
- A number of definitions exist for metabolic syndrome but all include glucose intolerance, raised triglycerides, low HDL levels, hypertension, microalbuminuria, small dense LDL particles, and central obesity
- JBS2 guidelines suggest tight glycaemic control with an HbA1c less than 6.5%.

Novel risk factors

- Large numbers of novel risk factors for CVD have been considered
- Widespread adoption of these risk factors is often limited by a combination of paucity of data and the lack of a standardized commercial assay for measurement/detection
- High sensitivity C-reactive protein (hs-CRP), lipoprotein (a), and homocysteine have the greatest amount of data supporting their value in risk assessment
- Hs-CRP:
  - Is a marker of inflammation but may also directly influence plaque vulnerability
  - Its role in risk assessment that is most likely limited to individuals with moderate or high risk, defined by conventional risk factors
- Homocysteine:
  - Homocysteine is a sulfhydryl-containing amino acid derived from demethylation of dietary methionine
  - A genetic defect in methionine metabolism can result in severe hyperhomocysteinaemia and associates with premature CAD
  - In the general population, elevated homocysteine levels tend to associate with poor dietary intake of folic acid
  - Elevated homocysteine levels are linked with an increased incidence of premature CAD and rate of venous thromboembolism
- Lipoprotein:
  - Lipoprotein (a) is composed of an LDL particle with its apolipoprotein B-100 component linked to apolipoprotein (a)
  - Lipoprotein (a) is a complex molecule and has over 25 heritable forms
  - Lipoprotein shares many of the structural characteristics with plasminogen, strengthening the link with atherothombosis.

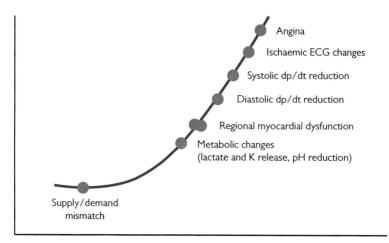

Figure 1.4 'The ischaemic cascade'. Sequence of events following mismatch between oxygen supply and demand.

Reprinted with permission from the *ESC Textbook of Cardiovascular Medicine* 2nd edition, ed. John Camm, Thomas Lüscher and Patrick Serruys, copyright Oxford University Press 2009.

The natural history, pathophysiology, and presentations of coronary artery disease

- Myocardial ischaemia commonly driven by:
    - Coronary atherosclerosis
    - Coronary vasoconstriction
    - Coronary artery thrombosis
- Ischaemia is the result of a mismatch between oxygen demand and supply and a cascade of events that ensues (see Figure 1.4)
- Initially ischaemia impacts at a cellular level with cell swelling, glycogen depletion, and apoptosis; ongoing tissue hypoxia results in ATP depletion, increased lactate levels, and acidosis
- Myocardial contractility diminishes and the loss of intracellular potassium and a reduction in the transmembrane potassium gradient drives ECG change
- Ischaemic chest pain is a late feature; an afferent pathway of non-medullated small sympathetic nerve fibres runs parallel to coronary arteries and enters the spinal cord from C8–T4
- Impulses are transmitted to corresponding spinal ganglia and then through the spinal cord to the thalamus and cerebral cortex
- Angina pectoris, like other pain of visceral origin, is often poorly localized and is commonly referred to the corresponding segmental dermatomes.

The severity of anginal symptoms has been classified as outlined in Box 1.1.

1.3 The pharmacology of drugs currently used in the treatment of stable angina

Aspirin (acetylsalicyclic acid)
Pharmacology
- Aspirin acetalyses cyclo-oxygenase irreversibly
- There is preferential inhibition of COX-1 isoform

BOX 1.1 CANADIAN CARDIOVASCULAR SOCIETY FUNCTIONAL CLASSIFICATION OF ANGINA PECTORIS

I Ordinary physical activity, such as walking and climbing stairs, does not cause angina. Angina results from strenuous or rapid or prolonged exertion at work or recreation.

II Slight limitation of ordinary activity. Walking or climbing stairs rapidly, walking uphill, walking or climbing after meals, in cold, in wind, or when under emotional stress, or only during the few hours after awakening. Walking more than two blocks on the level and climbing more than one flight of ordinary stairs at a normal pace and under normal conditions.

III Marked limitations of ordinary physical activity. Walking one to two blocks on the level and climbing more than one flight under normal conditions.

IV Inability to carry on any physical activity without discomfort—anginal syndrome may be present at rest.

Reproduced from 'Letter: Grading of angina pectoris', L. Campeau, *Circulation* 54, 522–3, copyright 1976, with permission of Wolters Kluwer Health.

- COX-1 inhibition blocks thromboxane A2 generation
- Aspirin inhibits production of prostacyclin.

Side effects

- Gastric irritation and gastrointestinal bleeding are significant risks.

Evidence

- In SAPAT (Swedish Angina Pectoris Aspirin Trial), addition of low-dose aspirin to Sotalol showed significant benefits in terms of cardiovascular events and significant reduction in incidence of first MI
- Current evidence suggests that aspirin should not be used for primary prevention even in patients with raised blood pressure or diabetes mellitus.

Beta-receptor antagonists (beta blockers)

Pharmacology

- See Figure 1.5
- There are three receptor types (β1– β3) all coupled to adenyl cyclase via the activated stimulatory G-protein and enhancing calcium ion entry to the cell via cyclic AMP activation of protein phosphate kinase A and phosphorylation of the calcium channel
- β1 limited to heart muscle—located on cardiac sarcolemma; stimulation results in increased sinus node activity (positive chronotropic effect), increased contractility (positive inotropic effect), and an increase in the rate of conduction (positive dromotropic effect)
- β2 located in bronchial and vascular smooth muscle
- β3 located in adipose tissue
- β-blockade results in reduced oxygen demand through a reduction in heart rate and blood pressure, and myocardial contractility
- Additionally, β-blockade lengthens diastolic filling time through slowing myocyte relaxation—enhancing myocardial perfusion
- Multiple indications for use—post-infarction protection, exertional angina, heart failure, arrhythmia, and hypertension—so drug choice in patients with angina pectoris is often determined by the presence of concomitant conditions
- Chronic therapy leads to an increased β-receptor density and consequently abrupt withdrawal can result in exacerbation of angina and MI.

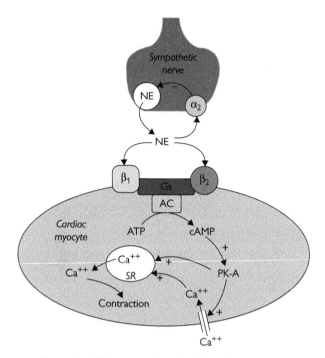

Abbreviation: NE, norepinephrine; Gs, G-stimulatory protein;
AC, adenylyl cyclase; PK-A, cAMP-dependent protein kinase;
SR, sarcoplasmic reticulum

Figure 1.5 Mechanism of action of beta-blockers.
Reproduced from www.cvpharmacology.com, with kind permission from Richard Klabunde.

Side effects

- β2-mediated bronchospasm or vascular smooth muscle spasm, resulting in cold extremities
- β1-related bradycardia/AV-nodal block and negative inotropic effect, and CNS effects, leading to depression and insomnia; β-blockade has been linked with inducing diabetes.

Evidence

- Beta blockers (BBs) were shown to provide similar outcomes in meta-analysis of trials comparing them to calcium channel antagonists and nitrates and were associated with fewer adverse events than calcium channel blockers (CCBs) in patients with stable angina.

Calcium channel antagonists

Pharmacology

- Calcium channel blockade primarily induces peripheral vasodilation and a reduction in peripheral vascular resistance
- Two groups within the family—dihydropyridines and non-dihydropyridines (NDHPs)—the NDHPs have an additional effect on nodal tissue with a resultant reduction in the heart rate and reduction in myocardial contractility
- Anti-anginal properties include the reduction of afterload, and negative chronotropic and inotropic effect.

Side effects

- Related to vasodilation: dizziness, flushing, headaches, and ankle oedema
- Contraindications include pre-existing sinus or AV node disease, antegrade Wolf-Parkinson White syndrome (WPW), and LV systolic failure.

Angiotensin-converting enzyme inhibitors

Pharmacology

- Angiotensin-converting enzyme (ACE) inhibition appears to stabilize the endothelium through bradykinin-linked nitric oxide production, enhances fibrinolysis, and offers a 'pre-conditioning' effect.

Side effects

- Side effects are hypotension, bradykinin-related cough, hyperkalaemia, renal failure, angioedema, and neutropenia.

Evidence

- HOPE (Heart Outcomes Prevention Evaluation) and the EUROPA study showed the benefits of ACE inhibitors in patients with high risk for cardiovascular events with a history of coronary heart disease.

Antianginals

The latest NICE guidance (July 2011) suggests:

- BBs or CCBs as first-line treatment
- If a person can't tolerate one consider switching to the other (BB or CCB)
- If symptoms not controlled consider switching to other options or a combination of BB and CCB
- If using a combination, use dihydropyridine CCB, e.g. nifedipine, amlodipine, or felodipine
- If either BB or CCB not tolerated or both contraindicated, considering monotherapy with long-acting nitrate or ivabradine or nicorandil or ranolazine
- For people on BB or CCB in whom the other option (BB or CCB) is contraindicated, choosing from the above options for a combination
- Aiming for a target heart rate <70 bpm; if not achieved despite maxmimal dose of BB or CCB consider adding ivabradine
- That symptoms not controlled on two anti-anginals warrant further investigations
- That a third anti-anginal should only be offered to people whose symptoms are not controlled on two anti-anginals *and* are awaiting revascularization or revascularization is not deemed appropriate.

Nitrates

Pharmacology

- Nitrates are exogenous source of vasodilator nitric oxide
- Chronic use produces tolerance—prolonged treatment inhibits endothelial nitric oxide synthase (one mechanism to explain tolerance)
- They dilate large coronary arteries and arterioles >100 μm, enhancing collateral supply and relieving dynamic stenoses/coronary spasm
- They reduce afterload and preload of the heart— they increase venous capacitance and thereby reduce venous return and myocardial wall stretch—in turn reducing myocardial oxygen demand
- Nitroglycerin is quick acting and has a half-life of only a few minutes because of extra-hepatic metabolism; it gets converted to longer acting dinitrate

- Dinitrates are converted in liver to mononitrates, which have half-life of 4–6 h and are renally excreted
- Mononitrates have almost 100% bioavailablity without any hepatic metabolism
- Nitrates often lose efficacy over time, giving rise to the phenomenon of nitrate tolerance
- Poor function of mitochondrial enzyme aldehyde dehydrogenase is one of the hypotheses
- Production of excess free radicals (toxic superoxides and peroxynitrites) also inhibits the enzymes (guanyl cyclase and cyclic GMP), which in turn affects the activity of aldehyde dehydrogenase. All these enzymes play an important role in nitrate metabolism
- Nitrate-free interval of approximately 10 h is advised to prevent this from happening
- Modified/extended release preparations can also overcome this problem
- Side effects are headache and hypotension
- Contraindications are hypertrophic obstructive cardiomyopathy (HOCM) amd critical aortic stenosis (AS).

Nicorandil
Pharmacology
- Nicorandil is a potassium channel activator (opens mitochondrial ATP-sensitive potassium channels) with a nitrate component and has both arterial and venous vasodilating properties.

Side effects
- Headache, flushing, nausea, and oral/anal ulceration.

Evidence
- IONA (Impact of Nicorandil in Angina) study showed benefits in patients with stable angina with regard to major cardiovascular events.

Ranolazine
Pharmacology
- Ranolazine acts through modulating the trans-cellular late sodium current
- It indirectly prevents the calcium overload via an effect on sodium-dependent calcium channels
- The drug is licensed as an adjunct for use in patients with uncontrolled symptoms or intolerance to first-line agents.

Side effects
- Prolongation of the QT interval, which can be exacerbated through drug interactions and hepatic impairment.

Evidence
- MARISA (Monotherapy Assessment of Ranolazine in Stable Angina) trial showed that ranolazine was well tolerated and increased exercise performance without any meaningful haemodynamic side effects
- In CARISA trial, additional anti-anginal effect of ranolazine was demonstrated in patients already taking atenolol, amlodipine or diltiazem
- ERICA (Efficacy of Ranolazine in Chronic Angina) trial showed significantly reduced frequency of angina and nitroglycerin consumption when ranolazine was compared against placebo.

Ivabradine
Pharmacology
- Ivabradine acts on the I_f ion current, which is highly expressed in the sinoatrial node

- I_f is a mixed Na^+–K^+ inward current, activated by hyperpolarization and modulated by the autonomic nervous system. It is one of the most important ionic currents for regulating pacemaker activity in the sinoatrial node
- Ivabradine selectively inhibits the pacemaker I_f current in a dose-dependent manner
- Blocking this channel reduces cardiac pacemaker activity, slowing the heart rate and allowing more time for blood to flow to the myocardium.

Side effects
- Similarity between the I_f channels and I_h ion channels found in the retina can lead to visual field disturbance
- Bradycardia and headache.

Evidence
- INITIATIVE study showed greater anti-ischaemic efficacy of heart rate reduction than with beta-blockers. It also showed that ivabradine provides powerful anti-anginal efficacy
- ASSOCIATE trial confirmed ivabradine is safe and well tolerated in patients receiving BBs
- BEAUTIFUL study showed reduced risk of cardiovascular death, hospitalization for MI, and heart failure of 24% in patients with limiting angina and also that ivabradine has maximum efficacy on MI, with a 42% reduction.

Cholesterol-lowering agents

Statins
Pharmacology
- Statins decrease hepatic cholesterol synthesis via inhibition of 3-hydroxy-3-methyl-glutaryl-coenzyme A (HMG-CoA) reductase
- They reduce total cholesterol and LDL
- They increase HDL
- Their pleiotrophic effects include improving endothelial function, stabilization of platelets, and anti-inflammatory effects.

Side effects
- Liver enzyme elevation and myopathy/rhabdomyolysis well reported. Myopathy = Creatine Kinase × 10 normal
- Co-admininstration with certain agents increases risk of myopathy/rhabdomyolysis: fibrates, niacin, cyclosporine, erythromycin, and azole antifungal agents.

Evidence
- 4S (Scandinavian Simvastatin Survival Study) demonstrated that use of statins in secondary prevention reduced overall mortality and cardiac events
- The Health Protection Study (HPS) suggested those at high risk of CVD benefit from statins regardless of cholesterol level.

Fibrates
- Fibrates are agonists for nuclear transcription factor peroxisome proliferator-activated receptor-α (PPAR-α)
- They decrease triglycerides with consequent increase in HDL
- They increase particle sizes of small, dense LDL.

Others

- Bile sequestrants
  - Bind bile acids to promote secretion into the intestinal tract
  - Increase loss of hepatic cholesterol with a compensatory increase in hepatic LDL-cholesterol receptor and consequent reduction in blood LDL levels
  - Lead to a transient rise in triglyceride levels
- Ezetimibe
  - Inhibits cholesterol absorption from intestine
  - Binds to Niemann-Pick C1 Like 1(NPC1L1) protein on gastrointestinal tract epithelial cells and hepatocytes
  - Has an indirect effect on increased LDL uptake in cells, leading to decreased LDL blood plasma level
- Nicotinic acid
  - Decreases mobilization of free fatty acids from adipose tissue—consequently less substrate for hepatic synthesis of lipoprotein lipid
  - Increases HDL
  - Side effect profile can be minimized by cautious titration of the dose but includes flushing, dizziness, and palpitations.

1.4 Indications, limitations, risks, and predictive value of non-invasive and invasive investigations

Guidance on the investigation of chest pain has recently undergone a major review, with publication of NICE guidelines (see Figure 1.6).

- Table 1.3 offers some guidance on the pre-test probability of a diagnosis of CAD defined by age, symptom quality, and risk profile
- Investigation for CAD can be defined as functional, anatomical, or a combination of the two. The available tests, their sensitivity, specificity, pros, and cons are detailed in Table 1.4

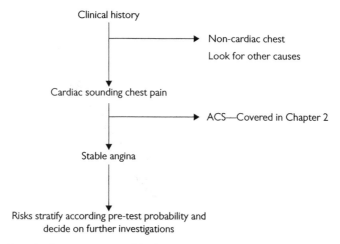

Figure 1.6 Algorithm for assessment and further investigation.

Table 1.3 Percentage of people estimated to have coronary disease according to typicality of symptoms, age, sex, and risk factors

	Non-anginal chest pain				Atypical angina				Typical angina			
	Men		Women		Men		Women		Men		Women	
Age (years)	Lo	Hi	Lo	Hi	Lo	Hi	Lo	Hi	Lo	Hi	Lo	Hi
35	3	34	1	19	8	59	2	39	30	88	10	78
45	9	47	2	22	21	70	5	43	51	92	20	79
55	23	59	4	25	45	79	10	47	80	95	38	82
65	49	69	9	29	71	86	20	51	93	97	56	84

For men older than 70 with atypical or typical symptoms, assume an estimate >90%. For women older than 70, assume an estimate of 61–90% *except* women at high risk *and* with typical symptoms, for whom a risk of >90% should be assumed. Values are percentage of people at each mid-decade age with significant CAD. Hi, high risk—diabetes, smoking and hyperlipidaemia (total cholestrol >6.47 mmol/litre); Lo, low risk—none of these three. These results are likely to overestimate CAD in primary care populations. If there are resting ECG ST-T changes or Q waves, the likelihood of CAD is higher in each cell of the table.

National Institute for Health and Clinical Excellence (2010) CG 95, 'Chest pain of recent onset: assessment and diagnosis of recent onset chest pain or discomfort of suspected cardiac origin', London: NICE. Available from www.nice.org.uk/guidance/CG95 Reproduced with permission. Information was accurate at the time of going to press.

Table 1.4 Functional and anatomical tests for coronary artery disease

Diagnostic test		Sensitivity	Specificity	Advantages	Disadvantages
Functional	Exercise stress test	68%	77%	Cheap Easily accessible Technician-led No radiation	Lacks diagnostic accuracy LBBB precludes ECG assessment
	Stress echocardiography	85%	81%	Cheap Determines LV and valvular function Offers territory of ischaemia No radiation	Body habitus can prevent adequate windows Requires specialist reporting
	Myocardial perfusion imaging (SPECT)	85%	81%	Determines LV function Defines territory of ischaemia	Radiation Body habitus can lead to false positives Balanced ischaemia can give false negatives Requires specialist reporting
	Stress perfusion cardiac magnetic resonance	83%	86%	Determines LV function & viability Defines territory of ischaemia No radiation	Requires specialist reporting Time-consuming Contrast exposure

(Continued)

Table 1.4 (Continued)

Diagnostic test		Sensitivity	Specificity	Advantages	Disadvantages
Anatomical	Coronary angiography	100%	100%	Offers accurate detail of anatomy Facilitates immediate intervention	Radiation exposure Invasive procedure Requires specialist operator No functional information Contrast exposure
	CT coronary angiography (128-slice imaging)	97%	87%	Non-invasive Fast Offers extra-cardiac information	Radiation exposure Contrast exposure Limited by heart rate Requires specialist reporting
	Cardiac magnetic resonance imaging	87%	70%	Non-invasive No radiation Offers functional information	Poor resolution Limited by heart rate Requires specialist reporting

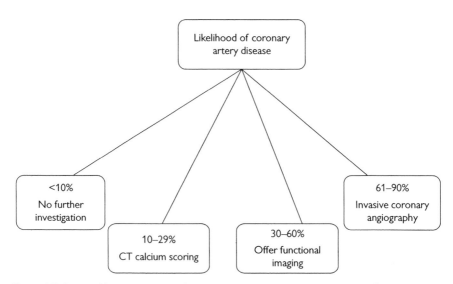

Figure 1.7 Protocol for investigation of choice according to pre-test probability of underlying coronary artery disease.

- Further investigation must take into consideration the likelihood of disease and the risks/ predictive value of the test selected (see Figure 1.7)
- The current NICE guidance has generated a useful protocol for investigation choice based upon the pre-test probability of underlying CAD.

Table 1.5 Recommendations for myocardial revascularization to improve prognosis

Evidence and/or general agreement that revascularization is beneficial

Significant left main stem disease or its equivalent (i.e. severe stenosis of ostial/proximal segment of left descending and circumflex coronary arteries)

Three-vessel disease with significant proximal stenoses: the survival benefit is greater in patients with abnormal left ventricular function or with extensive reversible ischaemia on non-invasive testing

Two-vessel disease with significant proximal LAD disease in patients with reversible ischaemia on non-invasive testing

Significant stenoses in patients with left ventricular dysfunction and a large area of viable myocardium

Conflicting evidence and/or a divergence of opinion that revascularization is beneficial, but weight of evidence/opinion is in favour

One- or two-vessel disease without significant proximal LAD coronary artery stenosis in patients who have survived sudden cardiac death or sustained ventricular tachycardia

Significant stenoses in patients with reversible ischaemia on non-invasive testing and evidence of frequent episodes of ischaemia during daily activities

Evidence or general agreement that revascularization is not useful/effective and in some cases may be harmful

One or two vessel-disease without significant proximal LAD coronary artery stenosis in patients who have mild or no symptoms and have not received an adequate trial of medical therapy or have no demonstrable ischaemia or a limited area of ischaemia/viability only on non-invasive testing

Borderline (50–70%) coronary stenoses in locations other than left main stem and no demonstrable ischaemia on non-invasive testing

Non-significant (<50%) coronary stenoses

High risk of procedure-related morbidity or mortality unless the risk of the procedure is balanced by an expected significant improvement in survival or the patient's quality of life

LAD, left anterior descending. Reproduced from the *ESC Textbook of Cardiovascular Medicine* 2nd edition, ed. John Camm, Thomas Lüscher and Patrick Serruys, copyright 2009 with permission of Oxford University Press.

1.5 Which patients should be investigated further and referred for intervention?

- NICE suggests that all patients should undergo a trial of medical therapy
- Consider revascularization when (Table 1.5):
  - There are persisting symptoms despite maximal medical therapy
  - There is high-risk anatomy, e.g. proximal vessel stenoses, especially left anterior descending (LAD), multivessel disease, and left main stem (LMS) disease
  - There are significant territories of ischaemia on non-invasive testing.

Further reading

Camm AJ, Lüscher TF, and Serruys PW (eds). *The European Society of Cardiology Textbook of Cardiovascular Medicine*. Oxford University Press, 2009.
NICE guidance: Stable angina.
NICE guidance: Chest pain of recent onset.

Acute coronary syndromes and myocardial infarction

2.1 Pathology of atherosclerosis

Introduction and clinical relevance

- Atherosclerosis is the major underlying pathology of CVD
- It accounts for 35% of all deaths in the UK and 4.35 million deaths in Europe each year
- The main clinical sequelae of atherosclerosis are:
  - Stable angina and ACS secondary to coronary artery disease (CAD)
  - Cerebral infarction secondary to cerebrovascular disease (CVD)
  - Limb ischaemia secondary to peripheral vascular disease (PVD).

The natural history of atherosclerosis

- Atheroma formation is now understood to be a chronic inflammatory disease of the vascular intima
- Characterized by infiltration of the sub-endothelial space of large arteries by inflammatory cells
- Formation of foam cell macrophages by monocyte invasion of the intima and ingestion of modified cholesterol esters
- Ongoing accumulation of inflammatory cells and mediators leading to evolution of atherosclerotic plaques.

Initiation of atherogenesis and vulnerable arterial segments

- The earliest stage of atheroma formation is endothelial injury and dysfunction in response to a variety of insults
- Factors contributing to endothelial activation include circulating levels of cholesterol and its derivatives, genetic variations, homocysteinaemia, hyperglycaemia, and levels of reactive oxygen species (ROS), and there has been much debate about the contribution of past and present infectious microorganisms, e.g. *Chlamydia pneumonia* in promoting atherosclerotic inflammation
- Histopathological examination of the human vasculature has shown subtle eccentric intimal thickenings at vulnerable parts of the arterial tree

- It is seen from as early as 36 weeks gestation and present in nearly all humans to some degree by 1 year of age
- It is these regions that correlate with the locations of future advanced atherosclerotic lesions.
- Atherosclerosis-prone segments of the vascular tree tend to have typical patterns of haemodynamic shear stress
- Typically seen at branch points where there is low average shear but high oscillatory shear stress.

Low-density lipoprotein and the oxidative modification hypothesis

- The most critical steps in atherogenesis are the accumulation and modification of cholesterol esters in the sub-endothelial space
- For almost 50 years the relationship between hyperlipidaemia, and in particular raised LDL portions of the lipid profile, and atherosclerotic disease has been appreciated.

Vascular smooth muscle cells and atherosclerosis

- Vascular smooth muscle cells (VSMCs) play an important role in both the initiation of atherosclerotic lesions at vulnerable points of the arterial tree and later on in the stability of these lesions by contributing to the protective fibrous caps of plaques
- Intimal VSMCs interact and bind macrophages directly via a number of adhesion molecules including VCAM-1, ICAM-1, and the fractalkine ligand CX_3CL_1
- As the fibrous cap is subjected to shear stress from the luminal blood flow, the tensile strength of the cap determines the likelihood of rupture and subsequent clinical events
- The effectiveness with which VSMCs migrate into the cap is a vitally important contributor to the stability of individual lesions.

Monocyte recruitment and foam cell macrophage formation

- Initial steps in monocyte recruitment involve the expression and secretion of a variety of chemo-attractant factors (fractalkine, MCP-1 etc) by endothelial and smooth muscle cells as well as recently recruited leukocytes
- Activated endothelial cells also express several types of leukocyte adhesion molecules (e.g. VCAM), which cause circulating monocytes rolling along the vascular endothelium to adhere
- Activation of these recently recruited monocytes occurs due to the local influence of pro-inflammatory cytokines (eg TNF-α and IFN-γ) secreted by a variety of intimal cells including recently recruited T cells
- Recruited monocytes then undergo differentiation into macrophages and there is an intense upregulation of scavenger receptors capable of taking up oxidized LDL (oxLDL)
- Accumulation of oxLDL as cytoplasmic droplets ultimately leads to the morphological characteristics of these macrophages, known as foam cell macrophages
- Build up of foam cell macrophages eventually contributes to the formation of an atheromatous core
- Cell fragments and toxic intracellular debris contributes to necrosis of surrounding cells, including other leukocytes and smooth muscle cells, which all contribute to the expansion of the necrotic core and further pro-inflammatory stimulation.

Histopathological definition of plaque type

- To date, most of our knowledge of plaque progression comes from immunohistochemical examination of surgically removed plaques, post-mortem specimens, and animal models of disease

- Two major classification structures for human atherosclerotic plaques have emerged. These two classification systems are complementary
  - Stary et al. produced a numerical classification system in 1995 (updated in 2000) endorsed by the American Heart Association (AHA) (see Figure 2.1)
  - Virmani and colleagues produced a more descriptive classification system in 2000.

Atherosclerotic plaque rupture

- Plaque rupture is the commonest atherosclerotic event that leads to clinically relevant arterial ischaemia
- Plaque ruptures are identified as the underlying aetiology in 60% of individuals who die suddenly from thrombotic arterial occlusion
- It is the most frequent cause of death in men <50 years old and women >50 years old.

Definition

- Atherosclerotic plaque rupture is an area of plaque with fibrous cap disruption whereby the overlying thrombus is in continuity with the necrotic core
- Fracture of the fibrous cap allows platelets, circulating clotting factors, and inflammatory cells to come into contact with the thrombogenic necrotic core and promote thrombus formation.

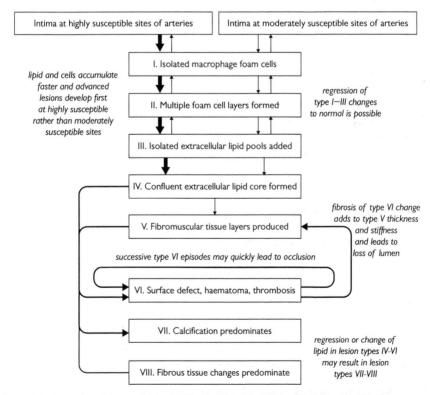

Figure 2.1 Stary classification of atherosclerotic plaque histology. Classification of human atherosclerotic plaques according to their histological characteristics.

Adapted from Stary, H.C., 'Natural history and histological classification of atherosclerotic lesions: an update', Arterioscler. Thromb. Vasc. Biol., 2000. 20(5): p. 1177–8, with permission of Wolters Kluwer Health.

Vulnerable plaque characteristics

Thin-capped plaques are the lesions that are most prone to cap disruption and thrombus formation, and subsequent clinical events. These are termed **'thin-capped fibro-atheromas'** (TCFAs). Characteristics include:

- Thin fibrous caps, defined by Virmani and colleagues as <65 μm thick:
  - Thinning of the fibrous cap may occur due to VSMC apoptosis, reduced matrix synthesis, and therefore tensile strength of the cap
  - Rarefaction of the fibrous cap by a variety of extracellular proteases secreted from macrophages, e.g. serine proteases, cathepsins, and matrix metalloproteinases, contributes to the likelihood of plaque rupture
- **Large necrotic lipid-rich core**
- **High macrophage numbers**
- **Paucity of smooth muscle cells**: such plaques have been shown to be at high risk of such rupture
- **Intraplaque haemorrhage**: neoangiogenesis is more prevalent in unstable plaques and subsequent intraplaque haemorrhage due to microvessel incompetence is associated with plaque instability.

Effect of shear stress

The most important dynamic that defines likelihood of rupture is the balance between tangential stresses exerted on the fibrous cap by luminal blood flow and the innate mechanical strength of the cap itself; a change in either one of these factors can shift the balance towards cap rupture.

Patient characteristics

- Thrombophilic propensities of individual patients are important in determining the extent of thrombosis and may be affected by lifestyle factors such as cigarette smoking
- **Platelet function**: platelet interaction with the endothelium, circulating coagulant factors, and inflammatory cells is of key importance in the promotion of thrombus in association with plaque rupture.

Clinically silent plaque rupture

- In many cases plaque rupture alone is not enough to cause thrombosis that leads to luminal occlusion and clinical events
- Post-mortem studies have shown the prevalence of clinically silent plaque ruptures of up to 10% in patients who have died from other causes
- Using intravascular ultrasound (IVUS) of coronary arteries, evidence of previous plaque ruptures has been shown in up to 70% of non-culprit vessels.

Atherosclerotic plaque erosion

- Plaque erosion is far less well understood than rupture
- It contributes to about a third of all sudden thrombotic coronary deaths identified on post-mortem studies
- **Definition**: loosely defined as luminal thrombus in an arterial segment without evidence of plaque rupture
- **Plaque characteristics**: typical plaque characteristics underlying erosions are stenotic fibrous lesions with little or no atheromatous core; the endothelium is usually absent at the site of erosion
- **Patient characteristics**: erosions are more common in young men and women <50 years old and are associated with smoking, especially in premenopausal women.

2.2 Risk factors for atherosclerosis

Male gender

- In the UK, one in five men die from coronary disease under the age of 75 (one in seven women)
- After the menopause, female risk increases greatly, with a 55-year-old woman having an identical risk of cardiovascular death to a 45-year-old man.

Genetic predisposition

- Increased risk associated with a family history of early ischaemic heart disease (IHD) (male <55 years and female <65 years) ranges between 1.5 and 1.7 times the normal population and is independent of other risk factors
- There appear to be vulnerable genotypes, which are intrinsically related to the pathophysiology of IHD, i.e. those affecting dyslipidaemia, endothelial dysfunction, diabetes, and hypertension
- Candidate genes have been investigated, but in isolation have little effect on overall risk stratification above that of traditional risk factors.

Hypertension

- Hypertension is an independent risk factor for CVD, heart failure, PVD and renal failure
- Framingham data shows BP of 130–139/85–89 is associated with a >2-fold increase in relative risk compared to BP below 120/80.

Dyslipidaemia

- Dyslipidaemia has established causality with CVD
- A 10% reduction in total cholesterol is followed by a 25% reduction in coronary events at 5 years
- A reduction of LDL by 1 mmol/l is associated with a 20% reduction in coronary events.

Diabetes mellitus

- Hyperglycaemia promotes atherosclerosis by a number of mechanisms, most importantly by decreasing endothelium-derived NO availability
- In the context of an ACS, high blood-sugar concentrations independent of previous diagnosis of diabetes are highly predictive for poorer outcomes either in hospital or at 12 months
- Data exists on glycaemic control and primary and secondary prevention of cardiovascular events:
  - The UKPDS trial showed that intensive glucose-lowering therapy reduced the incidence of cardiovascular events by 25%
  - The DIGAMI trial, which targeted acute hyperglycaemia in the context of an ACS, showed an absolute mortality reduction of 11% with a number needed to treat (NNT) of nine patients to save one life.

Tobacco smoking

- Tobacco smoking has a clear association with cardiovascular risk, which is reversed on smoking cessation
- Effects include endothelial activation, enhanced inflammatory response promoting atherosclerosis, and induced thrombophilia in the host.

Body weight

- Intra-abdominal visceral fat is associated with increased secretion of free fatty acids, hyperinsulinaemia, insulin resistance, hypertension, and dyslipidaemia
- Excess visceral abdominal fat has been strongly associated with metabolic and cardiovascular risk.

2.3 Acute presentations of coronary artery disease

- The spectrum of ACSs represents the clinical expression of atherosclerotic plaque pathology
- At one end of the spectrum is occlusive thrombus associated with plaque rupture or erosion causing epicardial coronary obstruction and transmural infarction
- At the other end is slow, progressive coronary luminal obstruction caused by increasing plaque bulk. Typically produces increasing symptoms of ischaemia at decreasing workload or rest
- The European Society of Cardiology has categorized ACS patients into two major groups:
  - **Patients with typical acute chest pain and persistent (>20 min) ST segment elevation on the ECG.** This is termed ST elevation ACS (STE-ACS) and generally reflects an epicardial coronary occlusion
  - **Patients with acute chest pain but without persistent ST segment elevation.** They have transient or persistent ST segment depression or T wave inversion, flat T waves, pseudo-normalization of T waves, or no ECG changes at presentation. If this is associated with a rise in cardiac biomarkers then this is termed a non-ST elevation ACS (NSTE-ACS)
  - If the patient has ischaemic chest pain without a rise in cardiac biomarkers they may be labelled as having unstable angina.

2.4 Pharmacotherapy in acute coronary syndromes

Antiplatelet agents

- The event that leads to clinical presentation in ACSs is the formation of flow-limiting thrombus
- The mainstay of pharmacological treatment for these conditions consists of antiplatelet and antithrombotic agents
- Pharmacological inhibition of platelet function has been shown to have both symptomatic and prognostic benefit in patients with ACS.

Acetylsalicylic acid (aspirin)

- Irreversible inhibition of COX-1 reduces thromboxane A2 production thereby reducing platelet aggregation
- Its antiplatelet effect is saturable with doses of 75–100 mg
- Meta-analysis has shown a 46% reduction in subsequent vascular events in patients with ACS
- 75–100 mg appears to be as effective as higher doses, with fewer side effects than 150 mg or more
- GI intolerance, including bleeding, is the major reason for discontinuation
- The CAPRIE study reported a 0.93% incidence of GI bleeding leading to discontinuation.

Thienopyridines (clopidogrel/prasugrel/ticlopidine)
- Thienopyridines cause irreversible inhibition of the platelet P_2Y_{12} ADP receptor, thus reducing platelet activation and aggregation.

Ticlopidine
- Ticlopidine is now virtually redundant due to GI intolerability, neutropaenia (2.4% of patients), thrombocytopaenia, and a slower onset of action as compared to clopidogrel.

Clopidogrel
- Clopidogrel is a pro-drug that is converted to its active metabolite by hepatic cytochrome enzyme (CYP3A4) pathway
- This may explain why some patients do not achieve expected levels of platelet inhibition and may be prone to further thrombotic events including catastrophic stent thrombosis
- CURE trial showed additive benefit to conventional therapy in treatment of NSTE-ACS, reducing major adverse cardiovascular events (MACE) rates from 11.4% to 9.3% ($p < 0.0001$)
- The trade off was an increase in major bleeding from 2.7 to 3.7% ($p = 0.001$)
- CLARITY trial showed additive benefit to aspirin alone in STEMI patients receiving fibrinolytic therapy
- CHARISMA trial showed that, in patients with documented CVD but without recent ACS, treatment with clopidogrel in addition to aspirin reduced the composite endpoint of MACE from 7.9% to 6.9% ($p = 0.046$) as compared to aspirin alone
- Although this benefit is modest, current ESC guidelines recommend 12 months of aspirin and clopidogrel only for those patients with ACS
- Evidence of substantial benefit of dual antiplatelet therapy with aspirin and clopidogrel in patients with ACS undergoing PCI and stent insertion
- ARMYDA-2 trial showed a reduction in cardiovascular events in patients undergoing PCI who received a 600-mg loading dose as opposed to 300 mg up to 8 h pre-procedure.

Prasugrel
- Prasugrel is also a pro-drug but its pharmacodynamics differ to clopidogrel
- It is converted to its active form faster and more consistently; it gives more reliable platelet inhibition
- TRITON-TIMI 38 showed that, in a large cohort of ACS patients undergoing PCI, patients receiving prasugrel had lower rates of the combined end-points of MACE (9.9% vs 12.1%; $p < 0.0001$) than those receiving clopidogrel at 15 months
- Within this there was a significant reduction in non-fatal MI but no difference in rates of death or stroke
- As expected this was offset by an increase in significant bleeding complications in the prasugrel group.

Glycoprotein IIb/IIIa inhibitors (abciximab/eptifibatide/tirofiban)
- Glycoprotein IIb/IIIa inhibitors bind to fibrinogen and von Willebrand factor thus blocking the final common pathway of platelet activation
- Indications include 'upstream' in the management of high risk ACS and as an adjunct agent during PCI
- In patients at intermediate to high risk, particularly with elevated troponins, ST depression, or diabetes—eptifibatide or tirofiban are recommended in addition to antiplatelet therapy 'upstream' in the treatment of ACS

- In high-risk patients not pre-treated with IIb/IIIa inhibitors and proceeding to PCI, abciximab is recommended immediately following angiography
- IIb/IIIa inhibitors must be combined with an anticoagulant
- Bivalirudin may be used as an alternative to IIb/IIIa inhibitors plus UFH/LMWH.

Newer P2Y$_{12}$ inhibitors

Ticagrelor

- Ticagrelor is an oral, reversible direct acting inhibitor of the P2Y$_{12}$ ADP receptor
- Since it is active in its native form it has a more rapid onset and achieves more pronounced platelet inhibition than clopidogrel
- PLATO trial showed that in a large cohort of ACS patients, treatment with ticagrelor reduced the incidence of MACE at 12 months as compared to patients treated with clopidogrel (9.8% vs 11.7%; $p < 0.001$)
- Importantly there was significantly lower mortality in the ticagrelor group
- Interestingly there was no difference in the rate of overall major bleeding between the two groups but there was an increase in the rate of non-CABG-related bleeding in the ticagrelor group (4.5% vs 3.8%; $p = 0.03$).

Anticoagulants

Unfractionated heparin

- Antithrombotic effects achieved through a number of different pathways—most importantly by accelerating the effect of antithrombin on factor Xa
- Due to poor subcutaneous absorption, intravenous administration is the route of choice
- A narrow therapeutic window means regular APTT monitoring is mandatory
- Whilst evidence exists as to the benefit of UFH versus placebo in the treatment of patients with ACS, due to the practical limitations of administration UFH has largely been superseded by the agents listed below.

Low molecular weight heparin

- The antithrombotic effect of low molecular weight heparin (LMWH) is achieved through inhibition of factors IIa and Xa
- Its major advantages over UFH are in ease of administration, as there is almost complete subcutaneous absorption, and a predictable weight-adjusted dose–effect relationship
- There is a lower incidence of heparin-induced thrombocytopaenia with LMWH as opposed to UFH
- Due to partial renal excretion, dose adjustment or alternative anticoagulants should be used in patients with significant impairment of renal function
- FRISC trial demonstrated significant reduction in death and re-infarction in ACS patients treated with LMWH versus placebo (2.5% vs 6%; $p < 0.05$)
- A large meta-analysis of trials comparing LMWH to UFH (21,946 patients) showed that whilst there was no significant difference in death at 30 days between the two, there was a significant reduction in the combined endpoint of death or MI for patients treated with LMWH (10.1% vs 11%; $p < 0.05$). There was no significant difference in major bleeding between the two groups.

Factor Xa inhibitors (fondaparinux)

- Fondaparinux is a synthetic pentasaccharide inhibitor of factor Xa
- It has 100% bioavailability after subcutaneous injection and a standard dosing of 2.5 mg is recommended for all patients with ACS

- As with LMWH, excretion is mainly renal and therefore care is advised in patients with significant renal impairment
- OASIS-5 trial of 20,078 patients showed that fondaparinux was non-inferior to LMWH at preventing future MACE following NSTE-ACS, with the added advantage of halving major bleeds (2.2% vs 4.1% p < 0.001).

Direct thrombin inhibitors (bivalirudin)

- HORIZONS-AMI trial showed that in the treatment of patients undergoing primary PCI for acute STE-ACS, bivalirudin treatment was associated with a significant reduction in all cause mortality (3.5% vs 4.8%; p = 0.037) and major bleeding (5.8% vs 9.2%; p < 0.0001) as compared to those treated with UFH and a IIb/IIIa inhibitor.

Beta blockers

- Beta blockers have been consistently shown to have a beneficial effect in patients with ACS
- ISIS-1 and MIAMI trials demonstrated a significant mortality benefit in patients with STEMI, although these trials were performed before the advent of modern reperfusion therapy
- Data suggest that beta blockers have beneficial effects for some years post MI, with a mortality benefit seen up to 3 years
- Although contemporary data is somewhat lacking, meta-analysis has suggested a 13% relative risk reduction in NSTE-ACS patients progressing to STEMI when treated with beta blockers.

Statins

- In all subgroups of patients with CAD, statins improve outcomes
- As well as their beneficial effect on altering the lipid profile, it is increasingly clear that statins have other powerful anti-inflammatory or pleiotropic effects
- The benefits of statins can be demonstrated very early after ACS, suggesting that these non-cholesterol lowering properties are dominant in this context
- Studies such as MIRACL, PROVE-IT, and IDEAL have demonstrated clinical benefit for early aggressive statin therapy in ACS
- The effect of statins is largely mediated by favourably altering the lipid profile of patients in favour of HDL and reducing LDL
- ASCOT trial showed a 36% reduction in death and non-fatal MI in hypertensive patients taking 10 mg of atorvastatin versus placebo at 3 years (p = 0.0005)
- PROVE-IT trial showed a significant reduction in both measured LDL levels and clinical endpoints in patients taking 80 mg atorvastatin versus those taking 40 mg pravastatin (22.4% vs 26.3%; p = 0.005).

ACE inhibitors

- ACE inhibitors prevent conversion of angiotensin I to angiotensin II
- They are potent vasoconstrictors and prevent aldosterone release
- Benefit to patients with CAD both with or without LV systolic dysfunction has been shown:
  - HOPE trial showed that in patients with preserved LV function and CVD, patients taking 10 mg ramipril had a significant reduction in death, MI, and stroke at 5 years as compared to placebo (14% vs 17.8%; p < 0.001)
  - The benefit of ACE inhibition was only seen at 2 years and continued to increase over time, suggesting that long-term therapy is the gold standard for patients with CVD
  - SMILE trial showed that in patients with LV dysfunction after an anterior MI, those randomized to receive an ACE inhibitor had a significant reduction in death and CCF at 6 weeks as compared to placebo (7.1% vs 10.6%; p = 0.018).

Angiotensin receptor blockers

- Angiotensin receptor blockers (ARBs) block the angiotensin II AT1 receptor producing benefits similar to ACE inhibitors
- Unlike ACE inhibitors they do not inhibit the breakdown of bradykinin, which causes cough and discontinuation of treatment in up to a quarter of patients:
  - ONTARGET trial demonstrated non-inferiority of telmisartan as compared to ramipril in the reduction of cardiovascular endpoints in patients with established CVD
  - With equivalent benefit this leaves ARBs mainly for patients who are ACEi intolerant.

2.5 Invasive and non-invasive investigations and management of patients with ACS

ST elevation ACS

- Reperfusion therapy is recommended for all patients with cardiac chest pain <12 h and ST segment elevation or new left bundle-branch block
- In patients with chest pain of more than 12 h duration, reperfusion should be considered if there is evidence (clinical/ECG) of ongoing ischaemia
- The goal of any treatment in STEMI must be to restore flow in the occluded coronary artery
- There are two options: administration of a fibrinolytic to dissolve thrombus or PCI with adjuvant pharmacotherapy.

Fibrinolytic therapy

- The benefit of fibrinolytic therapy is well established as compared to routine medical therapy, with 30 deaths prevented per 1000 patients treated
- Early fibrinolysis (<2 h) is supported by meta-analysis of 22 relevant trials
- Intracranial haemorrhage occurs in approximately 1% of the treated population, with age, female gender, low BMI, and previous CVA increasing that risk
- Significant non-cerebral bleeds occur in 5–15% of patients.

Percutaneous coronary intervention

- Primary percutaneous coronary intervention (PPCI):
  - Angioplasty/stenting without prior or concomitant fibrinolysis
  - A meta-analysis by Keeley et al. of relevant randomized clinical trials showed the superiority of primary PCI over in-hospital fibrinolysis, with the combined endpoint of death, non-fatal MI, and CVA being 8% in the primary PCI group vs 14% in the fibrinolytic group (p < 0.0001)
  - The time from first medical contact to balloon inflation should be <2 h in any case and <90 min in patients presenting within 2 h
  - Indicated for patients with shock or those with contraindications to fibrinolytic therapy irrespective of time delay.
- PPCI vs fibrinolysis:
  - A series of studies has compared thrombolysis with PPCI (DANAMI, PRAGUE2) and shown benefit for PPCI
  - The main benefit is a reduction in infarct size
  - PPCI is now the most common method for treating STEMI in the UK

- NRMI2–4 registry demonstrated a benefit of PPCI over fibrinolysis up to a time point of 114 min, when mortality rates for both strategies became equal
- Current ESC guidelines recommend that if PCI is not possible within 2 h of first medical contact then fibrinolysis should be initiated
- Facilitated PCI:
    - Facilitated PCI is fibrinolysis prior to planned PCI, as a bridge to definitive therapy
    - Keeley et al. performed a meta-analysis of 17 relevant trials in 2006, which suggested no significant benefit as compared to primary PCI at the expense of increased rates of stroke (1.1% vs 0.3%; p = 0.0008).

Coronary artery bypass grafting

- Possible if PCI has failed or if there are refractory symptoms, cardiogenic shock, or mechanical complications such as ventricular rupture, acute mitral regurgitation, or VSD.

Non-ST elevation ACS

- A heterogenous group of patients with variable prognosis
- Risk stratification is imperative to balance the benefits of invasive investigations (coronary angiography and angioplasty) against the morbidity and mortality associated with those procedures.

Percutaneous coronary intervention

- ECG changes in combination with angiographic appearances may identify culprit lesions
- The data overwhelmingly support invasive assessment with appropriate revascularization in patients with NSTEMI
- In the majority of cases this revascularization is with PCI
- PCI is recommended in the NICE guidance for unstable angina and NSTEMI (March 2010)
- A meta-analysis by Fox et al. has shown that an early invasive strategy is associated with a reduction in cardiovascular endpoints, including death and MI, at 5 years
- ST depression and elevated troponin appear to be the most powerful individual predictors of benefit from invasive treatment
- FRISC II trial showed a reduction in death or MI (12.1 vs 9.4%; p = 0.03) at 6 months in patients undergoing early invasive revascularization as opposed to medical therapy
- At 5 years there was an even greater reduction in the composite endpoint from 24.5 to 19.9% (p = 0.009) within the invasive arm
- RITA 3 trial similarly showed the benefit of an early invasive strategy
- There is a significant reduction in both death and MI at 4 months, continuing to 5 years, as compared to a conservative strategy.

Risk stratification

- ESC has adopted the GRACE risk score as a predictor of individual patient risk for use in daily clinical practice. ESC recommend that in NSTE-ACS patients:
    - With GRACE score >140, use an early invasive strategy within 24 h of presentation
    - With GRACE score <140, use a later invasive strategy within 72 h
    - With refractory angina, haemodynamic instability, arrhythmia, or heart failure, consider emergent angiography within 2 h of presentation.

CABG

- Indicated if the distribution and severity of CAD warrants surgical revascularization.

Non-invasive investigation of patients with suspected CAD

- In troponin-negative patients at intermediate or low risk who have an uncertain diagnosis, non-invasive ischaemia testing (functional testing) or coronary imaging (anatomical testing) may be the most appropriate management
- Patients with a significant burden of ischaemia (>10% ischaemic myocardium) are at lower risk of death and MI with revascularization as opposed to medical therapy
- In patients with poor LV function myocardial viability assessment may help to guide appropriateness of revascularization:
  - Exercise ECG is commonly used to document objective evidence of inducible ischaemia due to high availability and low cost
  - Defining a positive test as inducing 1 mm ST depression or more, meta-analysis has shown variation in sensitivity and specificity of 23–100%
  - Excluding patients with prior MI and studies without work-up bias, the sensitivity was 50% and specificity 90%
- Because of this there are important concerns about the sensitivity and specificity of exercise testing to determine ischaemia, and other tests have become increasingly relevant.

Non-invasive anatomical testing

Multidetector computed tomography coronary angiography (MDCT)

- MDCT is excellent in excluding significant CAD due to high negative predictive values (NPV)
- It produces moderate positive predictive values (PPVs), i.e. only approximately 50% of stenoses classified as significant on MDCT are associated with ischaemia on interrogation during coronary angiography.

Magnetic resonance imaging coronary angiography (MRCA)

- MRCA has the advantages of no radiation and high soft-tissue contrast without a need for synthetic contrast agents
- It requires ECG gating (acquisition of images in diastole) to reduce cardiac motion artifact and breath holding to reduce respiratory movement artifact
- Its spatial resolution is still inferior to MDCT and therefore currently has limited clinical use.

Functional testing

Stress echocardiography

- Stress echocardiography involves exercise on a treadmill or bicycle ergometer. If unable to physically exercise then a pharmacological stressor such as dobutamine or dipyridamole may be used
- Intravenous contrast agents help to identify the true endocardial border, making inducible regional wall motion abnormalities easier to detect
- The technique has a pooled sensitivity of 80–85% and specificity of 84–86%.

Perfusion scintigraphy

- Perfusion scintigraphy has a sensitivity of 85–90% and specificity of 70–75%
- ECG gating may improve these parameters in women, diabetics, and elderly patients.

Cardiac MRI (CMR)

- **Assessment of inducible ischaemia**
  - Perfusion imaging identifies myocardium subtended by significantly stenosed coronary arteries
  - Following administration of a vasodilator (typically adenosine), the dynamic passage of a contrast agent (typically gadolinium) is imaged through the cardiac chambers and myocardium. The hypoperfused myocardium is exposed relative to a normal segment

- Recent meta-analysis has shown a 91% sensitivity and 81% specificity of this technique
- Dobutamine stress imaging (DSCMR)
- By standard agreement the LV is divided into 17 segments, and images at rest and under stress are compared for inducible regional wall motion abnormalities
- Recent meta-analysis has shown an 83% sensitivity and 86% specificity of this technique
- **Myocardial viability** can be assessed by late gadolinium enhancement (LGE). This is based on the principle that an irreversibly damaged myocardium holds up gadolinium for longer than a normally functioning myocardium, appearing brighter on T-1 weighted images.

Multidetector computed tomography perfusion
- There is little contemporary data on this technique at present.

Positron emission tomography
- Positron emission tomography is expensive and limited to few UK centres
- The technique has a sensitivity of 92% and specificity of 85% in the detection of CAD.

Further reading

Bassand JP, Hamm CW, Ardissino D, et al., Guidelines for the diagnosis and treatment of non-ST-segment elevation acute coronary syndromes. Eur Heart J, 2007; 28: 1598–660.

Falk E. Why do plaques rupture? Circulation, 1992; 86: III30–42.

Fox K, Garcia MAA, Ardissino D, et al., Guidelines on the management of stable angina pectoris: executive summary: The Task Force on the Management of Stable Angina Pectoris of the European Society of Cardiology. Eur Heart J, 2006; 27: 1341–81.

Hobson A, Curzen N. Current status of oral antiplatelet therapies. In: Redwood S, Curzen N, Thomas M (eds). Oxford Textbook of Interventional Cardiology, pp. 379–94. Oxford University Press, 2010.

NICE guidance on unstable angina and NSTEMI 2010. www.nice.org.uk.

Patrono C, Bachmann F, Baigent C, et al. Expert consensus document on the use of antiplatelet agents. The Task Force on the Use of Antiplatelet Agents in Patients with Atherosclerotic Cardiovascular Disease of the European Society of Cardiology. Eur Heart J, 2004; 25: 166–81.

Redwood S, Curzen N, Thomas M (eds). Oxford Textbook of Interventional Cardiology. Oxford University Press, 2010.

Ross R. Atherosclerosis—an inflammatory disease. N Engl J Med, 1999; 340: 115–26.

Ross R. The pathogenesis of atherosclerosis: a perspective for the 1990s. Nature, 1993; 362: 801–9.

Stary HC. Natural history and histological classification of atherosclerotic lesions: an update. Arterioscler Thromb Vasc Biol, 2000; 20: 1177–8.

Van de Werf F., Ardissino D, Betriu A, et al. Management of acute myocardial infarction in patients presenting with persistent ST-segment elevation: the Task Force on the Management of ST-Segment Elevation Acute Myocardial Infarction of the European Society of Cardiology. Eur Heart J, 2008; 29: 2909–45.

Wijns W. Guidelines on myocardial revascularization. The Task Force on Myocardial Revascularisation of the ESC and the EACTS. Eur Heart J, 2010; 31: 2501–55.

Heart failure

All information from the ESC guidelines for the diagnosis and treatment of heart failure is from 2008 and 2010 unless otherwise stated. (See Further Reading section.)

3.1 Definitions

Heart failure is defined by the European Society of Cardiology as a clinical syndrome of:
- Symptoms typical of heart failure (HF)

with
- Signs of HF

with
- Reduced left ventricular ejection fraction (LVEF).

Ejection fraction

- Ejection fraction (EF) is defined as follows

$$\text{Ejection fraction} = \frac{\text{stroke volume (end diastolic volume} - \text{end systolic volume)}}{\text{end diastolic volume}}$$

- HF with preserved ejection function (HFPEF) involves:
  - Presence of symptoms
  - Signs of HF
  - Prevalence of normal or only mildly abnormal LV systolic function (LVEF $\geq$ 45–50%) and LV non-dilated
  - Evidence of relevant structural heart disease (LV hypertrophy/LA enlargement) and/or diastolic dysfunction (abnormal LV relaxation or diastolic stiffness).

3.2 Prevalence

- The incidence and prevalence of HF increase steeply with age
- The average age at first diagnosis is 76 years

- The incidence of HF in the UK is 140 per 100,000 men and 120 per 100,000 women
- Around 3% of people aged 65–74 years have HF; this increases to ≥10% of those 75 years and older
- The prevalence of HF in the UK is 40 per 1000 in men and 30 per 1000 in women.

3.3 Prognosis

- 50% patients will be dead at 4 years
- 40% of those admitted to hospital with HF will be dead or readmitted in 1 year
- More severely ill patients are more likely to die because of congestive HF
- Those with less severe HF are more likely to experience sudden cardiac death.

3.4 Predictors of poor prognosis in heart failure

- Advanced age
- Ischaemic aetiology
- Resuscitated sudden death
- Hypotension
- NYHA (New York Heart Association) functional class III–IV
- Prior HF hospitalization
- Wide QRS
- Complex ventricular arrhythmias
- Low peak VO_2
- Marked elevation of BNP/NT-proBNP
- Hyponatraemia
- Elevated troponin, neurohumoral activation
- Low LVEF.

See Table 3.1 for common causes of HF.

3.5 Symptoms

- Breathlessness
- Fatigue
- Paroxysmal nocturnal dyspnoea
- Orthopnoea
- Anorexia
- Confusion
- Weakness
- Cold peripheries
- Peripheral oedema.

See Table 3.2 for symptoms by NHYA classification and Table 3.3 for signs of HF.

3.6 Investigations

ECG

- An ECG should be performed in all patients with suspected HF
- If ECG is normal, HF is unlikely.

Table 3.1 Causes of heart failure

Coronary artery disease	
Hypertension	
Cardiomyopathies	Familial/genetic or non-familial/non-genetic (including acquired e.g. myocarditis) Dilated cardiomyopathy, restrictive cardiomyopathy, hypertrophic cardiomyopathy, arrhythmogenic right ventricular cardiomyopathy
Drugs	Beta blockers, calcium antagonists, antiarrhythmics, cytotoxic agents
Toxins	Alcohol, medication, cocaine, trace elements
Endocrine	Diabetes mellitus, hypo/hyperthyroidism, Cushing's syndrome, adrenal insufficiency, excessive growth hormone, pheochromocytoma
Nutritional	Deficiency of thiamine, selenium, carnitine, obesity, cachexia
Infiltrative	Sarcoidosis, amyloidosis, haemochromatosis
Others	Chagas disease, HIV infection, peripartum cardiomyopathy, end-stage renal failure

Adapted from ESC guidelines for acute and chronic heart failure 2008

Table 3.2 New York Heart Association functional classes

NYHA class	Symptoms
I	No limitation of physical activity
II	Slight limitation
III	Marked limitation
IV	Symptoms at rest

Table 3.3 Signs of heart failure

Appearance	Alertness, nutritional status, weight
Pulse	Rate, rhythm, character
Blood pressure	Systolic, diastolic, pulse pressure
Fluid overload	JVP, peripheral oedema, hepatomegaly, ascites
Lungs	Respiratory rate, rales, pleural effusion
Heart	Apex displacement, gallop rhythm, third heart sound, murmurs suggesting valvular dysfunction

Adapted from ESC guidelines for acute and chronic heart failure 2008

See Table 3.4 for ECG abnormalities in HF.

CXR

- Apart from congestion, findings predictive of HF only in context of typical signs and symptoms of HF
  See Table 3.5 for CXR abnormalities in heart failure.

Laboratory tests

B-type natriuretic peptide and N-terminal pro-BNP

- Evidence supports the use of B-type natriuretic peptide (BNP) and N-terminal pro-BNP (NT-proBNP) in diagnosis, staging, making hospitalization/discharge decisions, and identifying patients at risk for clinical events

Table 3.4 ECG abnormalities

ECG abnormality	Causes
Sinus tachycardia	Decompensated HF, anaemia, fever, hypothyroidism
Sinus bradycardia	Beta blocker, digoxin, hypothyroidism, sick sinus syndrome
Atrial tachycardia/fibrillation/ flutter	Hyperthyroidism, infection, MV diseases, decompensated HF, infarction
Ventricular arrhythmias	Ischaemia, infarction, cardiomyopathy, myocarditis, hypokalaemia, hypomagnasemia, digitalis OD
Ischaemia/infarction	Coronary artery disease
Q waves	Infarction, HCM, LBBB, pre-excitation
LV hypertrophy	Hypertension, AV disease, HCM
AV block	Infarction, drug toxicity, myocarditis, sarcoidosis, Lyme disease
Microvoltage	Obesity, emphysema, pericardial effusion, amyloidosis
QRS >120 ms	Desynchrony

Adapted from ESC guidelines for acute and chronic heart failure 2008

Table 3.5 CXR abnormalities

CXR abnormality	Causes
Cardiomegaly	Dilated LV, RV, atria, pericardial effusion
Ventricular hypertrophy	Hypertension, AS, HCM
Pulmonary venous congestion	Elevated LV filling pressures
Interstitial oedema	Elevated LV filling pressures
Pleural effusions	Elevated LV filling pressures, non-cardiac
Kerley B lines	Increased lymphatic pressures

Adapted from ESC guidelines for acute and chronic heart failure 2008

- BNP is co-secreted along with the 76-amino-acid NT-proBNP, which is biologically inactive
- BNP and NT-proBNP are mainly produced in the cardiac ventricles and serum levels rise in response to an increase in myocardial wall stress
- In patients presenting with acute onset or worsening of symptoms, cut off exclusion is: BNP, 100 pg/ml; NT-proBNP, 300 pg/ml
- For non-acute patients exclusion cut off is: BNP <35 pg/ml; NT-proBNP, 125 pg/ml.

Troponin

- Troponin I or T should be sampled when the clinical picture suggests ACS
- Increased troponin indicates myocardial necrosis, acute myocarditis, severe HF, and other conditions such as sepsis
- Elevated troponin is a strong prognostic marker in HF especially in the presence of raised BNP.

Echocardiography

- Per the British Society of Echocardiography *Guidelines for Chamber Quantification*, confirmation of the diagnosis of HF by echocardiography is mandatory
  See Tables 3.6–3.8 for BSE Guidelines for Chamber Quantification.

Table 3.6 Left Ventricle Chamber Quantification

	Normal	Mild	Moderate	Severe
LV wall thickness (IVSd/PWd) mm	6–12	13–15	16–19	≥20
LV dimension (cm/m²)				
Women LVIDd/BSA	2.4–3.2	3.3–3.4	3.5–3.7	≥3.8
Men LVIDsd/BSA	2.2–3.1	3.2–3.4	3.5–3.6	≥3.7
LV volume index				
Diastole (ml/m²)	35–75	76–86	87–96	≥97
Systole (ml/m²)	12–30	31–36	37–42	≥43
LV function (%)				
Ejection fraction	≥55	45–55	36–44	≤35
Fractional shortening	25–43	20–24	15–19	<15

For non-indexed see BSE reference charts.

Table 3.7 Left ventricle diastolic function

	Normal	Grade 1	Grade 2	Grade 3
		↓Relaxation *Abnormal relaxation*	↓Relaxation ↓Compliance ↑LVEDP *Pseudo-normal*	↓Relaxation ↓Compliance ↑↑ LVEDP *Restrictive filling*
LV inflow Doppler				
E/A ratio	1–2	<1	1–2	>2
DT (ms)	150–200	>200	150–200	<150
Mitral annular tissue Doppler				
E/E$_m$ (septum)	<8		>15	
E/E$_m$ (lateral)	<10		>10	
Left atrial size				
Diameter cm/m²	1.5–2.3	2.4–2.6	2.7–2.9	≥3.0
Volume ml/m²	16–28	29–33	34–39	≥40

Table 3.8 Right Ventricle Chamber Quantification

	Normal	Mild	Moderate	Severe
RV dimensions (A4Ch) cm				
Basal RV diameter (RVD1)	2.0–2.8	2.9–3.3	3.4–3.8	≥3.9
Mid RV diameter (RVD2)	2.7–3.3	3.4–3.7	3.8–4.1	≥4.2
Base-to-apex length (RVD3)	7.1–7.9	8.0–8.5	8.6–9.1	≥9.2
RV area (cm²)				
Diastole	11–28	29–32	33–37	≥38
Systole	7.5–16	17–19	20–22	≥23
RV function				
Fractional area change (%)	32–60	25–31	18–24	≤17
TAPSE (mm)	16–20	11–15	6–10	≤5

Cardiac magnetic resonance (CMR)

- CMR is the gold standard for determining LV/RV volumes, regional wall motion abnormalities, myocardial thickness, thickening, and myocardial mass
- It assesses tumours, cardiac valves, congenital defects, and pericardial disease
- It predicts prognosis in inflammatory and infiltrative disease
- It is the imaging method of choice in complex congenital heart disease
- Gadolinium contrast agent is contraindicated in patients with GFR <30 ml/min/m^2 due to risk of nephrogenic systemic fibrosis.

CT scan

- CT scan provides a non-invasive diagnosis of CAD
- It may be considered in patients with low-risk CAD and in equivocal stress testing.

Radionucliatide ventriculography

- Myocardial perfusion scanning can provide information on viability and ischaemia
- It has limited value for assessing volumes and subtle abnormalities in systolic and diastolic function.

Pulmonary function tests

- Pulmonary function tests are of limited value in the diagnosis of HF
- They are useful in assessing lung disease as a cause for breathlessness.

Exercise testing

- Exercise testing provides an objective evaluation of exercise capacity
- A 6-min walk test is reproducible and assesses response to intervention
- Cardiopulmonary exercise testing:
    - Gas exchange analysis provides a highly reproducible measurement of exercise limitation and insights into the differentiation between respiratory or cardiac causes of breathlessness, assesses ventilatory efficiency, and carries prognostic information
    - Peak VO$_2$ (oxygen uptake) and the anaerobic threshold are useful indicators of patients' functional capacity
    - The VE/VCO$_2$ (ventillatory response to exercise) is the major prognostic variable.

Ambulatory ECG

- Ambulatory ECG is valuable in patients with symptoms suggestive of arrhythmia
- Ambulatory ECG can monitor rate control in AF
- Episodes of symptomatic non-sustained ventricular tachycardia are frequent in HF and carry a poor prognosis.

Cardiac catheterization

- Unnecessary for routine diagnosis and management of patients with HF.

The indications for coronary angiography are:

- A history suggestive of angina
- Suspected ischaemic LV dysfunction
- Reversible ischamia on non-invasive testing
- ACS
- Recent cardiac arrest
- Patient not responding to treatment

- Refractory HF of unknown aetiology
- Evidence of severe MR or aortic valve disease potentially correctable with surgery.

Endomyocardial biopsy

Considered in:

- Patients with acute or fulminant HF of unknown aetiology who deteriorate rapidly with ventricular arrhythmias and or AV block
- Patients unresponsive to conventional HF treatment
- Patients with chronic HF with suspected infiltrative process, eosinophyllic myocarditis, and restrictive cardiomyopathy.

Genetic testing is indicated in:

- Idiopathic dilated cardiomyopathy (DCM) and hypertrophic cardiomyopathy (HCM)
- DCM with AV block or a family history of sudden cardiac death, as a prophylactic ICD may be indicated.

3.7 Treatments

For treatment algorithm as advised by the ESC see Figure 3.1.

Drugs

ACE inhibitors

Indications:

- ACE inhibitors should be used in patients with HF and EF ≤40% in addition to beta blockers (BB).

Contraindications:

- History of angioedema
- Bilateral renal artery stenosis
- Serum potassium >5 mmol/l
- Serum creatinine >220 μmol/l
- Critical AS.

Important studies:

- CONCENSUS (enalapril) 27% RRR mortality
- SOLVD-treatment (enalapril) 16% RRR mortality
- ATLAS (lisinopril) 15% RRR mortality and hospitalization in high dose vs low dose
- Post MI: SAVE (captopril), AIRE (ramipril), TRACE (trandolapril) 26% RRR mortality, 27% RRR death or hospitalization.

Adverse effects:

- Check renal function and electrolytes before initiation; recheck 1–2 weeks post starting. Consider dose up titration after 2–4 weeks
- An increase in creatinine of up to 50% or total 265 μmol/l is acceptable
- If creatinine 265 μmol/l–310 μmol/l or K^+ >5.5 halve the dose of ACE inhibitor and monitor blood chemistry closely
- If creatinine rises to more than 310 μmol/l or K^+ >6.0 mmol/l stop ACE inhibitor and monitor blood chemistry closely
- If ACE inhibitor causes a troublesome cough switch to an ARB.

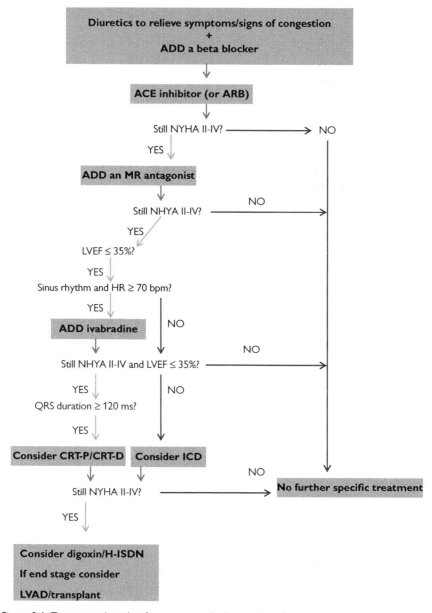

Figure 3.1 Treatment algorithm for patients with chronic heart failure.

Adapted with permission from 'The ESC guidelines for the diagnosis and treatment of acute and chronic heart failure 2012,' *European Heart Journal* (2012) 33, 1787–1847. McMurray *et al.*, with permission of Oxford University Press.

Beta blockers (carvedilol, bisoprolol, metoprolol succinate, nebivolol)

Indications:

- LVEF≤40%
- NYHA II–IV
- Asymptomatic LVSD post MI

- Instead of an ACE inhibitor
- Patient clinically stable.

Contraindications:

- Asthma (COPD not a contraindication)
- Second- or third-degree heart block, sick sinus syndrome, sinus bradycardia (<50 bpm).

Key studies:

- CIBIS II (bisoprolol), COPERNICUS (carvedilol), MERIT-HF (metorolol succinate CR) 34% RRR mortality, 28–36% RRR hospital admission for worsening HF with one year of starting treatment
- SENIORS (nebivolol >70 years) 14% RRR mortality or hospital admission for cardiovascular cause).

Mineralocorticoid/aldosterone antagonists (MRA)

Indications:

- LVEF ≤35%
- NYHA II–IV
- Optimal dose of ACE inhibitor and BB.

Contraindications:

- Serum potassium >5.0 mmol/l
- Serum creatinine >220 μmol/l
- Concomitant potassium-sparing diuretic or potassium supplement
- Combination ACE inhibitor and ARB.

Key studies:

- RALES (spironolactone, LVEF ≤35%, and NYHA III) 30% RRR mortality, 35% hospital admission within 2 years, improved NYHA class)
- EPHESUS (epleronone, post MI, LVEF ≤40%, and HF or diabetes) 15% RRR mortality
- EMPHASIS-HF (epleronone, LVEF ≤30%, and NHYA II) 37% RRR, CV death or hospitalization).

Adverse effects:

- If potassium rises to >5.5 mmol/l or creatinine >220 μmol/l halve the dose of spironolactone/epleronone
- If potassium rises to >6.0 mmol/l or creatinine >310 μmol/l stop spironolactone/epleronone
- If breast tenderness/gynaecomastia switch spironolactone to epleronone.

Angiotensin receptor blockers (ARB)

Indications:

- LVEF ≤40%
- An alternative in patients NYHA II–IV who are intolerant of ACE inhibitors.

Contraindications:

- Patients taking an ACE inhibitor and an aldosterone antagonist
- Renal dysfunction and/or raised serum potassium.

Key studies:

- Val-HEFT (valsartan) 24% RRR hospital admission for worsenening HF, improved symptoms and quality of life
- CHARM-Added (candesartan) 17% RRR hospital admission for worsening HF, improved symptoms and quality of life.

Ivabradine

Indications:

- Sinus rhythm
- EF ≤35% and HR >70 bpm with persisting symptoms (NYHA II–IV) despite optimal-dose BB, ACE inhibitor (or ARB) and MRA (or ARB)
- EF ≤35% and HR >70 bpm with persisting symptoms (NYHA II–IV) on ACE inhibitor (or ARB) and MRA (or ARB) who are unable to tolerate BBs.

Contraindications:

- AF.

Key studies:

- SHIFT (NYHA II–IV, EF ≤35%, bpm >70) RRR CV death or hospitalization 18%
- BEAUTIFUL (CAD and EF <40%).

Hydralazine and isosorbide dinitrate (H-ISDN)

Indications:

- H-ISDN is an alternative to ACE inhibitor/ARB when both not tolerated if EF ≤45% and dilated LV (or EF ≤35%). On BB and MRA EF ≤45% and dilated LV (or EF ≤35%) and persisting symptioms despite treatment with BB and ACE inhibitor (or ARB) and MRA (or ARB)
- The evidence is strongest in African-American patients.

Contraindications:

- Symptomatic hypotension
- Lupus
- Severe renal failure.

Key studies:

- V-HeFT (placebo, pravastatin, or H-ISDN added to diuretic and digoxin); H-ISDN indicated
- A-HeFT (African-American in NYHA III–IV, randomized to placebo or H-ISDN added to diuretic, digoxin, ACE inhibitor, ARB, BB and spironolactone) RRR mortality 43%.

Digoxin

Indications (in HF):

Atrial fibrillation

- Ventricular rate at rest >80 bpm, at exercise >110–120 bpm.

Sinus rhythm

- LVEF ≤40%
- NYHA II–IV
- Optimal dose ACE inhibitor or ARB, BB and MRA or ARB.

Key studies:

- DIG trial 28% RRR for hospital admission for worsening HF.

Diuretics

- Used for relief of symptoms and signs of pulmonary and systemic venous congestion in patients with HF
- Loop diuretic usually required in moderate or severe HF
- Thiazide diuretic (e.g. metolozone) may be used in addition to loop diuretic for resistant oedema with caution.

Revascularization

Indications:

- Angina
- LMS stenosis
- Two- or three- vessel disease including LAD disease
- Viable myocardium >10% more likely to benefit.

Key studies:

- STITCH (EF ≤35% and CAD randomized to CABG plus medical therapy or medical therapy alone). All-cause death not reduced. CV death RRR 19%, CV hospitalization RRR 26%.

Valvular surgery

Indications:

- Aortic stenosis:
  - Eligible patients with severe AS and HF symptoms
  - Severe AS and LVEF <50%
- Aortic regurgitation
  - Severe AR and symptoms of HF
  - Asymptomatic patients with severe AR and LVEF ≤50%
- Organic mitral regurgitation
  - Severe MR when coronary revascularization is an option
  - Severe MR when LVEF >30% and valve repair possible
- Functional mitral regurgitation
  - May be considered in selected patients with severe functional MR and severely depressed LV function who remain symptomatic despite optimal medical therapy
- Ischaemic mitral regurgitation
  - Severe MR and LVEF >30% when CABG planned
  - Moderate MR undergoing CABG if repair possible.

CRT-D (ESC guidelines)

CRT-D/CRT-P is recommended to reduce morbidity and mortality in:

- NYHA functional class II–IV on optimal medical therapy with LVEF ≤35%, QRS ≥120 ms (LBBB morphology) in SR
- NYHA functional class II–IV on optimal medical therapy with LVEF ≤35%, QRS ≥150 ms (irrespective of QRS morphology) in SR.

CRT in AF

- NYHA functional class III/IV on optimal medical therapy with EF <35%, QRS >120 ms provided BiV pacing as close to 100% as possible can be achieved
- AV junction ablation should be added in cases of incomplete BiV pacing.

CRT (NICE guidance)

Cardiac resynchronization therapy with a pacing device (CRT-P) is recommended as a treatment option for people with HF who fulfil all of the following criteria:

- Currently experiencing or have recently experienced NYHA class III–IV symptoms
- In sinus rhythm:
  - *Either* with a QRS duration of 150 ms or longer estimated by standard ECG

- *Or* with a QRS duration of 120–149 ms estimated by ECG *and* mechanical dyssynchrony that is confirmed by echocardiography
- LVEF ≤35%
- Receiving optimal pharmacological therapy.

The addition of a defibrillator (CRT-D) may be considered for those with no worse than class III HF:

- Primary prevention: ischaemic aetiology (prior MI) with EF <30% or EF <35% with documented NSVT
- Secondary prevention: cardiac arrest/sustained spontaneous VT (syncope suggestive).

See Chapters 8 and 30.

Key studies:

- CRT-P compared with optimal pharmacological therapy:
  - CRT-P with optimal pharmacological therapy (CARE-HF, COMPANION, MIRACLE and MUSTIC-SR) demonstrated a statistically significant reduction in all-cause mortality for CRT-P compared with optimal pharmacological therapy alone. All four RCTs showed consistent improvements in exercise capacity and health-related quality of life for CRT-P compared with optimal pharmacological therapy alone
- CRT-D versus optimal pharmacological therapy alone:
  - COMPANION and CONTAK-CD: a meta-analysis demonstrated a statistically significant reduction in all-cause mortality for CRT-D compared with optimal pharmacological therapy alone (HR 0.65, 95% CI 0.49–0.85)
  - COMPANION also reported improvements in the effectiveness of CRT-D compared with optimal pharmacological therapy alone for rate of death from HF (HR 0.73, 95% CI 0.47–1.11, p = 0.143), rate of sudden cardiac death (HR 0.44, 95% CI 0.23–0.86, p = 0.02) and NYHA class (pooled RR 1.40, 95% CI 1.13–1.75, p <0.0001)
  - COMPANION reported a significant improvement in the number of patients hospitalized due to HF with CRT-D (rate ratio 0.59, 95% CI 0.49–0.70, p <0.0001)
- CRT-D versus ICD:
  - MADIT CRT (NYHA I/II, EF <30%, QRS >130 ms) showed a 41% reduction in the risk of heart-failure events with CRT. This was in a subgroup of patients with a QRS duration of 150 ms or more. There was no significant difference between the two groups in the overall risk of death, with a 3% annual mortality rate in each treatment group
- CRT-ON versus CRT-OFF:
  - Reverse (NYHA I/II, QRS ≥120 ms, EF ≤40%) showed that CRT, in combination with optimal medical therapy (±defibrillator), reduces the risk for HF hospitalization and improves ventricular structure and function in NYHA I/II patients with previous HF symptoms
- CRT-D versus CRT-P:
  - COMPANION was the only RCT that provided a direct comparison between the effectiveness of CRT-P and CRT-D. CRT-D was associated with a statistically significant reduction in the incidence of both cardiac death (12.8% for CRT-D compared with 17.1% for CRT-P) and sudden cardiac death (2.9% for CRT-D compared with 7.8% for CRT-P, p = 0.0001) compared with CRT-P.

Risks:

- Perioperative death associated with CRT (CRT-P and CRT-D pooled) in the RCTs was 0.8% (95% CI 0.5–1.2%)
- CRT devices were implanted successfully on average in 90.8% of patients (95% CI 89.6–92.0%)

- CRT device implanted successfully without an improvement in patient condition ranges from 11–46% (patient condition is assessed by NYHA class and echocardiographic parameters).

Left ventricular assist device

In patients with severe HF ineligible for transplantation, a left ventricular assist device (LVAD) may be considered as a bridge to transplantation or a destination treatment to reduce mortality in patients with severe symptoms despite optimal medical and device therapy plus one of:

- NYHA functional class IIIB/IV, LVEF ≤25%, peak VO$_2$ <12 ml/kg/min
- ≥3 HF hospitalizations in three months without an obvious precipitating cause
- Dependence on IV inotropic therapy
- Progressive end organ dysfunction due to reduced perfusion and not inadequate filling pressure (PCWP ≥20 mm Hg and SBP ≤80–90 mmHg or CI ≤2 l/min/m^2)
- Deteriorating RV function.

Cardiac transplant

See 'UK guidelines for referral and assessment of adults for heart transplantation', in the Further Reading section.

Indications:

- Impaired LV systolic function
- NYHA III or IV HF
- Receiving optimal medical therapy
- CRT, ICD, or CRT-D device implanted (if indicated)
- Evidence of poor prognosis:
  - Cardiorespiratory exercise testing (VO$_2$ max <12 ml/kg/min if on beta blockade, <14 ml/kg/min if not on beta blockade, ensuring respiratory quotient ≥1.05)
  - Markedly elevated BNP (or NT-proBNP) serum levels despite full medical treatment
  - Established composite prognostic scoring system (HF survival score, Seattle Heart Failure Model).

Absolute contraindications:

- Irreversible renal dysfunction
- Pulmonary hypertension irreversible despite treatment with pulmonary vasodilators (pulmonary vascular resistance >5 Woods units, transpulmonary gradient >15 mmHg, pulmonary artery systolic pressure >60 mmHg)
- Microvascular complications of diabetes (except non-proliferative retinopathy)
- Chronic/active current systemic infection, including endocarditis
- Active malignancy (except non-melanoma skin cancer)
- Unable to give informed consent
- History of prior non-compliance to treatment or follow up (require psychological/psychiatric evaluation).

Relative contraindications:

- Age >65 (incremental risk factor and associated with co morbidity)
- Obesity (BMI >32 kg/m^2)
- Symptomatic peripheral and cerebrovascular disease
- Autoimmune disorders
- Infiltrative cardiac disease
- Aggressive skeletal myopathies

- Chronic viral infections
- History of prior non-compliance to treatment or follow up (require psychological/psychiatric evaluation)
- Substance abuse (including smoking and excessive alcohol consumption)
- Recent pulmonary embolus.

Further reading

Banner NR, Bonser RS, Clark AL, et al. UK guidelines for referral and assessment of adults for heart transplantation. Heart, 2011; 97(18): 1520–7.

Brignole M, Auricchio A, Baron-Esquivias G, et al. 2013 ESC Guidelines on cardiac pacing and cardiac resynchronization therapy. Eur Heart J, 2013; 34(29): 2281–329.

British Society of Echocardiography. Guidelines for Chamber Quantification.

Dickstein K, Cohen-Solal A, Filippatos G, et al. ESC guidelines for the diagnosis and treatment of acute and chronic heart failure 2008, Eur Heart J, 2008; 29: 2388–442.

Dickstein K, Vardas PE, Auricchio A, et al. Focused update of ESC guidelines on device therapy in heart failure 2010. Eur Heart J, 2010; 31: 2677–87.

McMurray J, Adamopoulos S, Anker SD, et al. ESC guidelines for the diagnosis and treatment of acute and chronic heart failure 2012. Eur Heart J, 2012; 33: 1787–847.

National Institute for Health and Clinical Excellence. CRT-D (Adapted from TA 120 Cardiac Resynchronisation Therapy for the Treatment of Heart Failure). London: NICE.

Cardiomyopathy

4.1 Primary cardiomyopathy

- Patients with primary disorders of the myocardium tend to have a genetic component
- The conditions fall broadly under five categories (Figure 4.1):
    - Dilated cardiomyopathy (DCM)
    - Hypertrophic cardiomyopathy (HCM)
    - Restrictive cardiomyopathy (RCM)
    - Arrythmogenic cardiomyopathy (ACM)
    - Unclassified cardiomyopathy (UCM or left ventricular non-compaction)
- An inflammatory cardiomyopathy may also exist and is defined as inflammation of the myocardium and its structures by infectious or non-infectious agents.

4.2 Hypertrophic cardiomyopathy

Four cardinal features are key to diagnosis:

1. Unexplained hypertrophy of the left ventricle
2. Cardiac myocyte disarray
3. Familial occurrence
4. Association with sudden cardiac death.

- Concentric, asymmetric, and apical patterns of hypertrophy are all well recognized
- The presence of left ventricular outflow tract obstruction (LVOTO), although not essential for diagnosis, occurs in around a quarter of patients with clinical and prognostic implications.

Genetics

- Hypertrophic cardiomyopathy is an inherited disorder with mutation of the sarcomeric proteins
- Sarcomere is the contractile apparatus within the myocardial cells
- Mutation leads to myocyte disarray and fibrosis, myocardial hypertrophy, and small vessel coronary artery disease.

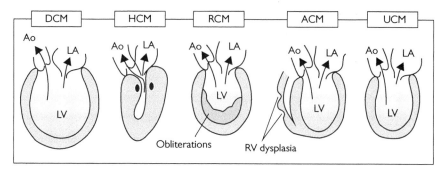

Figure 4.1 Classification of cardiomyopathies based on a report of the World Health Organization and International Society and Federation of Cardiology. DCM, dilated cardiomyopathy; HCM, hypertrophic cardiomyopathy; RCM, restrictive cardiomyopathy; ACM, arrhythmic cardiomyopathy; UCM, unclassified cardiomyopathy.

Reproduced from Richardson et al. Report of the 1995 World Health Organization/International Society and Federation of Cardiology Task Force on the definition and classification of cardiomyopathies. *Circulation* 1996; 93: 841–2, with permission of Wolters Kluwer Health.

BOX 4.1 MUTATIONS

β-myosin heavy chain

α-tropomyosin

Troponin T

Troponin I

Myosin-binding protein C

Regulatory myosin light chain

Essential myosin light chain

Cardiac actin

Titin

α-cardiac myosin heavy chain

Troponin C

- Autosomal dominant mode of inheritance is most common, with increasing penetrance with age
- Most common mutation is the gene for β-myosin heavy chain but many other mutations have been implicated (see Box 4.1)
- Prevalence is estimated at 1 in 500
- Only 60% are estimated to have a detectable mutation in sarcomeric genes
- Some patients have phenocopies of HCM, i.e. a phenotype suggestive of HCM but an alternative underlying condition (e.g. Fabry's disease, glycogen storage disorder, disorders of metabolism)
- Phenocopies tend to have extra-cardiac manifestations and an increased incidence of conduction disease, cavity dilation, and heart failure.

Pathophysiology

- Diastolic dysfunction (several mechanisms):
  - Normal calcium uptake required for early diastole is disrupted
  - Hypertrophy and interstitial fibrosis decrease compliance and cause the failure of passive relaxation

- Small vessel ischaemia:
  - Changes occur in the microcirculation, with reduced arteriolar luminal size and capillary density
  - There is also a reduction in coronary flow reserve
- LVOT obstruction:
  - Outflow tract obstruction occurs in 25% of patients (it can occur in the mid cavity and apex as well as at the sub-aortic level)
  - Systolic anterior motion of the mitral valve caused by abnormal mitral apparatus and abnormal haemodynamics leads to further obstruction as well as a degree of mitral regurgitation.

Clinical presentation

- Asymptomatic:
  - Screening due to family history or abnormal ECG
- Angina:
  - Small vessel coronary disease
- Breathlessness:
  - Diastolic dysfunction due to left ventricular hypertrophy (LVH)
- Raised pulmonary pressures:
  - Ischaemia ± mitral regurgitation
- Dizziness/syncope:
  - Left ventricular tract obstruction
  - Ventricular arrhythmia

Physical signs include:

  - Rapid upstroke to pulse
  - Forceful left ventricle at apex ('double impulse')
  - Mid-late systolic murmur (no carotid radiation), which can be provoked with exercise or valsalva manoeuvre.

Diagnosis

Echocardiography

See Box 4.2.

- Caution should be used to distinguish HCM from athlete's heart in young, fit individuals
- Athletes tend to have milder degrees of left ventricular hypertrophy (LVH) (septal thickness of 13–14 mm), the LV cavity tends to be enlarged, and diastolic parameters are normal or enhanced.

ECG

See Box 4.3.

Cardiac magnetic resonance imaging

- Permits accurate assessment of left ventricular hypertrophy and left ventricular mass
- Late gadolinium studies are helpful in distinguishing from other forms of cardiomyopathy.

Screening investigations

- Patients screened for HCM with echocardiography if family history or symptoms:
  - Pre-pubescent children only if symptomatic, have a high risk family history, undertake competitive sport, or there are high levels of parental anxiety

BOX 4.2 ECHOCARDIOGRAPHIC GUIDELINES FOR THE DIAGNOSIS OF HYPERTROPHIC CARDIOMYOPATHY

Major criteria

LV wall thickness ≥13 mm in the anterior septum or ≥15 mm in the posterior septum or free wall.

Severe SAM (septum–leaflet contact).

Minor criteria

LV wall thickness of 12 mm in the anterior septum or posterior wall or of 14 mm in the posterior septum or free wall.

Moderate SAM (no septum–leaflet contact).

Redundant mitral valve leaflets.

Guidelines are applicable only to first-degree relatives of index cases with confirmed hypertrophic cardiomyopathy, all of whom have a 50% probability of carrying the mutation. Diagnosis is established in the presence of one major criterion, or two minor echocardiographic criteria, or one minor echocardiographic plus two minor electrocardiographic criteria. Other causes of left ventricular hypertrophy (e.g. athletic training and hypertension) may confound diagnosis.

LV, left ventricular; SAM, systolic anterior motion of the mitral valve. Reproduced from the *ESC Textbook of Cardiovascular Medicine* 2nd edition, ed. John Camm, Thomas Lüscher and Patrick Serruys, copyright 2009 with permission of Oxford University Press.

BOX 4.3 ECG GUIDELINES FOR THE DIAGNOSIS OF HYPERTROPHIC CARDIOMYOPATHY

Major criteria

Left ventricular hypertrophy and repolarization changes.

T wave inversion in leads I and aVL (≥3 mm) (with QRS–T wave axis difference ≥30°), V3–V6 (≥3 mm) or II and III and aVF (≥5 mm).

Abnormal Q (>40 ms or >25% R wave) in at least two leads from II, III, aVF (in absence of left anterior hemiblock), V1–V4; or I, aVL, V5–V6.

Minor criteria

Complete bundle branch block or (minor) interventricular conduction defect (in LV leads).

Minor repolarization changes in LV leads.

Deep S V2 (>25 mm).

Reproduced from the *ESC Textbook of Cardiovascular Medicine* 2nd edition, ed. John Camm, Thomas Lüscher and Patrick Serruys, copyright 2009 with permission of Oxford University Press.

- Adolescents: annual review from early adolescence, as clinical manifestations occur during puberty
- In later life, five-yearly screening of relatives due to incidence of late onset HCM.

Prognosis and outcome

- Clinical course is variable—annual mortality estimated at 1% for asymptomatic patients; 5% for symptomatic (overall 2–3%). See Box 4.4
- Symptoms tend to be due to left ventricular outflow tract obstruction (LVOTO) and diastolic dysfunction due to LVH
- Left ventricular thinning also occurs secondary to abnormal haemodynamics, leading to myocyte loss and fibrosis.

BOX 4.4 RISK FACTORS FOR SUDDEN CARDIAC DEATH IN HYPERTROPHIC CARDIOMYOPATHY

- Family history of premature death (first degree relative)
- Recurrent syncope (exercise related)
- Septal thickness >30 mm
- A genetic phenotype associated with sudden cardiac death (SCD)
- Non-sustained ventricular tachycardia (VT) (especially if under 30 years old)
- Inadequate rise in blood pressure during exercise
- Resting LVOTO >30 mmHg.

Risk stratification for patients with confirmed HCM

- Risk stratification should be performed annually
- Echocardiography to assess LV thickness and LVOTO
- Exercise testing: inadequate Bp response defined as <20 mmHg rise in response to exercise
- 24-h Holter monitor:
    - ≥3 beats of VT at rate of ≥120 bpm
    - Presence of AF (refer for formal anticoagulation)
    - Consider implantable loop recorder if suspicious history for malignant arrhythmia.

Management

Aims of management

- Alleviate symptoms
- Prevent complications, e.g. atrial fibrillation
- Reduce risk of SCD.

Medical therapy

- Asymptomatic patients:
    - Mild LVH—no treatment
    - Severe LVH—verapamil to improve relaxation and diastolic dysfunction
- Symptomatic patients:
    - Calcium antagonists (verapamil or diltiazem) or BBs act as negative inotropes and reduce systolic LVOT gradient
    - Diuretics should be used with caution as patients can be very volume sensitive
    - Disopyramide can be used to alter calcium kinetics in the myocytes and is associated with reduced symptoms and reduced systolic pressure gradient
    - Amiodarone to reduce the burden of atrial fibrillation; formal anticoagulation should be strongly considered.

Additional therapy

- **Septal myectomy:**
    - Marrow procedure is treatment for patients with refractory symptoms and obstructive HCM
    - Good long-term results but remodeling and cavity dilation seen in 15–20%
    - Complications include pacemaker implantation (3%) and ventricular septal defect (VSD; 1%)

- **Septal ablation:**
  - Septal ablation is performed with LVOT gradient >30–50 mmHg (rest); 60–100 mmHg (with provocation)
  - The site of injection is identified by contrast echocardiography and alcohol injected into the first or second septal perforator leading to a limited infarction
  - In a third of cases, the pressure gradient disappears immediately; two thirds in weeks/months
  - Complications include pacemaker implantation (3–5%)
- **Implantable cardiac defibrillator implantation:**
  - Implantable cardiac defibrillator implantation is indicated in patients at high risk of SCD
  - There is no evidence that medical therapy reduces the risk of SCD.

Special considerations

- Pregnancy:
  - Cardiomyopathy generally well tolerated with low maternal mortality if asymptomatic with no high risk features
  - Joint cardiac and obstetric care is recommended
- Exercise:
  - Patients with HCM should not undertake competitive sport
  - Burst exertion (e.g. sprints) and isometric exercise (e.g. weight lifting) should be discouraged
- Elderly patients:
  - Elderly patients with HCM should be distinguished from those with non-genetic hypertensive heart disease. Hypertrophy tends to be milder in hypertensive disease
  - In the absence of a genotype, the presence of LVOTO, a disproportionate level of hypertrophy compared to the degree of hypertension, or an unusual pattern of hypertrophy, suggests HCM.

4.3 Dilated cardiomyopathy

- Dilated cardiomyopathy (DCM) is a chronic heart muscle disease with cavity enlargement and impaired systolic function of the left or both ventricles
- The diagnosis is made once other specific cardiomyopathies have been excluded (see Table 4.1)
- Around 30–40% of cases are genetically transmitted
- Prevalence of familial DCM is likely underestimated due to poor disease expression and a variability of phenotype for the same genetic abnormality leading to a number of presentations, e.g. arrhythmia, stroke, conduction system disease, and sudden cardiac death
- Inheritance is commonly autosomal dominant but recessive, X-linked and mitochondrial forms are recognized
- Proteins affected include dystrophin, desmin, cardiac actin, β myosin heavy chain, cardiac troponins C and T, and lamin A/C proteins
- Some environmental factors may unmask incomplete genetic penetrance, e.g. alcohol excess
- Other causative factors include anthrocyclines, malnutrition, thiamine, and protein deficiencies
- In patients with no family history, the mechanism is felt to be an acute myocarditis, e.g. secondary to a viral insult
- There follows chronic inflammation and a possible exaggerated immune response leading to LV remodeling and dysfunction.

Table 4.1 Diagnostic criteria for dilated cardiomyopathy

Diagnostic criteria	Exclusion criteria
LV ejection fraction <45%	Blood pressure >160/100
Fractional shortening <25%	Coronary artery disease (>50% luminal stenosis)
	Chronic alcohol excess
LV End-diastolic diameter >117% of predicted (age and body surface area corrected)	Clinical sustained and rapid tachycardia
	Systemic disease
	Pericardial disease
	Congenital heart disease
	Cor pulmonale

Reproduced from 'Guidelines for the study of familial dilated cardiomyopathies', L. Mestroni, B. Maisch, W. J. McKenna, et al., Collaborative Research Group of the European Human and Capital Mobility Project on Familial Dilated Cardiomyopathy, *Eur. Heart J.*, 20, 93–102, copyright 1999 with permission of Oxford University Press.

Clinical course and prognosis

- The course is heterogenous
- Better outcomes are associated with young age, shorter clinical history, improvement in LV function with medical therapy, a worse NYHA class on presentation, and a history of hypertension
- Demonstrable genetic mutations are associated with a worse prognosis.

Diagnostic testing

- Neurohormones:
  - Brain natriuretic peptide (BNP) relates to myocardial stretch
  - A value twice the upper limit of normal range is predictive of long-term mortality
- ECG:
  - Atrial fibrillation and prologation of QTc are associated with increased mortality and heart failure progression
  - Prolongation of QRS duration (>120–150 ms) implies dyssynchrony and allows consideration for cardiac resynchronization therapy (CRT)
  - Ventricular arrhythmias detected on Holter monitoring are associated with increased mortality and allow consideration of implantable defibrillator (ICD)
- Cardiopulmonary exercise testing:
  - Assessment of anaerobic threshold and ventilatory efficiency are reliable markers of mortality as well as part of the assessment for cardiac transplantation
- Echocardiographic assessment of ejection fraction:
  - ≤30% indicates severe LV systolic impairment
  - 30–45%, moderate
  - >45% mild
  - >60% is normal
- Cardiac MRI:
  - Cardiac MRI is the gold standard test for LV size, function, myocardial mass, and regional wall motion
  - Late gadolinium enhancement imaging can be helpful to identify scar and other patterns of uptake

- Cardiac catheterization:
  - Cardiac catheterization excludes coronary artery disease and invasive assessments of cardiac output, pulmonary capillary wedge pressure, and trans-pulmonary gradient
- Endomyocardial biopsy:
  - Endomyocardial biopsy is usually non-specific in DCM.

Management and prognosis

1. Treatment for heart failure:
   - ACE inhibitors/ARBs
   - Beta blockers (BBs)
   - Aldosterone antagonists
   - Heart rate controlling drugs such as If channel blockers should be considered
2. Discontinuation of cardiotoxics, e.g. alcohol, anthrocyclines
3. Assessment for device therapy:
   - Risk assessment for SCD (Box 4.5)
   - QRS >120 ms and NYHA >Class II for consideration of CRT
4. Exercise training/cardiac rehabilitation
5. Left ventricular assist device as bridge to transplant or to recovery
6. Cardiac transplantation.

Risk assessment for SCD in DCM

See Box 4.5.

- First-degree relatives of patients with DCM should be screened with ECG and echocardiography for early detection
- Tests should be performed every 3–5 years
- Medical therapy with ACE inhibitors and BBs improve pump function in 50% of patients; normalization occurs in 16%
- Death occurs in around one-fifth of cases probably secondary to SCD; the remainder have terminal heart failure
- Five-year survival is estimated at 30–35%
- Optimized medical therapy has improved LV ejection fraction, NYHA class, risk for SCD, and transplant-free survival.

BOX 4.5 RISK FACTORS FOR SUDDEN CARDIAC DEATH ON DCM

- Unexplained syncope
- LV end-diastolic diameter >7 cm and NSVT on Holter monitor
- LV ejection fraction <35% and NSVT on Holter monitor.

NSVT: non-sustained ventricular tachycardia.

4.4 Restrictive cardiomyopathy

- In restrictive cardiomyopathy (RCM) there is abnormal diastolic function due to rigid or thickened ventricular walls leading to elevated right- and left-sided filling pressures
- Unlike constrictive cardiomyopathy, there is dissociation between the right and left chambers with respiration, i.e. there is ventricular discordance.

Classification

Primary RCM

i.   Loffler's endocarditis (acute)
ii. Endomyocardial fibrosis (chronic)
iii. Idiopathic.

- Pathophysiology is associated with inflammation (hypereosinophilia)
- This is secondary to a chronic inflammatory process, e.g. parasitic infection, autoimmune disease, eosinophilic leukaemia
- It is rare in the Western world but endemic in African and South American countries.

Secondary RCM

This is due to specific material deposition within the myocardium by infiltrative disease, e.g. amyloid, storage disorders, or replacement by other molecules.

Loeffler endocarditis

Pathophysiology

- Due to presence of a sustained hypereosinophilia secondary to an autoimmune state, parasitic infection, or an eosinophilic leukaemia leading to tissue infiltration
- Eosinophilic endomyocardial fibrosis occurs secondary to an inflammatory response from cytotoxic and growth factor release
- The severe eosinophilia also leads to a hyperviscosity syndrome
- Myocardial fibrosis occurs at the left and/or right ventricular apices. It extends to the outflow tracts and involves the chordae leading to mitral and or tricuspid regurgitation
- Histology demonstrates acute eosinophilic myocarditis.

Clinical features

- Patients can present with weight loss, fever, cough, a rash. and congestive cardiac failure
- Systemic embolization frequently occurs. causing renal and neurological complications
- Cardiac dysfunction occurs in >50% of patients and mitral/tricuspid regurgitation is commonly seen
- Death is secondary to congestive cardiac failure.

Diagnosis

- CXR:
    - Radiological evidence of heart failure, biatrial dilatation
- ECG:
    - Non-specific ST segment abnormality; AF common
- Echo:
    - Localized apical thickening with chordal involvement
    - Mitral/tricuspid regurgitation
    - Biatrial enlargement
    - Preserved systolic function
    - Restrictive filling patterns
    - Reduction in mitral and tricuspid inflow velocities with inspiration

- Cardiac catheterization:
    - High LV end-diastolic pressure
    - Thick obliterated ventricle
    - Mitral/tricuspid regurgitation
- Biopsy:
    - Eosinophilic endomyocardial fibrosis.

Management

Treat the underlying cause: steroids for autoimmune disease, anti-parasitics for infection, disease modifying drugs for rheumatoid arthritis, chemotherapy for eosinophilic leaukaemia.

- Heart failure management:
    - Diuretics (with caution as can lower filling pressures further by hypovolaemia)
    - ACE inhibitors/ARBs
    - BBs
    - Digoxin for AF
- Anticoagulation:
    - LMWH/warfarin is mandatory
- Surgery:
    - Endocardial decortication can be used in medically stable patients
- Prognosis:
    - Death at 6–12 months from diagnosis; better if underlying disease can be treated.

Endomyocardial fibrosis

- Endomyocardial fibrosis involves intense endocardial thickening leading to similar presentation to Loeffler endocarditis
- Fibrosis leads to both restriction and constriction (if both ventricles affected)
- There are three types: left ventricular (40%), right ventricular (10%), and biventricular (50%)
- There are two forms:
    - African form: age 30–40 years with male:female ratio of 2:1. Secondary to parasitic disease (filarisis)
    - European form: age 30–50 years with male:female ratio of 1:2; secondary to autoimmune disease, particularly associated with glomerulonephritis, rheumatoid arthritis
- Pathophysiology is similar to Loffler endocarditis but is less acute
- Clinical course is chronic. Diagnostic tests give similar results to Loffler endocarditis.

Management

- Heart failure treatment is as above but BBs are used with caution as bradycardias are poorly tolerated in patients with small ventricles and high filling pressures, giving significant diastolic dysfunction
- Endocardial decortication is used, with or without mitral/tricuspid valve replacement
- Transplantation is usually excluded due to pulmonary hypertension.

Prognosis

- Patients remain stable for years but can deteriorate suddenly.

Differential diagnosis

- Post-viral constrictive pericarditis
- Carcinoid of the right ventricle
- Amyloidosis.

Secondary restrictive cardiomyopathy

Amyloid heart disease

- Amyloid is deposition of a soluble extracellular protein as an insoluble fibril causing loss of tissue architecture and function:
    - **Acquired amyloid (AL or 1°)** is deposition of fibril proteins from immunoglobulin light chains produced by plasma cells. It is associated with myeloma or monoclonal gammopathies
    - **Secondary amyloid (AA)** is associated with chronic inflammatory conditions such as rheumatoid arthritis, ankylosing spondylitis, and familial Mediterranean fever. The amyloid fibrils consist of protein A. Nephrotic syndrome and renal failure are common at presentation
    - **Senile systemic amyloidosis** (TTR amyloid) involves the deposition of a fibril precursor of the protein transthyretin. Heart failure, heart block, and atrial fibrillation are recognized manifestations. It is slowly progressive and has a better prognosis than acquired forms
    - **Hereditary amyloid** is typically autosomal dominant. It is a mutation in any of the fibril precursor proteins for transthretin, apolipoprotein AI or AII, lysozyme, fibrinogen Aa chain, gelsolin, and cystatin C
- Cardiac amyloid is mainly seen in primary, senile systemic (TTR), and certain hereditary forms
- Cardiovascular involvement is seen in AA forms of the disease but is an unfavorable marker if present
- Amyloid fibrils deposit within the myocardium, papillary muscles, valves, conduction tissue, and in the vessels
- Suspicion of amyloid should be raised if there is
    - Cardiac disease in the presence of established AL amyloid ± plasma cell dyscrasia
    - Ventricular dysfunction/arrhythmia in patients with long-standing connective tissue disease or chronic inflammatory disorder
    - Any restrictive cardiomyopathy without explanation
    - Thickened ventricle on echocardiography but low-voltage ECG
    - Heart failure of unknown cause or refractory to treatment.

Investigations
See Table 4.2.

Management
- Management aims at treatment of the underlying condition—hence identification of subtype is crucial
- Treatment of heart failure is mainly with diuretics
- ACE inhibitors/ARBs should be used with caution due to the frequency of hypotension
- Digoxin is contraindicated as it binds to amyloid fibrils
- BBs can promote AV blockade so should be used with caution
- Ventricular arrhythmias can predict SCD
- Cardiac transplantation is relatively contra-indicated in AL amyloid.

Prognosis
- Prognosis for AL amyloid is very poor
- Systemic senile amyloid is slowly progressive and requires no specific treatment
- Reactive AA amyloid may improve with anti-inflammatory treatments.

Table 4.2 Investigations for cardiac amyloid

12-lead ECG	Low voltage (though this is not always seen)
	Varying degrees of atrioventricular block
	Interventricular conduction delay/bundle branch block
	Left-axis deviation
	Poor R-wave progression*
Holter	Atrial fibrillation
	Other tachyarrhythmia or bradyarrhythmia
Two-dimensional echocardiography	Concentric or asymmetric thickening of the left ventricular wall
	Occasional thickening of the right ventricle
	Thickened interatrial septum*
	Sparkling/granular appearance of myocardium*
	Thickened valves and/or papillary muscles
	Left atrial or biatrial dilation
	Diastolic dysfunction in early disease (E/A reversal)
	Restrictive physiology (E >> A)
	Pericardial effusion
	Systolic impairment with normal end-diastolic volume
Histology	Apple-green birefringence under polarized light microscope after staining with Congo red* Immunoperoxidase stains to differentiate light chains/transthyretin/protein A, etc.
Cardiac catheterization	Raised filling pressures
Protein electrophoresis	Serum and urine electrophoresis for presence of monoclonal protein in patients with suspected AL amyloidosis
Genetic testing	Commercially available to detect common mutations

* Features considered relatively more specific for amyloidosis.
Reproduced from the *ESC Textbook of Cardiovascular Medicine* 2nd edition, ed. John Camm, Thomas Lüscher and Patrick Serruys, copyright 2009 with permission of Oxford University Press.

Sarcoid heart disease

- Sarcoid is a multisystem disorder characterized by deposition of non-caseating granuloma
- It most commonly affects the lungs and lymphatics
- Cardiac involvement is seen in around a quarter of cases, affecting mainly the LV free wall and septum
- Right-sided and atrial involvement is recognized
- Sarcoid should be considered in
  - Young people presenting with conduction disease
  - Patients with unexplained DCM and AV block and features of abnormal wall thickness, regional wall motion abnormality, or apical/septal perfusion defects that improve with stress nuclear imaging
  - Patients with sustained VT with no obvious cause
  - Pateients with RCM of unknown cause
  - Presumed ARVC or AV block in patients with chronic respiratory disease.

Clinical presentation

- Arrhythmia/conduction abnormality
- Heart failure
- Pericardial effusions, constriction, and valvular disease recognized
- SCD can be first presentation
- Isolated cardiac involvement is rare—presentation usually follows systemic manifestation of the disease.

Table 4.3 Guidelines for diagnosis based on study report on diffuse pulmonary disease for Japanese Ministry of Health and Welfare, 1993

Histology	Endomyocardial biopsy demonstrating epitheloid granulomata without caseating granulomata
Clinical	Exclusion of other aetiologies and the presence of complete RBBB, LAD, AV block, VT, ventricular ectopy on ambulatory ECG plus one of the following: 1. Abnormal wall motion, regional wall thinning of dilatation of the left ventricle 2. Perfusion abnormality on perfusion imaging 3. Abnormal intracardiac pressure, low cardiac output, abnormal wall motion or reduced left ventricular ejection fraction 4. Evidence of interstitial fibrosis or cellular inflammation

Adapted from Hiraga H, Yuwai K, Hiroe M. et al., 'Guideline for diagnosis of cardiac sarcoidosis', published in 'Cardiac sarcoidosis', Abdul R. Doughan, Byron R. Williams, *Heart* 92, 282–288, copyright 2006 with permission of BMJ Publishing.

Diagnosis

- Investigations can include:
  - Serum ACE
  - 12-lead ECG
  - Holter monitoring
  - Chest X-ray
  - Echocardiography
  - Myocardial perfusion imaging
  - Cardiac MR
  - Cardiac catheterization
  - Endomyocardial biopsy
- See Table 4.3 for guidelines on diagnosis.

Management

- Early treatment with corticosteroids is first-line treatment
- Other treatments include chloroquine, hydoxychloroquine, and methotrexate
- Resolution of arrhythmia and conduction disease can be seen, as well as some resolution in LV function
- Treatment should be started prior to standard heart failure treatment if possible
- Pacemaker implantation should be performed in patients with high-grade AV block
- Defibrillators should be used in patients who survive cardiac arrest or have refractory ventricular arrhythmia
- Pacemaker/ICD implantation and steroid treatment improve prognosis
- Catheter ablation can be used to treat recurrent VT
- Transplantation is rare.

4.5 Storage diseases

- Storage diseases are inborn errors of metabolism resulting in the abnormal accumulation of the substrate or byproduct in tissues (see Table 4.4)
- Intracellular deposition distinguishes them from infiltrative disease, where deposition is within the interstitium
- Within the myocytes, the presence of these metabolites is toxic, causing either concentric (HCM-like phenotype) or eccentric (DCM-like phenotype) changes

Table 4.4 Summary of cardiovascular manifestations of some inborn errors of metabolism.

	Mechanism	Genetics	Presentation	Diagnosis	Management
Haemachromatosis	Iron overload and deposition	Mutation on HFE gene encoding for transferrin receptor. AR inheritance with variable penetrance.	Liver, pancreas, joints and heart affected. Heart failure, SVTs, AV blockade, raised atrial pressures (restrictive filling)	Echo: normal LV thickness CMR Histology: stainable iron within the sarcoplasm	Regular phlebotomy Serial EMB ± CMR, FBC and iron studies to assess treatment. Standard heart failure and arrhythmia management Screening of first-degree relatives
GSD Type II (Pompe's Disease)	Acid α galactosidase (acid maltase) deficiency	AR inheritance	Within first few months—failure to thrive, hypotonia, macroglossia, hepatomegaly	CXR: cardiomegaly Raised cardiac enzymes ECG: short PR, LAD, high voltage QRS Enzyme assay of muscle or skin fibroblasts shows no acid maltase activity Echo: bilateral ventricular hypertrophy; HCM phenotype ± SAM	Previously poor prognosis with death. New treatment with recombinant acid maltase (acid α galactosidase) enzyme replacement now promising.
GSD Type III (Corbi or Farbe's disease)	Amylo-1,6,-glucosidase deficiency causing phosphorylase limit dextran accumulation	AR inheritance with variable phenotype	Fasting hypoglycaemia and hepatomegaly. Many patients asymptomatic but recurrent sustained VT and SCD seen	Echo: HCM-type phenotype ± SAM. CMR: late gadolinium suggestive of late fibrosis	
GSD Type IV	Amylo 1,4–1,6 transglucosidase deficiency with accumulation of polyglucosan bodies in the liver		Liver dysfunction, skeletal myopathy and heart failure		

GSD = glycogen storage disorders.

Anderson-Fabry's disease

- Fabry's disease is an X-linked genetic disorder causing a deficiency in α-galactosidase
- It leads to a deposition of glycosphingolipids (particularly globotriaosylcermide) in the skin, endothelium, kidneys, liver, pancreas, and central nervous system
- Patients may present a multi-system disease (see section on 'Cardiovascular presentations') with obstructive airways disease, proteinuria, end-stage renal disease, or stroke
- Cardiovascular deposition is within the myocardium, conduction tissue, valves, and vascular endothelium.

Cardiovascular presentations

- Patients present with heart failure, conduction disease, arrhythmia and angina
- It is an incidental finding on echocardiography with unexplained LVH
- Endothelial involvement is associated with subendocardial ischaemia
- LVH and reduced coronary flow reserve may also be the cause of angina
- Renal involvement increases the incidence of hypertension and hypercholesterolaemia and leads to premature coronary artery disease
- Increased prevalence of smoking in this population also contributes to this higher risk of premature coronary artery disease
- Stroke is seen as a consequence of deposition within the cerebral endothelium.

Extra-cardiac features

- Cutaneous:
  - Angiokeratomas
  - Lympoedema
- Neurological:
  - Tinnitus
  - Vertigo
  - Headache
  - TIA/stroke
  - Chronic arm and leg pain
  - Fabry crisis (severe acute pain precipitated by emotional or physical stress)
- Gastrointestinal:
  - Diarrhea
  - Abdominal discomfort or vomiting
- Renal:
  - Proteinuria
  - Renal failure.

Investigations

- Echocardiography reveals increased wall thickness (concentric and septal patterns) with associated systolic anterior motion of the mitral valve and LVOTO
- Systolic function is preserved whilst mild–moderate diastolic dysfunction is seen
- Restriction is rare
- Thickened papillary muscles and mitral valve leaflets occur in over 50% of patients
- The diagnosis is made by demonstration of reduced α-galactosidase activity in the plasma or peripheral leukocytes
- 6% of patients with 'late-onset HCM' have Fabry's disease

- Women have relatively high levels of α-galactosidase which can limit the assay in its use (women express varying phenotypes due to random inactivation of an X-chromosome)
- Genetic testing can be helpful.

Management

- Treatment is with enzyme replacement therapy, which can reduce the overall tissue and serum load of glycosphingolipids leading to a reduction in pain symptoms, renal complications, and improved quality of life
- There is currently limited evidence in the regression of cardiac disease
- Anginal symptoms should be treated with antiplatelet agents and calcium antagonists
- BBs are used with caution due to the incidence of conduction disease and bradycardia
- Heart failure is treated with standard treatments; transplant can be considered in severe cases.

Post-radiation disease

- Radiation damage can affect any part of the heart (see Table 4.5) and is seen after treatment for lymphoma as well as breast, lung, and testicular malignancy
- Symptoms are associated with the area affected
- Regular assessment with 12-lead ECG, echocardiography, exercise testing, Holter monitoring, and cardiac MR is useful for occult disease
- Newer radiotherapy techniques involve smaller doses as well as shielding

Table 4.5 Summary of cardiac complications from radiation

Structure	Mechanism	Clinical features
Myocardial	Damage occurs due to microcirculatory damage and free radical toxicity. Acute inflammation of small/medium sized arteries is followed by latent phase of thrombosis and ischaemia. Myocyte death and fibrosis follows.	Clinically overt cardiomyopathy (restrictive CM) is uncommon. Anthrocycline induced DCM-like phenotype does occur with more frequency when associated with radiation exposure.
Pericardial	Early complications are associated with radiation induced necrosis of tumour masses adjacent to the heart. Treatment is usually continued with no long-term sequelae. Late presentation is due to a chronic constrictive pericarditis and presence of a chronic pleural effusion	Acute symptoms of pericarditis—fever, chest pain. Chronic constriction leads to right-sided heart failure. Pericardectomy is treatment of choice in intractable cases.
Conduction disease		Sick sinus syndrome and AV block have been reported
Valve disease		Around a third of patients had valve demonstrable valve disease (mainly aortic) post radiation therapy
Coronary artery disease		Ostial left main stem and left anterior descending disease can be seen in patients who have had mediastinal radiotherapy. Often, other risk factors for CAD are present

Reproduced from the *ESC Textbook of Cardiovascular Medicine* 2nd edition, ed. John Camm, Thomas Lüscher and Patrick Serruys, copyright 2009 with permission of Oxford University Press.

- Cardiovascular risk assessment and aggressive treatment can reduce the risk of coronary disease
- The use of cardiotoxic chemotherapy with radiotherapy should be avoided.

4.6 Arrhythmogenic cardiomyopathy

The WHO classification
- A group of heart muscle disorders characterized by structural and functional abnormalities of the right ventricle due to localized or diffuse atrophy, with replacement of the myocardium by fatty and fibrous tissue
- Areas affected are the outflow tract, apex, and subtricuspid areas of the free wall
- The septum is spared
- There is replacement of myocardial tissue with fibro-fatty infiltrates (mainly diffuse) with increase wall thickness
- Saccular aneurysms are present in 50% of cases
- Genetic predisposition plays a part—familial component in 30–50% of cases with several genes implicated (autosomal dominant and recessive).

Clinical presentation
- Exercise-induced symptomatic VT of RV origin (LBBB pattern)
- Palpitations/syncope/pre-syncope
- Sudden cardiac death
- Some patients present with heart failure and ventricular arrhythmia and misdiagnosed as DCM.

Diagnosis
- The ECG is abnormal in 90% of cases with the presence of an epsilon wave being a distinct marker of disease (Figure 4.2)
- Imaging (echocardiography, cardiac MR and RV angiography) demonstrates RV dilatation, segmental or regional wall motion abnormality. and the presence of saccular aneurysms
- Diagnosis based on two major criteria, one major plus two minor criteria, or four minor criteria (Box 4.6).

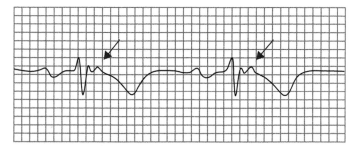

Figure 4.2 ECG lead in V1 with T wave inversion and epsilon-wave (arrows) in a patient with arrhythmogenic right ventricular cardiomyopathy.

Reproduced from the *ESC Textbook of Cardiovascular Medicine* 2nd edition, ed. John Camm, Thomas Lüscher and Patrick Serruys, copyright Oxford University Press 2009.

BOX 4.6 DIAGNOSTIC FEATURES OF ARRHYTHMOGENIC RIGHT VENTRICULAR CARDIOMYOPATHY

Major criteria

Familial disease confirmed at necropsy or surgery.

Epsilon wave or QRS duration >110 ms in V1–V3.

Severe RV dilatation and systolic dysfunction with no/mild LV involvement.

Localized RV aneurysms (akinetic/dyskinetic areas with diastolic bulgings).

Severe segmental RV dilatation.

Fibrofatty replacement of myocardium (endomyocardial biopsy).

Minor criteria

Family history of premature sudden death (<35 years).

Family history based on clinical diagnostic criteria.

Late potentials (signal-averaged ECG).

Inverted T waves in V2 and V3, no RBBB, in patients >12 years.

LBBB-type tachycardia (sustained or non-sustained) on ECG, Holter monitoring, or during exercise testing.

Ventricular extrasystoles (>1000 in 24 h) on Holter monitoring.

Mild global reduced RV dilatation and/or RV dysfunction with preserved LV function.

Mild segmental RV dilatation.

Regional right-heart hypokinesia.

LBBB, left bundle branch block; LV, left ventricle; RBBB, right bundle branch block; RV, right ventricle. Reproduced from 'Diagnosis of arrhythmogenic right ventricular dysplasia/cardiomyopathy', Task Force of the Working Group Myocardial and Pericardial Disease of the European Society of Cardiology and of the Scientific Council on Cardiomyopathies of the International Society and Federation of Cardiology. W. J. McKenna, G. Thiene, A. Nava, et al., *British Heart Journal*, 71, 215–218, copyright 1994 with permission from BMJ Publishing Group Ltd.

Table 4.6 Arrhythmia management

Good systolic function Non-life-threatening arrhythmias	Medical therapy with amiodarone, beta blockers or propafenone
Reduced systolic function	Amiodarone, beta blockers or class I agents
Syncope, cardiac arrest, documented VT/VF and a family history of sudden cardiac death	Implantable defibrillator

Management

- Use standard heart failure treatment with ACE inhibitors/ARBs, BBs, aldosterone antagonists, and digoxin (see Table 4.6)
- Transplantation should be considered in those patients with refractory symptoms despite full standard therapy
- ICD use may be limited due to the abnormal RV myocardium giving low endocardial signals and increased pacing thresholds
- Catheter ablation can be used but new foci arise in around half of cases
- Sustained VT refractory to drug treatment may require transplantation.

Prognosis and outcome

- Biventricular dysplastic involvement leading to a DCM is rare
- Progressive right ventricular failure occurs in some patients
- Untreated sustained or non-sustained VT may be well tolerated but can degenerate to VF in 1–2% of cases.

4.7 Unclassified cardiomyopathy

- Unclassified cardiomyopathy is also known as left ventricular non-compaction (LVNC)
- It is a genetic-based disease where there is a two-layer myocardium: a thin compacted layer adjacent to the epicardium and a thicker non-compacted layer adjacent to the endocardium.

Aetiology

- The myocardium is a loose network of fibres separated by deep recesses during embryogeneisis
- At weeks 5–8, these fibres compact down, with the intratrabecular recesses becoming capillary networks
- LVNC is the arrest of normal myocardial maturation by unknown mechanisms
- Isolated LVNC has been associated with a Z protein seen in cardiac muscle on the X chromosome; autosomal dominant inheritance is more commonly seen.

Pathophysiology

- Subendocardial ischaemia due to compression of intramural coronary vessels may cause areas of ischaemia and fibrosis
- It leads to remodeling and dilatation causing systolic impairment, and substrate for arrhythmia
- Excess trabeculation limits myocardial compliance and causes diastolic dysfunction
- Thromboembolism (cerebral, mesenteric, or pulmonary) is seen due to stagnation of blood within the trabeculae.

Clinical presentation

- Patients present at any age with heart failure, arrhythmia, or thromboembolic complications
- It can also be an incidental finding or be observed as part of family screening for SCD
- ECG can show high-voltage QRS and repolarization abnormality and shifts in QRS axis
- High-quality transthoracic echo, with or without the use of contrast, or cardiac MR is used to confirm the diagnosis.

Diagnostic criteria

- The ratio of N/C ≥2 in adults (N/C ≥1.4 in children) where N and C are the maximal end-systolic thickness of the non-compacted and compacted layer respectively
- The ratio of the depth of the intratrabecular recesses and overall wall thickness is also significantly high
- Other features include:
  1. Prominent and excessive trabeculation in the non-compacted layer
  2. Deep intratrabecular recesses that fill completely with blood
  3. Localization of the non-compacted regions at the apex, lateral, and inferior walls

- Although left ventricular dilatation and systolic impairment is seen, it is not essential for diagnosis
- LVNC can be misdiagnosed as apical HCM, DCM, apical thrombus, or apical infarction.

Management

1. Standard heart failure treatment is used for LV dysfunction
2. Arrythmia management: ICD implantation is used for patients with:
   - Sustained VT
   - Recurrent unexplained syncope
   - LV ejection fraction <35% on optimal medical therapy with non-sustained VT on Holter monitor
3. Thromboprophylaxis: formal anticoagulation in patients with ventricular dilatation and systolic impairment, or previous embolic event
4. Cardiac transplantation in patients refractory to treatment.

Prognosis and outcome

- Initially felt to have high mortality but increase in diagnosis rates has demonstrated patients at lower risk
- Timely detection, appropriate treatment, and ICD implantation may also improve prognosis.

4.8 Inflammatory myocardial disease

- Inflammatory cardiomyopathy is characterized by myocarditis in association with cardiac dysfunction
- The underlying cause may be idiopathic, autoimmune, or infectious (Box 4.7).

Pathophysiology

- There are various hypotheses regarding the mechanism of myocarditis
- It may be secondary to a virus triggered inflammation in those patients with a genetic predisposition to myocardial inflammation
- The virus can cause a direct toxic effect or cause a secondary immune response, which can persist despite elimination of the virus

BOX 4.7 CARDIOTROPIC VIRUSES INVOLVED IN MYOCARDITIS AND INFLAMMATORY CARDIOMYOPATHY

Coxsackie virus	Adenovirus	Parvovirus B19
Human herpesvirus type 6	Epstein–Barr virus	Cytomegalovirus
Echovirus	Mumps virus	Influenza A and B viruses
Flavovirus	Human immunodeficiency virus	Measles virus
Polio virus	Hepatitis C virus	Rabies virus
Rubella virus	Variola virus	Varicella-zoster virus
Borrelia burgdorferi	Parastitic infection	

Reproduced from the *ESC Textbook of Cardiovascular Medicine* 2nd edition, ed. John Camm, Thomas Lüscher and Patrick Serruys, copyright 2009 with permission of Oxford University Press.

- Alternatively there may also be persistent chronic infection driving a continued inflammatory response. This could be in the form of antibodies cross-reacting with myocardial antibodies or the release of cardiodepressive cytokines causing myocardial dysfunction.

Clinical presentation

- Patients present with heart failure, chest discomfort, palpitations, syncope, or SCD
- There can be a temporal relationship with a viral infection, although this is quite often subclinical
- Acute fulminant myocarditis: acute and rapid onset with severe LV dysfunction which may need inotropic or mechanical support
- Acute non-fulminant myocarditis: usually presents with chest pain, non-specific ECG changes, and a rises in serum troponin and C reactive protein
- The coronary arteries are normal
- Echo shows preserved systolic function but may demonstrate regional wall motion abnormality
- Pericardial effusion and wall oedema is seen on echo and cardiac MR
- In both clinical scenarios, arrhythmias can be seen. Patients can present with SCD.

Management

- Secondary causes of heart failure should be excluded
- Standard heart failure treatment including ICD and LVAD, either as bridge to recovery or transplantation
- If patients improve they should be closely monitored with serial echo, ECG, and Holter monitoring
- If there is progressive LV dysfunction, immunomodulatory treatment and transplantation should be considered
- Endomyocardial biopsy and immunohistology may be necessary to help with aetiology (Figure 4.3)

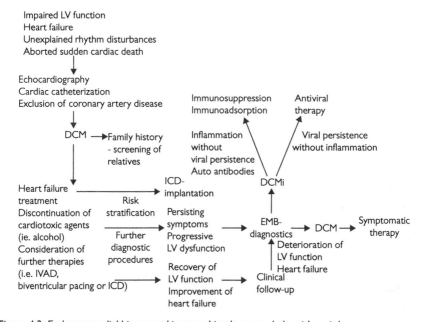

Figure 4.3 Endomyocardial biopsy and immunohistology may help with aetiology.

- Immunomodulatory treatment strategies are dependent on the absence of viral persistence by immunohistology
- Persistent inflammation due to an autoimmune response in the absence of any virus may respond to immunosuppression.

Prognosis and outcome

- No clinical parameter predicts outcome
- The presence of viral persistence and chronic inflammation is associated with an adverse prognosis
- 5-year survival is estimated at around 35%; initial presentation of fulminant myocarditis and heart failure is associated with a better outcome.

HIV cardiomyopathy

- Cardiac involvement can be seen in 50% of HIV positive patients (usually sub-clinical)
- The pathogenesis is felt to be a result of either continued infection by HIV-1 of the myocardial cells, further opportunistic infection of the myocardium by other organisms, or as a result of nucleoside analogue treatment
- Management is with standard heart failure treatment but caution should be used given the interactions with protease inhibitors.

Chagas disease

- Chagas disease is a protozoal myocarditis after infection with *Trypanosoma cruzi*
- It is endemic in south and central America and is transmitted by realuvid bug, but an be from animal reservoirs, blood transfusion, and vertical transmission
- Patients present with fatigue, fluid retention, conduction disease, progressive left ventricular dysfunction, ventricular arrhythmia, sudden cardiac death, and thrombo-embolic disease
- Investigations include the Machado-Guerreiro complement fixation test, indirect immunofluorescence or ELISA, 12-lead ECG, and echocardiography
- Echo can demonstrate global LV systolic dysfunction but can show septal sparing, posterior wall hypokinesia, and apical aneurysm formation.

Treatment

1. Antiparasitics, e.g. benzidazole, which reduces but does not eradicate the organism
2. Heart failure treatment
3. Antiarrhythmics, e.g. amiodarone
4. Anticoagulation.

Lyme disease

- Lyme disease is an infection with a tick borne spirochete, *Borrelia burgdorferi*
- Patients present with erythema migrans and general malaise
- Cardiac and neurological features occur after weeks and months
- It is more common in females but men tend to suffer more complications
- Cardiac sequelae include conduction disease, myo-pericarditis, and a self-limiting cardiomyopathy
- Other complications include cranial nerve palsies and a migratory polyarthiritis
- Diagnosis is made on the basis of the history of tick bite, clinical findings, and serological studies
- Treatment should be in an expert centre
- The antibiotic of choice is doxycycline
- Intravenous ceftriaxone is used for 2–4 weeks if there are cardiac or neurological signs.

4.9 Secondary myocardial diseases

Ischaemic cardiomyopathy

- Ischaemic cardiomyopathy is the most common cause for heart failure in the Western world
- There is conflicting data on the benefits of revascularization
- The mechanism of injury can be due to:
  - Myocardial infarction—irreversible damage; neurohormonal activation can lead to further adverse remodeling
  - Myocardial ischaemia—stunning and hibernation
- Viability assessments can help distinguish between those areas of myocardium that are dead and those that are alive and may improve by revascularization.

Management

- Management uses standard heart failure treatment with medical and device therapy
- Revascularization can be considered. In patients with anginal symptoms there is data to support improved symptoms and prognosis with severe left ventricular dysfunction and three-vessel coronary artery disease
- In patients without chest pain revascularization is contentious. A number of small studies have shown improvement in left ventricular function, symptoms, and prognosis with surgical revascularization (CABG). The current AHA/ACC guidelines (see Further Reading section) recommend CABG being offered to patients with:
  - Proven significant regions of hibernation
  - Left main stem/equivalent disease
  - Severe three-vessel coronary disease
- Surgery in this group is, however, high risk, particularly in those with an LV end-diastolic diameter of >7 cm.

Hypertensive cardiomyopathy

- Hypertension-induced LVH is independently associated with ventricular dysfunction, arrhythmia, and sudden cardiac death.

Pathophysiology

- The condition involves enlargement and proliferation of cardiac myocytes and interstitial fibrosis
- An increase in collagen content leads to ventricular non-compliance and diastolic dysfunction
- The abnormal myocardial microcirculation fails to enlarge at the same rate as the increase in muscle mass
- This, together with endothelial dysfunction and perivascular fibrosis, leads to ischaemic symptoms despite normal epicardial coronary arteries.

Clinical presentation

- Patients may complain of chest pain and breathlessness (from diastolic dysfunction) but some remain asymptomatic
- There is high prevalence of atrial fibrillation
- Frequent ventricular ectopics are seen; sustained VT is unusual but some patients do present with SCD.

Management

- Treatment with antihypertensives can reduce the degree of LVH hence reducing cardiovascular risk
- ACE inhibitors/ARBs are the treatment of choice (in combination with standard antihypertensives).

Alcoholic cardiomyopathy

- Ethanol at a level of >90 g daily for >5 years is felt to unmask a genetic predisposition to dilated cardiomyopathy via a direct toxic effect on myocytes and function
- Two phases of the disease are recognized:
  i. Initial asymptomatic phase with isolated LV cavity enlargement and diastolic dysfunction
  ii. Clinically overt phase with signs and symptoms of heart failure and LV systolic dysfunction
- Incidence of arrhythmia such as AF and non-sustained VT are similar to those patients with DCM
- SCD rates are also comparable but this figure can be attenuated by abstinence
- Standard heart failure treatment improves ventricular function
- Therapy is more effective when the patient abstains from alcohol.

Metabolic cardiomyopathy

- Metabolic cardiomyopathy is myocardial dysfunction secondary to a derangement in metabolism
- It includes nutritional disorders such as thiamine deficiency, which is a cause of cardiomyopathy worldwide
- The most common metabolic disorder is diabetes.

Beri-beri (Vitamin B1 deficiency)

- Thiamine deficiency (Vitamin B1) is prevalent in Asia due to the consumption of thiamine-deplete polished rice
- Diagnostic criteria include:
  - Cardiomyopathy whilst in normal sinus rhythm
  - Dependant oedema
  - Signs of a neuritis and/or pellagra
  - A history of over three months of thiamine deficiency
- Patients have a reduced serum thiamine, raised pyruvate and lactate, and a low red cell transketolase
- Patients present with either high-output cardiac failure and a peripheral neuropathy ('dry' beri-beri) or fatigue, malaise, and oedema ('wet' beri-beri)
- Other features include an anaemia, painful glossitis, and hyperkeratinized skin lesions
- Treatment is with intravenous followed by oral thiamine deficiency and is associated with good recovery.

Diabetic cardiomyopathy

- Diabetes affects ventricular function independent of its effect on the coronary arteries and concurrent hypertension
- Prevalence of heart failure is higher and patients have a poorer prognosis
- Patients tend to have more extensive coronary disease as well as small vessel disease
- There is thickening of the basement membrane, myocellular atrophy and hypertrophy with myocardial and interstitial fibrosis leading to ventricualr dysfunction

- Standard heart failure treatment may attenuate remodeling and improve prognosis
- Optimal glycaemic control is mandatory.

Takotsubo cardiomyopathy

- Takotsubo cardiomyopathy is characterized by LV dysfunction with severe impairment of the apical and mid segments and sparing of basal segments
- It predominately affects women (usually in their sixties) and is often triggered by emotional or physical stress
- Patients present with chest pain or breathlessness
- ECG demonstrates ST elevation, usually in the anterior chest leads, and patients are commonly treated for STEMI/ACS, but normal coronary arteries are seen on cardiac catheterization
- LV angiography and echocardiography show the characteristic features of severe LV impairment with sparing of the basal segments ('apical ballooning')
- Some patients have basal segment involvement ('reverse Takotsubo')
- Low–moderate tropinin elevation is seen
- The pathophysiology is incompletely understood—catecholamines appear central, either via vasospasm or other toxic effect. The result is significant but usually transient LV dysfunction
- Treatment with aspirin, ACE inhibitors/ARBs and BBs and nitrates is used to reduce afterload, heart rate, and vasospasm
- Clinical outcomes are generally good, with resolution of LV dysfunction in hours/days
- Treatment can be stopped at 3–6 months but recurrence can occur in around 5% of patients.

Tachycardiomyopathy

- Incessant arrhythmia, such as SVT or AF (heart rates 180–200 bpm), can lead to LV dysfunction
- The restoration of sinus rhythm improves left ventricular function
- Heart rate reduction: BBs and ivabradine have demonstrated prognostic benefit in patients with heart failure
- Catheter ablation to restore sinus rhythm has been beneficial in restoring LV function in patients with incessant tachycardia.

Muscular dystrophy cardiomyopathy

- Primary disorders of skeletal muscle may affect cardiomyocytes
- There are many disorders associated with myocardial disease (Table 4.7)
- Skeletal deformity of the chest also leads to raised pulmonary pressures, leading to secondary cardiomyopathy
- Patients with muscular dystrophy should be periodically monitored with ECG, Holter monitoring, and echocardiography.

Peripartum cardiomyopathy

- Peripartum cardiomyopathy occurs in around 1/3000–1/10000 pregnancies
- It is defined as left ventricular systolic impairment with the following:
    1. Presentation one month prior to delivery or five months post partum
    2. Absence of pre-existing cardiac disease
    3. No other cause for cardiac dysfunction
- Aetiology is unclear, with hypotheses including an inflammatory component, malnutrition, or a familial DCM that is unmasked by the cardiovascular burden of pregnancy
- There are some features that predispose patients to developing the disease (Box 4.8)

Table 4.7 Cardiac manifestations in muscular dystrophies

Type	Inheritance	Mechanism of disease expression	Extracardiac manifestations	Cardiac manifestations
Duchenne	X-linked	Absence of dystrophin leads to disruption of the mechanical link between the sarcolemma and the extracellular matrix	Childhood onset Progressive proximal myopathy	Dilated cardiomyopathy
Becker	X-linked	Dystrophin present but at reduced levels	Onset age >12 years with slowly progressive proximal myopathy	Dilated cardiomyopathy
Emery-Dreifuss	X- linked AD, rarely AR	Loss of emerin (inner nuclear protein) Lamins A and C (nuclear envelope proteins)	Ankle, elbow and neck contractures Slowly progressive myopathy	Absent/reduced p waves refractory to atrial pacing; require V pacing AF/A flutter Massive atrial dilatation requiring anticoagulation Dilated cardiomyopathy SCD
Myotonic (Type A)	AD	Abnormal expansion of trinucleotide repeat sequence on myotonin protein kinase gene (DMPK) which modifies actin cytoskeleton. Demonstrates genetic anticpation	Myotinia Facial, pharyngeal and distal limb muscles Diabetes and thyroid dysfunction Cataracts	Conduction disease—may require pacing AF/flutter Ventricular arrhythmia SCD LV dilatation ± systolic impairment Mitral valve prolapse Left ventricular hypertrophy

Adapted from the *ESC Textbook of Cardiovascular Medicine* 2nd edition, ed. John Camm, Thomas Lüscher and Patrick Serruys, copyright 2009 with permission of Oxford University Press.

BOX 4.8 RISK FACTORS FOR DEVELOPING PERI-PARTUM CARDIOMYOPATHY

Increasing maternal age	Multiparity
Multiple pregnancy	Pre-eclampsia
Gestational hypertension	Afro-Caribbean
Familial occurrence	Malnutrition
Cocaine use by mother	Long-term tocolytic therapy
Selenium deficiency	Chlamydia infection
Enterovirus infection	

Data from 'Peripartum cardiomyopathy: a condition intensivists should be aware of', E. de Beus, W. N. van Mook, G. Ramsay *et al., Intensive Care Med.*, 29, 167–74, copyright 2003 with kind permission from Springer Science and Business Media; and 'A review of peripartum cardiomyopathy', P. R. James, *Int. J. Clin.* Pract. 58, 363–5, copyright 2004 with permission from John Wiley and Sons.

- Physical examination can be difficult as third heart sound and systolic murmurs can be heard as part of normal pregnancy
- ECG: sinus tachycardia and left axis deviation are normal for pregnancy
- Echocardiography is the investigation of choice. The definition of LV systolic dysunction is LVEF <45% or fractional shortening of <30% with an end-diastolic diameter of 2.7 cm/m^2 body surface area.

Management
- Standard heart failure therapy is used, e.g. diuretics and supportive measures including intra-aortic balloon pumps for cardiogenic shock
- ACE inhibitors/ARBs are contraindicated in the first trimester—they cause oligohydramnios
- Thrombo-prophylaxis: increased risk from prolonged bed rest, diuretic use, and impaired left ventricular function.

Prognosis and outcome
- Mortality and transplant rates are around 7%. Most patients have resolution of systolic function
- Death is usually from pump failure
- Counselling is important after the event:
  - Subclinical LV systolic dysfunction exists and another pregnancy is likely to cause decompensation thus risk of recurrence must be emphasized
  - Incidence of complication is higher, e.g. maternal death, foetal prematurity, and loss
  - Women with completely normalized LV function are at low risk but heart failure will occur in 20% of those patients with residual LV impairment
- All patients with previous peripartum cardiomyopathy need close monitoring in the event of subsequent pregnancies.

4.10 Cardiac transplantation

- Cardiac transplantation is the final option for those patients with progressive heart failure despite optimal medical and device therapy
- Patients considered for transplantation should not only have severe disease, but should have no significant co-morbidity
- As well as major surgery, physical and psychological suitability for long-term immunosuppression should be considered
- Primary indication worldwide is split equally between cardiomyopathy of ischemic and non-ischaemic origin
- The most commonly performed procedure is orthotopic transplant where the heart is replaced by the donor's.

Indications for cardiac transplantation
- Advanced heart failure refractory to maximum tolerated medical/device or surgical treatment with
  - Expected mortality of >25%
  - Limiting symptoms attributable to heart failure
- Life-threatening acute heart failure unresponsive to treatment
- Refractory life-threatening arrhythmia
- Intractable angina not ameanable to revascularization.

Contraindications to transplantation

- Irreversible pulmonary hypertension (raised pulmonary pressures, raised transpulmonary gradient)
- Irreversible hepatic or lung dysfunction (FEV1 <50% predicted)
- Cerebrovascular disease
- Active infection
- Systemic disease, e.g. amyloid, vasculitis, sarcoid
- Inability to comply with immunosuppresion
- Continued alcohol/substance misuse.

Relative contraindications

- Age >70 years
- Renal dysfunction with eGFR <40 ml/min
- Diabetes with end-organ damage
- Peripheral vascular disease not amenable to revascularization
- Malignancy
- Learning difficulties/dementia
- Hep B/C or HIV
- BMI >30
- Recent pulmonary embolism (within three months)
- Active peptic ulcer disease
- Osteoporosis
- Current smoker.

Further reading

Camm AJ, Lüscher TF, and Serruys PW (eds). *The European Society of Cardiology Textbook of Cardiovascular Medicine.* Oxford University Press, 2009.

Dubrey SW, Hawkins PN, Falk RH. Systemic disorders in heart disease: Amyloid diseases of the heart: assessment, diagnosis, and referral. *Heart,* 2011; 97: 75–84.

Eagle KA, Guyton RA, Davidoff R, *et al.* Guideline Update for Coronary Artery Bypass Graft Surgery: a report of the American College of Cardiology/American Heart Association Task Force on Practice Guidelines (Committee to Update the 1999 Guidelines for Coronary Artery Bypass Graft Surgery). ACC/AHA, 2004.

Elliott P. Cardiomyopathy: diagnosis and management of dilated cardiomyopathy. *Heart,* 2000; 84: 106.

Gardner RS, Mconagh TA, Walker NL. *Heart Failure. Oxford Specialist Handbooks in Cardiology.* Oxford University Press, 2007.

Linhart A, Elliott P. The heart in Anderson-Fabry disease and other lysosomal storage disorder. *Heart,* 2007; 93: 528–35.

Maron BJ, McKenna WJ, Danielson GK, *et al.* ACC/ESC Clinical Expert Consensus Document on Hypertrophic Cardiomyopathy: a report of the American College of Cardiology Task Force on Clinical Expert Consensus Documents and the European Society of Cardiology Committee for Practice Guidelines (Committee to Develop an Expert Consensus Document on Hypertrophic Cardiomyopathy). *Eur Heart J,* 2003; 24: 1965–91.

McKenna, WJ, Thiene G, and Nava A. Diagnosis of arrhythmogenic right ventricular dysplasia/ cardiomyopathy. *Br Heart J*, 1994; 71: 215–8.

Mestroni L, Maisch B, and McKenna WJ. Guidelines for the Study of Familial Dilated Cardiomyopathies. Collaborative Research Group of the European Human and Capital Mobility Project on Familial Dilated Cardiomyopathy. *Eur Heart J*, 1999; 20, 93–102.

Richardson P, McKenna W, Bristow M, *et al*. Classification of cardiomyopathies based on a report of the World Health Organization and International Society and Federation of Cardiology. *Circulation*, 1996; 93:841–2.

Valvular heart disease

5.1 Epidemiology

Changes with time

The western world:

- Degenerative disease is the most common cause (mainly calcific aortic valve disease and degenerative mitral valve disease)
- Rheumatic is the second most common: young immigrants or older patients exposed during childhood to rheumatic fever.

Developing countries:

- Rheumatic is the most frequent cause.

5.2 Aortic valve

Anatomy:

- The aortic valve has three cusps, which overlap each other by 1 mm
- The lines where the valve cusps meet are known as the commisures
- The sinus of valsalva surrounds the aortic valve cusps and act to pool blood to allow improved coronary flow during diastole
- The cusps and associated sinus are named with the associated coronary artery that arises from it (right, left, and non).

5.3 Aortic stenosis

Aetiology
Supravalvular aortic stenosis
There are two main forms:

- Constriction of a thickened ascending aorta at the superior aspect of the sinuses of valsalva ('hour glass deformity'): 60–75%
- Diffuse narrowing along the ascending aorta: 35–40%.

Valvular aortic stenosis
Causes include:

- Calcific 'degenerative' aortic stenosis—the most common cause in the West
- A congenitally abnormal valve (unicuspid or bicuspid) with superimposed calcification
- Rheumatic valve disease.

Subvalvular aortic stenosis
- Subvalvular aortic stenosis usually results from a variety of fixed lesions such as a thin membrane (most common) or a thick fibromuscular ridge.

Rare causes
- Familial hypercholesterolemia: lipid infiltration causes thickening of the aortic cusps
- Hyperparathyroidism: characterized by disturbed mineral metabolism and associated inflammation/calcification of the aortic cusps
- Paget's disease: increased cardiac output causes increased turbulence across the valve, increasing the incidence of calcific aortic stenosis
- Lupus erythematosus: characterized by thickening of valvular leaflets and distortion with fibrocalcific nodules.

Pathophysiology
Calcific degenerative disease
This is characterized by:

- Subendothelial accumulation of low density lipoprotein (LDL) and subsequent production of angiotensin II together with inflammation of T lymphocytes and macrophages
- Local production of proteins causing tissue calcification and activation of inflammatory signalling pathways (such as tumour necrosis factor alpha, C reactive protein, and the complement system)
- Microscopic accumulation of extracellular calcification in the early disease stage, progression as disease advances culminating in areas of frank bone formation in end-stage disease.

Rheumatic valve disease
- Rheumatic valve disease is characterized by fusion of the commisures between the leaflets with a small central orifice.

Natural history
- Rheumatic disease often presents earlier (second to fourth decades)
- Congenitally abnormal aortic valve stenosis presents in the fifth to sixth decades
- Degenerative calcific trileaflet aortic stenosis usually presents in more elderly patients (seventh to eighth decades).

Asymptomatic patients with severe aortic stenosis:

- Rate of sudden death without surgery is less than 1% per year
- Likelihood of remaining free from cardiac death and aortic valve replacement at 1, 2 and 5 years was approximately 80%, 63%, and 25% respectively
- In symptomatic patients, average survival following symptom onset is 2–3 years and there is a high risk of sudden death.

Symptoms

Heart failure

- Obstructed outflow causes increase in LV filling pressures and compensatory hypertrophy
- As diastolic dysfunction progresses there is an inability of the LV to sustain cardiac output during exercise
- Systolic heart failure occurs late and can often be an end-stage finding.

Pre-syncope/syncope

This reflects decreased cerebral perfusion and may manifest due to:

- Exercise induced vasodilation in conjunction with a fixed obstruction resulting in hypotension
- Transient bradyarrhythmia or arrhythmia such as atrial fibrillation post exertion
- Increased left ventricular (LV) pressures causing stimulation of LV baroreceptors and then a fall in arterial pressures causing reduced venous return.

Angina

- Angina occurs in up to two thirds of patients. In those without underlying coronary artery disease, angina can occur via several mechanisms:
  - Increased left ventricular mass causing increased oxygen demand
  - Compression of intra myocardial coronary arteries from prolonged contraction
  - Outflow obstruction causing a compensatory tachycardia to augment cardiac output but with reduced diastolic coronary perfusion time.

Examination

Carotid pulse palpation

- The quality reflects the degree of obstruction to blood flow into the circulation. A slow rising carotid pulse occurs due to prolonged ejection through the narrowed aortic valve.

Precordial palpation

- A sustained apex due to outflow obstruction. In later stages as LV failure occurs the cardiac impulse becomes displaced.

Cardiac auscultation

- Heart sounds:
  - Aortic valve closure becomes progressively delayed with progression, and S2 is soft and single (occurring simultaneously with P2)
  - With increasing severity the closing aortic valve sound may disappear
  - Fourth heart sound due to vigorous left atrial contraction into a stiff non-compliant LV
  - Bicuspid valve: an aortic ejection click may be heard following S1 in the early stages of aortic stenosis when the leaflets have some stiffness but are still mobile
- Heart murmur:
  - Classically an ejection systolic murmur is audible, loudest at the base of the heart in the second right intercostal space and radiating to the carotid arteries

- With increasing severity the maximum outflow and gradient occur late in systole; later murmurs signify worse disease.

Investigations

Chest radiograph

- In moderate aortic stenosis the chest radiograph is usually normal
- With advancing disease calcification of the aortic valve leaflets and dilatation of the ascending aorta can be seen.

Electrocardiogram

- LVH with or without repolarization changes are seen in approximately 80% with severe aortic stenosis.

Echocardiography

- Echocardiography is the main diagnostic tool used
- It allows visualization of the aortic valve morphology, leaflet mobility, and the degree of commissural fusion, and estimation of severity of the disease
- The severity is commonly judged by estimating the valve area via the continuity equation (see Table 5.1)
- In LV dysfunction and severe aortic stenosis, as measured by valve area but mild–modest peak aortic valve gradient, it can be difficult to establish whether the reduced valve area is due to 'true' severe aortic stenosis or a consequence of impaired left ventricular function with reduced valve opening ('pseudo-severe'). Low-dose dobutamine stress echocardiography can help to differentiate between the two
    - True aortic stenosis: there is little change in valve area (<0.2 cm^2) and increasing aortic valve gradient (mean gradient >30 mmHg at any point during infusion)
    - Pseudo-severe aortic stenosis: the valve area becomes bigger with little change in aortic valve gradient
- On average the various echocardiographic parameters of aortic stenosis vary as follows:
    - Valve area declines by 0.1 cm^2 per year
    - Aortic valve gradient increases by 7 mmHg per year
    - Aortic valve velocity increases by 0.25 m/s per year.

Table 5.1 Aortic stenosis: echocardiography ranges

	Mild	Moderate	Severe
Peak velocity (m/s)	1.7–2.9	3.0–4.0	>4.0
Peak gradient (mmHg)	<36	36–64	>64
Mean gradient (mmHg)	<20	20–40	>40
Valve area (cm^2)	>1.5	1.0–1.5	<1.0

Exercise tolerance test

- Exercise tolerance test is used in the risk stratification of the asymptomatic individual by monitoring the development of symptoms and for abnormal haemodynamic changes with exercise (fall in resting blood pressure with exercise or failure to augment resting blood pressure by >10 mmHg)

- ST depression during exercise is common in asymptomatic patients and has no known prognostic significance
- The test is contraindicated in symptomatic patients.

Cardiac catheterization
- Cardiac catheterization is usually undertaken to establish the presence of coronary artery disease prior to surgery. The 2006 ACC/AHA guidelines recommend cardiac catheterization for haemodynamic assessment in aortic stenosis in patients where non-invasive tests are inconclusive.

Cardiac computed tomography
- Multislice cardiac computed tomography (CT) is able to provide quantitative estimation of the amount of valvular calcification
- The correlation between this and clinical decision making has not been defined
- It allows assessment of the ascending aorta.

Cardiac magnetic resonance
- Cardiac magnetic resonance (CMR) is able to detect the presence of aortic stenosis, the antegrade velocity, and allows assessment of the ascending aorta.

Management
Medical management
- The development of symptoms, or progressive worsening haemodynamic parameters, are indications for surgery
- The role of medical therapy is to alleviate symptoms of advanced disease such as heart failure.

Surgical management
- Asymptomatic patients. Consider surgery if:
    - Markedly calcified valve with a rapid increase in velocity of >0.3 m/s per year
    - Symptoms, failure of appropriate haemodynamic response, or increasing valve velocity during exercise-tolerance testing
    - Reduced LV function (ejection fraction <50%) without another cause
- Symptomatic patients:
    - Valve replacement is recommended for all
- Special populations:
    - Aortic valve replacement should be considered in patients requiring coronary artery bypass grafting with at least moderate aortic stenosis
    - Transcatheter aortic valve implantation is currently indicated in high-risk surgical candidates.

Follow-up
- Asymptomatic severe aortic stenosis: follow up every 6 months–1 year
- Figure 5.1 shows a flow chart for the most recent ESC guidelines.

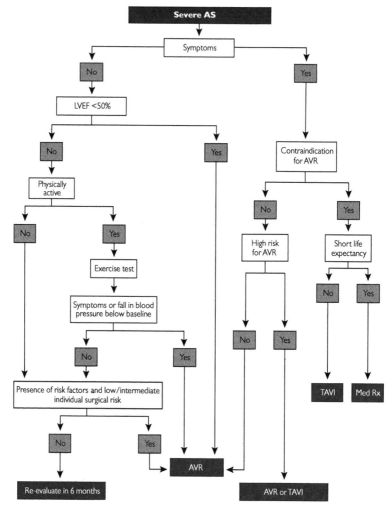

AS = aortic stenosis; LV = left ventricle; EF = ejection fraction; BSA = body surface area
Note: The management of patients with low gradient and low ejection fraction is detailed in the text

Figure 5.1 Management of severe aortic stenosis.

Reproduced from 'Guidelines on the management of valvular heart disease', *European Heart Journal* (2012) **33**, 2451–96. Alec Vahanian, Ottavio Alfieri, Felicita Andreotti et al., with permission of Oxford University Press.

5.4 Aortic regurgitation

Aetiology

Primary valve disease

- Degenerative valve disease is the most common form in the western world, accounting for >50% of cases
- Bicuspid valve is affected in 15–30%
- Rheumatic disease is the most common form in developing countries
- Endocarditis causes 10% of cases
- Rarer causes:

- Trauma
- Ankylosing spondylitis
- Acromegaly
- Fenfluaramine.

Disease of the aorta

Most often due to:

- Systemic hypertension
- Aortic dissection
- Aortitis
- connective tissue disease:
    - Marfan syndrome
    - Ehlers–Danlos syndrome
    - pseudoxanthoma elasticum.

Pathophysiology

Acute severe aortic regurgitation

- There is an abrupt increase in end diastolic volume, whilst a normal left ventricular size is maintained causing an increase in end diastolic pressure
- Ventricle is unable to dilate acutely to compensate for this increased volume and there is a reduction in forward-stroke volume.

Chronic severe aortic regurgitation

- Slowly increasing end diastolic volume causes a gradual increase in LV size
- Increase in LV wall stress occurs together with initial compensatory myocardial hypertrophy
- The combination of hypertrophy and increased LV volumes increases stroke volume—net forward flow is maintained despite the regurgitant lesion and so patients may remain asymptomatic for some time
- Decompensation and symptoms occur due to the onset of LV dysfunction leading to an inability to maintain the stroke volume.

Natural history

- Acute severe AR: poor prognosis unless surgical correction used
- Asymptomatic severe AR with preserved LV function
    - Development of LV dysfunction: <1.3% per year
    - Sudden death <0.2% per year
    - Development of symptoms with LV dysfunction or death <4.3% per year
- Predictors of outcome in these individuals include:
    - Age
    - End systolic volume
    - Ejection fraction.

Symptoms

- The onset of symptoms are related to increased left ventricular size
- Symptoms of heart failure are dyspnoea, orthopnoea, and paroxysmal nocturnal dyspnoea
- Palpitations due to tachycardia or premature beats are seen
- Angina (in the absence of coronary artery disease) seen due to reduced myocardial perfusion pressure or as a result of subendocardial ischemia due to left ventricular hypertrophy.

Examination

Peripheral signs

- Water hammer or Corrigan pulse:
    - Initial distension of the peripheral arteries occurs due to increased stroke volume and an elevation in systolic pressure
    - The regurgitation leads to a fall in pressure and rapid collapse of the arteries and a low diastolic pressure (creating a wide pulse pressure)
- Other findings associated with a hyperdynamic pulse include
    - Traube's sign: systolic and diastolic sounds heard over femoral arteries
    - Duroziez sign: systolic and diastolic bruit heart over femoral arteries
    - DeMusset's sign: head bobbing with heart beat
    - Quincke's pulse: capillary pulsations in finger tips.

Precordial palpation

- As a consequence of left ventricular enlargement the apical pulse is displaced laterally and is more diffuse.

Cardiac auscultation

- Heart sounds:
    - A third heart sound (gallop) is heard due to severe LV systolic impairment in decompensated disease
- Heart murmur:
    - High-pitched diastolic murmur is audible following A2; best heard in the third/fourth intercostal space at the left sternal edge
    - The duration of the murmur in diastole correlates with severity of regurgitation
    - Austin Flint murmur is a mid-to-late diastolic murmur audible at the apex due to anterior mitral valve leaflet displacement from the regurgitant flow and also turbulence due to mixing of the antegrade mitral flow with retrograde aortic flow
    - An ejection systolic murmur can often be heard, similar to that of aortic stenosis, due to the increased stroke volume across the aortic valve.

Investigations

Chest radiograph

- Cardiomegaly can be apparent due to dilatation of the left ventricle.

Electrocardiogram

- Changes due to increase in left ventricular size or hypertrophy (increasing amplitude of the QRS complex) with or without repolarization abnormalities may be seen.

Echocardiography

The severity of aortic regurgitation can be graded in several ways (see Table 5.2):

- Vena contracta: measurement of the narrowest part of the jet as it passes through the valve
- Jet width to outflow tract diameter ratio in central, non-eccentric jets of aortic regurgitation

Table 5.2 Echocardiographic parameters for assessing severity in aortic regurgitation

	Vena contracta	Regurgitant volume	Regurgitant fraction	AR/LVOT ratio	ERO	Pressure half time
Mild	<0.3 cm	30 ml	30%	<25%	0.1 cm^2	>500 ms
Severe	>0.6 cm	60 ml	50%	≥65%	>0.3 cm^2	<200 ms

- The presence of retrograde diastolic flow in the descending aorta, measured by placing the pulsed wave Doppler in the centre of the descending aorta
- Pressure half-time of the aortic regurgitation measured by continuous wave Doppler
- Calculation of regurgitant volume and effective regurgitant orifice (ERO).

Cardiac catheterization

- The 2006 ACC/AHA guidelines recommend cardiac catheterization only be used for haemodynamic assessment in patients where non-invasive tests are inconclusive
- It is usually undertaken to establish the presence of coronary artery disease prior to aortic valve surgery
- Left ventricular and aortic root contrast angiography can be used to assess:
  - LV size and function
  - Aortic root dimensions
  - Aortic valve movement
  - Visual semi-quantitative severity of aortic regurgitation.

Cardiac MRI

- AHA guidelines (2006) state that cardiac MRI maybe used to assess AR in those with suboptimal echocardiography. CMR allows quantification of left ventricular function, stroke volumes, and assessment of regurgitant volume.

Exercise stress testing

- For chronic asymptomatic AR exercise stress testing can be used to assess functional capacity (AHA 2006).

Management

Medical management

- ACE inhibitors (vasodilatation) can be used in those with LV systolic dysfunction or hypertension.

Surgical management

- Aortic regurgitation due to aortic root dilatation:
  - Aortic diameter >55 mm (trileaflet aortic valve)
  - Aortic diameter >50 mm (bicuspid aortic valve)
  - Aortic diameter >45 mm in patients with Marfan syndrome
- Asymptomatic severe aortic regurgitation:
  - LV ejection fraction <50% or
  - LV end diastolic diameter >70 mm or
  - LV end systolic diameter >55 mm
- Symptomatic severe aortic regurgitation:
  - Recommend surgery.

Follow up

- Mild–moderate AR should have clinic review yearly and biannual echocardiography (see Figure 5.2)
- Asymptomatic severe AR should have 6-monthly follow up after initial examination
- If echocardiographic parameters change then 6-monthly follow up until time of surgery should occur
- If all is stable then 1-yearly follow up is sufficient
- In those with a dilated aortic root, follow-up should be at yearly intervals at least.

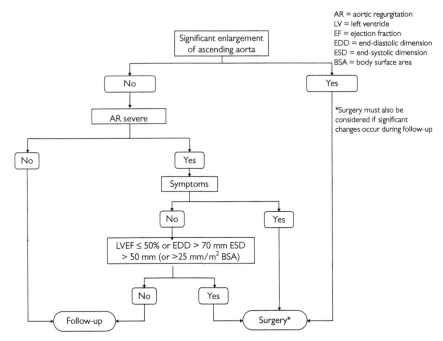

Figure 5.2 Flowchart for management of aortic regurgitation.

Reproduced from 'Guidelines on the management of valvular heart disease', *European Heart Journal* (2012) **33**, 2451–96. Alec Vahanian, Ottavio Alfieri, Felicita Andreotti et al., with permission of Oxford University Press.

5.5 Mitral valve

Anatomy

The mitral valve consists of two leaflets (anterior and posterior).

- Each leaflet has three scallops, with A1 and P1 being adjacent to the antero-lateral commisures; A3 and P3 are adjacent to the postero-medial commisures
- The valve leaflets are supported by the mitral valve annulus
- The leaflets are attached to the papillary muscles by chordae tendinae.

5.6 Mitral regurgitation

Aetiology
Primary mitral regurgitation

Main causes:

- Degenerative MR—most common cause
- Infective endocarditis
- Rheumatic valve disease
- Trauma causing ruptured chordae.

Secondary mitral regurgitation

Main causes:

- Ischemic heart disease: MR can occur as a complication of ischemic heart disease usually due to damage to the papillary muscle (mainly posteromedial) following myocardial infarction
- LV systolic dysfunction: annular dilatation can occur due to left ventricular enlargement causing poor leaflet coaptation.

Pathophysiology

Acute severe mitral regurgitation

- If the left ventricle and atrium have not had a chance to adapt to the MR, its compliance is usually normal (and there has been no compensatory LVH)
- Acutely: forward stroke volume and cardiac output are reduced
- Increased LA volumes cause a marked rise in LA pressure, which is reflected back to the pulmonary circulation
- Cardiogenic shock can quickly develop. Tachycardia occurs to try to compensate for the fall in left ventricular ejection volume, and the ventricle can appear 'hyperdynamic'.

Chronic severe mitral regurgitation

- The LV adapts to the chronic increase in LV volume by enlarging to deliver a larger stroke volume (whilst systolic function is maintained)
- Eccentric LVH contributes to the increase in LV size whilst better LA compliance allows moderation of left atrial pressure, a feature not seen in acute severe mitral regurgitation
- Patients may remain asymptomatic for some time.

Natural history

Acute severe mitral regurgitation

- Without intervention acute severe mitral regurgitation carries a poor prognosis.

Chronic asymptomatic mitral regurgitation

- With medical management, end points and 5-year rates are:
  - Death from any cause: 22%
  - Death from cardiac causes: 14%
  - Cardiac events (death from cardiac causes, heart failure, or new AF): 33%
- Predictors of poor outcome include ERO, left atrial dilatation, LV enlargement, and reduced LV ejection fraction.

Symptoms

- Exertional dyspnoea
- Palpitations
- Atrial fibrillation is a common presentation due to increased LA volume and pressure.

Examination

Precordial palpation

- Chronic MR (LV dilatation)—apex pulse laterally displaced
- Acute MR—the apex beat is hyperdynamic and not displaced
- Apical thrill indicates severe disease.

Cardiac auscultation

- Heart sounds:
  - S1 can be reduced as the mitral valve leaflets do not coapt properly
  - Wide splitting of S2 can happen as A2 occurs earlier due to the reduced LV ejection time
  - In patients with pulmonary artery hypertension, P2 will be increased and delayed, further accentuating splitting of S2
  - In severe MR with LV systolic impairment, the increased flow into a dilated left ventricle produces an S3
- Heart murmur:
  - Holosystolic murmur is most easily audible at the apex, radiating to the axilla
  - With mitral valve prolapse a systolic click occurs in mid–late systole (time of maximum prolapse) when the chordae are under peak tension
  - In acute MR (fall in LV filling pressure together with the acutely raised LA pressure): intensity of the murmur does not correlate with severity.

Investigations

Chest radiograph

- Chronic severe MR: LV and LA dilatation
- Acute severe MR: Normal cardiac silhouette with evidence of pulmonary congestion.

Electrocardiogram

- The chronicity of MR and adaptation of the LV and LA are reflected in the ECG by features of LVH and LA dilatation
- AF is commonly seen
- In ischaemic MR, ischaemic features are seen most commonly in the inferolateral leads.

Echocardiogram

Echocardiography allows MR severity to be quantified in several ways:

- Vena contracta: the narrowest region of the regurgitant jet (usually just below the valve in the left atrium)
- Flow convergence (PISA): a measurement of how much blood travels through a valve
  - Get a good image of the mitral valve (usually the apical four chamber view is best) and ensure you are in the plane of the regurgitant jet
  - Check what the colour scale is set to, i.e. aliasing velocity—$V_{aliasing}$. You can use this velocity if the flow convergence is obvious but to optimize the colour contrast at the boundary layer it is normal to shift the zero of the baseline so that the aliasing velocity is 40 cm/s
  - Acquire a loop of the cardiac cycle and scroll through to identify the mid-systolic hemisphere shell (Figure 5.3)
  - Measure the radius (r) from valve orifice to point of colour change. If the colour flow is obscuring the valve orifice on your loop, place a caliper at the aliasing zone then suppress the colour flow and position the second cursor on the valve
- Regurgitant volume and fraction: $2\pi r^2 \times V_{aliasing}$
- Effective regurgitant orifice area:

$$EROA = \frac{\text{regurgitant flow}}{\text{peak velocity on CW}}$$

0–20 mm^2: mild, 20–40 mm^2: moderate, >40 mm^2: severe

- Jet area/left atrial area ratio
- Visual density of continuous wave Doppler trace through MR

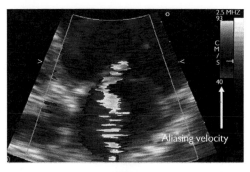

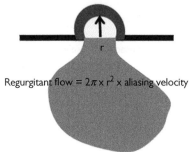

Regurgitant flow $= 2\pi \times r^2 \times$ aliasing velocity

Figure 5.3 Scroll through a loop of the cardiac cycle to identify the mid-systolic hemisphere shell.

- In more severe disease the density of the regurgitation matched that of the forward flow from LA to LV
- Supportive measures:
  - E wave >1.2 m/s is indicative of severe MR. With severe MR and increased LA volumes blood leaves the atrium more rapidly at the start of diastole resulting in increased early diastolic velocities (see Table 5.3)
  - Pulmonary vein flow systolic reversal.

Table 5.3 Quantification of mitral regurgitation severity by echocardiography

	Mild	Severe
Vena contracta	<0.3 cm	>0.7 cm
Jet area/LA area ratio	<20%	>40%
ERO	<0.2 cm^2	>0.4 cm^2
RV	<30 ml	>60 ml
RF	<30%	>50%

Cardiac catheterization
- This is usually undertaken to establish the presence of coronary artery disease prior to mitral valve surgery. Haemodynamic measures should be undertaken only when non-invasive tests are inconclusive (AHA 2006).

Cardiac MRI
- If there is a discrepancy between echocardiographic and clinical findings then CMR allows calculation of MR regurgitant volumes and ERO as well as LV/LA size and LV function.

Management

Medical management

- Acute MR:
  - Management is aimed at stabilizing haemodynamics in preparation for surgery
  - Nitrates and diuretics can reduce filling pressures
  - Inotropic agents may be needed in those with cardiogenic shock
- Chronic asymptomatic MR:
  - There are no long-term studies to indicate any prognostic benefit from the use of vasodilators in patients with chronic MR and preserved LV ejection fraction
  - ACE inhibitors and vasodilators are recommended in those with chronic severe MR and LV systolic dysfunction
  - If heart failure occurs then beta blockers and spironalactone are recommended as per heart failure guidelines
  - Anti-coagulation with warfarin is used for those with atrial fibrillation.

Surgical management

- Acute severe mitral regurgitation:
  - In symptomatic patients urgent surgery is recommended
- Chronic severe mitral regurgitation:
  - Mitral valve repair (with artificial chord replacement and annuloplasty) is preferred to valve replacement
  - If repair not possible then replacement is undertaken (ideally with chordal preservation)
- Symptomatic chronic severe mitral regurgitation:
  - Surgery indicated if LV ejection fraction >30% and end systolic diameter <55 mm
  - If LV ejection fraction <30% and/or end systolic diameter >55 mm and symptoms persist despite medical therapy then surgery (repair preferably) is recommended if likelihood of success is good and comorbidity low
- Asymptomatic chronic severe mitral regurgitation:
  - There are no randomized controlled trials assessing the prognostic benefit of valve surgery in asymptomatic patients
  - ESC guidelines recommend surgery in the following circumstances:
    - LV ejection fraction <60% and/or LV end systolic diameter >45 mm
    - LV ejection fraction >60% and LV end systolic diameter >45 mm with atrial fibrillation or systolic pulmonary artery pressure >50 mmHg at rest
  - For patients undergoing coronary revascularization, mitral valve surgery (for ischaemic asymptomatic mitral regurgitation) is recommended:
    - In those with severe mitral regurgitation, when ejection fraction >30%
    - In those with moderate mitral regurgitation, if repair is possible.

Functional mitral regurgitation

- In patients with functional (or secondary) mitral regurgitation the papillary muscles, chordae and valve leaflets are normal. The two major causes of functional mitral regurgitation are ischaemia and any cause of a dilated ventricle
- There is limited data available on the role of surgery in this subgroup of patients
- Medical therapy is the preferred treatment and if symptoms are ongoing then mitral valve surgery with LV reconstruction can be considered in those with severe mitral regurgitation and LV systolic dysfunction (see Figure 5.4).

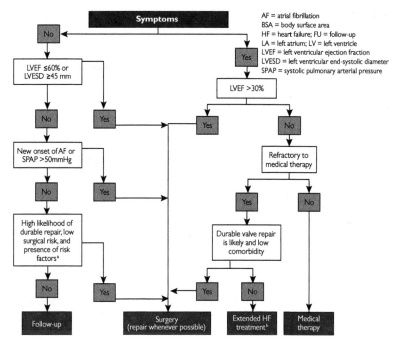

[a]When there is a high likelihood of durable valve repair at a low risk, valve repair should be considered (IIaC) in patients with flail leaflet and LVESD ≥40 mm; valve repair may be considered (IIbC) if one of the following is present: LA volume ≥60 mL/m² BSA and sinus rhythm or pulmonary hypertension on exercise (SPAP ≥60 mmHg).

[b]Extended HF management includes the following: cardiac resynchronization therapy; ventricular assist devices; cardiac restraint devices; heart transplantation.

Figure 5.4 Flowchart for management of mitral regurgitation.
Reproduced from 'Guidelines on the management of valvular heart disease', *European Heart Journal* (2012) **33**, 2451–96. Alec Vahanian, Ottavio Alfieri, Felicita Andreotti et al., with permission of Oxford University Press.

Follow-up

- Asymptomatic patients with moderate MR and normal LV function should have annual clinic follow up with biannual echocardiography
- Asymptomatic patients with severe MR and normal LV function should have 6-monthly clinic follow up with echocardiography annually
- In those with borderline indications for surgery then follow-up should be more frequent.

5.7 Mitral stenosis

Aetiology

Rheumatic heart disease is responsible for the majority of cases. Rarer causes include:

- Degenerative mitral valve disease
- Muchopolysaccahridosis
- Gout
- Lupus erythematousus
- Stenosis due to obstruction from vegetations or tumour.

Pathophysiology

- Leaflets thicken with a loss of normal valve morphology due to deposition of fibrin
- As disease progresses there is fusion of the leaflet commisures and thickening/shortening of the chordae tendinae
- Ultimately calcification of the mitral valve apparatus

- Reduced LV diastolic filling and subsequently left atrial pressures increase
- A diastolic pressure gradient between the LA and LV exists
- Increase in LA pressure is transmitted through the pulmonary circulation causing an increase in pulmonary capillary and arterial pressures
- Pulmonary oedema ensues as the pulmonary capillary wedge pressure approaches 25 mmHg
- With chronic mitral stenosis, LV systolic dysfunction occurs in around 25% of cases
- Atrial fibrillation is common in advanced disease due to:
  - Chronically increased LA size
  - The fibrotic effects of rheumatic disease on the left atrium and intermodal and interatrial tracts as well as damage to the sinus node.

Natural history

- MS is slowly progressive disease and patients remain asymptomatic for years
- Disease progression has been noted to increase following the onset of symptoms
- The mean rate of progression is estimated to be 0.1 cm^2 per year and the mean interval between rheumatic fever and the onset of symptoms is 16–20 years
- In symptomatic patients, without intervention 5-year survival rates were estimated at 44%.

Symptoms

The normal mitral valve area is 4–6 cm^2 and clinical symptoms may occur with moderate narrowing (<2 cm^2). The most frequent symptoms encountered are:

- Dyspnoea
  - Left ventricular systolic dysfunction
  - Inability to increase left ventricular ejection with increased physiological demands
- Haemoptysis
  - Increased LA pressures causing rupture of thin dilated bronchial veins
  - Pulmonary oedema causing pink frothy sputum
- Palpitations
  - Atrial fibrillation is commonly seen with advanced disease
- Dysphonia
  - Compression of the recurrent laryngeal nerve by the dilated LA
- Oedema/ascites
  - Due to right-sided heart failure.

Examination

Precordial palpation

- In advanced disease an apical diastolic thrill may be palpable
- With pulmonary hypertension a right ventricular heave and palpable S2 occurs.

Cardiac auscultation

- Heart sounds
  - Opening snap
    - Due to leaflet tip fusion—rapid initial opening of the valve followed by a sudden reduction in motion
    - In more advanced stenosis the increasing LA pressure brings mitral valve opening earlier and reduces the interval between S2 and the opening snap
  - First heart sound
    - In non-calcified MS the leaflets are still patent at the onset of ventricular contraction and S1 is loud

- As the leaflets become more restricted due to calcification their movement is limited and S1 is soft
  - Second heart sound
    - P2 is loud in those with pulmonary hypertension
- Heart murmur
  - Low-pitched diastolic rumble loudest at the apex
  - The duration of the murmur correlates with disease severity
  - In severe MS the increased LA to LV pressure gradient and longer duration of blood flow across the mitral valve results in longer murmur duration
- Right heart failure
  - Chronically raised pulmonary pressures are reflected by signs of right-sided heart failure with changes in the JVP, peripheral oedema, and sometimes ascites present (see 'Heart failure' section).

Investigations

Chest radiograph

- Enlarged left atrium with a double contour
- Straightening of left heart border
- Calcification of the mitral valve annulus
- Pulmonary congestion.

Electrocardiogram

Common ECG features seen include:

- Broad and bifid P wave due to left atrial enlargement and hypertrophy
- Atrial fibrillation
- Changes due to pulmonary hypertension: right ventricular hypertrophy, right axis deviation.

Echocardiogram

The following echocardiographic parameters allow grading of severity of MS (see Table 5.4):

- Plannimetry of the valve
- Measurement of pressure half time
- Mean transmitral diastolic pressure gradient
- Estimation of pulmonary artery systolic pressure.

In asymptomatic patients with borderline parameters then stress echocardiography can be performed to evaluate the post-stress transmitral gradient and pulmonary artery systolic pressures.

Table 5.4 Echocardiographic parameters for assessing severity in mitral stenosis

	Mild MS	Moderate MS	Severe MS
MV area	1.6–2.0 cm^2	1.0–1.5 cm^2	<1.0 cm^2
Pressure half time	71–139 ms	140–219 ms	>219 ms
Mean transmitral diastolic gradient	<5 mmHg		>10 mmHg
PASP	<30 mmHg		>50 mmHg

Exercise stress test/dobutamine stress echocardiography

- In patients who have symptoms but whose parameters of severity do not correlate, stress testing may be considered to estimate heart rate, blood pressure response, transmitral gradient, and pulmonary artery pressure at rest and upon stress

- Those with a rise in PASP to >60 mmHg or increase in transmitral gradient to >15 mmHg during exercise should be considered for intervention (AHA 2006).

Cardiac catheterization

- The 2006 ACC/AHA guidelines recommend cardiac catheterization only be used for haemodynamic assessments in patients where non-invasive tests are inconclusive.

Management

Medical management

- Prophylaxis against rheumatic fever if appropriate
- Diuretics
- BBs/calcium antagonists for heart-rate control
- Anticoagulation for those with AF
- Anticoagulation can be considered if LA diameter >55 mm or if spontaneous contrast on echocardiography is seen (AHA 2006, level of evidence C).

Surgical management

If possible percutaneous mitral commisurotomy (PMC) is performed. The suitability for this procedure depends on the mobility of the leaflet and degree of thickening/calcification. One such scoring system is the Wilkins score (see Table 5.5).

Table 5.5 Wilkins classification

Grade	Mobility	Subvalvular thickening	Thickening	Calcification
1	Highly mobile valve with only leaflet tips restricted	Minimal thickening just below the mitral leaflets	Leaflets near normal in thickness	A single area of increased echo brightness
2	Leaflet mid and base portions have normal mobility	Thickening of chordal structures extending to one-third of the chordal length	Mid-leaflets normal, considerable thickening of margins (5–8 mm)	Scattered areas of brightness confined to leaflet margins
3	Valve continues to move forward in diastole, mainly from the base	Thickening extended to distal third of the chords	Thickening extending through the entire leaflet (5–8 mm)	Brightness extending into the mid-portions of the leaflets
4	No or minimal forward movement of the leaflets in diastole	Extensive thickening and shortening of all chordal structures extending down to the papillary muscles	Considerable thickening of all leaflet tissue (>8–10 mm)	Extensive brightness throughout much of the leaflet tissue

Scores >8 are not suitable for PMC. Reproduced from *Am. J. Cardiol.* 83, Luis R. Padial, Vivian M. Abascal, Pedro R. Moreno, *et al.*, 'Echocardiography can predict the development of severe mitral regurgitation after percutaneous mitral valvuloplasty by the Inoue technique', 1210, copyright 1999 with permission of Elsevier.

Symptomatic MS (valve area <1.5 cm²)

PMC for those with:

- No contraindications to PMC (left atrial thrombus, >mild MR)
- No unfavourable anatomical or clinical characteristics, defined as the presence of several of the following:
  - Clinical characteristics
    - Old age
    - History of PMC

- NYHA IV
- Atrial fibrillation
- Severe pulmonary hypertension
  - ■ Anatomic characteristics
    - Echo score >8
    - Calcification of mitral valve
    - Severe tricuspid regurgitation
    - Contraindications to surgery
- Valve replacement for those with:
  - Contraindications to PMC
  - Unfavourable anatomical characteristics, unfavourable clinical characteristics for PMC.

Asymptomatic MS (valve area <1.5 cm²)

PMC for those with high risk of embolism or haemodynamic decomponsation, i.e. those with:

- Previous embolism
- Atrial spontaneous echo contrast
- Recent or paroxysmal AF
- Systolic pulmonary pressure >50 mmHg
- Need for major non-cardiac surgery or desire for pregnancy.

In those without high risk for embolism or haemodynamic decomponsation, exercise tolerance testing is recommended. The development of exertional symptoms would be an indication to PMC (unless any unfavourable anatomical or clinical characteristics are present).

Follow-up

In asymptomatic patients with significant MS yearly follow-up is recommended (see Figure 5.5).

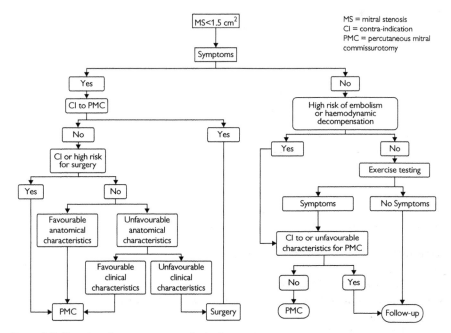

Figure 5.5 Flowchart for management of mitral stenosis.

Reproduced from 'Guidelines on the management of valvular heart disease', *European Heart Journal* (2012) **33**, 2451–96. Alec Vahanian, Ottavio Alfieri, Felicita Andreotti et al., with permission of Oxford University Press.

5.8 Tricuspid valve

Anatomy
- The valve is made up of three cusps: anterior, posterior, and septal
- Chordae tendinae attach the cusps to papillary muscles on the septum and right ventricular free wall and the valve is seated in its own annulus.

5.9 Tricuspid regurgitation

Aetiology
Primary tricuspid regurgitation
This is as a consequence of a disruption to the valve, papillary muscles, or chordae. Causes include:
- Infective endocarditis
- Trauma from pacemaker lead
- Rheumatic valve disease
- Carcinoid syndrome
- Ebstein's anomaly
- Iatrogenic, e.g. anorectic drugs.

Functional tricuspid regurgitation:
- Accounts for the majority of cases
- Is due to a consequence of volume ± pressure overload with structurally normal valve chords and leaflets.

There is dilatation of the RV and RA with dilatation of the annulus.

Pathophysiology
- In mild–moderate TR the RA adapts relatively well (good compliance)—patients remain asymptomatic for some time
- Onset of symptoms usually coincides with the onset of right-sided heart failure
- RA decompensates with the increasing volumes
- It is reflected by high right atrial pressure and increased right ventricular pressures/volume overload.

Natural history
- Primary TR—poor prognosis unless corrected
- Functional TR—remain asymptomatic for some time and the degree of TR may improve as RV failure improves.

Symptoms
- Symptoms of right-sided heart failure or the underlying disease process.

Examination
Jugular veins
- Elevation of right atrial pressure causes distension of the jugular veins and the JVP has characteristic features.

Palpation
- A right ventricular heave may be present due to RV dilatation and raised pulmonary pressures

- Right heart failure:
    - This manifests by the presence of peripheral oedema and ascites
    - Hepatomegaly
    - Pulsatile hepatomegaly can be present in severe TR.

Cardiac auscultation
- Heart sounds:
    - P2 component is increased with pulmonary hypertension
    - Third heart sound occurs with right heart failure and a dilated right ventricle
- Heart murmur:
    - A pan systolic murmur is heard, loudest in the left sternal border and accentuated by inspiration.

Investigations

Chest Radiograph
- Right atrial and right ventricular enlargement.

Electrocardiogram
- If TR is due to right ventricular infarction the ischaemic changes may be seen inferiorly/posteriorly
- If TR is due to pulmonary hypertension then features of right ventricular hypertrophy may exist (right axis deviation, tall R waves V1 and V2, right bundle branch block).

Echocardiogram
- This is the main imaging tool used, allowing assessment of the valvular structure and quantification of severity using:
    - Vena contracta
    - Hepatic vein flow
    - CW trace
    - RV/RA/IVC size (see Table 5.6)
- Assessment of pulmonary hypertension: RV to RA pressure gradient estimated form TR jet plus RA pressure (estimated from the size and respiratory variation of IVC).

Table 5.6 Echocardiographic parameters for grading severity of tricuspid regurgitation.

	Mild	Severe
Qualitative		
Valve structure	Normal	Abnormal
Jet (Nyquist 50–60 cm/s)	<5 cm^2	>10 cm^2
CW trace	Soft and parabolic	Dense and triangular
Semi-quantitative		
Vena contracta	—	>0.7 cm
PISA r (Nyquist 40 cm/s)	<0.5 cm	>0.9 cm
Tricuspid inflow	Normal	E wave dominant >1m/s
Hepatic vein flow	Normal	Systolic reversal
Quantitative		
EROA	Not defined	>/40 mm^2
R vol	Not defined	>45 ml
RV/RA/IVC	Normal size	Usually dilated

Management

Medical

- Diuretics.

Surgical

- ESC guidelines recommend early repair (rather than valve replacement) with preserved RV function prior to irreversible dysfunction
- Current recommendations (class 1C) for TV surgery due to TR include:
  - Severe TR in a patient undergoing left-sided valve surgery
  - Severe primary TR and symptoms despite medical therapy without severe right ventricular dysfunction
  - Moderate organic TR in a patient undergoing left-sided valve surgery
  - Moderate secondary TR with dilated annulus (>40 mm) in a patient undergoing left-sided valve surgery
  - Severe TR and symptoms after left-sided valve surgery in the absence of left-sided myocardial valve or right ventricular dysfunction and without severe pulmonary hypertension
  - Isolated TR with mild or no symptoms and progressive dilatation or deterioration of right ventricular function.

5.10 Tricuspid stenosis

Aetiology

- Rheumatic valve disease (most common)
- Congenital atesia or stenosis of valve
- Carcinoid
- Right atrial tumours
- Bacterial endocarditis.

Pathophysiology

- Persistent pressure gradient between the right atrium and right ventricle—increases during inspiration and exercise (as venous return increases)
- Pressure gradient of up to 5 mmHg is sufficient to cause an increase in mean right atrial pressure.

Symptoms

- Fatigue due to obstruction of tricuspid flow limiting cardiac output.

Examination

- Jugular venous pressure: large A wave and rate of Y descent
- Signs of pulmonary hypertension and right heart failure: hepatomegaly/hepatic pulsation, ascites, peripheral oedema, right ventricular parasternal heave.

Auscultation

- Heart sounds:
  - Opening snap localized to lower left sternal border
  - S2. Loud P2 in pulmonary hypertension

- Heart murmur:
  - Low-frequency diastolic murmur audible at the lower left sternal border, fourth intercostal space.

Investigations

Chest Radiograph
- Right atrial dilatation and right ventricular enlargement may be evident.

Electrocardiogram
- Right atrial hypertrophy
- Atrial fibrillation is a common presentation.

Echocardiogram
- Measurement of peak velocity across the valve and substitution into the Bernoulli equation
- Pressure half time cannot be used to measure valve area as the appropriate constant has not been identified (see Table 5.7).

Table 5.7 Echocardiographic assessment of tricuspid stenosis

	Normal	Severe
Mean pressure drop		≥5 mmHg
Valve area	>7.0 cm²	<1.0 cm²

Management

Medical management
- Diuretics when heart failure present
- Anticoagulation if AF present.

Surgical management
- Percutaneous balloon dilatation can be performed in cases of pure tricuspid stenosis (TS)
- Due to the higher risk of thrombosis, biological prostheses are the preferred choice
- Current ESC recommendations for surgical intervention in those with TS are:
  - Severe TS (±TR) with symptoms despite medical therapy
  - Severe TS (±TR) in patient undergoing left-sided valve intervention.

5.11 Pulmonary valve

Anatomy
- The pulmonary valve (PV) consists of three cusps: anterior, left, and right.

5.12 Pulmonary stenosis

Aetiology
- Congenital pulmonic stenosis
- Congenital rubella syndrome

- Tetralogy of Fallot
- Noonan syndrome
- Supravalvular/subvalvular pulmonic stenosis.

Pathophysiology

- Fibrous thickening and fusion of the commisures. Two main morphological types exist:
  - Commissural fusion leaving an effectively bicuspid pliable valve (90%)
  - No commissural fusion but valves are dysplastic and thickened
- The obstruction leads to right ventricular hypertrophy and pulmonary hypertension
- Increasing right heart pressures in the presence of a patent foramen ovale (PFO) or septal defect will cause cyanosis
- Ultimately right ventricular failure will ensue.

Natural history

- Symptoms usually begin with more than mild pulmonary stenosis (PS)
- With moderate pulmonary stenosis both medical and surgical treatment has been shown to be effective
- Severe pulmonary stenosis, when detected early in life, will require surgical treatment to avoid right ventricular failure.

Symptoms

- Asymptomatic or may present with exertional dyspnoea progressing to symptoms of right heart failure
- Exercise induced symptoms—inability to augment pulmonary flow during physical activity. May present as syncope or chest pain
- Palpitations are common due to atrial arrhythmias.

Examination

In severe pulmonary stenosis several key clinical features are apparent.

Precordial palpation

- A left parasternal lift indicates a prominent right ventricular systolic impulse.

Cardiac auscultation

- Heart sounds:
  - Systolic ejection click is audible if leaflets are thin and pliable
  - Splitting of the second heart sound may occur due to delay in the pulmonary component
  - A right fourth heart sound due to right ventricular hypertrophy and a 'stiff' ventricle
- Heart murmur:
  - Ejection systolic murmur loudest at the left upper sternal edge.

Investigations

Chest radiograph

- Dilatation of the main pulmonary artery may be evident together with reduced vascular pulmonary markings.

Electrocardiogram

- Depending on the severity of obstruction the following may be present: P pulmonale, RVH, right axis deviation.

Table 5.8 Echocardiographic parameters for assessing pulmonary stenosis

	Mild	Moderate	Severe
Peak gradient (mmHg)	10–25	24–40	>40
Valve area (cm²)	>1.0	0.5–1.0	<0.5

Echocardiogram
- Severity of PS is estimated by:
  - Measuring peak gradient across PV (see Table 5.8)
  - Calculating the effective orifice area.

Cardiac MRI
- Can be very useful because of its ability to image in any plane to get accurate flow measures.

Management
- Balloon valvuloplasty is the preferred option (if leaflets are pliable) upon symptom development or at rest when the pulmonary valve gradient exceeds 30 mmHg
- Valve replacement is usually reserved for dysplastic/calcified leaflets or in those with significant PR.

Follow-up
- Mild PS: discharge following echocardiogram
- Mild PS or presence of PR: 1–3 yearly follow up.

5.13 Pulmonary regurgitation

Aetiology
- Pulmonary hypertension
- Tetralogy of Fallot
- Infective endocarditis
- Rheumatic heart disease
- Carcinoid.

Pathophysiology
- The regurgitation occurs usually by one of the following mechanisms:
  - Dilatation of the pulmonary valve ring
  - Acquired alteration of the valve leaflet morphology
  - Congenital absence or malformation of the valve
  - Increasing regurgitation causing RV volume overload.

Symptoms
- Dyspnoea
- Fatigability
- Right-sided heart failure: oedema
- Symptoms related to the underlying disease process.

Examination

- Raised jugular venous pressure
- Precordial palpation
  - Right ventricular heave may be palpable due to pulmonary hypertension
  - Cardiac auscultation
- Heart sounds:
  - Loud delayed P2 in the presence of pulmonary hypertension
  - Absent P2 if regurgitation is due to congenitally absent valve or surgical resection
- Heart murmur:
  - Classically there is a high-pitched early diastolic murmur audible in the left upper sterna area.

Investigations

Chest radiograph

- Features of pulmonary hypertension / right heart failure may be present.

Electrocardiogram

- Features reflect increasing RV volume and pressure overload: right bundle branch block (RBBB), right axis deviation, right atrial dilatation, and RVH.

Echocardiogram

- The severity of PR can be assessed by
  - Jet to outflow tract ratio (see Table 5.9)
  - Continuous wave Doppler: intensity, shape, and deceleration time estimation
  - Flow reversal in main pulmonary artery.

Table 5.9 Echocardiographic parameters for assessing pulmonary regurgitation

	Mild	Severe
Jet size on colour flow	<10 mm long	Large and wide origin
CW density and shape	Soft and slow	Dense and steep
Pulmonary valve	Normal	Abnormal
Pulmonary artery flow	Increased	Greatly increased

Management

Medical

- Treatment of the underlying cause (e.g. with secondary pulmonary hypertension)
- Treatment of heart failure.

Surgical

- When symptoms continue despite medical therapy then surgical intervention can be considered either by surgical reconstruction or valve replacement.

5.14 Prosthetic valves

Biological prosthesis

- Do not require long-term anticoagulation
- Homograft/autograft

- Xenograft, e.g. porcine valve
- Bioprosthesis: uses biological tissue (usually harvested from the pericardial sac of either horses or cows) that is sewn into an artificial stent.

Mechanical valve

- Require long-term anticoagulation
- Ball and cage (Starr Edwards)
- The cage. consisting of a sewing ring made from three or four struts. contains a silastic ball occluder
- Tilting disc (e.g. Medtronic-Hall): a singular disc suspended within a frame
- Bileaflet (e.g. Carbomedics): two leaflets hinged in the centre of the prosthesis.

Choice of prosthetic valve

- The choice of prosthesis type should be individualized
- Mechanical prosthesis are recommended if
  - It is the desire of an informed patient
  - A mechanical valve is implanted on another valve
  - The patient is already on anticoagulation
  - No contraindications to anticoagulation
  - Age <65–70 and long life expectancy
- Patients for whom future redo valve surgery would be at high risk
- Bioprosthetic valves are recommended:
  - If it is the desire of an informed patient
  - If there are contraindications/high risk/unwillingness to anticoagulation
  - For reoperation for mechanical valve thrombosis in a patient with proven poor anticoagulant control
  - If there is limited life expectancy, severe comorbidity or age >65
  - For young women contemplating pregnancy.

Anticoagulation

- The target INR for mechanical valves depends on a combination of prosthesis thrombogenicity and patient related risk factors (see Table 5.10).

Table 5.10 Anticioagulation for prosthetic valves

Prosthesis thrombogenicity[a]	Patient-related risk factors[b]	
	No risk factor	≥1 risk factor
Low	2.5	3.0
Medium	3.0	3.5
High	3.5	4.0

[a] Prosthesis thrombogenicity: low = Carbomedics (aortic position), Medtronic Hall, St Jude Medical (without Silzone); medium = Bjork-Shiley, other bileaflet valves; high = Lillehei-Kaster, Omniscience, Starr-Edwards.

[b] Patient-related risk factors: mitral, tricuspid, or pulmonary valve replacement; previous thrombo-embolism; atrial fibrillation; left atrial diameter >50 mm; left atrial dense spontaneous contrast; MS of any degree; LVEF <35%; hypercoagulable state. Reproduced from 'Guidelines on the management of valvular heart disease: The Task Force on the Management of Valvular Heart Disease of the European Society of Cardiology', (2012) **33**, 2451–96. Alec Vahanian, Ottavio Alfieri, Felicita Andreotti, copyright 2012 with permission of Oxford University Press.

Complications

Prosthetic valve thrombosis

Obstructive thrombus:

- If haemodynamically unwell and no immediate surgery available, proceed with fibrinolysis (see Figure 5.6)
- If haemodynamically well and recent inadequate anticoagulation, give heparin ± aspirin (regular follow-up if this is successful). If unsuccessful then ideally proceed to surgery; if patient too high risk for surgery then give fibrinolysis
- If haemodynamically well and recent adequate anticoagulation, proceed to surgery or if too high risk for surgery then give fibrinolysis.

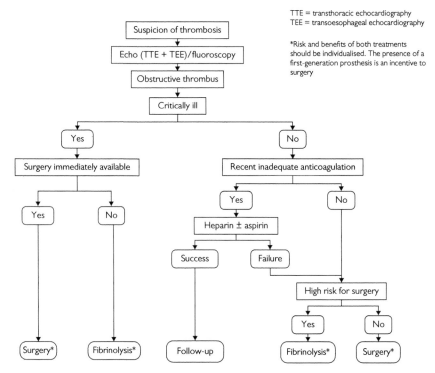

TTE = transthoracic echocardiography
TEE = transoesophageal echocardiography

*Risk and benefits of both treatments should be individualised. The presence of a first-generation prosthesis is an incentive to surgery

Figure 5.6 Flowchart for management of obstructive thrombus.

Reproduced from 'Guidelines on the management of valvular heart disease', *European Heart Journal* (2012) **33**, 2451–96. Alec Vahanian, Ottavio Alfieri, Felicita Andreotti et al., with permission of Oxford University Press.

Non-obstructive thrombus:

- Optimize anticoagulation and follow up for evidence of thromboembolism (either clinically or cerebral imaging) (see Figure 5.7)
- If evidence of thromboembolism and
    - >10 mm thrombus: proceed to surgery
    - <10 mm thrombus: optimize anticoagulation and proceed to surgery (or fibrinolysis if high risk) if thrombus persists and there is evidence of recurrent thromboembolism
- If no evidence of thromboembolism and large thrombus: optimize anticoagulation and proceed to surgery (if not high risk) if thrombus persists or there is evidence of recurrent thromboembolism.

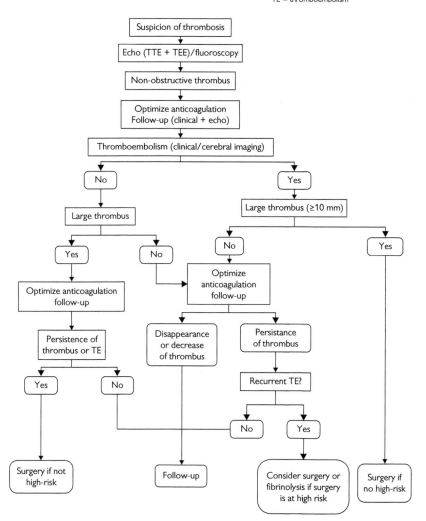

TTE = transthoracic echocarsiography
TEE = transoesophageal echocardiography
TE = thromboembolism

Figure 5.7 Flowchart for management of non-obstructive thrombus.

Reproduced from 'Guidelines on the management of valvular heart disease', *European Heart Journal* (2012) 33, 2451–96. Alec Vahanian, Ottavio Alfieri, Felicita Andreotti *et al.*, with permission of Oxford University Press.

Haemolysis and paravalvular leak

- There is limited data with regards to therapeutic options. Current ESC recommendations are to recommend reoperation if there is haemolysis requiring repeated blood transfusions or if the leak is related to endocarditis.

Follow-up

- Bioprosthesis and homografts should be followed up yearly after having been implanted for 5 years
- Endocarditis: as per guidelines (see Chapter 15).

Further reading

Camm J, Lüscher TF, Serruys PW (eds). *The European Society of Cardiology Textbook of Cardiovascular Medicine*, 2nd edn. Oxford University Press, 2009.

Hayes CJ, Gersony WM, Driscoll DJ, *et al*. Second natural history study of congenital heart defects. Results of treatment of patients with pulmonary valvular stenosis. *Circulation*, 1993; 87: I28.

Lancellotti P, Triboulilloy C, Hagendorff A, *et al*. European Association of Echocardiography recommendations for the assessment of valvular regurgitation. Part 1: aortic and pulmonary regurgitation (native valve disease). *Eur J Echocard*, 2010; 11: 223–44.

Leeson P, Augustine D, Mitchell A, Becher H. *Echocardiography*, 2nd edn. Oxford University Press, 2012.

Libby P, Bonow R, Zipes D, Mann D (eds). *Braunwald's Heart Disease: A Textbook of Cardiovascular Medicine*. Elsevier, 2007

Otto C. *Textbook of Echocardiography*. Elsevier, 2009.

Pellikka PA, Sarano ME, Nishimura RA, *et al*. Outcome of 622 adults with asymptomatic, haemodynamically significant aortic stenosis during prolonged follow up. *Circulation*, 2005; 111(24): 3290–5.

Vahanian A, Alfieri O, Andreotti F, *et al*. ESC guidelines on the management of valvular heart disease. *Eur Heart J*, 2012; 33: 2451–96.

Presyncope and syncope

6.1 Overview

Syncope

A **transient** loss of consciousness (T-LOC) due to **global cerebral hypoperfusion** characterized by **rapid onset, short duration,** and **spontaneous complete recovery**.

Presyncope

A state that resembles the prodrome of syncope but which is not followed by loss of consciousness.

6.2 Glossary of terms

See Box 6.1.

- The terminology in patients with T-LOC and related symptoms is very muddled
- The use of the same terms by different doctors/in different settings can lead to a different diagnosis
- The misdiagnosis of epilepsy affects at least 74,000 patients in England alone, all of whom are taking anticonvulsants inappropriately
- Getting the terminology right is a major part of getting the assessment and the treatment right
- 'Syncope' is often used synonymously with T-LOC in the USA, and this is quite wrong.

6.3 Prevalence

- Frequent: >50% experience one episode per lifetime in general population
- 30% experience at least one episode of T-LOC with a peak between the ages of 10 and 30 years

BOX 6.1 GLOSSARY

T-LOC	A **transient** loss of consciousness
Blackout	A **transient** loss of consciousness, and a term used commonly by patients, relatives and neurologists
Syncope	A **transient** loss of consciousness (T-LOC) due to **global cerebral hypoperfusion** characterized by **rapid onset, short duration,** and **spontaneous complete recovery**.
Presyncope	A state that resembles the prodrome of syncope but which is not followed by loss of consciousness.
Collapse	An abrupt loss of postural control, with or without T-LOC
Fall	An episode of collapse where there is no T-LOC, and contributory factors include musculo-skeletal infirmity, inability to adjust against gravity when over-balancing, failure of postural aids, e.g. a walking stick.
Apparent fall	Up to 30% of falls are actually T-LOC with collapse interpreted by the patient or the doctor as a fall. Patients may forget the blackout or choose to minimize it. Many of these patients need pacing.
Epilepsy attack	This is defined by the International League Against Epilepsy as 'manifestation(s) of epileptic (excessive and/or hypersynchronous), usually self-limited, activity of neurons in the brain'.
Epilepsy	'A chronic neurological condition characterized by recurrent epileptic seizures'.
Seizure	An episode of T-LOC accompanied by convulsive features. In the USA epilepsy is confusingly referred to as a 'seizure disorder'. Syncope may be convulsive, and be accompanied by abrupt collapse, abnormal limb movements, tongue-biting, and incontinence due to cerebral anoxic irritation. Generalized epilepsy may also be accompanied by these features. 'Seizure' should not be used to imply that the mechanism of T-LOC is epilepsy.

- First episode commonly occurs in patients presenting between 10 and 30 years
- Frequency increases with age, rapidly after 70 years
- The 10-year cumulative incidence of syncope is 11% for both men and women at age 70–79, and 17% and 19% respectively for men and women at age ≥80
- Approximately one-third of patients have recurrences of syncope at three years of follow up.

6.4 Classification and pathophysiology

- T-LOC can be classified as traumatic (caused by concussion) and non-traumatic (caused by syncope, epileptic seizures, psychogenic blackouts, and other rare miscellaneous causes, e.g. cataplexy)
- Syncope is the most common subset of T-LOC
- Syncope can be classified broadly according to its underlying cause
- Reflex syncope is by far the most common cause of T-LOC, and easily mimics an epileptic seizure if there are convulsive features
- Nevertheless, arrhythmic and cardiac causes should always be considered.

Reflex syncope (neurally-mediated)

- Vasovagal
  - Mediated by emotional distress, fear, pain
  - Mediated by orthostatic stress

- Situational
  - Cough, sneeze, gastrointestinal stimulation post-prandial, micturition, post micturition, post-exercise, others (e.g. laughter, bass instrument playing, weightlifting)
- Carotid sinus syncope
- Atypical forms (without apparent triggers and/or atypical presentation).

Orthostatic hypotension syncope

- Primary autonomic failure
  - Pure autonomic failure, multiple system atrophy, Parkinson's disease with autonomic failure, Lewy body dementia
- Secondary autonomic failure
  - Diabetes, amyloidosis, uraemia, spinal cord injuries
- Drug induced orthostatic hypotension
  - Alcohol, vasodilators, diuretics, phenothiazine, antidepressants
- Volume depletion
  - Haemorrhage, diarrhoea, vomiting, etc.

Cardiac syncope

- Arrhythmia
  - Bradycardia: sinus node dysfunction, atrioventricular conduction system disease, implanted device malfunction, drug-induced
  - Tachycardia: supraventricular, ventricular
  - Drug-induced bradycardia/tachycardia
- Structural disease
  - Valvular disease, acute myocardial ischaemia, hypertrophic cardiomyopathy, cardiac masses, pericardial disease/tamponade, anomalous coronary arteries
  - Others: pulmonary embolus, acute aortic dissection, pulmonary hypertension
- Syncope is caused by cerebral hypoperfusion; largely results from a fall in systemic blood pressure
- Experience from tilt testing shows that a decrease in systolic blood pressure to 40–60 mmHg is associated with syncope
- When upright, the blood pressure in the cerebral cortex is far lower than this, overcoming autoregulation of cerebral perfusion
- Systemic blood pressure is the product of cardiac output and total peripheral vascular resistance
- A fall in either component can contribute to syncope
- A number of mechanisms are involved in regulating systolic blood pressure and in maintaining cerebral perfusion:
  - Arterial baroreceptor-induced adjustment of heart rate, cardiac contractility, systemic vascular resistance
  - Rennin-angiotensin and vasopression vasoconstriction
  - Renal-body-fluid pressure control system
  - Cerebrovascular autoregulator system.

Reflex syncope

- A heterogeneous group of functional disturbances characterized by episodic vasodilation and/or bradycardia resulting in transient failure of blood pressure control (autonomic 'hypersensitivity')
- Vasodepressor type: vasodilatation predominates

- Cardioinhibitory type: bradycardia or asystole predominates
- Mixed type: both mechanisms are involved
- Often has an identifiable trigger or triggers
- May occur with uncertain or even apparently absent triggers
- Usually proceeded by prodromal symptoms of autonomic activation.

Orthostatic hypotension syncope

- Classical orthostatic hypotension is defined by BP decrease $\geq$20 mmHg and/or 10 mmHg in diastolic pressure within 3 min of standing
- Common in elderly with autonomic dysfunction; more commonly associated with presyncope than syncope.

Sub-types

- Initial orthostatic hypotension
  - BP decrease immediately upon standing up, $\leq$30 s
  - Mismatch between cardiac output and systemic vascular resistance (SVR)
  - Passive tilting has no diagnostic value, as only standing up actively causes the condition
  - Syncope rare
- Delayed (progressive) orthostatic hypotension
  - Common in the elderly
  - BP decrease slowly upon standing, 3–30 min
  - Reflex bradycardia 'vagal' may be present or absent
  - Diagnostic by tilt table test
  - Syncope more common
- Reflex syncope triggered by standing
  - Initial normal adaptation of reflex followed by rapid fall in venous return and vasovagal reaction (reflex bradycardia and vasodilation)
  - Common in the young and healthy, women > men
  - Syncope often preceded by prodromal symptoms
- Postural orthostatic tachycardia syndrome (POTS)
  - Clear mechanisms uncertain
  - Inadequate venous return or excessive blood venous pooling
  - Symptomatic marked heart rate increase (>30 bpm) and instability of blood pressure on postural changes
  - Associated with dizziness, palpitation, and presyncope; not usually accompanied by syncope
  - Common in young females.

6.5 Evaluation of patients

- The EGSYS study (*Evaluation of Guidelines in Syncope Study*) established a definite diagnosis in 98% of patients (2% unexplained):
  - 66% neurally mediated syncope
  - 10% orthostatic hypotension
  - 11% arrhythmia
  - 5% structural cardiac or cardiopulmonary disease
  - 6% non-syncopal attacks
- Initial evaluation (history and examination) can establish a diagnosis in 50% of cases.

Purpose

- Consider all causes of collapse, (abrupt loss of postural control)
- Confirm that T-LOC did occur
- Establish by careful history-taking that syncope/pre-syncope occurred
- Establish aetiology
- Undertake risk stratification.

Diagnose syncope

- History:
  - LOC complete? Transient with rapid onset and short duration? Spontaneous complete recovery? Loss of postural tone? Prodromal symptoms?
  - Convulsive features are quite common in syncope.

Establish aetiology

- History
  - Circumstances: posture position, activity, predisposing factors
  - Symptoms at onset: autonomic symptoms
  - Symptoms at offset
  - History from eyewitness is essential
  - Past history: cardiac disease, neurological disease, medication (including eye drops), family history
  - Facial pallor is a critical clue; loss of facial skin perfusion in the upright person indicates the abrupt vascular changes of syncope (not epilepsy)
- Examination
  - Physical examination
  - Orthostatic blood pressure measurements
- Investigation
  - 12-lead ECG the most important investigation for all T-LOC patients; most are normal because most patients have reflex syncope (ECG establishes a diagnosis in 5% cases. Only about 5% of patients attending neurology clinic with T-LOC have an ECG)
  - Carotid sinus message (patients >40 years old, avoid if bruits present and duplex required to exclude significant stenosis)
  - Echocardiography
  - Tilt table test
  - Ambulatory ECG monitor: in-hospital telemetry, Holter, implantable loop recorders
  - Exercise test
- Further evaluation in cases of doubt about the mechanism of T-LOC
  - Neurological evaluation
  - Psychiatric/psychological evaluation
  - Some tests will only be needed when there is clearly an electrical or structural cardiac abnormality, and it is deemed very likely to be the cause of T-LOC
    - Cardiac catheterization
    - Electrophysiological study.

Risk stratification

High risk of death and life-threatening events.

- Cardiovascular
  - Abnormal 12-lead ECG*
  - History of cardiovascular disease especially structural disease, ventricular arrhythmia, and heart failure
  - Family history of sudden cardiac death under 40 years of age
  - Syncope occurring without prodrome/during effort/supine (predictors of arrhythmia cause)
  - Unexplained new onset of breathlessness
- Neurological
  - Features that strongly suggest epilepsy: tonic-clonic movements at the onset, facial cyanosis, head-turning, lateral tongue-biting, incontinence (faecal)
  - A history of brain injury, (birth/infection/infarction/tumour etc.)
  - New or evolving neurological deficit
- Other
  - Anaemia
  - Electrolyte disturbance
- High risk of syncopal recurrence
  - Number of episodes of syncope and frequency are strongest predictor of recurrence
  - 20% probability of recurrence during next two years in low-risk patient with <3 episodes of syncope with unclear diagnosis
  - 42% probability of recurrence during the next two years in low risk patients with ≥3 episodes of syncope with unclear diagnosis.

* Bifascicular block or other intraventricular conduction abnormalities with QRS ≥120 ms, inappropriate sinus bradycardia or sino-atrial block, pre-excited QRS complex. long or short QT interval, Brugada/ARVC pattern ECG.

6.6 Investigations

See Table 6.1.

Carotid sinus massage (CSM)

- Indicated in patients >40 years with unexplained aetiology after initial evaluation
- Avoid:
  - In patients with previous transient ischaemic attack (TIA) or stroke <3 months
  - In patients with suspected carotid disease
- Diagnostic: if syncope is reproducible in the presence of asystole >3 s and/or a fall in systolic BP >50 mmHg.

Orthostatic challenge: active standing

- Recommended methodology
  - Manual intermittent BP measurement with lying and active standing for 3 min
  - Continuous beat-to-beat non-invasive BP measurement may be helpful if in doubt
- Diagnostic
  - Drop of a systolic BP of ≥20 mmHg or diastolic BP ≥10 mmHg, or:
  - Drop of a systolic BP to <90 mmHg, especially associated symptoms.

Table 6.1 Clinical features suggestive of diagnosis on initial evaluation

Type of syncope	Clinical features
Reflex syncope (neurally mediated)	• Absence of heart disease • Long history of recurrent episodes • Triggers, e.g. stress, sound, smell, or pain • Prolonged standing or crowded, hot places • Nausea and vomiting associated with syncope • During a meal or post-prandial • Head rotation or pressure on carotid sinus • After exertion • Always check that the ECG is normal
Orthostatic hypotension	• Proceeded by standing up • Temporal relation to taking medication • Prolonged standing or crowded, hot places • Presence of autonomic neuropathy or Parkinsonism • Standing after exertion

Cardiovascular syncope	• Structural cardiac disease
	• Family history of unexplained sudden death or channelopathy
	• During exertion or supine
	• Abnormal ECG:
	  ■ conduction defect, bifascicular block, QRS duration ≥120 ms, Mobitz I second degree AV block
	  ■ inappropriate bradycardia or sinus pause ≥3 s
	  ■ non-sustained VT
	  ■ pre-excited QRS complexes
	  ■ long or short QT intervals
	  ■ early repolarization
	  ■ Brugada ECG pattern
	  ■ ARVC ECG pattern
	  ■ ischaemic changes
	• Palpitation precedes syncope

Orthostatic challenge: tilt testing

- It has become recognized that tilt-table testing has less value as a tool in the investigation of syncope than was thought in the past
- Patients likely to have reflex syncope have the highest yield (patients with other causes low yield)
- Using more aggressive provocation in the protocol results in more false positive tests and therefore increases sensitivity at the expense of specificity
- This may add confusion, when a detailed and careful history independently suggests a very confident feel for the diagnosis
- Tilt-table testing should not be used as a first-choice discriminator in patients with T-LOC, as the predictive value for different causes of T-LOC is unknown
- It can be useful where it is thought a patient may gain confidence from having their symptoms reproduced, as long as the doctor and patient are prepared for a false-negative test
- It is useful in suspected psychogenic blackouts when suggestibility to a psychogenic blackout can be used to reproduce symptoms during tilt (while monitoring ECG, BP, and EEG).

Recommended methodology

- Patient usually fasted
- Supine pre-tilt phase of >5 min when no venous cannulation, and >20 min when cannulation is undertaken
- Measure supine HR and BP (at least every minute during test with continuous ECG monitor)
- CSM can be performed in the supine and head-up position
- Tilt angle between 60° and 80°
- Passive phase of ≥20 min and ≤40 min
- For nitroglycerine challenge, a fixed dose of 300–400 µg sublingually administered in the upright position
- For isopreterenol challenge, an incremental infusion rate from 1 up to 3 µg/min in order to increase average heart rate by approx. 20–25% over baseline (avoid in patients with ischaemic heart disease).

Traditional indications

- Unexplained single syncopal episode in high-risk settings after cardiac syncope has been excluded
- When it is of clinical value to demonstrate susceptibility to reflex syncope to patient
- To discriminate between reflex and orthostatic hypotension syncope
- To differentiate syncope with jerking movements from epilepsy
- To evaluate patients with recurrent unexplained falls
- To evaluate patients with frequent syncope and psychiatric disease.

Diagnostic criteria

- Induction of reflex hypotension/bradycardia with reproduction of symptom is diagnostic
- Induction of reflex hypotension/bradycardia without reproduction of symptom may be diagnostic.

Added value of tilt testing

- The subject of much debate
- Many centres have stopped using routine tilt testing because the sensitivity and specificity are probably quite poor
- Positive tilt tests are usually obtained in patients with a typical clinical profile for reflex syncope, so a careful and detailed history is better than a tilt test, which may introduce doubt about the diagnosis
- It is of value in suspected psychogenic blackouts.

Electrocardiographic monitoring

- **In-patient telemetry** for high-risk patients where cardiovascular syncope and arrhythmia are suspected
- **Holter monitor** for patients with frequent symptoms, continued for 1 week as appropriate
- Longer periods of monitoring are associated with poor compliance and technical problems
- On average syncope occurs about three times per year, so that long-term implantable monitoring should be considered when:
  - Diagnosis is reflex syncope with frequent and disabling symptoms that cannot be controlled
  - Pacemaker is being considered and asystole is being sought or contribution of bradycardia to symptoms

- Unexplained and recurrent symptoms/infrequent symptoms (particularly occurring ≥4-week intervals)
- Structural heart disease but the clinical history is not diagnostic; implantable loop recorder (ILR) may be used to guide therapy.

Exercise stress test

- Indicated in patients who have experienced episodes of syncope during and shortly after exertion
- If Mobitz type II second degree or third degree AV block develops during exercise the test is diagnostic even without syncope.

Electrophysiology study

- Indicated in patients with high index of suspicion of arrhythmogenic syncope
- Sensitivity and specificity of the electrophysiology study is not very good
- Questionable use for diagnosis of sinus node disease
- Very occasional use for assessment of HV-interval where paroxysmal atrioventricular block is suspected as the cause of T-LOC
- May be useful in suspected tachycardia, although an ECG recording during symptoms is far more useful.

6.7 Treatment of reflex syncope and orthostatic hypotension

Lifestyle measures
- Education and reassurance
- Trigger avoidance
- Avoidance of volume depletion
- Sufficient salt and water intake, 2–3 l of fluids per day and 6 g of NaCl, useful in orthostatic hypotension.

Physical counterpressure manoeuvres
- Useful in reflex syncope/vasovagal syncope
- Leg crossing, hand grip, arm tensing
- Tilt training, i.e. progressively prolonged periods of enforced upright posture
- Compression stocking.

Pharmacological therapy
- This is adjunctive therapy to salt and water intake
- Midodrine (alpha agonist): this drug is by far the most useful in reflex syncope. The reasons are unclear, since even low doses (2.5 mg tds) are often very effective but without any affect on blood pressure
- Doses of up to 15 mg tds may be needed
- The drug is not licensed in the UK (causes patients problems with repeat prescriptions)
- Midodrine may also be effective in conditions with autonomic failure
- Fludrocortisone sometimes used in orthostatic hypotension (recent evidence suggests ineffective)
- Evidence also suggests beta blockers ineffective in reflex syncope (ivabradine has also been used for patients with pronounced tachycardia).

Cardiac pacing

Only recommended where brady-arrhythmia is the predominant cause of syncope.

- Recurrent syncope reproducible by carotid sinus massage, associated with ventricular asystole of >3 s
- Patients with current severe vasovagal syncope who show prolonged asystole during ECG recording and/or tilt testing *and* after failure of other therapeutic options (patient need to be informed of the current conflicting evidence)
- This may include young patients whose symptoms cannot be controlled any other way.

Implantable cardioverter defibrillator

- As per guidelines for ICD implant (see Chapter 8)
- Patients with previous myocardial infarction, poor LVEF, and syncope may have syncopal VT. These patients have a 1-year mortality of 44%.

Driving and syncope

- The doctor's duty is to advise his/her patient when they should cease to drive and notify the DVLA
- Where the doctor is uncertain he/she should consult 'At a Glance Guide to the Current Medical Standards of Fitness to Drive', DVLA
- The DVLA classifies neurocardiogenic syncope into
    - Simple faints
    - 'Loss of consciousness, likely to be *unexplained* syncope'
- 'Unexplained' means that no relevant cardiac or neurological abnormality has been found during examination
- 'Unexplained syncope' is sub classified into low and high-risk groups (see Table 6.2)
- A special distinction is made about 'cough syncope'.

6.8 Bradyarrhythmia: anatomy and electrophysiology of the heart rhythm

Sinus node

- A collection of specialized cells located in the right atrial sulcus terminalis, between superior vena cava and right atrium (RA)
- P (pacemaker) cells have regular spontaneous depolarization (autonomicity) to initiate the depolarization, activation, and subsequent contraction of the surrounding atrial myocardial cells
- They are the only cells in the heart where cell membranes exhibit the I_f current, which causes fast spontaneous depolarization
- Blood supply usually from a branch that arises from proximal right coronary artery.

Atrium conduction

- Electrical impulses propagate through the atrial tissue and pathways of preferential conduction from the right atrium to the atrioventricular node as well as to the left atrium

Table 6.2 Driving restrictions associated with syncope

	Group 1 Entitlement ODL—Car, M/Cycle	Group 2 Entitlement VOC—LGV/PCV
1. Simple faint—definite provocation factors with associated prodromal symptoms and unlikely to occur whilst sitting or lying. '3 Ps' (provocation/ prodrome/postural).	No driving restrictions. DVLA need not be notified.	No driving restrictions. DVLA need not be notified.
2. Unexplained syncope and *low risk* of recurrence. No clinical evidence of structural heart disease and a normal ECG.	Can drive four weeks after the event.	Can drive three months after the event.
3. Unexplained syncope and *high risk* of recurrence. Factors indicating high risk: (a) abnormal ECG (b) structural heart disease (c) syncope causing injury, occurring at the wheel or whilst sitting or lying (d) >1 episode in previous six months.	Can drive four weeks after the event if the cause has been identified and treated. If no cause identified, licence refused/revoked for six months.	Can drive three months after the event if the cause has been identified and treated. If no cause identified, then licence refused/revoked for one year.
Cough syncope	Driving must cease until liability to attacks has been successfully controlled, confirmed by medical opinion.	Driving must cease. If there is any chronic respiratory condition, including smoking will need to be free of syncope/pre-syncope for five years. Individuals identified as having asystole in response to coughing can be considered once a pacemaker has been implanted.

- Normal atrial conduction occurs in the sequence of high right atrium, mid right atrium, low right atrium, atrioventricular junction, and coronary sinus
- Intra-atrial conduction delay leads to broad P wave
- This may be largely due to enlarged atrial size and is often associated with congenital heart disease, such as endocardial cushion defects and Ebstein's anomaly.

Atrioventricular node

- Located in the low atrial septum, anterior to the ostium of coronary sinus and above the insertion of the septal leaflet of the tricuspid valve, in the anatomically defined Triangle of Koch (see Section 7.5)
- It accounts for the major component of time in normal AV conduction
- Delays in the AV node account for the major source of prolonged AV conduction
- AV conduction varies greatly with autonomic influence
- Blood supply from atrioventricular nodal artery, a branch of the posterior descending artery, which arises from right coronary artery (80%) and from the circumflex artery (20%).

Bundle of His

- Passes through the annulus fibrosus and penetrates the membranous interventricular septum before division of the left and right bundle branches
- Blood supply predominantly from the AV nodal artery, and sometimes from the septal peforators from the left anterior descending coronary artery.

Infra-His conduction

- Right bundle branch crosses the anterior part of the interventricular septum and reaches the apex of the right ventricle and the base of the anterior papillary muscle
- Left bundle branch is less anatomically discrete and 'fans' into an anterior (superior) and a posterior (inferior) fascicle
- The bundle branches ramify and give rise to the endocardially located terminal Purkinje fibres, ensuring the activation of the both ventricles.

6.9 Bradycardia

Defined as inappropriately low heart rate in relation to age, gender, activity level, and physical training status.

Causes of bradycardia

Intra-cardiac

- Degeneration
- Ischaemic heart disease
- Infiltrative disease: sarcoidosis, amyloidosis, haemochromatosis
- Collagen vascular disease: systemic lupus erythematosus, rheumatoid arthritis
- Myotonic muscular dystrophy
- Surgical trauma: valve replacement, heart transplant
- Ablation therapy
- Congenital disease
- Infectious disease: endocarditis, Gram-negative sepsis, typhoid, dipheria, Chagas disease.

Extra-cardiac

- Physical training
- Vagal hypertonicity: vasovagal syncope, carotid-sinus hypersensitivity
- Vagal hyper-reactivity: reflex syncope
- Electrolyte imbalance: hypokalaemia or hyperkalaemia
- Metabolic disturbances: hypothermia, hypothyroidsm, anorexia nervosa
- Neurological disorders: raised intracranial pressure
- Drugs
- Obstructive sleep apnoea.

6.10 Conduction system defects

Sinus node dysfunction—'sick sinus syndrome'
Sinus bradycardia

- Classically defined sinus node rate <60 bpm with normal P waves before each QRS complex
- Usually benign finding.

Sinoatrial block and sinus arrest
- Sinus pause of >150% of cardiac cycle length
- May be due to failure sinus node impulse or failure of the impulse to exit the sinus node and reach the atrium (SA exit block), (on ECG the P–P interval maybe be multiples of baseline P–P interval).

Tachy-brady syndrome
- Sinus pause following the cessation of paroxysmal supraventricular tachyarrhythmias (often atrial fibrillation) that occur in the setting of sinus bradycardia (see Figure 6.1)
- This is due to overdrive suppression of the sinus automaticity during the tachycardic phase
- Commonly associated with syncope with prolonged pause.

Atrioventricular conduction disturbances
- Atrioventricular (AV) conduction disturbances can be classified by criteria combining implications about anatomic site, mechanism and prognosis
- Traditionally they are classified as first-, second-, or third-degree
- Depending on the anatomical point of the conduction defect can be described as supra-Hisian, intra-Hisian, or infra-Hisian.

First-degree AV block (prolonged conduction)
- Every atrial stimulus is conducted to the ventricles, but the PR interval is prolonged (traditionally classified as to be >200 ms)
- Does not lead to bradycardia unless progress to second or third degree AV block or association with SA node disease.

Second degree AV block (intermittent conduction)
- Failure to conduct one or more atrial stimuli to the ventricles
  - Mobitz type I (Wenckebach block): PR intervals increases progressively until a P wave is not conducted. The PR interval then resumes its original value after the failed conduction
  - Mobitz type II: PR interval is constant before and after the abrupt blocked P wave.

Third degree AV block (no conduction)
- Complete dissociation of the atrial and ventricular activity: there is no conduction of the atrial activity to the ventricle.

Likely sites of AV conduction disturbances
- There is considerable overlap in the location of the disturbances and pattern of block
- Surface ECG also may not be able to identify the site of block
  - First degree heart block: commonly occurs at the level of the atrium, AV node, intra-His or infra-His regions

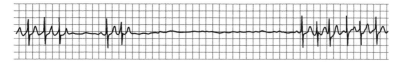

Figure 6.1 Rapidly conducted atrial fibrillation with pause.

- Second degree heart block: virtually never occurs in the atrium
- Type 1 second degree commonly occurs at the level of the AVN and uncommonly at the intra- or infra-His levels
- Type 2 second degree commonly occurs below the level of AVN, in the intra-His or infra-His levels
- Third degree heart block: commonly occurs at the levels of AVN, intra-His or infra-His.

Intraventricular block

- Conduction delays can occur at any level between the His and Purkinje system
- Bifascicular block refers to the ECG appearance of complete right bundle branch block with left anterior (more common) or left posterior fascicular block (see Figure 6.2). (Complete left bundle branch block is regarded technically bifascicular block by some)
- Trifascicular block refers to bifascicular block + first-degree AV block (see Figure 6.3)
- Alternating bundle branch block refers to ECG demonstration of conduction disturbances in either left or right bundle branches on the same or successive ECG recording.

6.11 Evaluation of bradycardia patients

Aims

- Identify inappropriate bradycardia
- Assess impact of bradycardia upon quality of life
- Assess risk of series complication such as syncope, heart failure, arrhythmia with embolic risk, or sudden death.

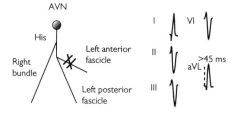

Left anterior fascicular block

- Left axis deviation –30 to –90 degrees
- qR in lateral limb leads (I and aVL)
- rS in the inferior leads (II, III and aVF)
- Prolonged R wave peak time in aVL >45 ms
- QRS mildly prolonged, but less than 120 ms

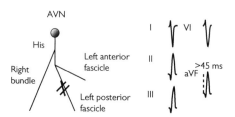

Left posterior fascicular block

- Right axis deviation +90 to +180 degrees
- rS in lateral leads (I and aVL)
- qR in leads inferior leads (II, III and aVF)
- Prolonged R wave peak time in aVF >45 ms
- QRS mildly prolonged, but less than 120 ms

Figure 6.2 Left anterior and left posterior fascicular blocks.

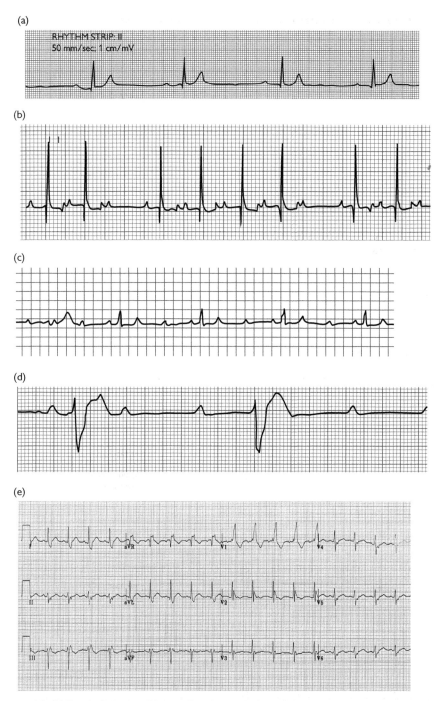

Figure 6.3 ECGs of conduction delays. a, first degree; b, second degree Mobitz type I; c, second degree Mobitz type II; d, third degree heart block; e, bifascicular block, RBBB with left axis deviation (left anterior fascicular block).

History and examination

- Identify symptoms of inappropriate bradycardia, i.e. failure to respond to physiological demand = chronotropic incompetence, e.g. breathlessness, fatigue, syncope
- Identify potentially reversible causes of bradycardia.

Investigation

- 12-lead ECG, bloods, carotid sinus message
- Ambulatory ECG (Holter, event recorder, implantable loop recorder)
- Electrophysiological testing is useful in:
  - Assessing sinus node function
  - Assessing the level of the block along the conduction system
  - Risk stratification in those asymptomatic patients with bifascicular block or trifascicular block.

6.12 Clinical implication of electrophysiology study in patients with suspected conduction disturbances

Sinus node dysfunction

- Normal corrected sinus node recovery time (cSNRT) <550 ms
- Marked prolongation of cSNRT and an absence or blunted response to atropine and exercise suggest impaired sinus node function.

Atrioventricular conduction

- Identification of concealed His extrasystoles, which may render part of the conduction system refractory resulting in first or second degree AV block
- More accurate determination of the site or sites of conduction block, AV node, intra-His and infra-His, especially in the presence of co-existent bundle branch block
- Atrial pacing or introduction of premature stimuli may reveal latent prolongation or failure of conduction (it maybe physiological or pathological).

Intraventricular conduction

- In patients with bi- or trifascicular block, His-ventricular (H–V) conduction time >100 ms (normal H–V is 35–55 ms), or the demonstration of intra- or infra-His block during incremental atrial pacing at a rate of <150 bpm, is predictive for the development of high-grade AV block
- Electrophysiology study allows the determination of VA conduction, accessory pathway, and risk of ventricular arrhythmia, which may account for the symptoms other than bradyarrhythmia.

6.13 Treatment of bradyarrhythmia

- Permanent cardiac pacing implant rates are comparatively low in the UK
- Western European nations implant approximately 1000 new pacing systems per million population per annum, whilst the UK implants about 500 new pacing systems per million population per annum

- It has been unclear why this difference exists, but recently more evidence has been provided
- Major factors include: a generally high threshold for pacing (which may be due to a misunderstanding of the complexity of the procedure), acute medical services not identifying indications for pacing, money, and targets being directed to other areas of cardiology
- 52% of UK pacing cases present to acute medical services, and CCAD records 'syncope' or 'pre-syncope' as the indication for pacing in 70% of cases
- Temporary pacing is generally performed badly and should be avoided unless absolutely necessary
- Patients should receive a permanent pacemaker as soon as possible after presentation (ideally without temporary pacing).

Evaluation

- Identify and correct reversible causes such as drugs, ischaemia, metabolic or electrolyte disturbances
- In the absence of reversible causes, drug therapy or cardiac pacing may be required.

Drug treatment

- For symptomatic significant bradycardia, intravenous atropine or isoprenaline may be used in acute setting (paradoxical effect may sometimes occur, e.g. in intra-His or infra-His conduction disturbances).

Pacing

- Route: transoesophagus (atrium only), transcutaneous, and transvenous
- Temporary or permanent implantable pacemakers.

Pacing indications in sinus node disease

- Class I ESC recommendations:
    - Where there is documented correlation between symptoms and rhythm
    - Symptomatic bradycardia/chronotropic incompetence
    - Syncope with sinus node disease
- Class II ESC recommendations:
    - Where there is no documented correlation between symptoms and rhythm (Class IIa)
    - Symptomatic bradycardia/chronotropic incompetence
    - Resting heart rate <40 bpm
    - Unexplained syncope with abnormal EP findings
    - cSNRT >800 ms
    - Minimal symptoms with sinus node disease (Class IIb)
    - Resting heart rate <40 bpm when awake
    - No evidence of chronotropic incompetence.

Pacing indications in atrioventricular conduction block

- Class I ESC recommendations:
    - Chronic symptomatic third or second degree AV block
    - Neuromuscular diseases (e.g. myotonic muscular dystrophy, Kearns-Syre syndrome, etc.)
        - With third or second degree AV block

- Third or second degree AV block
  - Post catheter ablation of the AV junction
  - Post valvular surgery when the block is not expected to resolve
- Syncopal patients with bundle branch block with His-Purkinje conduction defect on EP study
- Class II ESC recommendations:
  - Asymptomatic third or second degree AV block
  - Symptomatic prolonged first degree AV block
  - Syncopal patients with bundle branch block
  - Neuromuscular diseases (e.g. myotonic muscular dystrophy, Kearns-Syre syndrome, etc) with first degree AV block.

Others

Pacing recommended in:

- Symptomatic patients with bifascicular or trifascicular block
- Asymptomatic patients with bifascicular or trifascicular block with:
  - Intermittent second or third degree AV block, or
  - Signs of severe conduction disturbances below the level of the AV node (HV >100 ms, (or >75 ms in some expert opinions), or intra or infra-His block during rapid atrial pacing) during EP study
- Patients with neuromuscular disease and any degree of fascicular block, with or without symptoms
- Congenital third degree AV block with:
  - Symptoms
  - Ventricular rate <50–55 bpm in infants
  - Ventricular rate <70 bpm in congenital heart disease
  - Ventricular dysfunction
  - Wide QRS escape rhythm
  - Complex ventricular ectopy
  - Abrupt ventricular pauses >2–3 times of the basic cycle length
  - Prolonged QTc
  - Presence of maternal antibodies-mediated block.

Pacing modes

- Current evidence support the trend towards dual-chamber pacing with minimization of right ventricular pacing
- Incidence of AF was generally found to be greater in VVI(R) paced patients than in patients with atrial-based pacing (AAIR or DDDR)
- In isolated sinus node dysfunction AAIR may be considered, as the annual incidence of second and third degree atrioventricular block is <1% (although this maybe higher in older population)
- In sinus node dysfunction and concomitant conduction disturbance:
  - A dual-chamber is more appropriate
  - DDD if chronotropic competence of the sinus node is preserved
  - DDD(R) if chronotropic competence of the sinus node is not preserved
  - DDI(R) or a device with mode-switching function is preferred in bradycardia –tachycardia syndrome
- In AV or multi-fascicular block:

- DDD or DDD(R) is appropriate
- VVI(R) may be considered in the elderly
- VVI or VVI(R) should be used in AF
- In heart failure patients with significant impairment of LV function, cardiac resynchronization therapy should be considered.

Clinical trials

- DANPACE (2010)
  - DDDR vs AAIR in sick sinus syndrome
  - No difference in all cause mortality between the pacing modes detected
  - AAIR pacing is associated with higher incidence of atrial fibrillation and risk of reoperation
- UKPACE (2005)
  - DDD(R) versus VVI(R) in AV block
  - In elderly patients with high-grade atrioventricular block, the pacing mode does not influence the mortality from all causes during the first five years or the incidence of cardiovascular events during the first three years after pacemaker
- DAVID (2005)
  - DDDR (pacing at 70 ppm) versus VVI (pacing at 40 ppm) in patients with LV dysfunction
  - More frequent RV pacing was associated with worsened outcomes in patients with LV ejection fraction ≤40%
- Andersen et al. (1997)
  - AAI versus VVI in sinus node disease and normal AV conduction
  - Atrial pacing is associated with higher survival, lower incidence of atrial fibrillation, fewer thromboembolic complications, and less heart failure in sinus node disease.

Further reading

Brignole M, Blanc J-J, Sutton R, Moya A. Syncope. In: J Camm, TF Lüscher, PW Serruys (eds) *The European Society of Cardiology Textbook of Cardiovascular Medicine*. Oxford University Press, 2009.

DVLA. DVLA at a glance guide to the current medical guidelines. Available at: http://www.dft.gov.uk/dvla/medical/ataglance.aspx

ESC guidelines for the diagnosis and management of syncope. *Eur Heart J*, 2009; 30: 2631–71.

Josephson ME. *Clinical Cardiac Electrophysiology: Techniques and Interpretation*, 3rd edn. Lippincott Williams & Wilkins, 2001.

Vardas PE, Mavrakis HE, Toff WD. Bradycardia. In: J Camm, TF Lüscher, PW Serruys (eds) *The European Society of Cardiology Textbook of Cardiovascular Medicine*. Oxford University Press, 2009.

Vardas PE, Auricchio A, Blanc JJ, et al. ESC guidelines for cardiac pacing and cardiac resynchronization therapy. *Europace*, 2007; 9: 959–98.

Supraventricular tachycardia

7.1 Overview

- Supraventricular tachycardia (SVT) requires the structures prior to the division of the His bundle either for their origin or transmission (propagation) of the tachycardia
- From north to south these include:
  - Inappropriate sinus tachycardia (IST)
  - Atrial tachycardia (AT)
  - Atrial flutter
  - AF (see relevant chapter)
  - AV junctional tachycardia:
    - Atrioventricular nodal re-entrant tachycardia (AVNRT)
    - Atrioventricular re-entrant tachycardia (AVRT)
    - Junctional tachycardia (JT)
    - Persistent junctional reciprocating tachycardia (PJRT).

7.2 Classification

ECG features can be useful for classification and to aid differential diagnosis (see Figure 7.1).

Long RP tachycardia

- Sinus tachycardia/IST
- AT
- Atypical AVNRT
- PJRT.

Short RP tachycardia

- Typical AVNRT
- AV re-entry.

Before proceeding to describe key features of the more common SVTs, it is necessary to outline some EP basics.

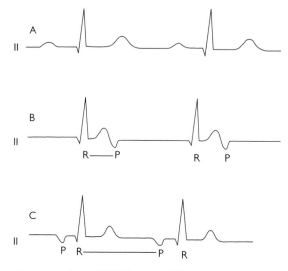

Figure 7.1 Descriptive terminology of SVT. A, normal SR; B, short RP tachycardia with RP < PR interval; C, long RP tachycardia with RP >= PR.

Reproduced from *Current Problems in Cardiology*, (9), Lee, K.W., N. Badhwar, and M.M. Scheinman, Supraventricular tachycardia—Part I, 467–546, Copyright 2008 with permission from Elsevier.

7.3 EP study (EPS) basics

- The typical EP study consists of insertion of four electrodes, usually via the femoral veins
- Standard positions are the high right atrium, coronary sinus, His bundle, and the right ventricle, providing electrical insight into the:
    1. Right atrium
    2. Left atrium (and ventricle)
    3. AV junction
    4. The ventricles (see Figure 7.2)
- Timing intervals between these sites are measured, e.g. the AH interval, which gives a measure of conduction to and through the AV node
- Typically, cycle lengths are expressed in milliseconds rather than beats per minute (600 ms is 100 bpm, 300 ms is 200 bpm and so on)
- After measuring the basic intervals, depending on the indication, different protocols are employed
- Common protocols involve either programmed stimulation with burst pacing; a drive train of 8–10 beats at a fixed cycle length ~<100 ms of the intrinsic cycle length, or an extra-stimulus technique; a drive train of 6–10 fixed cycle length stimuli with an added on extra-stimulus at the end (S1–S2 protocol)
- The extra-stimulus at the end (the S2) can be brought forward by 10–20 ms until the refractory period (RP) is reached (decremental coupling intervals); additional extra-stimuli (S3 or S4) can also be added, for example in VT stimulation studies.

7.4 Basics of a re-entrant tachycardia

- To favour re-entry:
    - Two pathways must be linked (e.g the AV node and an accessory AV pathway)

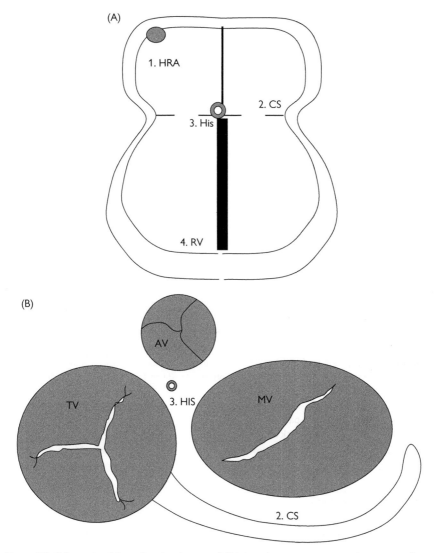

Figure 7.2 Schematic of four-chamber heart and AV ring, demonstrating typical positions of diagnostic EP catheters.

- These two pathways must have different conduction velocities and different refractory characteristics
- 'Timing' is critical (excitable gap).

See Figure 7.3.

- Slower pathways have shorter RPs and fast pathways have longer RPs. (Useful analogy; a fast sprint requires greater recovery time than a gentle stroll)
- A premature complex that finds the faster pathway refractory will instead travel via the slower pathway

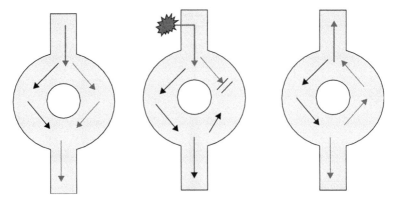

Figure 7.3 Schematic demonstrating re-entry. The faster conduction pathway (grey) has a longer refractory period, and following a critically timed premature electrical impulse, (middle) is found to be refractory. The slower path (black) is able to conduct and, by the time the impulse has travelled around to the fast pathway, it has recovered and is able to conduct retrogradely, thus instigating re-entry.

TIP

The patho-physiological nature of AV re-entry gives rise to the characteristic description in the history of 'sudden onset and sudden offset' palpitations, reflecting the critically timed beats of initiation and termination, often from atrial or ventricular extras. This history is often distinct from the more gradually onset and offset of non- re-entrant or focal tachycardia, as described.

- If it then reaches the faster pathway during the 'critical time' when it has recovered from refractoriness, it can travel back retrogradely
- By the time it comes round to the slower pathway, which has now recovered from refractoriness, re-entry will continue.

7.5 Common SVTs

- AVNRT
- AVRT: accessory pathways, ventricular pre-excitation, and pathway mediated tachycardia
- Atrial flutter
- Atrial tachycardia (AT).

AVNRT

- Up to 20% of the general population have dual AV nodal physiology
- Most common SVT; about two thirds of all SVTs
- Onset relatively late in life, c.f. most pathway-mediated AVRTs
- Twice as common in females
- Understanding AVNRT requires some insight into the function of the AV node (AVN) (see Figure 7.4)
- The AVN (usually a right atrial structure) receives input from the right atrium, and in a certain proportion of individuals this seemingly consists of two distinct pathways, one slow and one fast, thus providing the ingredients for potential re-entry

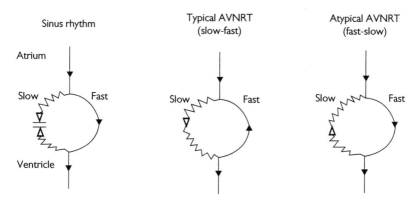

Figure 7.4 Cartoon illustrating AV nodal re-entry.

Reproduced from *Current Problems in Cardiology*, **33** (9), Lee, K.W., N. Badhwar, and M.M. Scheinman, Supraventricular tachycardia—Part I, 467–546, Copyright 2008 with permission from Elsevier.

- In SR (left panel of Figure 7.4), impulses will travel down both the slow and fast AVN pathways
- In typical AVNRT (middle panel of Figure 7.4) the premature impulse will propagate via the slow pathway as the faster pathway is initially refractory
- By the time the impulse comes around, *if* the faster pathway recovers from its RP it can allow conduction retrogradely and initiate re-entry
- As the retrograde limb back to the atrium is fast, the tachycardia is short RP
- In atypical AVNRT the anterograde limb of conduction for the impulse is the fast pathway (right panel of Figure 7.4, in fast-slow AVNRT) or two slow pathways in both the anterograde and retrograde limbs (not shown; slow–slow AVNRT)
- As the retrograde limb back to the atrium is slow, the tachycardia is usually long RP.

Types of AVNRT
- Typical AVNRT (~90%): also termed 'slow–fast', as the anterograde limb of conduction is via the slow pathway and the retrograde limb via the fast pathway. See Figure 7.5
- Atypical AVNRT constitutes the rest; could be either 'fast-slow' or 'slow-slow'
- The slow–slow AVNRT would require two slow pathways of different conduction and refractory properties.

Different types may coexist but this is less common.

ECG features
- Narrow complex
- Rates may vary between 120 and 250 bpm
- P wave is often buried within the QRS complex or early after the QRS (one of the 'short RP' tachycardias) as retrograde conduction is via the fast pathway; VA interval is short
- This is often seen as pseudo r' in V1 or pseudo s wave in the inferior leads; both these features are highly suggestive of AVNRT
- P waves if seen are almost always negative in the inferior leads (atrial depolarization is from bottom to top, i.e. away from the inferior leads)
- Atypical AVNRT may manifest as long RP tachycardia
- Other features such as ST segment depression or T wave changes can be seen and do not necessarily predict ischaemia 'rate-related changes'.

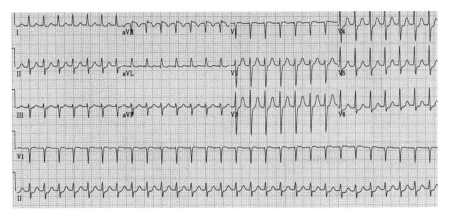

Figure 7.5 Usual ECG pattern of typical AVNRT. 12-lead ECG shows a regular narrow complex tachycardia (sweep speed 25 mm/sec). Note the pseudo r' in V1 (arrow) and accentuated S waves in II, III, aVF (arrow) suggestive of AVNRT.

TIP

Symptomatic neck pulsation in tachycardia is highly suggestive of typical AVNRT (simultaneous activation of atria and ventricles).

EP features

- 'AH jump': sudden increase in the AH interval (>50 ms) during atrial pacing with 10 ms decremental coupling intervals of the extrastimulus
- This is due to critical premature atrial stimulus (extrastimulus, or S2) which then finds the fast pathway to be refractory. The impulse will thus travel only down the slow pathway
- This finding means dual AVN physiology is present but does not necessarily mean the clinical tachycardia is AVNRT (the AH interval is the time it takes the atrial impulse to travel to and through the AVN)
- Typical AVNRT is more likely to be initiated from the atrium rather than the ventricle
- A diagnostic feature of AVNRT is initiation of tachycardia following a critical interval with an 'AH jump'
- VA conduction is very short in typical AVNRT (retrograde conduction via the fast pathway); a VA interval<70 ms is highly suggestive of typical AVNRT.

Management

- Acute management is AV node blockade: if physical vagal manoeuvres fail, adenosine is first choice; may need higher doses with patients taking theophyllines and careful with patients taking dypiridamole (reduces adenosine elimination)
- Transplant recipients and pregnant women can be very sensitive to adenosine, so use a smaller dose
- Alternative AVN blockade can be achieved with CCBs or BBs
- If need for long-term anti-arrhythmic drugs (AADs), use with the usual cautions in patients with hypotension and severe left ventricular dysfunction
- Long-term management often rests with the patient; choice between AADs and catheter ablation
- Catheter ablation (Figure 7.6) is often curative with high success rate (~95–99%)

- Risks of inadvertent AV block necessitating PPM are small (<1%), even less with use of cryo-energy instead of radio-frequency (if risks of AV block is deemed high), although success rates with cryotherapy are considered lower and recurrences more common
- Oral BBs and CCBs are commonly used
- Class 1 drugs such as flecainide and propafenone can be effective
- More toxic pharmacological agents (e.g. amiodarone) are not warranted
- Intervention with catheter ablation should be considered before subjecting an individual to long-term drug therapy.

AVRT: accessory pathways, ventricular pre-excitation and pathway mediated tachycardia

- 'Manifest' accessory pathway: the resting ECG demonstrates ventricular pre-excitation and represents the ventricle being depolarized earlier than it would be by AVN conduction (short PR and delta wave), as anterograde conduction via an accessory pathway (AP) is faster than the AVN
- The AP can provide the substrate for re-entrant tachycardia (see Section 7.4)
- AVRTs can thus be orthodromic (antegrade limb is via normal, or *orthodox*, AV nodal conduction axis) or antidromic (5–10%). See Figure 7.7
- These are also known as orthodromic or antidromic reciprocating tachycardia, respectively.

'Concealed' accessory pathways

- These are able to conduct only retrogradely; therefore the ECG in SR is normal with no delta waves (the ventricle is not pre-excited)
- These represent around 25% of SVTs.

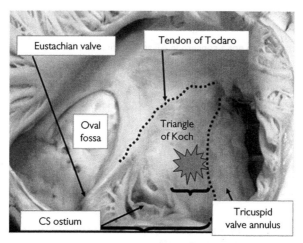

Figure 7.6 The triangle of Koch (looking in from the lateral RA). The compact AVN sits at the upper apex. The triangle of Koch is bordered on three sides by the TV annulus, the CS os and the tendon of Todaro. The slow input to the compact AVN usually runs just anterior to the CS os and cautious mapping and ablation (shaded shape) of this area can result in termination of slow pathway conduction in the AVN, with modification or elimination of dual AVN physiology and thus AVNRT. Care has to be taken not to damage the fast input or the compact AVN thus risking heart block. (The brackets represent potential routes of ablation for typical right atrial flutter; see subsection on 'Atrial flutter').

Adapted from 'The structure and components of the atrial chambers', Anderson R and Cook A, *Europace* 9 (S6), vi3–vi9, 2007, with permission of Oxford University Press.

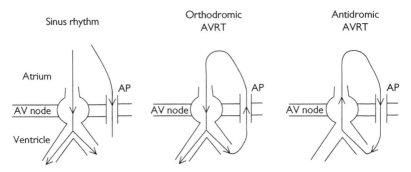

Figure 7.7 Orthodromic or antidromic tachycardia.

Reproduced from *Current Problems in Cardiology*, **33** (9), Lee, K.W., N. Badhwar, and M.M. Scheinman, Supraventricular tachycardia—Part I, 467–546, Copyright 2008 with permission from Elsevier.

Other points on accessory pathways

- Left-sided APs are most common (Figure 7.7)
- In descending order of frequency:
  - i. Left free wall
  - ii. Left posterior wall
  - iii. Left or right postero-septal wall
  - iv. Right free wall
  - v. Antero-septal region
- The anatomical position influences the likelihood of successfully ablating the pathway (Figure 7.8)
- Concealed pathways are not a concern in AF as by definition the AP only conducts only retrogradely
- Wolf Parkinson White (WPW) syndrome: requires a manifest AP that has anterograde conduction reflected in ventricular pre-excitation on the ECG
- The WPW 'syndrome' only exists if there is re-entrant tachycardia; otherwise it is simply a manifest (i.e. visible) AP
- 20% patients with Ebstein's anomaly; often multiple APs
- Reported familial incidence of 3%.

ECG features of manifest accessory pathways

- Short PR interval
- Broad QRS and delta waves
- Often more obvious with right-sided pathways (AP closer to the SAN so the ventricle pre-excites earlier relative to a left sided AP)
- Localization of AP can be estimated from the surface ECG, e.g. positive delta and R wave in V1 likely left sided as the ventricular depolarization wavefront moves from left to right across the chest leads (Figure 7.9)
- Relative conduction velocity of the AV node can influence degree of pre-excitation, which can thus be intermittent (slicker AVN, less pre-excitation).

Risk stratification (difficult)

- As well as symptomatic AV re-entrant tachycardia, there is a risk of sudden death due to AF (which occurs in a third of WPW patients) being rapidly conducted via the AP (APs typically do not decrement like the AVN, and conduct 'all or nothing') thus degenerating into VF

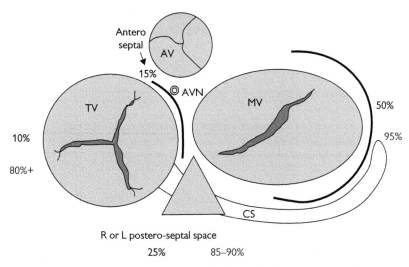

Figure 7.8 Schematic demonstrating the relative frequency of AP on the AV ring (black) along with the likelihood of successful ablation (dark grey). Note most pathways are left-sided and lateral. Anterior septal pathways are close to the normal conduction system and thus provide a challenge to treat with catheter ablation without causing harm. Modified with kind permission from Dr CB Pepper.

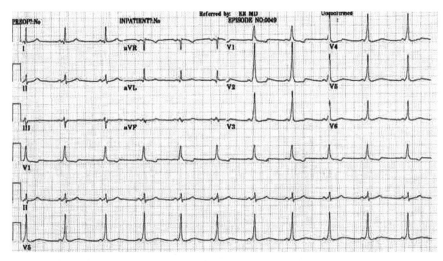

Figure 7.9 12-lead ECG demonstrating clear ventricular pre-excitation, with a strongly positive delta wave and R wave in lead V1 (wavefront moving from left to right across the chest leads suggests left sided) and a small negative delta wave in the lateral limb leads I and aVL (i.e. wavefront passes away from lateral LV wall) suggesting this is a left lateral AP.

- Risk of SCD is 1 in 1000 WPW patients per year (0.15–0.39%)
- Higher risks of SCD in patients of WPW with the following:
  - The shortest pre-excited RR interval <200 ms during spontaneous or induced AF (>300 bpm) (see Figure 7.10)
  - Multiple APs
  - Documented AF and AVRT
  - Ebstein's anomaly
  - EPS confirmed APs with rapid anterograde conduction time (<250 ms)
- Non-invasive tests like exercise treadmill testing (ETT) or drug challenges such as flecainide, procainamide, or ajmaline are not reliable tests to risk-stratify WPW.

Management
Usual principles apply, with some cautions:

- AV node blocking agents should be avoided with pre-excited AF
- Small risk of inducing AF with adenosine so use with caution (theoretical risk of rapidly conducting this AF to the ventricle—VF; wise to keep defibrillator nearby) when treating re-entrant arrhythmia if patient has history of pre-excitation
- Intravenous flecainide will usually preferentially slow pathway conduction, and thus can be used in pre-excited AF.

Definitive treatment
- RF ablation of the AP should be first choice in *symptomatic* WPW or AVRT
- Particularly offer ablation first-line to women considering pregnancy (i.e. to avoid drugs), or where profession (e.g. professional sports people, pilots) or lifestyle present risk
- RF ablation success rate varies (80–95%) depending on pathway locality (see Figure 7.8)
- Class Ic drugs, e.g. flecainide, will likely slow pathway conduction
- Digoxin, verapamil, and diltiazem are best avoided

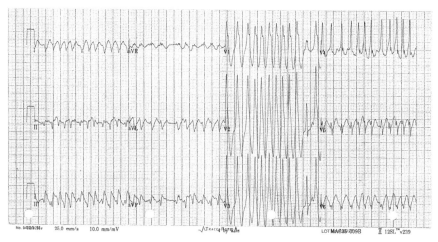

Figure 7.10 ECG showing pre-excited AF; note the short RR interval (shortest approx. 160 ms). V1 positive thus likely left sided AP (wavefront from left to right), and probably left lateral (negative in limb lead I).

- BBs do not usually affect the AP conduction but can often reduce the rate of re-entrant tachycardia.

Treatment strategy in asymptomatic pre-excited ECG

Treatment strategy in *asymptomatic* pre-excited ECG (i.e. not WPW *syndrome*) is as follows:

- Controversial: ESC/AHA/ACC guidelines consider catheter ablation a class IIa indication, with B level of evidence in this group of patients
- Initial evaluation of patients with ECG to look for structural abnormalities such as Ebstein's anomaly, a period of monitoring to look at rate profile and asymptomatic AF, as well as a treadmill test to look for sudden disappearance of delta waves; these may give some information about risk stratification, but they are poorly predictive
- Routine EP study has not been routinely recommended unless patient deemed to be in high-risk categories, though it is increasingly becoming routine in some centres due to the uncertainty in non-invasive risk stratification and the relatively low-risk nature of invasive EPS (<1%)
- Presence of multiple pathways, rapidly conducting AP, and inducibility of AVRT or AF during EPS are felt to be most predictive of future events, though none is perfect
- Current guidelines could be summarized as:
  - Ablate if:
    - Ayomptomatic (AF or AVRT)
    - Rapid pathway conduction (<250 ms)
    - High-risk occupation, e.g. high-level sportsman
    - Occupation threatened by diagnosis, e.g. pilots
  - Don't ablate if:
    - Asymptomatic and none of above
    - Patient declines
    - High-risk of complications, e.g. anteroseptal pathways and minimal symptoms
- Note that risk of AV block low with cryo-ablation
- It is reasonable to offer an EP study.

Special notes
- 'Mahaim' physiology:
  - A misnomer, but sometimes used to describe an AV bypass tract (AP) on the right side with decremental conduction properties acting as an accessory His-Purkinje system
  - Presents with a broad QRS AVRT (usually LBBB, as inserts into the right ventricle)
- Persistent junctional reciprocating tachycardia (PJRT):
  - An incessant form of long RP tachycardia due to an atypical AV junction bypass tract (atypical as the AP has decremental retrograde conduction properties)
  - ECG features are thus similar to AT and its relentless nature (due to a large excitatory gap) can result in tachycardiomyopathy if left untreated.

Atrial flutter
- Right atrial flutter (AFL) is the commonest form of macro-re-entrant atrial tachycardia
- The most common is described as 'typical' *and* counter-clockwise
- Typical AFL is cavo-tricuspid-isthmus (CTI)-dependent (see Figure 7.11)
- The direction of travel through the CTI gives rise to the counter-clockwise (most frequent) or clockwise label.

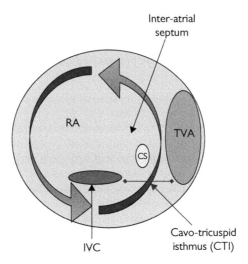

Figure 7.11 Schematic of the RA looking in from lateral wall. Diagram shows typical (i.e. CTI-dependent) RA flutter moving in a counter-clockwise direction. This gives rise to the typical ECG changes shown in the accompanying figure. Ablation of the CTI (dark grey) will eliminate the critical isthmus of conduction on which this macro re-entrant circuit depends, thus eliminating tachycardia.

ECG features

- These can vary widely, though classically there is no isoelectric point due to continuous atrial activity
- Typical counter-clockwise AFL appearance has:
    - Negative saw-tooth pattern in the inferior leads, as atrial depolarization moves up the inter-atrial septum (the main structural muscle bulk) from the low CTI (see Figures 7.11 and 7.12)
    - Positive flutter waves in V1, as the depolarization wave-front moves from the septal side (back) to the front of the RA
- Note that not all CTI-dependent AFLs have a counter-clockwise pattern of atrial activation. A CTI-dependent RA flutter going the other way (i.e. clockwise) is still 'typical' (CTI-dependent), but clockwise; the P wave axis is now positive in the inferior leads, as atrial depolarization progresses down the inter-atrial septum towards the CTI in a clockwise fashion. This is sometimes called 'reverse typical'. The semantics can cause confusion, as discussed in the next subsection
- Organized atrial rate in typical AFL can vary widely (it is typically 200 ms or 300 bpm), often influenced by RA size, disease, scarring, or AADs
- This may also manifest with varying degrees of block.

Atypical versus typical AFL

- Atypical AFL is usually related to surgical or non-surgical scars
- Atypical AFL should be used to describe any flutter that is *not* dependent on the CTI
- **Semantics** can sometimes confuse
    - Some texts will refer to typical clockwise atrial flutter as either 'reverse typical AFL', or 'atypical AFL'. However, a true atypical flutter is one not involving the CTI

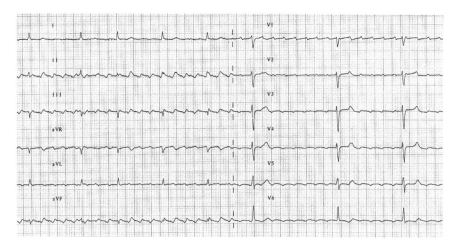

Figure 7.12 A 12-lead ECG: typical counter-clockwise AFL. Note the negative saw-tooth pattern in the inferior leads as atrial depolarization moves up the main muscle bulk of the inter-atrial septum from the low CTI (see Figure 7.11), and positive flutter waves in V1, as the depolarization wavefront moves from the septal side (back) to the front of the RA.

Reproduced from 'Consensus statement of the European Heart Rhythm Association', Johan Vijgen, Gianluca Botto, John Camm et al., Europace 11(8), 1097–1107, 2009, with permission of Oxford University Press.

- ■ LA flutter is best referred to as LA tachycardia, as conventionally flutter suggests a RA circuit
- ● 'Lone' AFL is rare. AFL is almost always secondary to some organic disease (i.e. rare in the young healthy heart).

Treatment

- ● Acute treatment with vagal manoeuvres, adenosine, or verapamil do not usually convert AFL to SR but might slow AV conduction allowing flutter waves to manifest
- ● Class 1C drugs (such as flecainide) can retard the atrial conduction velocity (i.e. AFL rate can reduce) but do not necessarily prolong the AV nodal RP
  - ■ This can lead to an increased liklihood of 1:1 AV conduction, and a sudden increase in ventricular rate
  - ■ Patients don't like this and it could even be life-threatening
- ● Therefore AV node blocking agents such as BB, CCB, or digoxin should generally be used with AADs in AFL
- ● Amiodarone is only effective in a third of cases, mainly in reducing flutter rate in the atrium and supplying a degree of AVN control
- ● Generally other management strategies should be considered before resorting to long-term amiodarone for AFL. However, as rate control can be challenging, amiodarone is often added
- ● DCCV is best to cardiovert acute AFL to SR, although its timing can be difficult as precautions similar to those taken regarding anti-coagulation in AF cardioversion should be observed
- ● Thromboembolic risk from AFL is theoretically smaller than that from AF due to preserved 'atrial kick', although the guideline evidence suggests risk stratification similar to AF both in the acute or chronic settings

- Chronic management with rate control is usually not successful unless there is concomitant AV node disease
- **Ablation:**
  - Paroxysmal AFL after single recurrence, or symptomatic rate-control refractory AFL, is recommended to be referred for ablation
  - Success rates for ablation of CTI-dependent AFL are high (>90%)
  - It involves delivering high-dose radiofrequency energy into a thick structure
  - The trabeculation and anatomical variations in the CTI mean success rates can never be 100%
  - Non-CTI-dependent AFLs are difficult to ablate and success rates vary from 50 to 88%
  - Patients do not necessarily need to be in AFL at the time of ablation (see Figure 7.6 for ablation lines)
- See Table 7.1 for the recommendations for the long-term management of AFL from the ACC/AHA/ESC 2003 guidelines.

Risk of AF

- Another issue to consider is co-existence of AFL with AF
- Data suggests that 25–50% of AFL patients ablated will go on to develop AF within five years
- If AFL is the pre-dominant rhythm then there is evidence to support the use of RF ablation to the CTI whilst continuing with the AADs for AF (AFL is often more symptomatic and less well tolerated than AF). If AFL is not the pro-dominant rhythm then recurrence of AF after AFL ablation is high
- The best results for ablations are in patients with AFL alone.

Atrial tachycardia (AT)

- AT can be focal or macro-re-entrant
- Atrial flutter (AFL) is the commonest macro-re-entrant AT

Table 7.1 Recommendations for the long-term management of AFL from the ACC/AHA/ESC 2003 guidelines

Clinical status/proposed therapy	Recommendation	Classification	Level of evidence
First episode and well-tolerated atrial flutter	Cardioversion alone	I	B
	Catheter ablation	IIa	B
Recurrent and well-tolerated atrial flutter	Catheter ablation	I	B
	Dofetilide, amiodarone, sotalol, flecainide, quinidine, propafenone, procainamide, disopyramide	IIa IIb	C C
Poorly tolerated atrial flutter	Catheter ablation	I	B
Atrial flutter appearing after use of class IC agents or amiodarone for treatment of AF	Catheter ablation	I	B
	Stop current drug and use another	IIa	C
Symptomatic non-CTI-dependent flutter after failed antiarrhythmic drug therapy	Catheter ablation	IIa	B

- The term AFL conventionally implies a macro-re-entrant atrial tachycardia circuit dependent on the cavo-tricuspid isthmus, or CTI, of the RA
- AT could be 'incision', i.e. scar-related, following surgery or catheter ablation
- Multifocal ATs are common in patients with COPD; usually focal
- Focal ATs are often (appoximately 50%) adenosine sensitive

- AADs generally considered first line, as AT can be more of challenge in the EP lab
- Useful agents include:
    - β-blockade to reduce ventricular rate as well as automatic and triggered features
    - Stabilizing agents such as flecainide or amiodarone, although considerations will have to be given to side effect profile on an individual basis
- Catheter ablation can be challenging (see subsection on 'EP features'), though has a role for those unable to or unwilling to take/tolerate AADs, or in whom AADs have failed.

ECG features
- Usually long RP tachycardia; often will be >1:1 A:V
- Variation in cycle length
- Variation in VA (RP) time
- About 50% of AT can be terminated with adenosine, which can further increase the diagnostic difficulty in differentiating AT from AV re-entrant SVT (see Section 7.4)
- Morphology of P wave can be useful to localize the AT (e.g. negative P wave in inferior leads suggests origin from low down in the atria; negative in V1 suggests RA)
- Increasingly seen as an unfortunate and difficult-to-treat complication of extensive LA ablation for AF.

EP features
- Usually started with extra stimulus pacing or burst overdrive pacing in the atrium
- Often need isporenaline to initiate
- Can be unpredictable and difficult to initiate and sustain during EPS, thereby making mapping challenging
- Mapping AT has improved through use of 3D electro-anatomical mapping systems (see Section 7.6), particularly if multiple ATs
- These considerations make catheter ablation less likely successful (c.f. AV re-entry tachycardia) and generally a second-line choice after drug therapy has failed.

7.6 3D electro-anatomic mapping

- One of the most significant advances in cardiac EP has been the evolution of 3D electro-anatomic mapping (EAM) techniques
- 3D EAM allows recording of the intra-cardiac electrical activation and propagation in relation to the anatomical structures
- These rapidly evolving systems have been proven to reduce radiation dose (fluoroscopy time) and procedure time as well as increasing the success rates of more complex procedures
- Commonly used mapping systems are described in the next sections.

CARTO® (Biosense Webster)

Function: magnetic sensor in catheter tip allows localization within external magnetic field.

Strengths: accurate reconstruction and activation mapping; user-friendly propagation maps; simultaneous anatomic, activation, and voltage acquisition; scar and tagging functions.

Weaknesses: Only compatible with own brand diagnostic and ablation catheters, limited utility for non-sustained arrhythmia.

EnSite NavX® (St Jude Medical)

Function: catheter located through voltage impedance changes relative to skin patches.

Strengths: accurate anatomical reconstruction; ability to locate and display multiple catheters at once; compatibility with any catheter; simultaneous multi-electrode collection of activation, voltage, and anatomical mapping.

Weaknesses: limited utility with non-sustained arrhythmia, prone to reference shift.

EnSite Array; non-contact mapping (St Jude Medical)

Function: a balloon covered in 64 electrodes producing high-density virtual unipolar array to rapidly map electrical signals off a single beat; 'non-contact mapping'.

Strengths: useful in non-sustained or poorly tolerated arrhythmia.

Weaknesses: accuracy depends on activation being within a certain distance from the balloon; prone to reference shifts; balloon can be obtrusive to ablation if small chamber.

Further reading

Fogoros RN. *Electrophysiologic Testing*, 5th edn. Wiley-Blackwell, 2012.

Murgatroyd F, Krahn AD, Klein GJ, Skanes AC, Yee RK. *Handbook of Cardiac Electrophysiology: A Practical Guide to Invasive EP Studies and Catheter Ablation*. Remedia, 2002.

Ventricular tachycardia and sudden cardiac death

8.1 Definitions

Ventricular tachycardia (VT)	Tachycardia arising from the ventricle with a rate of >100 bpm.
Non-sustained VT	Lasting for three or more beats and up to 30 s
Sustained VT	Lasting for more than 30 s
Monomorphic VT	The QRS pattern is consistent from beat to beat implying that the tachycardia is arising from a single consistent focus
Polymorphic VT	The QRS complexes vary in morphology from beat to beat with a rate between 100–333 bpm (cycle length 600–180 ms)
Ventricular fibrillation	Chaotic ventricular activation without discrete ventricular complexes
Sudden cardiac death	Death from an unexpected circulatory arrest, usually due to a cardiac arrhythmia, occurring within an hour of the onset of symptoms

8.2 Diagnosis of ventricular tachycardia

Differential diagnosis of a broad complex regular tachycardia can be grouped into three categories (see Figure 8.1):

- ventricular tachycardia
- SVT with aberrancy
  - Pre-existing bundle branch block
  - Rate-related bundle branch block
- pre-excited tachycardia
  - Antidromic AVRT (i.e. AVRT where antegrade conduction is over the pathway and retrograde conduction is over the AV node; the more typical orthodromic AVRT has antegrade conduction over the AV node and is narrow)
  - Atrial fibrillation etc. with an accessory pathway.

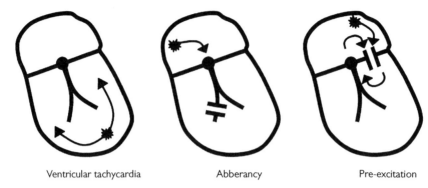

| Ventricular tachycardia | Abberancy | Pre-excitation |

Figure 8.1 Diagram demonstrating the initial site of activation for the three causes of a regular broad complex tachycardia. In aberrancy and pre-excitation the rhythm is supraventricular whereas in VT it is from within the ventricle.

Note that aberrancy refers to bundle branch block, which may be permanent or rate related. It does not have anything to do with accessory pathways.

- The history is key: a broad complex tachycardia in the context of any conditions that pre-dispose to VT, such as coronary artery disease or CCF, makes the diagnosis very likely to be VT
- The haemodynamic status of the patient is not a good guide as to whether the rhythm is VT.

ECG diagnosis

- Evidence of independent atrial activity is diagnostic of VT (pathognomonic) (see Figure 8.2)
  - P waves 'walk-through' the ECG
  - Fusion beats: the independent P waves are timed so that they are able to penetrate the AV node and begin depolarizing down the His-Purkinje system, but the VT continues and the two complexes fuse together
  - Capture beats: the independent beats timed perfectly to activate the His-Purkinje system and depolarize the entire ventricular myocardium before the next beat of VT
- Often the above features are not present and therefore additional clues are required to make a diagnosis of VT.

How broad is the QRS?
- The broader the QRS complex the more likely it is to be VT
- QRS >140 ms in RBBB and >160 ms in LBBB make VT likely
- Note: a specific form of VT, termed 'fascicular ventricular tachycardia', has a relatively narrow QRS (see Section 8.7).

Is the bundle branch block typical?
- If the rhythm is SVT with bundle branch block then the QRS morphology should look like a typical bundle branch block in sinus rhythm
- In RBBB this means an RsR' pattern with the R' larger than the R wave and a relatively small S wave in V6
- In LBBB this means a sharp initial downwards deflection in V1 and a positive deflection in V6

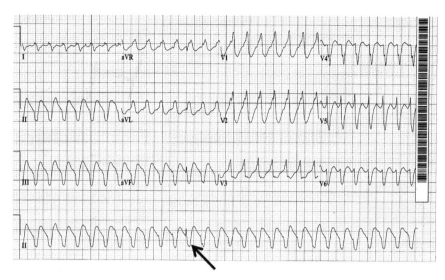

Figure 8.2 ECG showing several diagnostic features of VT. 1. QRS duration approximately 200 ms. 2. The arrow points to a fusion beat which demonstrates independent p wave activity. 3. The morphology is 'RBBB like' (positive in V1, negative in V6) but the appearance is highly atypical, with a deep S wave in V6, suggesting the left ventricle is origin for the VT. 4. The inferior leads are negative further localizing the origin of the VT to the inferior portion of the left ventricle. 5. aVR is positive and the frontal ECG axis is 210 degrees.

- The morphology of the VT can be used to give clues as to from where the VT originates; if the VT has a 'LBBB-like' morphology then it implies the right ventricle was activated first, and vice versa for a 'RBBB-like' morphology.

What is the QRS axis?

- If the axis is markedly deviated such that aVR is predominantly positive it indicates that activation is unlikely to be coming antegradely through the AV node and therefore the tachycardia is likely to be VT
- The QRS axis can also be used to give clues to the origin of the VT. If the inferior leads are positive the VT must originate superiorly and propagate downwards and vice versa (if the inferior leads are negative the VT originated inferiorly and propagates superiorly).

Is there concordance across the chest leads?

- If all the chest leads show a negative deflection—**there is negative concordance**—this demonstrates that the impulse is initiated in the apex and therefore the rhythm must be VT (see Figure 8.3)
- If all the chest leads show a positive deflection—**positive concordance**—it implies that the rhythm may be VT originating from the left basal area, but it is also possible that the rhythm is an SVT with conduction across a left-sided pathway
- **Note that concordance means that the predominant QRS deflection is in the same direction in all the chest leads, i.e. in positive concordance all the chest leads are positive, in negative concordance all the chest leads are negative.**

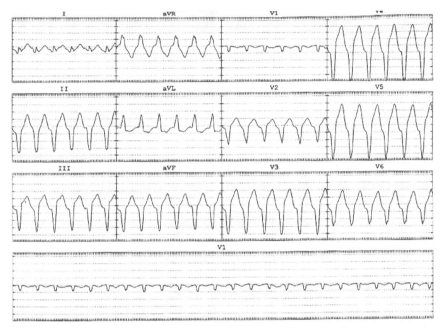

Figure 8.3 ECG demonstrating negative concordance across the chest leads, i.e. V1–V6 all have a predominantly negative deflection. This rhythm was mapped to the apex of the left ventricle on EP study.

Is the QRS narrower in tachycardia than in sinus rhythm?

- If the patient has a conduction defect on their resting ECG it will not rectify itself during tachycardia
- QRS complexes in a supraventricular tachycardia should be the same duration or longer
- If they can be demonstrated to shorten during tachycardia this shows that the rhythm is VT.

Is the morphology the same in other ECGs?

- Compare the broad complex tachycardia (see Figure 8.4a) with the ECG in sinus rhythm (see Figure 8.4b). If the morphology of the broad complex in tachycardia is identical to that in sinus rhythm it is likely that the diagnosis is SVT with pre-existing branch block, i.e. aberrancy.

Are there ventricular ectopic beats on the 12-lead ECG?

- If there are ventricular ectopic beats that are identical in morphology to the broad complex tachycardia it is very likely that the diagnosis is VT.

8.3 Acute treatment of ventricular tachycardia

- **Lost output**—advanced life support (ALS) algorithms for cardiac arrest with a shockable rhythm
- **Haemodynamically compromised**—rapid assessment adopting an ABC (airway, breathing, circulation) approach is required. In order to restore adequate circulation an urgent synchronized DC cardioversion should be performed; normally this will require

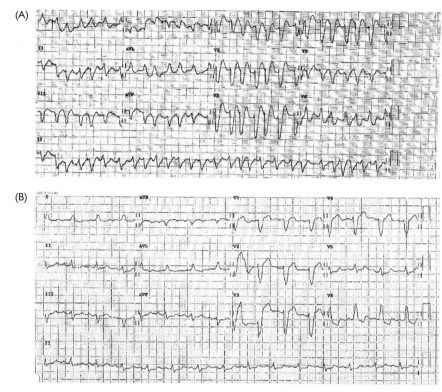

Figure 8.4 ECG of patient with AF, before and after returning to sinus rhythm. A. ECG showing an irregular broad complex tachycardia demonstrating that it is AF. The LBBB morphology is also typical with a sharp downstroke in V1 and positivity in V6. aVR is negative and the axis is −60°, which is consistent with LBBB. B. This ECG is in the same patient after they have returned to sinus rhythm. It can be seen that the QRS morphology is the same confirming that the original rhythm was AF with pre-existing LBBB.

anaesthetic support to manage appropriate sedation and analgesia for the patient during the cardioversion. The energy chosen for the cardioversion will depend on the defibrillator used but should be the same as in a cardiac arrest

- **In a more stable patient** consider medical treatment with i.v. amiodarone or lignocaine (i.v. amiodarone is very irritant to the veins and central venous access is optimal)
- Oral or intravenous beta blockers can be tried, particularly if VT in a structurally normal heart such as RVOT VT (see Section 8.7)
- Once stabilized, consider adding regular oral BBs
- If VT is recurrent or the administered medication has led to significant bradycardia a temporary pacing wire may be required; this enables the ongoing administration of medication and overdrive pacing to terminate VT
- If an ICD is *in situ* it is possible to access its anti-tachycardia pacing and shock functions directly through the appropriate programming device if suitable expertise is available (see Section 8.4)

- Once the patient has been stabilized they should be moved to the coronary care unit and monitored
- Correct reversible factors:
  - Aim for a K^+ of >4.5
  - Check Mg and aim for a level of 1.0
  - Look for ischaemia
  - Stop culprit medications, e.g. QT-prolonging drugs
- The patient will need an echo to identify structural heart disease (particularly LV and RV size and function)
- The long-term management of VT depends on the cause of the VT and the degree of compromise (discussed with reference to the different conditions that have led to the VT).

Polymorphic ventricular tachycardia versus torsades de pointes

- The nomenclature is confusing. The term 'torsades de pointes' should be reserved for the specific combination of QT prolongation with a distinct form of polymorphic VT in which the axis of ventricular complexes moves progressively from beat to beat in such a way that there is a transition from positive to negative complexes within a single ECG lead
- The most common cause of polymorphic VT with a normal QT interval is acute ischemia
- Management is different for the two conditions.

Torsades de pointes

- **Torsades de pointes VT is often initiated by a 'short–long–short' sequence:**
  - A ventricular ectopic beat leads to a compensatory pause before the next sinus beat
  - This pause means that the QT interval of the next sinus beat is further prolonged
  - A further ectopic beat therefore has a greater chance of falling within the end of the T wave and leading to the 'R on T' phenomenon and resulting in polymorphic VT
- **Torsades de pointes is promoted by bradycardia.** Bradycardia, particularly in relation to high grades of AV block, leads to QT prolongation, which can lead to torsades.

Management

- Correct the K^+ and Mg^{2+}. Magnesium can be very beneficial, and if the QT interval is prolonged it is reasonable to administer it before the lab results are back
- If torsades de pointes continues consider a temporary pacing wire. This can increase the heart rate, which will shorten the QT interval. The temporary wire also breaks the short–long–short cycle described and is often effective in stabilizing the patient
- Consider BBs. If there are no problems with bradycardia or once the temporary wire is *in situ*, BBs can be added to further reduce polymorphic VT
- Long-term management depends on the underlying condition:
  - If there is significant bradycardia, particularly if high-grade AV block has led to the polymorphic VT, then permanent pacing is appropriate
  - If there has been no significant bradycardia long-term treatment with BBs may be appropriate.

Polymorphic ventricular tachycardia in ischaemia

- In previous infarction the scar formation generally causes a stable pattern of re-entry and monomophic VT
- In the context of acute ischaemia (even without infarct) polymorphic VT can occur
- Management is as for other forms of VT in the acute setting, but urgent revascularization may be required.

8.4 Implantable cardiac defibrillators

- Implantable cardiac defibrillators (ICDs) have revolutionized the management of ventricular arrhythmias
- They are implanted in a manner similar to standard pacemakers (apart from new subcutaneous ICDs)
- In their simplest form they may have a single lead to the right ventricle or they may be dual chamber or biventricular
- The two essential features of all ICDs are:
  - First detect ventricular arrhythmias
  - Then deliver appropriate therapy.

Detection

- Typically ICDs have two zones of detection: the VF zone and the VT zone
- These are determined by rate. Typical values are:
  - VT zone: 170–200 bpm
  - VF zone >200 bpm
- For example, for the VF zone, the device simply monitors the ventricular R–R intervals. If it measures enough beats with a short enough cycle length (i.e. a fast enough rate) such as 300 ms (200 bpm) the device diagnoses VF and begins instigating therapy **without looking at other criteria**
- If the rate is slower and there are sufficient R–R intervals within the VT zone the device will then examine the rhythm according to several different algorithms to determine whether it an SVT or a VT
- The terms for these algorithms are often copyrighted by the individual manufacturers, which can make things confusing. The principles described for interpreting ECGs can help in developing an understanding of the concepts:
  - i. Onset: VT should be sudden onset (compare with sinus tachycardia and poorly controlled AF)
  - ii. Stability: VT should be regular (compare with AF)
  - iii. P wave activity: if there are more ventricular beats than atrial beats then the atria can not be driving the tachycardia and therefore it must be VT/VF; if there are equal numbers of ventricular and atrial beats, further parameters looking at the stability of the intervals can be used
  - iv. QRS morphology: the ICD stores a template of the normal QRS morphology and looks for a significant change
- Looking at these criteria it can be seen that a dual-chamber device has more parameters to discriminate with than a single-chamber device, although they will be unhelpful if the patient is in AF as the atrial rate will always be high. The risks and benefits of an extra lead need to be considered on a patient-by-patient basis.

Therapy

- The ICD has two types of therapy: anti-tachycardia pacing (ATP) and delivery of a shock
- ATP involves a short burst of pacing at a rate faster than the VT
- The aim is to deliver an appropriately timed stimulus to enter into the VT re-entry circuit in such a way that it disrupts the circuit and terminates the tachycardia
- Burst pacing: each paced impulse is at the same speed (around 88% of the tachycardia cycle length)

- Ramp pacing: paced impulse starts at around 88% of cycle length and each impulse is delivered 10 ms faster than the last
- If the ATP is ineffective it can be tried again at a slightly faster rate but this does come with an increased risk of accelerating the VT or pushing the patient into VF
- Shock: these are typically around 35 J and are experienced as a painful jolt by the patient but are usually effective at restoring a stable rhythm.

Programming

- ICDs have a wide range of settings that can be tailored to the patient's risks and previously documented VTs
- There is no standard setup that can be applied to all ICDs but there are a few simple concepts to consider:
  - Shocks are unpleasant and should be minimized as far as possible
  - Fast rates are more likely to be VF, which will not be terminated by ATP
  - Fast rates are likely to be less well tolerated if they are VT, therefore a shock should be delivered without delay
- This means that for fast rates the device may try ATP while it is charging but will default early to a shock
  - Slower rates are more likely to be VT and therefore ATP may be successful
- This means that the device will try ATP for longer, possibly going through a sequence of burst and then ramp pacing
  - Slower rates are more likely to be non-ventricular arrhythmias
- This means that discriminators other than just rate, such as onset, stability, P wave monitoring and morphology parameters, are used to avoid inappropriate shocks
- A typical setup is shown in Table 8.1.

Implantable cardiac defibrillator interrogation and follow up

- Routine follow up every 6 months, either in an ICD clinic or via remote download of data over phone lines/internet, e.g. the 'care-link' system
- Interrogation and appropriate follow up as soon as possible within normal working hours for a single shock in an otherwise well patient
- If there have been multiple shocks or the patient is otherwise unwell they should be admitted via the Accident and Emergency department and assessed urgently
- Interrogation of the device should enable the physician to determine if the shock was appropriate or inappropriate
- ICD setup can be changed to avoid inappropriate shocks
- The findings of interrogation can guide drug management to avoid both appropriate and inappropriate shocks.

There are two essential components to look at when examining an event: the box plot and the electrograms recorded by the device.

Table 8.1 A typical programming setup of an ICD

Zone	Rate, bpm (cycle length, ms)	Discriminators	Therapy
VF	>200 (300)	Off	ATP while charging then shock at 35J (Max 6 shocks)
VT	171–200 (300–350)	On	ATP x 4, if ineffective shock at 35J (max 2 shocks)

Box plots

- Box plots show the R–R and A–A intervals for each of the leads (note that in a single chamber device there will only be R–R intervals)
- Look at the onset (see Figure 8.5): it is sudden, suggesting VT vs gradual, suggesting sinus tachycardia or AF with poor rate control
- Look at regularity of the rhythm: regular rhythm suggests VT, versus irregular for AF
- Look at the discordance between the V rate and A rate:
  - If there are more Vs than As this shows the rhythm is ventricular
  - It should be noted that an equal number of Vs and As could be an AVRT, AVNRT, atrial tachycardia, sinus tachycardia, or VT with 1:1 retrograde conduction.

Intracardiac electrograms

- Information similar to that obtained from the box plot can be gained by looking at the intervals on the recording (see Figure 8.6)
- The relative timings between the A and V lead can be determined
- The device can monitor an electrogram between the can of the generator and the RV shock coil. This can provide useful information about the morphology of the QRS complex (see Figure 8.7).

IDs	Date/Time	Type	V. Cycle	Last Rx	Success	Duration
4	07 Oct 2006 09 08 06	VI	290 ms	VF Rx 1	Yes	19 sec

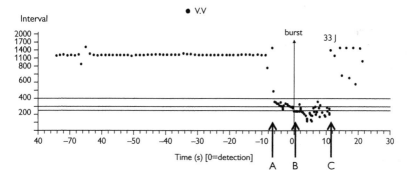

Figure 8.5 Box plot from a single chamber ICD (no data from the atrium). A. Sudden onset of a regular tachycardia with an R–R interval of 310 ms (i.e. a rate around 194 bpm). This falls within the VT zone (programmed to an R–R interval of 300–400 ms). B. The time at detection is set at 0 s. At this point burst ATP is delivered marked 'burst'. This results in eight regular beats that have a shorter R–R interval (and are therefore faster) than the VT—these are the burst pacing beats. C. After the burst pacing has finished the rhythm becomes irregular and the cycle length shortens with R–R intervals of around 200 ms (i.e. 300 bpm); this indicates that the burst pacing has degenerated the rhythm to VF. This is correctly detected and the device delivers a shock which restores sinus rhythm (this is annotated with '33J' indicating the energy of the shock). At this point the R–R interval returns to baseline and there are occasional beats with a short R–R interval, which are likely to be ectopic beats.

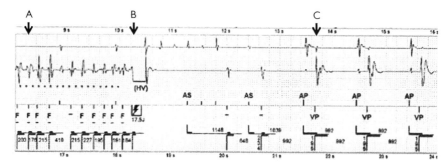

Figure 8.6 This recording has the atrial lead at the top, ventricular lead next, markers for the device sensing and then the intervals on the bottom line. A. At the beginning of the trace it can be seen that there is a regular relatively slow rate in the atrial lead but a fast irregular rate in the V lead. B. This has correctly been detected as VF and a shock is delivered (note the 'lightning' icon that documents the delivery of the shock). C. Following on from the shock there is some atrial and ventricular ectopy before settling to a paced rhythm in which the A lead is clearly paced first followed by a paced beat in the V. This is a successful shock for VF and has restored a normal-paced rhythm.

Complications

Complications can occur either early or late, with an estimated incidence of up to 30% in some series.

- Early complications
  - Pneumothorax: 1%
  - Lead displacement: 1%
  - Pericardial effusion
- Late complications
  - Infection: 1%
  - Lead failure: up to 30% at 10 years although this was with older leads
  - Inappropriate shocks: (more common than appropriate shocks).

Driving regulations

The DVLA has strict driving regulations for patients with ICDs:

- For class 2 licenses (HGV) an ICD results in a permanent ban
- Note that an EF of <40% or any arrhythmia that has caused or is likely to cause incapacity also results in a permanent ban.

For class 1 drivers the rules are summarized as follows.

- Primary prevention ICD leads to one month off driving
- Secondary prevention ICD leads to six months off driving
- Appropriate shock or symptomatic ATP leads to
  - Six months off driving (for both primary and secondary prevention) provided that steps have been taken to prevent recurrence (e.g. new medications or VT ablation)
  - Two years off driving if no changes to treatment are made

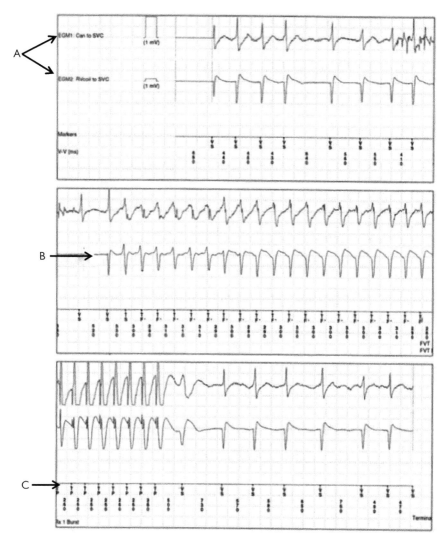

Figure 8.7 Intracardiac electrograms showing successful treatment of VT with ATP A. This recording comes from a single chamber but there are two traces which can cause confusion. The top trace is measured from the ICD can to the SVC coil and the lower trace is recorded from the RV coil to the SVC coil. The RR intervals are irregular, demonstrating AF. B. It can be seen that there is a sudden onset regular tachycardia with a clear change in morphology that is easiest to see in the can-to-SVC lead. The device marks the each event with a TF' to denote that they fall within the fast VT zone. C. After 18 consecutive events the device marks the diagnosis of FVT and delivers a burst of 8 beats of ATP, marked as TP, which successfully terminates the VT and the rhythm returns to AF.

- If inappropriate therapy is delivered (e.g. a shock for AF), driving may resume 1 month after this has been completely controlled to the satisfaction of the cardiologist (DVLA do not need to be notified)
- Revision of electrodes will necessitate one month off driving
- Box change leads to one week off driving.

8.5 Sudden cardiac death/arrest

- Sudden cardiac death/arrest is defined as an unexpected circulatory arrest, usually due to a cardiac arrhythmia occurring within one hour of onset of symptoms
- The term 'sudden cardiac arrest' has been suggested when death has been avoided by medical intervention. This is in preference to the difficult term 'aborted sudden cardiac death'.

8.6 Managing the risk of sudden cardiac death in specific conditions

- Secondary prevention trials have demonstrated that ICDs are effective in patients who have been resuscitated from VF and VT with haemodynamic compromise compared with amiodarone, metoprolol, and propafenone
- ICDs are indicated, regardless of the underlying condition, when the patient is known to have had a VF or VT cardiac arrest, i.e. for secondary prevention
- Due to the poor success rate of out-of-hospital resuscitation the aim of primary prevention is to identify patients who are at an increased risk of cardiac arrest and to implant an ICD prophylactically.

Left ventricular impairment: ischaemic and non-ischaemic

There are three main trials of patients with impaired LV function that have influenced current guidelines. These are summarized in Table 8.2.

ACC/AHA/ESC guidelines

These studies have led to the ACC/AHA/ESC guideline recommendations for LV dysfunction due to MI and also non-ischemic causes. They make reference to the need for:

- Optimal medical therapy
- Revascularization if appropriate
- Secondary prevention ICDs for resuscitated VF/unstable VT.

With specific reference to primary prevention ICDs in ischaemic heart disease are indicated:

- 40 days post-MI, in NYHA class II or III, with EF <40% on maximal treatment, with reasonable expectation of survival of more than one year (class 1)

Table 8.2 Trials dealing with primary prevention of SCD by an ICD in patients with impaired LV function

Trial	Aetiology of LV impairment	Inclusion criteria	Results
MADIT -I	Ischaemic (Q wave MI >4 weeks)	EF <35%, NSVT on monitoring, EP study postive	ICD better than conventional medical therapy
MADIT II	Ischaemic (Q wave MI >4 weeks)	EF <30% (no need for document arrhythmias or EP testing)	ICD better than conventional medical therapy
SCD-Heft	Ischaemic and non-ischaemic	EF <35% or less	ICD better than conventional medical therapy and amiodarone

- 40 days post MI, in NYHA class I, with EF <35% on maximal treatment with reasonable expectation of survival of more than one year (class IIa).

With reference to primary prevention for dilated cardiomyopathy:

- EF <35%, NYHA II to III, with expectation of survival of more than one year (class 1)
- EF <35%, NYHA class I, with expectation of survival of more than one year (class IIb).

These guidelines do not stipulate the QRS duration, need for ambulatory monitoring, or invasive EP testing in these primary prevention settings.

NICE guidelines

The National Institute of Clinical Excellence (NICE) have performed an economic analysis of the data and have identified the highest risk groups in order to ensure maximum cost-effectiveness of ICD implantation. These guidelines state that ICDs are indicated for primary prevention for patients with ICD only for patients with prior MI >4 weeks and:

- EF <35%, NHYA III or less, NSVT on monitoring, and VT on EP study

or

- EF <30%, NHYA III or less, and QRS >120 ms.

Secondary prevention ICDs are indicated for:

- VF/VT arrest
- VT with compromise
- EF <35% and sustained VT, NHYA III or less.

No specific guidance is given on other causes of LV impairment such as dilated cardiomyopathy although it is noted that ICDs may be indicated for genetic conditions with a high risk of SCD.

Hypertrophic cardiomyopathy

Key facts:

- Hypertrophic cardiomyopathy incidence is 1 in 500
- Echo is the key to diagnosis
- ECG often shows marked changes in QRS morphology and non-specific ST segment deviations
- Normal ECGs are very unusual and suggest other diagnosis should be considered
- Inheritance is autosomal dominant
- Most patients will not suffer from SCD.

There is no single tool to risk-stratify patients, but the ACC/AHA/ESC guidelines suggest that:

- Patients with sustained VT or VF should receive an ICD (class 1)
- Patients with one or more major risk factors may be considered for ICD, namely:
  - A family history of SCD
  - Unexplained syncope
  - LV thickness >30 mm
  - BP reduction on exercise testing
  - Non-sustained VT on monitoring
- Amiodarone use may be considered instead of ICD
- Genetic screening should be considered.

Suggested further risk factors are:

- AF
- Myocardial ischaemia
- LV outflow obstruction
- High-risk mutations
- Intense physical exercise.

Arrhythmogenic right ventricular cardiomyopathy (ARVC)

Key facts:

- Fibro-fatty replacement in the RV free wall is the characteristic histological finding
- It is a genetic defect in cell adhesion proteins
- Inheritance is normally autosomal dominant
- Genes are identified in only approximately 30% of cases
- The diagnostic guidelines have recently been reviewed. Diagnosis of ARVC requires either two major criteria, one major and two minor criteria, or four minor criteria as assessed in several categories:
    - Global or regional wall motion abnormalities, particularly affecting the RV (on either echo or MRI)
    - Tissue histology
    - ECG abnormalities (in both depolarization and repolarization)
    - Arrhythmias
    - Family history
    - Invasive EP testing.

Management:

- ICD is used for secondary prevention
- ICD should be considered for patients with
    - Extensive disease
    - Family history of SCD
    - Syncope
- VT ablation is useful as adjunctive therapy for patients with ICD *in-situ*.

Long QT syndrome

Key facts:

- There is an incidence of 1 in 7000 to 1 in 10,000
- It involves multiple mutations in the K^+ and Na^+ channels
- Long QT 1–3 accounts for approximately 80% of patients with clues in the ECG (see Figure 8.8)
    - LQT 1 is characterized by a broad-based T wave:
        - Arrhythmias often occur on exertion
        - QT fails to shorten with exercise

LQT 1 　　　　　　 LQT 2 　　　　　　 LQT 3

Figure 8.8 Examples of QT morphology in LQT 1–3.

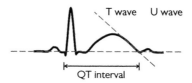

T wave   U wave

QT interval

Figure 8.9 A tangent is taken from the steepest downslope of the T wave and the QT interval is measured to the point where it crosses the isoelectric baseline.

- LQT 2 is characterized by a notched, biphasic T wave:
  - Arrhythmias often occur on exertion or with a sudden noise
- LQT 3 is characterized by a prolonged isoelectric baseline:
  - Arrhythmias often occur during sleep
- It is usually autosomal dominant with incomplete penetrance
- Measuring the QT interval is difficult (see Figure 8.9):
  - It is generally best performed lead II or V5
  - Care should be taken so as not to incorporate the U wave in the measurement
- Normal values are
  - Male <440 ms
  - Female <460 ms
- A QTc interval of more than 500 ms is a risk marker for SCD.

Management:

- Avoid all prolonging drugs; there is a useful list at www.qtdrugs.org
- BBs are first-line therapy
- ICD is indicated for patients with previous cardiac arrest or if the patient has a cardiac arrest whilst on BBs.

Brugada syndrome

Key facts:

- Brugada syndrome involves a mutation in the Na^+ channel
- Genes are identified in approximately 30% of cases
- Inheritance is autosomal dominant
- There are characteristic ECG changes (see Figure 8.10):
  - Type 1 has J point elevation of more than 2 mm, down-sloping ST elevation, and T wave inversion. It is described as 'coved'

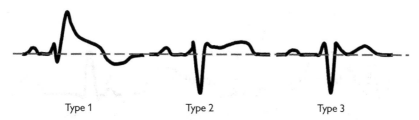

Type 1   Type 2   Type 3

Figure 8.10 Example of Brugada ECGs in the right precordial chest leads.

- Type 2 has J point elevation of more than 2 mm, a saddleback ST segment remaining more than 1 mm above the baseline, and the T wave is positive or biphasic
- Type 3 has a saddleback or coved ST segment elevation less than 1 mm above the baseline, and the T wave is positive
- It can be provoked by class 1 antiarrhythmics, which can therefore be used as a diagnostic test. This can be either:
  - Ajmaline challenge (generally preferred because of its short half-life), or
  - Flecainide challenge
- The role of a VT stimulation study to risk stratify is controversial (class IIb ESC guidelines)
- ECG changes can be provoked by fevers.

Management:

- No medications are proven
- ICDs are used for secondary prevention
- ICD is 'reasonable' for patient with syncope and Brugada syndrome according to AHA/ESC guidelines
- Avoid high fevers, treating them aggressively with paracetamol.

Catecholamingergic polymorphic ventricular tachycardia

Key facts:

- Catecholamingergic polymorphic ventricular tachycardia (CPVT) was recently discovered
- Patients have a high risk of SCD
- It is usually autosomal dominant but may be recessive
- The gene is identified in approximately 80% of cases. Calcium handling problems are secondary to a mutation of the ryanodine receptor
- Resting ECG may be normal
- Testing with ETT, ambulatory monitoring, or adrenaline infusion may demonstrate ventricular salvos. Bidirectional VT may be seen.

Management:

- Secondary prevention is with ICDs combined with BBs
- ICD may be considered for patients with syncope or sustained VT whilst on BBs
- BBs should be given to all patients in whom a clinical diagnosis of CPVT has been made
- BBs should be considered for asymptomatic patients who have had a genetic diagnosis of CPVT.

8.7 Ventricular tachycardia in structurally normal hearts

- VT can occur in structurally normal hearts
- In contrast to the conditions listed in Section 8.6 patients generally have a much more stable rhythm and tolerate their arrhythmias well
- Therapy is therefore focused on relieving symptoms and an ICD is very rarely indicated.

Right ventricular outflow tract ventricular tachycardia

- Usually the VT originates from the RVOT but can also be from the LVOT
- Typically the ECG shows an 'LBBB-like' morphology with positive QRS complexes in the inferior leads (see Figure 8.11)

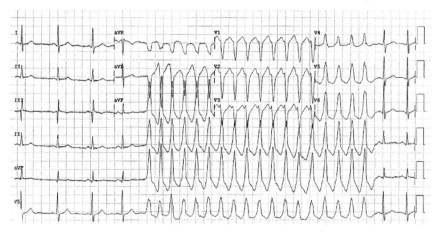

Figure 8.11 NSVT consistent with RVOT VT. 'LBBB'-like morphology indicates the tachycardia originates in the right ventricle. Leads II and aVF are strongly positive indicating that the tachycardia originates superiorly and propagates inferiorly. The patient was investigated with a cardiac MR and echo to look for evidence of ARVC. These were both normal and the patient was commenced on beta blockers.

- It may terminate with adenosine or verapamil
- There is normal ECG in sinus rhythm
- There is normal echo/cardiac MRI.

Treatment:

- Medical therapy is with BBs or calcium channel blockers
- VT ablation is used for patients in whom medications are ineffective or poorly tolerated
- ICD's are **not** normally required.

Fascicular ventricular tachycardia

- Fascicular ventricular tachycardia arises within the fascicles of the left bundle and has a relatively narrow QRS (120–140 ms)
- Left posterior fascicle is most common; ECG shows RBBB and LAD
- Left anterior fascicle is less common; ECG shows RBBB and RAD
- It may terminate with verapamil but is not usually adenosine sensitive.

Treatment:

- Calcium channel blockers and BBs may be tried but are often ineffective
- Catheter ablation is used.

8.8 Risk of sudden cardiac death with accessory pathways

- In patients with a manifest accessory pathway (i.e. one allowing antegrade conduction with a delta wave on the ECG) there is a small risk of SCD (approx 0.2–0.4%)
- There is an increased risk of AF
- In AF the rapid atrial rates can be conducted via the accessory pathway to the ventricle, leading to dangerously high ventricular rates

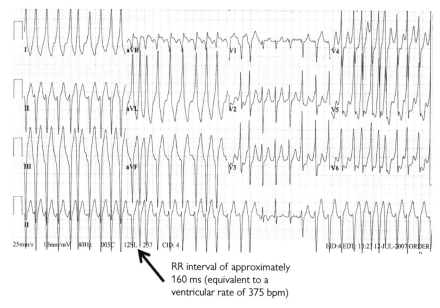

RR interval of approximately
160 ms (equivalent to a
ventricular rate of 375 bpm)

Figure 8.12 Pre-excited atrial fibrillation. Key to the diagnosis is the irregular R–R intervals. Note that the shortest R–R intervals show maximal pre-excitation because there is no time for conduction across the AV node and therefore all conduction is across the pathway. There are several very short R–R intervals here (<250 ms ; one example arrowed) indicating that this a high-risk pathway and ablation of the pathway is indicated. If in doubt deliver a shock.

- ECG shows a broad complex, but irregular rhythm, with varying degrees of fusion (see Figure 8.12)
- **AV blocking drugs should be avoided.** They will have no effect on the conduction down the accessory pathway and if they are negatively inotropic may lead to death. **Intravenous calcium channel blockers in particular should be avoided**
- **It is often safest to perform urgent synchronized DC cardioversion** but i.v. flecanide can be considered
- There is no consensus on how to risk stratify:
  - Non-invasive testing is generally with Holter monitoring; if there is spontaneous loss of delta wave a good prognosis is implied
  - Asymptomatic patients are at lower risk
  - Invasive EP testing is the gold standard; pathways with refractory periods of <250 ms (able to sustain rates of >240 bpm) are high risk and will generally be ablated at the time of testing.

Further reading

Garratt CJ, Elliott P, Behr E, et al. Heart rhythm, UK position statement on clinical indications for implantable cardioverter defibrillators in adult patients with familial sudden cardiac death syndromes. *Europace*, 2010; 12: 1156–75.

Moss AJ, Jackson Hall W, Cannom DS, *et al.*, for the MADIT investigators. Improved survival with an implanted defibrillator in patients with coronary disease at high risk for ventricular arrhythmia. *N Engl J Med.* 1996; 335: 1933–40.

Moss AJ, Zareba W, Jackson Hall W, *et al.*, for the MADIT II investigators. Prophylactic implantation of a defibrillator in patients with myocardial infarction and reduced ejection fraction. *N Engl J Med,* 2002; 346: 877–83.

Wellens HJJ. Ventricular tachycardia: diagnosis of broad RS complex tachycardia. *Heart,* 2001. 86: 579–83.

Zipes DP, Camm AJ, Borggrefe M, *et al.* ACC/AHA/ESC 2006 guidelines for management of patients with ventricular arrhythmias and the prevention of sudden cardiac death—executive summary. *Eur Heart J,* 2006; 27: 2099–140.

Atrial fibrillation

9.1 Overview

- Atrial fibrillation (AF) is a common arrhythmia that may be asymptomatic
- Paroxysmal and persistent AF may become permanent
- AF may cause stroke, heart failure, sudden death, reduced exercise capacity and quality of life
- Treatment involves thromboprophylaxis, rate control, and rhythm control in appropriate patients
- Many clinical trials have, however, shown no advantage in pursuing either rhythm-control or strict rate-control strategies.

9.2 Epidemiology

General population
- Irregular ventricular rhythm without consistent P waves (see Figure 9.1)
- 1–2% prevalence
- Increases with age (5–15% of 80 year olds affected).

ESC atrial fibrillation definitions
- First diagnosed AF—presenting for the first time irrespective of duration of AF
- Paroxysmal AF (PAF)—recurrent and self-terminating, lasting <7 days. Usually lasts <48 h and >30 s (usual clinical trial definition)
- Persistent AF—lasts >7 days or terminated by chemical or electrical cardioversion (term implies rhythm-control strategy pursued)
- Permanent AF—longstanding AF (term implies rate-control strategy pursued)
- Silent AF—asymptomatic AF that it is found by chance on an ECG or because of an AF-related complication such as stroke.

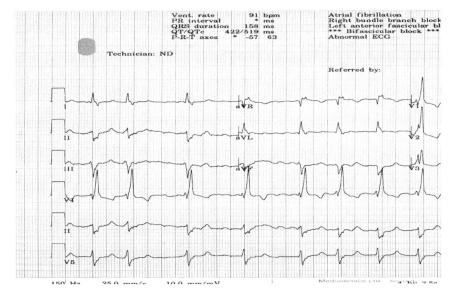

Figure 9.1 ECG showing atrial fibrillation.

Progression

- 10% AF recurrence rate in first year after diagnosis then 5%/year
- 30–70% recurrence of AF in first month after cardioversion
- Asymptomatic AF common even in symptomatic patients.

Predisposing clinical conditions

- **Hypertension**—occurs in approximately two thirds of patients. ACEI and ARBs most effective in preventing incident AF in hypertensive patients
- **Heart failure**—30% AF patients NYHA class II–IV. AF found in 30–40% of heart failure patients (50% of NYHA IV patients). May be cause or consequence of AF. ACE inhibitors and BBs may prevent new-onset AF
- **Tachycardiomyopathy**—LV dysfunction caused by AF with fast ventricular response. LV function may be restored with adequate rate control or return to sinus rhythm
- **Valvular heart disease**—especially mitral stenosis and mitral regurgitation. Some degree of valvular disease in 30% of AF patients
- **Cardiomyopathies**—high risk of AF. Includes hypertrophic cardiomyopathy, dilated cardiomyopathy, arrhythmogenic right ventricular cardiomyopathy as well as 'channelopathies' such as long and short QT syndromes and Brugada syndrome
- **Atrial septal defects (ASDs)**—associated with AF in 10–15% of patients. AF may be due to pressure and volume overload due to septal defect itself or common abnormality e.g. genetic cause
- **Other congenital defects**—patients with single ventricles, atrial repair, transposition of the great arteries, or Fontan procedure are at especially high risk of AF
- **Coronary artery disease**—present in 20% of AF patients. Unclear if CAD itself predisposes to AF—association may be secondary to other shared risk factors, e.g. heart failure, hypertension. AF indicates poor prognosis after MI
- **Obesity**—25% of AF patients
- **Chronic renal disease**—present in 10–15% of patients

- **Diabetes mellitus**—20% of AF patients
- **COPD**—10–15% of AF patients
- **Sleep apnoea**—associated with increased atrial pressure and dilatation
- **Thyroid dysfunction**—hyperthyroidism and hypothyroidism may cause AF.

Consequences of atrial fibrillation

- **Death**—AF associated with a doubled mortality risk independent of other known predictors of death. Only anti-thrombotic treatment and dronedarone have been shown to affect AF-related deaths and reduce thrombo-embolic strokes
- **Stroke**—risk is the same for paroxysmal, persistent, and permanent AF. Strokes often severe, result in death or permanent disability, and more likely to recur than strokes of other causes
- **Reduced quality of life and exercise capacity**—AF is one of the most common reasons for hospitalization. Even otherwise asymptomatic patients report lower quality of life than subjects in sinus rhythm
- **LV function**—often impaired by fast ventricular rate and loss of atrial contractile function with reduced diastolic filling
- **Cognitive dysfunction**—asymptomatic embolic events without overt stroke may contribute.

9.3 Pathophysiology

- The causes of AF are multi-factorial and complex
- Familial component exists, especially in AF of early onset
- AF associated with inherited cardiac conditions such as hypertrophic cardiomyopathy (HCM), Brugada and long and short QT syndromes
- AF episodes (especially in 'lone AF') may be initiated by rapid focal electrical activity originating from within or near the pulmonary veins
- Rapid atrial rates may create a vicious circle whereby 'electrical remodelling' occurs; this makes the atrium more likely to support sustained AF
- Remodelling can be electrical (e.g. changes in action potential duration) but later in the process can be structural (e.g. fibrosis), involving shortening of the atrial action potential duration and refractoriness. This may prevent calcium overload-induced cell death but the reduction in wave length contributes to AF recurrence
- Reduced atrial contractile function persists for several weeks after restoration of sinus rhythm ('atrial stunning') and is a reason to maintain anticoagulation in the first weeks after cardioversion
- AF also induces atrial fibrosis resulting in slowed conduction and electrical isolation of atrial cardiomyocytes, further maintaining AF or provoking recurrence
- Chronic dilatation of the atria secondary to chronic pressure or volume overload may induce the structural changes that predispose to AF, e.g. secondary to valvular disease or heart failure
- High-level endurance sports may predispose to AF via chronic atrial dilatation
- Protein mutations seen in inherited cardiomyopathies such as the long and short QT syndromes may cause AF.

9.4 Diagnosis

- ECG diagnosis of AF confirmed by complete irregularity of R–R intervals and loss of discernible P waves (small atrial waves may be seen in the right precordial leads, however)—see Figure 9.1
- Differential diagnosis includes atrial tachycardia, atrial flutter, and frequent atrial ectopy, but the atrial cycle length of these tachycardias is usually slower than the <200 ms found in AF (AF cycle length may be longer if on conduction-slowing or action-potential-prolonging drugs)

- Differential diagnosis for AF with a slow ventricular response includes severe sinus node disease with changing ectopic pacemakers and higher-degree AV block. The ventricular rate may be regular if AF occurs with complete heart block
- Silent AF (incidental finding) accounts for around 25–30% of cases of all AF patients
- Vagal AF usually occurs at evening, night, and weekends, especially after heavy meals and alcohol consumption. Usually sinus bradycardia or sinus pauses precede the AF and the ventricular rate is slow
- Adrenergic AF is less common and provoked by physical or mental stress.

Investigations

- 12-lead ECG—look for evidence of MI, LVH, bundle branch block, ventricular pre-excitation, cardiomyopathy, ischaemia, and other arrhythmias that may provoke AF
- CXR—look for cardiomegaly, evidence of pulmonary disease
- Echocardiography—look for LVH, LA enlargement, slow flow in LAA, thrombi (may need TOE), ventricular function, valve function
- Lab tests—thyroid function tests (TFTs), BNP, electrolytes, haemoglobin, renal function, fasting glucose
- Holter monitoring—may be used for diagnosis of AF (and initiating arrhythmia) or monitoring of ventricular rate control. Relevance of AF burden (percentage of time in AF) is unclear
- Exercise testing—to determine ventricular rate control during exercise in symptomatic patients with normal resting heart rate.

9.5 Thromboprophylaxis

- Only antithrombotic therapy has been shown to reduce AF-related deaths
- AF is the cause of 1 in 5 strokes
- 2–7-fold increased relative risk (RR) of stroke and thromboembolism for non-valvular AF (no signs of rheumatic mitral valve disease) compared to arrhythmia-free controls
- 17-fold increased RR of thromboembolism in those with rheumatic mitral valve disease.

Risk stratification

Stroke risk factors include:

- Prior stroke/transient ischaemic attack (TIA) (RR 2.5)
- Increasing age (RR 1.5/decade)
- Hypertension (RR 2.0)
- Diabetes mellitus (RR 1.7)
- Heart failure (LVEF <40%)
- Mitral stenosis
- Prosthetic heart valve.

CHADS2 and CHA$_2$DS$_2$VASc

- CHADS$_2$ score well validated and simple assessment of stroke risk:
  - Age >75 years (1 point)
  - Hypertension (1 point)
  - Diabetes mellitus (1 point)
  - Heart failure (1 point)
  - Prior stroke or TIA (2 points)

- Less well validated risk factors include female gender, age 65–74, cardiovascular disease (MI, PVD, aortic plaque)
- Stroke risk with PAF similar to persistent/permanent AF
- 'Lone AF' patients aged <60 years and no other risk factors have a low cumulative risk (1.3% over 15 years)
- A recent refinement of the $CHADS_2$ risk stratification system is CHA_2DS_2VASc
- CHA_2DS_2VASc improves on the predictive power of $CHADS_2$ by putting fewer patients in an intermediate risk category and having very low event rates if categorized as low risk (see Table 9.1).

Table 9.1 CHA_2DS_2VASc score and stroke rate.

(a) Risk factors for stroke and thrombo-embolism in non-valvular AF

'Major' risk factors	'Clinically relevant non-major' risk factors
Previous stroke, TIA, or systemic embolism Age ≥75	Heart failure or moderate to severe LV systolic dysfunction (e.g. LVEF ≤40%) Hypertension—diabetes mellitus Female sex—age 65–74 years Vascular disease

(b) Risk factor-based approach expressed as a point based scoring system, with the acronym CHA_2DS_2VASc (note: maximum score is 9 since age may contribute 0, 1 or 2 points)

Risk factor	Score
Congestive heart failure/LV dysfunction	1
Hypertension	1
Age ≥75	2
Diabetes mellitus	1
Stroke/TIA/thrombo-embolism	2
Vascular disease	1
Age 65–74	1
Sex category (i.e. female sex)	1
Maximum score	9

(c) Adjusted stroke rate according to CHA_2DS_2VASc score

CHA_2DS_2VASc score	Patients (n = 7329)	Adjusted stroke rate (%/year)
0	1	0
1	422	1.3
2	1230	2.2
3	1730	3.2
4	1718	4.0
5	1159	6.7
6	679	9.8
7	294	9.6
8	82	6.7
9	14	15.2

Good evidence for antithrombotic therapy in AF:

- If $CHADS_2$ or CHA_2DS_2VASc score ≥2 then treat with vitamin K antagonist (VKA) such as warfarin with target INR 2–3
- Anti-coagulate if one major risk factor (age>75, stroke, mitral stenosis, prosthetic heart valve) or two non-major risk factors (Class 1A evidence)
- Patients with one non-major risk factor should be considered for VKA or anti-platelet agent such as aspirin
- If no risk factors then aspirin (class 1B) or nothing (Class 2A).

Bleeding risk

- A patient's bleeding risk must be considered before commencing anti-coagulation
- Major bleeding risk with VKA is similar to aspirin
- The HAS-BLED system can be used to assess the bleeding risk in patients (see Table 9.2)
- HAS-BLED score of ≥3 indicates high risk and thus caution required if initiating VKA or anti-platelet therapy.

Vitamin K antagonist versus anti-platelets

- Theoretical increased risk of haemorrhage with VKA versus aspirin but BAFTA study found no difference in major bleeding between warfarin and aspirin in elderly AF population
- Meta-analysis suggests 67% relative risk reduction in ischaemic stroke/systemic embolism with warfarin versus placebo and 39% versus aspirin in patients with non-valvular AF
- Meta-analysis of eight RCTs suggests aspirin reduces stroke risk by 22%
- Studies used doses of 50–1300 mg/day but 75 mg od gives nearly complete platelet inhibition with low bleeding risk
- Aspirin less effective in those >75 years and does not prevent severe or recurrent strokes
- Absolute increased risk of intracranial haemorrhage with warfarin versus aspirin is small
- No evidence for combination of VKA with anti-platelet in preventing thromboembolism/death/MI but there is increased risk of bleeding
- Aspirin + clopidogrel worse than warfarin alone in preventing stroke in AF patients
- Aspirin + clopidogrel reduces stroke compared to aspirin alone but at the expense of increased haemorrhage.

Vitamin K antagonist dosing

- INR of 2.0–3.0 is optimal for preventing stroke and systemic embolism yet keeping bleeding risk to a minimum in non-valvular AF patients (see Figure 9.2)
- No evidence for using a lower target INR range.

Table 9.2 HAS-BLED scoring system

Letter	Clinical characteristic	Points awarded
H	Hypertension	1
A	Abnormal renal and liver function (1 point each)	1 or 2
S	Stroke	1
B	Bleeding	1
L	Labile INRs	1
E	Elderly	1
D	Drugs or alcohol (1 point each)	1 or 2

Hypertension, systolic BP>160 mmHg; abnormal renal function, dialysis/transplant/creatinine ≥200 μmol/l; abnormal liver function, chronic liver disease or bili >2 × upper limit of normal and ALT/AST/ALP >3× upper limit of normal; bleeding, bleeding history or predisposition; elderly, age>65; drugs, e.g. anti-platelets/NSAIDs; alcohol = alcohol abuse.

Vitamin K antagonist in special situations

- Treat PAF and atrial flutter patients as for persistent and permanent AF i.e. anti-coagulate depending on risk score
- Stop warfarin approximately five days prior to surgery and aim to restart usual maintenance dose (without loading) on evening of surgery
- If mechanical heart valve or AF with high risk of thromboembolism then can consider 'bridging' therapy with UFH or LMWH
- Post elective PCI aim to use non-drug-eluting stents and use triple therapy (VKA, aspirin + clopidogrel) for four weeks followed by life-long VKA (see Table 9.3)
- Post ACS/PCI with drug eluting stent then triple therapy for at least a month then consider VKA with one or two antiplatelets for up to 12 months depending on bleeding risk (VKA alone after 12 months) (see Table 9.3)
- Stable vascular disease (no ischaemic events or PCI in the previous year) should be treated with VKA alone as it is at least as effective as aspirin in the secondary prevention of CAD
- In survivors of thromboembolic stroke with AF, reasonable to start warfarin after 2 weeks (possible increased risk of intracranial haemorrhage/haemorrhagic transformation of the infarct)

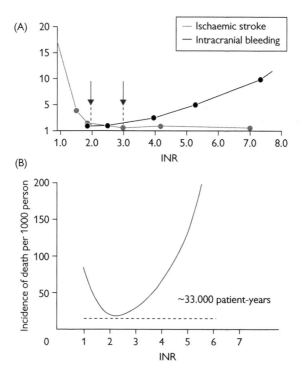

Figure 9.2 (A) Adjusted odds ratio for ischaemic stroke and intracranial bleeding in relation to international normalized ratio (INR). (B) Risk of death during the month following an INR test in relation to the INR value. The blue line represents the mortality.

Figure A reproduced with permission from 2nd edition, ed. John Camm, Thomas Lüscher and Patrick Serruys, copyright Oxford University Press 2009. Figure B reproduced from 'Oral anticoagulation and risk of death: medical record linkage study', Anders Odén, Martin Fahlén, **325**: 1073–5, copyright 2002 with permission from BMJ Publishing Group Ltd.

Table 9.3 Guidance on anti-thrombotics post PCI in AF patients at moderate to high thrombo-embolic risk

Haemorrhagic risk	Clinical setting	Stent implanted	Anticoagulation regimen
Low or intermediate (e.g. HAS-BLED score 0–2)	Elective	Bare-metal	*1 month*: triple therapy of VKA (INR 2.0–2.5) + aspirin ≤100 mg/day + clopidogrel 75 mg/day *Lifelong*: VKA (INR 2.0–3.0) alone
	Elective	Drug-eluting	*3 (-olimus group) to 6 (paclitaxel) months*: triple therapy of VKA (INR 2.0–2.5) + aspirin ≤100 mg/day + clopidogrel 75 mg/day (or aspirin 100 mg/day). *Lifelong*: VKA (INR 2.0–3.0) alone
	ACS	Bare-metal/ drug-eluting	*6 months*: triple therapy of VKA (INR 2.0–2.5) + aspirin ≤100 mg/day + clopidogrel 75 mg/day *Up to 12th month*: combination of VKA (INR 2.0–2.5) + clopidogrel 75 mg/day (or aspirin 100 mg/day) *Lifelong*: VKA (INR 2.0–3.0) alone
High (e.g. HAS-BLED score ≥3)	Elective	Bare-metal	*2–4 weeks*: triple therapy of VKA (INR 2.0–2.5) + aspirin ≤100 mg/day + clopidogrel 75 mg/day *Lifelong*: VKA (INR 2.0–3.0) alone
	ACS	Bare-metal	*4 weeks*: triple therapy of VKA (INR 2.0–2.5) + aspirin ≤100 mg/day + clopidogrel 75 mg/day *Up to 12th month*: combination of VKA (INR 2.0–2.5) + clopidogrel 75 mg/day (or aspirin 100 mg/day) *Lifelong*: VKA (INR 2.0–3.0) alone

Adapted from G. Y. H. Lip, K. Huber, F. Andreotti et al., 'Management of antithrombotic therapy in atrial fibrillation patients presenting with acute coronary syndrome and/or undergoing percutaneous coronary intervention/stenting', *Thrombosis and Haemostasis*, 103(1), 13–28, copyright 2010 with permission from Schattauer Publishers.

- In pregnancy VKAs may be teratogenic and should be avoided in first trimester (use UFH or LWMH instead)
- Full anti-coagulation for at least 3 weeks prior to chemical or electrical cardioversion required if AF for >48 h. Typically embolism occurs in the initial few days following reversion to sinus rhythm. Continue anti-coagulation for minimum of 4 weeks post cardioversion
- If transoesophageal echocardiography (TOE) confirms no thrombus in left atrial appendage (LAA) or LA then give LMWH and cardiovert without need for 3 weeks anti-coagulation prior (but do need to anti-coagulate for 4 weeks after).

Dabigatran
- Dabigatran is a new direct thrombin inhibitor
- RE-LY study showed that 110 mg dabigatran non-inferior to VKA for the prevention of stroke and systemic embolism and had lower rates of bleeding
- RE-LY also showed 150 mg dabigatran bd associated with similar rates of major haemorrhage. but lower rates of stroke and systemic embolism compared with VKA.

Non-pharmacological methods
- LAA is the source of thromboembolism in >90% of non-valvular AF
- LAA resection in those undergoing other cardiac surgery significantly reduces risk of stroke

- Percutaneous LAA closure devices may be as good as warfarin at preventing stroke and death with a low haemorrhage risk but increased risk of pericardial effusion. NICE allows the use of such devices in non-valvular AF.

9.6 Drugs

- Aim, apart from anti-coagulation, is termination of arrhythmia and maintenance of sinus rhythm with control of ventricular rates during AF episodes
- Treatment of conditions associated with AF such as hypertension and CCF may prevent occurrence, reduce recurrence rate, or delay progression to permanent AF
- Treatment of underlying conditions to prevent atrial remodelling and substrate for AF is called 'upstream' therapy
- Long-term maintenance of sinus rhythm difficult to achieve, with high recurrence rate and adverse effects associated with anti-arrhythmic medication
- Virtually all studies have shown that a primary rate-control strategy is not inferior to rhythm control
- Rhythm-control strategy reasonable in symptomatic patients, in those with recent onset of AF, and in the young and active
- In the RACE II study, strict rate control (target resting HR <80) versus lenient (HR <110) was not shown to improve symptoms, adverse events, or quality of life (the lenient control group actually had fewer hospital visits).

Cardioversion

- Many episodes of AF will terminate spontaneously in the first few hours or days
- Indeed, if AF onset <24 h, two thirds spontaneously revert to sinus rhythm
- Pharmacological cardioversion (see Table 9.4 and Figure 9.3) is slower and the success rate lower compared to DC cardioversion but does have the advantage of not requiring sedation or general anaesthesia

Table 9.4 Antiarrhythmic drugs for pharmacological cardioversion of atrial fibrillation

Drug	Route	Dose	Adverse effects
Flecainide	Oral/i.v.	2 mg/kg i.v. over 10 min or 200–300 mg p.o.	Rapidly conducted atrial flutter; QT prolongation; unsuitable for patients with structural heart disease
Propafenone	Oral/i.v.	2 mg/kg i.v. over 10 min or 450–600 mg loading p.o.	Rapidly conducted atrial flutter; QT prolongation; unsuitable for patients with structural heart disease
Amiodarone	i.v.	5 mg/kg i.v. over 1 h followed by 50 mg/h	Hypotension; bradycardia; QT prolongation; torsade de pointes; phlebitis (intravenous); multiorgan toxicity in the long term
Ibutilide	i.v.	1 mg over 10 min with further 1 mg after waiting 10 min	QT prolongation and significant risk of polymorphic VT
Vernakalant	i.v.	3 mg/kg over 10 min followed by 2 mg/kg over 10 min after 15 min	

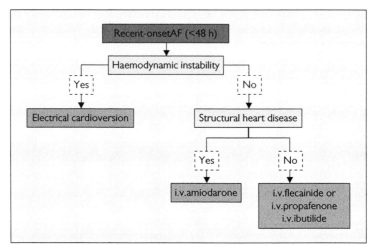

Figure 9.3 DC or pharmacological cardioversion for recent-onset AF.

Reproduced from 'Guidelines for the management of atrial fibrillation', The Task Force for the Management of Atrial Fibrillation of the European Society of Cardiology (ESC) *European Heart Journal* (31):2369–2429, 2010, with permission of Oxford University Press.

- If no proarrhythmia concerns (those with prolonged QT interval or those at risk of tachy-brady syndrome) can commence anti-arrhythmic outside of hospital, for example flecainide, propafenone in combination with an AV-blocking drug to prevent fast ventricular rates if atrial flutter occurs
- Pharmacological cardioversion usually successful if commenced within a week of AF onset. Within 72 h around 45% of patients may convert spontaneously and 70% with medication
- Flecainide or propafenone iv cardiovert 80–90% of patients within 1 h if AF duration <72 h; figures are 70–80% at 8 h if these drugs are taken orally
- 'Pill in the pocket' strategy, using flecainide or propafenone loading doses within 5 min of PAF onset, has been shown to reduce hospitalizations
- Atrial flutter occurs in 5–7% of patients receiving oral loading doses of flecainide or propafenone for AF cardioversion (AV nodal blocking drug also required)
- Class IC drugs (e.g. flecainide and propafenone) are ineffective at cardioverting atrial flutter (13–40% success)
- Class IC and III (sotalol and ibutilide) agents are not recommended for cardioversion in patients with history of MI/CCF/significant LVH or LV dysfunction
- **Amiodarone** can be used in heart failure patients, who can be safely commenced as out-patients
- Amiodarone has no negative inotropic effect and low incidence of torsade. Intravenous followed by oral maintenance increases likelihood of conversion but takes longer than with flecainide or propafenone. 600 mg/day for 4 weeks restored sinus rhythm in 34% of patients with long-standing AF (mean 2 years) versus 0% for placebo
- **Ibutilide** (class III anti-arrhythmic) has been shown to cardiovert around 50% of recent onset AF patients within 90 min but is more effective at converting atrial flutter
- Vernakalant (class III anti-arrhythmic) has been shown to cardiovert 52% of AF of <7 days, but is ineffective at converting persistent AF or atrial flutter
- **Sotalol** not effective for acute cardioversion. It may facilitate conversion to sinus rhythm but can cause torsade
- Class 1A drugs procainamide (iv) and quinidine (oral) similarly effective to flecainide for cardioversion of AF of <48 h (60–80%) but side effects mean it is less commonly used

- Magnesium sulphate may potentiate effect of other anti-arrhythmics for cardioverting AF
- BBs, calcium antagonists, and digoxin are usually ineffective for acute cardioversion of AF and digoxin may even be profibrillatory. Short-acting iv betablockers may be useful for rate control (e.g. esmolol).

Maintenance of sinus rhythm

- After cardioversion around 25–50% patients will have a recurrence of AF within 1–2 months and thereafter the recurrence rate is about 10% per year
- Propafenone and flecainide are first-line therapy in patients without structural heart disease (CCF, LV dysfunction, LVH, MI, or CAD). Both reduce recurrence rate by two thirds
- BBs are mainly used for rate control but may be slightly better than placebo at preventing AF recurrence post cardioversion; similar to sotalol. No evidence that any one BB is better than another for prevention of AF
- BBs often used as first-line therapy because of their safety, their AV node effect during AF with fast ventricular response, and, in those with CCF, BBs may reduce the incidence of new onset AF. Also first line in thyrotoxicosis and adrenergically medicated AF
- **Quinidine** effective in maintaining sinus rhythm but associated with ventricular arrhythmias even at low doses and with increased mortality and sudden death at higher doses
- **Disopyramide** rarely used because of its negative inotropic effect and poor tolerance because of anti-muscarinic side effects
- **Sotalol** reduces recurrence rate but not as effective as amiodarone at preventing AF post electrical cardioversion (30% in sinus vs 60% at 2 years and only 10% with placebo). May see hypotension, bradycardia, or prolongation of QT
- **Amiodarone** best drug for maintaining sinus if structural heart disease present
  - Better than sotalol and propafenone
  - Low risk of torsade but multiple other side effects including skin toxicity, thyroid disease, pulmonary toxicity, liver damage, peripheral neuropathy, and visual disturbances
  - Therefore not first line if no structural heart disease
- **Dronedarone** is structural analogue of amiodarone but without iodine atoms and thus lower risk of skin, lung, and eye side effects
  - It is moderately effective in preventing AF recurrence post electrical cardioversion
  - Dronedarone reduces the ventricular rate response during AF by 10–15 bpm
  - The ATHENA study showed a 24% relative risk reduction of the combined endpoint of cardiovascular hospitalisation and death when compared to placebo (mainly driven by a reduction in cardiovascular hospitalisations especially for AF)
  - The more recent PALLAS study, however, showed a significant excess of CV-related deaths, stroke, and hospitalisations due to CV events compared to placebo
  - Dronedarone is recommended by NICE as an option in patients whose AF is not controlled by first-line therapy and who have at least one of the following risk factors: hypertension (requiring at least two different drugs), diabetes, previous TIA/stroke/LA $\geq$50 mm, LVEF $\leq$40%, $\geq$70 years old
  - Dronedarone is contraindicated in patients with:
    - Unstable haemodynamic conditions
    - History of, or current, heart failure or left ventricular systolic dysfunction
    - Permanent AF (duration $\geq$6 months or unknown, and attempts to restore sinus rhythm no longer considered by physician)
    - Liver and lung toxicity related to previous use of amiodarone (liver and renal function need to be monitored).

Drugs post left atrial ablation

- AF or atrial tachycardia incidence is 45% in first 3 months after LA ablation despite antiarrhythmic medication
- Early recurrence may be transient and related to inflammation secondary to RF injury and may subside after 3 months when the inflammation has resolved and autonomic regulation has been restored
- Thus antiarrhythmic therapy is often used for the first 1–3 months post ablation and is associated with a 30% increase chance of remaining in sinus rhythm.

Rate control

Acute rate control

- Initial target ventricular rate should be <110 bpm but this may be lowered if patient remains symptomatic
- Intravenous BBs, diltiazem and verapamil are commonly used and are equally effective in dropping the ventricular rate by 20–30% in 20–30 min. BBs probably better for thyrotoxic or post-MI patients, CCBs in those with airways disease
- Digoxin takes >60 min to work but may be a useful adjunct to BBss in those with impaired LV function given its positive inotropic effect
- Avoid AV nodal-blocking drugs in those with pre-excitation as they will have no effect on the accessory pathway (use iv sodium channel blockers, such as flecainide or ajmaline, instead)
- Intravenous amiodarone can be used when other agents are ineffective or contraindicated but it has a slow onset and may cause phlebitis
- Sotalol has a negative inotropic effect and may cause torsade so not as useful as other drugs.

Rate control in paroxysmal atrial fibrillation

- BBs, verapamil and diltiazem are the drugs of choice for controlling ventricular rate in PAF and they may be used in combination with class IC agents such as propafenone and flecainide to control ventricular rates if AF evolves into flutter
- Digoxin is pro-fibrillatory and therefore should be avoided in PAF or if DC cardioversion is planned.

Rate control in persistent atrial fibrillation

- Aim for rate of 60–80 at rest and 90–115 bpm during exercise
- BBs, verapamil and diltiazem are first-line drugs
- Digoxin prolongs AV node conduction and refractoriness through vagal stimulation. Its effects are negated during exercise because its effect on vagal tone is lost and its effect on AV conduction is counteracted by increased sympathetic tone. Therefore its use is recommended as an adjunct to BBs or CCBs or as monotherapy, mainly in older, sedentary patients.

Congestive cardiac failure and atrial fibrillation

- Amiodarone or dofetilide are the drugs of choice as neither is associated with a deterioration in LV function or proarrhythmia if used carefully (need to monitor QTc, however)
- Standard heart failure medication of BBs, ACE inhibitors and ARBs may delay atrial remodelling and thus reduce risk of AF.

9.7 Electrical cardioversion

Method

- Usually synchronize shock with QRS to avoid shocking during the ventricular vulnerable period when there is a risk of inducing VF
- Current intensity depends on output waveform, selected energy level, and transthoracic impedance
- The higher the impedance, the less current delivered
- Transthoracic impedance is determined by body habitus, skin/electrode interface, and position of electrode paddles
- Antero-posterior paddle position may be more successful at electrically cardioverting patients than the anteroapical position
- Waveforms may be monophasic (max 360 J output) or biphasic (max 200 J output) with biphasic being more efficacious, requiring fewer shocks and less energy
- If cardioversion unsuccessful with maximum energy in both paddle positions, should consider using antiarrhythmic therapy before administering further shocks or internal cardioversion
- Internal cardioversion can be performed with a catheter in the right atrium and a backplate (200–300 J) or between right atrium and coronary sinus/pulmonary artery (around 20 J)
- Transoesophageal cardioversion has also been shown to be safe and effective
- Serum potassium should be within normal range prior to cardioversion because of the risk of ventricular arrhythmia post shock in hypokalaemic patients
- Cardioversion is contraindicated in patients with digitalis toxicity
- Must anticoagulate patients prior to shock as risk of thromboembolism is otherwise 1–2%
- Following electrical cardioversion, CK may rise but not troponin T or I.

Success and recurrence

- Success rate for persistent AF cardioversion is usually around 80%
- Pre-treatment with iv ibutilide, flecainide and sotalol have been shown to lower the energy requirement for DC cardioversion by around 30% and increase the success rate of the procedure. There is also some evidence for oral amiodarone, propafenone, verapamil, and diltiazem but this is inconsistent
- Recurrence risk higher in the first couple of months post cardioversion and antiarrhythmics should therefore be continued in patients at high risk of reversion (e.g. previous reversion)
- Factors increasing recurrence risk are age, increased duration of AF prior to cardioversion, previous recurrences, increased LA size or reduced LA function, and underlying cardiac disease.

9.8 Device therapy

Device based therapy for AF is based on the following:

- Avoiding AF initiation by alleviating bradycardia-induced dispersion of atrial activation and repolarization and atrial overdrive suppression of premature atrial beats (preventative pacing)
- High-rate pacing once arrhythmia has started (anti-tachycardia pacing)
- Atrial or dual chamber pacing reduces risk of AF compared to ventricular pacing alone and may reduce stroke risk

- Algorithms that reduce ventricular pacing reduce the risk of AF
- Biatrial stimulation in patients with sinus node disease has been shown to increase AF-free survival compared to support pacing or high right atrial pacing.

Preventative pacing algorithms

- AF most commonly initiated by premature atrial complexes (PACs) (48%) and sinus bradycardia (33%) rather than spontaneous sudden onset (17%)
- Algorithms have therefore been developed to prevent bradycardia and avoid significant atrial rate variations associated with PACs
- These work by pacing just above the intrinsic rate and elevating the rate after spontaneous PACs, with transient overdrive pacing after mode-switch episodes and increased pacing post-exercise to prevent abrupt drops in heart rate
- Atrial pacing algorithms have only a small overall benefit in preventing AF, and AF alone is not an indication for preventative pacing
- There is no trial evidence that any pacing algorithms provide long-term prevention or termination of AF
- Atrial defibrillator use is hampered by the fact that even low-energy shocks are painful.

9.9 Ablation

Atrioventricular node ablation

- Useful strategy in permanent AF if rate control difficult with drugs
- This may improve exercise tolerance, LVEF, and quality of life
- Risk of sudden death at 1 year is 2%, with 6% overall mortality, similar to medical therapy for AF
- AV node ablation with CRT implant in those with AF and heart failure has been shown to improve LVEF but smaller gains seen in NYHA/6MWT/quality of life compared to those in sinus rhythm
- Nonetheless, an 'ablate and pace' strategy in these patients may have a better outcome than pharmacological rate control.

LA catheter ablation

- First reports of catheter ablation appeared in 1994
- Pulmonary veins are dominant source of AF triggers in 60–94% of PAF
- Sleeve of atrial muscle extends into PVs allowing preferential conduction, unidirectional conduction block, and re-entry
- Initial approach of direct focal ablation of PVs difficult and led to scarring of the ablated tissue with PV stenosis and possible occlusion
- Next approach was to isolate all PVs using circumferential mapping catheters close to or within the PV ostia; there was still a risk of ostial stenosis. AF recurrence rates remained high
- Currently ablation has moved more into the atrium to reduce risk of PV stenosis. Long linear lesion may be made around each PV or around both ipsilateral PVs together
- AF may terminate during PVI in up to 75% of patients and around half of PAF patients can no longer sustain AF following PVI suggesting the PVs are the substrate in maintaining AF in these patients
- Circumferential ablation is a purely anatomical approach that does not require electrical disconnection of the encircled areas. Only a single trans-septal puncture is required

(no mapping needed). Procedure time shorter as no waiting after successful isolation is required. Up to 45% of PVs not isolated with this approach
- Vast majority of AF recurrence post AF ablation is in patients with PV–LA re-conduction. Repeat PVI may eliminate AF in 90% of patients. Thus important to achieve complete PV isolation.

Additional lines
- The multiple wavelet hypothesis suggests that AF is maintained by multiple re-entrant wavelets propagating simultaneously in the atria and there must be a minimum mass of electrically continuous myocardium present to sustain the re-entry wavelets
- Additional lines prevent this re-entry, e.g. roof line (connecting upper PVs), left isthmus line (connecting inferior left PV to MV annulus; 68% require ablation from within the CS with subsequent risk of damaging the close-lying circumflex artery), anterior line (roof to MV annulus), posterior line (between septal and lateral PVs across posterior LA—risk of atrio-oesophageal fistula)
- Linear lesions should be trans-mural but there is therefore a risk of tamponade, stroke, and fistulae. Incomplete linear lesions may be arrhythmogenic, allowing rapid AV conduction of gap-related atrial tachycardia
- Initially 'complete' lines may develop conduction gaps later.

Alternative approaches
- Complex fractionated electrogram ablation without PVI has been shown to be favourable in single-centre studies
- Ablating ganglionic plexuses at atrial sites where vagal response is observed after local stimulation is currently being evaluated.

Imaging
3D imaging (CT or MR) requires careful registration. Accuracy may reach 2 mm.

Complications
See Table 9.5.

Indications and success rate for LA ablation
- For PAF, should have frequent symptomatic episodes of AF resistant to at least one anti-arrhythmic drug. 70–90% success rates reported at 1 year but patients may have required more than one attempt and some remained on anti-arrhythmic medication
- For persistent or permanent AF, ablation is more difficult. Should have significant symptoms. Patients with LVEF may have particular benefit even if not symptomatic. Procedure may be long and difficult. Reported success rates at 1 year range from around 55–80%. As for PAF, patients in studies may have had more than one procedure and remained on anti-arrhythmic medication.

Surgical ablation
- Involves compartmentalizing the atria into segments too small to sustain AF
- Now usually involves PV isolation
- Commonly used in patients who need cardiac surgery for another reason (e.g. CABG, valve surgery).

Post ablation
- Should resume anti-coagulation post ablation for a minimum of 2 months and then maintain if CHADS2 score of ≥2.

Table 9.5 Complications of left atrial ablation

Complication	Symptoms	Acute onset	Late onset	Incidence	Prevention/treatment
Thromboembolic events	Stroke TIA	Yes	With AF recurrence postablation	~1%	Periprocedural anticoagulation Exclusion of pre-existing intracardiac thrombi Continuous flush of trans-septal sheaths Use of irrigated tip catheters
PV stenosis/ occlusion	Cough Pneumonia Dyspnoea Haemoptysis	Yes	Yes	~2%	Avoid intra-PV ablation Imaging of PV ostium; 3D imaging when typical symptoms Dilatation of symptomatic PV stenosis/recanalization if needed
Atrio-oesophageal fistula formation	Unexplained fever Dysphagia Neurologic signs (seizures)	Typically within 48 hours	Possible after penetration of an oesophageal ulceration	<1%	Avoid excessive energy delivery at sites close to posterior LA wall. Immediate 3D imaging Avoid endoscopy Emergency surgery
Air embolism	ST elevation Pressure drop and bradycardia Cardiac arrest	Within seconds	Only with fistula formation	Transient event, probably underreported	Check sheaths for air leak. Continuous flush of all trans-septal sheaths Perform CPR if necessary
Tamponade	Hypotension Cardiac arrest	Within minutes	Rare	Up to 6% of cases	Avoid direct mechanical trauma during trans-septal puncture. Avoid 'pops' and excessive contact force. Treat with pericardiocentesis or surgical intervention if percutaneous approach unsuccessful
Phrenic nerve injury	Diaphragm palsy with subsequent dyspnoea	Within seconds to minutes		~0.5% Mostly transient event Incidence higher in balloon devices	Avoid ablation in vicinity of phrenic nerve (especially at RSPV)

Gastropathy	Dysphagia pyloric spasm gastric hypomotility	No	Yes	Probably underreported	Avoid excessive energy deployment
Vascular complication (AV fistula formation, groin haematomas, aneurysms)	Local pain Swelling Bruising	Yes	Yes	~1% in WW survey	Careful puncture technique Sheath removal after restored haemostasis
Death overall				0.7%	

9.10 Special situations

Wolff–Parkinson–White syndrome

Most accessory pathways (AP) do not have decremental properties and thus patients with pre-excitation are at risk of rapid conduction across the AP, which may degenerate into VF and SCD.

- Catheter ablation of overt APs are recommended to reduce risk of SCD (efficacy of 95%)
- Survivors of SCD with an overt AP should be referred for catheter ablation
- Patients with AP and high risk of AF or in high-risk profession (e.g. pilot, bus driver) should be offered catheter ablation
- Avoid AV nodal-blocking drugs in these patients as this encourages conduction down the accessory pathway.

Pregnancy

- AF in pregnancy rare
- Avoid all anti-arrhythmic medication if possible
- DC cardiovert if haemodynamic compromise (safe in all stages of pregnancy)
- BBs particularly harmful in first trimester
- Amiodarone has harmful foetal effects
- Warfarin teratogenic so avoid in first trimester and for 1 month before due date (use LMWH or UFH instead).

Post-operative atrial fibrillation

- Peak incidence 2–4 days post cardiac surgery
- Atrial flutter and ATs also common
- BBs effective at preventing AF especially if given pre and post surgery
- Amiodarone and sotalol also effective at preventing post-op AF
- Most post-op AF spontaneously converts to sinus within 24 h
- Amiodarone or DCC can be used to cardiovert patients who develop AF post surgery.

Pulmonary disease

- Treat underlying disease
- Avoid non-selective BBs, sotalol, adenosine, propafenone if evidence of bronchospasm
- Can give verapamil/diltiazem
- Can give small doses of β-1 selective BBs such as bisoprolol
- Can give flecainide to chemically cardiovert.

9.11 Summary

- AF is a common arrhythmia that may reduce exercise capacity and quality of life
- Complications include stroke, heart failure, and sudden death
- Paroxysmal AF may progress to persistent and permanent AF
- Predisposing conditions include hypertension, heart failure, structural heart disease, diabetes, thyroid disease, and COPD
- Cause of AF is multi-factorial and complex

- Anticoagulation is only treatment proven to reduce AF-related death
- The risk of thromboembolism is the same for PAF as for persistent/permanent AF
- The $CHADS_2$ and CHA_2DS_2VASc scoring system can be used to risk-stratify patients with regards to thromboembolic risk
- HAS-BLED scoring system can be used to risk-stratify patients with regards to bleeding risk when considering thrombophrophylactic therapy
- No advantage to VKA + anti-platelet in majority of patients
- Many drugs available for pharmacological cardioversion, maintenance of sinus rhythm, and ventricular rate control
- DC cardioversion more successful at cardioverting patients than drugs
- Risk of reversion to AF post cardioversion dependent on age, previous recurrences, LA size, and underlying cardiac disease
- Pacing algorithms have been developed to prevent or terminate AF but limited with limited success
- AV node ablation is an option in symptomatic patients refractory to drugs
- LA catheter ablation an option in symptomatic patients with drug refractory AF
- Success rate of LA catheter ablation around 70–90% at 1 year for PAF and 55–80% for persistent AF (may require several attempts, however)
- Special care needs to be taken when treating patients with accessory pathways, who are pregnant, have pulmonary disease, or are post-op.

Further reading

Camm AJ, Lüscher TF, Serruys PW (eds). *The European Society of Cardiology Textbook of Cardiovascular Medicine* (2nd edn). Oxford University Press, 2009.

Gage BF, Waterman AD, Shannon W, Boechler M, Rich MW, Radford MJ. Validation of clinical classification schemes for predicting stroke: results from the National Registry of Atrial Fibrillation. *JAMA*, 2001; 285(22): 2864–70.

Lip GY, Nieuwlaat R, Pisters R, Lane DA, Crijns HJ. Refining clinical risk stratification for predicting stroke and thromboembolism in atrial fibrillation using a novel risk factor-based approach: the euro heart survey on atrial fibrillation. *Chest*, 2010; 137(2): 263–72.

NICE. IPG349. Blocking the left atrial appendage of the heart to prevent stroke in non-valvular atrial fibrillation, using a catheter. NICE, 2010.

NICE. Technology appraisal guidance TA197. Dronedarone for the treatment of non-permanent atrial fibrillation. NICE, 2010.

Pisters R, Lane DA, Nieuwlaat R, de Vos CB, Crijns HJ, Lip GY. A novel user-friendly score (HAS-BLED) to assess 1-year risk of major bleeding in patients with atrial fibrillation: the euro heart survey. *Chest*, 2010; 138(5):1093–100.

Pericardial disease

10.1 Anatomy of the pericardium

- The pericardium is a thin, predominantly fibrous layer of tissue encapsulating the heart and roots of the great vessels
- It is attached via ligaments to the sternum and vertebrae, anchoring it in place
- It covers the entire heart other than a small posterior part of the left atrium
- It extends upwards to cover the proximal parts of the great vessels.

The components of the pericardium are as follows:

Viceral pericardium

- Monolayer of ciliated mesothelial (serosal) cells adherent to the surface of the epicardium. It is of microscopic thickness.

Parietal pericardium

- Collagen and elastin layer lined with mesothelial (serosal) cells
- Contains both elastic and collagenous matrices, which result in the physical properties of compliance and stiffness
- Anatomically, the parietal layer of pericardium is only 1 mm thick (although current imaging modalities detect it at 2 mm thick).

Pericardial space and fluid

- The continuity of the mesothelial visceral and parietal pericardial layers establishes the pericardial space, completely lined by a layer of serosal cells
- 15–50 ml of a high phospholipid ultrafiltrate fluid acts as a lubricant between these two layers
- The visceral and parietal layers can move up to 1.5 cm over each other per cardiac cycle
- There is continuous production and absorption of pericardial fluid
- Pericardial fluid usually drains via the thoracic and right lymphatic ducts.

The pericardial sac forms a complex shape as it envelopes the chambers of the heart and forms sleeves around the roots of the great vessels. See Figure 10.1.

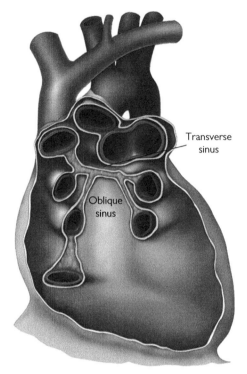

Copyright © 2009 by Saunders, an imprint of Elsevier Inc.

Figure 10.1 Posterior parietal pericardial anatomy.

Reprinted from 'Pericardial diseases: clinical diagnostic imaging atlas', Stuart J. Hutchison, copyright 2008 with permission from Elsevier.

10.2 Physiology of the pericardium

The functions of the pericardium and pericardial fluid include the following:

- It is predominantly made of collagen, which results in a tough physical barrier to the spread of infection and malignancy from adjacent organs
- It is attached via ligaments to the sternum and vertebrae, anchoring the heart, preventing excessive cardiac movement, and protecting it from acceleration/deceleration forces
- It reduces friction between the heart and adjacent tissues
- It has limited ability to stretch, thereby preventing acute volume distension and myocardial stretch, preserving sarcomere architecture and maintaining myocardial systolic function
- It acts to distribute hydrostatic forces over the heart.

Intrapericardial pressure

- Intrapericardial pressure is usually slightly negative and is an important determinant of the filling pressure of the cardiac chambers

> **The true (transmural) filling pressure of the cardiac chambers is diastolic pressure less intrapericardial pressure.**

- As the intrapericardial pressure elevates over 0 mmHg, the true (transmural) filling pressure of the chamber reduces—the chamber will underfill during diastole

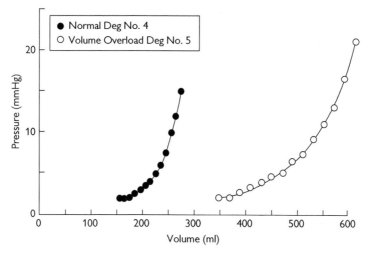

Figure 10.2 Pericarial pressure/volume relationship.

Reproduced from GL Freeman, M M LeWinter, 'Pericardial adaptations during chronic cardiac dilatation in dogs', *Circulation Research* 54 (3):294 (1984), with permission from Wolters Kluwer Health.

- When the intrapericardial pressure exceeds the diastolic pressure of a cardiac chamber, the chamber wall will compress inwards and collapse during diastole
- Once the pericardial reserve volume is exceeded pressure rise is rapid
- Equally (in these situations) removal of a small volume of fluid results in a rapid drop in pressure
- The transition from compliance to non-compliance happens more gradually in a chronically volume-overloaded pericardium
- Figure 10.2 shows pressure/volume relations in an animal with no previous pericardial effusion (closed circle) and an animal with a chronically volume overloaded pericardium (open circle).

Ventricular interdependence

- The parietal pericardium is compliant within the range of usual cardiac filling but can only stretch a limited further amount beyond this
- Overfilling of one ventricle will result in reduced filling of the other: ventricular interdependence
- In physiological states, during inspiration, RV filling increases with a parallel reduction in filling of the LV; during expiration this is reversed
- When the pericardium reaches its maximum 'stretch' and intrapericardial pressures begin to elevate, the phenomenon of ventricular interdependence becomes pathological
- The increased filling of one ventricle results in underfilling of the other. This is seen in the following disease states:
  - Constrictive pericarditis (non-compliant pericardium)
  - Effuso-constrictive pericarditis (non-compliant pericardium and fluid)
  - Pericardial tamponade
  - Right ventricular infarction with acute severe dilatation of the RV
  - Tumour encasement of the heart (non-compliant tumour mass).

10.3 Acute pericarditis

- Pericarditis is a clinical syndrome caused by inflammation of the pericardium
- It encompasses a vast spectrum from mild, clinically silent disease to fulminant purulent inflammation

- In acute pericarditis, there is a thickening of both the parietal and serosal pericardium with rough irregularity of the surfaces
- The approach to patients with suspected acute pericarditis involves:
    - Establishing the clinical diagnosis of acute pericarditis
    - Establishing the aetiology of the acute pericarditis
    - Assessing for complications (such as pericardial effusion and tamponade)
    - Treatment.

Establishing a clinical diagnosis

Acute pericarditis is characterized by:

- Chest pain
- Pericardial friction rub (seen in 60–80%)
- Typical ECG repolarization changes (seen in 80%).

The diagnosis of acute pericarditis requires at least two of these three elements.

- Acute pericarditis usually presents with subretrosternal chest pain (may be pleuritic), exacerbated by lying flat, or twisting
- A minority of patients experience a more visceral type of pain, which is readily confused with ischaemic pain
- Other symptoms depend on the aetiology of the pericarditis but often include prodromal fever, malaise, and myalgia.

Physical signs are shown in Table 10.1.

- The ECG is abnormal in 80% of patients with acute pericarditis; characteristic ECG findings are outlined in Table 10.2
- All four stages are only seen in 50% of cases and only if the underlying ECG is normal
- Baseline abnormalities render changes much less sensitive and specific for acute pericarditis

Table 10.1 Physical signs in pericarditis

Physical sign	Characteristic features
Pericardial rub (Described in some texts as being pathognomic of acute pericarditis). Found in up to 80% of cases of acute pericarditis. Optimal positioning may be required to increase detection (Supine, left lateral position with arms above head or sitting and leaning forward. Listening at end-expiration with the diaphragm). Note: pericardial rubs are often transient, therefore repeated examination may be required to detect them.	Typically made up of three components related to the motion of the heart: 1) systolic motion 2) early diastolic filling 3) late diastolic atrial contraction when in sinus rhythm. If only 2 or 1 component audible then may be confused with cardiac murmur. Note: pericardial rub can be audible even in the presence of a pericardial effusion.
Pericardial effusion (May be absent in 50% of cases) or tamponade	See Section 10.5
Pleural effusion	Particularly of the left side in patients with pleuropericarditis
Ewarts' sign	Bronchial breathing at the left base caused by compression of the left lower lobe of the lung.

Table 10.2 ECG changes found in pericarditis

ECG in pericarditis	Characteristic findings	ECG example
Stage I May be confused with acute MI or early repolarization (normal variant of repolarization)	Anterior and inferior concave ST segment elevation (usually less then 5 mm) with positive T waves in several leads. PR segment depression (indicating atrial injury).	
Early stage II **Late stage II**	ST segments return to baseline. PR remains deviated. T waves progressively flatten and invert.	
Stage III (an ECG at this stage on its own cannot be reliably differentiated from diffuse myocardial injury, biventricular strain or myocarditis.)	Generalized T wave inversion	
Stage IV (occasionally this stage does not occur and there are permanent T wave changes on the ECG.)	ECG returns to pre-pericarditis state.	

Typical lead involvement includes I, II, aVL, aVF, and V3-V6. The ST segment is always depressed in aVR, frequently in V1, and occasionally in V2. Pericarditis is likely if in V6 the J point is >25% of the height of the T wave apex (using the PR segment as baseline). Reproduced with permission from ECGpedia.org.

- Pericarditis is a clinical diagnosis and cannot be made echocardiographically
- Most cases of pericarditis do not develop a significant pericardial effusion
- The role of an echocardiogram is to: identify pericardial effusion, identify pericardial thickening, and assess LV function
- Routine blood analyses usually only provide non-specific information of raised inflammatory markers

- Small troponin elevation is seen in 35–50% of patients indicating epicardial involvement
- Additional blood tests should be tailored to identifying the aetiology of the suspected pericarditis depending on the nature of patient's presentation
- A CXR will show cardiomegaly when effusions exceed 250 ml
- The classic features of pericardial effusion are described as a 'water bottle' or 'globular' heart shadow
- Evidence of left pleural effusion should be sought and the CXR is useful in identifying additional pulmonary/mediastinal pathology, which may point towards aetiology.

Establish the aetiology of acute pericarditis

Acute pericarditis is usually either associated with an obvious clinical condition—making a cause–effect relationship likely—or is idiopathic (routine diagnostic tests fail to uncover the aetiology—the majority of these cases are likely to be viral). Figure 10.3 outlines the aetiological classification of acute pericarditis.

Idiopathic and viral

- In the western world (immunologically competent patients with no predisposing diseases) 90% of cases of acute pericarditis are idiopathic (presumed viral)
- If the clinical features of acute pericarditis fade over a few days then the likelihood of the aetiology being idiopathic approaches 100%
- The most common specific viral causes include coxsachievirus, echovirus, adenovirus, mumps virus, varicella zoster virus, and Epstein-Barr virus
- A diagnosis can be made by comparing acute and convalescent neutralising antibodies

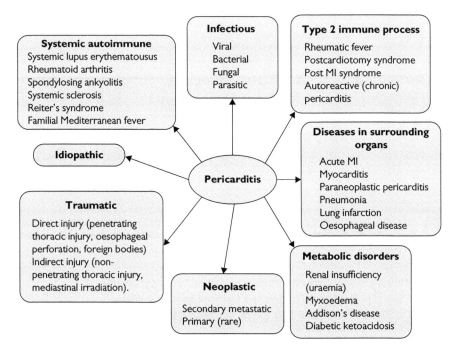

Figure 10.3 Aetiological classification of pericarditis.

- Because viral pericarditis is usually a self-limiting disease, viral serology and invasive pericardial procedures in order to clarify the exact aetiology are not usually undertaken.

Bacterial

- Purulent bacterial pericarditis is most commonly caused by streptococci, staphylococci, pneumococci, Gram-negative rods, *Haemophilus influenza, Mycoplasma*, and *Legionella*
- Patients more likely to develop bacterial pericarditis include those with pneumonia, empyema, those recently having undergone chest surgery, and the immunocompromised
- Patients with bacterial pericarditis are more likely to develop tamponade
- TB pericarditis is rare in the western world. Its incidence is increased in immunocompromised patients, especially those with HIV infection.

Systemic disease

- In patients who are known to suffer from a disease predisposing them to pericarditis (renal failure, recent MI, autoimmune disease, widespread neoplasia) it is very likely that acute pericarditis is caused by that disease
- Of patients with autoimmune disease, up to 30% with SLE, 30% with rheumatoid arthritis and over 50% with systemic sclerosis have evidence of episodes of pericarditis
- Pericarditis caused by systemic autoimmune disease is often clinically mild or silent
- Some form of pericardial inflammation in patients with uraemia is common and up to 30% of myxedematous patients develop pericarditis
- Other metabolic causes of pericarditis are rare.

Post myocardial infarct and myocarditis

- Early post-infarction pericarditis develops in approximately 10% of patients 2 to 3 days after a transmural infarction
- Delayed post-infarction pericarditis (Dressler's syndrome) occurs 2 weeks or so after MI
- Up to 30% of patients with myocarditis develop an associated pericarditis.

Diagnostic pathway in acute pericarditis

Figure 10.4 is a pragmatic diagnostic pathway.

Management of acute pericarditis

Inpatient versus outpatient management

Consider the risk of an immediate complication, adverse aetiology, and long-term sequlae when considering which patients need inpatient care (see Table 10.3).

- Patients with acute idiopathic or viral pericarditis should rest until the symptoms abate
- Pain and fever should be managed with paracetamol and either aspirin (500 mg–1 g QDS) or NSAIDs such as ibuprofen (300–800 mg QDS)
- Treatment should continue whilst pain and fever are present and should be tapered gradually over 3–4 weeks
- Concurrent use of anticoagulation during pericarditis increases the risk of developing effusion and tamponade. Consider changing from warfarin to heparin during the acute phase
- Additional administration of colchicine may prevent relapses and manage symptoms (see COPE trial—colchicine for acute pericarditis—see Further Reading section)
- Systemic cortosteriod therapy should be avoided—it is probably associated with an increased risk of relapse

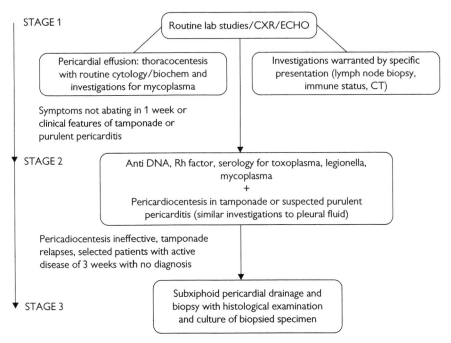

Figure 10.4 Protocol for routine diagnostic approach to patients with acute pericarditis.

Table 10.3 Features recommending a patient for inpatient investigation and treatment

- Pericardial effusion >2 cm
- History of anticoagulation use
- History of concurrent malignancy
- Chest trauma
- Fever >38°C
- Subacute onset over days
- Immunosuppressed
- Elevated troponin or leucocyte count

Adapted from 'Risk prediction in pericarditis: who to keep in hospital?', David H. Spodick, *Heart* 94, 398–399, copyright 2008 with permission from BMJ Publishing Group Ltd.

- Its use should be restricted to connective tissue diseases, autoreactive, or uremic pericarditis (intrapericardial administration of corticosteroids is highly effective and avoids systemic side effects)
- To avoid rebound pericarditis as steroids are tapered, NSAIDS or cochicine should be introduced early.

Recurrent pericarditis

Recurrent pericarditis occurs in 10–25% of cases and includes the following types:

- Incessant—discontinuation of anti-inflammatory therapy results in relapses
- Intermittent—symptom-free intervals without therapy of >6 weeks.

Relapses may be accounted for by inadequate courses of anti-inflammatories as well as the use of corticosteroids.

- There is no definitive treatment for the prevention of relapses
- Long-term colchicine may be advantageous (i.e. for one year)
- Pericardectomy may be considered as a last resort
- Serious complications, such as the development of constrictive pericarditis, are rare.

10.4 Pericardial effusion

Many pericardial effusions are incidental findings on ECHO and CT. They consist of increased pericardial fluid, pus, or blood. The causes of pericardial effusions are:

- Any cause of acute pericarditis; most commonly idiopathic due to high incidence
- Malignancy: pericardial tumour involvement
- Iatrogenic: post cardiac surgery or perforation of coronary artery post PCI
- Acute bleed into pericardium from cardiac rupture or dissection of ascending aorta
- Hydrostatic forces: heart failure, lymphatic obstruction, raised central pressure.

Pericardial effusions are qualified as small, moderate, or large (Table 10.4).

- Sizing of the pericardial effusion may be misleading, as often effusions are not uniformly distributed
- Importantly, the size of an effusion often has a poor association with its haemodynamic consequences and is more of a marker of its chronicity.

Diagnostic evaluation

- History, examination, and investigations should be focused on elucidating the cause of the pericardial effusion and identifying any haemodynamic consequence
- In the majority of patients presenting with a moderate or large pericardial effusion, an obvious causal disease will be present
- Inflammatory features associated with pericardial effusion are highly suggestive of acute idiopathic pericarditis
- Moderate–large pericardial effusions persisting for longer then 3 months are considered chronic. In most cases, the cause is unknown
- A large pericardial effusion without tamponade is likely to be an idiopathic, chronic pericardial effusion
- Even in asymptomatic patients, intrapericardial pressures are usually elevated and patients are at an increased risk of developing unexpected tamponade

Table 10.4 Quantification of pericardial effusions

Size	Depth	Volume	Approach
Minimal/'no effusion'	<5 mm	50–100 ml	
Small	5–15 mm	100–400 ml	If asymptomatic and effusion stable at 6 months, long-term follow up not needed
Moderate	15–30 mm	400–1000 ml	Aetiological diagnosis should be sought and patient followed up
Large	>30 mm	>1000 ml	Aetiological diagnosis should be sought and patient followed up

Table 10.5 Assessment of patients with pericardial effusion

Assessment	Comments
History and physical examination	Focused on elucidating the cause and haemodynamic consequence
ECG	Assess for evidence of low voltage, electrical alternans, pericarditis, recent MI
CXR	Assess for associated pleural or parenchymal lung disease, abnormal hilar, or abnormal aortic contours
Serum biochemistry	Renal function, thyroid function
Serum haematology	FBC
Blood cultures	If infection suspected
Troponin	If recent MI is suspected
Immunological testing	If autoimmune disease suspected, e.g. SLE, RA
PPD skin testing	If TB is suspected
CT	If malignancy is suspected

- In patients presenting with tamponade and no inflammatory features, the effusion is likely to be neoplastic
- Echocardiography is the diagnostic test of choice for evaluating pericardial effusions
- ECHO can establish the presence of pericardial fluid, identify important underlying causes (MI, masses, aortic dissection), evaluate haemodynamic consequence of the pericardial effusion, evaluate optimal drainage method if needed, and guide drainage.

Minimum assessment of a pericardial effusion should include the following (see Table 10.5):

- Analysis of pericardial fluid has a low aetiological detection rate when undertaken in the absence of features of tamponade (5%)
- In the context of tamponade aetiological detection rates may be up to 40%.

The haemodynamic consequence of a pericardial effusion is far more important than its size. Only a small subset of pericardial effusions result in tamponade.

10.5 Tamponade

- Tamponade is a clinical syndrome with an eventual low-output, high venous state
- The diagnosis is made using bedside clinical signs and objective testing (echocardiography).

In a patient presenting with cardiac tamponade, the clinical goals are to:

- Establish the diagnosis
- Establish the aetiology
- Stabilize the patient.

Establish the diagnosis

Clinical features may include:
- Chest discomfort, pericardial rub, quiet heart sounds, dyspnoea, tachycardia
- Raised JVP with loss of y descent
- **Kussmauls' sign** (elevation of JVP during inspiration)

Table 10.6 Indications of cardiac tamponade

Imaging modality	Features indicating tamponade
ECG	Low voltage if there is significantly sized pericardial effusion. Electrical alternans (specific but insensitive sign—only seen in 20% of tamponade—only seen in large effusions where the heart responds to tamponade with dynamic contraction resulting in swinging in the fluid—seen in large malignant effusions).
CXR	200–250 ml fluid accumulation is required before the CXR starts to show signs of effusion. Useful to look for adjacent lung and mediastinal disease.
ECHO	TTE is usually adequate. ECHO should be used to confirm tamponade, determine cause (if possible), and determine the safest and most logical method of drainage.

- **Pulsus paradoxus** (detected as a fall in BP and pulse pressure of >10 mmHg occurring during inspiration); total pulsus paradoxus is where no pulse can be felt during inspiration
- Falling BP (once the elevation in heart rate and vasoconstriction fail to compensate for the low stroke volume)
- **Beck's triad** (hypotension, quiet heart sounds, raised JVP with absent y descent).

Investigations

See Table 10.6. ECHO features may include:

- Loss of cardiac transmural distension pressure, which results in inward displacement of chamber walls (RA and RV) and eventual compression
- RA collapse, which only has a 30% positive predictive value of tamponade
- RA and RV collapse, which is more specific, with a positive predictive value of 74%
- Increase in RV volumes during inspiration and leftward movement of the septum during diastole (exaggeration of normal)
- IVC distension with <50% reduction on inspiration. In large pericardial effusion there may be marked swinging of the heart beat to beat
- Increased tricuspid and pulmonary flow velocities (>50%) with decreased mitral and aortic flow velocities (>25%) during inspiration (exaggeration of normal). See Figure 10.5.

Stabilize the patient

- The definitive management of patients with features of cardiac tamponade associated with life-threatening haemodynamic changes is pericardiocentesis (see Box 10.1)
- Pericardiocentesis and drainage in the context of tamponade is life saving
- The diagnostic yield of both pericardiocentesis and drainage with biopsy is significantly higher when done in the context of tamponade rather then purely for diagnostic purposes (35% vs 6%)
- It is important to recognize intrapericardial thrombus vs fresh blood, as pericardiocentsis cannot be used to drain thrombus and can result in chamber perforation during attempts
- Surgical pericardial drainage is the preferred method of stabilization in cardiac tamponade caused by thrombus
- Thrombus may be caused by the following:
  - Open cardiac surgery
  - Trauma (penetrating, blunt, iatrogenic)
  - Myocardial rupture post infarct
  - Aortic dissection with intrapericarial rupture.

(A)

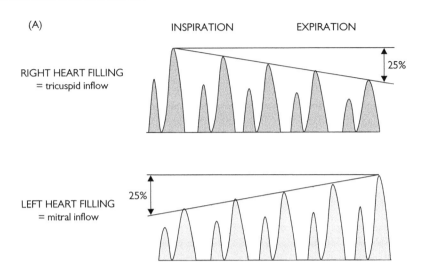

(B)

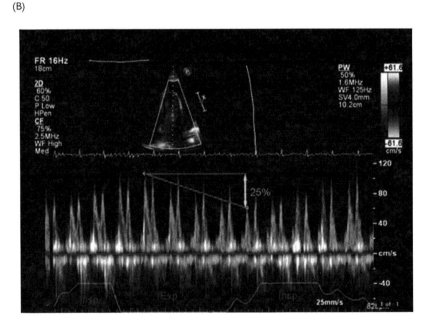

Figure 10.5 Tricuspid and mitral inflow Doppler velocities.

10.6 Constrictive pericardial disease

Constrictive pericardial disease refers to the syndrome of pathophysiological compression of the heart caused by rigid, thickened, and often fused pericardial membranes.

- The stiff, non-compliant pericardium resists deformation outwards resulting in increased diastolic pressures with reduced diastolic filling

BOX 10.1 PROCEDURE FOR PERICARDIOCENTESIS

The following information is not intended to outline step by step the practical skill of performing pericardiocentesis. Rather, it is intended to summarize key points for consideration before, during, and after undertaking this practical procedure.

Pericardial fluid drainage can be achieved by:

- Pericardiocentesis tap (with needle)
- Pericardiocentesis catheter drainage (Seldinger techniques or chest tube techniques via surgical approaches)
- Percutaneous balloon percardiostomy
- Pericardial window
- Surgical percardiectomy.

Considerations pre-procedure

- Avoid positive pressure ventilation (invasive or non-invasive) as this will reduce cardiac output
- If tamponade occurs in the context of trauma then surgical drainage is required
- Where possible, formal consent should be sought from the patient before undertaking pericardiocentesis. The risk of the procedure in experienced hands is as follows:
  - 1% major complications (death, cardiac arrest, vascular or cardiac cavity laceration requiring surgery, pneumothorax requiring chest drain)
  - 4% minor complications (sepsis, vasovagal reflex, pneumothorax not requiring chest drain, non-sustained VT, pleuropericardial fistulae).

Considerations during the procedure

- Whenever possible, pericardiocentesis should be performed with imaging support. However, in the context of circulatory collapse, pericardiocentiesis should not be delayed and should be done immediately
  - Echocardiography should be used to establish the safest and easiest access site. Agitated saline can be used to confirm position within the pericardial space
  - Fluroscopy can be used to visualize the guide wire to ensure it is within the pericardium. The guide wire should be seen wrapping around the inside of the pericardial space and not advancing into the SCV or pulmonary trunk
- Position the patient at 30° to allow maximum fluid accumulation posteriorly
- As with all invasive procedures, it is essential to use sterile technique.

Considerations post-procedure

- It is important for further management that the cause of pericardial fluid accumulation is identified. Pericardial fluid should be sent to the labs for analysis; including cytology, microbiology, and biochemistry for glucose, amylase, protein, and haemoglobin if relevant.

- Eventually the cardiac chamber diastolic pressures become equal to each other
- The reduced diastolic filling initially limits stroke volume, and then reduces stroke volume
- The stroke volume becomes fixed and thus the cardiac output is reliant on heart rate (tachycardia).

The stiffened pericardium also resists deformation inwards resulting in exaggerated ventricular recoil outward in early diastole on cessation of ventricular contraction. Due to the phenomena of ventricular interdependence, inspiration results in increased right ventricular diastolic pressures with the consequence of a fall in left ventricular venous return and pressure.

The approach to a patient with suspected pericardial constriction is:

- Establish the diagnosis
- Establish the aetiology
- Treatment.

Establish the diagnosis

Patients usually present with:

- Symptoms secondary to right sided heart failure
- Symptoms secondary to low cardiac output.

There is often a delay in diagnosis (typically 1–2 years) due to the insidious onset of symptoms. Physical signs are shown in Table 10.7.

Diagnostic approach

See Table 10.8.

Table 10.7 Physical signs of constrictive pericarditis

Physical signs	Features associated with physical signs
Features of right sided heart failure	• Enlarged liver • Ascites • Peripheral oedema • Pleural effusions
JVP	• Increased V wave (due to increased RA diastolic filling pressures) • Prominent y descent (due to brisk early diastolic recoil) • Kussmaul's sign (failure of JVP to fall during inspiration or increase in JVP during inspiration indicating severe non-compliance of right sided cardiac chambers)
Proto-diastolic pericardial knock	• As the ventricles relax and 'knock' against the stiffened pericardium (may be confused clinically with the opening snap heard in mitral stenosis)

Table 10.8 Diagnostic approach in constrictive pericarditis

Diagnostic tool	Possible findings in constrictive pericarditis
ECG	May be normal • Atrial arrhythmias common (incidence 25%) • P wave abnormalities (due to atrial enlargement) • Low voltage complexes (if pericardium is thickened impairing surface reading of ECG) • Pseudo-infarction pattern (rare—associated with penetration of fibrotic process into myocardium
CXR	May be normal • Mild cardiac silouhette enlargement with LA enlargement is common • Perciardial calcification • Pleural plaques • Pleural effusions common

(Continued)

Table 10.8 *(Continued)*

Diagnostic tool	Possible findings in constrictive pericarditis
ECHO • ECHO measurements should be taken with concurrent respirometry tracings • ECHO features will be compounded by concurrent AF, abnormal breathing effort as well as valvular/myocardial disease • TTE is not a good imaging tool for measuring pericardial thickening. Although TOE can be used to assess pericardial thickening, CMR and CT are the preferred tests	*Mitral inflow* • Exaggerated interventricular interdependence with >15% reduction in mitral inflow during inspiration *Tricuspid regurgitation velocity* • Exaggeration of interventricular interdependence with >25% reduction in tricuspid inflow velocities during expiration *Elevated central pressure* • Dilated IVC • Failure of IVC collapse during inspiration • Spontaneous contrast in IVC *Interventricular septum* Classically the septum appears to flutter during diastole • Early diastolic motion towards the left ventricle (due to early diastolic pressure dip). Best appreciated using M mode *Tissue Doppler* • Lateral mitral annulus E prime >8cm/sec • Features of diastolic dysfunction as myocardial relaxation is inhibited by the stiffened pericardium—E/A ratio exaggeration with shortening of deceleration time
Cardiac CT and cardiac MRI • Cardiac CT and MRI are not used to assess the complex haemodynamics found in constrictive pericarditis • Note: not all patients with pericardial constriction have pericardial thickening and not all patients with pericardial thickening have pericardial constriction	• Useful in measuring pericardial thickness and assessing for calcification • Tube like configuration of one or both ventricles • Enlargement of one or both atria • Narrowing of AV grooves and congestion of the caval veins • Useful if assessing underlying myocardial fibrosis (a poor prognosticator for pericardectomy)
Right and left cardiac catheterization • Measurements should be taken with simultaneous respirometer • Pacing may be needed to overcome R–R interval variability in patients in AF	• Interdependence of filling. Simultaneous increase in RV systolic pressure and decrease of LV systolic pressure during the first or second beats of inspiration • Pulmonary capillary wedge pressure/LV diastolic pressure gradient increase of >5% during inspiration. • Elevated RV diastolic pressure >1/3 of RV systolic pressure • Pulmonary artery pressure <50 mmHg • LV end diastolic pressure: RV end diastolic pressure equalization within a pressure range difference of <5 mmHg • Kussmaul's sign on RA pressure recording • Early diastolic dip followed by plateau in pressure curve of RV and LV (see Figure 10.6)

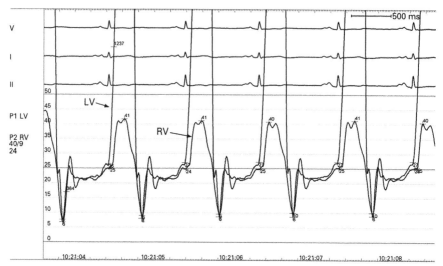

Figure 10.6 Dip and plateau sign as seen in constrictive pericarditis.
Reproduced from *The BMJ Case Reports*, Imran Patanwala, Jenifer Crilley, Peter N Trewby,
copyright 2009 with permission from BMJ Publishing Group Ltd.

Establish the aetiology

Idiopathic pericardial constriction is the most common aetiology. Other causes of pericardial constriction include the following:

- Trauma
  - Post open heart surgery
  - Post trauma
  - Post radiation
- Inflammation
  - Post pericarditis
  - Post uremia
  - Post Dressler's
  - Associated with inflammatory disease
  - Associated with infiltrative disease
- Infection
  - Tuberculous
  - Fungal.

Management

- Widespread pericardectomy is the only effective treatment
- Involves resection of the parietal pericardium as well as visceral pericardium if it is found to be thickened
- Once severe constrictive pericarditis has been diagnosed, surgery should not be delayed as mortality and poor outcome increase with age and advanced functional class
- Outcomes are worse if there is severe calcified adhesions between the peri and epicardium or if there is significant thickening of the epicardium
- Surgery in these patients carries a higher risk of incomplete success or significant damage to the myocardium

- Mortality in patients undergoing pericardictomy for constrictive pericarditis ranges between 6 and 12%
- Major operative complications include perioperative heart failure (low output syndrome as a consequence of right ventricular dilatation) and ventricular wall rupture
- Normalization of haemodynamics occurs in 60% of patients
- Patients who fail to improve post pericardectomy often have underlying myocardial atrophy or fibrosis.

Factors predicting worse prognosis include:

- Radiotherapy (there is often concurrent fibrosis in the underlying myocardium)
- Calcification
- Increasing NYHA classification
- Increasing age.

10.7 Rare causes of pericardial disease

Primary pericardial tumours

Primary pericardial tumours are exceptionally rare. They are often detected when presenting with pericardial effusions. Surgery is indicated in benign neoplasms (lipomas, fibromas).

Congenital abnormalities

Congenital abnormalities include the following:

- Absence of the pericardium
  - Complete absence—requires no treatment; it may present with atypical chest pain but is usually asymptomatic
  - Partial absence—may require surgery; it increases the risk of cardiac herniation presenting with severe, non-exertional chest pain
- Pericardial cysts
  - Usually benign and asymptomatic malformations located in the right costophrenic angle. No treatment is required.

Further reading

Imazio M. Colchicine in addition to conventional therapy for acute pericarditis: results of the COlchicine for acute PEricarditis (COPE) trial. *Circulation*, 2005; 112: 2012–6.

Maisch B, Seferović PM, Ristić AD, *et al.* The Task Force on the Diagnosis and Management of Pericardial Diseases of the European Society of Cardiology. Guidelines on the diagnosis and management of pericardial diseases. *Eur Heart J*, 2004; 25: 587–610.

Primary and secondary prevention of cardiovascular disease

CONTENTS

11.1 Overview

- Cardiology benefits from the largest evidence base of all medical specialties
- A growing number of cardiovascular risk factors have been identified since the original Framingham Heart Study
- Modification of reversible risk factors (rather than interventional procedures) has been largely responsible for the decline in age-adjusted cardiovascular mortality in the western world, and large global geographical variations in cardiovascular disease (CVD)
- Despite improvements, an unacceptable number of individuals are not adequately risk-controlled and suffer premature cardiovascular events (CVEs).

11.2 Cardiovascular risk

- Prevention strategies are based on identification and modulation of risk
- These can either target whole populations (the 'Rose model') or individuals most at risk (the 'high-risk' approach)
- The National Institute for Health and Clinical Excellence (NICE) and American Heart Association (AHA) have published guidelines on population-wide public health measures for preventing CVD
- These are based on education, with cooperation from government, industry, and commercial bodies
- More relevant to the practising cardiologist is identification of those individuals in whom intervention (lifestyle or pharmacological) will prevent CVEs and/or the need for interventional or surgical procedures, extending duration and quality of life (QOL). See Table 11.1 for a list of major modifiable and non-modifiable risk factors, as well as more novel emerging biomarkers of cardiovascular risk

- Medications are associated with variable risks and costs; therefore risk stratification is necessary to quantify those most at risk, with consideration of numbers needed to treat (NNT) and numbers needed to harm (NNH)
- There is no diagnostic challenge in secondary prevention—these individuals are at the highest risk and will benefit the most from appropriate intervention.

Table 11.1 List of established major modifiable and non-modifiable cardiovascular risk factors, in addition to emerging biomarkers currently being investigated

Non-modifiable	Major modifiable	Emerging
Genetic factors	Lipids	Highly sensitive CRP
Gender	Blood pressure	Fibrinogen
Family history	Metabolic (glycaemic)	Coronary calcium scores
Age	Smoking	Homocysteine
	Alcohol	Apolipoprotein B
	Diet and salt	Aortic pulse wave velocity
	Sedentary lifestyle	
	Obesity	

11.3 Risk estimation charts

- There are a number of multivariable risk-scoring systems in operation, including the Framingham, SCORE, QRISK, PROCAM, REYNOLDS, and WHO/ISH models
- These tools stratify individuals according to risk, quantified as the 10-year likelihood of a defined outcome
- The Framingham equation is the most widely used and has been adapted by a number of different societies, including the Joint British Societies (JBS), illustrated in Figure 11.1, and National Cholesterol Education Program Adult Treatment Panel (NCEP ATP) guidelines
- The NCEP ATP III system calculates risk of coronary heart disease (CHD) events, whilst JBS 2 broadened their focus to assess total and comprehensive cardiovascular risk and estimates of CVD events
- The JBS 2 modified version uses information on gender, age, ratio of total cholesterol (TC) to high-density lipoprotein cholesterol (HDL-C), systolic blood pressure (SBP) and smoking status to calculate risk scores: a 10-year CVD risk of >20% is defined as 'high' and requires therapeutic intervention
- The Joint European Guidelines on the prevention of CVD in clinical practice used the Systematic Coronary Risk Evaluation (SCORE) (Figure 11.2), as this was derived from a large pool of European cohort studies and may therefore be more relevant to northern European populations than Framingham data
- SCORE predicts 10-year risk of CVD mortality, which provides a well-standardized hard end-point, but provides no information on non-fatal CVEs
- A 10-year risk of >5% using SCORE is classified as 'high' risk
- Comparator studies of the various systems have shown differences but failed to demonstrate a single system as superior
- Risk tools are based on combined global risk and risk continuum—concepts central to the underlying multifactorial atherosclerotic process—where individual risk factors are multiplicative, rather than additive, interacting and amplifying harm when present in combination
- For example, a given blood pressure will be more damaging to an individual with Type 2 diabetes mellitus (T2DM) than equivalent pressures in a non-diabetic person

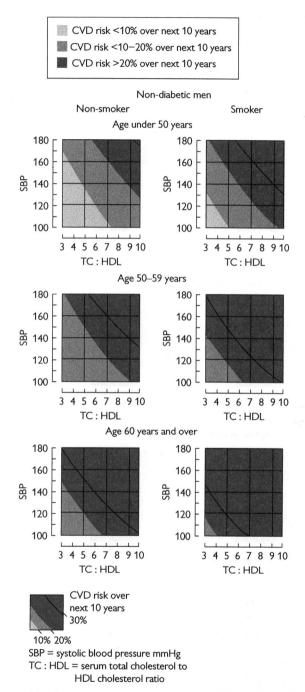

Figure 11.1 The modified Framingham risk chart used by JBS 2. Non-diabetic individuals are stratified according to their likelihood of CVD over 10 years. Diabetic individuals are not included, as they are automatically high risk.

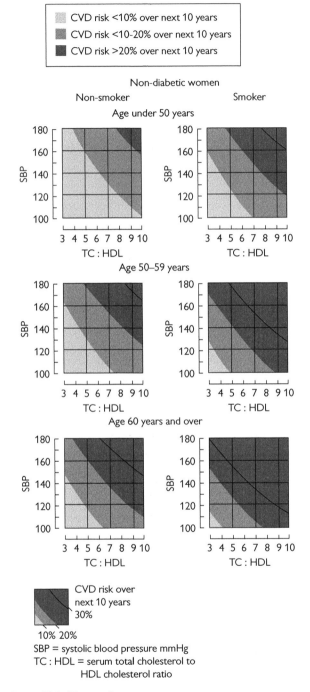

Figure 11.1 *(Continued)*

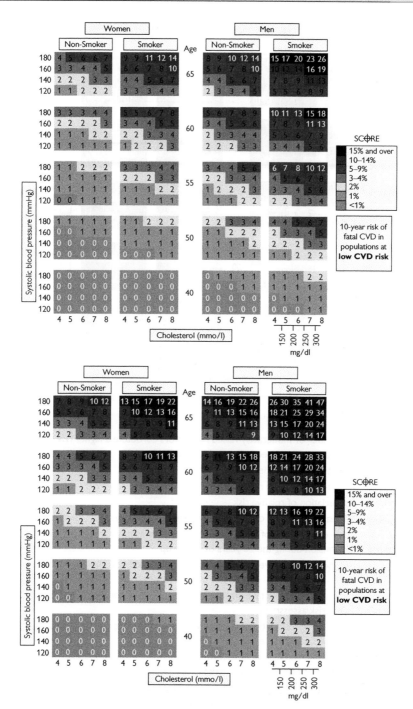

Figure 11.2 SCORE—chart model for CVD risk assessment. Different charts are used for high- and low-risk European regions.

Reproduced with permission from 'Estimation of ten-year risk of fatal cardiovascular disease in Europe: the SCORE project', R. M. Conroy, K. Pyorala, A. P. Fitzgerald et al., Eur Heart J., 24, 987–1003, copyright 2003 Oxford University Press.

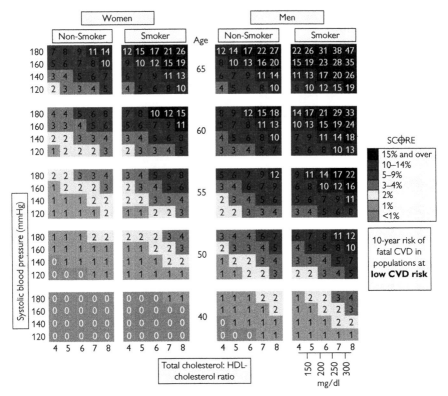

Figure 11.2 *(Continued)*

- Furthermore, a number of moderately raised risk factors constitute a higher risk than a single very elevated risk factor (illustrated in Figure 11.3 and Table 11.2)
- Risk scoring systems have a number of limitations:
    - Over-emphasis of absolute risk
    - Under-appreciation of relative risk
    - Short (10-year) time frame of risk may not represent lifetime risk
- In the Framingham cohort, 90% of individuals normotensive at the start of the study developed hypertension during the 20 years of follow up
- Recent data has shown that 10-year risk scores may underestimate lifetime risk by a factor of 4
- Updated Framingham risk scores take into consideration the relation between age and CVD risk, with a 30-year risk assessment
- Significant under- and overestimation of risk may result form ethnic and socio-economic variations, and other parameters excluded from charts
- Although over 200 CVD risk factors have now been identified, scoring systems remain focused on modulation of three 'classical' risk factors: cholesterol, diabetes, and hypertension
- Addition of novel risk factors, such as HDL-C, emerging biomarkers, HsCRP, and HbA1c have added very little discriminating value to current scoring systems, although they may have value in those at intermediate or borderline risk.

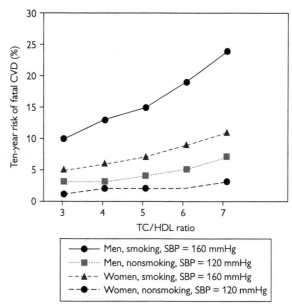

Figure 11.3 Graphical representation of the multiplicative actions of risk factors on total CVD risk. The relationship of total cholesterol (TC):HDL cholesterol ratio to 10-year fatal CVD events in men and women aged 60 years with and without risk factors, based on a risk function derived from the SCORE project. SBP = systolic blood pressure

Reproduced with permission from 'European guidelines on cardiovascular disease prevention in clinical practice: The Fourth Joint Task Force of the European Society of Cardiology and other societies on Cardiovascular Disease Prevention in Clinical Practice', Ian Graham, Daniel Atar, Knut Borch-Johnsen et al., Eur Heart J, **28**, 2375–2414, copyright 2007 Oxford University Press.

Table 11.2 Table demonstrating the interaction between cholesterol, blood pressure and smoking in amplifying combined risk.

Sex	Age (years)	Cholesterol (mmol/l)	BP (mmHg)	Smoker	Risk (%)
F	60	8	120	No	**2**
F	60	7	140	Yes	**5**
M	60	6	160	No	**8**
M	60	5	180	Yes	**21**

Reproduced from 'European guidelines on cardiovascular disease prevention in clinical practice: Fourth Joint Task Force of the European Society of Cardiology and other societies on Cardiovascular Disease Prevention in Clinical Practice', Ian Graham, Dan Atar, Knut Borch-Johnsen et al., Eur Heart J 28,2375–2414, copyright 2007 with permission from Oxford University Press.

KEY CLINICAL EVIDENCE

The Bogalusa Heart Study demonstrated the progressive multifactorial nature of atherosclerotic risk, with number of risk factors closely correlating with the extent of atherosclerotic burden. The INTERHEART study showed that 90% of cases of acute MI could be related to nine easily identifiable and modifiable risk factors. The multiple risk factor intervention trial was a landmark primary prevention trial, which randomized 12,866 high risk asymptomatic middle aged men to multi-factor risk reduction looking at the four major end points of death from CHD, CVD, any cause, and a combination of fatal CHD and non-fatal MI. It confirmed the graded continuous relationship between cholesterol concentration and CHD mortality rates and demonstrated the multiplicative interplay between individual risk factors.

11.4 Management

- JBS 2: comprehensive CVD assessment in all those >40 years of age, as well as younger patients with a family history of premature CVD (a first-degree male relative <55 years or female <65 years of age)
- Individuals at high risk (>20% 10 year risk of CVD) meet the threshold for therapeutic treatment to address global cardiovascular risk with intensive lifestyle measures and pharmacotherapy
- Updates of JBS, NCEP ATP, and the Joint European Guidelines have all seen progressively lower thresholds for intervention
- Those not deemed high risk should have the assessment repeated within 5 years
- Intervention is automatically advised in those with:
  - Clinical evidence of, or established CVD
  - Diabetes mellitus (DM)
  - TC:HDL-C ratio ≥6
  - Familial dyslipidaemia
- Over the age of 70 years (particularly in men) CVD risk will be high, but a comprehensive assessment should still be performed
- In addition to the risk score, clinical assessment should also give consideration to:
  - Ethnicity
  - Smoking history
  - Family history
  - Weight
  - Waist circumference
  - Non-fasting lipids
  - Non-fasting glucose
  - Fasting triglycerides (Tg)
  - Physical activity
  - Alcohol consumption
  - Impaired fasting glucose (IFG)
  - Impaired glucose tolerance (IGT)
  - Salt intake
  - Renal profile
- These parameters may be useful to determine treatment in those with borderline risk, who do not otherwise meet thresholds for intervention

- The AHA guidelines for prevention of CVD in women recommend a modified algorithm, stratifying risk into three categories:
  1) High risk: known CVD, DM, chronic kidney disease (CKD), or a 10-year CHD risk >20%
  2) At risk: one major CVD risk factor, metabolic syndrome (MetS) or evidence of subclinical vascular disease (e.g. coronary calcification), or poor exercise tolerance on treadmill testing
  3) Optimal risk: 10-year CHD risk <10%, absence of major CVD risk factors, and engagement in a healthy lifestyle.

11.5 Lifestyle

- Guidelines recommend 'therapeutic lifestyle change' (TLC) in both primary and secondary prevention of CVD (see Table 11.3)
- Recommendations are centered on maintaining a healthy diet (in accordance with the DASH, dietary approaches to stop hypertension, AHA Step 2 or Mediterranean diet), regular exercise, and smoking cessation
- Appropriate advice, support and follow up should be provided to asssit individuals in achieving and maintaining these goals.

Table 11.3 Summary of therapeutic lifestyle changes that should be instituted in both primary and secondary prevention of CVD.

Lifestyle factor	Goal
Smoking	Counselling
	Intensive behavioral support
	Opportunistic advice
	Nicotine replacement therapy
Diet	≥5 portions fresh fruit and vegetables daily
	≥3 servings whole grain foods daily
	≥2 portions of fish per week, including oily fish (≥7 g omega-3 fatty acids)
	Increased nut, seed, and legume consumption
	20–30 g/day fiber
	Intake of plant sterols/stenols and viscous fibers (NICE do not recommend routine supplementation for primary prevention)
	Reduce salt intake <1.5 g/day
	Total calories: ≤30% total fat intake
	<7% saturated fats; up to 10% polyunsaturated and 15% monounsaturated
	15% protein and 50–60% carbohydrates <200 mg/day dietary cholesterol
Alcohol	Reduce alcohol intake in accordance with recommended daily limits
Exercise	Increase physical activity to at least 30 min of physical activity per day, of at least moderate intensity (or graded as able), at least 5 days a week

11.6 Blood pressure

- Hypertension is the level of blood pressure above which treatment reduces development or progression of disease

- The most recent recommendations come from the joint British Hypertension Society and NICE guidelines released in 2011
- Randomized controlled trials and meta-analyses have failed to show any class benefit in antihypertensive regimens in CVD prevention
- Although ASCOT and CAFÉ showed CCBs to be superior to BBs, this may have been due to differences in blood pressure variability
- BBs have been associated with less benefit in stroke prevention and have not been included as first-line agents in the most recent NICE guidelines, although they still have clear indications in the setting of ischaemic heart disease and heart failure
- It has become clear that combination therapy is frequently required to achieve optimal blood pressure levels
- Guidelines set target blood pressures at <140/85 mmHg, with lower target levels of <130/80 mmHg for selected high-risk individuals (established CVD, DM, or CKD) (see Figure 11.4)
- These recommendations have not yet been supported by RCT data and the updated NICE guidelines have not advised blood pressure lowering below proven targets
- NICE have made specific changes for diagnosing hypertension, with use of ambulatory blood pressure monitoring (ABPM) and home blood pressure monitoring (HBPM) (see Chapter 12)
- In severe hypertension antihypertensive drug treatment should be considered immediately (without waiting for results of ABPM/HBPM) and patients should undergo comprehensive

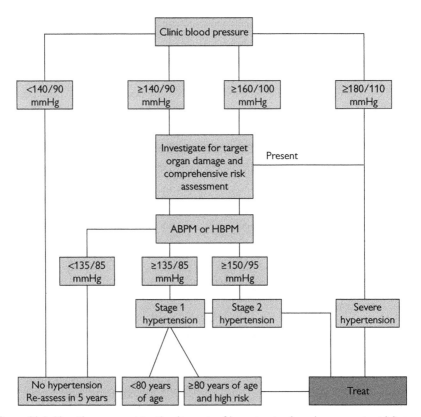

Figure 11.4 Algorithm summarizing the diagnosis of hypertension based on current guidelines.

cardiovascular risk assessment and detailed screening for target organ damage (such as LVH, CKD, and hypertensive retinopathy)

- Individuals >80 years of age with Stage 1 hypertension should be offered antihypertensive therapy if high risk, defined as any of the following characteristics:
  - Target organ damage
  - Established CVD
  - Renal disease
  - Diabetes mellitus
  - 10-year cardiovascular risk ≥20%
- Treatment is divided into four steps, with the goal of achieving a clinic blood pressure <140/90 mmHg in people aged <80 years and <150/90 mmHg in people aged >80 years:
  - Step 1: offer those <55 years of age an ACE inhibitor or a low-cost ARB
    - If an ACE inhibitor is prescribed and not tolerated (e.g. due to cough), offer a low-cost ARB
  - Step 2: offer those >55 years of age or black people of African or Caribbean descent of any age a CCB
    - If a CCB is not suitable, offer a thiazide-like diuretic
    - If diuretics are initiated, chlortalidone (12.5 mg–25.0 mg once daily) or indapamide (1.5 mg modified-release or 2.5 mg once daily) are preferred
  - Step 3: if antihypertensive treatment with three drugs is required, combinations of an ACE inhibitor or ARB, CCB, and thiazide-like diuretic should be used
  - Step 4: clinic blood pressure that remains >140/90 mmHg after treatment with the optimal or best tolerated doses of an ACE inhibitor or ARB + CCB + diuretic is classified as *resistant hypertension*, and a fourth antihypertensive agent should be considered and/or expert opinion sought. Consider further diuretic therapy with low-dose spironolactone (25 mg once daily)—if contraindicated or ineffective, consider an alpha- or beta-blocker
- If hypertension is not diagnosed, measure the person's clinic blood pressure at least every 5 years subsequently, and possibly more frequently depending on how high their original readings were
- All those with accelerated hypertension (blood pressure >180/110 mmHg with signs of papilloedema and/or retinal haemorrhage) or suspected phaeochromocytoma (labile or postural hypotension, headache, palpitations, pallor and diaphoresis) should be referred to a hypertension specialist
- Investigations should include testing for proteinuria, albumin to creatinine ratio, haematuria, plasma glucose, electrolytes, creatinine, eGFR, TC and HDL-C, fundoscopy, and obtaining an electrocardiograph.

KEY CLINICAL EVIDENCE

The Anglo-Scandinavian Cardiac Outcome Trial-Blood Pressure Lowering Arm (ACOT-BPLA) was a large trial of 19,342 hypertensive subjects with ≥3 other CVD risk factors randomized to amlodipine +/- perindopril and atenolol +/- bendroflumethiazide. Although there was not a significant difference in the primary endpoint of non-fatal MI and fatal CHD, the trial was stopped early due to differences in secondary outcomes, with favoured benefits for CCBs and ACE inhibitors for fatal and non-fatal stroke, total CVEs and all-cause mortality. The Antihypertensive and Lipid-Lowering Treatment to Prevent Heart Attack Trial (ALLHAT) also failed to show any difference in the primary endpoint of CHD events for diuretic based treatment versus ACE inhibitors or CCBs but with significant benefits in the secondary endpoints of reduced heart failure and stroke events with diuretic treatment.

11.7 Lipids

- There is a strong linear relation between elevated TC and CHD death with TC >4 mmol/l (180 mg/dl)
- Every 1 mmol/l (38.7 mg/dl) reduction in LDL-C is associated with a 12% reduction in all-cause mortality, 19% reduction in coronary mortality, and 21% reduction in any major vascular event
- Management is focused on comprehensive cardiovascular risk assessment and treatment
- All guidelines recommend initiating pharmacological treatment in those with established atherosclerotic CVD
- NICE and JBS 2 recommend treating those with 10-year Framingham risk >20% (or equivalent high risk using another scoring system) and familial hypercholesterolaemia/monogenic disorder of lipid metabolism
- There are certain cohorts who have a propensity to CVD but are not included in risk-stratifying tools. NICE recommends clinical assessment to determine the need for lipid-lowering therapy in these individuals, e.g. HIV, DM, systemic lupus erythematosus (SLE), CKD, rheumatoid arthritis, age, ethnicity, BMI, and family history of premature CVD
- JBS 2 stipulates commencing pharmacotherapy in the following individuals with T2DM:
  - >40 years of age
  - 18–39 years with at least one of:
    - Retinopathy (pre-proliferative, proliferative, maculopathy)
    - Nephropathy, including persistent microalbuminuria
    - Poor glycaemic control (HbA1c >9%)
    - Hypertension
    - Raised TC ≥6
    - MetS
    - Family history of premature CVD in a first-degree relative
- The Joint European Guidelines recommend treatment in diabetics with microalbuminuria or severe hyperlipidaemia
- All other individuals should be risk stratified using SCORE—those with a 10 year risk >5% should commence TLC for 3 months
- After 3 months, individuals should be reassessed with repeat SCORE risk calculation and fasting lipids: if TC <5 mmol/l, LDL-C <3 mmol/l and SCORE <5%, they should continue with TLC and have regular follow up. Otherwise they should commence pharmacological intervention
- Pharmacotherapy should be offered with a focus on reducing LDL-C
- JBS 2 set targets for TC <4 mmol/l and LDL-C <2 mmol/l, regardless of degree of individual risk (or a 25% reduction in TC and a 30% reduction in LDL-C, depending on which gives the lowest absolute value), whilst NSF lipid-lowering goals for LDL-C were <3 mmol/l (115 mg/dl)
- In contrast, NCEP ATP III set different lipid targets depending on risk, and NICE did not set target lipid levels at all for primary prevention
- Joint European Guidelines recommend TC <5 mmol/l, LDL-C <3, and in the highest-risk individuals TC <4.5, or <4 if possible, with LDL-C <2.5, or <2.

Five classes of lipid-lowering agents are available:

1) statins
2) fibrates
3) niacin
4) bile acid sequestrants
5) cholesterol absorbers

- NICE recommend starting drug therapy with statins, and without the need for subsequent lipids levels to be checked

- NICE does not recommend routine use of fibrates, nictonic acid, or anion exchange resins individually or in combination for primary prevention
- These agents can be considered when statins are not tolerated
- Individuals with primary hypercholesterolaemia should be considered for ezetimibe treatment in combination with a statin, or in instances when a statin is not tolerated
- Secondary hyperlipidaemia should be considered: hypothyroidism, nephrotic syndrome, primary biliary cirrhosis, and anorexia nervosa in those with elevated LDL-C, and screening for DM, CKD, alcoholism, and hypothyroidism in those with elevated Tg levels

KEY CLINICAL EVIDENCE

The HPS trial showed simvastatin 40 mg effective in reducing death from vascular causes by 17% in a cohort of individuals without dyslipidaemia but with CAD, DM, non-occlusive CAD, or treated hypertension. The CARDS study demonstrated 10 mg atorvastatin effective in prevention of major CVEs in a cohort of individuals with T2DM without dyslipidaemia but with at least one of hypertension, smoking, or diabetic complication (retinopathy, maculopathy, micro- or macroalbuminuria). These trials together set the path for statin therapy in preventive cardiology and have subsequently been supported by large meta-analyses.

- Statin treatment can slow progression and even regress athermoatous plaques/volume based on clinical studies using intravascular ultrasound.

11.8 Secondary prevention

- Statins should be prescribed in all individuals following ACS, cerebral infarction, or transient ischaemic attack (TIA) (but not haemorrhagic strokes)
- Large trials have consistently shown benefit of intensive statin therapy post ACS (meta-analysis—16% reduction in CVEs and CHD death)
- Fasting lipids should be estimated at least 8 weeks after an acute CVE and if necessary, doses titrated up to achieve cholesterol targets
- JBS 2 recommends an 'audit' level of TC <5 mmol/l to assess progress in populations or groups of people with CVD, in recognition that more than a half of patients will not achieve a total cholesterol of <4 mmol/l or an LDL-C <2 mmol/l
- NICE advises that fibrates, nicotinic acid, and anion exchange resins may be considered for secondary prevention in people with CVD who are not able to tolerate statins
- People who have liver enzymes (transaminases) that are raised but are less than three times the upper limit of normal should not be routinely excluded from statin therapy.

KEY CLINICAL EVIDENCE

Treat New Targets (TNT) was a double-blind RCT, which showed that intensive lipid lowering (80 mg atorvastatin) was associated with a 22% relative risk reduction in major CVEs compared with standard treatment (10 mg atorvastatin) in a cohort with stable CHD. The Justification for Use of Statins in Prevention, an Intervention Trial Evaluating Rosuvastatin (JUPITER) randomized men ≥50 years old and women ≥60 years without a history of CVD, with LDL-C <130 mg/dl and HsCRP ≥2 mg/l to 20 mg rosuvastatin, demonstrating a significant reduction of 44% in the composite endpoint of non-fatal MI, stroke, hospitalization for unstable angina, revascularization, and cardiovascular death (as well as reduced incidence of venous thromboembolism). No trial has yet shown a cut off below which LDL-C lowering ceases to benefit CVD protection. Sub-analysis of PROVE-IT TIMI 22 showed levels below target (<40 mg/dl) were not associated with an increase in adverse effects.

11.9 High density lipoprotein and triglycerides

- Meta-analyses of prospective cohorts have demonstrated elevated Tg levels as a risk factor for CHD
- Triglycerides are not directly atherogenic but are biomarkers of metabolic health and CVD, due to their association with remnant lipoprotein particles and apo CIII
- LDL-C lowering and weight reduction is the first-line treatment in hypertriglyceridaemia
- A recent scientific statement from the AHA reviewed the role of Tg, with a consistent therapeutic emphasis on TLC
- A 5% to 10% reduction in body weight can result in a 20% reduction in triglyceride levels, with further improvements from low carbohydrate, low calorie diets, reduced sugars, and increased proportion of unsaturated fat
- Elimination of trans fats, restriction of SFA, and increasing consumption of marine-based omega-3 products, coupled with aerobic activity, were recommended for further Tg lowering and, taken together, TLC can result in reductions of 50% or more in Tg levels
- Trial data for pharmacotherapy targeting Tg is lacking, and specific triglyceride-lowering medication is only recommended to prevent pancreatitis in those with very high Tg levels (>5.6 mmol/l)
- Elevated triglycerides and low HDL-C closely correspond with insulin resistance and obesity—a cluster of risk factors which, when present together, form MetS.

11.10 Pre-diabetes and metabolic syndrome

- Around a third of patients with CAD have abnormal oral glucose tolerance tests (OGTT), and 22% (acute) and 14% (stable) have newly diagnosed DM
- JBS 2 and Joint European Guidelines recommended optimal fasting plasma glucose (FPG) ≤ 6 mmol/l in high-risk individuals
- If FPG is ≥6.1, fasting glucose measurements are advised, to look for IFG or new DM
- If FPG is 6.1–6.9 mmol/l, a repeat sample on a separate occasion or an OGTT is advised, and a second abnormal value confirms IFG
- If FPG is ≥7 mmol/l with symptoms (polyuria, polydipsia, weight loss), DM is diagnosed, otherwise two separate readings are needed
- An OGTT is the only way to diagnose IGT (2-h glucose ≥7.8 but <11.1 mmol/l) and is the conventional standard for the diagnosis of DM (2-h glucose ≥11.1 mmol/l)
- The ADA recommends screening for diabetes in asymptomatic individuals ≥45 years of age, or in those with BMI ≥25 and one additional risk factor for DM. Appropriate tests include HbA1c, fasting plasma glucose, or 2-h 75 g oral glucose tolerance test
- The ESC and European Association for the Study of Diabetes guidelines did not make specific recommendations regarding screening. Both Diabetes UK and the WHO support the use of HbA1c in diagnosing diabetes
- Pre-diabetes is defined in Table 11.4
- Individuals with pre-diabetes should undergo intensive TLC, with appropriate follow up, counseling, and support, with annual reviews to monitor for progression to DM
- Repeat trial evidence has shown that intensive lifestyle interventions are efficacious in long-term reduction in conversion of pre-diabetes to diabetes
- Metformin is the only drug therapy approved for pre-diabetes and can be considered for those at highest risk with progressive hyperglycaemia despite lifestyle interventions (greater benefit has been shown in obese individuals)

- Those with DM need rigorous glycaemic control: fasting or preprandial glucose of 4–6 mmol/l and an HbA1c <6.5%
- High-risk individuals should receive pharmacotherapy at doses proven in clinical trials
- MetS describes a cluster of risk factors which predict and promote atherosclerotic CVD and T2DM
- There are various definitions but all are based on the combination of atherogenic dyslipidaemia, elevated blood pressure, and pre-diabetes
- Different definitions have been proposed—with varying degrees of emphasis on insulin resistance and obesity as the predominant underlying abnormalities driving further disease (see Table 11.5)

Table 11.4 American Diabetes Association (ADA) and World Health Organization (WHO) criteria for the diagnosis of pre-diabetes and diabetes mellitus.

Glucometabolic category	Guidelines	Classification criteria (mmol/l)
Impaired fasting glucose (IFG)	WHO	FPG ≥6.1 and <7 + 2-h PG <7.8
	ADA	FPG ≥5.6 and <6.1
Impaired glucose tolerance (IGT)	WHO	FPG <7 + 2-h PG ≥7.8 and <11.1
	ADA	OGTT 7.8–11
Impaired glucose homeostasis (IGH) and pre-diabetes	WHO	IFG or IGT
	ADA	IFG or IGT or HbA1c 5.7–6.4%
Diabetes mellitus	WHO	FPG ≥7 or 2-h PG ≥11.1
	ADA	FPG ≥7 or OGTT ≥11.1 or HbA1c ≥6.5% or random blood glucose ≥11.1 with classical symptoms

FPG = fasting plasma glucose; 2-h PG = two-hour post-load plasma glucose. OGTT is performed in the morning after 8–14-h fast: one sample is taken before and one 120 min after intake of 75 g glucose dissolved in 250–300 ml water for 5 min.

Adapted from 'Guidelines on diabetes, pre-diabetes, and cardiovascular diseases: executive summary: the Task Force on Diabetes and Cardiovascular Diseases of the European Society of Cardiology (ESC) and of the European Association for the Study of Diabetes (EASD)', L. Ryden, E. Standl, M. Bartnik et al., Eur Heart J 28: 88–136, copyright 2007 with permission of Oxford University Press.

Table 11.5 Metabolic syndrome. MetS requires any three of the five criteria to be present according to the AHA/NHLBI modified NCEP ATP III classification.

Parameter	Criteria
Elevated waist circumference	≥102 cm men ≥88 cm women
Elevated Tg	≥1.7 mmol/l or requiring treatment
Reduced HDL-C	≤0.9 mmol/l men <1.1 mmol/l women or requiring treatment
Elevated blood pressure	≥130/85 or requiring treatment
Elevated FPG	≥100 mg/dl or requiring treatment

Adapted from 'Diagnosis and management of the metabolic syndrome: an American Heart Association/National Heart, Lung, and Blood Institute Scientific Statement', Scott M. Grundy, James I. Cleeman, Stephen R. Daniels et al., Circulation 112, 2735–2752, copyright 2005 with permission of Wolters Kluwer Health.

- First-line therapy for individuals with MetS is directed towards improving LDL-C, hypertension, and preventing diabetes (or controlling DM if present)
- Prime emphasis is on TLC to target obesity, sedentary lifestyle and atherogenic diet, improvements of which can result in significant benefit of all the metabolic factors involved
- TLC measures should be implemented, with specific aims to reduce weight and decrease calorie intake by approximately 500–1000 calories per day, aiming for 7–10% weight loss in 6–12 months to achieve a BMI ≤25 and waist circumference <40 and <35 inches in men and women respectively
- If the absolute risk remains high, as calculated using risk estimation scores, drug therapy can be initiated
- MetS may have a significant lifetime risk of CVD but disproportionately low 10-year risk estimates
- Interestingly, the Framingham investigators found little or no benefit in predictive scores by addition of abdominal obesity, triglycerides, or FPG
- For IFG, weight reduction and increased physical activity should be strongly encouraged with modification of other CVD risk factors as necessary
- Although MetS is recognized as a state of systemic low-grade inflammation, C-reactive protein (CRP) has not yet been proven as a therapeutic target.

KEY CLINICAL EVIDENCE

The STENO-2 study tested multifactorial intervention in a cohort with T2DM. Systolic blood pressure was reduced from 147 to 130 mmHg, LDL-C and triglyceride goals were achieved in the majority (fasting TC <4.5 mmol/l and triglyceride <1.7 mmol/l), and HbA1c reduced from 8.4 to 7.7%. Together, these interventions were associated with a 20% absolute reduction in CVD and 53% relative risk reduction.

11.11 Antithrombotic therapy

- The role of aspirin in primary prevention remains contentious
- JBS 2 recommend aspirin therapy in primary prevention for all individuals >50 years of age with a 10-year Framingham CVD risk >20%, as well as some individuals with DM (all >50 years, and younger individuals who have had DM >10 years, or already receiving treatment for hypertension) once blood pressure control is achieved
- NICE similarly recommends aspirin in all those >50 years of age with hypertension or T2DM or other significant CVD risk
- These recommendations were predominantly based on data from a large meta-analysis of a heterogeneous group of individuals of varied CVD risk by the Anti-Thrombotic Trialists (ATT) collaboration in 2002, which concluded that low-dose aspirin should be considered for those at intermediate–high risk for CVD
- Following an updated analysis by the ATT collaboration in 2009—looking at primary prevention data from 95,000 individuals—the absolute risk reduction was 0.06%, with NNT of 1667 per year
- This was supported in a RCT of at-risk individuals with asymptomatic atherosclerosis, which showed no protection for the primary composite endpoint (fatal/non-fatal coronary events, stroke, or revascularization) in individuals treated with aspirin versus placebo
- These small benefits have to be weighed against the risk of extra-cranial haemorrhage or gastrointestinal bleeding

- The FDA in the USA has not approved aspirin for primary prevention
- A recent statement from the AHA/ADA recommends low-dose aspirin in diabetic individuals at increased risk of CVD, with a 10-year risk score >10% and not at increased risk of bleeding (e.g. absence of previous bleed, ulcer, or concomitant medication increasing risk)
- Men >50 years and women >60 years of age, with ≥1 of: smoking, hypertension, dyslipidaemia, family history of premature CVD, or albuminuria should also be treated
- Consideration can be made for intermediate-risk individuals (e.g. young with risk factors, or old without risk)
- A very recent meta-analysis of nine randomized placebo-controlled trials with a total of 100,000 individuals and mean follow-up of six years found that aspirin treatment reduced total CVEs by 10%, but at the cost of a 30% increased risk of nontrivial bleeds.

11.12 Secondary prevention (post myocardial infarction)

- Clear guidance has been put forward for the importance of a rehabilitation programme post MI, with TLC measures as previously listed
- Additionally, the following pharmacotherapy should be initiated:
  - ACE inhibitors (if intolerant of ACE inhibitors substitute ARBs)
  - BBs (diltiazem or verapamil may be considered if BBs are contraindicated and in patients without pulmonary congestion or LV systolic dysfunction)
  - Statins and/or fibrates or niacin (as previously detailed)
  - Aldosterone antagonists if evidence of LV systolic dysfunction (ideally within 3–14 days, and preferably after ACE inhibitors)
  - Dual anti-platelets should be commenced and continue for 1 year after acute coronary syndromes
  - Patients unable to tolerate aspirin or clopidogrel after MI should be considered for warfarinization (target INR 2–3) for up to 4 years
  - Consider 1 g daily omega-3-acid ethyl esters post MI (within 3 months) for up to 4 years, in those unable to achieve a sufficient dietary intake of 7 g omega-3 fatty acids per week
- The use of low-dose aspirin has proven benefits in secondary prevention
- NICE recommends 75 mg aspirin therapy for all people with CHD or peripheral vascular disease
- If contraindicated, 75 mg clopidogrel and/or anticoagulation for people at risk of systemic emboli from large MIs, heart failure, LV aneurysm, or paroxysmal tachyarrhythmia
- The ESPS2 and ESPRIT trials showed that aspirin 75–150 mg daily plus dipyridamole M/R 200 mg twice daily was superior for stroke risk reduction compared with aspirin alone, in individuals with previous cerebral infarction, or TIA, in sinus rhythm
- The CAPRIE trial showed that clopidogrel was better than aspirin for prevention of the composite endpoint of stroke, MI, or vascular death
- The MATCH and CHARISMA studies showed no benefit with combination therapy of aspirin and clopidogrel, and with increased incidence of bleeding in stroke
- In individuals with previous stroke or TIA, the PRoFESS trial found no significant difference beteween clopidogrel monotherapy or aspirin and dipyridamole in combination, for recurrent stroke or the composite outcome of stroke, MI, or vascular death, although the study was unable to prove clopidogrel as statistically non-inferior

- In response to PRoFESS, NICE recommended clopidogrel as first line treatment for prevention of occlusive vascular events in individuals with a previous ischaemic stroke, or with peripheral arterial or multivascular disease
- If clopidogrel is contraindicated or not tolerated, combination therapy with aspirin and dipyridamole should be used
- Those in atrial fibrillation with a CHADS2 score >1 should commence anticoagulation and those at intermediate risk (CHADS2 = 1) should be assessed using CHADS2-VASc2 and HAS-BLED scores to determine whether to initiate antithrombotic or anticoagulant therapy
- ACE inhibitors should be considered in combination with a thiazide diuretic in all those with established stroke, as shown by HOPE and PROGRESS.

11.13 Special populations

The young

- In risk prediction charts such as SCORE, age is the most important factor in estimating absolute risk of CVD
- All young individuals will therefore be at low absolute risk, irrespective of risk factor levels and potentially a high lifetime risk (up to 12 times higher than those of the same age with 'optimal' risk)
- Some European guidelines have suggested extrapolating risk to age 60 years, to demonstrate to younger individuals that without modification, they would become high risk by 60 years of age
- New scoring systems have been introduced, which calculate heart age and CVD risk age (expressed as life-years lost or gained for individuals' actual age)—to communicate and quantify future risk to younger patients
- NICE hypertension guidelines recommend that individuals <40 years of age with Stage 1 hypertension (without target organ damage, CVD, CKD, or DM) be referred for specialist evaluation for secondary causes of hypertension and a more detailed assessment of potential target organ damage, in acknowledgement that 10-year CVD risks may underestimate lifetime risk.

Older adults

- Most risk estimation systems are not applicable >75 years of age
- This is partly a result of limited data for very elderly cohorts and in part due to the fact these individuals will automatically be classified as high risk
- Risk factors do continue to apply to elderly individuals, although with different relative risks
- The INTERHEART study showed that measures such as physical activity have greater predictive value in these groups
- Recent RCTs have shown benefit in lipid lowering and BP lowering in the elderly and very elderly
- Recent studies have shown that CCBs might reduce progression to dementia in hypertensive elderly patients over 70 years and may help in stroke prevention through stabilizing blood pressure variability
- Non-morning dipping and orthostatic hypotension (OH) have been observed in a quarter of an unselected cohort of ambulatory older patients without CVD, and this was associated with a 2.4-times increased risk of major CVE

- Recent ACC guidelines for management of high blood pressure in the elderly recommend target systolic pressures of 140 mmHg in those <80 years of age and 140–145 mmHg in those >80 years, comparable to NICE targets of <140/80 and <150/80 mmHg, respectively
- INVEST looked at older hypertensive individuals with stable CAD, and showed adverse affects with intensive blood pressure lowering
- ACCORD BP also found no benefit in reducing SBP to 120 mmHg versus 140 mmHg, and with greater adverse effects, in a cohort of high-risk diabetics
- Blood pressure measurements should be repeated while standing to identify OH, as a measure of autonomic dysregulation and risk for CVD
- In elderly individuals with CKD and CCF, blood pressure targets of <130/80 may be of benefit
- Reversible factors should be sought in the first instance and non-pharmacological therapies tested prior to initiating medications
- A small proportion of older adults will display pseudohypertension due to hardened and stiff vessels
- Consideration should be made for polypharmacy, QOL, and cognitive function when managing blood pressure in elderly individuals
- Elderly hypertensives with CVA should be treated with diuretic and ACE inhibitors but achieving BP targets is more important than antihypertensive class
- Drug therapy should be started at a low dose and titrated up as necessary and as tolerated—combination therapy can be given to achieve target doses.

KEY CLINICAL EVIDENCE

The HYVET (HYpertension in the Very Elderly Trial) randomized individuals with persistent hypertension ≥80 years of age to once daily treatment with placebo or indapamide 1.5 mg SR, with the addition of perindopril 2–4 mg as necessary, to reach a target blood pressure of 150/80 mmHg. The trial was stopped early due to significant reductions in overall mortality (21%), stroke-related deaths (39%), heart failure (64%), and CVEs (34%) in those receiving treatment. Indapamide was not associated with significant adverse effects on glycaemic or lipid profiles.

Women

- A number of stratification tools (such as the Framingham Score) remain based on predicting risk of CHD
- It is now appreciated that in middle and older age, in contrast to men, women's risk for stroke and heart failure exceeds that of CHD
- Only a small fraction of women therefore achieve the threshold (10-year risk of 20%) for pharmacological intervention based on CHD prediction models, likely underestimating total CVD events and mortality in women
- New Framingham equations, in addition to SCORE, which predict total CVD risk, may therefore be preferable
- The metabolic insult which pregnancy confers provides an insight to future risk and women with pre-eclampsia should therefore be referred to a cardiologist post-partum
- Systemic inflammatory states such as SLE have also been shown to be associated with significant cardiovascular risk and should therefore be taken into consideration in risk stratification

- The Euro Heart study showed similar risks for acute MI in women and men for lipids, current smoking, abdominal obesity, high-risk diet, and psychosocial stress factors, but an increased risk associated with hypertension, diabetes, and low physical activity
- There is also some evidence to suggest that triglyceride levels may be more useful in predicting CVEs in women, compared with men
- The AHA has released specific guidelines for CVD prevention in women.

Diabetes mellitus

- Diabetes represents such a powerful risk factor for CVD (CHD risk equivalent) that guidelines have recommended intensive risk factor control to reduce future CVEs
- In the UKPDS, dyslipidaemia, hypertension, and elevated HbA1c accounted for 45%, 33%, and 22% of CVD risk, respectively, in patients with T2DM
- JBS 2 and the Joint European Guidelines made empirical recommendations for blood pressure targets <130/80 mmHg in diabetic individuals, along with tight glycaemic control
- Several RCTs have subsequently addressed intensive risk factor modulation in diabetes: in ACCORD, intensive blood pressure control with combination therapy to achieve pressures of 119/64.4 mmHg did not provide any protection from the composite endpoint of non-fatal stroke or MI compared with standard blood pressure control (133.5/70.5 mmHg) in individuals with T2DM
- There was a reduction of stroke in the intensive arm, but with a NNT of 89 over 5 years. Intensive blood pressure control was also associated with improved eGFR but with no change in renal endpoints, and increased adverse hypotensive episodes
- These findings were supported by ADVANCE and INVEST, which did not support blood pressure lowering below 130 mmHg systolic
- As such, NICE have not recommended blood pressure lowering below 140/80 mmHg
- First-line drugs are ACE inhibitors, with addition of a thiazide diuretic if dual therapy is needed to achieve target levels (or a loop diuretic if eGFR <30 ml/min/l)
- Despite the linear association between HbA1c and CVD in the general population, glycaemic targets in DM are contentious
- Several studies have failed to show any benefit of intensive glycaemic control for CVEs or mortality
- In comparison UKPDS did show a reduction in mirovascular complications over a 10-year follow up, with differences in macrovascular disease becoming apparent long term (in those treated aggressively early in the disease)
- Meta-analyses have failed to show significant benefits for CVEs
- Furthermore, tight glycaemic control is associated with weight gain, increased hypoglycaemic episodes, and cerebral complications
- There is therefore no clear evidence that HbA1c <7% provides any benefit in established T2DM
- In contrast to blood pressure and glycaemia, intensive lipid modification has been effective in reducing LDL-C, with associated improvements in mortality, although with a small increase in the incidence of new diabetes
- The FIELD study demonstrated the benefit of fenofibrate in reducing triglycerides in T2DM, with reduced coronary revascularization and microvascular complications.

Chronic kidney disease

- Individuals with renal disease are extremely susceptible to CVD
- Individuals with CKD have been overlooked in some risk-scoring systems, in part due to their exclusion from clinical trials and the paucity of relevant data

- Prevention strategies are largely consistent with those in non-renal patients at high risk of CVD
- In addition to TLC, this includes good glycaemic control with HbA1c between 6.5% and 7.5%, in accordance with NICE and JBS guidelines
- Patients with CKD have profoundly altered lipid profiles
- Statin use in CKD stages I–IV has consistently been shown to reduce CVD mortality, and even slow the rate of progression to more advanced CKD
- The use of statins in end-stage renal disease is less certain
- There remains a lack of evidence for optimal blood pressure targets in CKD
- Updated NICE guidelines recommend initiating anti-hypertensive treatment in all individuals <80 years of age with Stage 1 hypertension but do not recommend lower blood pressure targets
- BBs and ACE inhibitors should be commenced in accordance with indications for non-renal patients, although with caution and monitoring.

11.14 Summary

- The wealth of observational and trial data in cardiology has allowed for identification of robust cardiovascular risk factors and effective interventions
- Despite numerous novel biomarkers and technological developments, the mainstay of treatment in primary and secondary prevention of CVD remains focused on modulation of dyslipidaemia, blood pressure, and glycaemia
- As an increasing body of data identifies the early, sub-clinical insults and damage that predate overt disease, guidelines from learned societies have recommended progressively earlier therapeutic intervention, through lifestyle and pharmacotherapy
- As our understanding of the pathophysiology and natural history of these diseases improves, distinguishing between primary and secondary prevention will become of less importance
- Cholesterol and blood pressure represent continuums of cardiovascular risk
- Whilst lower target boundaries have now been identified in hypertension and dysglycaemia, cholesterol lowering thus far has shown that the lower the LDL-C the better the outcome
- Very intensive glycaemic and blood pressure control has failed to show a benefit in RCTs of individuals with T2DM
- Primordial prevention targetting IFG/IGT may provide a window to halt and reverse this vascular damage, which becomes so challenging in later stages of disease
- Therapeutic lifestyle changes have been proven to be effective in reversing all the metabolic abnormalities comprising MetS
- It remains uncertain whether Tg levels and HDL-C should be pharmacotherapeutic targets in CVD prevention
- Many guidelines are almost a decade old. ATP 4, JNC 8, Obesity 2 and the Cardiovascular Risk Reduction Guidelines from the National Heart, Lung, and Blood Institute are all now some years overdue. It has been suggested that the delay in releasing these guidelines can be attributed to a fundamental change in the manner recommendations are made, with a shift towards RCT-level evidnce only, and dose titration to individual risk
- With the birth of personalized medicine, the future of cardiovascular risk will become increasingly focused on the risk of the individual
- Cardiovascular risk, treatment targets, and therapeutic options represent moving targets, which are constantly changing.

Further reading

Aronow WS, Fleg JL, Pepine CJ, et al. ACCF/AHA 2011 expert consensus document on hypertension in the elderly: a report of the American College of Cardiology Foundation Task Force on Clinical Expert Consensus documents developed in collaboration with the American Academy of Neurology, American Geriatrics Society, American Society for Preventive Cardiology, American Society of Hypertension, American Society of Nephrology, Association of Black Cardiologists, and European Society of Hypertension. *J Am Coll Cardiol*, 2011; 57: 2037–114.

Chobanian AV, Bakris GL, Black HR, et al. Seventh report of the Joint National Committee on Prevention, Detection, Evaluation, and Treatment of High Blood Pressure. *Hypertension*, 2003; 42: 1206–52.

Graham I, Atar D, Borch-Johnsen K, et al. European guidelines on cardiovascular disease prevention in clinical practice: full text. Fourth Joint Task Force of the European Society of Cardiology and other societies on cardiovascular disease prevention in clinical practice (constituted by representatives of nine societies and by invited experts). *Eur J Cardiovasc Prev Rehabil*, 2007; 14(Suppl 2): S1–113.

Grundy SM, Cleeman JI, Merz CN, et al. Implications of recent clinical trials for the National Cholesterol Education Program Adult Treatment Panel III guidelines. *Circulation*, 2004; 110: 227–39.

Grundy SM, Cleeman JI, Daniels SR, et al. Diagnosis and management of the metabolic syndrome: an American Heart Association/National Heart, Lung, and Blood Institute Scientific Statement. *Circulation*, 2005; 112: 2735–52.

JBS 2: Joint British Societies' guidelines on prevention of cardiovascular disease in clinical practice. *Heart*, 2005; 91: v1–52.

Mancia G, Laurent S, Agabiti-Rosei E, et al. Reappraisal of European guidelines on hypertension management: a European Society of Hypertension Task Force document. *J Hypertens*, 2009; 27: 2121–58.

Miller M, Stone NJ, Ballantyne C, et al. Triglycerides and cardiovascular disease: a scientific statement from the American Heart Association. *Circulation*, 2011; 123: 2292–333.

Mosca L, Benjamin EJ, Berra K, et al. Effectiveness-based guidelines for the prevention of cardiovascular disease in women—2011 update: a guideline from the American Heart Association. *J Am Coll Cardiol*, 2011; 57: 1404–23.

National Institute for Health and Clinical Excellence. *Hypertension: Clinical management of primary hypertension in adults [CG127]*. London: National Institute for Health and Clinical Excellence, 2011.

Hypertension

12.1 Classification of blood pressure

See Table 12.1.

Table 12.1 The 1999 WHO and International Hypertension Society classification

Classification	Blood pressure (SBP/DBP)
Optimal	<120/80
Normal	120–129/80–85
High normal	130–139/85–89
Grade 1	140–159/90–99
Grade 2	160–179/100–109
Grade 3	$\geq 180/\geq 110$
Isolated systolic hypertension	≥ 140

Reproduced from 'The World Health Organization–International Society of Hypertension guidelines for the management of hypertension', Guidelines Subcommittee, *Journal of Hypertension* 17(2), 151–83, copyright 1999 with permission of Wolters Kluwer Health

12.2 Assessing cardiovascular risk

- Risk of adverse cardiovascular events (stroke and CHD) show a continuous relationship with BP
- It is one of the most correctable risk factors
- Hypertension should not be treated in isolation but considered on the basis of the total CVD risk.

Classification of risk

- The JBS cardiovascular risk chart is based on the Framingham risk function (see Table 12.2)
- Framingham data can be applied to a northern European population and is related to CHD
- The JBS risk chart assesses 10-year CVD risk in non-diabetics.

Table 12.2 The British and European CVD risk scores

Risk	JBS CVD	SCORE (CV death)
Low	<15%	<4%
Moderate	15–20%	4–5%
High	20–30%	5–8%
Very high	>30%	>8%

Data from the European SCORE model.

Risk model limitations include:

- Under-estimation of lifetime risk
- Under-treatment of low risk groups (women and young)
- Over-treatment of high risk groups (male and elderly)
- They take no account of social deprivation
- They are for populations without CV events (primary not secondary prevention).

The European SCORE model uses similar risk factors based on a population of 250,000 and calculates 10-year risk of death from CVD.

Diabetes mellitus risk assessment:

- Type 1: Use UK PDS 'risk engine' or JBS assessor
- Type 2: Treat all as if 'secondary prevention' for a stroke or MI
- The evidence for treatment and CVD risks (lipids etc) in Type 1 diabetes is limited
- The risks for patients with type 2 diabetes for over 10 years or >50 years old is equivalent to having had a cardiovascular event
- As most T2 diabetic patients are over 50 all should be treated as high risk.

12.3 The measure of the problem

The British Hypertension Society recommends:

- 5-yearly BP measurements for all adults
- Annual measurements if previous high recording
- Seated and standing measurement in elderly
- Use of calibrated sphygmamometer and correct cuff size
- Diastolic BP at the disappearance of sound (phase V)
- Use of the mean of two readings.

The National Institute for Clinical Excellence (NICE) recommend clinic BP *and* subsequent ambulatory BP monitoring for diagnosis.

Ambulatory blood pressure monitoring (ABPM)

- Gives mean daytime (0700–2200) and night-time measurements and variability
- When using to confirm diagnosis ensure a 24-h recording, a minimum of 2 daytime readings per hour and use the average of 14 daytime measurements
- Diagnosis of grade 1 hypertension = 135/85.

Can also be used in:

- Variable blood pressure
- Suspected white coat syndrome

- Assessment of drug efficacy or resistance
- Pregnancy related hypertension
- Symptomatic hypotension.

Home measurements can be accurately used. Threshold for management is approximately 10/5 mmHg less than office BP sitting reading.

White coat (isolated office or clinic) hypertension: diagnosis should be reserved for those patients with consistently high clinic BP but normal ABPM. It occurs in 10% population but is <10% of grade 2–3 hypertension recordings. See Table 12.3.

12.4 Patient assessment

The clinical assessment of a patient should include the four Cs:

- **Contributory** factors and risk factors (CVD) (see Treatment section)
- **Causes,** i.e. secondary causes
- **Complications**—target organ damage (TOD)
- **Contraindications** to drugs.

Clinical and family history, examination, and laboratory investigations

Routine

Urinary albumin:creatine ratio, creatinine, and electrolytes, fasting glucose, lipids, an ECG and the European Guidelines recommend an echocardiogram (LVH).

Sensitivity for LVH is low (50%); that is, there are many 'false negatives', but positivity of Sokolow-Lyons index (SV1 + RV_{5-6} > 38 mm) is independently prognostic of adverse cardiovascular events.

Table 12.3 Risk stratification according to ESH/ESC guidelines

Other risk factors and disease history	Blood pressure (mmHg)				
	Normal SBP 120–129 or DBP 80–84	High normal SBP 130–139 or DBP 85–89	Grade 1 SBP 130–139 or DBP 90–99	Grade 2 SBP 160–179 or DBP 100–109	Grade 3 SBP≥180 or DBP≥110
No other risk factors	Average risk	Average risk	Low added risk	Moderate added risk	High added risk
1–2 risk factors	Low added risk	Low added risk	Moderate added risk	Moderate added risk	Very high added risk
3 or more factors or TOD or diabetes	Moderate added risk	High added risk	High added risk	High added risk	Very high added risk
ACC	High added risk	Very high added risk	Very high added risk	Very high added risk	Very high added risk

ACC, associated clinical conditions; TOD, target organ damage; SBP, systolic blood pressure; DBP, diastolic blood pressure. Reproduced from 'The European Society of Hypertension–European Society of Cardiology guidelines for the management of arterial hypertension', Guidelines Committee, *Journal of Hypertension.* 21(6), 1011–1053, copyright 2003 with permission of Wolters Kluwer Health.

Secondary causes (5–80%)

More likely if severe BP, rapid onset, and unresponsive to medication.

Renal parenchymal disease (5% all hypertension):

- Normal urinalysis and creatinine usually exclude renal parenchymal disease
- Blood and protein could suggest either glomerulonephritides or polycystic kidney disease
- Renal ultrasound (USS) and specialist referral would be appropriate next steps.

Renovascular disease (1–2%):

- Renal USS (difference of >1.5 cm between kidney length) or contrast MRA for diagnosis with selective X-ray renal angiography for certainty.

Aortic coarctation:

- Post ductal stenosis of thoracic aorta
- Associated bicuspid aortic valve and aortopathy
- Murmur of mid-systole- anterior chest to interscapular area
- Cardiac MRI allows non-invasive, non-ionizing assessment of anatomy, severity, and routine follow up (including post-operative complications).

Cushing's syndrome:

- Obese, diabetic, striae, cushingoid facies, and hypertension
- Hypercortisolaemia diagnosed by 24-h urine collection (>40 mcg)
- Low-dose dexamethasone suppression test can confirm Cushing's syndrome and a high-dose test may differentiate pituitary and adrenal cause
- Pseudocushings is associated with alcohol excess, and obese and depressed individuals.

Conn's disease (<1%):

- Muscle fatigue, hypokalaemia
- Low renin activity (<1 ng/ml/h), raised aldosterone and a renin-aldosterone ratio of >50 (a ratio driven by a high aldosterone is more meaningful than one dependent on low renin)
- Drugs that affect renin activity ideally should be withdrawn (4 weeks) prior to testing.

Phaeochromocytoma (0.1%):

- Tumour with raised urinary and plasma catecholamines
- Diagnosed with MRI, CT, USS, or m-iodobenzoic acid (^{131}I; MIBA)
- The 10% tumour (10% bilateral, 10% extra-adrenal, 10% malignant) Up to 10% are familial and these are usually bilateral
- Malignancy can only be confirmed by secondary spread, not histology
- The currently favoured diagnositic test is excess urinary secretion of the metabolites of catecholamines (normetadrenaline/normetanephrine or metadrenaline/metanephrine) over a 24-h period.

12.5 Complications—target organ damage (TOD)

- LVH: ECG (Sokolow-Lyons) or echocardiography (LV mass index; men >125 g/m^2, women >110 g/m^2) or most accurately MRI
- Carotid intimal thickening >0.9 mm
- Ankle brachial pressure index <0.9
- Carotid-femoral pulse wave velocity >12 m/s
- Microalbuminuria 30–300 mg/24 h

- eGFR <60 ml/min
- CV event
- Hypertensive retinal changes.

12.6 Anti-hypertensive treatment

Questions:

- When to start?
- What to start?
- Target of treatment?

When to start

European, BHS, and NICE guidance all focus on:

1. Cardiovascular risk
2. Grade of blood pressure.

Cardiovascular risk

- Low and moderate risk: lifestyle measures with BP assessment for 3 months then medication if indicated
- High and very high risk (see Figure 12.1): lifestyle measures and medication commenced immediately.

Grade of blood pressure

- Grade 1 and 2 hypertension (<180 systolic and/or 110 diastolic): assess risk for lifestyle or medication as initial choice
- Grade 3 hypertension (180 systolic and/or 110 diastolic or above): automatically high risk, therefore commence drug treatment.

Lifestyle measures

In primary prevention, lifestyle measures reduce overall CVD risk, reduce the incidence of hypertension and need for medication.

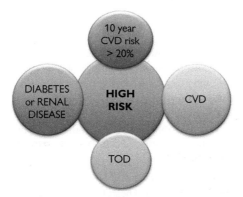

Figure 12.1 Cardiovascular risk. The presence of diabetes, target organ damage, or more than three risk factors indicate the individual is high risk.

Table 12.4 Contributory factors to hypertension, their respective targets, and important CVD risk factors.

Contributory factor	Target	Modifiable CVD risk factor
Weight	BMI 20–25 kg/m²	Hypercholesterolaemia
Alcohol#	Men <21, women <14 units	Smoking
Exercise	30 min/day	Diabetes
Salt excess	<100 mmol(2.4 g)/day	
Diet	DASH*	

#Chronic alcohol excess causes an increase in blood pressure; binge drinking is associated with stroke, BP may be very high during alcohol withdrawal. * DASH = Dietary Approaches to Stop Hypertension.
See: http://www.nhlbi.nih.gov/health/public/heart/hbp/dash

In established hypertension, lifestyle measures reduce need for medication, enhance medication effect, benefit CVD risk *and* have been proven by clinical trials to reduce BP by 2–10 mmHg.

Lifestyle interventions should be targeted at contributory and modifiable CVD risk factors: see Table 12.4.

Cigarette smoking does not cause hypertension but increases BP (acutely), stroke mortality, and CVD risk.

Anti-hypertensive medication

- Several classes of anti-hypertensive medications have been shown to reduce BP with equal efficacy
- When choosing the type of anti-hypertensive medication to use there are special indications, considerations, cautions, and contraindications to consider
- The response of the individual patient to any individual treatment in terms of efficacy or side effects is difficult to predict.

The evidence for medication

Anti-hypertensive vs placebo

Most trials are CVD outcome trials rather than specific hypertension endpoints.

- ACE inhibitors:
  - Blood Pressure Lowering Treatment Trialists Collaberation (BPLTT) was a meta-analysis of 29 trials (including ALLHAT, ANBP-2, SCOPE, LIFE). 162,341 patients comparing treatment regimes against placebo studies. 4 ACE inhibitor trials; risk reduction in stroke (30%), CHD (20%), and major cardiovascular events (21%)
  - Heart Outcomes Prevention Evaluation (HOPE)
  - Perindopirl Protection Against Recurrent Stroke Study (PROGRESS)
  - EUropean trial on Reduction Of cardiac events with Perindopril in stable Angina (EUROPA)
- Beta blockers:
  - Majority of evidence is based on atenolol
  - Reduced risk of stroke (RR 0.71) and heart failure (RR 0.58) but not CHD (RR 0.93) or mortality (RR 0.95)

- Given the evidence of BB benefit in CHD patients regardless of their BP, the lack of reduced CHD evidence in hypertension is confusing
- One explanation is the use of atenolol; as in CHD studies mortality benefit with metoprolol (RR 0.8), propanolol (RR 0.71), and timolol (RR 0.59) were far superior to atenolol (RR 1.02)
- Calcium channel blockers:
  - BPLTT examined two trials showing a risk reduction in stroke (39%) and major cardiovascular events (28%)
- Diuretics (thiazide-like):
  - This 'older' diuretic has good evidence of reducing risk of stroke (RR 0.66), CHD (RR 0.72), heart failure (RR 0.58), and mortality (RR 0.9)
  - It is particularly effective at BP lowering as a combination therapy
- Angiotensin receptor blockers:
  - SCOPE trial compared candesartan to placebo (many already had a different anti-hypertensive agent), found a RR reduction of 11% for stroke, MI, and CV death, and 28% risk reduction in non-fatal stroke
  - Irbesartan and losartan have been shown to improve renal dysfunction in addition to absolute BP reduction in Type 2 diabetics.

Comparison trials

Several trials have looked to answer the question of whether one drug is superior to another.

- Anti-hypertensive and Lipid Lowering Treatment to prevent Heart Attack Trial (ALLHAT) compared chlortalidone (thiazide-like drug) to doxazosin, amlodipine, and lisinopril
- Limitations in study design favouring chlortalidone, but it is still important due to large size (40,000 patients):
  - Doxazosin was stopped at 3 years due to inferiority
  - Other 3 arms showed no significant difference in non-fatal MI and fatal CHD
  - Lisinopril was inferior for heart failure (vs chlortalidone) and stroke (vs amlodipine) but this was attributed to a lower BP response
- Australian National Blood Pressure Study (ANBP2): hydrochlorthiazide vs ACE inhibitor:
  - Equivocal findings with borderline superiority of ACE inhibitors, but several limitations
- Losartan Intervention For End point reduction in hypertension (LIFE) trial examined losartan versus atenolol:
  - ARB had reduced cardiovascular events due to reduced risk of stroke with similar BP levels
  - This could reflect inferior action of BB in stroke rather than ARB superiority as a class
- Outcomes in hypertensive patients at high cardiovascular risk treated with regimens based on valsartan or amlodipine (VALUE):
  - Heart failure was included in the primary outcome with a RR of 1.04
- International Verapamil Trandolapril Study (INVEST) examined verapamil versus atenolol with an RR of 0.98; heart failure was not a primary outcome
- Anglo-Scandinavian Cardiac Outcomes Trial (ASCOT) examined amlodipine versus atenolol:
  - Stopped early as the secondary endpoints favoured amlodipine
  - Limitations include that heart failure was not in the primary outcomes and that the atenolol arm received sub-optimal BP therapy in 45%.

Summary of the evidence

- Cardiovascular outcomes are more dependent upon total BP lowering rather than class of drug used
- Individual response to treatment is, however, variable, with all classes of drug having similar effects except in the instance of age and ethnicity
- Monotherapy has been shown to rarely achieve target BP—most people will require combination therapy
- Complementary combinations of medications are outlined in Figure 12.2
- Depending upon patient preference and drug side effects low-dose monotherapy may be the initial therapy
- At higher levels of BP or where there is evidence of TOD, commencement with low-dose combination therapy is highly advisable
- The British Hypertension Society recommend an AB/CD approach based on levels of renin activity (see Figure 12.3)
- 'High-renin' individuals (<55 years and Caucasian) should receive an ACE inhibitor or ARB, or if resistant add in a BB or spirinolactone
- 'Low-renin' individuals (>55 years and Afro-Caribbean) should receive CCB and thiazide-like diuretic combination therapy (see Figure 12.4)
- NICE guidelines (2011) recommend that if a diuretic is required use a thiazide-like diuretic (chlortalidone or indapamide) in preference to bendroflumethiazide.

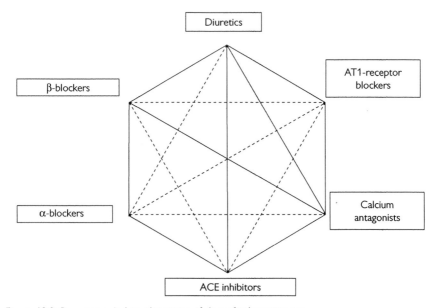

Figure 12.2 Recommended combinations of drugs for hypertension.

Reproduced from 'The European Society of Hypertension–European Society of Cardiology guidelines for the management of arterial hypertension', Guidelines Committee, *Journal of Hypertension*, 21(6), 1011–1053, copyright 2003, with permission of Wolters Kluwer Health.

- Block angiotensin 1 conversion to angiotensin 2
- Cough at 10–20%, angiodema in 1%
- Do not give in pregnancy (oligohydramnios and IUGR)

- Dihydropyridines (nifedipine and amlodopine), block L-type calcium channel of smooth muscle
- Nondihydropyridines (verapamil and diltiazem) block myocyte calcium channels
- Peripheral oedema (DHP) and bradycardia (NDHP)

- Negative ionotropic and chronotropic action and partial block of renin
- Lethargy, PVD
- Increase likelihood of diabetes
- Dyslipidaemia (high HDL low TG)

- Thiazide diuretics (bendroflumethiazide)
- Thiazide like diuretics (indapamide). Similar metabolic effects as BB (potentiate effect)
- Potassium sparing (spirinolactone and amiloride): only use secondary to thiazide

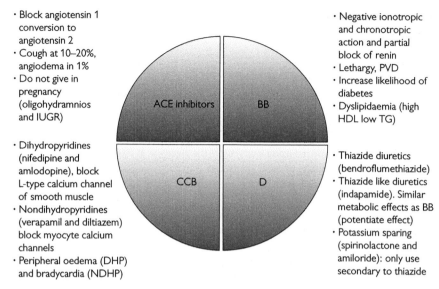

Figure 12.3 Flow-chart summary of diagnosis and treatment guidelines.

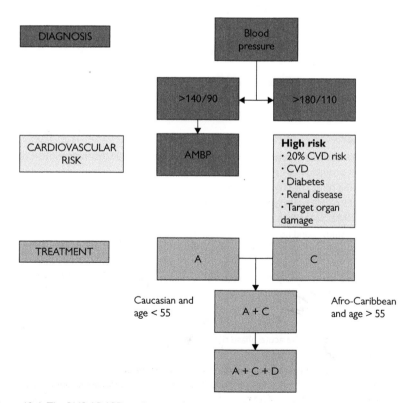

Figure 12.4 The BHS AB/CD guidance with common side effects of the medications

Special considerations

These considerations will affect the choice of medication.

Elderly

- Ageing results in a continuous SBP increase and a DBP increase until age 65
- DBP plateaus, with loss of arterial compliance causing an increased pulse pressure in the elderly
- BP is also more variable so that several measurements (including postural BP) should be made in the elderly prior to diagnosis
- The relative benefit in BP reduction is as great in the elderly as in the young, but their overall risk is usually higher because of other risk factors
- Results in greater absolute benefit, with proven benefit in individuals >80 years old (Hypertension in the Very Elderly Trial)
- There is also good evidence that BP reduction provides cognitive advantages and protects against vascular dementia and Alzheimer's disease.

Young

- Pulse pressure in the young tends to be narrower because of their compliant large blood vessels
- Diastolic hypertension rather than systolic elevation is sometimes more prominent
- The young may have a relatively low 10-year CVD risk but substantial lifetime risk, and there is concern that their treatment may be inappropriately delayed based on conventional risk tables.

Diabetes

- Commence treatment in high–normal BP patients with a BP target of <130/80 by lifestyle and any class of medication
- There is good evidence that blockade of the renin-angiotensin system provides renoprotection
- Use an ACE inhibitor (or ARB) as the first-line drug in hypertensive diabetic patients; they are strongly indicated in the presence of microalbuminuria or diabetic nephropathy.

Renal disease

- Threshold of treatment remains >140/90 with a BP target of <130/80, reduced to <125/75 if evidence of proteinuria ≥1 g in 24 h
- Blockade of the renin-angiotensin system is renoprotective (either ACE inhibitor or ARB)
- The CO-OPERATIVE study appeared to show additional benefit from a combination of ACE inhibitor and ARB but its findings have been challenged
- ON-TARGET study found no additional benefit but more adverse effects from the combination.

Stroke

- Hypertension is the most important treatable risk factor in stroke, with half of stroke patients having a history of hypertension
- BP can rise markedly around the time of a stroke and then usually improves gradually over 2 weeks
- Advice for treatment in the acute phase remains controversial but is usually advocated by 48 h if the pressure remains elevated
- Treatment reduces the risk of fatal and non-fatal stroke recurrence and all major cardiovascular events (The Perindopril Protection Against Recurrent Stroke Study (PRO-GRESS)).

Pregnancy

Hypertension occurs in 8–10% of pregnancies. The types of hypertension and the threshold levels to commence treatment are:

- Pre-existing hypertension: prior to pregnancy or before 20 weeks and persisting 42 days postpartum. Treatment at >150/95
- Gestational hypertension: occurs after 20 weeks gestation and resolves within 42 days. If the presence of proteinuria (++ dipstix or 300 mg/24 h) then it is known as pre-eclampsia. Treat if >140/90 or evidence of proteinuria
- Pre-existing hypertension and proteinuria (≥3 g/24 h).

The evidence for drug use in pregnancy is limited:

- Methyldopa, labetolol and CCBs are commonly used
- ACE inhibitors, angiotensin II antagonists, and renin inhibitors are absolutely contraindicated
- Traditionally diuretics have been avoided more on theoretical arguments than any evidence of adverse effect
- If breastfeeding, the following antihypertensive medications are considered safe:
  - Labetolol
  - Nifedipine
  - Enalapril
  - Captopril
  - Atenolol
  - Metoprolol
- There is an increased risk of long-term hypertension and CVD in patients who have suffered gestational hypertension or pre-eclampsia
- Low-dose aspirin has some protective effect and magnesium sulphate reduces the risk of developing eclampsia (Magpie trial), although its use is not universal.

Target of treatment

- The BPLTT, ABCD (Appropriate Blood pressure Control in Diabetes), and HOT (Hypertension Optimal Treatment) studies provide good evidence that intense treatment regimes reduce the CVD risk
- HOT additionally demonstrated that a J-shaped curve response with treatment did not occur, supporting a lower target level of BP control.

Blood pressure targets

- Hypertensive <140/85
- Diabetic <130/80
- Renal disease <130/80.

Other targets

Other measures to reduce cardiovascular risk should be implemented:

- Aspirin: 75 mg for the primary prevention in individuals with treated BP and a 10 year CVD risk >20%, and secondary prevention in all existing CVD patients
- Statin therapy: should be commenced as primary prevention in individuals with a 10 year CVD risk of 20% and total cholesterol >3.5 mmol/, or as secondary prevention in all CVD patients.

Further reading

British Hypertension Society. The British Hypertension Society guidelines for hypertension management 2004 summary. *BMJ*, 2004; 328: 634–40.

British Hypertension Society. Guidelines for the management of hypertension: report of the Fourth Working Party of the British Hypertension Society 2004 – BHS 4. *J. Human Hypertens.* 2004; 18: 139–85.

Calhoun DA, Jones D, Textor S, *et al.* Resistant hypertension: diagnosis, management and treatment. A scientific statement from the American Heart Association Professional Education Committee of the Council for High Blood Pressure Research. *Hypertension,* 2008; 51: 1403–19.

Camm, AJ, Lüscher, TF, Serruys, PW (eds). *The European Society of Cardiology Textbook of Cardiovascular Medicine.* Oxford University Press, 2009.

European Society of Hypertension, European Society of Cardiology. Guidelines for the management of arterial hypertension. *J. Hypertens,* 2003; 21: 1011–53.

NICE guidelines (2011), available at http://guidance.nice.org.uk

Lipids

13.1 Overview of lipid molecules and metabolism

- Provide fat and muscle with a steady source of fatty acids for storage and energy utilization respectively
- Provide hepatic and peripheral tissues with cholesterol for synthesis of bile salts, cell membranes, and steroid hormones.

Cholesterol and cholesterol esters

- Cholesterol and cholesterol esters are carried by all lipoproteins but predominantly by low-density lipoprotein (LDL)
- Cellular cholesterol demands are met through:
    - Uptake of cholesterol esters from LDL via the LDL receptor or
    - Intracellular synthesis pathway that involves HMG CoA reductase as its rate-limiting step.

Triglycerides

Are hydrolysed to free fatty acids, providing an important energy source.

- Triglyceride demands are met through:
    - Intestinal uptake
    - Endogenous hepatic synthesis
- Stored as adipose tissue
- Carried by all lipoproteins but predominantly by very low-density lipropoteins (VLDL) and chylomicrons.

13.2 Plasma lipoproteins and apolipoproteins

- Lipids are hydrophobic and cannot circulate freely in water-based plasma
- Apolipoproteins are a group of lipid binding proteins that transport water-insoluble lipids and regulate their metabolism, forming lipoproteins

- Apolipoprotein A forms high-density lipoprotein (HDL) ('good cholesterol'/anti-atherogenic)
- Apolipoprotein B forms 'bad cholesterol' (atherogenic)—mainly LDL (but also IDL, VLDL).

Lipoproteins are large molecules with:

- A core of triglycerides and cholesteryl esters
- An outer layer of phospholipids, free cholesterol and apolipoproteins (see Figure 13.1).

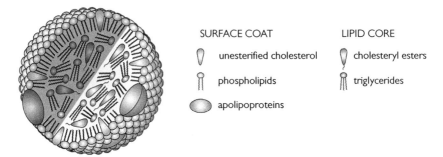

SURFACE COAT

    unesterified cholesterol

    phospholipids

    apolipoproteins

LIPID CORE

    cholesteryl esters

    triglycerides

Figure 13.1 Lipoprotein structure.

This figure was published in *The Williams Textbook of Endocrinology*, Henry M. Kronenberg, Shlomo Memed, Kenneth S. Polonsky *et al.*, copyright Elsevier 2011.

Five major groups of lipoproteins exist—separated on the basis of their densities into high, intermediate, low, or very low-density lipoproteins (see Figure 13.2).

- In order of descending size, they are chylomicrons, VLDL, IDL, LDL and HDL
- This forms the basis of the Fredrickson classification of dyslipidaemias.

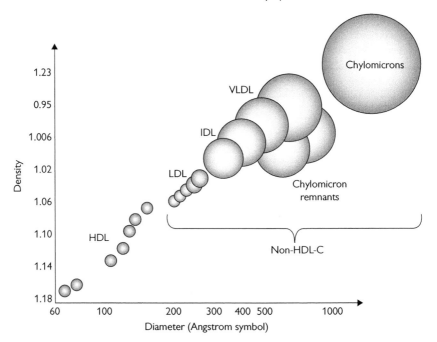

Figure 13.2 Relative size of lipoprotein fractions.

HDL

HDL is anti-atherogenic via multiple mechanisms including:

- Reverse cholesterol transport: transfer of peripheral cholesterol to the liver for breakdown and excretion in bile
- Inhibition of thrombosis and LDL oxidation.

LDL

- The main carrier of cholesterol
- LDL receptor mutations result in the familial hypercholesterolaemia phenotype
- Oxidized LDL can be internalized by macrophages leading to the formation of foam cells and plaque development
- Oxidized LDL plays a pivotal role in atherogenesis via a number of mechanisms including:
  - Endothelial damage
  - Macrophage recruitment
  - Increased platelet aggregation
- Triglyceride levels affect LDL composition and measurement
- When triglyceride levels are high, the triglyceride content of LDL can increase and becomes more atherogenic
- This qualitative difference in LDL to a degree explains the increased likelihood of atherosclerotic disease for any given LDL concentration in individuals with the metabolic syndrome
- At high triglyceride concentrations (>5 mmol/l), LDL measurements maybe inaccurate.

VLDL and chylomicrons

- VLDL and chylomicrons are the largest lipoproteins and contain proportionally the most triglyceride
- Both chylomicrons and VLDL may undergo metabolism to become smaller lipoproteins including LDL.

13.3 Cardiovascular risk associated with dyslipidaemia

- Hypercholesterolaemia acts in a multiplicative manner with other risk factors to produce an individual's overall risk
- Combinations of small elevations in various risk factors increase cardiovascular risk—often referred to as 'global risk'
- May be estimated from several risk equations such as FRAMINGHAM (inaccurate in European populations and ethnic minorities) or SCORE
- Risk calculators are only intended for use in a non-high-risk primary prevention population, i.e. *those not known to have CAD or a coronary risk equivalent* such as:
  - Cerebrovascular disease
  - Peripheral arterial disease
  - Aortic aneurysms
  - Diabetes
- CKD, although not strictly a CAD equivalent, is also associated with substantially increased cardiovascular mortality and morbidity

- Global risk estimation guides treatment thresholds: *NICE recommend the use of a ≥20% 10-year risk of developing CVD as a threshold for the initiation of statin therapy in primary prevention*
- Lipid-lowering therapy therefore should be viewed as aiming to *lower cardiovascular risk rather than lipid levels per se*
- Therefore, even patients without particularly high lipid indices should be treated with lipid-lowering therapy.

LDL and cardiovascular risk

- Strongly positive continuous and independent relationship of LDL-C (the amount of cholesterol contained in LDL) concentrations with the risk of major cardiovascular events (CVEs)
- This relationship is apparent over a wide range of concentrations (with no apparent threshold) and patient ages and is present in both sexes
- Statin therapy is associated with a linear relationship between the absolute LDL cholesterol reduction achieved and the proportional reduction in CVEs
- A sustained reduction of LDL-C concentration of 1 mmol/l produces a proportional reduction in major vascular events of almost a quarter.

Currently the lowering of LDL-C concentrations is the primary target of lipid-lowering interventions recommended by all consensus guidelines.

HDL and cardiovascular risk

- HDL-C concentrations have a strong continuous and independent *inverse* relationship with cardiovascular risk, which displays no apparent threshold
- An increase of 0.03 mmol/l in HDL-C levels is associated with a 6% reduction in coronary mortality
- Low HDL is often associated with other lipid profile abnormalities, such as increased LDL and triglyceride concentrations, as is found in the metabolic syndrome
- HDL's relationship with CAD risk is independent and present throughout a range of LDL concentrations
- Low HDL-C levels (<1.03 for men and <1.3 for women) are found in almost half of patients with known CHD
- Most interventions that increase HDL-C also decrease triglycerides and LDL-C
- This complicates the assessment of the impact of pharmacologically mediated HDL increases on CVEs
- Indirect evidence suggests therapeutic increases in HDL levels may reduce CVEs
- There have been no large-scale trials that have been designed to show that increasing HDL will result in lower event rates
- Therefore LDL-C reduction remains the primary target of lipid-lowering strategies in primary and secondary prevention of CVD.

Non-HDL cholesterol, apolipoprotein B and cardiovascular risk

- All the atherogenic lipoproteins (LDL mainly, but also IDL and VLDL) are associated with apolipoprotein B
- Apolipoprotein B levels represent all cholesterol present in serum that is not bound as HDL-C and therefore it conveys the full atherogenic potential of a given lipid profile

- Non-HDL-C concentrations carry similar prognostic information to apolipoprotein B (see Figures 13.3 and 13.4), with the added advantage of being easily calculated from the standard lipid profile:

Non-HDL cholesterol concentration = total cholesterol − HDL-C.

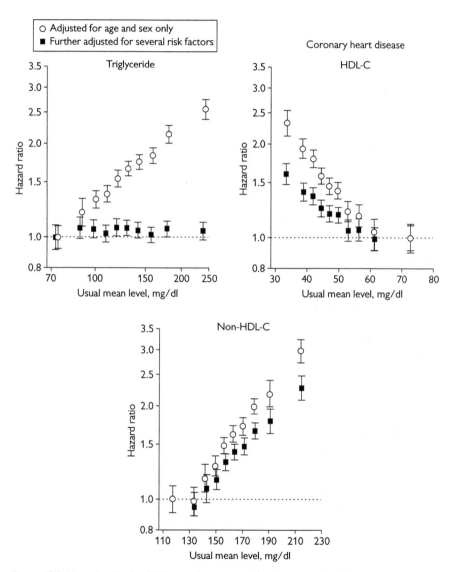

Figure 13.3 Hazard ratios for CHD or ischaemic stroke across quantiles of usual triglyceride, HDL-C, and non-HDL-C levels.

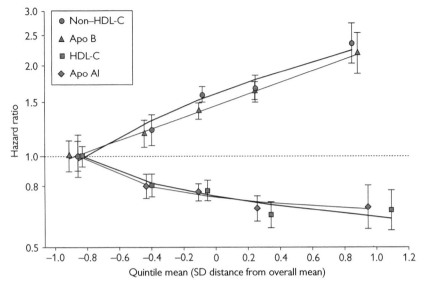

Figure 13.4 Hazard ratios for CHD across fifths of usual lipids or apolipoproteins.

Triglycerides and cardiovascular risk

- High triglyceride levels are often found with other disorders of lipid metabolism producing either increased LDL/VLDL/IDL or decreased HDL
- The decision to treat an elevated triglyceride level should be guided by likely aetiology
- After adjustment for lipid and non-lipid factors, elevated triglycerides do not confer additional risk for the development of CAD
- Severe elevations in triglyceride level (>10) may mandate treatment to reduce the risk of pancreatitis, which is itself a condition with a high mortality.

13.4 The dyslipidaemias

Classification systems

- Traditionally the Fredrickson classification system (see Table 13.1) was used to categorize familial (primary) lipid profile abnormalities on the basis of which lipoproteins and lipids were elevated
- Fredrickson groups are genetically non-specific and the classification does not account for aetiology or HDL levels
- Phenotypes IIb, 3, 4, and 5 are polygenic
- The Fredrickson classification has largely been replaced by a simpler focus on primary/secondary and isolated/combined dyslipidaemias

Table 13.1 Fredrickson classification system

Fredrickson type	Example conditions	Lipoprotein phenotype	Prevalence	Association with premature CAD	Comments
I	Familial chylomicronaemia	Severely raised triglycerides Cholesterol normal or mildly elevated	Rare	No	Often leads to pancreatitis
IIa	Familial hypercholesterolaemia	Severely raised LDL	Common	Yes	Monogenic disorder due to decreased LDLR function
IIb	Familial combined hyperlipidaemia	TC/LDL increased ± Increased triglycerides	Common	Strong	VLDL and LDL increased so TG and TC increased Need at least one first degree relative to make the diagnosis
III	Familial dysbetalipoproteinemia	Increased TC Increased triglycerides (Often reduced HDL)	Uncommon	Strong	Accumulation of remnant lipoprotein particles such as IDL/partially metabolized VLDL. A necessary, but not sufficient, condition of the receptor deficient ApoE2 mutation is required. Usually a second factor such as alcohol or diabetes is required for expression of the phenotype
IV	Familial hypertriglyceridemia	Cholesterol normal or elevated depending on VLDL levels Increased triglycerides Often reduced HDL	Common	Weak	Genetically heterogenous condition Due to increased VLDL production and VLDL breakdown may be normal or reduced VLDL increased and HDL decreased LDL relatively normal and TG levels respond well to dietary modification
V	Familial mixed hypertriglyceridemia	Severely raised triglycerides Cholesterol mildly or moderately elevated	Rare	Weak	VLDL and chylomicrons increased due to increased synthesis/decreased catabolism of both

- Primary or secondary dyslipidaemias:
  - Primary causes of dyslipidaemia are genetic in origin
  - Secondary causes are acquired either through environmental factors or through the effect of another disease process, e.g. hypothyroidism
  - This is also is an oversimplification as those with a genetic predisposition towards dyslipidaemia may only manifest it in the presence of secondary causes
- Isolated or combined dyslipidaemias:
  - Isolated dyslipidaemias affect one component of the plasma lipids
  - Combined dyslipidaemias affect multiple components of the lipid profile.

Primary disorders of LDL metabolism

Elevations in LDL cholesterol result from one or both of:

- Increased lipoprotein synthesis
- Impaired clearance due to:
  - Abnormal lipoproteins
  - Abnormal lipoprotein receptors.

Familial hypercholesterolaemia

- The most common of the autosomal dominant hypercholesterolaemias—significant risk of premature CAD
- Mutation of LDLR gene (encodes LDL receptor protein which removes LDL from circulation) or apolipoprotein B (which is the part of LDL that binds with the receptor)
- Results in reduced LDL clearance and elevated LDL:
  - The excess LDL is deposited in skin, tendons and arteries resulting in the development of xanthalesma, xanthoma, and atheroma
  - The phenotype is dependent on total LDL receptor activity (depends on how many defective copies of the LDLR gene are inherited), i.e. homozygotes have a more severe phenotype
  - Overall cardiovascular risk is determined primarily by LDL levels in homozygotes and by LDL levels and conventional risk factors in heterozygotes.

Diagnosis

Diagnosis made using the Simon Broome criteria.

- Definite FH (adult)
  - TC >7.5 or LDL >4.9 + tendon xanthomas in patient or first/second degree relative or
  - DNA evidence of defective LDL receptor, Apo B, or PCSK9 mutation
- Possible FH (adult)
  - TC >7.5 or LDL >4.9 + FHx of MI (<50 years in second degree relative, <60 years in 1st degree relative) or TC>7.5 first/second degree relative.

Treatment

- A statin is the first-line treatment, with the aim to reduce LDL-C by 50%
- Additional lipid-lowering agents maybe used as an adjunct—despite achieving lower LDL levels, data on reduction in CV risk with non-statins is limited
- For refractory or intolerant patients there are more invasive options, such as LDL apheresis.

Familial combined hyperlipidaemia

Familial combined hyperlipidaemia (FCHL) is a relatively common (probably oligogenetic) condition and is responsible for up to half of all cases of familial CAD and ~10% of premature CAD.

- LDL-C concentrations maybe normal or elevated whereas HDL is usually lowered and triglycerides are often raised
- Caused by an overproduction of apoliproprotein B
- Increases in *small dense* LDL particles, serum apolipoprotein B, triglycerides, and reduced HDL, confers a threefold risk for development of CAD
- Small dense LDL particles (as opposed to large or intermediate size) are associated with increased atherogenecity.

Diagnosis

- A diagnostic difficulty with FCHL is its phenotypic heterogeneity. It has been associated with multiple lipoprotein phenotypes (IIa, IIb and IV)
- A compatible family history, together with LDL:apo B ratio of less than 1.2, is suggestive of the condition
- In cases where the predominant abnormality is hypertriglyceridemia it can be difficult to distinguish from FH. Elevated apolipoprotein B levels (a marker of the total number of atherogenic particles including LDL, VLDL, and IDL particles) supports a diagnosis of FCH.

Treatment
- Treatment of FCHL depends on the relative rises in LDL and triglyceride levels. Those with predominantly raised triglycerides maybe treated with a fibrate to reduce risk of pancreatitis.

Polygenic hypercholesterolemia
- This poorly understood condition is suggested by the presence of moderate hypercholesterolaemia in a number of family members with premature CAD
- Unlike FH, it is not associated with the formation of xanthomata.

Diagnosis
- Is primarily one of exclusion and relies primarily on the distinction from heterozygous FH, in which LDL-C concentrations are usually higher
- Triglyceride levels tend to remain relatively undisturbed.

Treatment
- Statin therapy.

Disorders of HDL metabolism
- Low HDL levels are frequently found in CAD patients, particularly in those who develop the disease prematurely
- Low HDL levels may be caused by:
    - Impaired apo A-I synthesis
    - Increased breakdown of HDL-C
- Secondary causes of low HDL are common and should always be excluded. They include:
    - Metabolic syndrome and Type II DM (particularly in those with associated visceral obesity)
    - Cigarette smoking
    - Elevated triglycerides

- Sedentary lifestyle
- High carbohydrate diet (in particular foods with a high glycemic index)
- Medications (e.g. progestins and anabolic steroids)
- Hypothyroidism.

Disorders causing isolated severely low HDL levels are rare.

Familial primary hypoalphalipoproteinemia

This is relatively common autosomal dominant condition and is usually due to decreased apo A-I production or increased apo A-I catabolism. It is associated with premature CAD.

- Defined by a low HDL with relatively normal VLDL and LDL, with no secondary causes of low HDL and the presence of a similar lipid profile in a first degree relative
- It is sometimes associated with increased triglyceride levels
- LDL-C maybe predominantly of the atherogenic B type in this condition.

Disorders of triglyceride metabolism

- The major carriers of triglycerides in plasma are VLDL (derived predominantly from endogenous hepatic synthesis) and chylomicrons (derived predominantly from exogenous sources of fat)
- Hypertriglyceridemia is associated with elevations in these lipoproteins as a result of their increased synthesis (most commonly) and/or decreased catabolism
- Hypertriglyceridemia features in all the Fredrickson classification scheme dyslipidaemias, except for FH
- Severe elevations in triglycerides are most frequently due to heritable genetic disorders acting in concert with secondary causes (see Table 13.2).

The two main reasons to treat elevated triglyceride levels are:

- Prevention of CAD
- Prevention of pancreatitis.

Table 13.2 Causes of hypertriglyceridaemia

Common primary disorders of triglyceride metabolism that are associated with premature CAD	Common causes of elevated triglycerides encountered in clinical practice	Other common causes of elevated triglycerides
Familial combined hyperlipidaemia Residual dyslipidaemia in well controlled type II DM Familial hypoalphalipoproteinaemia	Increased caloric intake Obesity Diabetes Alcohol	Metabolic syndrome/obesity Uncontrolled or untreated DM Medications and alcohol Hypothyroidism ESRF Nephrotic syndrome HIV
These are mixed dyslipidaemias that each affect 1–5% of the population and together are thought to be responsible for half of all premature CAD.	*Most of these patients will also have an abnormality of another component of the lipid profile*	

- Whereas lifestyle measures have modest effects in lowering LDL they have a significant role to play in the management of hyperlipidaemia
- Dietary modification together with reduction/cessation of alcohol intake can produce profound reductions in triglyceride levels.

Secondary causes of dyslipidaemia

- See Table 13.3. Reversible secondary causes of dyslipidaemia should always be considered and often treated prior to the commencement of lipid lowering therapy
- Additionally, many secondary causes of dyslipidaemia also independently contribute to overall cardiovascular risk and as such should be identified and addressed as part of an overall risk-reduction strategy.

Table 13.3 Secondary causes of dyslipidaemia

Endocrine	Hepatic	Renal	Miscellaneous
Type 2 diabetes	Cholestatic liver	Nephrotic syndrome	Cigarette smoking
Hypothyroidism	disease	Chronic renal failure	SLE
Cushing's syndrome	Primary biliary		Medications
Obesity	cirrhosis		

Hypothyroidism

- Approximately 90% of patients with hypothyroidism will have an abnormality of triglycerides or LDL levels
- Hypothyroid patients are more likely to suffer from statin-induced myopathy
- NICE recommends the routine measurement of TSH for all patients with dyslipidaemia
- In general, thyroxine replacement corrects the dyslipidaemia.

Type II diabetes mellitus

- Insulin resistance is strongly associated with quantitative and qualitative changes of all aspects of the lipid profile, specifically
  - Increased triglycerides and VLDL
  - Increased LDL concentrations which tend to be small and dense
  - Decreased HDL concentrations
- Overall, metabolic syndrome/insulin resistance frequently produces a lipid phenotype that is particularly atherogenic.

13.5 Treatment of dyslipidaemia

Lifestyle measures

Dietary modification, exercise, smoking cessation, and moderate alcohol intake all have been demonstrated to positively affect cardiovascular outcomes with minimal adverse effects (see Tables 13.4 and 13.5).

Pharmacological intervention

- Reasonable to attempt lifestyle measures for between 6 months and 1 year prior to pharmacological intervention (primary prevention)

- The decision to initiate therapy is based on overall global cardiovascular risk, particularly as there are no 'normal' values in lipid indices but rather a continuum of risk associated with rising values
- In secondary prevention, these measures should be considered in tandem with pharmacological intervention
- Patients who do not respond to lipid-lowering therapy, are intolerant to multiple agents, or who have a significant family history of dyslipidaemia should be considered for referral to a lipid specialist.

Table 13.4 Effect of lifestyle measures on lipid parameters

	Dietary modification, weight loss	Exercise	Smoking cessation	Moderate alcohol intake
LDL	Mild decrease (5–7%) Can take 6 months	Mild decrease with regular exercise	No effect on levels but less oxidation	Variable
TG	High levels associated with obesity Moderate weight loss associated with decrease of up to a quarter	Small decrease with regular exercise	No effect	Increased Abstention recommended in those with severe hypertriglycerdimia
HDL	HDL levels inversely proportional to BMI Increase of 0.01 mmol/l per 1 kg lost Low-carb diet increases HDL Low-fat diet decreases both HDL and LDL	Up to 10% increase with regular exercise (particularly in those with metabolic syndrome)	Average increase of 0.10 mmol/l	Up to 8% increase and translates into lowered MI risk

Table 13.5 NICE lifestyle measures recommendations

Dietary modification and weight loss	Exercise	Smoking cessation	Moderate alcohol intake
A diet which contains <30% total fat and avoid saturated fats At least two portions of fish per week, including a portion of oily fish Five portions of fruit and vegetables per day Appropriate advice and support to work towards achieving and maintaining a healthy weight	Moderate intensity exercise for 30 minutes/day, five days a week	Cessation advice and support ± pharmacotherapy	Men: 3–4 units/day Women: 2–3 units/day

General overview of evidence and indications for non-statin lipid-lowering agents

See Table 13.6 for a general overview.

Fibrates

- Bezafibrate and fenofibrate (most common)
- Most trials of fibrate therapy have *not* demonstrated reductions in cardiovascular or all-cause mortality despite reductions in coronary events and major adverse CVEs
- This has been confirmed in a recent meta-analysis
- The benefits that have been demonstrated appear to be in specific subsets of patients with features of the metabolic syndrome, such as elevated triglycerides and low HDL
- NICE do not recommend the routine use of fibrate monotherapy as a primary or secondary prevention agent. It maybe considered in those intolerant to statins
- NICE do not recommend the use of fibrate in combination therapy with statins for primary prevention
- In moderate-to-severe hypertriglyceridemia fibrates are highly effective in lowering the risk of pancreatitis
- Fibrates have microvascular benefits, reducing the risk of diabetic retinopathy and albuminuria.

Niacin

- The first lipid-lowering agent but has been largely superseded by statins due to their better tolerability and a considerable body of evidence for both primary and secondary prevention
- The growing emphasis on the concept of 'residual risk' (see Section 13.6) together with improved strategies for minimising side effects has renewed interest in the use of niacin, mainly as an adjunctive therapy
- The majority of trials examining niacin are relatively small secondary prevention trials/imaging studies and have assessed it as a combination therapy
- The landmark Coronary Drug Project trial (monotherapy) was the first study to demonstrate a positive effect of any lipid-lowering agent in reducing coronary events (secondary prevention in hypercholesterolaemic men post MI)
- A late benefit in all-cause mortality reduction became apparent in the 15-year follow up study
- At present there are no reported trials comparing niacin/statin combination therapy or niacin monotherapy to intensive statin therapy
- There is very little available data on the use of niacin in primary prevention and, as such, NICE does not recommend its use for this indication.

Bile acid sequestrants

- Cholestyramine, colestipol, and the newer agent colesevelam
- There is some evidence to indicate a reduction in coronary events with the use of bile acid sequestrants
- The Lipid Research Clinics Coronary Primary Prevention trial examined cholestyramine as a primary prevention agent
- There was a statistically significant reduction in the composite primary end point of coronary mortality and non-fatal coronary events of almost a fifth. All-cause mortality was not reduced

Table 13.6 Pharmacology, efficacy, important side effects and interactions of non-statin lipid-lowering drugs

	Pharmacology	Efficacy	Important side effects and interactions
Fibrates	Mimic free fatty acids structure, thereby are agonists for the PPAR α family of nuclear hormone receptors, which control transcription of lipid metabolism genes • Increases breakdown of triglyceride-rich particles • Reduces hepatic secretion of VLDL (the most triglyceride rich lipoprotein) • Increases HDL synthesis • Increases LDL removal	Depends on baseline lipid levels, those with high triglycerides and low HDL derive the greatest benefit • Significantly lowers triglyceride levels (30–50%) • Mildly to moderately elevates HDL levels (5%, variable effect depending on population) • Mildly lowers LDL and total cholesterol levels (5%)	• Increases serum creatinine (with fenofibrate and maybe delayed, clinical significance unclear but to be avoided in patients with severe renal impairment) • Myopathy (More commonly when used concomitantly with a statin due to inhibition of CYP3A4 system–dependent statin metabolism) • Inhibits warfarin metabolism • Fenofibrate increases cyclosporine metabolism
Niacin	Multiple sites of action • Reduces adipocyte lipolysis through inhibition of cAMP production, which lowers free fatty acid levels reducing available substrate for VLDL production • Lowers LDL mainly as a secondary effect of reduced VLDL (as LDL is largely derived from VLDL) • Reduces LDL oxidation • Prevents HDL breakdown • Reduces hepatic triglyceride synthesis via inhibition of DGAT2 (the rate-limiting enzyme for triglyceride synthesis)	• At a dose of 1.5 g/day the rule of 20% approximates the magnitude of niacin's effect; reduction in LDL and triglycerides by 20% and an increase in HDL by 20%	The frequency and severity of many of its side effects vary considerably between the different preparations (immediate, prolonged, and sustained-release niacin) but are largely reversible and dose dependent • Flushing Prostaglandin mediated side effect that is the major reason for patient discontinuation of the drug, reduced by pretreatment with aspirin; tends to decrease in frequency and severity with consistent repeat dosing • Nausea and pruritis • Gastrointestinal upset • Hepatic dysfunction (commonly associated with elevations in liver enzymes but rarely significant hepatotoxicity; regular LFT measurement is recommended) • Hyperglycaemia (particularly in diabetics and those with insulin resistance, the clinical significance of this is unclear)

Bile acid sequestrants	Multiple sites of action	• LDL-C reduced by 9–20%
	• Reduces adipocyte lipolysis through inhibition of cAMP production, which lowers free fatty acid levels reducing available substrate for VLDL production	• HDL-C increased by 3–11%
		• These effects are synergistic with the statins and niacin
	• Lowers LDL mainly as a secondary effect of reduced VLDL (as LDL is largely derived from VLDL)	• Moderate elevation of triglycerides
		• Malabsorption of fat soluble vitamins
	• Reduces LDL oxidation	• Absorption of verapamil, metoprolol, digoxin, warfarin, levothyroxine, valproate and oral contraceptives affected by concomitant administration of bile acid sequestrants and, as such, bile acid sequestrants should not normally be ingested within 3–4 h of these drugs
	• Prevents HDL breakdown	
	• Reduces hepatic triglyceride synthesis via inhibition of DGAT2 (the rate limiting enzyme for triglyceride synthesis)	• Diarrhoea, constipation, belching, cramping and ALP rise
Selective cholesterol absorption inhibitors (ezetimibe)	• Selectively inhibits the absorption of cholesterol through binding the intestinal and hepatic Niemann–Pick C1-like transporter protein	• LDL-C reduced by 15–20%
		• Triglycerides—negligible effect
		• HDL-C increased by ~3%
	• Decreases cholesterol delivery to hepatocytes, which leads to upregulation of LDL-C receptors with consequent enhanced clearance of LDL-C resulting in reduction of LDL-C concentrations	• When used as combination therapy with statins, incremental improvements of 14–23% and 2–7% in LDL and HDL levels are seen respectively
		• Main side effect is diarrhoea
		• Associated with transaminitis and is not recommended in those with moderate or severe hepatic dysfunction
		• Does not affect the cytochrome P450 enzymes and appears to have few adverse drug interactions

- Due to problems with tolerability and drug interactions, bile acid sequestrants are currently not commonly prescribed but may have a role as adjunctive therapy and in those who are statin intolerant
- There has however been renewed interest in their use in diabetics due to their hypoglycaemic effects.

Selective cholesterol absorption inhibitors

- Ezetimibe is the first member of a new class of lipid-lowering agents
- At present there are no reported trials examining the efficacy of ezetimibe on hard clinical endpoints, except for the recently reported SHARP trial of combination therapy with simvastatin/ezetimibe in patients CKD
- The SHARP trial randomized patients to either combination therapy or placebo and therefore at present there is no long-term clinical endpoint data available on the effect of ezetimibe monotherapy
- SHARP demonstrated that a lipid-lowering strategy results in a reduction of major vascular events in patients with significant renal impairment. Previous studies addressing this question had been inconclusive
- Trials assessing the use of ezetimibe using surrogate endpoints of intima-medial thickness on ultrasonography have shown no statistically significant benefits despite substantial lowering of LDL-C levels
- At present the main role of ezetimibe appears to be as an adjunctive therapy in those who have either failed to meet target LDL levels (such as those with monozygous FH) or are intolerant of other agents.

13.6 Statins

Mechanism of action

- Statins reduce the de novo hepatic synthesis of cholesterol through competitive inhibition of HMG-CoA (the enzyme responsible for catalysing the rate limiting step in the mevalonate pathway) (see Figure 13.5), causing:
  - Decrease in intracellular cholesterol concentration
  - Up-regulation of LDL receptor expression
  - Increased clearance of VLDL and LDL
  - Lowered triglyceride (modest) and LDL-C concentrations
- Also reduce apolipoprotein B100 and triglyceride-rich lipoprotein synthesis. Enhanced lipoprotein lipase activity
- There is growing evidence that statins exert beneficial effects on plaque biology through additional mechanisms separate to lipid lowering—pleiotropism:
  - They mediate plaque stabilization, improve endothelial function as well as reducing thrombogenicity and systemic inflammation
  - Event rate plots from the TIMI 22 PROVE IT trial of intensive statin therapy after an ACS show a significant reduction of event frequency after just 30 days of intensive therapy. This timeframe is much shorter than would be expected from plaque regression alone and indicates the presence of other attributable mechanisms.

Efficacy

- Major effect is the reduction of LDL levels—most potent agents available for routine prescription
- Overall moderate effect in lowering triglyceride levels. The degree of reduction in triglyceride levels is variable and proportional to the baseline level and potency of the statin

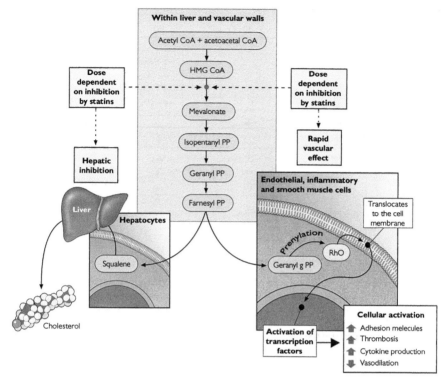

Figure 13.5 Molecular pathway of mevalonate metabolism and statin site of action.

Reprinted from *The Journal of the American College of Cardiology*, 46(8), Kausik K. Ray and Christopher P. Cannon, 'The potential relevance of the multiple lipid-independent (pleiotropic) effects of statins in the management of acute coronary syndromes', 1425, copyright 2005 with permission from Elsevier.

- Exert only mild effects on HDL levels
- The various statins have differing comparative efficacies with regards to the reduction of LDL concentrations:
  - Where the goal is moderate LDL reduction—equivalent dosages of various statins maybe utilized
  - For intensive reduction LDL it can be seen from the dose–response curve in Figure 13.6 that even the maximum dose of older statins such as pravastatin and simvastatin will not achieve the degree of LDL-lowering achievable with newer generation potent agents such as atorvastatin and rosuvastatin
  - There is no convincing evidence to suggest the superiority of any specific agent in the reduction of clinical endpoints by mechanisms other than through the lowering of LDL.

Important side effects and interactions

Hepatic

- Mild elevations in transaminase levels (<2–3 × ULN) are not uncommon (<1% in those on low/moderate doses)
  - Overt hepatic failure is extremely rare
  - The likelihood of transaminitis is dose-related and transient and more common in diabetics and the elderly (usually resolves with dose reduction or cessation)

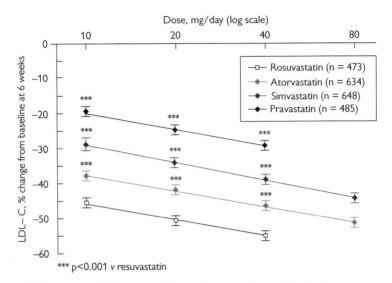

Figure 13.6 Comparative LDL lowering efficacy of commonly prescribed statins.

Reproduced from 'Management of dyslipidaemia', Gilbert R. Thompson, *Heart*, **90**(8):949–55, copyright 2004 with permission from BMJ Publishing Group Ltd.

- NICE recommend the measurement of liver enzymes prior to initiating statin therapy and once more at 3 months post initiation
- Mild elevations in transaminases (<1–3 × ULN) in asymptomatic individuals may simply be monitored and the statin continued
- More significant elevations in transaminases may necessitate dose reduction, cessation, and further investigation as appropriate.

Myopathy and rhabdomyolysis

- Muscle pain, weakness, or cramps have been associated with statin therapy
- With standard-dose statin monotherapy, the risk of significant myopathy is very low and progression to rhabdomyolysis is very rare
- Current UK and American guidelines do not advocate routine measurement of CK levels in asymptomatic individuals
- In patients who have a pre-existing muscle disorder or are deemed to be at high risk of developing myopathy, baseline and surveillance CK levels maybe helpful (see Table 13.7)
- CK levels <10× ULN: patient can be monitored and the statin continued, potentially with a dose reduction
- More significant elevations should prompt cessation of statin therapy, rehydration, and monitoring of renal function with attention to the possibility of ensuing rhabdomyolysis.

Primary prevention with statins

Primary prevention and global risk

- NICE recommends the use of statins as a primary prevention measure in those who are estimated to have a 20% or greater 10-year risk of developing CVD as assessed by the use of an appropriate risk calculator such as SCORE
- The outcome of the non-statin trials have been largely disappointing in that they lowered coronary events but not coronary mortality; more worryingly they appeared to increase non-coronary mortality

Table 13.7 Factors influencing the risk of statin induced myopathy

Statin	Patient	Concomitant drug therapy
• Dosage Dose-dependent likelihood of myopathy. But this risk is not related to statin potency. • Agent Pravastatin and fluvastatin exhibit less muscle toxicity whereas simvastatin appears to be associated with slightly higher risks of myopathy	Risk are higher in those with • Hypothyroidism At increased risk of dyslipidaemia and myopathy in general. Recommended that all dyslipidemic patients are screened for thyroid dysfunction prior to the initiation of therapy. • Renal failure • Obstructive liver disease • Genetic polymorphisms (SLCO1B1and CYP2D6)	Significant CYP3A4 inhibitors increase the likelihood of adverse effects with statins metabolized by that system (Mainly simvastatin and atorvastatin) • Cyclosporine Significantly elevated risk of myopathy in patients receiving simvastatin/atorvastatin but not with pravastatin Important in cardiac transplant patients as are at risk of accelerated atherogenesis, pravastatin is associated with substantial reductions in mortality and morbidity. • Fibrates Increase the risk of non-pravastatin/fluvastatin related myopathy (less so with fenofibrate)

- None of the early non-statin primary prevention trials lowered overall mortality
- Statin trials have demonstrated reduction in coronary events, coronary mortality, and overall mortality without the increased non-cardiovascular mortality seen in the earlier non-statin trials.

Primary prevention statin trials

The major primary prevention statin trials have demonstrated consistent reductions in composite CVEs in those at elevated CVD risk because of:

- Elevated total cholesterol and gender (WOSCOPS)
- Multiple CVD risk factors (ASCOT-LLA)
- Diabetes (CARDS)
- Elevated hsCRP (JUPITER).

Collectively the trials have shown benefit across a range of LDL values with no lower limit of benefit yet demonstrated.

NICE guidance

- At present NICE do not recommend a specific target for total cholesterol/LDL-C concentration with statins in a primary prevention context
- The decision to pursue a quantitative goal is left to the discretion of the physician and patient
- Routine lipid measurements are not mandated but should be considered in the context of baseline lipid values and global risk.

Secondary prevention with statins

- Significant reductions in mortality and event rates (see Table 13.8)
- Recommended for virtually all patients who have known CAD
- The absolute risk reduction for major CVEs achieved by statin therapy is greater in those with known coronary disease or coronary risk equivalents than in the primary prevention population.

Table 13.8 Secondary prevention statin trials of stable coronary artery disease

Trial	Population	Intervention	Outcomes
4S	Hypercholesterolaemic patients (total cholesterol: 5.5–8, mean total cholesterol 6.75, mean LDL 4.87) with angina or previous MI	Simvastatin 40 mg vs placebo	• Reduced all cause mortality—11.5 vs 8.2% • Reduced coronary mortality—8.5 vs 5.0% • Reduced non-fatal coronary events—22.6 vs 15.9%
CARE	Moderate hypercholesterolaemics (total cholesterol <6.2, mean TC 5.4, mean LDL 3.6) with previous MI	Pravastatin 40 mg vs placebo	• Primary endpoint of fatal or non-fatal coronary events was significantly reduced by an absolute difference of 3% (13.2 vs 10.2%). • Despite similar rates of non-coronary death, all-cause mortality did not appear to be significantly reduced.
LIPID	Similar to CARE, moderate hypercholesterolaemics (total cholesterol: 4–7, median TC 5.6, median LDL 3.88)	Pravastatin 40 mg vs placebo	• Reduced risk all cause mortality of 14.1 vs 11% (The LIPID trial was better powered than CARE to detect an effect on all cause mortality due to its greater event rate and sample size)
HPS	Total cholesterol >3.5 and an elevated risk of coronary events on the basis of • previously diagnosed CAD • other occlusive arterial disease (such as peripheral arterial disease) • stroke or endarterectomy • diabetes or hypertension	Simvastatin 40 mg vs placebo	• Reduced all-cause mortality—14.7% vs 12.9% • Reduced coronary mortality—6.9% vs 5.7% • Reduced non-fatal coronary events—5.6% vs 3.5%

NICE guidance

• In stable CAD, NICE recommend the use of simvastatin 40 mg (or a drug of a similar cost) initially with up-titration/switch to higher efficacy statin of similar cost if total cholesterol remains >4 and LDL >2 (a substantial proportion will not reach this level)
• The recent EAS/ESC guidelines recommend a slightly more aggressive approach—in patients with a very high CV risk the treatment target for LDL-C is 1.8 mmol/l or a ≥50% reduction from baseline LDL-C.

Intensive statin therapy

Residual risk

• The absolute event rates of recurrent MI and mortality are much more likely in patients with established CAD
• Even when treated with standard dose statin therapy (achieving a low LDL) they still remain at higher absolute risk of adverse events than those with equivalent LDL levels without known CAD

- There appears to be no lower limit for the linear relationship between LDL concentrations and coronary event risk
- Therefore, by extrapolation, further lowering of LDL translates into a lower residual risk
- As such these patients warrant earlier and more intensive statin therapy.

Intensive statin therapy in stable coronary artery disease

- Three major trials have examined intensive statin therapy in stable CAD patients
- TNT and IDEAL both used atorvastatin 80 mg (a higher efficacy statin) in their intensive therapy arm
- They demonstrated a significant reduction in major adverse CVEs using intensive therapy
- The SEARCH trial employed high dose simvastatin (a moderate efficacy statin) in its intensive arm without a significant reduction in MACE rates
- Rates of statin-related myopathy were increased tenfold in the high-dose simvastatin arm
- Mean LDL concentrations were lower in TNT/IDEAL when compared to SEARCH and this is likely to account for the differences in outcomes.

Early intensive statin therapy post acute coronary syndrome

- The incidence of death and recurrent ischaemia exhibits a marked time-dependent course following ACS

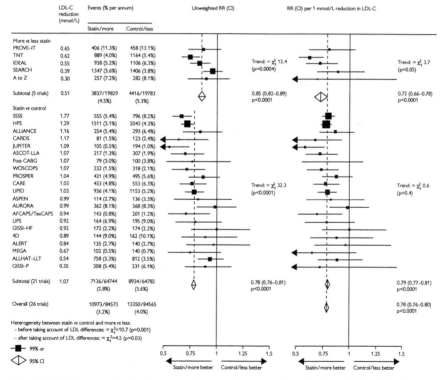

Figure 13.7 Meta-analysis of effects on major vascular events by reduction of LDL-C in the major statin trials.

Reprinted from *The Lancet*, 376, no. 9753, Cholesterol Treatment Trialists' CTT Collaboration 'Efficacy and safety of more intensive lowering of LDL cholesterol: a meta-analysis of data from 170,000 participants in 26 randomised trials', Copyright 2010 with permission from Elsevier.

- The highest risk of events occurs in the first few weeks, before substantially dropping over the next 1–2 months
- A to Z and PROVE IT examined the use of early intensive statin therapy following ACS and demonstrated significant reductions in major adverse cardiovascular event rates (see Figure 13.7).

NICE guidance
- In ACS, NICE recommend the early use of a higher-intensity statin regimen.

Further reading

Cholesterol Treatment Trialists' CTT Collaboration. Efficacy and safety of more intensive lowering of LDL cholesterol: A meta-analysis of data from 170 000 participants in 26 randomised trials. *Lancet,* 2010; 376: 1670–81.

Conroy RM, Pyörälä K, Fitzgerald AP, et al. Estimation of ten-year risk of fatal cardiovascular disease in europe: The SCORE project. *Eur Heart J,* 2003; 24: 987–1003.

Di Angelantonio E, Sarwar N, Perry P, et al. Major lipids, apolipoproteins, and risk of vascular disease. *JAMA,* 2009; 302: 1993.

National Institute for Health and Clinical Excellence. Lipid modification: cardiovascular risk assessment and the modification of blood lipids for the primary and secondary prevention of cardiovascular disease. CG67. NICE, 2008.

National Institute for Health and Clinical Excellence. Clinical guidelines and evidence review for familial hypercholesterolaemia: the identification and management of adults and children with familial hypercholesterolaemia. CG71. NICE, 2008.

Ray KK, Cannon CP. The potential relevance of the multiple lipid-independent (pleiotropic) effects of statins in the management of acute coronary syndromes. *J Am Coll Cardiol,* 2005; 46: 1425.

Reiner Z, Catapano AL, de Backer G, et al. ESC/EAS guidelines for the management of dyslipidaemias: the Task Force for the Management of Dyslipidaemias of the European Society of Cardiology (ESC) and the European Atherosclerosis Society (EAS). *Eur Heart J,* 2011; 32: 1769–818.

Thompson GR. Management of dyslipidaemia. *Heart* 2004; 90: 949–55.

Adult congenital heart disease

14.1 The basics and key concepts

Sequential segmental approach

Describes anatomy based on the cardiac components and connections:

- Atria (via AV valve)
- Ventricles
- Great arteries.

Atria

- Start at the atria (the morphological left and right atria are distinguished by the appendage, i.e. the 'left' atrium is not always on the left side; see Figure 14.1)
- The atrial location usually reflects the thoracic and abdominal visceral structures, e.g. morphological left atrium is associated with the left bronchus (left lung) and the stomach and spleen (isomerism more complex)
- Situs solitus is usual.

Atrial → ventricular connections (AV)

Connections can be **concordant** (e.g. left atrium connects to left ventricle) or **discordant** e.g. left atrium connects to right ventricle.

Ventricular → great artery connections

Great arteries (VA) can be:

- **Concordant** e.g. LV to aorta
- **Discordant** e.g. LV to pulmonary artery
- Double outlet—usually RV to both great arteries
- Common trunk.

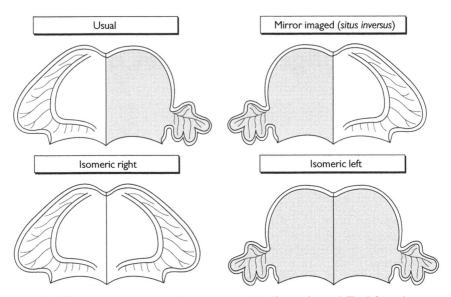

Figure 14.1 Right atrial appendage is broad and resembles 'Snoopy's nose'. The left atrial appendage is long and finger-like.

Reproduced with permission from the *ESC Textbook of Cardiovascular Medicine* 2nd edition, ed. John Camm, Thomas Lüscher and Patrick Serruys, copyright 2009 Oxford University Press.

For example, transposition of the great arteries (TGA) (see section on TGA):

- AV concordance with VA discordance
- Aorta arises from RV and aortic root is anterior to right pulmonary artery
- PA arises from LV.

Isometric right:

- More common in males
- Unoperated survival to adulthood rare
- Asplenic with severe cyanotic heart disease lesions (e.g. single ventricle physiology).

Isometric left:

- More common in females
- Polysplenia with absent sinus node and less severe spectrum of congenital cardiac lesions
- Interrupted IVC—does not connect to right atrium (RA)—Azygos vein (Azygos continuity) drains from IVC into SVC
- Note: embryologically the spleen is the only organ that is left sided from inception, and the IVC drains to the RA only which explains the above findings.

Distinguishing the morphological RV from the morphological LV

In congenital heart disease the morphological 'right' ventricle is not always on the right side, e.g. in congenitally corrected transposition of the great arteries the morphological LV is on the right and morphological RV is on the left.

- RV:
  - Increased trabeculations
  - Moderator band

- More apically inserted Tricuspid valve with *cordal attachment of the septal leaflet to the septum* (AV valve always follows the ventricle)—'offset of AV valve' on echo
- Discontinuity between AV valve and arterial valve
- LV:
  - Muscular wall is smoother
  - MV has a higher insertion (mitral valve follows LV)
  - Aorto-mitral continuity.

Other important anatomical terms

- **Dextrocardia:** heart on the right side of thorax (apex point to right)
- **Mesocardia:** heart centrally located with apex in midline
- **Levocardia:** heart on the left side of thorax (apex point to the left)
- Levocardia with situs inversus: heart on left with leftward pointing apex but mirror image of atria with thoracic and visceral structures.

Basic foetal circulation

See Figure 14.2.

- Oxygenated blood drains from umbilical vein via the **ductus venosus** to the IVC and then RA
- Foetal pulmonary vascular resistance is high so blood bypasses the lungs via the **foramen ovale** (FO) and **ductus arteriosus** (DA) into systemic circulation
- When the newborn inflates lungs for the first time, pulmonary resistance falls, flow increases, and LA pressure increases—FO closes
- DA flow reverses and closes
- Results in **parallel pulmonary and systemic circulations**.

14.2 Fundamental concepts in congenital lesions

Pulmonary blood flow

- Too little (low flow) results in hypoxia
- Too much (high flow) results in pulmonary oedema and adverse vascular remodeling
- The muscular pulmonary arterial tree changes in the newborn over the first few months and becomes elastic and compliant
- If the lungs are exposed to high pressure and flow (e.g. via a left-to-right shunt) then this change does not occur and progressive irreversible adverse remodelling and pulmonary hypertension develop

KEY CONCEPT

Protect the lungs from high pressures and flow (to prevent irreversible adverse remodelling).

- A cyanosed congenital patient has a right-to-left shunt (deoxygenated blood into systemic circulation)
- The combination of pulmonary blood flow (and size of right-to-left shunt) dictate the degree of cyanosis (systemic oxygenation):
  - **Low pulmonary flow:** greater cyanosis but lungs protected (blue but not breathless)
  - **High pulmonary flow:** less cyanosis but pulmonary congestion and damage to pulmonary vasculature (pink but breathless)

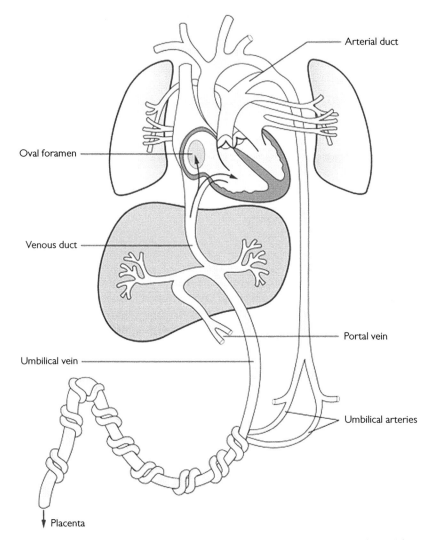

Arterial duct

Oval foramen

Venous duct

Portal vein

Umbilical vein

Umbilical arteries

Placenta

Figure 14.2 Venous circulation returning to the right heart bypasses the lungs via the oval fossa and arterial duct into the systemic arterial circulation.

Reproduced with permission from the *ESC Textbook of Cardiovascular Medicine* 2nd edition, ed. John Camm, Thomas Lüscher and Patrick Serruys, copyright 2009 Oxford University Press.

• In cyanosed congenital patients 'balancing' the pulmonary flow is essential, e.g. enough flow to achieve adequate systemic saturation whilst protecting the lungs

KEY CONCEPT

The degree of cyanosis reflects the balance between pulmonary blood flow and right-to-left shunt.

• In obligatory right-to-left shunt with 'balanced' pulmonary blood flow, systemic saturations will be around 85%

- Higher values suggest excess pulmonary blood flow and lower values inadequate flow.

If the flow is too high an intervention is required to limit the flow:

- For example, surgical banding of the PA protects distal vascular bed from high pressure whilst allowing adequate oxygenation
- Band is removed at definitive surgery (may develop PA stenosis at site of band).

If the flow is too little an intervention is required to increase the flow:

- Low flow due to a pulmonary valve obstruction is treatable by valvotomy/valvuloplasty
- Otherwise a surgical shunt (arterial blood from aorta/subclavian redirected to PA) is used.

Systemic arterial to pulmonary artery shunts
See Figure 14.3.

- Classical Blalock-Taussig (BT) shunt:
    - Usually right side via posterior thoracotomy
    - No longer used—subclavian ligated and redirected to PA
- Modified BT shunt (posterior thoracotomy):
    - Gortex tube between subclavian and PA
- Other shunts:
    - Waterston: direct communication between Ascending aorta and RPA
    - Potts: direct communication between descending aorta and LPA
    - Central: Gortex between brachiocephalic/aorta and PA
- After 6 months, infant pulmonary vascular resistance falls—systemic venous to pulmonary artery shunts become possible.

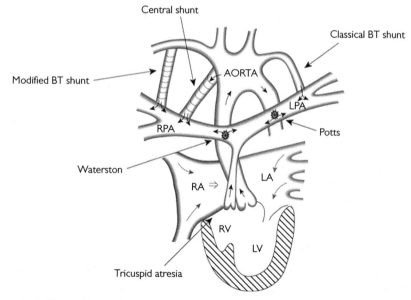

Figure 14.3 Blalock-Taussig shunt.

Systemic venous to pulmonary artery shunts

- Glenn shunt (cavopulmonary shunt)—SVC to PA anastomosis (Figure 14.4):
  - Classical Glenn—SVC anastomosis to RPA and RPA disconnected from main pulmonary artery (MPA)
  - Bidirectional Glenn—SVC anastomosis to RPA (RPA remains connected to MPA)
- If the IVC is also redirected to the PA then this constitutes a FONTAN circulation (discussed later)
- In childhood SVC return is 75%—Glenn provides adequate flow
- In adults SCV return is 25%—Glenn inadequate on its own
- Glenn shunts are associated with the development of AV malformations (can contribute to right-to-left shunt, causing additional cyanosis or pulmonary haemorrhage).

Cyanosis

Remember to consider if the pulmonary blood flow is high or low.

Aetiology in congenital heart disease

- Mixing of oxygenated and deoxygenated blood:
  - Right-to-left shunt
  - Bidirectional mixing via a univentricular heart or at great artery level
  - Discordant VA connections (uncorrected TGA)—parallel circulations—shunt required
- Inadequate pulmonary blood flow:
  - Obstructed or underdeveloped pulmonary vasculature
  - Pulmonary hypertension (cyanosis always associated with a right-to-left shunt).

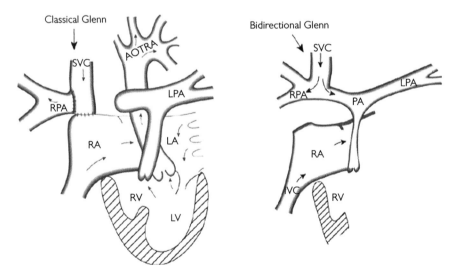

Figure 14.4 Glenn shunt.

Reproduced with permission from the *Oxford Specialist Handbook of Adult Congenital Heart Disease*, edited by Sara Thorne and Paul Clift, copyright 2011 Oxford University Press.

Important consequences of cyanosis

- Blood:
    - Polycythaemia, which can cause hyperviscosity:
        - **Venesection is not indicated unless there are clear clinical symptoms of hyperviscosity**
        - When appropriate, venesection should be perfomed via exchange transfusion with saline replacement of volume
        - Care to avoid excess volume loss, which can lead to circulatory collapse and worsening iron deficiency
    - Thrombocytopenia with impaired platelet function
    - Iron deficiency, exacerbated by venesection
    - Coagulopathy: dysfunctional low platelets and clotting impairment. **INR falsely elevated** due to increased ratio of blood tube anticoagulant to plasma (high haematocrit)—discuss with lab when sending samples
- Brain:
    - Stroke—usually secondary to paradoxical embolus (not due to hyperviscosity)
    - Cerebral abscess: risk related to arterial saturation. **Should be suspected if cyanotic patient has neurological deterioration, odd headache, unexplained sepsis**
    - Mental development is not significantly affected
- Kidney:
    - Renal impairment
    - Avoid nephrotoxic drugs
- Other:
    - Gout (urate excess) and pigment gallstones
    - Acne
    - Clubbing/scoliosis
    - Haemoptysis—secondary to collaterals or pulmonary hypertension (PHT)—may be catastrophic and requires emergency investigation (CT) and preparation for aggressive resuscitation
    - Paradoxical embolus—use line filters to reduce risk
    - Arrhythmias—poorly tolerated—require prompt rhythm control; low threshold for direct current cardioversion (DCCV)
    - Avoid vasodilators as worsen cyanosis; beta-blockers acutely to reduce hypertension if required.

Other basic concepts related to congenital lesions

- Cardiac and arterial structures develop relative to the amount of blood flow
- If there is an interruption to blood flow then the structure will remain rudimentary/ atretic
- If there is increased flow the structure will dilate and enlarge
- Illustrations of the concept: tricuspid atresia—no blood flow to RV—RV remains small and rudimentary
- Aortic stenosis and large ventricular septal defect (VSD)—coarctation often present, with hypolastic ascending aorta due to reduced aortic flow
- Volume-loaded cardiac chambers or arteries enlarge (note: PAs remodel/hypertrophy in response to high degrees of flow).

14.3 Atrial septal defects and patent foramen ovale

The atrial septum is made up of layers: **primum septum** (LA side) and **secundum septum** (RA side) with overlap flap in the region of the **fossa ovalis** (Figure 14.5).

Patent foramen ovale (PFO)

- Present in 25–30% of general population
- Clinical presentations:
  - Cryptogenic stroke in patients at low cardiovascular risk (paradoxical venous embolus)
  - Diving decompression illness (DCI; shunting of nitrogen bubbles)
  - Platypnoea-orthodeoxia syndrome
  - Association with migraine (particularly with visual aura)
- Transthoracic echo (TTE) is usually normal unless the shunt is large (colour flow across septum) but PFO should be suspected if there is a significantly aneurysmal septum

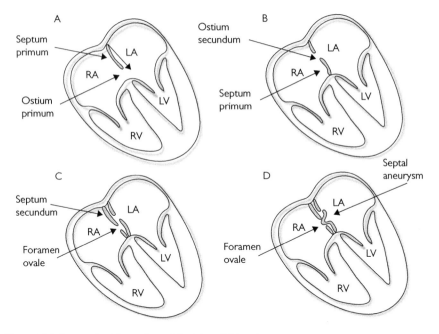

Figure 14.5 Summarized formation of the intra-atrial septum.
A - first the septum primum comes down. If it does not complete then an ostium primum defect is created (defect involves atrial component of atrioventricular septum).
B - a hole develops in the middle of the primum septum = ostium secundum.
C - a second muscular septum (septum secundum) forms on the RA side covering the hole. A large oval hole forms at the bottom = fossa ovalis. If the ositum secundum is not covered a ostium secundum ASD is created.
D - at birth, increasing pressure in the LA pushes the two laminar septa together. In 25–30% the septa do not fuse and there is a flap or tunnel between the septa called a patent foramen ovale. If the septa are large and mobile a septal aneurysm results, which is almost always associated with PFO and confers an increased risk of paradoxical embolus stroke (compared to PFO on its own).

- PFO does not result in anatomical haemodynamic change, e.g. right volume load
- Investigation of choice: microbubble contrast transthoracic echo
- Good technique requires repeated injection with high-quality Valsalva release (bubbles should cross on release of Valsalva manoeuvre) and sniff/cough manoeuvres
- Transcatheter closure indications:
  - Stroke without identifiable cardiovascular risk factors *and* no indication for long-term anticoagulation (e.g. intrinsic hypercoagulability) *and* no suspicion of left cardiac embolic focus (e.g. AF)
  - Patient with DCI who wishes to continue diving
  - ? migraine sufferers (controversial and subject of current research)
  - Platypnoea-orthodeoxia syndrome.

Platypnoea-orthodeoxia syndrome

Dyspnoea and **desaturation** when changing from lying to sitting/standing positions as a result of **right-to-left intra-atrial shunting** (against the normal pressure gradient).

- Requires an intra-atrial communication (includes PFO and atrial septal defects; ASD) **and** a functional component that produces a deformity of the intra-atrial septum with the postural change, which results in redirection of normal left-to-right shunt to a transient right-to-left shunt
- Functional components: aortic dilatation/aneurysm, emphysema (crossover with lung disease), pericardial effusion/constriction.

Atrial septal defects

See Figure 14.6. The 'true' atrial septum consists of the fossa ovalis. Atrial septal defects are categorized into:

- **Secundum** (most common; 60%)
- **Partial atrioventicular septal defects** (20%; for atrioventricular septal defects (AVSDs) Section 14.5). Sometimes referred to as 'primum ASD', these defects are usually associated with an abnormality of the left AV valve and are *not* related to the primum septum. Due to a deficiency in the atrial component of the atrioventicular septum
- **Sinus venosus**
  - Superior (overriding SVC, defect at junction of vein into both atria; 15%)
  - Superior sinus venosus defects associated with partial anomalous pulmonary venous drainage—this represents an additional left-to-right shunt; most commonly right upper PV to RA or SVC
  - Inferior (rare)
  - Sinus venosus defects difficult to detect on transthoracic echocardiogram (TTE) and require transoesophageal echocardiogram (TOE) assessment ('bicaval' 90° TOE view)
- **Coronary sinus** (rare).

Atrial septal defect physiology

Chronic left-to-right shunting causes right heart volume overload and increased pulmonary arterial flow (with ageing, LA pressure increases—reduced LV compliance—and so the left-to-right shunt increases).

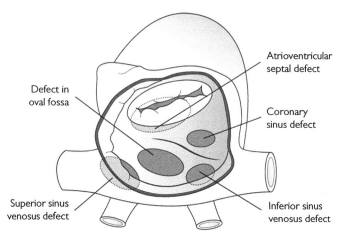

Figure 14.6 ASD locations.

Reproduced with permission from the *ESC Textbook of Cardiovascular Medicine* 2nd edition, ed. John Camm, Thomas Lüscher and Patrick Serruys, copyright 2009 Oxford University Press.

- Increased flow across PV and tricuspid valve (TV) can cause a murmur (signs can be confused with PS). Fixed split S2 classical
- Symptoms in childhood can be recurrent chest infections, failure to thrive, exercise intolerance
- Adults usually present in third or fourth decade with breathlessness and palpitations (or incidental; for example, investigation of chest pain)
- Right heart volume loading causes right heart dilatation
- Right and left sided atrial arrhythmias common
- Increased pulmonary flow can result in increased pulmonary vascular resistance (PVR) and PHT (late)
- Paradoxical embolus possible
- Endocarditis rare (low risk) with isolated secundum ASD
- ECG = right axis + incomplete RBBB (except primum or AVSD = left axis and RVH)
- One third of cases associated with genetic syndrome e.g. Down's, Holt-Oram
- The association of first degree heart block with a secundum ASD is suggestive of the familial (autosomal dominant) form and the family should be offered screening.

Closure indications

1. ASD with 'haemodynamic consequences'—right heart dilatation
2. Symptoms—breathlessness or arrhythmia (may improve afterwards)
3. Protection of pulmonary vasculature (remodeling and progressive PHT)
4. Paradoxical embolus
    - Secundum defects (without other surgical lesions e.g. anomalous PV drainage) up to 40 mm; anatomy usually suitable for transcatheter closure (Amplatzer device most common)
    - All other defects are currently only amenable to surgical intervention
    - In ASDs with established pulmonary hypertension caution is required—the ASD may act as a 'blow-off' valve to limit pulmonary pressure loading—closure may cause decompensation. Should still be possible with pressures <2/3 systemic, shunt >1.5:1 and demonstrated reversibility of PVR.

14.4 Ventricular septal defects

Ventricular septal defects (VSDs) are the most common form of congenital heart disease after bicuspid aortic valve.

The ventricular septum is composed of:

- Muscular septum—subdivided into
  - Inlet
  - Trabecular
  - Outlet
- Membranous septum—small area lying just below aortic valve.

VSDs are classified according to their location within the septum and borders as viewed from the RV (Figure 14.7), e.g. muscular VSDs are bordered entirely by myocardium whereas perimembranous VSDs are bordered in part by the fibrous continuity of the AV valves and doubly committed VSDs border the fibrous continuity of the arterial valves.

Restrictive ventricular septal defects

- Significant pressure gradient across left-to-right ventricle (high-velocity jet on echo)
- Shunt small (Qp/Qs <1.5/1.0)
- No haemodynamic consequence
- Spontaneous closure in childhood common

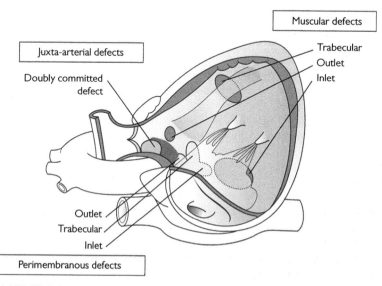

Figure 14.7 VSD locations.

Reproduced with permission from the *ESC Textbook of Cardiovascular Medicine* 2nd edition, ed. John Camm, Thomas Lüscher and Patrick Serruys, copyright 2009 Oxford University Press.

- Asymptomatic (high pitched murmur)
- Not always benign—restrictive perimembranous (including subarterial) VSD jet can 'suck' aortic valve leaflets via venturi effect into the defect and the turbulence can cause leaflet damage/thickening
- Usually right coronary cusp of AV with signs of prolapse and progressive AR (requires close follow-up and is an indication for closure of VSD before irreversible valve damage results)
- A small perimembranous VSD may close while developing significant muscular right ventricular outflow tract obstruction
- Risk of endocarditis is not related to the size of defect.

LEARNING POINT

A VSD-type murmur that recurs in a patient whose VSD was thought to have closed may represent the development of right ventricular outflow tract obstruction.

Unrestricted ventricular septal defects

- The spectrum of clinical effect is dependent on the size of shunt and pulmonary versus systemic vascular resistance
- The haemodynamic burden and volume loading is on the **left ventricle—LV dilatation and failure, not RV dilatation, as RV is in systole during shunting**
- Pressure load affects the pulmonary vascular bed (and subsequently the RV)—increased flow/volume leads to increased PA pressure
- Moderate shunts lead to left heart dilatation and failure with atrial arrhythmias
- Large shunts lead to irreversible pulmonary vascular change and systemic pulmonary pressures unless pulmonary bed protected by pulmonary stenosis. End result is **Eisenmenger syndrome**.

Management

The key indications for intervention are symptoms or progressive haemodynamic consequences of the shunt:

- LV dilatation or increasing PA/RV pressures (usually when Qp:Qs >2:1)
- Repair should be undertaken prior to irreversible pulmonary vascular change
- In established PHT, repair may still be considered if there is evidence of pulmonary pressure reversibility associated with a moderate shunt
- Previous endocarditis and signs of AV valve prolapse/progressive AR (in perimembranous defects) are other indications to prevent recurrence or valve damage.

Intervention

- Generally surgical repair
- Perimembranous—conducting tissues are vulnerable
- RBBB is common post-operatively and complete heart block (CHB) is possible
- Low threshold for permanent pacemaker (PPM) if there are persistent rhythm disturbances as there is a risk of late sudden death
- Transcatheter closure of muscular defects is possible in selected cases (requires no associated lesions and amenable anatomy)
- Perimembranous defects are also technically possible but rarely performed due to the higher incidence of unpredictable conduction problems (which can lead to late SCD)
- The aortic valve is also vulnerable and so highly specialist assessment is required.

14.5 Atrioventricular septal defects

Consist of a defect of the AV septum with associated defect of the AV valve(s). There is a common AV junction (no offset on echo) and common AV ring.

Note: in AVSD the correct terminology is **left** and **right AV** valve as the valve anatomy is no longer 'mitral' or 'tricuspid'.

Spectrum of anatomy (see Figures 14.8 and 14.9):

1. **Partial:** primum ASD + 'cleft' left AV valve but intact ventricular septum
2. **Intermediate:** primum ASD + restrictive VSD + separate but abnormal AV valves
3. **Complete:** continuous primum ASD and non-restrictive VSD + common AV valve (5 leaflets)

- **No AV offset on four-chamber echo = hallmark feature**
- 50% = trisomy 21 (Down's syndrome) but most partial AVSD are non-Down's (>90%) and most complete AVSD are Down's (>75%)
- Physiology relates to whether the anatomy is ASD- or VSD-predominant and the degree of AV valve regurgitation, which is universal—partial/intermediate defects behave as large ASD physiology + left AV valve regurgitation
- Complete AVSDs present with heart failure
- Down's patients may present with established PHT (appear to have a propensity to developing PHT early possibly due to other intrinsic lung problems)
- ECG: first degree AV block/higher degrees of AV block (defect effects the AV node)
- Instead of two AV rings there is a common AV ring and so the aorta is displaced from its normal position between the two AV rings—LVOT is displaced anterosuperiorly and is elongated ('goose-neck') and narrowed—predisposes to obstruction
- All require surgical correction (unless established severe irreversible PHT)
- Long-term outcome is related to recurrence of left AV valve regurgitation ('cleft' is sutured to create bi-leaflet left AV valve)
- Patients with operated AVSD who present with arrhythmia should have haemodynamic assessment, as the arrhythmia may be a manifestation of a structural lesion.

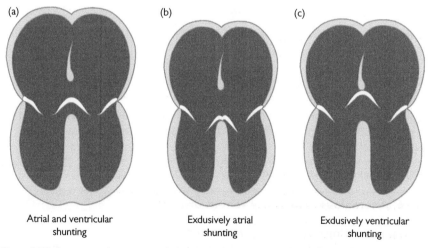

| (a) Atrial and ventricular shunting | (b) Exdusively atrial shunting | (c) Exdusively ventricular shunting |

Figure 14.8 Spectrum of anatomy and physiological consequences in AVSD relates to whether defect is ASD or VDS predominant and degree of left AV valve regurgitation.

Reproduced from 'Atrioventricular septal defect: from fetus to adult', Brian Craig, *Heart,* 92, 1879–1885, copyright 2006 with permission from BMJ Publishing Group Ltd.

(a)

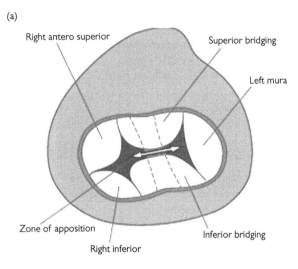

Common valvar orifice

(b)

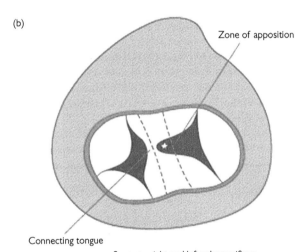

Separate right and left valvar orifices

Figure 14.9 Anatomy of atrial septal defects. (a) Complete AVSD with common AV valve and (b) partial AVSD with 'cleft' mitral valve. Note common AV ring and resultant anterior displacement of aorta.

Reproduced from 'Atrioventricular septal defect: from fetus to adult', Brian Craig, Heart, 92, 1879–1885, copyright 2006 with permission from BMJ Publishing Group Ltd.

14.6 Anomalous pulmonary venous drainage

Partial anomalous pulmonary venous drainage

Definition: at least one PV drains to the RA (directly or indirectly via SVC or IVC); most commonly right PVs to SVC or RA.

- Left PVs less common—usually drain to coronary sinus or left brachiocephalic vein
- **ASD physiology:** left-to-right shunt; symptoms, signs, and indications for intervention the same as ASDs

- Associated with sinus venosus ASD—suspect partial anomalous pulmonary venous drainage (PAPVD) in **superior sinus venosus ASD** (commonly RUPV to SVC or RA)
- If there is only a single anomalous vein patients are usually asymptomatic (but this may be associated with other congenital lesions).

Scimitar syndrome

- Type of PAPVD
- Right PV to IVC ('scimitar vein')
- Anomalous systemic arterial supply to right lung (usually descending aorta)
- Right lung hypoplasia and sequestration.

Characteristic chest X-ray
Often diagnosed incidentally by radiologists (See Figure 14.10).

Presentations
ASD physiology of left-to-right shunt (right heart volume loading/consequences of increased pulmonary flow):

- Breathlessness or palpitations (secondary arrhythmias)
- Frequent chest infections with possible haemoptysis due to lung sequestration
- Incidental—murmur/CXR.

Indications for surgical intervention similar to ASD/PAPVD—right heart/PA consequences/symptoms/right lung problems (25% associated lesions which may require correction—ASD, VSD, patent ductus arteriosus (PDA), coarctation, tetralogy of Fallot (ToF)). Intervention rarely required in adulthood.

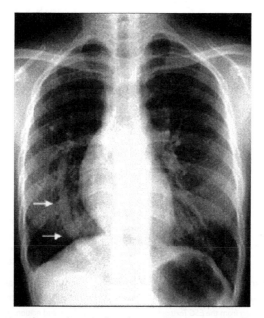

Figure 14.10 Scimitar syndrome. Arrows show 'scimitar' (curved middle-Eastern sword) vein and rightward displacement of the mediastinum.

Reproduced from 'Familial scimitar syndrome: three-dimensional visualization of anomalous pulmonary vein in young sisters', Kinya Ashida, Akira Itoh, Takahiko Naruko et al., Circulation 2001; 103, e126–e127, with permission from Wolters Kluwer Health.

Total anomalous pulmonary venous drainage (TAPVD)

PVs join a confluence behind the LA—confluence drains into the right heart via the systemic venous circulation or atrium (see Figure 14.11):

1. Supracardiac: drains to brachiocephalic vein, azygos vein, SVC
2. Cardiac: drains to coronary sinus
3. Infradiaphragmatic: to IVC; almost always with pulmonary venous obstruction (strongest predictor of poor outcome)

   - TAPVD is always associated with ASD as all systemic and pulmonary venous return drains to the RA (obligatory right-to-left shunt i.e. requires right-to-left shunt for life)
   - ASD physiology of left-to-right shunt: right heart volume load and elevated pulmonary flow (leads to congestion and increased PVR)
   - Requires early repair (no role for balloon septostomy); late results excellent, can be managed in primary care/general cardiology clinics:
     - Communication formed between confluence and LA
     - ASD closed
     - Anomalous vein to systemic circulation ligated.

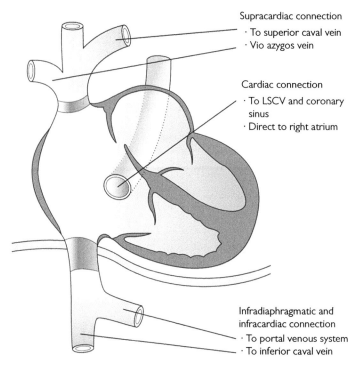

Figure 14.11 Total anomalous pulmonary venous drainage—entire pulmonary venous drainage is redirected to a confluence, which in turn drains into a right sided/venous structure.

14.7 Ebstein's anomaly

Failure of delamination of the TV leaflets. Results in (Figure 14.12):

1. Apical displacement of septal and posterol-lateral leaflets below the AV rings into the RV
2. 'Atrialization' of RV = smaller functional RV (large RA)
3. TV dysfunction
4. Atrial shunt (PFO or ASD) in 50%
5. Accessory pathways in 25% (increased risk arrhythmias); often multiple pathways

- Association with maternal lithium in first trimester may be false (majority of cases sporadic)
- There is a spectrum of Ebstein's malformation. Severity of the lesion dictates the natural history
- Adults present with consequences of TV/RV dysfunction or arrhythmia or complications related to a shunt (ASD/PFO; cyanosis, paradoxical embolus)
- Echo diagnosis: hallmark is apical displacement of septal leaflet (+/- post leaflet) >20 mm + elongated sail-like anterior leaflet
- Elevated JVP is a late sign due to the large compliant RA
- TV repair/replacement is indicated if there is significant TR with haemodynamic consequences (aim to intervene before significant right heart deterioration) or symptoms
- In addition to TVR the atrium can be 'plicated' to reduce the size, associated shunts closed, and arrhythmia surgery performed
- For high-risk patients, i.e. those with significant established right heart dysfunction, a bidirectional Glenn may be indicated to reduce RV preload
- Symptoms can be difficult to assess; regular objective functional testing is helpful (exercise testing).

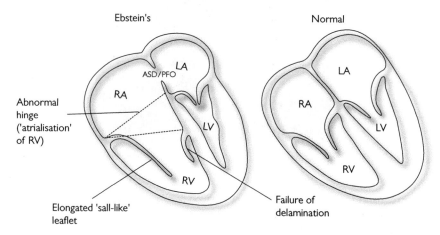

Figure 14.12 Ebstein's anomaly—elongated anterior leaflet and apical displacement of septal leaflet.

14.8 Coarctation of the aorta

Stenosis of the distal aortic arch usually at or beyond the site of the arterial duct (just distal to left subclavian; see Figure 14.13).

(a)

(b)

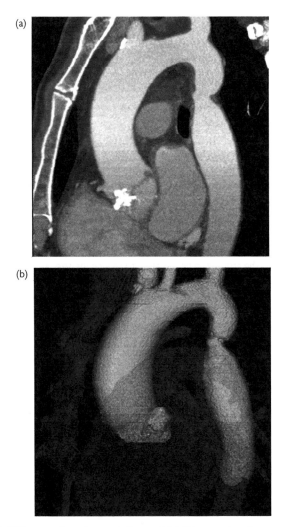

Figure 14.13   (a) CT image of aortic coarctation and (b) 3D reconstruction.

- Spectrum of severity varies from mild to interruption or hypoplasia of the arch (collateral supply from arch to descending aorta).

Associated with:

- Bicuspid aortic valve (80%)
- Berry aneurysms of circle of Willis
- Turner's syndrome

- Multiple left heart obstructive lesions (Shone's syndrome: parachute MV, subvalvular and valvular AS and coarctation).

If haemodynamically significant, infants present acutely and require surgery.

- Surgical repair of coarctation:
  1. End-to-end anastomosis
  2. Subclavian flap repair: left subclavian artery used to augment aorta (left arm pulse diminished)
  3. Dacron patch aortoplasty: now abandoned due to **risk of late aneurysm formation**
- Re-coarctation at the site of previous surgical repair is not uncommon (all patients require **lifelong follow-up** and may require transcatheter intervention)
- Adults usually present with uncontrolled hypertension or incidentally
- Claudication, cerebral haemorrhage, and heart failure are less common presentations
- Increasingly, the treatment of choice for adolescents and adults is transcatheter stenting (native and surgical recoarctation)
- Indication is uncontrolled hypertension with evidence of significant anatomical obstruction or significant gradient (>30 mmHg)
- Lifelong follow-up is required after transcatheter intervention as although relief of obstruction can reduce BP there is an inherent predisposition to hypertension and associated complications
  - Measure BP in the right arm
  - Ambulatory BP is commonly utilized to demonstrate hypertension
  - Aggressive BP treatment, with ACE inhibitors/ARBs (caution in females of reproductive age) and BBs as the preferred agents
  - Serial cross-sectional imaging is essential to assess the repair/stent—recoarctation, aneurysm formation, and stent fracture are all possible.

MRI is the usual modality in native or surgical repair due to the avoidance of radiation and provision of physiological data. Baseline scans should look for cerebral berry aneurysm. However, MRI cannot identify stent structure/fracture and luminal data is limited due to stent interference.

Low dose localized CT: higher resolution and useful in patients with stent follow-up.

Echo: suprasternal aortic arch view. Align continuous wave with colour flow in descending aorta. Look for increased velocity and diastolic tail (Figure 14.14).

14.9 Patent ductus arteriosus

Foetal connection between proximal left pulmonary artery to descending aorta (just distal to left subclavian); foetal circulation bypasses lungs (see Basic foetal circulation section).

Adult presentation

1. Incidental echo finding: very small, no murmur
2. Small: long ejection/continuous murmur radiating to back, no haemodynamic consequences, endocarditis risk
3. Moderate: continuous murmur, haemodynamic change (left-to-right shunt), increased pulmonary flow (risk of PHT) and left heart volume loading (left sided dilatation), collapsing pulses

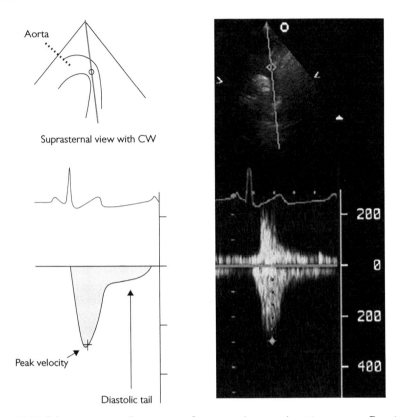

Figure 14.14 Echo assessment of coarctation. Suprasternal view and continuous wave Doppler trace demonstrating increased velocity with diastolic tail.

Reproduced with permission from the *Oxford Specialist Handbook of Echocardiography*, eds. Paul Leeson, Andrew Mitchell and Harald Becher, copyright 2007 Oxford University Press.

4. Large—Eisenmenger physiology with pulmonary hypertension, differential cyanosis (lower body sats < right arm), toe clubbing
   - Associated with aortic coarctation
   - Transcatheter closure is the treatment of choice for children and adults
   - Incidental (silent) PDAs do not need closure (unless associated with an episode of previous endocarditis)
   - Small PDAs can be closed to protect against endocarditis
   - Haemodynamic PDAs should be closed unless severe irreversible PHT (act as 'blow off' valve to limit pulmonary pressures).

14.10 Sinus of valsalva aneurysms

- Dilatation of one of the aortic sinuses
- Right coronary sinus most common site (75%)
- VSDs commonly associated
- Ruptured aneurysms can present acutely with chest pain and breathlessness (misdiagnosed as pulmonary embolus (PE) with loud continuous murmur or haemodynamic collapse and cardiac arrest/sudden death

- Presentation depends on the site of rupture/receiving chamber and associated compromise of the coronary ostium
- Requires emergency intervention—most commonly surgery but transcatheter closure feasible and successful in expert hands.

14.11 Transposition of the great arteries

See Figure 14.15.

- AV concordance with VA discordance (see segmental sequential approach)
- Aorta arises from RV and aortic root is anterior to RPA
- PA arises from LV.

Systemic and pulmonary circulations are in parallel rather than in series:

- **Systemic circulation** (deoxygenated blood is re-circulated): SVC and IVC venous return to RA via tricuspid valve to RV, to aorta, to peripheral circulation, and back to SVC and IVC
- **Pulmonary circulation** (oxygenated blood re-circulated): PVs to LA via mitral valve, to LV, to aorta, to PA, to lungs, and back to LA
- CXR: narrow cardiac 'pedicle' representing the great arteries' parallel arrangement (normalized with arterial switch operation) compared to the normal crossing great arteries
- In the absence of a septal defect the only way the two circulations can mix is via foetal shunts (foramen ovale and PDA). Otherwise the circulation is incompatible with life
- At birth the PDA can be maintained via prostoglandin and/or the intra-atrial communication via percutaneous balloon septostomy.

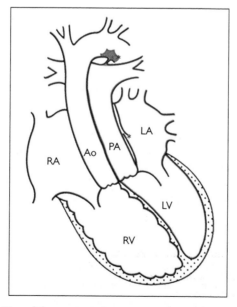

Figure 14.15 Transposition of the great arteries.

Atrial switch: Mustard or Senning operation

See Figure 14.16.

- The atrial switch has been superseded by the **arterial switch** (anatomical repair) since the late 1980s
- Intra-atrial baffles are used to re-route systemic and pulmonary circulation; systemic venous blood is redirected to the LV (pulmonary circuit pump) and oxygenated pulmonary venous return to the RV (systemic pump).

Definitions:

- Mustard operation uses prosthetic baffles (Dacron) or pericardium
- Senning operation uses baffles made of intrinsic atrial wall material
- Baffle is a saddle-shaped structure to redirect blood.

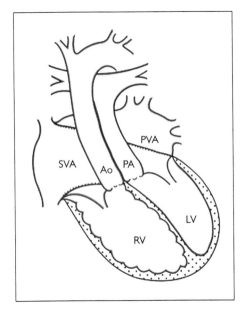

Figure 14.16 Atrial switch. Ao, aorta; LA, left atrium; LV, left ventricle; PA, pulmonary artery; RA, right atrium; RV, right ventricle; VC, valved conduit; PVA, pulmonary venous atrium; SVA, systemic venous atrium.

Reproduced with permission from the *Oxford Specialist Handbook of Adult Congenital Heart Disease*, edited by Sara Thorne and Paul Clift, copyright 2011 Oxford University Press.

TERMINOLOGY/NOMENCLATURE (POST-ATRIAL SWITCH)

Right sided atrium = pulmonary venous atrium

Left sided atrium = systemic venous atrium

Left ventricle = subpulmonary ventricle

Right ventricle = systemic ventricle

Long-term problems:

1. Venous pathway (SVC/IVC) stenosis/baffle leak; if this results in a right-to-left shunt will cause cyanosis
2. Atrial arrhythmias inevitable (focus is atrial surgical scar) and can cause circulatory collapse; **needs prompt DCCV**
3. Junctional rhythm common (AV node damage. PPM is indicated for symptomatic bradycardia or tachycardias secondary to the bradycardia. No proven prognostic benefit)
4. Eventual RV (systemic ventricle) or AV valve failure (not designed for systemic pressures). Options are transplant or arterial switch operation but LV needs to 're-trained' (as has been operating at pulmonary pressures) by banding PA.

Arterial switch (anatomical repair)

- Aorta reconnected to LV and PA reconnected to RV
- Issues with distortion of the great arteries/valves:
    - ('neo') aortic regurgitation/root dilatation
    - Supravalvular PS/RVOT obstruction
    - Coronary ostial stenosis.

Rastelli operation

In TGA with a VSD and PS (see Figure 14.17):

- Parallel circulation blood mixed across VSD
- Excessive pulmonary blood flow prevented by stenosis (otherwise leads to increased PVR and PHT, i.e. Eisenmenger's)
- 'Balanced' cyanotic circulation that may allow survival.

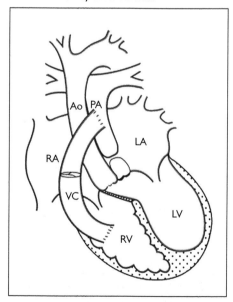

Figure 14.17 Rastelli operation in TGA with a VSD and PS. Ao, aorta; LA, left atrium; LV, left ventricle; PA, pulmonary artery; RA, right atrium; RV, right ventricle; VC, valved conduit; PVA, pulmonary venous atrium; SVA systemic venous atrium.

VSD is closed to in such a way to commit the aorta to the LV (across non-functional RVOT) and the RV is directed to the PA via a valved conduit. The PA is ligated.

- Issues:
    - Conduit stenosis
    - Subaortic obstruction as a result of VSD patch
    - Residual VSD (shunt and endocarditis risk).

14.12 Congenitally corrected transposition of the great arteries (ccTGA)

In ccTGA there is AV and VA discordance e.g. the ventricles are inverted (Figure 14.18).

- Associated lesions in the majority of cases:
    - VSD present in 75%
    - PS present in 75%
    - Left AV valve (tricuspid) abnormalities (Ebsteinoid)
- CXR: abnormally straight left heart border
- AV block is a very common complication (may be the presenting complaint); 2%/year incidence of CHB.

The problem with ccTGA is that the systemic circulation is supported by the RV and TV which are not designed for this purpose. The circulations are in series and mix normally.

If there are no associated lesions the patient may be asymptomatic until early adulthood or middle age. Usually present with:

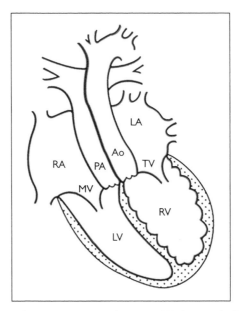

Figure 14.18 Isolated ccTGA. Ao, aorta; LA, left atrium; LV, left ventricle; PA, pulmonary artery; MV, mitral valve; RA, right atrium; RV, right ventricle; TV, tricuspid valve; **patent foramen ovale; *patent arterial duct.

- Progressive morphological RV and/or left AV valve failure
- Heart block/arrhythmias.

Management

- If asymptomatic and incidental it is reasonable to simply monitor the RV/TV (left AV valve) and treat with a PPM if CHB develops
- If significant TR develops early surgical intervention is indicated before the RV starts to fail
- **Anatomical surgical repair** or 'double switch' operation—Senning/Mustard and arterial switch, the LV becoming the systemic ventricle (LV may need to be 'retrained' with PA band)—considered if there is severe TR and RV dysfunction.

As documented at the start of this section, 75% of patients with ccTGA have associated VSDs and PS. In the case of ccTGA with VSD and PS the presentation is paediatric:

- Heart failure if the VSD is large (high pulomary flow and LV volume loading)
- Cyanosis if RVOT obstruction severe (low pulmonary flow but PAs protected).

Management: 'Classic repair'

- VSD patch closure
- LV redirected to the PA with a valved conduit
- TVR if significant valve problems.

i.e. the RV remains the systemic ventricle with associated future problems.

14.13 Tetralogy of Fallot

See Figure 14.19.

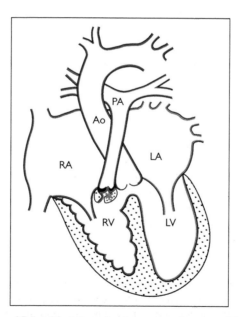

Figure 14.19 Tetralogy of Fallot. *deviation of outlet septum; Ao, aorta; LA, left atrium; LV, left ventricle; PA, pulmonary artery; RA, right atrium; RV, right ventricle.

1. RVOT obstruction—valvular and infundibular pulmonary stenosis
2. VSD
3. Overriding aorta
4. RVH as a consequence of pulmonary stenosis.

Should be considered as a primary problem of the outlet (subarterial) ventricular septal formation and migration (anterocephalad deviation), with subsequent RVOT obstruction and overriding aorta.

15% have a deletion of chromosome 22q11 (see Box 14.1).

BOX 14.1 DIGEORGE'S SYNDROME (CATCH 22, 22Q11 SYNDROME)

Due to a deletion of chromosome 22 (22q11).

C—cardiac defects (15% of ToF, interrupted aortic arch, truncus arteriosus)

A—abnormal facies (microagnathia, short philtrum, low-set ears)

T—thymic hypoplasia

C—cleft palate

H—hypocalcaemia

22—chromosome 22

Behavioural and psychiatric disorders.

Affected subjects have a 50% risk of passing the defect to offspring (e.g. if you have ToF with Catch 22 the implication is that there is a 50% of passing a congenital condition rather than 6% in isolated ToF). However, most cases sporadic.

FISH test for 22q11 should be offered to all patients with ToF considering pregnancy.

Presentation depends on the degree of RVOT obstruction, i.e. the 'balance' of systemic and pulmonary circulations:

• **Mild obstruction**—high pulmonary blood flow—cardiac failure and minimal cyanosis
• **Significant obstruction**—right-to-left shunt and cyanosis (majority).

Surgical management

• Palliative procedures to increase pulmonary blood flow—e.g. BT shunt—may be used if associated lesions complicate initial total repair
• Total repair (preferred treatment in infancy):
  ▪ VSD closed with a patch
  ▪ RVOT obstruction relieved by resection of infundibular muscle or transannular patch (literally cutting across the PV annulus and RVOT; almost always results in PR especially with associated dysplastic valves)
• With successful repair, survival approaches the general population
• Long-term PR is inevitable after transannular patch—essentially the RVOT/pulmonary valve annulus has been longitudinally cut open and the often dysplastic pulmonary valve will not coapt as the RVOT grows/enlarges (the converse is residual stenosis)
• The development of severe PR leads to RV dilatation and dysfunction—indication for intervention (increasingly transcatheter or 'injectable' off-pump surgical valves)
• ECG shows RBBB (right bundle runs in the floor of the VSD and is often damaged during surgery):

KEY CONCEPT

Change in QRS duration reflects RV size and is related to the risk of SCD and VT.

QRS >180 ms is a highly sensitive marker for SCD and VT in previous ToF repair (SCD accounts for one third of late deaths).

- Non-sustained VT is common but is not in itself an indicator of SCD risk
- Antiarrhythmics are not indicated if asymptomatic
- The VT is normally of RVOT origin (surgical scar from infundibulectomy or VSD patch)
- Development of major arrhythmias (AF/flutter and sustained VT) normally reflect haemodynamic deterioration (PR, RV dilatation), and therefore haemodynamic assessment and correction of the lesion can correct the arrhythmia (with the option of surgical/catheter ablation)
- CXR—'coeur en sabot' or boot-shaped heart (classical)
- Aortic root dilatation and AR are recognized: can be due to damage to the AV during VSD repair or intrinsic aortopathy (cystic medial necrosis type; root >55 mm is surgical indication).

Pulmonary atresia with VSD

Is part of the ToF spectrum but instead of pulmonary stenosis there is an interruption (atresia) of the pulmonary outflow.

- Associated with 22q11 micro-deletion
- Lack of PA flow results in different degrees of pulmonary vascular underdevelopment (cardiac structures develop relative to degree of blood flow)
- No blood passes directly from the right heart into the pulmonary tree (flow via VSD)
- Blood is redirected from systemic circulation back into PAs from either a large PDA or multiple systemic-to-pulmonary-artery collaterals—major aortopulmonary collateral arteries (MAPCAs)—usually from the descending aorta.

14.14 Functionally single ventricle and the Fontan circulation

Functionally single ventricle

Complex **cyanotic heart disease** with a functionally single ventricle *and* a biventricular surgical repair not possible.

Dominant ventricle can be morphologically right or left with an associated rudimentary ventricle. Common examples:

- **Tricuspid atresia** (no right AV connection = no blood flow = poor RV development = rudimentary RV); mixing via ASD
- **Pulmonary atresia** with intact ventricular septum (minimal flow into RV and so poor development = rudimentary RV)
- **Mitral atresia** (as per tricuspid atresia)
- **Double inlet ventricle:**
    - Both AV valves connected to a single dominant ventricle
    - Main ventricle connected to a rudimentary chamber via 'VSD'
    - One great artery arises from main chamber and one from the rudimentary chamber

- Left ventricle dominant in majority of cases
- VA discordance (TGA type) common (aorta arises from rudimentary right ventricle)
- Pulmonary obstruction protects the lungs from systemic pressures in 50%
- **Hypoplastic left heart syndrome**—varying hypoplasia of the LV, aorta and left-sided valves results in complex univentricular anatomy
  - Systemic and pulmonary blood is mixed in the dominant morphological right ventricle resulting in cyanosis
  - The degree of cyanosis and neonatal presentation depends on pulmonary blood flow (PA protected by PS or a restrictive 'VSD'—rare to have a balanced circulation)
  - **High pulmonary flow** = congestive heart failure and pulmonary vascular remodelling (mild cyanosis)—requires PA banding to protect lungs
  - **Low pulmonary blood flow** = severe cyanosis and circulatory collapse (requires emergency systemic-pulmonary shunt).

LEARNING POINT

There are now more adults than children with complex congenital heart disease. This reflects the success of paediatric cardiac surgery over the last 50 years.

Fontan surgery

- A **palliative procedure** when a two ventricle repair is not possible (Figure 14.20)
- There are a number of modifications but in simple terms the systemic venous blood from the IVC and SVC is redirected (bypassing right heart) directly to PAs
- Functionally single ventricle to support the systemic circulation
- End result is a palliative procedure, e.g. limited life expectancy but improved symptoms and functionality
- Is usually a staged approach. There are many historical technical variations:
  - Originally an **atrio-pulmonary connection (e.g. RA connected to PA);** leads to massive RA dilatation and risk of arrhythmias. RA can acts as a swirling reservoir wasting passive blood flow energy
  - Modern modification is the **total cavopulmonary connection (TCPC)**—SVC blood redirected via a Glenn shunt. IVC blood redirected via a lateral tunnel (within the RA) or an extracardiac conduit. The result is efficient laminar blood flow without RA loading. Note: as the SVC is usually disconnected from the RA the usual pacing lead route is not available.

Stage 1:

- Correct pulmonary blood flow (PA band if high flow vs systemic-arterial shunt if low flow).

Stage 2:

- Glenn operation—cavopulmonary shunt—SVC connected to PAs
- SVC flow accounts for 70% venous return in infant
- Only possible when PVR low (3–4 months of age).

Stage 3:

- Complete Fontan: modern approach TCPC (stages 2 and 3 may be combined)
- TCPC can be 'fenestrated'. This will result in a right-to-left shunt with mild desaturation. Acts as a 'blow off valve' for high venous pressures.

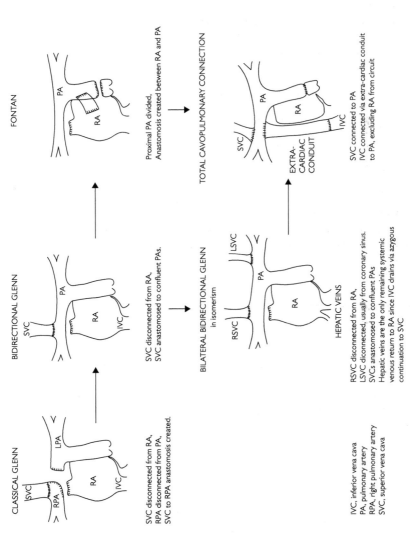

CLASSICAL GLENN

SVC disconnected from RA,
RPA disconnected from PA,
SVC to RPA anastomosis created.

BIDIRECTIONAL GLENN

SVC disconnected from RA,
SVC anastomosed to confluent PAs.

FONTAN

Proximal PA divided,
Anastomosis created between RA and PA

TOTAL CAVOPULMONARY CONNECTION

SVC connected to PA
IVC connected via extra-cardiac conduit
to PA, excluding RA from circuit

BILATERAL BIDIRECTIONAL GLENN
in isomerism

RSVC disconnected from RA,
LSVC disconnected, usually from coronary sinus.
SVCs anastomosed to confluent PAs
Hepatic veins are the only remaining systemic
venous return to RA since IVC drains via azygous
continuation to SVC

HEPATIC VEINS

IVC, inferior vena cava
PA, pulmonary artery
RPA, right pulmonary artery
SVC, superior vena cava

Figure 14.20 Glenn and Fontan operations. TCPC is the modern modification.

Reproduced with permission from the *Oxford Textbook of Medicine* 5th edition, ed. David A. Warrell, Timothy M. Cox, John D. Firth, copyright 2010 Oxford University Press.

KEY CONCEPT

By bypassing the RA (which acts as a reservoir with swirling blood) efficient laminar blood flow is redirected to the PAs.

Flow is passive—dependent on low pulmonary vascular resistance, good hydration/ systemic venous pressure and effective pulmonary venous atrium and systemic ventricular diastolic parameters (to 'suck' blood through the lungs)—therefore dehydration and arrhythmia can cause rapid life threatening decompensation.

Important consequences of Fontan circulation:

● Atrial arrhythmias—common due to atrial surgical scarring. Potentially lifethreatening due to slowing of passive flow—**acute arrhythmia in a Fontan patient is a medical emergency and requires immediate rhythm control**
● The single systemic ventricle and AV valve develop progressive dysfunction and eventual heart failure
● Any obstruction in the Fontan pathway or pulmonary circulation will obstruct passive flow
● At risk of thrombembolism and pulmonary embolus (PE)—all Fontan patients anticoagulated
● Chronic venous hypertension leads to hepatic dysfunction and *protein losing enteropathy* (5-year survival after diagnosis is 50%—test for low serum albumin but high stool alpha 1-antitrypsin (A1AT) in a 24-h collection)
● Progressive cyanosis (sats <90%) suggests right-to-left shunt (opening up of venous collateral/ pulmonary AVMs or shunting through Fontan fenestration). Patients without a Fontan fenestration should have sats >94%.

14.15 Truncus arteriosus

● Single great arterial trunk arises from the ventricle (always associated with large VSD for mixing)
● PAs come off ascending aorta
● 'Truncal' valve dysplastic—the degree of valve dysfunction dictates prognosis
● One third have DiGeorge's syndrome
● Early corrective surgery is required before irreversible PHT develops (PAs subject to systemic pressures).

Infective endocarditis

CONTENTS

15.1 Definition

Infective endocarditis (IE) is an infection of the endocardium of the heart. May involve:

- One or more valves (or valvular prostheses)
- Pacemaker/defibrillator leads
- Septal defects
- Mural endocardium (rare).

15.2 Epidemiology

- Despite significant advances in diagnosis and treatment, IE remains a dangerous disease
- Particularly for people at risk—prosthetic valve, congenital heart disease, or a history of IE—in whom morbidity and mortality approach 50%
- Annual incidence of 15–60 per million (significant variation between countries):
  - Male:female ratio 2:1
  - Significant increase with age
- Epidemiological profile has changed in recent decades, particularly in developed nations, due to changing risk factors:
  - Rheumatic heart disease now rare
  - More common in the elderly with native valve disease
  - More patients with prosthetic valves
  - More intravenous drug abuse
  - More cases of nosocomial infection (related to invasive procedures, haemodialysis)
  - *Staphylococcus aureus* has overtaken oral streptococci as the most common pathogen in developed nations.

15.3 Classification and terminology

Reflecting the 2009 ESC Guidelines (see 'Further Reading' section), IE is classified in the following areas:

According to localization of infection and presence/absence of intracardiac material:
- Left-sided native valve IE
- Left-sided prosthetic valve IE (PVE)
  - Early PVE <1 year after valve surgery
  - Late PVE >1 year after valve surgery
- Right-sided IE
- Device-related IE (pacemaker, defibrillator)

According to mode of acquisition:
- Healthcare associated IE
  - Nosocomial: signs/symptoms of IE developing >48 h after hospitalization
  - Non-nosocomial: signs/symptoms of IE developing <48 h after hospitalization in a patient with healthcare contact
  - Home-based nursing or i.v. therapy, haemodialysis, or i.v. chemotherapy <30 days before onset of IE
  - Hospitalization in acute care facility <90 days before onset of IE
  - Resident in nursing home or long-term care facility
- Community-acquired IE: signs/symptoms of IE developing <48 h after admission in a patient not fulfilling the criteria for health-care associated IE
- Intravenous drug abuse-associated IE

Active IE:
- Persistent fever and positive blood cultures or
- Active inflammatory morphology found at surgery or
- Patient still receiving antibiotic therapy or
- Histopathological evidence of active IE

Recurrence:
- Relapse: repeat episodes of IE caused by the same microorganism <6 months after the initial episode
- Reinfection: infection with a different microorganism or repeat episode caused by the same microorganism >6 months after the initial episode.

15.4 Microbiology

Infective endocarditis with positive blood cultures (85% of cases)

- Mainly staphylococci, streptococci, and enterococci
  - Staphylococci: S. aureus (more commonly native valve IE), coagulase-negative staphylococci (more commonly prosthetic valve IE)
  - Streptococci:
    - Oral (formerly viridians) streptococci: S. sanguis, S. mitis, S. salivarius, S. mutans, Gemella morbillorum—almost always respond to penicillin G
    - S. milleri or S. anginosus group (S. anginosus, S. intermedius, S. constellatus)—tend to form abscesses and haematogenous dissemination, requiring longer duration of antibiotic therapy

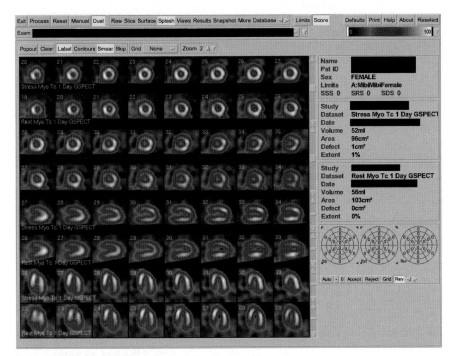

Figure 28.3 Normal study.

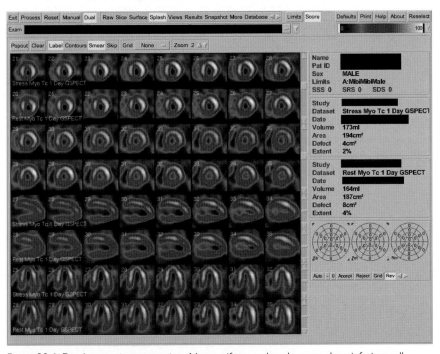

Figure 28.4 Diaphragmatic attentuation. Note uniform reduced counts along inferior wall, present both at rest and in stress. The gated study confirms normal wall thickening, which excludes a fixed inferior wall infarct.

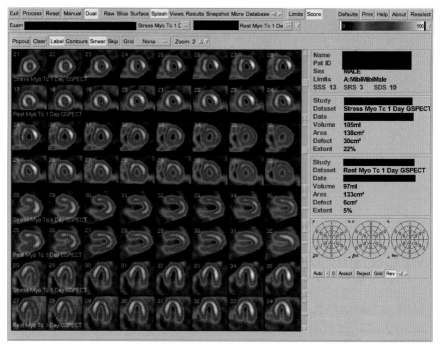

Figure 28.5 Abnormal study. There is evidence of a moderate sized inferior infarct with additional small volume of stress induced ischaemia in the anterior wall.

- Nutritionally defective streptococci: *Abiotrophia* and *Granulicatella*—often resistant to penicillin
- Group D streptococci: *S. bovis*, *S. equinus*—commensals of the human gastrointestinal tract (investigations should include colonoscopy to assess for colonic malignancy); usually sensitive to penicillin G
  - Enterococci: *E. faecalis*, *E. faecium*, *E. durans*.

Infective endocarditis with negative blood cultures because of prior antibiotic treatment

- Antibiotics given for unexplained fever before blood cultures performed
- Blood cultures may remain negative for many days after stopping antibiotics
- Causative organisms most commonly oral streptococci or coagulase-negative staphylococci.

Infective endocarditis frequently associated with negative blood cultures, usually due to fastidious organisms

- Nutritionally variant streptococci
- Gram-negative HACEK organisms (*Haemophilus*, *Actinobacillus*, *Cardiobacterium*, *Eikenella*, *Kingella*)
- Brucella
- Fungi.

Infective endocarditis always associated with negative blood cultures (5% of cases), usually due to intracellular organisms

- *Coxiella burnetii*
- *Bartonella*
- *Chlamydia*
- *Tropheryma whipplei*
- Diagnosis relies on serological testing, cell culture, or gene amplification.

15.5 Pathophysiology

Endothelial damage:
- Normal valve endothelium resistant to colonization and infection
- Mechanical disruption of endothelium results in:
  - Exposure of underlying extracellular matrix proteins
  - Production of tissue factor
  - Deposition of fibrin and platelets
  - Bacterial adherence forming a vegetation
- Endothelial damage may result from:
  - Turbulent blood flow
  - Cardiac instrumentation (catheters, pacing/defibrillator leads)
  - Inflammation (rheumatic carditis)
  - Degenerative changes (particularly in the elderly).

Transient bacteraemia:
- Magnitude and ability of pathogen to adhere to damaged endothelium are both important
- Occurs after invasive procedures (particularly dental procedures)

- However, also occurs following chewing or tooth brushing (short duration and low magnitude, but result in an annual cumulative exposure thousands to millions times greater than that caused by tooth extraction). This may explain why most cases of IE are unrelated to invasive procedures.

15.6 Diagnosis

- IE remains a diagnostic challenge
- Clinical history is very variable, depending on causative microorganism, presence/absence of pre-existing cardiac disease, and mode of presentation
- May present as acute, rapidly progressive infection or sub-acute/chronic disease with non-specific symptoms and low-grade fever
- As a result, patients may present to a variety of specialists
- Early involvement of a cardiologist and infectious diseases specialist is recommended
- A high index of suspicion is more important than strict adherence to diagnostic criteria (e.g. Duke criteria, Box 15.1)

BOX 15.1 DUKE AND MODIFIED DUKE CRITERIA FOR THE DIAGNOSIS OF IE

Duke criteria

Definite infective endocarditis

- Pathologic criteria:
  - Microorganisms: demonstrated by culture or histology in a vegetation, or in a vegetation that has embolized, or in an intracardiac abscess, or
  - Pathologic lesions: vegetation or intracardiac abscess present, confirmed by histology showing active endocarditis
- Clinical criteria:
  - 2 major criteria, or
  - 1 major and 3 minor criteria, or
  - 5 minor criteria.

Clinical criteria

- Major criteria:
  - Positive blood culture for infective endocarditis
  - Typical microorganism for infective endocarditis from two separate blood cultures
    - Viridans streptococci, *Streptococcus bovis*, HACEK group, or
    - Community-acquired *Staphylococcus aureus* or enterococci, in the absence of a primary focus, or
  - persistently positive blood culture, defined as recovery of a microorganism consistent with infective endocarditis from:
    - Blood cultures drawn more than 12 h apart or
    - All of three or a majority of four or more separate blood cultures, with first and last drawn at least 1 h apart

---

(Continued)

BOX 15.1 (CONTINUED)

- ■ Evidence of endocardial involvement
    - • Kositive echocardiogram for infective endocarditis
    - • Oscillating intracardiac mass, on valve or supporting structures, or in the path of regurgitant jets, or on implanted material, in the absence of an alternative anatomic explanation or
    - • Abscess or
    - • New partial dehiscence of prosthetic valve or
    - • New valvular regurgitation (increase or change in pre-existing murmur not sufficient).

- • Minor criteria:
    - ■ Predisposition: predisposing heart condition or intravenous drug use
    - ■ Fever: ≥38.0°C (100.4°F)
    - ■ Vascular phenomena: major arterial emboli, septic pulmonary infarcts, mycotic aneurysm, intracranial haemorrhage, conjunctival haemorrhages, Janeway lesions
    - ■ Immunologic phenomena: glomerulonephritis, Osler's nodes, Roth spots, rheumatoid factor
    - ■ Microbiologic evidence: positive blood culture not meeting major criterion or serologic evidence of active infection with organism consistent with infective endocarditis
    - ■ Echocardiogram: consistent with infective endocarditis but not meeting major criterion.

Possible infective endocarditis

- • Findings consistent with infective endocarditis that fall short of 'Definite,' but not 'Rejected.'

Rejected

- • Firm alternate diagnosis for manifestations of endocarditis or
- • Resolution of manifestations of endocarditis with antibiotic therapy for 4 days or less or
- • No pathologic evidence of infective endocarditis at surgery or autopsy, after antibiotic therapy for 4 days or less.

Modified Duke criteria (2000)

- • Duke criteria have a sensitivity of >80%, high specificity, and negative predictive value
- • However, they have shortcomings, particularly the broad nature of the 'possible' category
- • The modified Duke criteria proposed the following amendments:
    - ■ 'Possible' defined as 1 major criterion and 1 minor criterion or 3 minor criteria
    - ■ Removal of the minor criterion 'Echocardiogram: consistent with infective endocarditis but not meeting major criterion', given the widespread use of transoesophageal echocardiography
    - ■ Bacteraemia due to *Staphylococcus aureus* or positive Q-fever serology should both be adopted as major criteria.

Modified Duke criteria: Summarized from Li JS, Sexton DJ, Mick N. Proposed modifications to the Duke criteria for the diagnosis of infective endocarditis. *Clin Infect Dis*, 2000. 30(4): 633–8. Original Duke criteria reproduced from Hoen B, Selton-Suty C, Danchin N, *et al*. Evaluation of the Duke criteria versus the Beth Israel criteria for the diagnosis of infective endocarditis, *Clin Infect Dis*, 1995. 21: 905–9, with permission of Oxford University Press.

- IE should be suspected in the following clinical situations:
  - New regurgitant heart murmur
  - Embolic events of unknown origin
  - Sepsis of unknown origin (particularly if associated with an organism known to cause IE)
  - Fever (seen in up to 90% of cases of IE) associated with
    - Intracardiac prosthetic material (prosthetic valve, pacemaker/defibrillator, congenital heart disease repair)
    - Previous history of IE
    - Previous valvular or congenital heart disease
    - Immunocompromise
    - Intravenous drug abuse
    - Recent invasive procedure
    - Congestive heart failure
    - New conduction disturbance
    - Positive blood cultures with typical IE causative organism
    - Positive serology for chronic Q fever (*Coxiella burnetii*)
    - Embolic event, Roth spots, splinter haemorrhages, Janeway lesions, Osler's nodes
    - Focal or non-specific neurological signs/symptoms
    - pulmonary embolism or infiltration (right-sided IE)
    - Peripheral abscesses of unknown cause
    - Poor appetite, weight loss
  - elevated C-reactive protein or erythrocyte sedimentation rate, leukocytosis, anaemia, and microscopic haematuria (these lack specificity and are not included in current diagnostic criteria)
- Fever may be absent in the elderly and immunocompromised, after antibiotic therapy, and with less virulent or atypical organisms.

Echocardiography

- Should not be used indiscriminately
- The exception is *Staphylococcus aureus* bacteraemia, where routine echocardiography is justified, irrespective of the presence/absence of other features of IE (because of such potential for devastating consequences)
- If clinical suspicion of IE is low, a negative TTE with good image quality is sufficient
- In all other circumstances, where there is a suspicion of IE, TTE is the initial imaging modality of choice, but should be promptly followed by TOE if IE is confirmed or still suspected
- If initial TOE negative, should be repeated after 7–10 days if clinical suspicion of IE remains (earlier if *Staphylococcus aureus* bacteraemia)
- If TOE positive, follow-up echocardiography is mandatory to monitor response to treatment and detect complications
- 3D echo, CT, MRI, nuclear medicine, and PET may supplement (but not replace) TTE and TOE.

Microbiological diagnosis

- Blood cultures:
  - Remain the cornerstone of diagnosis
  - Three sets (aerobic and anaerobic) usually sufficient
  - Should be taken before starting antibiotic therapy
  - Sampling from central venous lines should be avoided due to high risk of contaminants

- No rationale for delaying sampling to coincide with peaks of fever
- A single positive blood culture should be viewed with caution, as it may be a contaminant
- In culture negative IE, antibiotics should be withdrawn and blood cultures repeated
- Histological/immunological examination:
  - Pathological examination of surgically resected tissue
  - Serological testing—*Coxiella burnetii*, *Bartonella* species, and probably staphylococci
  - Urinalysis—*Legionella*
- Molecular biology:
  - Polymerase chain reaction for fastidious organisms but limitations because of risk of contamination, false negatives, inability to provide antibiotic sensitivity information.

15.7 Complications

- Frequent and often severe
- Cardiac complications:
  - Heart failure (in 50–60% of cases)
  - Acute valvular regurgitation (valve stenosis much less common)
  - Abscess
  - Pseudoaneurysm
  - Fistula
  - Periprosthetic dehiscence
  - Ventricular septal defect
  - Conduction abnormalities
  - Acute coronary syndrome
  - Myocarditis
  - Pericarditis
- Non-cardiac complications:
  - Embolic events (in 20–50% of cases; silent in 20%)
    - Mainly spleen and brain
    - Lungs in right-sided IE (and device-related IE)
    - More likely with larger and more mobile vegetations
  - Ischaemic and haemorrhagic stroke
  - Acute renal failure.

15.8 Prognosis

- In-hospital mortality 10–26%
- Predictors of poor outcome:
  - Patient characteristics:
    - Older age
    - Prosthetic valve IE
    - Insulin-dependent DM
    - Significant comorbidity

- Presence of complications:
  - Heart failure
  - Renal failure
  - Stroke
  - Septic shock
  - Periannular abscess
- causative organism:
  - *S. aureus*
  - Fungi
  - Gram-negative bacilli
- Echocardiographic findings:
  - Periannular complications
  - Severe left-sided valve regurgitation
  - Low left ventricular ejection fraction
  - Pulmonary hypertension
  - Large vegetations
  - Severe prosthetic dysfunction
  - Premature mitral valve closure and other signs of elevated diastolic pressure.

15.9 Antibiotic treatment

- The early involvement of an infectious diseases expert is mandatory
- The key principles of antibiotic therapy in IE are:
  - Bactericidal agents
  - Synergistic combinations of antibiotics
  - High doses
  - Long duration
- Local guidelines should be used at all times, but suggested regimens are as follows:

Oral streptococci and group D streptococci

- Fully susceptible to penicillin (mean inhibitory concentration (MIC) <0.125 mg/l):
  - Standard treatment (4 weeks):
    - Penicillin G 12–18 million U/day i.v. in 6 doses or
    - Amoxicillin 100–200 mg/kg/day i.v. in 4–6 doses or
    - Ceftriaxone 2 g/day i.v./i.m. in 1 dose
  - 2-week treatment:
    - Penicillin G 12–18 million U/day i.v. in 6 doses or
    - Amoxicillin 100–200 mg/kg/day i.v. in 4–6 doses or
    - Ceftriaxone 2 g/day i.v./i.m. in 1 dose
  with
    - Gentamicin 3 mg/kg/day i.v./i.m. in 1 dose or
    - Netilmicin 4–5 mg/kg/day i.v. in 1 dose
  - Penicillin allergy:
    - Vancomycin 30 mg/kg/day i.v. in 2 doses (for 4 weeks)
- Relatively resistant to penicillin (MIC 0.125–2 mg/l):
  - Standard treatment (4 weeks):
    - Penicillin G 24 million U/day i.v. in 6 doses or
    - Amoxicillin 100–200 mg/kg/day i.v. in 4–6 doses

with
  - Gentamicin 3 mg/kg/day i.v./i.m. in 1 dose (for 2 weeks)
- Penicillin allergy:
  - Vancomycin 30 mg/kg/day i.v. in 2 doses (for 4 weeks)

with
  - Gentamicin 3 mg/kg/day i.v./i.m. in 1 dose (for 2 weeks).

Staphylococcus species

- Native valves:
  - Methicillin-susceptible staphylococci:
    - Flucloxacillin/oxacillin 12 g/day i.v. in 4–6 doses (for 4–6 weeks)

  with
    - Gentamicin 3 mg/kg/day i.v./i.m. in 2–3 doses (for 3–5 days)
  - Penicillin allergy/methicillin-resistant staphylococci:
    - Vancomycin 30 mg/kg/day i.v. in 2 doses (for 4–6 weeks)

  with
    - Gentamicin 3 mg/kg/day i.v./i.m. in 2–3 doses (for 3–5 days)
- Prosthetic valves:
  - Methicillin-susceptible staphylococci:
    - Flucloxacillin/oxacillin 12 g/day i.v. in 4–6 doses (for ≥6 weeks)

  with
    - Rifampicin 1200 mg/day i.v. or p.o. in 2 doses (for ≥6 weeks)

  and
    - Gentamicin 3 mg/kg/day i.v./i.m. in 2–3 doses (for 2 weeks)
- Penicillin allergy/methicillin-resistant staphylococci:
  - Vancomycin 30 mg/kg/day i.v. in 2 doses (for ≥6 weeks)

with
  - Rifampicin 1200 mg/day i.v. or p.o. in 2 doses (for ≥6 weeks)

and
  - Gentamicin 3 mg/kg/day i.v./i.m. in 2–3 doses (for 2 weeks).

Enterococcus species

- Beta-lactam and gentamicin susceptible:
  - Amoxicillin 300 mg/kg/day i.v. in 4–6 doses (for 4–6 weeks) or
  - Ampicillin 200 mg/kg/day i.v. in 4–6 doses (for 4–6 weeks) or
  - If penicillin allergic—vancomycin 30/mg/day i.v. in 2 doses (for 6 weeks)

with
  - Gentamicin 3 mg/kg/day i.v. or i.m. in 2–3 doses (for 4–6 weeks).

Blood culture negative IE

- *Brucella*: doxycycline 200 mg/day + cotrimoxazole 960 mg/12 h + rifampicin 300–600 mg/day for ≥3 months orally
- *Coxiella burnetii*: doxycycline 200 mg/day + hydroxychloroquine 200–600 mg/day orally OR doxycycline 200 mg/day plus quinolone (e.g. ofloxacin 400 mg/day) for >18 months orally
- *Bartonella*: ceftriaxone 2 g/day or ampicillin/amoxicillin 12 g/day i.v. *or* doxycycline 200 mg/day orally for 6 weeks + gentamicin 3 mg/kg/day or netilmicin i.v. for 3 weeks

- *Legionella:* erythromycin 3 g/day i.v. for 2 weeks then orally for 4 weeks + rifampicin 300–1200 mg/day or ciprofloxacin 1.5 g/day orally for 6 weeks
- *Mycoplasma:* newer fluoroquinolones for >6 months.

Empirical treatment (before or without pathogen identification)

- Native valves and prosthetic valves ≥12 months post surgery (4–6 weeks):
  - Penicillin tolerant:
    - Ampicillin-sulbactam 12 g/day i.v. in 4 doses or
    - Amoxicillin-clavulanate 12 g/day i.v. in 4 doses

with

    - Gentamicin 3 mg/kg/day i.v. or i.m. in 2–3 doses
  - Penicillin allergic:
    - Vancomycin 30 mg/kg/day i.v. in 2 doses

with

    - Gentamicin 3 mg/kg/day i.v. or i.m. in 2–3 doses

with

    - Ciprofloxacin 1000 mg/day orally in 2 doses or 800 mg/day i.v. in 2 doses
  - Prosthetic valves:
    - i. Vancomycin 30 mg/kg/day i.v. in 2 doses (for 6 weeks)

with

    - ii. Gentamicin 3 mg/kg/day i.v. or i.m. in 2–3 doses (for 2 weeks)

with

    - iii. Rifampicin 1200 mg/day orally in 2 doses (for 2 weeks).

15.10 Surgical treatment

- Almost 50% of patients with IE will undergo surgery
- Early surgery recommended in those with
  - Heart failure
  - Abscess
  - Perivalvular complications
  - Embolism
- 'Emergency' surgery (within 24 h):
  - Aortic or mitral IE with refractory pulmonary oedema or shock, due to acute regurgitation, valve obstruction, or formation of a fistula into a cardiac chamber or the pericardium
- 'Urgent' surgery (within a few days)
  - If heart failure persists or echocardiographic features suggest haemodynamic compromise
  - Should be considered in patients with persisting fever and positive blood cultures after 7–10 days despite appropriate antibiotic therapy (and in whom extracardiac infection has been excluded)
  - Should be considered in patients with locally uncontrolled infection and abscess, false aneurysm, fistula formation, or enlarging vegetation
  - In the absence of embolism, aortic or mitral vegetations >10 mm in size and with other factors suggesting a poor prognosis (heart failure, persistent infection or abscess); following one or more embolic events (which may be silent and detected radiologically), urgent surgery is indicated in the absence of these poor prognostic features

- 'Elective' surgery (within 1–2 weeks of commencing antibiotics) indicated if severe aortic or mitral regurgitation without heart failure
- Early surgery should also be considered if vegetation is very large (>15 mm) in the absence of other adverse clinical features. The patient's other comorbidities must be taken into consideration
- Intraoperative TOE is recommended in all cases
- Pre-operative coronary angiography is recommended in men >40 years, in post-menopausal women, and in patients with at least one cardiovascular risk factor or a history of CAD. The exception is a large aortic vegetation, which could be dislodged during cardiac catheterization or when emergency surgery is required.

15.11 Antibiotic prophylaxis

- The evidence in its favour is limited—no randomized trial
- Many cases of IE now arise in those without known pre-existing valvular heart disease, often with no clear preceding invasive medical or dental procedure
- *Staphylococcus aureus* is the most common organism, with fewer cases due to oral streptococci
- International organizations have significantly updated their guidelines in the past few years
- A careful approach is required in explaining these changes to patients, many of whom have taken antibiotic prophylaxis for years and have previously been warned of the dangers of IE.

National Institute of Health and Clinical Excellence guidelines (2008)

- See Table 15.1 and 'Further Reading'
- No longer indicated for dental or respiratory procedures
- Only indicated for gastrointestinal and genitourinary procedures where there is suspicion of pre-existing infection.

European Society of Cardiology guidelines (2009)

- See Table 15.2 and 'Further Reading'
- Antibiotic prophylaxis only for those with the highest risk of IE undergoing the highest-risk procedures
- No longer indicated for native valve disease
- No longer indicated for respiratory, gastrointestinal, or genitourinary procedures.

Table 15.1 National Institute of Health and Clinical Excellence guidelines (2008)

High-risk patients	Previous IE Prosthetic valve Acquired valvular heart disease with stenosis or regurgitation Structural congenital heart disease, including surgically corrected or palliated structural conditions. Excluding: • Isolated ASD • Fully repaired VSD/PDA • Endothelialized closure devices • HOCM
Procedures requiring prophylaxis	Gastrointestinal and genitourinary procedures where there is suspected pre-existing infection

National Institute for Health and Clinical Excellence (2008). Adapted from CG 64, 'Prophylaxis against infective endocarditis: antimicrobial prophylaxis against infective endocarditis in adults and children undergoing interventional procedures'. London: NICE. Available from www.nice.org.uk/guidance/CG64. Reproduced with permission.

Table 15.2 European Society of Cardiology guidelines (2009)

High-risk patients	• Previous IE • Prosthetic valve or prosthetic material used for valve repair • Cyanotic congenital heart disease (without surgical repair or with residual defects, palliative shunts, or conduits) • Congenital heart disease repaired with prosthetic material (for 6 months if complete repair, indefinite if residual defect)
Procedures requiring prophylaxis	• Dental procedures requiring manipulation of the gingival or periapical region of the teeth or perforation of the oral mucosa

Reproduced from 'Guidelines on the prevention, diagnosis, and treatment of infective endocarditis (new version 2009)', The Task Force on the Prevention, Diagnosis, and Treatment of Infective Endocarditis of the European Society of Cardiology (ESC), *Eur. Heart J.*, 30 (19), 2369–2413, 2009.

Table 15.3 Guidelines from the European Society of Cardiology for prophylaxis before dental procedures

	Oral	Intravenous or intramuscular
Penicillin tolerant	Amoxicillin 2 g or ampicillin 2 g	Amoxicillin 2 g or ampicillin 2 g
Penicillin allergic	Clindamycin 600 mg	Clindamycin 600 mg

Reproduced from 'Guidelines on the prevention, diagnosis, and treatment of infective endocarditis (new version 2009)', The Task Force on the Prevention, Diagnosis, and Treatment of Infective Endocarditis of the European Society of Cardiology (ESC), *Eur Heart J.*, 30 (19): 2369–2413, copyright 2009 with permission from Oxford University Press.

Antibiotic regimens

- Single dose to be given 30–60 min before procedure
- See Table 15.3 for guidelines from the European Society of Cardiology (ESC) for prophylaxis before dental procedures (local antibiotic guidelines and guidelines for other procedures may differ).

Non-antibiotic prevention of infective endocarditis

In patients with high-risk cardiac lesions, the risk of IE can be reduced by simple measures:

- Meticulous skin and dental hygiene
- Avoidance of unnecessary invasive procedures (including intravenous cannulae and urinary catheters)
- Institutional hygiene.

Further reading

Guidelines on the prevention, diagnosis, and treatment of infective endocarditis (new version 2009), The Task Force on the Prevention, Diagnosis, and Treatment of Infective Endocarditis of the European Society of Cardiology (ESC), *Eur Heart J*, 2009; 30: 2369–413.

NICE Guideline CG 64: *Prophylaxis against infective endocarditis: antimicrobial prophylaxis against infective endocarditis in adults and children undergoing interventional procedures.* London: National Institute for Health and Clinical Excellence 2008. Available online at www.nice.org.uk/guidance/CG64.

Diseases of the aorta and trauma to the aorta and heart

CONTENTS

16.1 Aetiology of aortic aneurysm and dissection

Risk factors:

- Atherosclerosis
    - Smoking
    - Dyslipidaemia
    - Hypertension
- Bicuspid aortic valve (BAV)
- Genetic defects
    - Marfan syndrome
    - Ehler's-Danlos
    - Familial connective tissue diseases ('overlap' syndromes); familial clustering occurs in about 20%
- Aortitis/inflammatory
    - Microbial disease
        - Syphilis
        - *Staphylococcus aureus*
    - Multisystem vasculitis
        - Kawasaki's syndrome
        - Behçet's disease
        - Giant cell arteritis
- Drugs
    - Cocaine
    - Amphetamines
- Aortic stenosis
- Previous surgery
- Trauma.

16.2 Pathology

Aortic wall is up to 4 mm thick and made up of the intima, media, and adventitia.
   Vessel weakness is typically due to abnormal composition of medial layer:

- Cystic medical degeneration—present in BAV and Marfan syndrome
    - Matrix metalloproteinases (MMPs): MMP-2 and MMP-9 have been found in higher levels in Marfan patients; thought to result in breakdown in elastin within the medial layer and result in aneurysm formation
- Loss of vascular smooth muscle
- Loss of elastic fibres
- Inflammatory response with T-cell clonal expansion, increased cytokine activity, and subsequent granuloma formation seen only in aortitis.

This leads to reduced wall strength and vessel dilatation. The law of Laplace can be used to calculate circumferential wall stress (W):

$$W = \frac{Pr}{2h}$$

where P is the pulse pressure, r is the radius, and h is the wall thickness.
   Important factors increasing wall stress and leading to dissection or rupture (see Figure 16.1) are:

- Hypertension
- Wall thinning
- Aortic enlargement
- Aortic diameter (although not always, especially in connective tissue diseases)
    - 6 cm—critical diameter of ascending aorta (30% rupture/dissection rate/annum)
    - 7 cm—critical diameter of descending aorta (40% rupture/dissection rate/annum).

16.3 Non-invasive and invasive investigations

Aim is:

- Confirm the presence of thoracic aortic disease
- Identify the anatomical extent of the diseased segment
- Identify the underlying pathological process
- Provide supplementary information potentially of value in treatment planning, i.e. aortic valve competence/entry tear, side branch involvement.

No single imaging modality can do all the above (see Table 16.1). An average of 1.8 modalities are needed for the diagnosis of aortic dissection.
   Modalities available:

- Computed tomography (CT)
- Magnetic resonance imaging (MRI)
- Transthoracic echocardiography (TTE)
- Transoesophageal echocardiography (TOE).

Aortography is available but rarely used. Choice depends on local availability, urgency, safety, relative and absolute contraindications, and question that needs answering. The 2010 AHA/ACC guidelines detail the benefits and drawbacks of each modality.

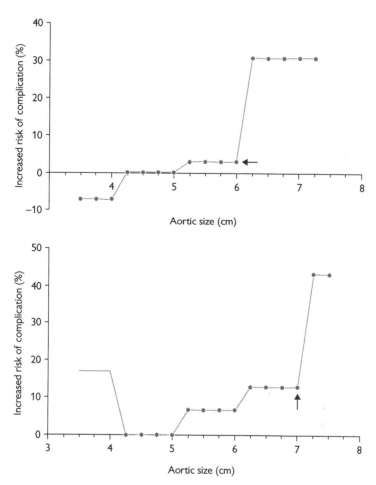

Figure 16.1 The influence of aortic size on the risk of complications. Beyond a critical diameter of 6 cm in the ascending aorta and 7 cm in the descending aorta, the risk of future complications increases significantly.

Reproduced from *Annals of Thoracic Surgery*, John A Elefteriades, 74, S1877–S80, 'Natural history of thoracic aortic aneurysms: indications for surgery, and surgical versus nonsurgical risks', copyright 2002 with permission from Elsevier.

CXR

- Helps exclude other causes of acute chest pain, e.g. pneumothorax
- Lacks specificity
  - Pooled analysis of predictive sensitivity of a widened mediastinum/abnormal cardiac contour with significant thoracic aortic disease of 64% and 71% respectively
- Helpful in very low risk patients
  - A completely normal CXR is unlikely to be associated with significant thoracic disease.

TTE

- Artefacts may mimic dissection flap (need to scan in two orthogonal views, use colour and presence of independent motion to help exclude artefact)
- Relatively low sensitivity and specificity of 77–80% and 93–96% for TTE in proximal aortic dissection; less for distal dissection

Table 16.1 Strengths and weaknesses of the commonly used imaging modalities in the assessment of aortic disease

Modality	CXR	TTE	TOE	CT	MRI
Emergency use	+++	+++	++	+++	+
Accuracy	+	+	++	+++	+++
Image quality of aorta	–	+	++	+++	+++
3D images	–	–	–	+++	+++
Image entire length of aorta	–	–	–	+++	+++
Radiation	+	–	–	++	–
Supplementary data on cardiac status	–	++	++	++	++
Long-term follow up use	–	–	–	++	+++
Expense	+++	+++	++	++	+

+++ strength; – weakness

- Limited by patient factors, e.g. habitus and acoustic windows
- Distal ascending and proximal aortic arch not well seen.

TOE
- Sensitivity and specificity with TOE of 88–98% and 90–95% in proximal aortic dissection
- Can be performed intraoperatively
- TOE often requires sedation
- Distal ascending and proximal aortic arch not well seen
- Artefacts may mimic dissection flap (need to scan in two orthogonal views, use colour and presence of independent motion).

CT
- Able to distinguish between causes of acute aortic syndromes
- ECG gating has improved sensitivity and specificity and should be used when motion artefact are likely to occur, e.g. proximal aorta and coronary arteries
- Sensitivity and specificity of 100% and 98–99% respectively
- Good in trauma with sensitivity, specificity, and accuracy of 96%, 99%, and 99% respectively
- Excellent negative predictive value for trauma of 100%
- Can image proximal coronary arteries
- Drawback of requiring contrast and exposing the patient to radiation; not ideal for multiple follow up scans.

MRI
- Highly sensitive and specific for thoracic aortic disease
- Prolonged duration of acquisition—limits use in emergencies
- Unable to use gadolinium in patients with renal impairment
- Claustrophobia and presence of metal implants/devices can limit its use
- Not widely available out of hours.

Table 16.2 Normal diameters of the aorta

	Male (cm)	Female (cm)
Aortic annulus (TTE)	2.6 (+/− 0.3)	2.3 (+/− 0.2)
Sinus of valsalva (TTE)	3.4 (+/− 0.3)	3.4 (+/− 0.3)
Aortic root (TTE)	<3.7	<3.7
Ascending aorta (TTE)	<3.7	<3.7
Descending aorta (CT)	<2.8	<2.8

16.4 Thoracic aortic aneurysm (TAA)

Definition and classification

Localized aneurysm is defined as a >50% dilatation compared to the diameter of the adjacent normal vessel (see Table 16.2). Ascending aorta measuring >5.5 cm is therefore generally considered aneurysmal.

Indexing the aortic size to body surface area is recommended. Normal vessel:

- Ascending 2.1 cm/m^2
- Descending 1.6 cm/m^2.

Normal growth of 1 mm/decade during adulthood.

- True aneurysm: enlargement of the inner lumen due to vessel wall expansion (see Figure 16.2)
- False/pseudoaneurysm: due to a defect in the vessel wall with the resultant extravasation of blood (see Figure 16.3). The pseudoaneurysm is not lined by vascular endothelium.

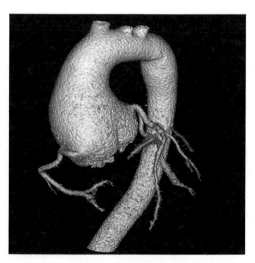

Figure 16.2 3D reconstruction of a huge aneurysm of the aortic root and ascending aorta with normal coronary arteries.

Used with permission from Dr N Manghat, Consultant Radiologist Bristol Heart Institute.

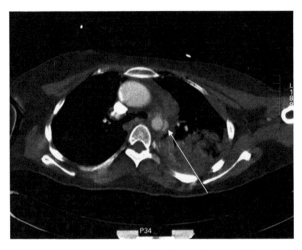

Figure 16.3 Post-traumatic pseudoaneurysm of the descending aorta (arrow) with associated hydropneumothorax of the left lung in a 41-year-old construction worker following a 10-m fall.
Reproduced from *Emerg. Med. J.*, M. Ballesta Moratalla, 'Aortic post-traumatic pseudoaneurysm', 25:533, copyright 2008 with permission from BMJ Publishing Group Ltd

Epidemiology

- Mean age 65 years for men and 77 years for women. 55% ascending, 11% arch, 38% descending
- Death from aneurysms and dissection—1.5/100,000 per year. 22% do not reach hospital and rupture occurs in 74% with mortality rate of 94.3%
- Male: female 1:1, unlike abdominal aortic aneurysm (AAA), which is more common in males
- Concomitant aneurysmal disease—25% infrarenal aneurysms up to 13% had multiple aneurysms.

Natural history

See Table 16.3.

- Rate of growth and risk of dissection/rupture depends upon aetiology and location of aneurysm
- Mean growth rate for TAA is significantly less than AAA (1–4 mm/year vs 2–5 mm/year respectively)

Table 16.3 Variables associated with increased rate of aneurysmal growth

Location	Descending aorta
Wall integrity	Dissected aorta
Initial size	<5 cm (2%)
	5–5.9 cm (3%)
	>6 cm (7%)
	(Annual rate of rupture)
Genetic	Marfan
Hormonal	Pregnancy

- 5-year survival of symptomatic TAA is 27% versus 58% in asymptomatic patients
- In 63 untreated patients with arteriosclerotic TAA, 40% died of rupture and 27% died of unrelated cardiovascular conditions.

Clinical features

Normally asymptomatic. Possible consequences due to compression/erosion/distortion of various structures:

- Vascular—SVC obstruction, aortic regurgitation, thromboembolic sequelae
- Neural—phrenic, vagus, or recurrent laryngeal nerve
- Airway compression and dysphagia.

Diagnostic procedures

See Chapters 29 and 30 for details.

Medical management

Generally reserved for asymptomatic aneurysms. Aortic size index (aortic diameter/m^2) may be useful to predict increasing rates of rupture, dissection or death:

- <2.75 cm/m^2: low risk (4%/year)
- 2.75–4.24 cm/m^2: moderate risk (8%/year)
- >4.25 cm/m^2: high risk (20%/year).

Reducing the aortic dp/dt (the rate of aortic pressure change over time) is the goal of medical management.

- Aggressive blood pressure control
  - <140/90
  - <130/80 for patients with diabetes or chronic kidney disease (see Box 16.1)
- Smoking cessation
- Beta blockers (ß blocker) are first line treatment—reduce rate of aortic dilatation in the young and in Marfan syndrome. Data from retrospective reviews or open label, randomized trial of 70 patients with Marfan syndrome using propanolol
- Evidence for ACE inhibitors from randomized, double-blind placebo-controlled trial of 17 patients with Marfan syndrome using perindopril followed up for 24 weeks
- Angiotensin receptor blockers (ARB): evidence supports valsartan (open label trial of 3081 adults) and losartan/irbesartan (18 Marfan syndrome paediatric patients). There is also evidence to suggest ARB have tissue granulating factor blocking properties and result in regression of aortic dilatation in Loeys-Dietz syndrome

BOX 16.1 AHA/ACC RECOMMENDATION 2010 FOR BLOOD PRESSURE CONTROL

- Antihypertensive to reduce risk of stroke, MI, heart failure, and cardiovascular death, with target <140/90 and 130/80 (diabetes and CKD)
- ß blocker should be given to all patients with Marfan syndrome and aortic aneurysm (unless contraindicated) to reduce rate of aortic dilatation
- Aim for the lowest tolerated BP achieved with ß blocker and ACE inhibitors for patients with thoracic aortic aneurysm
- Use losartan for Marfan syndrome patients to reduce rate of aortic dilatation.

Adapted from 'The 2010 ACCF/AHA/AATS/ACR/ASA/SCA/SCAI/SIR/STS/SVM guidelines for the diagnosis and management of patients with thoracic aortic disease', 121, e266–e369, copyright 2010 with permission of Wolters Kluwer Health.

- Statins shown to reduce mortality after endovascular repair in AAA repair but not in TAA
- Surveillance: important either CT/MRI generally annually
- Lifestyle: avoidance of manoeuvres that result in increased intra-thoracic pressure, e.g. weightlifting
- Screening: family screening in those with heritable conditions.

Surgical and endovascular management

The ESC has only issued guidance on thresholds for intervention in aortic root aneurysms. The AHA/ACC have expanded upon these, including recommendations for descending and thoraco-abdominal aneurysms, screening, management algorithms in general and high-risk groups (see Boxes 16.2 and 16.3).

Generally intervention (surgery/endovascular repair) is reserved for symptomatic or expanding aneurysms. As the risk of rupture increases significantly in ascending aortas >60 mm (see Figure 16.1), surgery is recommended in when the size reaches >55 mm. Importantly however, in higher risk populations the threshold is lower.

Features requiring consideration for intervention:

- Increasing size: >0.5 cm/year
- Aneurysm causing symptoms
- Size >5.5 cm in ascending aneurysm.

Operative mortality in ascending aneurysms:

- 1.5% for elective
- 2.6% for urgent
- 11.7% for emergency.

BOX 16.2 ESC AND AHA/ACC RECOMMENDATIONS FOR THRESHOLD OF THORACIC AORTIC ANEURYSM FOR INTERVENTION

Root aneurysm and aortic regurgitation (ESC)

- Root aneurysm >4.5 cm Marfan (ESC Class I indication)
- Root >5.0 cm bicuspid (ESC Class IIa indication)
- Root >5.5cm ascending (ESC Class IIa indication).

Descending aneurysms (AHA/ACC Class I indication)

- Open repair: chronic dissection >5.5 cm, especially with connective tissue disorder and without significant comorbidity
- Endovascular repair: degenerative/traumatic aneurysms >5.5 cm (saccular/post-operative pseudoaneurysms).

Adapted from 'The 2010 ACCF/AHA/AATS/ACR/ASA/SCA/SCAI/SIR/STS/SVM guidelines for the diagnosis and management of patients with thoracic aortic disease', *Circulation*, 121, e266–e369, copyright 2010 with permission of Wolters Kluwer Health.

BOX 16.3 AHA/ACC RECOMMENDATION FOR THRESHOLD OF THORACOABDOMINAL ANEURYSM SIZE FOR INTERVENTION

Thoracoabdominal aneurysms (AHA/ACC Class I indication)

- Open repair >6.0 cm if endovascular repair not feasible and elevated surgical morbidity
- Open repair >6.0 cm if connective tissue disorder present
- Additional revascularization procedure (e.g. endarterectomy/bypass) required if end organ ischaemia/significant stenosis present.

Adapted from 'The 2010 ACCF/AHA/AATS/ACR/ASA/SCA/SCAI/SIR/STS/SVM guidelines for the diagnosis and management of patients with thoracic aortic disease', *Circulation*, 121, e266–e369, copyright 2010 with permission of Wolters Kluwer Health.

Composite mechanical valve conduits (essentially tube with valve attached) preferred, especially if the aneurysm involves the aortic root or the sinus of valsalva.

Valve-sparing operation (Tirone David operation): localized aneurysms can be successfully resected, graft replacements and coronary buttons can be reimplanted, whilst keeping native valve (see Figure 16.4). Advantage of avoiding anticoagulation. Disadvantage of having a higher rate of residual regurgitation and they are not always technically possible.

Re-operation: more common in valve-preserving operations (16% vs 5%) and needed in 10–20% of all patients by 10–20 years. Indications same as above.

Risk factors for re-operation:

- Annulus diameter >2.5 cm
- Marfan syndrome
- Mitral valve prolapse
- AF
- Valve-preserving operation
- Concomitant procedures performed.

Predictors of late death:

- Female sex
- Older age
- Untreated with ß blocker
- Significant mitral regurgitation at presentation
- Mitral ring calcification
- Post-operative dysrhythmias
- Post-operative inotropes.

20 year survival rate 50%.

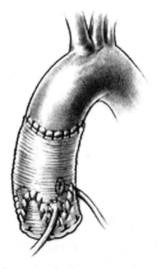

Figure 16.4 Reimplantation of the aortic valve in patients with annuloaortic ectasia and aortic root aneurysm, commonly called the Tirone David operation.

Endovascular repair

Graft-stent technology is developing fast and this is a rapidly changing field. Patients unfit for surgical repair may be candidates for endovascular repair.

There is an increasing amount of data to show that the risk of endovascular approaches is lower and the morbidity is less but the reintervention rate is higher than with open repairs.

The long-term durability of the stent-graft is currently unknown, though data up to now are promising.

In general the following should be considered when assessing a patient for endovascular repair both for aneurysms and dissection:

- What is the patient's surgical risk?
- Is the anatomy suitable for endovascular repair?
  - Do they have adequate vascular access (sheaths can be up to 20–25F)?
  - Is there an adequate 'landing zone' for the stent?
- Is there a risk of side branch occlusion and organ hypoperfusion as a result of the stent?
  - Will this require a debranching procedure (the sequential ligation of the supra-aortic vessels to allow a stent placement without risk of side branch compromise) before deployment of the stent?
  - Will this require placement of a fenestrated graft in order to preserve organ function?

Technique

- Mostly under general anaesthesia
- Peripheral access requires a surgical cut down for 22–24F sheaths
- Common femoral artery used most, though iliac and even retroperitoneal exposure to the abdominal aorta has been used in frail elderly women
- Graft-stent advanced using a stiff wire and positioning is confirmed with TOE. BP can be lowered either by rapid pacing of the right ventricle or pharmacologically if the BP is very high, allowing the stent to be deployed
- Endoleaks are secured with further balloon inflations.

Complications of endograft procedures

- Related to access:
  - Use of iliac or aorta is required in 15%
  - Bleeding: mean blood loss 371 ml and blood transfusion required in 3%
  - Thromboembolic complications
- Related to device:
  - Major adverse event in 10–12%
    - Stroke in 2.5–3.6%
    - Paraplegia 1.3–3%
    - MI 2–4%
    - Acute renal failure requiring dialysis 1.3%
    - Infection: very rare when performed electively
    - Endoleaks: classified I–V according to cause of perigraft blood flow
    - Aortic perforations/dissection: more common in uncovered or bare proximal attachment

- Beaking of the endograft, or partial collapse/infolding of the endograft can occur due to graft oversizing and can result in collapse of the endograft and vessel occlusion
- Conversion of a Type B dissection into a retrograde Type A dissection hence a surgical emergency
- Post-operative:
    - Pneumonia <5%
    - Endoleaks
    - Endograft failure, migration
    - Infection
    - Perforation and oesophageal fistula
    - Need for repeat interventions in 6–7%
    - Conversion to open operation in 1–2%.

Cost of endograft procedures has yet to be shown to be less than open procedures. Given all these factors patients should be carefully assessed and counselled with regard to pros and cons of both surgical and endovascular procedures and care individualized to them.

Aortic arch

Surgical repair has historically been the norm. Due to complex anatomy, with the head and neck vessels involved, mortality and significant morbidity are high (mortality 2–9%, paraplegia and stroke 4–13%).

Conventional surgical techniques either employ deep hypothermic circulatory arrest (15–18C) or a range of antegrade cerebral perfusion techniques.

16.5 Thoracoabdominal aneurysms

- Advances including permissive hypothermia have reduced the frequency of ischaemic complications, e.g. paraplegia and renal failure over the last 15 years
- 5-year survival is 75%
- Hybrid arch procedures, debranching bypass (supra-aortic vessel transposition) to establish cerebral perfusion and subsequent endovascular repair, are increasingly used
- Should be used in older patients with severe co-morbidities and redo surgery ineligible for open intervention
- Key to success is the quality of the unaffected ascending aorta as the site of the debranching bypass and landing site for the endograft
- Mortality rate, usually dependent upon premorbid condition of patient, 5% in-hospital mortality, follow up mortality 8.5%, persistent endoleak 15.2%, 1-year survival 92.5%.

See Figure 16.5.

16.6 Acute aortic syndromes

See Figure 16.6.

- Acute aortic dissection
- Intramural haematoma
- Penetrating aortic (atherosclerotic) ulceration.

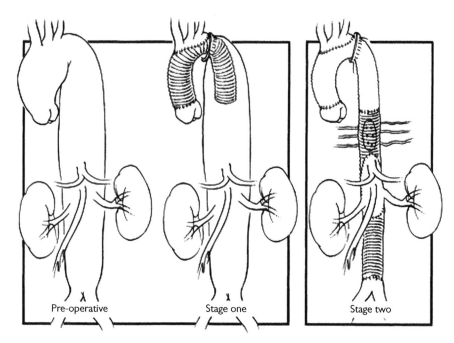

Figure 16.5 Artist's impression of the staged elephant's trunk technique.

Reproduced from *Circulation*, Hazim J. Safi, Charles C. Miller, Anthony L. Estrera, 104:2938, 'Staged repair of extensive aortic aneurysms: morbidity and mortality in the Elephant Trunk Technique', copyright 2001 Wolters Kluwer Health.

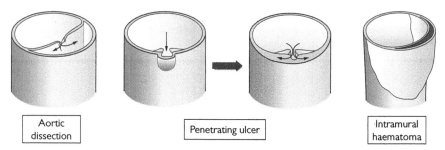

Figure 16.6 Representation of the acute aortic syndromes.

Reproduced with permission from the *ESC Textbook of Cardiovascular Medicine* 2nd edition, ed. John Camm, Thomas Lüscher and Patrick Serruys, copyright 2009 Oxford University Press.

16.7 Dissection of the thoracic aorta

Disruption and separation of the media layer of the aortic wall with bleeding along and within the wall resulting in separation of the layers.

- Acute dissection: within 2 weeks of onset of symptoms
- Subacute/chronic dissection: >2 weeks.

One in three patients have chronic dissection.

Classifications

Classified according to pathology or anatomy. The latter is more frequently used.

Pathological class I–V:

- Class I: classic aortic dissection subdivided into the DeBakey and Stanford classifications
- Class II: intramural haemorrhage/haematoma
- Class III: ulcerating aortic plaque
- Class IV: subtle/discrete aortic bulge; difficult to diagnose; typically seen in Marfan syndrome
- Class V: iatrogenic/traumatic, e.g. post cardiac catheter manipulation.

Anatomical:

- Proximal—involving aortic root or ascending aorta
- Distal—beyond left subclavian artery.

Stanford classification (see Figure 16.7):

- Type A: involves ascending aorta
- Type B: does not involve ascending aorta.

Surgery recommended for Type A dissections. Type B dissection that involves the aortic arch remains a Type B dissection. No consensus as to how to treat these cases (AHA/ACC guidelines 2010).

DeBakey classification (based on origin of the intimal tear):

- Type I: starts in the ascending aorta and extends distally, typically involving entire aorta
- Type II: starts in the ascending aorta and remains confined to the ascending aorta
- Type III: starts in the descending aorta and extends distally
    - Type IIIa: limited to descending aorta
    - Type IIIb: extends below diaphragm.

Surgery recommended in DeBakey Type I and Type II.

Pathology

Aortic dissection results from separation of aortic wall layers in the context of elevated blood pressure and degenerative changes in the aortic media.

The proximal aorta is a highest risk of dissection as it is subject to the steepest fluctuations in pressure.

Epidemiology

Rare:

- Incidence: 2.6–3.5 cases per 100,000 persons/year
- High prevalence in Italy; 4.04 cases/100,000/year
- 0.5% of admissions to A&E with chest/back pain are due to aortic dissection
- Male:female ratio 2:1
- Mean age 65 years
- Hypertension most common risk factor—seen in up to 72%.

Causes in the <40-year-old category due to connective tissue diseases.
Risk factors—as for aneurysm formation plus previous aortic/valvular surgery.

Clinical features

Characterized by rapid development of an intimal flap separating the true and false lumen, which in 90% is the site of communication between true and false lumen.

Anterograde or retrograde spread can occur—propagation of the dissection can causes signifi-cant morbidity.

Can involve side branches and result in malperfusion syndrome from obstruction of aortic flow, cardiac tamponade, and aortic regurgitation.

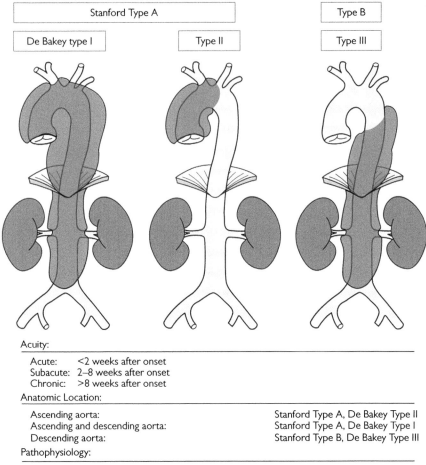

Acuity:

Acute:	<2 weeks after onset
Subacute:	2–8 weeks after onset
Chronic:	>8 weeks after onset

Anatomic Location:

Ascending aorta:	Stanford Type A, De Bakey Type II
Ascending and descending aorta:	Stanford Type A, De Bakey Type I
Descending aorta:	Stanford Type B, De Bakey Type III

Pathophysiology:

Class 1: Classical aortic dissection with initimal flap between true and false lumen

Class 2: Aortic intramural haematoma without identifiable intimal flap

Class 3: Intimal tear without haematoma (limited dissection)

Class 4: Atherosclerotic plaque rupture with aortic penetrating ulcer

Class 5: Iatrogenic or traumatic aortic dissection (intra-aortic catheterization, high-speed deceleration injury, blunt chest trauma)

Figure 16.7 Classification of aortic dissection.

Reproduced with permission from the *ESC Textbook of Cardiovascular Medicine* 2nd edition, ed. John Camm, Thomas Lüscher and Patrick Serruys, copyright 2009 Oxford University Press.

Typical features

- Onset: acute (most specific feature)
- Location: chest (73%; anterior 61%, posterior 36%), back pain (53%), abdomen (30%)
- Sharp, ripping, tearing, or knife-like in nature
- Syncope (20%) from tamponade, severe hypotension, and carotid obstruction.

Signs

Patients usually present in acute cardiac decompensation and shock. Other signs include:

- Hypertension
- Hypotension in 25% due to:
    - Haemopericardium and pericardial tamponade
    - Mediastinal bleeding
    - Acute aortic insufficiency in 50% of ascending dissections
    - Aortic rupture
    - Lactic acidosis
    - Spinal shock
- Malperfusion syndrome related to side branch obstruction with signs and symptoms secondary to organ involvement in one in three, e.g.
    - Cardiovascular
        - Ischaemia
    - Cerebrovascular manifestations
        - Paraplegia
        - Stroke
    - Limb ischaemia
    - Renal failure
    - Visceral ischaemia
    - Pulse differentials in 38% and most specific sign of dissection
- Aortic regurgitation (second most common cause of death).

Natural history

28–55% die without a correct diagnosis.

Predictors of in hospital mortality:
- Tamponade
- Coronary artery involvement
- Malperfusion of the brain or intestine
- Age >70 years
- Hypotension
- Renal failure
- Pulse deficits.

Risk of fatal rupture in untreated proximal aortic dissection is 90%.

Mortality with surgery is as follows: 10% day 1, 12% day 2, 20% week 2.

Acute dissection of descending aorta is less lethal.

Mortality with no treatment in type B dissection is 11% 1 month, 16% 1 year, 20% 5 years.

Diagnostic procedures

See Chapters 28 and 29.

Management

Lack of randomized controlled trials with long-term follow-up and comparison of medical to surgical techniques.

Rapid decompression of the false lumen followed by complete thrombosis of the false lumen is beneficial.

See Table 16.4.

Table 16.4 Management of dissection

Surgical management	Medical management	Interventional management
Type A aortic dissection	Uncomplicated, acute type B dissection	Unstable, acute type B dissection**
Type B dissection complicated by 1. retrograde extension 2. dissection in fibrillinopathies*	Stable, isolated aortic arch dissection	Stable type B dissection (under evaluation)
	Chronic type B dissection	Type B dissection with retrograde extension to ascending aorta
		Hybrid procedure for extended type A dissection

*e.g. Marfan syndrome, Ehler's-Danlos syndrome; **malperfusion, rapid expansion (>1 cm/year), critical diameter (≥5.5 cm), refractory pain.

Medical management

Admit to intensive care unit.

Target systolic BP of 110 mmHg:

- i.v. ß blocker (metoprolol, esmolol, or labetalol)
- Sodium nitroprusside 0.3 mcg/kg/min
- Angiotensin converting enzyme inhibitors
- i.v. verapamil, diltiazem if ß blocker contraindicated.

Occasionally dual therapy with ß blocker and sodium nitroprusside needed.

Normotensive patients need evaluating for potential blood loss/pericardial effusion/heart failure prior to volume administration.

Intubation and ventilation is required if there is profound haemodynamic instability.

Urgent imaging to characterize nature of the dissection with TOE/TTE/CT.

Pericardiocentesis as a temporizing measure often fails and can accelerate bleeding and shock so it is generally contraindicated.

Surgical management

The key to success is rapid surgery prior to any haemodynamic instability or deterioration.

Type A dissection (ESC class I indication):

- Emergency to avoid tamponade/rupture
- Valve-preserving surgery—tubular graft if normal sized aortic root and no pathological changes of valve cusps
- Replacement of aorta and aortic valve (composite graft) if ectatic proximal aorta and/or pathological changes of valve/aortic wall

Type A dissection (ESC class II indication):

- Valve-sparing operations with aortic root remodelling for abnormal valves
- Valve preservation and aortic root remodelling in Marfan patients

Type B dissection (ESC class I indication):

- Only in persistent pain and other complications.

Involvement of aortic arch

Management is more complicated, as either resecting of or leaving unrecognized intimal tears predisposes to later distal re-operation, which carries a substantial operative mortality (15–35%).

Arch tears occur in approximately 30% of patients with acute dissection.

Management of aortic arch involvement

- Consensus suggests that a dissected arch should be explored during hypothermic circulatory arrest
- When extensive tears are found, subtotal or total arch replacement may be required, with reattachment of the supra-aortic vessels with anterograde cerebral perfusion
- In the absence of a tear, an open distal anastomosis of the graft and the conjoined aortic layers at the junction of the ascending and arch portions is justified
- If dissecting and non-dissecting aneurysms extend to the descending aorta, an elephant trunk extension of the aortic graft can be used. This free-floating section of the graft can be connected to the distal descending aorta either surgically or using endovascular stent-graft techniques.

Endovascular therapy in aortic dissection

Endovascular therapy is currently the treatment of choice in complicated type B dissection. Use in type A dissection still experimental.

Principles and considerations:
- To cover the entry site of the false lumen
- Consider whether organs are perfused by the false lumen
  - Will occlusion of the false lumen result in hypoperfusion of an organ/limb?
  - Will stenting the 'at risk' vessel or creating a fenestration (window) improve perfusion to the organ?

Endovascular repair in dissection (ESC Class IIa indication):
- Stenting of obstructed branch origin for static obstruction of branch artery
- Balloon fenestration of dissecting membrane plus stenting of aortic true lumen
- For dynamic obstruction
- Stenting to keep fenestration open
- Fenestration to provide re-entry tear for dead-end false lumen
- Stenting of true lumen
  - to enlarge compressed true lumen
  - to seal entry (covered stent) (Class IIb indication).

Other possible indications (currently not clearly defined by ESC):
- Aortic aneurysms (with suitable morphology for repair)
- Rupture
- Type B dissections (acute and chronic)
- Giant penetrating ulcer
- Traumatic aortic tear
- Aorto-pulmonary fistulae.

Patient comorbities increase open surgical repair risk.

Combined surgical/endovascular repair:
- Often required when arch is involved and stent is used to seal distal end.

Follow up

- Data from the International Registry of Acute Aortic Dissection (IRAD) shows that the 3-year survival of patients discharged alive after repair of acute Type A dissection is approximately 90%
- For type B dissection 3 year mortality is 77.6 +/− 6.6% (treated medically), 82.8 +/− 18.9% (treated surgically), 76.2 +/− 25.2% (with endovascular therapy)
- Higher-risk patients are the elderly and those with hypertension, large aortic size, presence of patent false lumen, previous aortic aneurysm, female gender, and Marfan syndrome
- Aggressive treatment of hypertension with ß blockade is the cornerstone of medical therapy. Up to 40% develop resistant hypertension requiring up to six antihypertensive agents
- Target of <135/80 mmHg (<130/80 in patients with Marfan syndrome) and heart rate of <60/min
- Serial imaging is mandatory and has previously been recommended at 1, 3, 6, 9, and 12 months and then yearly thereafter. Choice of modality is dependent on local availability and expertise
- Repair is recommended if ascending aorta >5.5–6.0 cm (4.5–5.5 cm if Marfan syndrome present) and >6.0 cm in distal aorta
- Rate of change and risk factors should be taken into consideration when considering repair.

16.8 Intramural haematoma

- Precursor of classic dissection, with 30-day mortality of 20% and early death in 16%
- May be due to ruptured vasa vasorum in medial layers leading to secondary communication with the lumen
- See Figure 16.6 for a representation of acute aortic syndromes
- Can be initiated by aortic wall infarction
- Outcome:
  - Progress to dissection in 21–47%
  - Regress in 10%
  - Resorption.

Therapeutic options

- Type A → surgery
- Type B (uncomplicated) → medical management
- ß blocker use associated with improved outcome
- Age >55 years at diagnosis associated with improved outcomes, possibly due to more focal scars in the aortic wall limiting spread of haematoma
- Watchful waiting/graft stent placement appropriate if distal aorta affected (i.e. type B intramural haematoma) and if patient >65 years.

16.9 Atherosclerotic plaque rupture and ulceration

- Mostly in the descending thoracic and abdominal aorta in association with intramural haematoma
- Progressive erosion of mural plaque penetrates the elastic lamina—separation of medial layers
- Can lead to intramural haematoma, penetration, and dissection
- Symptomatic penetrating atherosclerotic ulcers imply impending complications and should prompt detailed imaging
- Treatment (surgery/graft/stent) if width >2 cm and depth >1 cm.

16.10 Genetic considerations

See Table 16.5.

Guidelines

See Boxes 16.4, 16.5, and 16.6.

Table 16.5 Genetic syndromes associated with thoracic aortic aneurysm and dissection

Genetic syndrome	Common clinical features	Genetic defect	Diagnostic test
Marfan syndrome	Facial, skeletal, eye, cardiac, skin, spinal features	FBN1 mutations	Ghent oncology DNA sequencing
Loeys-Dietz syndrome	• Bifid uvula/cleft palate • Arterial tortuosity • Hypertelorism • Skeletal features • Craniosynostosis • Aneurysms and dissections of other arteries	TGFBR1 TGFBR2	DNA for sequencing
Ehler's Danlos Type (IV vascular form)	• Thin, translucent skin • Gastrointestinal rupture • Rupture of the gravid uterus • Rupture of medium to large sized vessels • Short stature • Primary amenorrhoea • BAV • Aortic coarctation	COL3A1	DNA for sequencing
Turner syndrome	• Webbed neck • Low set ears • Low hairline • Broad chest • Wide carrying angle • Short stature	45,X karyotype	Karyotype analysis

Adapted from 'The 2010 ACCF/AHA/AATS/ACR/ASA/SCA/SCAI/SIR/STS/SVM guidelines for the diagnosis and management of patients with thoracic aortic disease', *Circulation*, 121, e266–e369, copyright 2010 with permission of Wolters Kluwer Health.

BOX 16.4 THE 2010 AHA/ACC GUIDELINES ON AORTIC DISEASE RECOMMENDATIONS FOR MARFAN SYNDROME

- Echocardiogram at the time of diagnosis and 6 monthly thereafter
- Annual imaging if aortic size is stable
- More frequent imaging is required if maximal diameter >45 mm or rate of change is increasing
- Surgery is reasonable in females considering pregnancy with aortic root/ascending aorta >40 mm
- Surgery is reasonable if maximal cross sectional area in cm^2 of aortic root or ascending aorta divided by patient's height in metres >10.

Adapted from 'The 2010 ACCF/AHA/AATS/ACR/ASA/SCA/SCAI/SIR/STS/SVM guidelines for the diagnosis and management of patients with thoracic aortic disease', *Circulation*, 121, e266–e369, copyright 2010 with permission of Wolters Kluwer Health.

BOX 16.5 THE 2010 AHA/ACC GUIDELINES ON AORTIC DISEASE RECOMMENDATIONS FOR LOEYS-DIETZ SYNDROME OR A CONFIRMED GENETIC MUTATION KNOWN TO PREDISPOSE TO AORTIC ANEURYSM AND DISSECTION

- Complete aortic imaging at the time of diagnosis and 6 monthly thereafter
- Yearly MRI from cerebrovascular circulation to pelvis
- Surgical repair if aortic diameter >4.2 (internal diameter echo) or >4.4–4.6 (internal CT/MRI).

Adapted from 'The 2010 ACCF/AHA/AATS/ACR/ASA/SCA/SCAI/SIR/STS/SVM guidelines for the diagnosis and management of patients with thoracic aortic disease', *Circulation*, 121, e266–e369, copyright 2010 with permission of Wolters Kluwer Health.

BOX 16.6 THE 2010 AHA/ACC GUIDELINES ON AORTIC DISEASE RECOMMENDATIONS FOR TURNER'S SYNDROME

- Imaging of the heart and aorta for assessment of BAV, coarctation, or dilatation of the ascending aorta
- If above imaging normal repeat imaging every 5–10 years, otherwise at least annually.

Adapted from 'The 2010 ACCF/AHA/AATS/ACR/ASA/SCA/SCAI/SIR/STS/SVM guidelines for the diagnosis and management of patients with thoracic aortic disease', *Circulation*, 121, e266–e369, copyright 2010 with permission of Wolters Kluwer Health.

16.11 Bicuspid aortic valve

- Common, affecting 1–2% of the population
- 9% of these have an affected first-degree relative and can been inherited in an autosomal dominant fashion (see Box 16.7)
- In these families, some have thoracic aortic disease without BAV
- 20% who underwent BAV at the Cleveland Clinic also had ascending aortic aneurysm repair
- 15% of patients with dissection have BAV.

BOX 16.7 THE 2010 AHA/ACC GUIDELINES ON AORTIC DISEASE RECOMMENDATIONS FOR BICUSPID AORTIC VALVE

- Screening of first-degree relatives of patients with premature onset thoracic aortic disease and BAV with minimal risk factors
- All patients with BAV should have the aortic root and ascending aorta evaluated for evidence of dilatation.

Other conditions associated with aortopathy:

- Aberrant right subclavian artery
  - Courses behind oesophagus and causes dysphagia as the artery enlarges (Kommerell diverticulum)
  - Aorta prone to aneurysm formation and dissection
- Coarctation of the aorta, associated with aortic dissection
- Right-sided aortic arch can cause either oesophageal or tracheal obstruction, and Kommerell diverticulum may form.

Adapted from 'The 2010 ACCF/AHA/AATS/ACR/ASA/SCA/SCAI/SIR/STS/SVM guidelines for the diagnosis and management of patients with thoracic aortic disease', *Circulation*, 121, e266–e369, copyright 2010 with permission of Wolters Kluwer Health.

16.12 Aortitis

Definition

Inflammation of the aorta categorized by underlying aetiology:

- Infective syphilitic
- Infective non-syphilitic (bacterial/fungal)
- Non-infective- due to large vessel vasculitis or atherosclerosis.

Determining the aetiology is critical as immunosuppressive therapy can worsen active infective processes.

Epidemiology

- Incidence of giant cell arteritis 18.8/100,000/year with male: female ratio of 2:1 and mean age 75 years
- Incidence of Takayasu arteritis much rarer: 0.4–1.0/1,000,000/year
- Non-infective large vessel vasculitis is the most common cause of aortitis.

Pathogenesis

- Infective aortitis
- Microorganisms gain entry via a number of mechanisms:
  - Haematogenous spread
  - Direct invasion of the aortic wall
  - Spread from nearby structures
  - Secondary infection following trauma
  - Septic emboli
- Bacterial and fungal infections can result in non-infectious vasculitis by generating immune complexes or cross reactivity. This tends to occur in atherosclerotic lesions or aneurysms
- Tertiary syphilis is now rare but may be seen in immunocompromised patients can present with aortitis
- S. aureus is the most common Gram-positive species. Gram-negative bacilli are less common but include Salmonella, Proteus and E. coli
- Autoimmune disorders can affect the blood supply to the vasa vasorum
- The causes of aortitis in Takayasu's and giant cell arteritis are unknown.

Clinical features

Difficult to assess due to non-specific features such as fatigue, malaise, arthralgia, and low-grade fever and raised inflammatory markers. Thoracic pain may be present in 60%.

- Look ill with mild fever
- Carotidynia suggests vascular inflammation
- Reduced/absent pulses, ocular disturbance, neurological deficits, claudication resulting in gangrene or myocardial infarction as a result of ostial involvement of a coronary artery
- Bruits over major arteries
- New aortic regurgitation (AR) due to aortitis related aneurysms of the ascending aorta.

Therefore, picture may mimic IE.

Diagnosis

- Suspect it based on clinical presentation and imaging
- Blood cultures important if infective causes, as these guide antibiotic choice
- Inflammatory markers usually raised
- CXR can demonstrate opacities of different sizes
- Angiography used to be the gold standard
- CT/MRI/TOE can all be used and have various advantages/disadvantages as already discussed.

Therapeutic management

- Prognosis related to aetiology and thus to potential complications
- Worst scenario is aneurysm formation with resultant rupture
- Treat according to cause with antibiotics or immunosuppressive therapy
- Optimal management of infective non-syphilitic aortitis is early surgical intervention with a prolonged course of antibiotics
- Mortality for infected aneurysms treated with antibiotics alone is approximately 90%
- Endovascular repair has yet to be used widely for non-infective vasculitic causes.

16.13 Aortic atheromatous disease: thrombotic or cholesterol emboli

- Tend to affect the aortic arch and descending aorta
- Aortic intimal can be classified as follows:
  - Grade I: normal
  - Grade II: increased intimal echo density without lumen irregularity
  - Grade III: increased intimal echo density with single or multiple well-defined atheromatous plaques of 3 mm
  - Grade IV: atheroma >3 mm or mobile or ulcerated plaque
- Reduced aortic compliance is thought to be an early expression of atheromatous disease
- Spontaneous emboli generally results from Grade IV intima
- Iatrogenic emboli (wires, catheters, or during surgery) can loosen mobile plaque—cholesterol crystal showers in 1–2% of cardiac catheterization cases with cutaneous signs or renal insufficiency
- Risk factors are same as for CHD
- Aortic plaque of 4 mm (measured as aortic wall thickness) is thought to be a major risk factor for stroke, with an annual occurrence of 12%.

Diagnosis

TOE is usually the first modality. CT and MRI can be used thereafter.

Management

- Risk factor modification and antiplatelet medication
- Anticoagulation is controversial
- Statins are superior to anticoagulation and antiplatelets in those with atheromatous disease in the aorta and at high risk of emboli.

16.14 Traumatic rupture of the aorta

Aetiology
21% mortality due to aortic rupture in 613 fatalities of road traffic accidents. 8000 victims per year in the USA.

Pathogenesis
- Any deceleration injury, e.g. fall from height, road collision, etc. can result in traumatic aortic rupture
- Airbags and seatbelts do not protect against lateral impact and this mechanism typically results in partial laceration of the lesser curve of the distal part of the aortic arch just above the isthmus (most common site of rupture: 80–95%).

Clinical presentation
- Signs may be non-specific and there are often other significant injuries that may require attention
- Symptoms: dyspnoea and chest pain, syncope, dysphagia, hoarseness
- Signs: hypotension, hypertension (17%), paraplegia, pulse differences, 'pseudo-coarctation' resulting from a flap, which acts as a ball valve resulting in partial obstruction and upper limb hypertension. Hypertension can also be due to stretching/stimulation of the cardiac plexus
- Normal physical findings are seen in 5–14% of cases.

Diagnosis
Clinical suspicion then confirm with CT.

Therapeutic management
- Early surgery carries high mortality (15–20%) and morbidity (most significant of which is paraplegia)
- There are two groups of populations with traumatic aortic rupture:
  - Unstable with signs of active bleeding
  - Stable
- Survival in the first group is low (17.7%) and is much higher in the second group (fatal rupture 4.5% in first 72 h) and therefore major intervention can be put on hold
- After diagnosis, therapeutic hypotension with vasodilators and ß blocker is mandatory
- In selected patients with pseudo-aneurysm or haematoma the risk of rupture is low (same as a 'normal pseudo-aneurysm) as a fibrous tissue will develop
- Blood pressure should be maintained at 90 mmHg (fluid replacement should be limited to prevent extension and rupture)
- Patients are often intubated
- Surgical repair of the aorta electively improves outcomes
- Operative measures include either a primary suture repair or Dacron graft repair
- Endovascular repair avoids thoracotomy and heparin and risk of destabilizing other traumatic lesions in the lungs, brain, and abdomen. Rapidly becoming the treatment of choice in traumatic aortic rupture.

16.15 Trauma to the heart

Most common cause of death for men <40 years:

- Penetrating trauma, e.g. stab wound to right ventricle resulting in haemopericardium (tamponade) or hypovolaemia and shock
- Blunt trauma (e.g. high speed deceleration injury): compression between sternum and vertebrae resulting in possible rupture of free wall, malignant arrhythmias, damage to epicardial coronary vessels.

1–20% of asymptomatic patients may develop complications of blunt cardiac trauma that require treatment.

Screening asymptomatic patients:

- Cardiac enzymes
- ECG: a normal ECG has a very good negative predictive value for complications; if abnormal further investigations are not necessary
- Echocardiography.

Symptomatic patients for diagnosis of tamponade:

- Subxiphoid access with TTE is standard
- Sternotomy/thoracotomy should be used if patients present with penetrating thoracic injury and diagnostic tools unable to show definitive evidence of cardiac penetration, e.g. in presence of haemopneumothorax.

Management

Penetrating trauma: surgical

Aimed at saving life.

- Life-threatening condition: may need thoracotomy in the emergency department
- Left anterolateral lateral thoracotomy incision of choice
- If mechanism due to stabbing and knife insitu it must only be removed in theatre
- Digital occlusion of haemorrhage if possible
- Simple closure if possible
- Transfer to operating room if injuries more complex, i.e. require CABG etc.

Classification: Scale I–VI according to American Association of Surgery of Trauma and its Organ Injury Scaling Committee. Uncertainties remain of its use in an emergency setting.

Prognosis dependent upon premorbid condition and nature of injury:

- Missile injury more severe than stab wounds 16 versus 65% 2-year survival
- In penetrating trauma, patients who are alive in the emergency department have 80% survival rate
- If young and without underlying cardiovascular disease fare better than patients with equivalent degree of necrosis due to coronary artery disease
- Myocardial contusion—benign
- Poor prognosis if thoracotomy required for blunt trauma.

Blunt trauma: medical

- Early mobilization and rehabilitation after monitoring if young and normal/slightly abnormal ECGs
- Anticoagulants/fibrinolytics are contraindicated due to increased risk of bleeding

- Arrhythmias, e.g. AF, treated with digoxin
- Analgesia: avoid NSAIDs
- Corticosteroids—only in Dressler's
- ACE inhibitors/ß blocker—no evidence to support use.

Further reading

Erbel R, Alfonso F, Boileau C, et al. Diagnosis and management of aortic dissection. Recommendations of the Task Force on Aortic Dissection. European Society of Cardiology. *Eur Heart J*, 2001; 22: 1642–81.

Hiratzka LF, Bakris GL, Beckman JA, et al. 2010 ACCF/AHA/AATS/ACR/ASA/SCA/SCAI/SIR/STS/SVM guidelines for the diagnosis and management of patients with thoracic aortic disease. A report of the American College of Cardiology Foundation/American Heart Association *Circulation*, 2010; 121: e266–369.

Nienaber CA, Haverich A, Erbel R. Diseases of the aorta and trauma to the aorta and the heart. In: Serruys PW, Camm AJ, Lüscher TF (eds). *The European Society of Cardiology Textbook of Cardiovascular Medicine*, 2nd edn. Oxford University Press, 2009.

Cardiac tumours

CONTENTS

17.1 Overview

- Primary cardiac tumours are uncommon; prevalence 0.05% at autopsy
- Most common: myxoma in adults and the rhabdomyoma in children
- Secondary tumours are more common; around 1% of autopsies
- 10% of primary cardiac tumours are malignant (majority sarcomas).

Present with some similar clinical features as follows:

Obstruction

- Atrial tumours can become very large and exert mass effect—ventricular inflow or pulmonary venous obstruction
- Ventricular tumours may outflow tract obstruction resulting in syncope, dyspnoea, or chest pain.

Embolization

- Tumour mass or associated thrombus—systemic or pulmonary.

Arrhythmia

- Reentrant circuits and other arrhythmia are common, with both intracavity and intramural tumours
- Some infiltrate the conductive tissue resulting in heart block or, occasionally, SCD.

17.2 Imaging of cardiac tumours

Echocardiography

- Mainstay of imaging: real-time images and haemodynamic data
- Management is often surgical; definition of location and boundaries essential to differentiate tumour from other structures (may avoid unnecessary surgery)
- Some masses have classic echo appearances but, ultimately, tissue diagnosis is gold standard.

Computed tomography

- Gated CT with intravenous contrast can help characterize a tumour—size, shape, site—and define the borders to assess infiltration into local structures
- Particular use in patients with poor echocardiographic windows who require urgent assessment
- Scan can be performed in a breath hold of less than 15 s
- Concomitant evaluation of the coronary arteries prior to surgical intervention.

Magnetic resonance imaging

- High spatial and temporal resolution imaging in any anatomical plane and therefore can offer an alternative imaging modality to echocardiography
- In addition to evaluation of tumour size, site and borders can aid characterization of tissue type
- No substitute for histological evaluation but can guide towards a particular diagnosis:
  - Thrombus can be differentiated from other masses due to its poor uptake of gadolinium (early variable TI scanning)
  - Lipomas have an almost identical T2 signal to subcutaneous fat
  - Malignant tumours tend to be extremely vascular and therefore will readily take up contrast when assessed with first-pass perfusion imaging
  - There is significant overlap between tumour types.

17.3 Benign tumours

Majority are myxomas, lipomas, and papillary fibroelastomas.

Myxoma

- Atrial myxoma is by far the most common cardiac tumour, with a slight female predominance
- Can occur from paediatric age to the elderly—peak prevalence in the sixth decade
- 90% are located in the left atrium and 90% are solitary.

Presentation is variable:

- Constitutional symptoms 30% (due to interleukin-6)
- Obstruction 60%: syncope, dyspnoea, and congestive cardiac failure
- Embolism 16%
  - Mid-diastolic plop is rarely heard; often mistaken for a third heart sound or opening snap
  - Clubbing and rash may be present
  - Signs of pulmonary hypertension (right-sided tumours that have embolized or obstructive left sided tumours) possible.

CARNEY COMPLEX

- Syndrome of endocrine adenomas, facial freckling, and (usually) multiple atrial myxoma
- Two acronyms: NAME and LAMB
- Autosomal dominant (deletion at gene *PRKAR1A* 17q24 locus, which codes for a tumour suppressor gene)
- Patients younger and have a higher chance of myxoma recurrence following surgery.

Diagnosis is ultimately made by histological examination following surgery. Imaging modalities have some characteristic features, which help decipher them from thrombus:

- The presence of a peduncle should be sought and its relationship with the intra-atrial septum and coronary sinus os carefully delineated (see Figure 17.1)
- Atrial myxoma diagnosis is almost assured if attachment to the intra-atrial septum is identified, together with evidence of tumour mobility and dispensability
- Typically heterogenous but may be homogeneous or have central areas of hyperlucency representing hemorrhage and necrosis, together with patches of calcification
- May appear villous (35% more prone to embolization) or smooth (65%)
- Usually large—mean size of 5–6 cm at time of detection
- Thrombus is homogenous and usually arises from the left atrial appendage but may exist as a large free-floating ball.

When a suspected atrial myxoma is identified (especially when a left-sided tumour has evidence of right-heart embarrassment) emergency surgery is considered mandatory.

Some advocate a more conservative approach in the elderly, with small tumours not causing haemodynamic compromises.

Lipoma

There are two main variants of lipoma, which are distinct entities:

Capsulated masses

- Usually subepicardial but may arise from any location in the heart
- Can occur from the endothelium of the valves
- Often have a broad peduncle

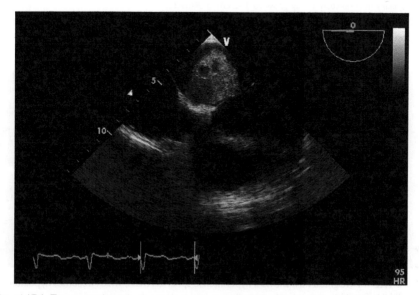

Figure 17.1 Transoesophageal echocardiography image of large heterogenous atrial myxoma. A broad-based peduncle is seen originating from the intra-atrial septum.

- Rarely symptomatic but may present with embolic phenomenon, arrhythmia, obstruction of valves, or compression of epicardial vessels
- Require surgical resection if symptomatic.

Lipoma of the intra-atrial septum

- Non-capsulated
- Common in obese, elderly patients
- Extension of the subepicardial fat through the right AV sulcus
- May present with palpitations; atrial arrhythmia, or AV block
- Lipomatous hypertrophy of the intra-atrial septum can be so extreme as to occlude the inflow of vena cava.

Echo appearance depends on location:

- In pericardium they range from being hypoechoic to hyperechoic
- Cavities always tend to be homogenous and hyperechoic.

Despite often being pedunculated not usually as mobile as myxomas.

Both true lipoma and lipoma of the intra-atrial septum are easily detected on CMR due to non-enhancing high fat signal (see Figure 17.2).

Papillary fibroelastoma

- Second most common primary cardiac tumour (excluding lipomatous hypertrophy of intra-atrial septum)
- Majority are incidental findings at autopsy
- When symptomatic, usually present with embolic phenomenon (typically too small to cause obstruction)—fourth to eighth decade
- Slightly more common in males
- Papillary fibroelastoma may grow to 1–2 cm in diameter
- Majority arise from the aortic or mitral valves but may originate from any endomyocardial tissue
- Sometimes mistaken for a giant Lambl excrescence

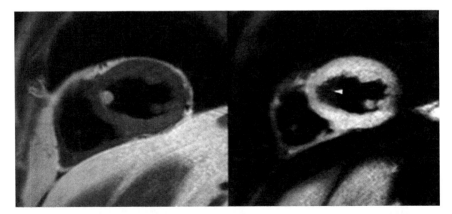

Figure 17.2 T1 weighted MRI shows a hyperintense spherical mass, which becomes hypointense with fat-suppression sequencing (arrowed).

Adapted from 'Cardiac lipoma diagnosed by cardiac magnetic resonance imaging', Javier Ganame, Jeremy Wright, Jan Bogaert et al., Eur. Heart J., 29, 697, copyright 2008, with permission of Oxford University Press.

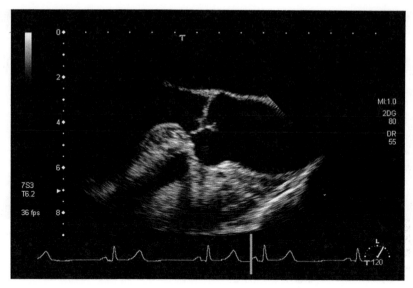

Figure 17.3 Papillary fibroelastoma seen on the tips of the aortic valve at transoesophageal echo.

Adapted from 'The role of intraoperative transoesophageal echocardiography in the diagnosis and management of a rare multiple fibroelastoma or aortic valve', Giovanni Truscelli, Concetta Torromeo, Fabio Miraldi *et al.*, *Eur. J. Cardiovascular Imaging* 10 (7): 884–886, copyright (2009) with permission of Oxford University Press.

- Histologically composed of a non-vascular fibroelastic axis surrounded by mixoid tissue and an endothelial cover
- Described as having a shimmering edge on echocardiography, which may help distinguish from thrombus (see Figure 17.3)
- Left-sided tumours should always be treated surgically in view of embolic risk whereas right-sided tumours may be treated conservatively.

Haemangioma

See Figure 17.4.

- A very rare tumour; can occur in adults and paediatric populations
- Principally comprised of neoplastic vessel proliferation
- There are three well described types:
  - arteriovenous haemangioma (infiltrative)
  - capillary haemangioma (capsulated)
  - cavernous haemangioma (infiltrative)
- Exist as subendocardial nodules, which can grow up to 4 cm in diameter
- 75% are intramural, which may result in arrhythmia and pericardial effusions
- 25% extend into cavities and may mimic myxoma, with obstructive symptoms
- The most common site is the left ventricle
- Despite often containing fat, haemangioma are readily distinguishable from lipoma on CMR as they appear heterogenous, with marked enhancement
- Natural history is variable; some tumours regress over time and others continue to proliferate
- Management is dependent on the site, size, history, and complications
- Mainstay of treatment is surgical
- Follow up is considered mandatory, with echo to detect tumour recurrence.

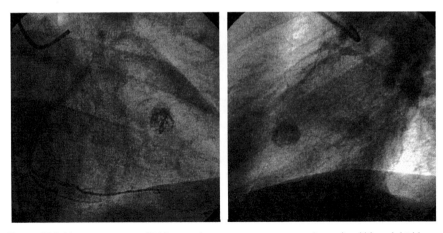

Figure 17.4 Haemangioma are highly vascular structures seen on angiography. Although highly suggestive of the haemangioma, myxoma and angiosarcoma may have similar appearances.

Adapted from 'Cardiac hemangioma presenting as atypical chest pain', Karim Serri, Philippe Schraub, Stephane Lafitte et al., Eur. J. Cardiovascular Imaging, 8, 17–8, copyright 2007 with permission of Oxford University Press.

BOX 17.1 TUBEROUS SCLEROSIS TRIAD

- Neurofibromatous lesions
- Mental slowing
- Cutaneous lesions.

Rhabdomyoma

- Most common cardiac tumour in the paediatric population
- 50–80% of cases associated with tuberous sclerosis (see Box 17.1)
- Consists of a non-proliferative hamartomatous lesion
- Commonly multiple
- Usually located within the ventricular myocardium
- Rarely arises from the subendocardium; pedunculated mass invading the cavity (can result in obstruction)
- Presents in the prenatal or neonatal group with hydrops, arrhythmia, heart block, and retarded growth
- Natural history is of spontaneous regression; possibly due to resorption of glycogen stores
- For this reason, management is usually conservative, surgical resection being reserved for obstructive lesions.

Fibroma

- Benign, low-grade, non-capsulated connective tissue tumours
- Account for around 20% of cardiac tumours in the paediatric population
- Usually present before the age of 15 with obstructive symptoms such as heart failure or re-entrant arrhythmia
- Firm, grayish tumours that can grow up to 10 cm in diameter
- Characteristic finding both to the naked eye and on echocardiography is the multiple foci of calcification

- Unlike many primary cardiac tumours, they have no evidence of cystic change, areas of haemorrhage, or necrosis
- Seen as large, solid, non-contractive masses on echocardiography and as a homogenous mass with soft tissue attenuation on CT
- Usually intramural within the interventricular septum or ventricular free wall
- Commonly interfering with the conductive system: heart block or SCD
- Fibromas with medically refractory arrhythmias or haemodynamically significant obstruction must be treated surgically.

Cystic tumour of the AV node

- Also known as a tawarioma
- Located in the triangle of Koch and can grow up to 2 cm in diameter
- Comprise multiple cysts filled with mucoid substance
- Through infiltration of the AV node, heart block and SCD can occur.

Pericardial cyst

- Congenital pericardial cysts are uncommon
- Both unilocular and multilocular forms and a diameter up to 5 cm
- Most patients are asymptomatic when cysts are detected incidentally on CXR, usually at the right cardiophrenic angle
- When symptomatic, pericardial cysts can cause chest discomfort, dyspnoea, cough, or palpitations due to compression of the heart
- Diagnosis is through echocardiography, CT, or MRI
- Percutaneous aspiration and ethanol sclerosis is often successful
- If this is not feasible, video-assisted thoracotomy or surgical resection may be necessary.

17.4 Malignant tumours

Ten percent of primary cardiac tumours can be considered malignant, of which around 95% are sarcomas and 5% are lymphomas.

Angiosarcoma

- Sarcoma of endothelial cell differentiation
- One third of primary cardiac malignancies
- More common in men
- Peak incidence third to fifth decade
- Found almost exclusively in the right atrium, near the AV groove
- Asymptomatic until advanced
- Commonly present with complications of lung metastasis
- Other symptoms include fever, chest pain, weight loss, and haemorrhagic pericardial effusion
- Like its benign cousin, the angioma, appears as a highly vascular mass on angiography
- Appearance on CT and MRI is of an irregular, heterogenous mass with areas of haemorrhage and necrosis
- Gross appearance is a lobulated brown neoplasm
- Invades local structures: commonly the right atrial wall, pericardium, and IVC
- Two thirds are moderately well differentiated

- One third are poorly differentiated and appear as anaplastic spindle cells on histology
- TP53 and K-ras mutations have been seen; the cells express factor VIII/vWF, CD31 and CD34
- Mean survival is 10 months.

Rhabdomyosarcoma

- Second most common primary cardiac malignancy; still very rare
- Arise from and infiltrate the muscle wall
- Rarely invade further than the parietal pericardium
- Usually of the embryological subtype: comprises mesenchymal cells with striated muscle differentiation
- Solid tumours; rarely impinge into the cavity.

Unlike other sarcomas, rhabdomyosarcoma usually present before the age of 20 with a male predominance.

Fibrosarcoma

- Malignant proliferation of mesenchymal cells showing fibroblastic features
- Accounts for 5% of primary cardiac malignancies
- Usually left sided
- Can be mural or protrude into cavities
- Median survival is 5 months.

Cardiac lymphoma

- 10% of primary cardiac malignant tumours
- Can occur at any age; median age of presentation around 60
- Three times more common in males
- Presents abruptly with heart failure, arrhythmia, heart block, chest pain, SVC obstruction and pericardial effusion
- Most common location is the right atrial wall (two out of three cases); any chamber can be affected
- In 75% of cases more than one cavity wall is affected, including the pericardium
- 80% are B-cell with CD20 positive cells and 20% are T-cell with CD3 positive cells
- Gross appearance is of multiple firm, white nodular masses
- On CT and MRI can have a variable non-diagnostic morphology presenting as a mass or as infiltrative disease
- Biopsy is required to confirm diagnosis, as pericardial fluid cytology is often negative
- Chemotherapy can lead to significant tumour regression
- Significant mortality may be related to massive pulmonary emboli, refractory heart failure, and cardiac arrhythmias
- In most cases, palliative therapy is indicated; prognosis is poor with mean survival of 7 months.

17.5 Metastatic spread to the heart

- Cardiac metastases were found in up to 25% of cases of metastatic disease in autopsy series
- Metastatic spread to the heart can be via four possible routes:
  - haematic spread
  - lymphatic spread

- direct infiltration
- transvenous extension

- Due to their incidence and location lung and breast carcinoma are the most common primaries leading to cardiac metastases
- Around half the cases of metastatic melanoma involve the heart
- Solitary cardiac metastases are rare; usually small and multiple
- Myocardial involvement is usually a result of haematic spread
- Lymphatic spread typically results in pericardial disease and may result in large effusions (or pericarditis)
- A constrictive picture may persist following draining of an effusion due to thickening and reduced compliance of the pericardium
- Majority of cases clinically asymptomatic and are only discovered at autopsy
- Pericardial effusions, heart failure, or rhythm disturbances in known cases of metastatic disease suggest cardiac spread.

Treatment of cardiac metastases is rarely surgical as it typically signifies advanced disease; usually palliative, sometimes involving chemotherapy and radiotherapy.

Cardiac rehabilitation

18.1 What is cardiac rehabilitation?

WHO DEFINITION

Cardiac rehabilitation (CR) is defined by the WHO as:

'The sum of activities required to influence favourably the underlying cause of the disease, as well as the best possible, physical, mental and social conditions, so that they (people) may, by their own efforts preserve or resume when lost, as normal a place as possible in the community. Rehabilitation cannot be regarded as an isolated form or stage of therapy but must be integrated within secondary prevention services of which it forms only one facet.'

Reproduced from 'World Health Organisation Needs and action priorities in cardiac rehabilitation and secondary prevention in patients with CHD', Geneva: World Health Organization, copyright 1993. Reproduced with permission.

- Meta-analysis of over 48 randomized controlled trials of exercise-based CR and comprehensive CR (8940 patients) has shown a reduction in total mortality of 27% and 13%, and a reduction in cardiac mortality of 31% and 26% respectively (Jolliffe et al., 2001, updated in 2009)
- The same analysis found significant improvement in cholesterol levels
- CR is also highly cost-effective with a cost per life year gained of under £2,000, which is four times better than PCI procedures (Fidan et al., 2007)
- In heart failure, a recent meta-analysis has shown a clear benefit in quality of life, fitness, and a substantial reduction in hospital readmissions following structured CR that includes exercise (Davies et al. 2010)
- Cardiac rehabilitation (CR) includes a range of interventions, from education and psychological support to practical exercise programmes, which aim to improve the prognosis, functional capacity, and quality of life for patients with an increasing range of cardiac pathologies.

CR plays a vital role in the secondary prevention of CHD. A high priority should be given to patients with a primary diagnosis of:

- Acute coronary syndrome (ACS), which includes STEMI, NSTEMI and unstable angina *and* those undergoing revascularization
- Chronic heart failure of new diagnosis, or chronic heart failure with a step change in clinical presentation.

Increasingly there is also evidence to support the benefit for other patient groups, including those with stable angina, congenital heart disease, post cardiac transplantation, and patients with implantable cardiac defibrillators or ventricular assist devices. In the UK the National Service Framework for CHD (2000) set the following goals:

- 85% of people discharged from hospital with a primary diagnosis of acute myocardial infarction (AMI) or after coronary revascularization should be offered cardiac rehabilitation
- 1 year after discharge, at least 50% of people should be non-smokers, exercise regularly, and have a BMI <30 kg/m^2.

The 2013 Cardiovascular Disease Outcomes Strategy for England calls for CR programmes to drive average uptake, across all indications, to >60%. One of the areas with the greatest scope for improvement is heart failure, which accounts for only 2% of the primary diagnoses on referral to CR.

CR is an essential part of the NICE 'Guideline for Secondary Prevention in Primary and Secondary Care for Patients Following a Myocardial Infarction', and the NICE 'Guideline for Chronic Heart Failure'. The NICE 'Commissioning Guide for Cardiac Rehabilitation Services' suggests that on average 0.2% of the UK population would be eligible for CR each year.

18.2 The structure of cardiac rehabilitation

- Traditionally, the NSF for CHD structured cardiac rehabilitation around four separate phases:
  - Phase 1: before discharge from hospital
  - Phase 2: early post discharge period
  - Phase 3: structured exercise four weeks post cardiac event
  - Phase 4: long-term maintenance of changed behaviour
- Aim to integrate CR services with primary and secondary care, and encourage the uptake of CR in both the short and long term.

The current model moves towards a more individualized cardiac rehabilitation pathway (see Figure 18.1).

18.3 Access to cardiac rehabilitation

- Despite the strong evidence for the efficacy of CR uptake remains low, with recent estimates showing an average of 43%
- There are some services where uptake is as high as 88% and others where it is as low as 13% (NACR 2013)
- One of the clear barriers to CR uptake is low referral from acute cardiology services
- Patients should have automatic referral that is supported by a cardiologist, stressing the importance of CR
  - Patients should begin cardiac rehabilitation as soon as possible after admission and before discharge from hospital
  - Patients should be invited to a cardiac rehabilitation session which should start within 10 days of their discharge from hospital.

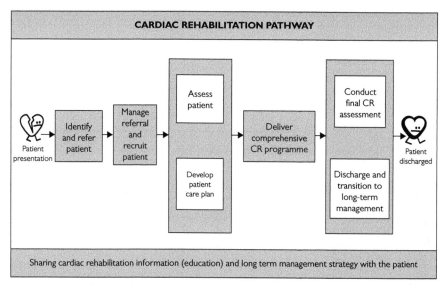

Figure 18.1 Cardiac rehabilitation pathway.

Adapted from the Department of Health Cardiac Rehabilitation Commissioning Pack Cardiac Rehabilitation, Strategic Commissioning Development Unit, Crown copyright 2010.

Accessibility

- Patients should be offered the choice of hospital-based or home-based programmes
- CR sessions should be held in more accessible community venues or transport provided whenever possible
- CR services should be able to adapt to an individual patient's gender, age, ethnicity, and mental and physical comorbidities
- CR programmes should be culturally sensitive with bilingual team members and resources for the visually and hearing impaired
- Efforts should be made to encourage uptake, particularly amongst women, the elderly, people from ethnic minority groups, and patients from lower socioeconomic groups, who currently underuse this resource
- Reminders such as telephone calls and motivational letters may help to improve uptake.

Staffing

- CR should be provided by an appropriately trained multidisciplinary team consisting of cardiologists, GPs, specialist nurses, physiotherapists and exercise specialists, psychologists, dieticians, occupational therapists, pharmacists, and with a designated team leader
- Staff should be trained to respond to emergency situations including basic life support and the use of a cardiac defibrillator where appropriate.

18.4 Core components of cardiac rehabilitation

The British Association for Cardiovascular Prevention and Rehabilitation recommends the following core components for a CR programme:

1. Health behaviour change and education
2. Lifestyle risk factor management

- Physical activity and exercise
- Diet
- Smoking cessation
3. Psychosocial health
4. Medical risk factor management
5. Cardioprotective therapies
6. Long-term management
7. Audit and evaluation.

The core components have been conceptualized into four areas within the new Department of Health Commissioning guidance (see Figure 18.2).

- Patient education and long-term management are key themes of the pathway
- The CR provider should offer choice and inform the patient of the available types of cardiac rehabilitation intervention (e.g. individual or group sessions or a combination) and locations (e.g. hospital, community or home)
- The CR provider should agree with the patient that they are ready and willing to commence cardiac rehabilitation in accordance with the care plan developed.

Recent guidance from the Department of Health (2010) suggests the measurement of baseline trends to inform patient agreed goals, which are then assessed for change post rehabilitation. The recommended measures include:

- Psychological wellbeing (HADs)
- Functional capacity (fitness) SWT, SMWT etc.
- BMI and waist circumference
- Quality of life (Dartmouth or MLWHF)
- Smoking cessation
- Compliance with medication
- Compliance with healthy eating plan.

Ongoing secondary risk factor measures should also be reported, e.g. BP and cholesterol.

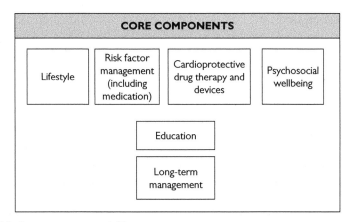

Figure 18.2 Core components of CR.
Adapted from the Department of Health Cardiac Rehabilitation Commissioning Pack Cardiac Rehabilitation, Strategic Commissioning Development Unit, Crown copyright 2010.

18.5 Physical activity and exercise

Evidence for the benefits of exercise training

Clinical evidence

- There is a strong evidence base for CR. This data has been brought together in a series of Cochrane reviews
- When looking at exercise training a Cochrane review (Joliffe et al., 2001) demonstrated that exercise-only CR reduced all-cause mortality by 27% and cardiac death by 31% for patients with previous MI, revascularization, or angina
- There was no effect on non-fatal MI alone and there was no apparent additional benefit from comprehensive cardiac rehabilitation
- The population studied included predominantly younger, low-risk, male patients
- A Cochrane review (Davies et al., 2010) of studies of exercise-based CR in patients with mild-to-moderate heart failure demonstrated a 28% reduction in heart-failure-related hospital admissions and an improvement in patients' quality of life, although no significant reduction in all-cause mortality was shown.

Physiological evidence

- In patients with CHD there are multiple suggested mechanisms for the clinical benefits seen from CR
- These partly relate to the modification of established risk factors, with evidence that exercise training can result in a reduced BP, weight loss, reduced insulin resistance, and an improved lipid profile
- Exercise training also has several neurohormonal effects:
  - Changes in the autonomic nervous system reduce the resting sympathicoadrenergic tone, and modifications within the renin-angiotensin-aldosterone system result in reduced plasma renin activity
  - On a microvascular level there is improved endothelium-dependent vasodilation, with increased expression and activity of endothelial NO synthase, as well as increased angiogenesis and collateralization
- In patients with heart failure, as well as the benefits of exercise training, studies have shown a reduction in circulating levels of angiotensin II, aldosterone, and atrial natriuretic peptide
- These patients also benefit from better respiratory function and improved skeletal muscle metabolism and function.

Exercise recommendations

- After an AMI, whilst awaiting CR, patients are advised to be physically active for 20–30 min per day to the point of slight breathlessness
- Patients who are not achieving this should be advised to increase their activity in a gradual, step-by-step way
- All physical activity and exercise sessions should start with a graded warm-up to enable physiological adjustments, and on completion of the main exercise there should be a graded cool-down period
- Coronary artery bypass graft (CABG) patients should be advised to avoid heavy lifting for 3 months
- Resistance training aimed at improving muscle strength and or muscle endurance should be incorporated into the exercise programme
- Patients should be advised to avoid short, sharp, strenuous activity

- Patients should be assessed and risk stratified prior to commencing exercise training:
  - Low-risk patients can be assessed via a history, examination, resting ECG, and functional testing (e.g. shuttle walking test or 6-min walking test)
  - High-risk patients should be assessed with a clinical history and examination, resting ECG, echocardiogram, and formal exercise testing
  - High-risk patients should participate in exercise sessions with appropriate staff-to-patient ratios (often) based in a hospital environment with access to a defibrillator and staff trained in advanced life support
  - High-risk patients include those with:
    - MI complicated by heart failure, cardiogenic shock, and/or complex ventricular arrhythmias
    - Angina or breathlessness occurring at a low level of exercise, e.g. inability to complete the first 4 min of the shuttle walking test
    - ST segment depression ≥1 mm on resting ECG
    - Exercise testing with marked ST depression ≥2 mm or angina at <5 METS (see Box 18.1), e.g. 3 min of a Bruce protocol
  - Patients unsuitable for exercise training include those with:
    - Decompensated heart failure
    - Severe valvular stenosis or regurgitation
    - Refractory arrhythmias
    - Other clinical conditions that worsen with exertion
- Exercise sessions:
  - Aerobic low-to-moderate intensity activity at least 2 times a week for a minimum of 8 weeks
  - Patients should be prescribed an individualized exercise regime adapted in respect of associated comorbidity, e.g. arthritis, COPD, stroke, etc.
  - Low-to-moderate risk patients can undertake resistance training
  - Exercise sessions usually last 1 h including:
    - 10 to 15 min warm-up
    - Aerobic phase for 20–30 min
    - 10-min cool-down
    - Period of relative rest, often in sitting position

BOX 18.1 METABOLIC EQUIVALENTS (METS) FOR SPECIFIC PHYSICAL ACTIVITIES

- A metabolic equivalent is a way of expressing the metabolic energy requirements of a task as multiples of the resting metabolic rate (RMR)
- 1 MET is equivalent to the RMR when sitting quietly, and has a conventional reference value of 3.5 ml $O_2 \cdot kg^{-1} \cdot min^{-1}$, which is equal to 1 kcal·kg^{-1}·h^{-1}.

Physical activities	METS
Sleeping	0.9
Light intensity activities (e.g., gentle stroll)	<3
Moderate intensity activities (e.g. moderate paced to brisk walking, gentle cycling and swimming)	3–6
Moderate- to high-intensity activities (e.g. hill walking, jogging, skipping, swimming at pace)	6 to 8
High-intensity activities (e.g. running, fast cycling)	>8

Table 18.1 Commonly used perceived exertion scales

Exercise training level	Rate of perceived exertion (Borg)	Borg CR 10 scale	Perceived breathing rate	% maximal heart rate from symptom limited exercise test
	6 No exertion at all	0		
	7 Very, very light	0.5		
	8	1		
	9 Very light	2		
	10	3		
LOW	11 Fairly light	4	SING	50–60
	12			
MODERATE	13 Somewhat hard	5	TALK	60–75
	14	6		
HIGH	15 Hard (heavy)	7	GASP	75–85
	16			
	17 Very hard	8		
	18			
	19 Very, very hard	9		
	20 Maximal exertion	10		

Adapted from 'A comparison between three rating scales for perceived exertion and two different work tests', E. Borg and L. Kaijser, *Scandinavian Journal of Medicine & Science in Sports*, 16, 57–69, copyright 2006 with permission of John Wiley and Sons.

- Monitor exercise intensity as a percentage of acquired maximal heart rate or maximal age predicated heart rate using a pulse monitor, or as a perceived level of exertion on the Borg scale (see Table 18.1)
- Long-term advice to continue with at least 150 min of moderate aerobic exercise per week.

18.6 Diet and weight management

On commencing cardiac rehabilitation:

- An assessment should be made of the patients BMI and waist circumference
- An assessment should be made of the patient's dietary habits.

Dietary advice:

- Eat a Mediterranean-style diet (more bread, fruit, vegetables, and fish, less meat, and replace butter and cheese with products based on vegetable and plant oils)
- Eat five portions of fruit and vegetables per day
- Reduce intake of saturated fats
- Reduce salt intake
- Do not routinely recommend eating oily fish for the secondary prevention of MI, although there is no evidence of harm from consuming oily fish, and fish may form part of a Mediterranean-style diet

- Do not offer or advise people to use omega-3 fatty acid capsules or omega-3 fatty acid supplemented foods for the secondary prevention of MI. This is amended from previous NICE guidance, following the results of the Alpha Omega Trial (Kromhout et al., NEJM, 2010) which showed no benefit from omega-3 fatty acids in the reduction of cardiovascular events (possible benefit in women and diabetic patients on subgroup analysis)
- Patients should be advised not to take supplements containing beta-carotene, antioxidant supplements (vitamin E and/or C) or folic acid to reduce cardiovascular risk
- Patients should keep within the advised safe limits for alcohol intake:
  - 21 units a week for a man
  - 14 units a week for a woman
- Patients should avoid binge drinking (>3 units of alcohol in 1–2 h)
- Aim for the whole family to improve their dietary habits.

18.7 Smoking cessation

- Smoking cessation should be advised
- Patients should be offered support, advice, and referral to a smoking cessation service
- When necessary, and ideally in association with counselling, pharmacotherapy with nicotine replacement therapy or bupropion should be offered.

18.8 Education

Patients should be given information about:

- Their diagnosis, the basic pathophysiology of CHD, symptoms of angina and AMI and a plan of action should these symptoms occur
- Common misconceptions about cardiac illness
- Physical activity, smoking, and diet
- Cardiac risk factors, including blood pressure, lipids, and glucose
- Psychosocial issues including:
  - Anxiety and depression
  - Stress management
  - Occupational factors
  - Sexual dysfunction
  - Driving and travel guidance
- Instructions for use, indications for, and potential side effects of any new medications
- Details of any cardiac investigations, interventions, devices, or surgery that may be required
- Training for the patient and family members in basic cardiopulmonary resuscitation.

18.9 Risk factor management

Cardiac rehabilitation sessions provide an ideal forum for assessing patient's cardiovascular risk and for providing ongoing patient education about risk reduction.

- As discussed patients should be given advice about smoking cessation and weight loss.

Hypertension

- Following a cardiac event patients should aim for a target blood pressure of 140/90 mmHg (or 130/80 mmHg in patients with diabetes or renal disease)

- In addition to continuing with any prescribed medications, hypertensive patients can be advised to:
  - Stop smoking
  - Lose weight
  - Manage stress
  - Reduce salt intake
  - Take regular exercise
  - Keep alcohol intake within recommended limits
  - Eat healthily.

Hypercholesterolaemia

- Following a cardiac event patients should aim for a total cholesterol of <4 mmol/l and LDL cholesterol <2 mmol/l. Even if premorbid cholesterol levels are low, patients will still benefit from reducing their cholesterol by 25%
- In addition to continuing any prescribed medications patients with an elevated cholesterol can be advised to:
  - Stop smoking
  - Take regular exercise
  - Keep alcohol intake within recommended limits
  - Lose weight/reduce waist circumference
  - Maintain a diet low in saturated fat
  - If diabetic, maintain their target HbA1c.

Diabetes mellitus

- Patients with pre-existing diabetes should be informed of the importance of good blood sugar control, and the potential long-term complications of poorly controlled diabetes
- The impact of exercise on circulating blood sugars should be talked through and patients should be encouraged to use their own monitoring kit to check sugars prior to exercise
- If not already registered patients should be referred to a diabetes specialist nurse for further advice, with secondary care input as required.

18.10 Psychological status and quality of life

- CHD risk has been related to five specific psychosocial factors: anxiety, depression, personality factors and character traits, social isolation, and chronic life stress
- As part of a comprehensive CR programme these issues should be identified and appropriate help and support offered
- Psychological interventions include individual and group counselling, stress management and relaxation, cognitive-behavioural approaches and goal setting.

Further support should incorporate the following:

- Assessment with the Hospital Anxiety and Depression Scale (HADS)
  - Treatment of anxiety and depression if identified, including specialist referral if appropriate
- Assessment of quality of life using the Dartmouth Coop Scales
- Identification and addressing of economic, welfare rights, housing, or social support issues
- Stress awareness and stress management approaches
- Driving and travel guidance:
  - For current DVLA regulations see Table 18.2

Table 18.2 DVLA guidance

Cardiovascular disorder	Group 1 entitlement (private car, motorcycle) Notify DVLA when specified	Group 2 entitlement (Vocational – large goods and passenger carrying vehicles) Notify DVLA in all cases
Angina	Stop driving if symptoms occur at rest, with emotion or at the wheel.	Refusal or revocation with continuing symptoms Re/licensing provided: • free from angina for >6/52 • functional test requirements met*
ACS - Unstable angina - NSTEMI - STEMI	If successful PCI, may drive after 1/52 provided: • No other urgent revascularization is planned • LVEF is >40% pre-discharge If not successfully treated by PCI can drive after 4/52.	Disqualified for 6/52 Re/licensing provided functional test requirements met*
Elective PCI	No driving for 1/52	Disqualified for 6/52 Re/licensing provided functional test requirements met*
Post CABG	No driving for 4/52	Disqualified for 3/12 Re/licensing provided: • LVEF is ≥40% • functional test requirements met 3 months post-op*
Arrhythmia	Stop driving if the arrhythmia has caused/is likely to cause incapacity. May drive when underlying cause has been identified and controlled for >4/52. Notify DVLA if there are distracting/disabling symptoms.	Disqualifies from driving if the arrhythmia has caused/is likely to cause incapacity. May drive when: • the arrhythmia is controlled for at least 3/12. • the LVEF is ≥40%
Successful catheter ablation	No driving for 2/7	For arrhythmia that has caused/would likely have caused incapacity, may drive after 6/52. When arrhythmia has not caused incapacity, may drive after 2/52
Pacemaker implant Includes box change	No driving for 1/52	Disqualifies from driving for 6/52
ICD implanted for ventricular arrhythmia associated with incapacity	Should not drive for: 1) 6/12 after the first implant 2) 6/12 after any shock therapy and/or symptomatic antitachycardia pacing 3a) 2 years if any therapy accompanied by incapacity unless 3b or 3c 3b) If due to inappropriate cause; 1/12 once controlled 3c) If appropriate and steps taken to prevent recurrence; 6/12	Permanently bars

(Continued)

Table 18.2 *(Continued)*

Cardiovascular disorder	Group 1 entitlement (private car, motorcycle) *Notify DVLA when specified*	Group 2 entitlement (Vocational – large goods and passenger carrying vehicles) *Notify DVLA in all cases*
	4) 1/12 off following any revision electrodes or alteration of anti-arrhythmic drugs 5) 1/52 off after a defibrillator box change. For 1, 2 and 3a/3c, DVLA should be notified.	
ICD implanted for ventricular arrhythmia which did **not** cause incapacity	Can drive 1/12 after ICD implantation providing all of the following conditions are met: • LVEF >35% • no fast VT induced on electrophysiological study (RR <250 ms) • any induced VT could be pace-terminated by the ICD twice, without acceleration, during the post implantation study	Permanently bars
Prophylactic ICD	Driving should cease for 1/12. DVLA need not be notified.	Permanently bars
CRT-P	1/52 following implantation.	Disqualifies for 6/52 after implantation
CRT-D	See ICD requirements	Permanently bars

*functional testing:

- ETT 48 h off antianginals + 3 stages/9 min of Bruce protocol with no significant symptoms/ECG changes
- Stress myocardial perfusion scan/stress echocardiography—demonstrating:
  - LVEF is 40% or more
  - (a) <10% reversible ischaemia on MPI
  - (b) <1 segment reversible ischaemia on stress echo.

Available from http://www.dft.gov.uk/dvla/medical/medical_drivers.aspx under Crown copyright 1993.

- Most patients are fit to fly 2–3 weeks after an uncomplicated MI; specialist advice required in more complex patients or those holding a pilots licence
- Sex guidance:
  - Patients can resume sexual intercourse 4 weeks after an uncomplicated MI
  - Erectile dysfunction is often due to underlying vascular disease but may relate to the use of BBs, ACE inhibitors, diuretics, etc.
  - Phosphodiesterase type 5 inhibitors (e.g. Viagra/sildenafil) may be considered in patients who had an MI more than 6 months earlier and who are now stable; avoid taking with nitrates and/or nicorandil because this can lead to dangerously low blood pressure.

18.11 Cardio-protective drug therapy and implantable devices

- Patients with CHD should be taking the following drug therapies for secondary prevention:
  - Aspirin
  - BBs

- ■ ACE inhibitor/ARB
- ■ Statin
- ■ +/− second antiplatelet agent (for up to 12 months post ACS/AMI depending on indication)
- ■ +/− aldosterone antagonist if left ventricular failure
- In patients with chronic heart failure
  - ■ Assess fluid status (weight, postural BP)
  - ■ Manage fluid status appropriately with diuretics
  - ■ Consider use of ACE inhibitor, ARB, BBs, aldosterone antagonist as appropriate
- Consider thrombotic risk management
- When indicated implantable devices are known to be clinically beneficial and reduce premature cardiovascular death yet, in some patients, they may impact negatively on psychological health and exercise ability. These components should be assessed and a tailored intervention delivered by appropriately trained staff.

18.12 Long-term management strategy

- There are two aspects to long-term management: patient self-management and GP-supported management
- On completion of a structured CR programme patients should be encouraged to maintain a healthy lifestyle
- Patients should be advised to continue with at least 150 min of moderate aerobic exercise per week.

Patient self-management could include:

- Community-based programmes such as Phase IV exercise groups
- Leisure centre and gym memberships
- Continuing diet and weight management support with specialized community initiatives
- Contact with voluntary groups/resources and self-help groups such as coronary support groups.

GP supported management should include:

- Patients entered onto GP practice CHD/CVD registers for structured follow up in primary care
- Continuation of smoking cessation services
- Risk factor management: blood pressure, lipids, glucose, and weight management
- Shared care for more complex patients or those awaiting intervention or surgery.

18.13 Audit and evaluation

All CR services should use clinical audit to: monitor and manage patient progress; evaluate clinical outcomes and benchmarking against local, regional, and national standards.

CR programmes are increasingly being asked to align with national clinical indicator measures and quality outcomes which are best achieved through registration on the National Audit of Cardiac Rehabilitation (NACR). The NACR is the official audit for CR in the UK and supports direct online data entry or third party data upload from locally based software.

Further reading

British Association for Cardiovascular Prevention and Rehabilitation. Standards and Core Components for Cardiac Rehabilitation. BACPR, 2012. Available at: http://www.bacpr.com

Camm AJ, Lüscher TF, Serruys PW. *The European Society of Cardiology Textbook of Cardiovascular Medicine*. Wiley-Blackwell, 2006.

Chow CK, Jolly S, Rao-Melacini P, *et al*. Association of diet, exercise, and smoking modification with risk of early cardiovascular events after acute coronary syndromes. *Circulation*, 2010. 121: 750–8.

Davies EJ, Moxham T, Rees K, *et al*. Exercise based rehabilitation for heart failure. *Cochrane Database of Systematic Reviews* 2010, Issue 4.

Department of Health. National Service Framework for Coronary Heart Disease, DoH, 2000.

Department of Health. Cardiovascular Disease Outcomes Strategy for England, DoH, 2013.

Department of Health. Commissioning a cardiac rehabilitation service. Available at: http://webarchive.nationalarchives.gov.uk/20130107105354/http:/www.dh.gov.uk/en/Publicationsandstatistics/Publications/PublicationsPolicyAndGuidance/Browsable/DH_117504

DVLA. At a glance guide to the current medical standards of fitness to drive. Drivers Medical Group, DVLA, 2012. Available at: www.dft.gov.uk/dvla

Fidan D, Unal B, Critchley J, *et al*. Economic analysis of treatments reducing coronary heart disease mortality in England and Wales, 2000–2010. *QJM*, 2007. 100: 277–89.

Jolliffe JA, Rees K, Taylor RS, Thompson D, Oldridge N, Ebrahim S. Exercise based rehabilitation for coronary heart disease, (Cochrane Review). *Cochrane Database of Systematic Reviews* 2001, Issue 2.

Mancia G, De Backer G, Dominiczak A, *et al*. Guidelines for the management of arterial hypertension. The Task Force for the Management of Arterial Hypertension of the European Society of Hypertension (ESH) and of the European Society of Cardiology (ESC). *Eur Heart J*, 2007; 28: 1462–1536.

National Audit of Cardiac Rehabilitation. Annual Statistical Report 2013. NACR, 2013. Available at: http://www.cardiacrehabilitation.org.uk/nacr/index.htm

NHS Improvement Programme. NHS Improvement: Heart. Available at: www.improvement.nhs.uk/heart/cardiacrehabilitation

NHS Lothian. The Edinburgh Heart Manual. Available at: http://www.theheartmanual.com

NICE Guideline for Secondary Prevention in Primary and Secondary Care for Patients Following a Myocardial Infarction, CG172. NICE, 2013.

NICE. Guideline for Chronic Heart Failure. CG108. NICE, 2010.

NICE. Commissioning Guide for Cardiac Rehabilitation Services. NICE, 2013.

NICE. Clinical Guideline 94; Unstable Angina and NSTEMI: the early management of unstable angina and non-ST-segment-elevation myocardial infarction. NICE, 2010.

Perk J, de Backer G, Gohlke H, *et al*. European Guidelines on cardiovascular disease prevention in clinical practice (version 2012) The Fifth Joint Task Force of the European Society of Cardiology and Other Societies on Cardiovascular Disease Prevention in Clinical Practice. *Eur Heart J*, 2012; 33: 1635–1701.

Reiner Ž, Catapano AL, de Backer G, *et al*. ESC/EAS Guidelines for the management of dyslipidaemias The Task Force for the management of dyslipidaemias of the European Society of Cardiology (ESC) and the European Atherosclerosis Society (EAS). *Eur Heart J*, 2011; 32: 1769–1818.

Rydén L Standl E, Bartnik M, *et al*. Guidelines on diabetes, pre-diabetes, and cardiovascular diseases. The Task Force on Diabetes and Cardiovascular Diseases of the European Society of Cardiology (ESC) and of the European Association for the Study of Diabetes (EASD). *Eur Heart J*, 2007; 28: 88–136.

Scottish Intercollegiate Guidelines Network. Cardiac rehabilitation. SIGN, 2002.

Assessment of patients with cardiovascular disease prior to non-cardiac surgery

CONTENTS

19.1 Why is assessment important?

- Prevalence of CVD increases with age
- Number of non-cardiac surgical procedures performed in older persons will increase from 6 million currently to nearly 12 million per year
- Nearly a quarter of these will be major intra-abdominal, thoracic, vascular, and orthopaedic procedures
- Associated with significant perioperative cardiovascular morbidity and mortality.

19.2 Myocardial ischaemia occuring in the perioperative period

This may be due to:

- Chronic mismatch in the supply-to-demand ratio of blood flow response to metabolic demand; clinically resembles stable ischaemic heart disease (IHD) due to a flow-limiting stenosis in coronary conduit arteries
- Coronary plaque rupture due to vascular inflammatory processes presenting as acute coronary syndromes.

19.3 What happens during surgery?

- Every operation elicits a stress response:
  - Initiated by tissue injury and mediated by neuroendocrine factors
  - Induces tachycardia and hypertension
- Fluid shifts in the perioperative period add to the surgical stress; this stress increases myocardial oxygen demand
- Surgery also causes alterations in the balance between prothrombotic and fibrinolytic factors, resulting in hypercoagulability and possible coronary thrombosis (elevation of fibrinogen and other coagulation factors, increased platelet activation and aggregation, and reduced fibrinolysis).

19.4 Can the risks be assessed?

- Several risk scores exist:
  - E.g. Goldman or Lee (see Table 19.1)
  - Poorly validated in general non-cardiac population
  - Lee risk index recommended in ESC guidelines
- Preoperative assessment tailored to circumstances:
  - Emergent versus elective surgery
  - Simple risks-versus-benefit assessment.

Functional capacity is critical in evaluation of patient:

- Measured in metabolic equivalents (MET)
- 1 MET = basal metabolic rate
- Exercise testing provides objective assessment
- Ability to perform activities of daily living can help estimate:
  - <4 METS = 2 flights stairs = poor functional capacity
  - >10 METS = swimming
- If functional capacity is
  - High (>4 METS), prognosis is excellent, even in the presence of stable heart disease or multiple risk factors
  - Poor (<4 METS), further risk assessment is needed.

Table 19.1 Lee's revised cardiac risk index

Clinical variable	Points
High-risk surgery, e.g. intraperitoneal, intrathoracic, or suprainguinal vascular surgery	1
Coronary artery disease	1
Congestive heart failure	1
History of cerebrovascular disease	1
Insulin treatment for diabetes mellitus	1
Preoperative serum creatinine level greater than 2.0 mg/dl (180μmol/l)	1
Total	

Interpretation of risk score

Risk class	Points	Risk of complications* (%)
I. Very low	0	0.4
II. Low	1	0.9
III. Moderate	2	6.6
IV. High	3+	11.0

*Myocardial infarction, pulmonary embolism, ventricular fibrillation, cardiac arrest, or complete heart block.

Reproduced from 'Derivation and prospective validation of a simple index for prediction of cardiac risk of major noncardiac surgery', Thomas H. Lee, Edward R. Marcantonio, Carol M. Mangione et al., *Circulation* 100,1047, copyright 1999 with permission of Wolters Kluwer.

19.5 How do patient factors affect cardiac risk assessment?

Major predictors

Mandate intensive management, may delay surgery unless urgent.

- Unstable coronary syndromes:*
  - Recent MI with evidence of important ischaemic risk by clinical symptoms or non-invasive study
  - Unstable or severe angina (CCS III or IV)
- Decompensated congestive cardiac failure
- Significant arrhythmias:
  - High-grade AV block
  - Symptomatic ventricular arrhythmias in the presence of underlying heart disease
  - Supraventricular arrhythmias with uncontrolled ventricular rate
- Severe valvular disease.

*Increased incidence of re-infarction after non-cardiac surgery if the prior MI was within 6 months of the operation and especially within 6–12 weeks.

Intermediate predictors

The following well validated markers of enhanced risk of perioperative cardiac complications justify careful assessment of patient's current status.

- Mild angina pectoris (CCS I or II)
- Prior MI by history or pathologic Q-waves
- Compensated or prior congestive heart failure
- DM
- Chronic renal insufficiency.

Minor predictors

The following are recognized markers for cardiovascular disease that have not been proven to independently increase perioperative risk:

- Advanced age
- Abnormal ECG (LVH, LBBB, ST-T abnormalities)
- Rhythm other than sinus (eg AF)
- Low functional capacity (although associated with worse outcome in thoracic surgery)
- History of stroke
- Uncontrolled systemic hypertension.

19.6 Preoperative testing

In patients without unstable cardiac features, the assessment of risk factors can guide the need for further diagnostic testing and perioperative management.

- Evidence suggests that in low or intermediate risk patients, non-invasive assessment does not alter outcome, provided optimal medical therapy is achieved
- Testing should not be performed unless the results would affect perioperative management.

What about non-invasive assessment?

- Resting ECG is recommended in all patients with cardiac risk factors undergoing intermediate or high-risk non-cardiac surgery
- Rest echocardiography should be considered in patients undergoing high-risk non-cardiac surgery:
  - LV ejection fraction of <35% has a sensitivity of 50% and a specificity of 91% for prediction of perioperative non-fatal MI or cardiac death
  - Should also be performed in known or suspected valve disease
- Exercise treadmill or bicycle are preferred method of non-invasive stress:
  - Good negative predictive value
  - Limited by functional consideration and ECG abnormalities
- Semi-quantitative nuclear myocardial perfusion scanning is well validated; normal scan indicates an excellent surgical prognosis
- Dobutamine stress echocardiography has good negative predictive value (probably equivalent to nuclear perfusion imaging)
- MRI and CT are not validated in perioperative setting
- Cardiopulmonary exercise testing can be useful, but is not widely available or established in this setting.

What about invasive assessment?

- Coronary angiography is considered for the same indication as a non-surgical setting; patients facing high-stress surgery who have unstable coronary syndromes, or decompensated ischaemic heart failure may benefit
- Intraoperative PA catheter or TOE may be helpful in ischaemic cardiomyopathy.

19.7 How do surgical factors affect cardiac risk stratification?

High (reported cardiac risk often >5%):

- Emergency major operations, especially in elderly
- Aortic and other major vascular
- Peripheral vascular
- Anticipated prolonged surgical procedures associated with large fluid shift and/or blood loss.

Intermediate (reported cardiac risk generally <5%):

- Carotid endarterectomy
- Head and neck
- Intraperitoneal and intrathoracic
- Orthopaedic
- Prostate.

Low (reported cardiac risk generally <1%):

- Endoscopic procedures
- Superficial procedure
- Cataract
- Breast.

Laparoscopic procedures carry a similar cardiac risk to open procedures since lesser pain, GI paralysis, and fluid shifts are offset by pneumoperitoneum and decreased venous return.

19.8 Which pharmacological therapies are validated?

Beta-blockers

- Large meta-analyses demonstrate reduction in perioperative myocardial ischaemia, MI, and cardiac mortality, with greater risk reduction in higher-risk patients
- POISE trial caused recent concern due to excess BB-associated mortality, but this was driven by hypotension, bradycardia, and stroke, presumably due to aggressive dosing strategy
- Target heart rate 60–70 bpm rather than dose-driven strategy preferred
- No clear benefit in low-risk patients scheduled for low-risk surgery
- BBs should not be withdrawn preoperatively
- Intermediate- and high-risk patients should be stabilized on BBs prior to surgery (surgery postponed if possible).

Lipid-lowering therapy

- Data (mostly observational) suggests perioperative use of statins offers protection against cardiac complications occurring during non-cardiac surgery
- Duration, dose, and patient group are unclear
- In patients with risk factors, statin therapy should be initiated preoperatively.

ACE inhibitors

- Some data suggesting a reduction in post-operative cardiovascular events
- Perioperative use of ACE inhibitors carries risk of severe hypotension during anaesthesia
- On balance it is recommended to commence and continue ACE inhibitors in patients with reduced LV function
- Transient discontinuation of ACE inhibitors prescribed for hypertension should be considered.

19.9 What about revascularization?

- Highest risk patients undergoing highest risk procedures may be functionally limited and therefore do not exhibit limiting cardiac symptoms; stress testing in this group may be useful if the outcome will affect management
- Stress testing in intermediate-risk patients has not been shown to alter outcome and is not recommended, but optimal management otherwise is required (including heart-rate control)
- Revascularization decision made on long-term risk/benefit analysis:
  - Stable angina should be worked up similarly to any other stable angina patient
  - No evidence to support prophylactic revascularization where it would not normally be indicated
- Post-surgical revascularization recovery before non-cardiac surgery is a matter of expert opinion and not evidence- or guideline-based
- Use of bare metal stent/drug-eluting stent needs to be considered in view of dual antiplatlet therapy: limited evidence from case series suggest use of pro-healing/biological stents may become useful in future
- Generally lack of benefit of preoperative revascularization in otherwise optimally treated patient
- Use of perioperative intraortic balloon pump should be considered in high-risk cases.

19.10 Specific cardiovascular conditions

Previous revascularization

- Single antiplatelet should continue following mandated period of dual agents
- Good functional capacity and adequate medical therapy does not need further stress testing.

Pacemaker/ICD

- Indications as for permanent pacing
- Bifasicular block, with or without first degree AV block, is not an indication for a temporary wire
- Electrocautery may interfere with permanent pacemaker sensing. A non-sensing mode is recommended
- Implantable cardioverter defibrillator devices should be deactivated if electrocautery is to be used.

Aortic stenosis

- Critical aortic stenosis is associated with a very high risk of cardiac decompensation in patients undergoing elective moderate to high risk non-cardiac surgery
- Symptomatic patients should be offered valve replacement prior to surgery; consider balloon valvuloplasty or transcatheter vascular aortic valve implantation in unsuitable patients
- Asymptomatic patients with severe aortic stenosis can have low- or intermediate-risk non-cardiac surgery safely; valve replacement should be offered if high-risk non-cardiac surgery planned.

Mitral stenosis

- Non-cardiac surgery considered low risk in:
  - Mitral valve area (MVA) >1.5 cm^2
  - MVA <1.5 cm^2 and PAP <50 mmHg if asymptomatic
- Heart-rate/rhythm control and fluid balance critical
- Non-cardiac surgery considered high risk for MVA <1.5cm^2 and PAP >50 mmHg; consider surgical repair or valvotomy.

Hypertension

- Presence of mild-to-moderate hypertension not an independent risk factor
- Severe chronic hypertension, e.g. DBP >110 mmHg, should be controlled before any elective non-cardiac surgery.

Pulmonary arterial hypertension

- Perioperative risks are high
- Acute right heart failure can occur due to increase in pulmonary vascular resistance
- Treatment should be optimized prior to non-cardiac surgery
- Diuretics and dobutamine should be considered in right heart failure
- Specific perioperative therapies not validated.

See Figure 19.1 for a summary of ESC guidelines for pre-operative cardiac risk evaluation and perioperative management.

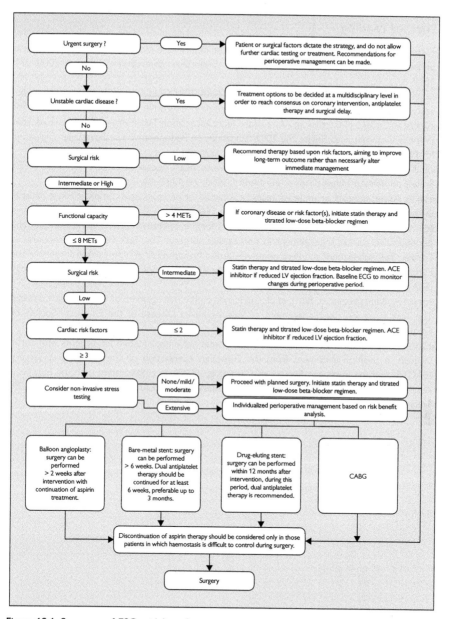

Figure 19.1 Summary of ESC guidelines for pre-operative cardiac risk evaluation and perioperative management.

Reproduced from 'Derivation and prospective validation of a simple index for prediction of cardiac risk of major noncardiac surgery', Thomas H. Lee, Edward R. Marcantonio, Carol M. Mangione et al., *Circulation*, 100, 1047, copyright 1999 with permission of Wolters Kluwer Health.

Further reading

Devereaux PJ, Yang H, Yusuf S, *et al*. Effects of extended-release metoprolol succinate in patients undergoing non-cardiac surgery (POISE trial): a randomised controlled trial. *Lancet*, 2008; 371: 1839–47.

Fleisher LA, Beckman JA, Brown KA, *et al*. ACC/AHA 2007 Guidelines on perioperative cardio-vascular evaluation and care for noncardiac surgery: Executive Summary: A Report of the American College of Cardiology/American Heart Association Task Force on Practice Guidelines (Writing Committee to Revise the 2002 Guidelines on Perioperative Cardiovascular Evaluation for Noncardiac Surgery). *Circulation*, 2007; 116: 1971–96.

Lung B. A prospective survey of patients with valvular heart disease in Europe: The Euro Heart Survey on Valvular Heart Disease. *Eur Heart J*, 2003; 24: 1231–43.

Kertai M. Aortic stenosis: an underestimated risk factor for perioperative complications in patients undergoing noncardiac surgery. *Am J Med*, 2004; 116: 8–13.

Poldermans D, Bax JJ, Boersma E, *et al*. Guidelines for pre-operative cardiac risk assessment and perioperative cardiac management in non-cardiac surgery: The Task Force for Preoperative Cardiac Risk Assessment and Perioperative Cardiac Management in Non-cardiac Surgery of the European Society of Cardiology (ESC) and endorsed by the European Society of Anaesthesiology (ESA). *Eur Heart J*, 2009; 30: 2769–812.

Vahanian A, Baumgartner H, Bax J, *et al*. Guidelines on the management of valvular heart disease: The Task Force on the Management of Valvular Heart Disease of the European Society of Cardiology. *Eur Heart J*, 2007; 28: 230–68.

Vahanian A, Alfieri O, Al-Attar N, *et al*. Transcatheter valve implantation for patients with aortic stenosis: a position statement from the European Association of Cardio-Thoracic Surgery (EACTS) and the European Society of Cardiology (ESC), in collaboration with the European Association of Percutaneous Cardiovascular Interventions (EAPCI). *Eur Heart J*, 2008; 29: 1463–70.

Assessment of patients prior to cardiac surgery

CONTENTS

20.1 Surgical risk

- Patient assessment for surgery should always involve a cardiac surgeon
- Best practice would dictate a multi-professional approach.

What are typical risks?

- Fourth European Association for Cardio-Thoracic Surgery adult cardiac surgery database reports mortality rate for CABG at 2.4% (England 1.8%)
- Typical risks for CABG include:
  - Permanent pacemaker, 1%
  - Stroke, 1%
  - Renal failure requiring dialysis, 3%
  - Reoperation within 24 h, 7%
  - Prolonged postoperative ventilation, 6%
- Operative risks vary according to exact procedure and premorbid status, for example:
  - Risk of permanent pacemaker up to 10% in patients with native aortic valve disease and pre existing conduction disease
  - Stroke risk is associated with atherothrombotic debris from the aortic arch, AF, low cardiac output, and hypercoagulopathy from tissue injury.

20.2 Risk scores

- Many different risk scores exist; none is perfect
- Useful in
  - Providing individual risk
  - Comparing internal and external performance
- Need to consider
  - Discrimination: accurate prediction between low and high risk
  - Calibration: do the observed risks reflect prediction?
  - Clinical performance: does it include important factors, and can they be measured in routine practice?

- Predictive value of older scores lessens as medical and surgical care improves, therefore affecting calibration
- STS (Society of Thoracic Surgeons) risk score algorithm based on North American database
  - Regularly updated, therefore accurately calibrated
  - Asks 50+ questions, therefore poor usability
  - Gives score for a number of interventions
- No widely used 'valve-specific' risk scores.

European system for cardiac operative risk evaluation (EuroSCORE)

(See Table 20.1.)

Table 20.1 European system for cardiac operative risk evaluation

euroSCORE II risk factors	
Patient related factors	
Age	
Gender	
Renal impairment	Normal, moderate, severe, on dialysis
Extracardiac arteriopathy	Claudication, >50% carotid stenosis, amputation, previous or planned vascular intervention
Poor mobility	Severe impairment of mobility secondary to musculoskeletal or neurological dysfunction
Previous cardiac surgery	
Chronic lung disease	Long term use of bronchodilators or steroids for lung disease
Active endocarditis	Patient still on antibiotic treatment for endocarditis at time of surgery
Critical preoperative state	Ventricular tachycardia or ventricular fibrillation or aborted sudden death, preoperative cardiac massage, preoperative ventilation before anaesthetic room, preoperative inotropes or IABP, preoperative acute renal failure (anuria or oliguria <10ml/hr)
Diabetes on insulin	
Cardiac related factors	
NYHA	
CCS Class 4 angina	Angina at rest
LV function	Good, moderate, poor, very poor
Recent MI	
Pulmonary hypertension	Moderate, severe
Operation related factors	
Urgency	Elective, urgent, emergency. Salvage
Weight of the intervention	Isolated CABG, non CABG, 2 or 3 including valve, aortic surgery, structural repair, maze, tumour resection
Surgery on the thoracic aorta	

With kind permission of EUROScore. Available at http://www.euroscore.org/escntcts.htm

- First presented in 1998
- Based on outcome database of nearly 20,000 patients across European countries
- Initially additive score giving approximate percentage predicted 30 day mortality for "all" cardiac surgery
- Logistic score (2003) recalibrated for high risk patients
- Validated for use in other populations (e.g. North America)
- Highest discriminatory power of several risk scores
- 2010 UK risk was approximately 50% euroscore therefore new dataset collected
- EuroSCORE II updated October 2011
  - Renal function more accurately assessed
  - Severe impairment of mobility now adjust score
  - Better weighting for urgency and type of intervention including valve, aorta, tumours and repair of structural defect
  - Yet to be validated worldwide
  - Calculate online at euroscore.org.

20.3 What happens during surgery?

Cardiopulmonary bypass

See Figure 20.1.

- Most cardiac operations rely on the heart-lung machine, which supports the patient's circulation
- During cardiopulmonary bypass (CPB) the heart beats empty but the coronary arteries are still perfused from the aorta, which itself is perfused by the heart-lung machine
- Clamping the aorta between the site of insertion of the aortic cannula and the origin of the coronary arteries produces a bloodless field
- The aorta is cannulated, ready to deliver oxygenated blood from the heart-lung machine (see Figure 20.2)
- Adequate heparinization is achieved and then the right atrium is cannulated, draining venous blood into the heart-lung machine (either one atriocaval cannulae, or two caval cannulae)
- The venous cannula is unclamped and the patient is put on bypass
- Once ready, the aorta is cross clamped; the heart is ischaemic during this period
- Myocardial protection is achieved with cardioplegia (blood or crystalloid, warm or cold):
  - Results in combination of electromechanical arrest and/or hypothermia
  - After cross-clamping the aorta, the cardioplegic solution is infused into the aortic root via a catheter inserted in the ascending aorta proximal to the cross-clamp; retrograde infusion into coronary sinus may be necessary e.g. aortic insufficiency
- De-airing:
  - If a main chamber has been opened as part of the procedure it is important to evacuate air from the heart (especially the left side) before the heart is put back into the circulation
- Clamp-off:
  - If myocardial protection is optimal, sinus rhythm should return
  - VF requires internal cardioversion
- Protamine to reverse heparinization, after de-cannulating.

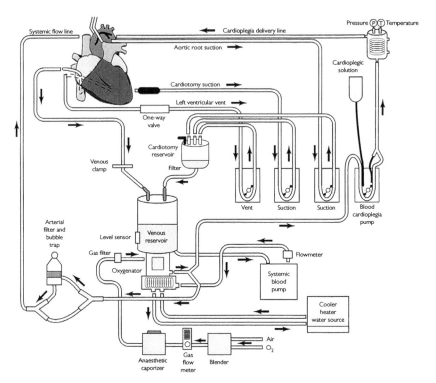

Figure 20.1 Diagram of a typical cardiopulmonary bypass circuit with vent, field suction, aortic root suction, and cardioplegic system. 1. Blood is drained from a single 'two-stage' catheter into the venous reservoir, which is part of the membrane oxygenator/heat exchanger unit. 2. Venous blood exits the unit and is pumped through the heat exchanger and then the oxygenator. 3. Arterialized blood exits the oxygenator and passes through a filter/bubble trap to the aortic cannula, which is usually placed in the ascending aorta. 4. Blood aspirated from vents and suction systems enters a separate cardiotomy reservoir, which contains a microfilter, before entering the venous reservoir. 5. The cardioplegic system is fed by a spur from the arterial line, to which the cardioplegic solution is added and is pumped through a separate heat exchanger into the antegrade or retrograde catheters. 6. Oxygenator gases and water for the heat exchanger are supplied by independent sources.

Reproduced from 'A practical approach to cardiac anesthesia', eds. Frederick A. Hensley, Jr., Donald E. Martin, Glenn P. Gravlee, 4th ed., Philadelphia: Lippincott Williams & Wilkins; copyright 2008 with permission of Wolters Kluwer Health.

Off-pump surgery

- Beating heart surgery avoids the need for cardiopulmonary bypass, but partial cross clamping is still needed to perform proximal anastomoses on a depressurized aorta
- Suction clamps help immobilize the heart and expose target vessels whilst maintaining haemodynamic stability
- Tension snares, silastic sutures and a misted CO_2 "blower" help maintain a bloodless field
- May be associated with reduced risk of stroke, AF, respiratory and wound infections, less transfusions and shorter length of stay when performed by experienced teams
- Still not clear evidence that off-pump surgery results in superior outcomes, mainly because large numbers would be needed to produce an adequately powered trial.

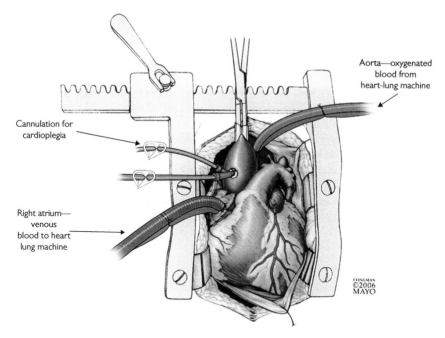

Figure 20.2 Typical cannulation sites for the heart lung machine. After full systemic heparinization, cannulation of the distal ascending aorta is performed. A two-stage venous cannula is used for access to the right atrium, usually through the right atrial appendage. An aortic root cardioplegia/vent is placed.

20.4 Airways disease

- Clinical history of airways disease is present in up to 25% of patients undergoing cardiac surgery
- Often misdiagnosed
- Diagnosis alone does not indicate severity
- Most risk scores do not include pulmonary function testing
- Moderate or severe obstruction and reduction in DLCO (<50% predicted) is independently associated with:
    - Operative mortality (up to 10× increase)
    - Prolonged ventilation time
    - Prolonged length of stay in the ICU and the hospital.

20.5 Myocardial revascularization and valve surgery

- 40% of patients with valve disease will have concomitant coronary disease
- Coronary angiography required in all cases except
    - Men <40 years old and premenopausal women with no cardiac risk factors
    - Where risks outweigh benefit, e.g. aortic dissection, aortic valve endocarditis

- Combined valve surgery and CABG:
  - Recommended in patients with a primary indication for aortic/mitral valve surgery and coronary stenosis ≥70%
  - Considered in patients with a primary indication for aortic/mitral surgery and coronary stenosis 50–70%
  - Combination of CABG and valve surgery for severe aortic stenosis reduces the rates of perioperative MI, perioperative mortality, late mortality, and morbidity when compared with patients not undergoing simultaneous CABG; carries an increased risk of mortality of 1.6–1.8% over isolated aortic valve replacement
- Combined CABG and mitral valve surgery:
  - Indicated in patients with a primary indication for CABG and severe ischaemic MR and EF >30%
  - Should be considered in patients with a primary indication for CABG and moderate ischaemic MR, provided valve repair is feasible; performed by experienced operators
- Combined CABG and aortic valve surgery should be considered in patients with a primary indication for CABG and moderate aortic stenosis.

20.6 Carotid artery stenosis and cardiac surgery

- Carotid bifurcation stenosis is
  - A marker for global atherosclerosis
  - Independent risk factor for neurological complications during CABG
- The incidence of coexisting coronary and carotid artery disease varies between 2–14%:
  - 8% of patients undergoing CABG have a significant stenosis in an extracranial carotid artery
  - ≤40% of patients undergoing carotid endartectomy (CEA) have significant CAD and may benefit from cardiac risk assessment
- Patients with previous TIA or non-disabling stroke and a carotid artery stenosis (50–99% in men or 70–99% in women) undergoing CABG have a high risk of stroke:
  - CEA may reduce the risk of stroke or death
  - Carotid revascularization may be considered in asymptomatic men with bilateral severe carotid artery stenosis or contralateral occlusion if the risk of post-procedural 30-day mortality or stroke rate <3% and life expectancy >5 years
  - In women the benefit is dubious
- No clear proof that staged or synchronous CEA or stenting is beneficial; individual assessment by a multidisciplinary team including a neurologist is recommended
- Duplex ultrasound scanning is recommended in patients with previous TIA/stroke or carotid bruit on auscultation.

Carotid revascularization

- Carotid endarterectomy or carotid artery stenting
  - Only performed by teams with demonstrated safety record
  - Indication should be individualized
  - Timing should be dictated by local expertise, targeting most symptomatic territory first
- If previous TIA/non-disabling stroke, carotid revascularization
  - Recommended in 70–99% stenosis
  - Considered 50–69% in men with symptoms <6 months
  - Not recommended <50% (men) and <70% (women)

- If no previous TIA/stroke, carotid revascularization
  - May be considered in men with bilateral 70–99% carotid stenosis or 70–99% carotid stenosis + contralateral occlusion
  - Is not recommended in women or patients with a life expectancy <5 years.

Further reading

Adabag AS, Wassif HS, Rice K, et al. Preoperative pulmonary function and mortality after cardiac surgery. Am Heart J, 2010; 159: 691–7.

Bonow RO, Carabello BA, Chatterjee K, et al. ACC/AHA 2006 guidelines for the management of patients with valvular heart disease: a report of the American College of Cardiology/American Heart Association Task Force on Practice Guidelines (writing Committee to Revise the 1998 guidelines for the management of patients with valvular heart disease) developed in collaboration with the Society of Cardiovascular Anesthesiologists endorsed by the Society for Cardiovascular Angiography and Interventions and the Society of Thoracic Surgeons. J Am Coll Cardiol, 2006; 48: e1–148.

Bridgewater B, Kinsman R, Walton P, Gummert J, Kappetein AP. The 4th European Association for Cardio-Thoracic Surgery adult cardiac surgery database report. Interact CardioVasc Thorac Surg, 2011; 12: 4–5.

Online euroSCORE calculator. Available from: http://www.euroscore.org/calc.html

Online STS Risk Calculator. Available from: http://209.220.160.181/STSWebRiskCalc261

Parsonnet V, Dean D, Bernstein AD. A method of uniformstratification of risk for evaluating the results of surgery inacquired adult heart disease. Circulation, 1989; 701: 13–112.

Shroyer AL, Grover FL, Hattler B, et al. On-pump versus off-pump coronary-artery bypass surgery. NEJM, 2009; 361: 1827.

Vahanian A, Baumgartner H, Bax J, et al. Guidelines on the management of valvular heart disease: The Task Force on the Management of Valvular Heart Disease of the European Society of Cardiology. Eur Heart J, 2007; 28: 230–68.

Wijns W, Kolh P, Danchin N, et al. Guidelines on myocardial revascularization: The Task Force on Myocardial Revascularization of the European Society of Cardiology (ESC) and the European Association for Cardio-Thoracic Surgery (EACTS). Eur Heart J, 2010; 31: 2501–55.

Management of critically ill patients with haemodynamic disturbances

CONTENTS

21.1 Shock

Shock is a common cause of admission to intensive care. It is defined as a hypotensive syndrome associated with an imbalance between tissue oxygen supply and demand.

Classically categorized as:

- Cardiac index normal or high, associated with reduced peripheral vascular resistance:
  - Septicaemia
  - Anaphylaxis
  - Neurogenic
- Cardiac index low, associated with increased peripheral vascular resistance:
  - Hypovolaemia: trauma, surgery; blood loss or loss of circulating volume via capillary leak (third space losses)
  - Cardiogenic—MI, myocarditis
  - Obstructive—tamponade, pulmonary embolus, pneumothorax.

In shock states, tissue perfusion is impaired at the microcirculatory level despite an adequate cardiac output:

- Obstruction to flow, secondary to thrombosis, neutrophil accumulation, platelet aggregation
- Shunting, possibly due to nitric oxide induced vasodilatation.

This results in

- Depletion of cellular ATP and anaerobic metabolism, resulting in lactic acidosis
- Cell swelling, secondary to loss of cell membrane integrity and sodium influx
- Mitochondrial dysfunction
- Progressive organ dysfunction associated with cell death and apoptosis.

BOX 21.1 COMMON NON-INFECTIVE CAUSES OF SIRS/MODS

Surgery
Transfusion/transfusion reaction
Trauma/burns
Hepatic failure
Visceral ischaemia
Renal failure
Ischaemia-reperfusion
Cardiopulmonary bypass
Pancreatitis
Cancer
Anaphylaxis
Lung injury, e.g. secondary to mechanical ventilation

Types of shock frequently overlap. Any event that significantly reduces tissue blood flow and oxygen delivery (particularly to the kidneys and GI tract) can trigger a set of cytokine responses that:

- Produce a systemic inflammatory response syndrome (SIRS), which can progress to multiple organ dysfunction syndrome (MODS) (see Box 21.1)
- Present many of the features of septic shock, without obvious infective causes in up to 50% of cases.

In MODS—three-organ failure is associated with 60% mortality.

Common complications of shock

- Peripheral vasoplegia: reduced sensitivity to vasoconstrictors is common, probably related to inappropriate nitric oxide production and endothelial injury in the microcirculation
- Acute respiratory distress syndrome (ARDS): initially a low-pressure pulmonary oedema associated with inflammatory infiltrates, which progresses to fibrosis over several days. Secondary infection is a common complication. Mechanical ventilation is usually required
- Myocardial depression: circulating factors in shock states can reduce cardiac performance in previously healthy hearts. Some improvement in cardiac function can usually be achieved with careful fluid administration, even in cardiogenic shock
- Renal failure: can be due to pre-renal factors, e.g. low cardiac output, or impaired autoregulation of blood flow within the kidney. Typically lasts 5–10 days, requiring temporary renal support. Associated with 40% excess mortality
- Hepatic dysfunction: reduced lactate clearance may exacerbate lactic acidosis
- Encephalopathy correlates with mortality. Reduced conscious level; may require intubation to protect the airway
- Disseminated intravascular coagulation.

21.2 Non-surgical cardiology admissions to intensive care

Common causes:
- Elective:
  - Preventative insertion of intra-aortic balloon pump (IABP)
  - Recovery and monitoring following percutaneous valvular procedures
  - Renal replacement therapy (RRT) in patients with renal impairment

- Emergency:
  - Invasive monitoring to establish diagnosis or titrate inotropic support
  - Invasive procedure such as IABP, RRT, or mechanical support
  - Pulmonary oedema and respiratory failure requiring ventilatory support
  - Life-threatening complications from catheter laboratory
  - Therapeutic hypothermia post-cardiac arrest.

Treatment of shock states

Philosophy of treatment is based around restoring effective tissue perfusion and oxygen delivery. Avoidance of secondary organ injury and infection is paramount.

- Initial resuscitation to restore mean arterial pressure of 60–70 mmHg. Fluid challenges, inotropic and vasopressor therapy address key components of circulatory function (see Figure 21.1)
- Invasive or non-invasive monitoring of cardiovascular performance to guide inotropic and vasopressor therapy—see Section 21.3
- Investigation and diagnostic testing; echocardiography may play a vital role
- Treatment of the underlying cause; may require surgery despite the shock state
- Maintenance of circulating volume; ongoing capillary leak may impair adequate circulating volume despite positive fluid balance
- Maintaining cardiac index to ensure adequate oxygen transport: a minimal value of 2.2 l/min/m². This may be achieved with volume alone or require inotropic support. Some advocate supra-normal values; this is controversial
- Ventilatory support for respiratory failure, a common consequence of shock states—see Section 21.6
- Support of individual organ systems, e.g. renal replacement therapy; continuous veno-venous haemofiltration or dialysis
- Control of hyperglycaemia, which may impair endothelial, mitochondrial, and immune function, using intravenous insulin to keep blood sugar <8–10 mmol/l
- Low-dose hydrocortisone reduces vasopressor requirements. Effect on survival remains controversial; increased infection rates have been reported
- Support of the circulation until recovery of organ function allows discharge from ICU; in practice this is until patients no longer require ventilator support or inotrope/vasopressor therapy

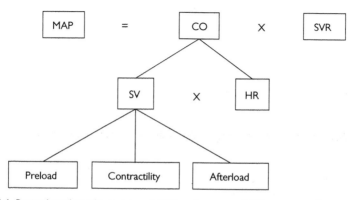

Figure 21.1 Basic physiological principles of CVS performance. MAP, mean arterial pressure; SV, stroke volume; CO, cardiac output; HR, heart rate; SVR, systemic vascular resistance.

● Discharge planning for long term support, e.g. renal unit for ongoing dialysis, cardiology service for management of impaired ventricular function
● **Cardiovascular management in shock is directed to each factor, guided by clinical examination, invasive monitoring, and relevant investigations.**

Causes of cardiac dysfunction in intensive care unit

Cardiology involvement in ICU is often required to delineate cardiac causes of shock or define extent of complications. Ventricular dysfunction may be:

● Diastolic or systolic
● Acute, or chronic following decompensation of long-standing pathology.

See Tables 21.1 and 21.2 for causes of dysfunction.

Other cardiovascular causes of shock:
  ● Pericardial compression
    ▪ Tamponade—pericarditis, aortic dissection, cardiac rupture
  ● Obstructed flow
    ▪ Dynamic LVOT obstruction
    ▪ Obstruction to venous return: tension pneumothorax, dynamic hyperinflation, ventilator dysynchrony.

Circulatory arrest

Cardiac arrest is treated according to current guidelines.

Treatment

Unconscious adults with return of spontaneous circulation after VF arrest should be cooled to 32–34°C as soon as possible for at least 24 h.

Table 21.1 Causes of left ventricular dysfunction

Acute causes	Chronic causes
Myocardial stunning	Myocardial ischaemia
Myocardial ischaemia	Valvular dysfunction
Myocardial infarction and mechanical complication post MI: VSD, free wall rupture	Cardiomyopathy
Drugs	
SIRS	
Hypertensive crisis	
Acute myocarditis	
Acute pericarditis	
Post-partum cardiomyopathy	
Arrhythmia	
Valvular dysfunction: endocarditis	

Table 21.2 Causes of right ventricular dysfunction

Systolic	Volume overload	Pressure overload (High PVR)	
		Acute	Chronic
Myocardial stunning	Excess fluid	PE	Chronic pulmonary disease
Myocardial infarction	Pulmonary or tricuspid regurgitation	Mechanical ventilation	Left heart valvular disease
Myocardial ischaemia	ASD	SIRS	Pulmonary vascular occlusive disease: Eisenmengers, chronic PE, primary pulmonary hypertension
	Ruptured sinus of valsalva aneurysm	Hypoxaemia	
		Hypercarbia	
		Acidaemia	Pulmonary valve stenosis

21.3 Specialized monitoring on the intensive care unit

Preload assessment

- Assessment of circulating volume remains controversial; studies have shown poor correlation with CVP and pulmonary artery occlusion pressure (PAOP)
- Assessment of cardiac preload remains controversial; studies have also shown a poor correlation between stroke volume (SV) response to fluid challenges and either CVP or PAOP measurements in intensive care patients
- Alternative means of assessing likelihood of an SV response to fluid loading are now well validated:
    - Variation in invasively measured systolic pressure or pulse pressure with mechanical ventilation; over 10% change predicts a positive response to fluid challenge. This is not valid if patients are breathing spontaneously
    - Passive leg-raising test; may be used in both mechanical ventilation and spontaneous breathing in association with cardiac output measurement.

Cardiac output assessment

- Cardiac output monitoring is an important part of assessment and management of shock states
- Inadequate cardiac output despite therapy is associated with high mortality.

Pulmonary artery catheters

- Pulmonary artery catheters enable both cardiac output and estimates of preload to be assessed (see Table 21.3). They remain the 'gold standard' against which other devices are compared. There is still no good evidence that pulmonary artery catheters improve outcome in any group of patients
- The catheter is inserted to 15 cm, where the CVP waveform is visible
- The balloon is then inflated and the catheter slowly advanced into the wedge position at 45–55 cm. The pressure waveform can be observed to confirm placement
- Once the measurements have been completed, the balloon is deflated to avoid damage to the vessels.

Measurement

- A thermodilution technique is used to calculate the cardiac output. A fast bolus of cold saline is injected into the right atrium and the temperature in the pulmonary artery is measured over time

Table 21.3 Types of lumen and uses

Lumen	Use
Distal	Measures pulmonary artery pressures and can be used for blood sampling.
Balloon	Proximal to catheter tip. Inflation with 1.5 ml air allows placement of the catheter in the pulmonary artery and measurement of the occlusion pressure.
Thermistor	Proximal to balloon lumen. Wires travel down the lumen enabling temperature measurement for the calculation of cardiac output.
Proximal	30 cm from tip. Measures CVP waveform and is used during measurements to inject fast bolus of cold saline.

- A high flow (cardiac output) dilutes the cold saline rapidly; there is a small temperature change detected at the thermistor. A low cardiac output state does not dilute the temperature; there is a large temperature drop detected at the thermistor
- Three consecutive measurements are averaged out to account for respiratory variation in right ventricular volumes
- Some values may be directly measured (see Table 21.4), others are calculated (see Table 21.5).

Indications for pulmonary artery catheters
- Diagnostic assessment of shock states (cardiogenic, distributive, hypovolaemic) and assessment of response to treatment

Table 21.4 Measured values

Direct measurement	Normal values	Implication
Right atrium	0–5 mmHg	CVP
Right ventricle	25/5 mmHg	
Pulmonary artery	25/10 mmHg	RV afterload
Pulmonary artery occlusion pressure	6–12 mmHg	LA pressure, LVEDP, i.e. preload
Cardiac output	3.5–7.5 l/min	
Mixed venous oxygen saturations	70–75%	Oxygen delivery and consumption

Table 21.5 Calculated values

Calculated variables	Normal range
Systemic vascular resistance	800–1600 dynes.s.cm^{-5}
Pulmonary vascular resistance	40–160 dynes.s.cm^{-5}
Stroke volume	60–90 ml
Mixed arterial oxygen content (CaO_2)	16–20 ml/dl
Mixed venous oxygen content (CvO_2)	13–15 ml/dl
Arteriovenous oxygen difference ($avDO_2$)	3–5 ml/dl
Oxygen delivery (DO_2)	600–1400 ml/min
Oxygen consumption (VO_2)	180–280 ml/min
Oxygen extraction ratio (ERO_2)	20–30%

- LV preload and LV performance, pulmonary vasomotor tone, intravascular volume status, especially in the context of acute lung injury
- Right heart pressures
- Intracardiac shunt.

Limitations

The PAOP only *approximates* left ventricular end diastolic pressure (LVEDP) and is based on the assumptions of:

- A continuous column from right-side heart to left-side heart
- A normal mitral valve
- Normal LV compliance.

There are problems of misrepresentation when:

- The catheter tip is outside West's zone 3 (i.e. $P_{alveolar} > P_{venous}$)
- There is mitral valve dysfunction, e.g. mitral stenosis, mitral regurgitation, atrial myxoma (PAOP > LVEDP)
- There is LV dysfunction (PAOP < LVEDP)
- Tricuspid valve regurgitation confounds cardiac output measurement: an unknown fraction of the cold injectate is not delivered to the thermistor.

Complications

These are uncommon, but can be catastrophic:

- Arrhythmias
- Thromboembolic events
- Lung infarction: obstruction to blood flow
- Mechanical complications
- Infective complications
- Pulmonary artery rupture.

Alternative cardiac output monitors

For cardiac output measurements see Table 21.6.

LiDCO (lithium dilution continuous cardiac output)

- Cardiac output is first measured by indicator dilution; a fixed dose of lithium is injected via a central or peripheral vein and detected by a sensor attached to a peripheral arterial cannula
- SV is then derived from a mathematical transformation of the arterial waveform and calibrated using the measured cardiac output
- Continuous cardiac output and SV are displayed from continuous arterial waveform analysis.

PICCO (pulse contour cardiac output)

For pulse contour cardiac output see Table 21.6.

- Cardiac output is calibrated using thermodilution. A fast bolus of cold saline is injected centrally and a thermistor attached to a peripheral arterial cannula detects the temperature change
- Continuous SV is derived from pulse contour analysis of the arterial pressure trace; the area under the systolic portion of the trace bears an indirect relationship with SV
- Aortic compliance is calculated from the rate of decline of the diastolic down-slope on the arterial pressure trace, which also provides a measure of pulse pressure. Systemic vascular resistance (SVR) can then be derived once the CVP is known
- Volumetric indices can be calculated, utilizing the mean transit times of the initial thermodilution curve measurement, to guide fluid therapy:
    - The intrathoracic thermal volume (ITTV)

Table 21.6 Measurements

Measurement	Normal values	Indices
Cardiac index	3.0–5.0 l/min/m²	Flow
Pulse pressure variation	<10%	Volume responsiveness
Stroke volume variation	<10%	Volume responsiveness
Global end-diastolic volume index	680–800 ml/m²	Preload
Intrathoracic blood volume index	850–1000 ml/m²	Preload
Systemic vascular resistance index	1700–2400 dynes.s/cm⁵/m²	Afterload
Cardiac function index	4.5–6.5 l/min	Cardiac contractility
Global ejection fraction	25–35%	Cardiac contractility
Extravascular lung water index	3.0–7.0 ml/kg	Pulmonary oedema
Pulmonary vascular permeability index	1.0–3.0	Pulmonary oedema
Oesophageal Doppler		
Flow time corrected	330–360 ms	Afterload
Peak velocity	50–120 cm/s	Cardiac contractility

- Extravascular lung water (EVLW)
- Pulmonary thermal volume (PTV)
- Subtraction of PTV from ITTV gives a measure of the volume of the heart, termed the global end-diastolic volume, an estimate of total cardiac filling.

Systolic pressure variation
(See Figure 21.2).

- Arterial pressure monitors are able to provide an index of fluid (preload) responsiveness by measuring the degree of variation or downward 'swing' in arterial pressure in response to intermittent positive pressure ventilation:
  - An increase in intrathoracic pressure inhibits venous return to the right ventricle
  - The effect of this reduction in preload depends on the position of the left ventricle on the Starling curve

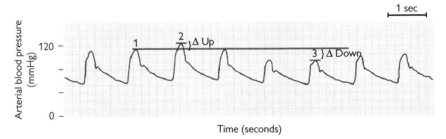

Figure 21.2 Systolic pressure variation in arterial waveform. Systolic pressure variation (SPV) during positive pressure mechanical ventilation. End-expiratory systolic blood pressure (1) serves as a baseline from which an early inspiratory increase (2, ΔUp) can be measured, followed by a delayed decrease (3, ΔDown). The large ΔDown and total SPV of nearly 30 mmHg suggests the diagnosis of hypovolemia, despite the fact that tachycardia and hypotension are not present. ART, arterial blood pressure.

Reproduced from the Oxford Specialist Handbook of Cardiac Anaesthesia, Matthew Barnard and Bruce Martin, copyright 2010 with permission of Oxford University Press.

■ On the plateau part of the curve, such a reduction has a minimal effect on SV, but on the ascending part of the curve it gives rise to a significant reduction in SV, indicated by a fall in both systolic and pulse pressure
■ Right ventricular failure and cardiac tamponade also cause arterial pressure variation, diagnosed with echocardiography
- Normal value <10%
- Measurement requires the patient to be fully ventilated and in sinus rhythm.

Oesophageal Doppler
See Table 21.6.
- Probe inserted into the oesophagus, which measures the change of frequency of an ultrasound beam transmitted and received from the probe in the descending aorta
- The frequency change measured directly correlates with the speed of blood travelling through the aorta. The integral of the blood velocity–time waveform represents stroke distance. If this is combined with the aortic cross-sectional area (estimated by weight, height, and age), the SV can be calculated
- Specific aspects of the velocity–time waveform correspond with pre-load, afterload, and contractility.

Thoracic impedance and bioreactance
- Electrodes attached to the chest deliver an electric current of known frequency and amplitude
- Bioimpedance: changes in blood volume throughout the cardiac cycle can be detected by changes in trans-thoracic current amplitude
- Thoracic bioreactance is an improvement on bioimpedance. Cardiac output is calculated using the change in frequency and phase of an alternating electrical current, which correlates with change in aortic flow
- Blood pressure and CVP are added to derive other cardiovascular variables.

21.4 Inotropes

Inotropes vary in their pharmacological profiles (see Tables 21.7 and 21.8). However, there are no randomized trials that demonstrate superiority of one over another in shock. Inotropes work predominantly by their effects on the autonomic nervous system (see Figure 21.3).

Dobutamine
- Inodilator
- Beta agonist: $\beta_1 >> \beta_2$
- Increases cardiac ouput by increased contractility and heart rate, but this may increase oxygen requirements
- β_2 effects cause vasodilatation, reducing SVR.

Dopamine
- Inoconstrictor
- α_1 effects cause vasoconstriction
- β effects increase cardiac output by increased heart rate and contractility
- Dopaminergic effects vasodilate the renal and mesenteric blood vessels.

Table 21.7 Pharmacological profiles of inotropes

Receptor	Cardiovascular action	Drugs
Acetylcholine		
Muscarinic	Bradycardia Reduced conduction velocity Vasodilatation	Atropine Glycopyrolate
Nicotinic	Ganglionic: not direct	
Adrenergic		
Alpha 1	Vasoconstriction	Noradrenaline, metaraminol, adrenaline
Alpha 2	Inhibit noradrenaline release	Clonidine
Beta 1	Inotropic Chronotropic	Dobutamine, adrenaline, dopamine, isoprenaline, dopexamine
Beta 2	Vasodilatation	Dobutamine, dopexamine
Dopaminergic		
DA 1	Vasodilatation of renal and mesenteric vascular beds	Dopamine, dopexamine
DA 2	Inhibits noradrenaline release	Dopamine, dopexamine

Table 21.8 Effect of inotropes on cardiac function

	HR	Inotrope	SVR	BP	CO	Bolus	Dose
Adrenergic agonists							
Dobutamine	↑↑	↑↑	↓	↑	↑↑	No	2–20 µg/kg/min
Dopamine	↑	↑	↑↑	↑	↑	No	2–10 µg/kg/min
Adrenaline	↑	↑↑↑	↑↑↑	↑↑	→	No	0.05–0.5 µg/kg/min
Noradrenaline	→	→	↑	↑↑	→	No	0.02–0.2 µg/kg/min
Metaraminol	→	→	↑	↑↑	→	No	0.2–1.0 µg/kg/min
Phosphodiesterase inhibitors							
Enoximone	↑	↑↑	↓	↓↓	↑↑	0.25–0.75 mg/kg	1.25–7.5 µg/kg/min
Milrinone	↑	↑↑	↓	↓↓	↑↑	25–75 µg/kg	0.375–0.750 µg/kg/min
Calcium sensitizers							
Levosimendan	↑	↑↑	↓↓	↓	↑↑	12–24 µg/kg	0.05–0.20 µg/kg/min
Other							
Vasopressin	→	→	↑↑↑	↑↑	↓	No	0.5–2.5 units/h

Noradrenaline

- Vasopressor
- Works by α_1 receptor action, although it does have some β effects

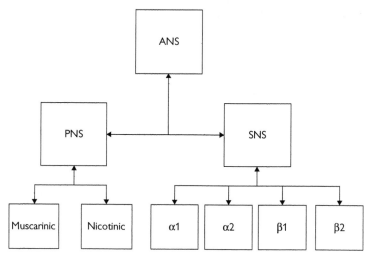

Figure 21.3 Basic physiology of the autonomic nervous system.

- It causes peripheral vasoconstriction of the afferent arterioles, which initially may cause a reflex bradycardia
- It causes a tachycardia in higher doses due to a small beta effect
- Reduces renal and hepatic blood flow.

Phosphodiesterase inhibitors
- Inodilators; increase cardiac output and decrease pulmonary artery pressure, PAOP, SVR, and PVR.

Levosimendan
- Has both anti-ischaemic and cardioprotective effects
- Sensitizes troponin C to calcium, enhancing myocardial contractility without substantial changes in oxygen consumption
- Activates the adenosine triphosphate-sensitive potassium channel, producing vasodilatory effects that decrease preload and afterload.

Vasopressin
- Antidiuretic hormone analogue
- Acts on V1 receptors located in the efferent arterioles to cause vasoconstriction.

21.5 Mechanical support devices

Intra-aortic balloon pump
- Placed in thoracic aorta distal to origin of left subclavian artery
- The catheter has two channels, one to inflate and deflate the helium balloon, the other to directly monitor aortic blood pressure.

Mechanism

- The timing of the inflation and deflation is triggered by the patient's ECG or arterial waveform (see Figure 21.4)
- During diastole the balloon is inflated
- At the end of diastole the balloon is deflated, before isovolumetric contraction
- The inflation ratio refers to the number of inflations to QRS complexes e.g. 1:1, 1:2. The augmentation percentage (10–100%) determines how fully the balloon is inflated
- In normal use, it is initiated with 1:1 and 100% augmentation
- The timings of the triggers should be checked regularly and adjusted to optimize the support provided (see Table 21.9).

Indications

Ischaemic myocardium:
- Unstable angina despite maximal medical therapy
- Ischaemia-induced ventricular arrhythmia
- Elective support in high-risk percutaneous coronary intervention, e.g. refractory angina post-MI.

Cardiogenic shock:
- After MI
- Acute myocarditis
- Acute deterioration of chronic heart failure
- After cardiotomy
- Acute donor organ failure.

Cardiac surgery:
- Assist weaning off cardiopulmonary bypass
- Treat haemodynamic instability after surgery
- Pre-operative placement in high-risk patients undergoing surgery, e.g. CABG with acute ischaemia or ejection fractions less than 25%
- Acute mitral valve dysfunction
- Acute ventricular septal defect.

All patients without contraindications should receive an IABP for at least 3 days, for recovery from myocardial stunning.

Contraindications

- Severe aortic regurgitation
- Aortic dissection
- Severe atheromatous disease of descending thoracic aorta
- Occlusive vascular disease involving the distal aorta or the femoral or iliac arteries.

Limitations

- Excessive tachycardia or irregular pulse → causes alterations in diastole length → reduced effectiveness.

Complications of insertion

- Position related: left arm ischaemia (too proximal) or renal ischaemia (too distal)
- Vascular injury 15%: dissection, rupture or haemorrhage, pseudoaneurysm

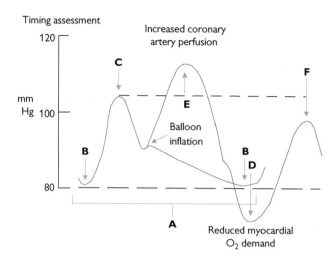

Figure 21.4 Mechanism of intra-aortic balloon pump. IABP: A, one cardiac cycle; B, unassisted end diastole; C, unassisted systole; D, assisted end diastole; E, augmented diastole; F, assisted systole.

Reproduced with kind permission from MAQUET Cardiovascular.

Table 21.9 Effects of IABP

Stage	Effect
Overall	Augments cardiac output Increases mean diastolic pressure Decreases mean systolic pressure Mean arterial pressure unchanged Reduces pulmonary capillary wedge pressure (LA pressure) Relieves pulmonary congestion
Inflation	Increases diastolic aortic pressure *Increases coronary perfusion pressure* Augments coronary blood flow Improves myocardial oxygen delivery
Deflation	Reduced LVEDP Reduces peak left ventricular wall stress and stroke work *Reduced left ventricular afterload* Increases left ventricular ejection i.e. cardiac output *Decreases myocardial oxygen demand* Reduces mitral valve regurgitation

- Thromboembolism: systemic anticoagulation often used
- Peripheral vasoconstriction and low CO state can cause distal limb ischemia
- Infection
- Thrombocytopenia
- Rupture of balloon causing gas embolism; blood seen tracking down the gas channel and IABP must be removed.

Weaning
- Inotropic support normally weaned first to avoid rhythm disturbances
- CI maintained above 2.2 l/min/m²
- Acceptable preload (PAOP <15 mmHg)
- Augmentation reduced to 50%, then inflation ratios to 1:3
- Heparin discontinued so that coagulation normal at the end of weaning for catheter removal.

Ventricular assist devices
- Take over ventricular systolic function; left, right, or biventricular
- Used as a bridge to recovery or transplantation, or as permanent support.

Mechanism
- Mechanical pump:
  - Inflow and outflow cannulas: parallel (atrial cannulation) or in series (ventricular cannulation) with the native ventricle
  - Pulsatile, displacing a 'stoke volume' from the chamber, or non-pulsatile, continuous flow using an axial pump
  - Extracorporeal or implantable pump
- External power source
- Control unit
- Anticoagulation.

Types
- Left ventricular assist device (LVAD):
  - Oxygenated blood from the left atrium/ventricle to aorta
  - Relies on adequate RV function to deliver adequate blood across the lungs into the left heart chambers
- Right ventricular assist device (RVAD):
  - Venous blood from right atrium/ventricle to pulmonary artery
  - Relies on adequate LV to generate enough stroke work
- Biventricular: two-VAD.

Indications
These patients fall into four categories:
1. Cardiogenic shock following heart surgery
2. Cardiogenic shock following acute myocardial infarction
3. Acute heart failure, usually following myocarditis, cardiomyopathy, or drug overdose
4. Decompensated chronic heart failure; most common indication for long-term VAD.

Patient criteria:
- Maximal medical therapy:
  - Maximal inotropic support, optimal ventricular filling and full IABP augmentation
- Haemodynamic parameters:
  - Cardiac output <2 l/min
  - PAOP >20 mmHg
  - SBP <90 mmHg with signs of impending organ dysfunction
  - Chronic heart failure: LV ejection fraction <25%, SBP <80 mmHg, VO_{2max} <12–14 ml/kg/min (peak oxygen consumption)

- Chance of recovery
- Patient would be a candidate for heart transplantation (unless permanent support implicated)
- Non-cardiac considerations:
  - Age <65 years
  - No significant neurological impairment
  - No significant liver dysfunction
  - No severe renal dysfunction
  - Absence of multiple organ dysfunction syndrome.

Complications

- Perioperative haemorrhage
- Low pump flows: right ventricular dysfunction, hypovolaemia, tamponade, obstruction to inflow of cannula
- Arrhythmias → thromboembolism (exclude ASD or PFO)
- Infection
- Neurological injury (CVE)
- Mechanical pump failure.

21.6 Haemodynamic effects of positive pressure ventilation

Intubation and mechanical ventilation is the mainstay of respiratory support in ICU. Non-invasive ventilation is an alternative in many situations, but shares many of the same indications and physiological consequences (see Table 21.10).

Types

- Volume controlled ventilation: predetermined volume delivered. Airway pressures dependent on lung compliance
- Pressure controlled ventilation: predetermined pressures delivered. Tidal volume dependent on lung compliance.

Table 21.10 Indications for Positive Pressure Ventilation

Respiratory	Non-respiratory
Pneumonia	Airway obstruction
Cardiogenic pulmonary oedema	Airway protection, e.g. reduced Glasgow Coma Scale
Acute lung injury, acute respiratory distress syndrome	Severe sepsis or shock
Control of CO_2, e.g. head injury	Post-operative hypothermia or acidosis
PE	Cardiogenic shock
Acute severe asthma	Therapeutic hypothermia post-cardiac arrest
Acute exacerbation of COPD	Neuromuscular disorders e.g. Guillain Barré syndrome
Impaired respiratory drive causing apnoea or hypoventilation, e.g. overdose	Severe anaemia where transfusion is contraindicated e.g. Jehovah's witness

Mode

- Spontaneous—patient drives own breathing
- Mandatory: ventilator drives breathing; uncomfortable for patient and relatively deep sedation is required
- Assisted/support/demand: patient drives inspiration, ventilator supports inspiration. More commonly used in lightly sedated patients because it is well tolerated and can assist weaning
- Positive end expiratory pressure (PEEP): minimizes airway and alveolar collapse during expiration, increasing FRC, therefore increasing lung compliance.

Physiological effects of positive pressure ventilation

The physiological consequences are largely the result of increased intrathoracic pressure compared with spontaneous breathing (see Table 21.11). The adverse effects positive pressure ventilation can be minimized by using spontaneous breathing or non-invasive modes.

Table 21.11 Physiological consequences of Positive Pressure Ventilation

Effect	Explanation
Cardiovascular	
↓ RV preload	Increased intrathoracic pressure reduces venous return, decreases RV volume (preload) but increases RV pressure
↑ RV afterload	Increased PVR
↔ RV contractility	No evidence of impaired contractility
↓ LV preload	Reduced filling due to increased PVR. Reduced compliance due to bulging of intraventricular septum with high PEEP as RV pressure increases.
↓ LV afterload	Circulatory reflexes reduce SVR and improve LV emptying
↔ LV contractility	May be impaired in IHD due to altered coronary blood flow
↔/↓ HR	Impaired baroreceptor reflexes
↓CO	Reduced preload + HR
Respiratory	
↓ Work of breathing	↑FRC, ↓transdiaphragmatic pressure + muscle activity →↑TV, ↓RR → ↑MV
↑ A-a gradient	Atelectasis in dependent lung and increased dead space
Other	
↑ ICP	Elevated CVP and pulmonary artery pressures Reduction in CO may reduce MAP
Renal	Reduced renal perfusion (low CO + increased venous pressure) GFR reduced and RAA stimulated ANP secretion lowered and vasopressin secretion increased → reduced UO and sodium retention
Gastrointestinal	Reduced CO and MAP → reduced splanchnic blood flow Ileus: mechanism unknown

RV, right ventricle; LV, left ventricle; HR, heart rate; CO, cardiac output; IHD, ischaemic heart disease; PVR, pulmonary vascular resistance; PEEP, positive end expiratory pressure; SVR, systemic vascular resistance; FRC, functional residual capacity; TV, tidal volume; RR, respiratory rate; MV, minute ventilation; ICP, intracranial pressure; CVP, central venous pressure; MAP, mean arterial pressure; CO, cardiac output; GFR, glomerular filtration rate; RAA, renal, angiotensin, aldosterone; ANP, atrial natriuretic peptide; UO, urine output.

Clinical consequences of physiological effects

- RV dysfunction or hypovolaemia:
    - Reduction in RV preload can precipitate hypotension. This is exacerbated by PEEP and can be treated by loading with IV fluids
    - Increased RV afterload can be caused by high lung volumes (high pressures or PEEP), which may compress the pulmonary capillaries, impacting cardiac output
    - Reduced LV preload may reduce cardiac output and BP
- LV dysfunction:
    - Cardiac output may improve because increases in intrathoracic pressure reduce transmural gradients across the LV, thereby reducing wall stress and LV afterload.

Care of the patient following cardiac surgery

CONTENTS

22.1 Introduction

- Cardiac surgery encompasses a number of procedures and a variety of patient types. However, many of the objectives in the post-operative period are common to all and are suitable for protocol driven care by the nursing staff of the Intensive Care Unit (ICU)
- The overall goal of the ICU after uncomplicated cardiac surgery is to discharge patients to the ward or step-down care within 24hrs
- Some cardiac surgery centres manage routine patients in recovery units, using fast track protocols that avoid intensive care admission for patients with good ventricular function and minimal co-morbidity.

A normal cardiac surgery time-course

- Admit to ICU
- Within 3 hours—warm to 36.5 °C
- Within 6 hours—extubate
- ICU overnight—wean vasoactive/inotropic drugs and analgese
- Next morning—multidisciplinary ward round. Remove drains, arterial lines and pulmonary artery catheter (if used)
- Midmorning/afternoon—transfer to ward or step-down unit.

Patients are (in general) reviewed every 2–4hrs by the medical staff during their time on the ICU.

Assessment and care

- The approach to the cardiac surgical patient on intensive care is essentially the same as any other critically ill patient
- Both assessment and care of the patient are best managed by a systems based approach under the following headings:
  - Airway and breathing
  - Circulation and fluids
  - Renal, electrolytes

- Neurology and analgesia
- GI and feeding
- Bleeding and anti-coagulation
- Infection and antibiotics
- Drugs.

22.2 Management of specific issues

Airway and breathing
Ventilation
- Mechanical ventilation is continued from the operating theatre and adjusted to maintain the pH, $PaCO_2$ and PaO_2 within normal limits for the patient
- There is frequently a pre-induction arterial blood gas for comparison
- Those with a balanced circulation and reactive pulmonary vasculature require extra care to maintain these close to normal to avoid profound falls in cardiac output and hypoxia.

Weaning ventilation and extubation
For the uncomplicated cardiac surgical patient this is protocol driven by the ICU nurse, without any specific intervention from the medical staff.
  Sedation is stopped when:

- The patient is haemodynamically stable, on little or no inotropic support.
- There is no metabolic derangement (pH within normal range, BE < -4, serum lactate <2)
- Core temperature >36.5°C
- There is adequate gas exchange (FiO_2 <0.50, PaO_2 >75mmHg (10kPa), $PaCO_2$ <53mmHg (7kPa)
- Chest drainage is <100mls/hr for 2 consecutive hours.

Criteria for extubation:

- Patient awake and obeying commands
- Adequate analgesia
- Respiratory rate 8–25 bpm
- Tidal volume (V_T) ≥6ml/kg
- PEEP 5cmH$_2$O
- Pressure support <10cmH$_2$O
- Patients should be extubated onto humidified oxygen, which should be continued for 48–72 hrs post-operatively to prevent desaturation
- Patients should be encouraged to deep breathe and cough to aid in lung recruitment and prevent sputum retention.

Respiratory failure
- The major determinant of outcome is cardiac function
- Some degree of respiratory failure is common (2–20%) following cardiac surgery and is a continuing source of morbidity and mortality
- Pathology ranges from sputum retention and atelectasis to acute lung injury (ALI), and acute respiratory distress syndrome (ARDS)
- Common causes of respiratory failure after cardiac surgery are shown in Figure 22.1.

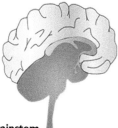

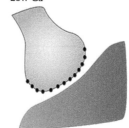

Peripheral nerves
- Neuropathy
- Critical care neuropathy

Neuromuscular junction
- Neuromuscular blockers
- Gentamicin
- High Mg^{2+} levels
- Low Ca^{2+}

Respiratory muscles
- Fatigue
- Disuse atrophy
- Myopathy
- Malnutrition
- Hypophosphataemia

Respiratory system
- Airway obstruction
  o upper or lower
- Decreased lung, pleural or chest wall compliance
- Cardiac failure
- Infection

Brainstem
- Haemorrhage, infarction, hypoxia, infection
- Metabolic encephalopathy
- Sedative drugs

Spinal cord
- Ischaemia
- Haemorrhage

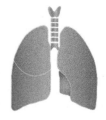

Figure 22.1 Causes of post-operative respiratory failure and failure to wean from the ventilator on the Cardiac Intensive Care Unit.

BOX 22.1 GOALS FOR TREATING RESPIRATORY FAILURE

- $SaO_2 > 90\%$ / $PaO_2 > 7kPa$ (55mmHg)
- pH > 7.25
- RR < 30
- Ability to speak in short sentences
- Ability to protect airway
- Haemodynamic stability.

Treatment of respiratory failure is essentially supportive and is aimed at reaching the goals shown in Box 22.1.

- These goals can be achieved using a stepwise progression through supplemental oxygen/ CPAP/non-invasive ventilation and tracheal intubation and ventilation
- Ventilation should follow a lung protective strategy, which has been shown to minimize ventilator induced lung injury:
  - $FiO_2 < 0.6$
  - Tidal volume <6ml/kg
  - Permissive hypercapnia where possible
  - Pressure limited ventilation (peak airway pressure <35cmH$_2$O).

Circulation

Pacing

- Epicardial pacing wires are placed in many cardiac surgical patients
- Some surgeons place them in all patients, some only when specifically indicated e.g. valve surgery (transient injury to the A-V node) or conducting system is more likely
- There is usually institution-specific coding as to which wires are atrial and which are ventricular
- Pacing wires are usually removed on day 3–6 post-op
- Patients who still require pacing 72hrs post-op should be considered for a permanent pacemaker
- Heparin should be stopped 4hrs prior to removal and the INR should be <2.5 for patients taking warfarin
- Tamponade is a real risk, even in patients with a normal coagulation profile and therefore patients should be closely observed for 4hrs following wire removal.

Vasoactive drugs and LV dysfunction

- Titrated to haemodynamic parameters or may be maintained at a constant level for a set period (such as 24hrs)
- Cardiac output falls immediately after cardiac surgery with cardiopulmonary bypass (CPB), but usually returns to normal over 24hrs when pre-operative LV function is normal (Fig. 22.2)
- In those with impaired LV function, this may be prolonged
- There is little information about what happens to postoperative cardiac output in those having 'off-pump' surgery
- LV dysfunction can occur for a number of remediable reasons and these should be corrected before starting vasoactive medicines
- Common causes of LV dysfunction after cardiac surgery are shown in Box 22.2
- The approach to the patient with post-operative LV dysfunction is the same as optimizing any patient's cardiac output. Namely optimization of:
    - Remove/reverse any precipitating factor
    - Heart rate—80–100bpm, paced if needed

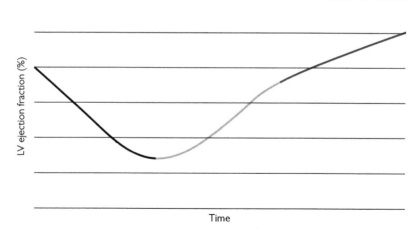

Figure 22.2 LV ejection fraction following 'on-pump' coronary artery surgery.

Adapted from 'Perioperative myocardial infarction and changes in left ventricular performance related to coronary artery bypass graft surgery', Arthur J. Roberts, Ann Thorac Surg. 1983 Feb; 35 (2): 208–25

BOX 22.2 COMMON REASONS FOR LV DYSFUNCTION AFTER CARDIAC SURGERY

- Metabolic abnormalities
- Low [Ca^{2+}] due to citrated blood
- Myocardial ischaemia/infarction
  - Stent/graft thombosis
  - Vessel/graft occlusion
  - Coronary vasospasm
- Drugs—β-blockers
- Prolonged bypass times (>2hrs)
- Myocardial stunning secondary to ischaemia reperfusion injury.

BOX 22.3 CAUSES OF POST-OPERATIVE RV DYSFUNCTION.

- **Systolic dysfunction**
  - Myocardial stunning
  - Myocardial ischaemia / infarction
- **RV volume overload**
  - Excess fluid administration
  - PV regurgitation
  - TV regurgitation
  - ASD
- **RV pressure overload**
  - Hypoxia
  - Hypercarbia
  - Acidosis
  - Over-PEEP
  - Pulmonary embolus
  - Chronic pulmonary disease
  - PV Stenosis
  - Pulmonary vascular occlusive disease.

- Heart rhythm— maintain sinus rhythm where able or A-V sequential pacing
- Pre-load—fluid challenges to assess responsiveness
- Afterload—reducing vasopressors/intra-aortic balloon pump
- Contractility— using inotropic drugs/intra-aortic balloon pumps and ventricular assist devices.

RV dysfunction
- This is extremely difficult to manage due to 'ventricular interaction' i.e. the failing RV can also impair LV function
- It accounts for about 20% of circulatory failure after cardiac surgery (Box 22.3)
- Diagnosis is based on a rising CVP in the face of falling blood pressure and cardiac output
- Echocardiography is useful to confirm the diagnosis and exclude tamponade.

Treatment is based on optimization of:

- Removal/reversal of precipitating causes
  - Thromboembolectomy/thrombolysis
  - Relief of tamponade (often manifests as RV dysfunction)
- Heart rate
- Heart rhythm
- Maintaining adequate pre-load
  - Do not aggressively fluid load patients with RV failure
  - It rarely improves either cardiac output or blood pressure and reduces the RV perfusion pressure by increasing RVEDP
- Maintaining RV perfusion pressure
  - Intra-aortic balloon pumps, although not specifically indicated for RV failure, will improve RV perfusion pressure and thus may help to support the RV as a bridging method
- Augmenting contractility
  - Inotropes will both improve RV perfusion pressure and augment contractility
  - An inodilator (dobutamine/milrinone/enoximone) in combination with low-dose noradrenaline reduces RV afterload as well as improving both contractility and blood pressure
- Reducing RV afterload
  - Simple measures such as reversing hypoxia, hypercapnia, acidosis and reducing PEEP to the lowest possible level are often extremely effective
  - Nitric oxide, nebulized or intravenous prostacyclin are specific treatments.

Tamponade

- This is characterized by falling blood pressure and cardiac output in the face of a rising CVP and tachycardia
- It can develop rapidly within the first 24hrs after cardiac surgery, although tamponade physiology can occur in a sub-acute fashion over several days
- The physiology, diagnosis and treatment of surgical tamponade differs from medical tamponade for the following reasons listed:
  - Rapid onset
  - Ability to for even small amounts of blood to cause localized compressive effects and significant haemodynamic compromise
  - This makes for difficult echocardiographic diagnosis
  - A *negative* TTE or TOE examination should not prevent return to theatre for suspected tamponade
  - Tamponade due to non-pericardial causes such as oedema of the thoracic structures
- Treatment of tamponade is aimed at maintaining cardiac output
- In the post-surgical population, return to theatre is required
- Percutaneous drainage is not indicated because of the need to identify and control the source of bleeding and because percutaneous removal of localized tamponade is unreliable.

Atrial fibrillation

- New onset AF occurs in about 30% of the post cardiac surgery population within 72hrs of surgery
- Risk factors for this are shown in Box 22.4

BOX 22.4 RISK FACTORS FOR NEW ONSET AF

Independent RF's:

- Age >65
- Male
- Pre-operative hypertension
- Previous episode of AF
- Valve surgery.

Associated factors:

- Prolonged Ao X-clamp
- Pulmonary vein venting
- Peri-op pneumonia
- COPD
- Prolonged ventilation.

- Pre-operative use of β-blockers (1st-line) and amiodarone (2nd-line) reduce the risk of post-operative AF and are cost effective
- Serum $[Mg^{2+}]$ >1.0mml/l and $[K^+]$ >4.5 reduce risk in the early post-operative period
- IV amiodarone followed up by oral maintenance controls rate and promotes cardioversion to sinus rhythm
- Digoxin rate controls in the context of amiodarone contraindication and provides a degree of positive inotropy
- DC cardioversion is an option
- All patients who do not revert to sinus rhythm should be anti-coagulated within 24–48hrs
- The need for dysrhythmics should be reviewed at 6–8wks post-operatively and stopped if the patient is in sinus rhythm.

Renal, fluids and electrolytes

Acute renal failure

- Renal dysfunction after cardiac surgery is common
- Acute renal failure (ARF) by the RIFLE criteria occurs in just over 1% of cardiac surgical procedures, but once established has a mortality of 60%
- ARF in this population is due to:
  - Renal hypo-perfusion outside auto-regulatory reserve
  - The systemic inflammatory response (SIRS) causing localized vasoconstriction, ischaemia and direct cell death from mediators
  - Embolic injury from atheroma during cross clamping along with air, lipid and tissue
  - Prolonged CPB causing haemolysis—intracellular contents cause renal failure directly
  - Nephrotoxic drug administration—particularly soon after the high contrast load of angiography.

Risk factors for renal failure after cardiac surgery are shown in Table 22.1.

- There are many indications for the use of renal replacement therapies after cardiac surgery. Only the absolute indications are listed in Box 22.5.

Table 22.1 Risk factors for renal failure after cardiac surgery

Pre-operative	Intra-operative	Post-operative
Increased age	Redo surgery	RBC transfusion
Female	Complex surgery	Low cardiac output
Peripheral vascular disease	Emergency surgery	Haemorrhage
Diabetes	CPB < 2hrs	Hypovolaemia
COPD	Intra-op radiocontrast	Sepsis
NYHA 3–4		Nephrotoxic drugs
LVEF <35%		
Other chronic disease		

BOX 22.5 ABSOLUTE INDICATIONS FOR RENAL REPLACEMENT THERAPIES

- Urea > 36 mmol (100mg/dl)
- K > 6 mmol
- pH < 7.10
- Urine output:
  - <200ml/12hr
  - Anuria
- Fluid overload
- Uraemic complications:
  - Pericarditis
  - Encephalopathy
  - Bleeding
- Mg^{2+} >4mmol
  - Absent tendon reflexes.

Fluid balance (following cardiac surgery)

- Patients following CPB are in a state of moderate sodium and water overload
- Although often polyuric for the first couple of hours after cardiac surgery, they often become oliguric later
- Oliguria can also be due to intravascular volume depletion or high circulating levels of anti-diuretic hormone (ADH)
- Patients are often intravascularly deplete due to bleeding, polyuria and 'third-space' losses secondary to capillary leak
- Treatment of oliguria is initially based on assessment of volume status
- Hypovolaemia requires fluid, hypervolaemia is treated with diuretics. Low cardiac output output states are treated with inotropes
- Post-operative weight gains of between 5–10% are common following cardiac surgery
- Frusemide is often given until the patient has returned to their pre-operative weight
- The urethral catheter is removed on post-operative day 2–3 when renal function has returned close to baseline and all intravenous vaso-active medicines have stopped.

Neurology and pain control

Neurological dysfunction

- Neurological dysfunction is common following cardiac surgery
- Rates vary by operation and outcome measured
- Stroke occurs in about 1–3% of patients after surgery, but up to 80% of patients have cognitive change
- In those with a stroke, about one-quarter will suffer long-term disability
- Many of these will be due to complications of prolonged intensive care.

The risk factors that predispose to neurological injury following cardiac surgery parallel those of mortality:

- Age
- Unstable angina
- Diabetes
- Neurological disease
- Previous CABG
- Vascular disease
- Pulmonary disease.

Prevention and management

- There is little specific treatment to prevent neurological injury after heart surgery short of good quality care
- No drugs have been proven to improve outcome
- The following factors may play a part in outcome:
  - Maintenance of cerebral perfusion pressure (see Box 22.6)
  - Maintaining higher MAP when 'on-bypass'
  - α-stat pH management
    - (Total CO_2 stores maintained at a constant level for measurement).

Delirium

- Delirium is often seen after cardiac surgery and on the intensive care unit
- Although often short lived, it is a risk factor for significant morbidity and mortality
- Early cognitive dysfunction following cardiac surgery is a risk factor for long-term cognitive dysfunction
- Treatment is aimed at excluding precipitating causes (hypoxia, hypoglycaemia and sepsis) and maintaining a normal cognitive environment (sleep/wake cycle, minimization of noise, early mobilization)

BOX 22.6 ALGORITHM TO FIND CEREBRAL PERFUSION PRESSURE

$$CPP = MAP - (ICP + CVP)$$

CPP = Cerebral perfusion pressure

MAP = Mean arterial pressure

ICP = Intra-cranial pressure

CVP = Central venous pressure

- Pharmacological treatment is based around traditional (haloperidol) and new-generation (quetiapine) anti-psychotics
- Benzodiazepines cannot be recommended for treatment of delerium on intensive care except those of the *delerium tremens* of alcohol withdrawal.

Analgesia

Aside from the humanitarian aims of treating pain, analgesia after cardiac surgery serves several functions:

- Reduction of sympathetic stimulation—and therefore reduction of tachycardia, hypertension, bleeding and ischaemia
- Improves respiratory effort—reducing atelectasis, sputum retention and chest infection
- Promotes early mobilization
    - Both sternotomy and thoracotomy are extremely painful
    - Intraoperative analgesia during cardiac surgery is usually provided by fentanyl
    - Postoperatively analgesia is provided by combinations of:
        - Intermittent boluses of morphine or PCA morphine
        - Oxycodone is an alternative for those who vomit with morphine
        - Regular paracetamol
        - Tramadol or codeine
- NSAIDs are often avoided unless there are specific indications and the renal function is known
- Patients kept sedated often have an infusion of short acting opiate such as alfentanil; in severely impaired renal function systemic accumulation of morphine and its active metabolites may occur
- Although some studies show improvements in postoperative respiratory function with neuraxial analgesia (epidurals/spinals), there are no consistent survival benefits
- There are, however concerns regarding neuraxial blockade and full systemic heparinization of patients for cardiac surgery—although this correlation has never been proved.

Gastro-intestinal issues

- Gastro-intestinal complications are relatively rare following cardiac surgery (<3%). See Box 22.7
- They are associated with significant morbidity and mortality (70% for mesenteric infarction)
- GI haemorrhage accounts for around 1/3 of GI complications
- The pathogeneisis in virtually all cases is impaired GI perfusion and mucosal ischaemia
- Following resuscitation surgical management is almost always warranted if endoscopic therapies fail.

BOX 22.7 COMMON GI PROBLEMS AFTER CARDIAC SURGERY

- GI haemorrhage
- GI perforation
- GI ischaemia
- Pancreatitis
- Acalculous cholecystitis
- Obstriction/ileus.

Feeding

- Most patients having straightforward cardiac surgery have few ill effects from interruption to their normal feeding habits
- Those who need prolonged intensive care or do not follow the normal pathways require nutritional assessment and possibly supplementation
- Enteral feeding is preferred as it maintains GI mucosal perfusion and as such maintains gut integrity and prevents bacterial translocation
- Early feeding of post cardiac-surgical patients is currently encouraged.

Glycaemic control

- Tight glycaemic control (blood glucose 4.4–6.6mmol/l) is controversial
- A study from Leuven in Belgium showed a significant mortality benefit by preventing hyperglycaemia in cardiac surgical patients
- Several well-conducted studies have subsequently shown potentially harmful hypoglycaemia episodes do occur, which often go unrecognized in sedated patients
- Individual critical care units generate their own policies—but all will try to prevent blood glucose concentrations rising above 10mmol/l.

Bleeding and anti-coagulation

Bleeding

- Post-operative bleeding is a common problem after cardiac surgery
- Most cardiac surgical units have a haematocrit transfusion trigger of around 23% (Hb 7–8)
- In the bleeding patient it is prudent to maintain the haematocrit around 30% (Hb 10), as a level around this is required for maximal clotting
- Causes of post operative bleeding:
  - Pre-operative drug induced platelet dysfunction (eg aspirin/clopidogrel)
  - Residual heparinization
  - CPB induced coagulopathy/fibrinolysis
  - 'Surgical bleeding' sternal wires/anastamoses/graft side branches.

Bleeding should be aggressively treated and investigated along the following lines:

- Appropriate clotting tests: FBC, APTT, PT, fibrinogen
- Red cell transfusion to maintain haematocrit
- Transfusion of blood components guided by:
  - Coagulation screen
  - Thromboelastograph (TEG) a near patient testing device which provides a dynamic assessment of clot strength
  - Clopidogrel and aspirin do not affect the TEG and so either use of the newer platelet mapping assay or empiric treatment with platelets will help overcome this problem
  - Platelets are the most common product used due to CPB induced dysfunction
  - FFP is often transfused unnecessarily, but *is* useful after long bypass times and in those with pre-existing coagulopathy (warfarin, liver disease)
  - Cryoprecipitate is guided by a fibrinogen assay (fibrinogen < 2.0)
  - Activated Factor VII is used off licence for patients with life threatening bleeding refractory to other treatments

- Administration of drugs
  - Protamine: The half-life of heparin is significantly longer than that of protamine and therefore there can often be a degree of residual heparinization, particularly if the 'pump blood' (blood salvaged from the CPB circuit) is given back to the patient
  - Many units give anti-fibrinolytics (usually tranexamic acid) as a routine, but if these have not been previously given then a single dose or infusion may be helpful
  - Aprotinin in cardiac surgery has essentially stopped due to an excess mortality in those in whom it was used
- Surgical re-exploration where appropriate
  - Approximately 2–5% of patients need re-exploration bleeding and this is associated with a significant increase in morbidity and mortality
  - As a general rule, the following chest drain losses should prompt re-exploration:
    - >400mls in the first hour
    - >200mls in 2 consecutive hours
    - >100mls in 4 consecutive hours
- Other factors to consider include:
  - Maintaining SBP around 100–120mmHg
  - Restoration of normothermia
  - Addition of PEEP—may reduce bleeding by increasing mechanical intrathoracic pressure, but may also reduce venous return and thus cardiac output in those who are hypovolaemic
  - A chest X-ray or TOE may show large pleural/pericardial collections which necessitate immediate return to theatre regardless of coagulation status.

Anti-coagulation
- Almost all patients will have a degree of residual coagulopathy on the day of cardiac surgery
- The incidences of DVT and PE after cardiac surgery are around 20% and 0.5% respectively
- Prevention follows NICE guidelines (see Box 22.8).

Anti-coagulation after specific operations
CABG:
- Aspirin is prescribed after bleeding has settled on the evening of surgery and daily thereafter
- Some surgeons use clopidogrel after 'off-pump' surgery—or in the presence of difficult anastamoses.

BOX 22.8 SUMMARY OF NICE GUIDELINES ON ANTI-COAGULATION PREVENTION

Patients undergoing cardiac surgery who are not anticoagulated should have VTE prophylaxis.

This starts with mechanical VTE prophylaxis at admission (choose one):

1. Anti-embolism stockings (thigh or knee length)
2. Foot impulse devices
3. Intermittent pneumatic compression devices (thigh or knee length).

In addition, pharmacological VTE prophylaxis should be started for patients who have a low risk of major bleeding:

1. LMWH
2. Unfractionated heparin (for patients with renal failure).

VTE prophylaxis should continue until the patient no longer has significantly reduced mobility (generally 5–7 days).

Valve surgery:

- Oral anticoagulation is usually started on the first post-operative day
- Since most patients have a degree of coagulopathy after surgery, there is usually no need to use heparin until the therapeutic range is reached (aside from routine thromboprophylaxis)
- The first post-operative month is the highest risk for valve thrombosis—so falls below the target INR should be avoided
- ESC guidance on anti-coagulation for prosthetic valves is listed in Box 22.9
- Mitral valve repairs require warfarin in the immediate post-operative phase. This may be discontinued at 6 weeks to 3 months.

Infection and antibiotics

- Cardiac surgery is generally regarded as being 'clean' surgery
- This is fortunate as deep-seated infections such as mediastinitis and infective endocarditis can have devastating consequences
- Common pathogens are *Staphylococci* (antibiotic prophylaxis policies are usually orientated towards this)
- Steps in preventing infection are outlined in Box 22.10.

BOX 22.9 ESC GUIDANCE ON ANTI-COAGULATION FOR PROSTHETIC VALVES

Oral anticoagulation is recommended in the following situations:

- Lifelong for all patients with mechanical valves
- Lifelong for patients with bioprostheses who have other indications for anticoagulation, e.g. atrial fibrillation, or with a lesser degree of evidence; heart failure and impaired LV function (EF <30%)
- For the first 3 months after insertion in all patients with bioprostheses (target INR 2.5). However, there is widespread use of aspirin (low dose: 75–100 mg) as an alternative to anticoagulation for the first 3 months, but no randomized studies to support the safety of this strategy.

Adapted from Vahanian A, Baumgartner H, Bax J, et al for the Task Force on the Management of Valvular Heart Disease of the European Society of Cardiology, the ESC Committee for Practice Guidelines. Guidelines on the management of valvular heart disease: the Task Force on the Management of Valvular Heart Disease of the European Society of Cardiology. Eur Heart J 2007; 28: 230–268

BOX 22.10 INFECTION PREVENTION

- Pre-op
  - All patients should be screened for MRSA
  - All patients should have intranasal muprocin and body wash with chlorhexidine in the 5 days prior to surgery
  - General prophylactic measures should be undertaken to reduce infection (diabetes control, weight loss etc.)
- Prophylaxis
  - Antibiotic prophylaxis is generally with flucloxacillin and gentamicin or cefuroxime
  - Prophylaxis usually continues for 24hrs post op although evidence suggests that intra-operative doses of antibiotics are adequate
- Post-op
  - Dressings should not be removed earlier than 48hrs post op.

Sternal wound infection

- Sternal wound infections occur in about 10% of cardiac operations (only about 4% are severe)
- The three most common causative organisms are:
    1. *Staphylococcus aureus*
    2. *Staphylococcus epidermidis*
    3. Coliforms
- Treatment of minor infection is with regular dressing
- Major infection will often require antibiotics, debridement and irrigation
- Mediastinitis is the most difficult to treat and requires radical debridement, irrigation and evacuation of all exudate
- Mortality is grossly increased in this group to around 25%.

Re-introduction of medicines

Cardiovascular:

- β-blockers re-introduced on the first post-operative day
- This prevents tachycardia and acts as prophylaxis against atrial fibrillation
- Mild bradycardia is not a contra-indication
- In those with heart failure β-blockers should be titrated carefully, when cardiac function is adequate and inotropes discontinued
- Rapid withdrawal of calcium channel blockers has been associated with coronary artery spasm after CABG surgery
- They should be re-introduced early in the post-operative period
- Angiotensin-converting enzyme inhibitors, angiotensin receptor blockers and spironolactone can cause problems in patients with low cardiac output and renal dysfunction
- Their re-introduction should be delayed until all inotropic drugs have been weaned and renal function is satisfactory
- Digoxin can be re-introduced on the first post-operative day.

Diabetes:

- Patients are usually on sliding scale insulin infusion throughout the perioperative period
- They can be restarted on their pre-operative dose of subcutaneous insulin and oral anti-hyperglycaemics when they are eating a full diet and their blood sugar is stable on the sliding scale insulin
- Metformin can cause fatal lactic acidosis in those with elevated creatinine; it should only be re-introduced when the creatinine is stable and less than 150µmol/l.

CNS:

- Medicines such as anti-epileptic and anti-parkinsonian drugs should not be missed and warrant placement of an NG-tube if the patient is not extubated immediately after surgery
- Psychiatric medicines may be introduced on the first post-operative day with the awareness that they may prolong the QT interval.

Long-term steroids:

- Those on long-term steroids require the intravenous equivalent to cover the stress response.

Early rehabilitation

- For the routine patient having cardiac surgery, there is little rehabilitation done on the Intensive Care Unit
- Patients are usually got out of bed and into the chair on the first post-operative day and begin walking the length of the ward from day 2 to day 3
- 'On-the-spot' walking is used as a therapeutic bridge between the two.

22.3 'Off-pump' coronary surgery

Interest in off-pump coronary artery bypass (OPCAB) has been driven by a need to try and minimize ill effects resulting from the CPB circuit, develop less invasive approaches and reduce costs.

Avoiding CPB should reduce activation of the immune system and the consequent inflammatory response, reduce bleeding and renal dysfunction and therefore improve recovery.

The absence of aortic cannulation brought expectations of reduced neurological complications.

Currently however, there is controversy about whether these benefits are realized in practice.

Post operative care of patients who have had off pump surgery is essentially the same as any cardiac surgical patient. The differences are:

- **Temperature:** Patients need to be actively warmed. Significant heat loss occurs from an open sternotomy and vein harvest wounds
- **Hypovolaemia:** Patients often require increased intravenous fluid compared to 'on-pump' CABG, in whom the bypass circuit priming fluid (1.5l) is reinfused at the end of the surgery before arrival in intensive care
- **Acidosis and lactataemia:** Patients can be more more acidotic in the immediate post-operative period than 'on-pump' cases due to the reductions in cardiac output that occur when the heart is moved to be grafted. This usually resolves when normal perfusion is restored at the end of the operation
- **Anticoagulation:** Off-pump CABG does not require full anticoagulation; therefore it is prudent to start thromboprophylaxis with a LMWH on the day of surgery, along with aspirin.

22.4 Risk scoring

- Risk scoring has moved on since its introduction in the 1950s
- This has taken on increasing importance in the UK since the publication of individual Surgeon's outcomes as part of a joint project between the Care Quality Commission and the Society of Cardiovascular and Thoracic Surgeons
- Each scoring system uses different variables to predict outcome (usually mortality)
- The only two variables that consistently appear in all scoring systems are renal failure and diabetes.

Examples of scoring systems are:

- **EuroSCORE**—regarded as the gold standard scoring system constructed from almost 20,000 patients across Europe. Presented as a simple numerical scoring system and a logistic (percentage mortality) system. It is generally thought to *overestimate* mortality now as care has progressed in the last decade. EuroSCORE II has recently been introduced to update this and presents its outcome as a percentage risk of death (see Table 22.2)

Table 22.2 Standard EuroSCORE

Patient factors	Notes	Score
Age	Per 5 years over 60	1
Sex	Female	1
Chronic pulmonary disease	Long term bronchodilator use	1
Extracardiac arteriopathy		2
Neurological dysfunction		2
Previous cardiac surgery		3
Serum creatinine	> 200 mmol/l	2
Active endocarditis	On ABx at time of surgery	3
Critical pre-operative state		3
Cardiac factors		
Unstable angina	Needing IV nitrates until AR	2
LV dysfunction	Moderate or poor	1 or 3
Recent MI	Within 90 days	2
Pulmonary hypertension	Systolic PA pressure >60mmHg	2
Operative factors		
Emergency	Surgery before next working day	2
Surgery other than isolated CABG		2
Surgery on thoracic aorta		3
Post-infact septal rupture		4

- **STS**—The Society of Thoracic Surgeons (USA) has a large database of over 1.5 million patients that is constantly updated and has a good predictive value
- **CARE**—The Cardiac Anaesthesia Risk Evaluation is a five-point score (plus an emergency class) similar to the ASA classification of general perioperative risk
- **Parsonnet**—This was one of the first models and is now not really used as current risk levels are incomparable to when it was produced.

Pregnancy and heart disease

23.1 Overview and epidemiology

- Heart disease complicates <1% of all pregnancies but this number is increasing
- Congenital heart disease occurs in 0.8% live births and 85% of these patients now reach adulthood due to improvements in surgical and intensive care
- In developed countries, congenital and inherited cardiac conditions account for most cases. In developing countries cases are mainly rheumatic heart disease, though this is also increasing in developed countries due to immigration
- Arrhythmias are the most common acquired problems
- Coronary disease is seen in older, obese women who smoke and have an increased risk of diabetes. Historically MI in pregnancy has been due to coronary dissection but is now more commonly due to atheromatous disease
- 'The Centre for Maternal and Child Enquiries' produced a triennial report of maternal deaths, now to be taken over by MBRRACE-UK (Mothers and Babies: Reducing Risk through Audits and Confidential Enquiries across the UK. The most recent report identified cardiac disease as the leading cause of maternal death for the second time. More than half of deaths were the result of substandard care
- Cardiac death in pregnancy is rare. The main causes have been the same for many years: peripartum cardiomyopathy, myocardial infarction, aortic dissection, and pulmonary hypertension. Morbidity is much more common.

23.2 Cardiovascular adaptations during pregnancy

- Characterized by significant haemodynamic changes to allow foetus to receive adequate blood supply for development and protect mother from blood loss at delivery
- Hormonally-mediated upregulation of nitric oxide synthesis and increases in prostaglandins and atrial natriuretic peptide seen
- See Figure 23.1 for a list of physiologic changes during pregnancy.

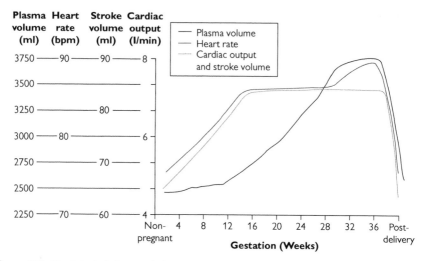

Figure 23.1 Physiological changes during pregnancy.

Reproduced from 'Pregnancy in heart disease', S. A. Thorne, *Heart*, 90 (4), 450–456, copyright 2004 with permission from BMJ Publishing Group Ltd and the British Cardiovascular Society.

Plasma volume and cardiac output

- Stimulation of the renin–angiotensin system results in an increase in plasma volume, which begins from 6 weeks' gestation, reaching a peak at 32–34 weeks, where it plateaus
- Results in a relative anaemia, in spite of an increase in red cell mass
- Returns to pre-pregnancy levels by 6–8 weeks post partum
- Cardiac output increases by 40% by around 25 weeks due to increased stroke volume and heart rate. Patients who decompensate from an increase in preload and heart rate tend to present at around 18–22 weeks
- Blood pressure falls to lowest level in the mid second trimester then rises gradually towards term
- In the supine position, IVC compression results in decreased venous return and can result in significant systemic hypotension. Pregnant women should be nursed in the left lateral decubitus position to avoid this
- Serum colloid osmotic pressure decreases resulting in physiological oedema of extremities; pulmonary oedema may occur more readily.

Therefore pregnancy may place significant additional burden on an already compromised cardiovascular system or unmask a pre-existing but undiagnosed cardiac abnormality.

Heart rate

- Heart rate increases from around 6 weeks' gestation, reaching a peak at 36 weeks. A rise of 10–20 bpm is seen
- Atrial tachyarrhythmias commonly seen in pregnancy due to increased circulating catecholamines, increased sensitivity to catecholamines, and increased atrial wall stretch secondary to an increased circulating plasma volume.

Vascular resistance

- Systemic and pulmonary vascular resistance both decrease; placenta is a low-resistance organ
- Peripheral arterial vasodilatation seen in pregnancy causes aldosterone-mediated retention of sodium and water.

Haemostasis

- Pregnancy induces a state of hypercoagulability to minimize haemorrhage post-partum. Women with atrial arrhythmias, surgical venous pathways, dilated cardiomyopathy, mechanical valves, and post-Fontan surgery are therefore at risk of thromboembolic events
- Red cell mass increases but haematocrit decreases due to increase in plasma volume
- Decreased tissue plasminogen activator (tPa); increased clotting factors.

Delivery and post-partum period

- Dramatic changes in haemodynamics during delivery and immediate post-partum period
- Each uterine contraction causes an increase in venous return
- Cardiac output increases by up to 25% during contractions in early labour, 50% during second stage, and 80% immediately post partum due to autotransfusion from contracted uterus and relief of caval compression
- Sympathetic stimulation caused by pain and anxiety also augment cardiac output and blood pressure
- Cardiac output and SVR return to normal at most by two weeks post partum, all by 12–24 weeks' post-partum
- Clotting changes take 6 weeks to return to normal.

23.3 Cardiac assessment

History

- The following are normal in pregnancy: dyspnoea, fatigue, reduced exercise tolerance, palpitations, syncope, dizziness and hyperventilation
- Syncope or the development or progression of dyspnoea may be abnormal
- Orthopnoea, exertional chest pain, and paroxysmal dyspnoea are not normal
- Condition-specific issues need to be addressed, e.g. anti-coagulation in prosthetic valves
- Drug history needs to be assessed for safety profile for mother and baby.

Examination

- Elevated jugular venous pressure, right ventricular heave, collapsing pulse, and ankle oedema are common
- More than 90% of patients will have a 2/6 systolic murmur heart, loudest at the left sternal edge, due to increased pulmonary flow. Continuous bruits heard over the breasts also common (mammary soufflés) and can be obliterated by pressure with the stethoscope
- Diastolic murmurs in pregnancy are abnormal
- 80% have an S3. S1 often loud with an exaggerated split S2.

Cardiac investigations in pregnancy

- ECG: the following may be seen:
  - Sinus tachycardia in third trimester (exclude thyroid problems and pulmonary embolus). Resolves by 2 weeks post partum
  - R wave can be increased V1 and V2
  - Apex beat seen to shift to the left in normal pregnancy in third trimester, so may see a slight leftward axis shift (small Q wave in lead III)

- ■ Inferolateral ST depression/T inversion
- ■ Isolated ventricular and supraventricular ectopics
- ■ T inversion in III. P may be inverted in III
- ■ First- and second-degree atrioventricular block and RBBB
- Echocardiography is a safe and non-invasive test that allows serial surveillance. In a normal pregnancy:
  - ■ All four chamber sizes increase
  - ■ Transvalvular velocities increase and mild atrioventricular valve regurgitation also common due to increased cardiac output and mild annular dilatation
  - ■ Reducing velocities in left-sided obstructive valve disease may indicate left ventricular decompensation
- CXR: avoid if possible, especially in early pregnancy. Pelvic shield recommended. In normal pregnancies, cardiac silhouette may be larger, lung markings more prominent, and small pleural effusions present
- MRI: few indications. Gadolinium is contraindicated
- CT: mainly used to diagnose pulmonary emboli. Avoid if possible and use techniques to minimize radiation dose otherwise. Iodine contrast can cause neonatal hypothyroidism, thus the infant must be screened at birth
- Exercise ECG: unhelpful in pregnancy as heart rate and cardiac output already increased by the pregnancy itself. Useful as part of the pre-pregnancy assessment of women contemplating pregnancy as risk stratification
- Ambulatory ECG: useful investigation to identify the cause of palpitations.

23.4 Maternal risk assessment in cardiac disease

Cardiac conditions can be thought of as low or high risk (see risk score, Box 23.1). Patients at highest risk of cardiac events are those with:

- Left-sided valvular obstructive lesions
- Reduced systemic ventricular function
- Aortopathy and mechanical valves
- Pulmonary hypertension (risk of death is very high; pregnancy should be avoided).

Other independent risk factors for adverse events are

- Severe AV valve regurgitation
- Severe pulmonary regurgitation and reduced subpulmonary ventricular dysfunction.

BOX 23.1 CARPREG RISK SCORE

Condition	Points	Total points	Risk (%)
Prior pulmonary oedema, transient ischaemic attack, stroke or arrhythmia	1	0	5
NYHA functional class >II or cyanosis	1	1	27
Left heart obstruction	1	>1	75
Systemic ventricular dysfunction (EF <40%)	1		

Adapted from 'Prospective multicenter study of pregnancy outcomes in women with heart disease', Samuel C. Siu, Matthew Sermer, Jack M. Colman et al., *Circulation* 104: 515–521, copyright 2001 with permission of Wolters Kluwer Health.

23.5 General principles of pregnancy care for the cardiac patient

Guidelines from European Society of Cardiology and the Royal College of Obstetricians describe ideal model of care:
- Individualized care is key
- Cases must be reviewed in a MDT meeting
- Have a birth plan in the notes and on labour ward
- Care should be in a joint clinic
- Balance the mother's need with those of the foetus
- Do not alienate the woman by overmedicalizing birth if not necessary
- Allow for mother's input into birth plan
- Those looking after patients should undergo formal training
- Formalize pre-pregnancy counseling.

In addition:
- All patients with heart disease planning assisted conception should have cardiological assessment and optimization of treatment
- Risks of assisted conception include multiple birth, and the consequent haemodynamic stress of this and the risk of ovarian hyperstimulation syndrome.

Where to deliver

If low risk delivery in local hospital is advised. Otherwise delivery should be in a tertiary centre with consultant obstetric, cardiology, and anaesthetic cover.

Wherever delivery planned, need to ensure that the resources for a safe delivery are in place including appropriately trained staff, equipment, and environment.

Mode of delivery

- Generally determined by obstetric indications
- Generally a vaginal delivery with good analgesia is optimal
- May need to limit active pushing due to the haemodynamic stress
- Caesarean section results in more dramatic and sudden hemodynamic shifts and is therefore not usually recommended. Reserved for those with a high risk of aortic dissection if the risk of requiring cardiac surgery is high, those in whom warfarin has been taken in the previous three weeks, or if the mother is acutely unwell and rapid delivery is required. Needed if baby is premature
- High-risk patients can be delivered with a carefully titrated combined spinal epidural and passive second stage, with lift-out ventouse or forceps if pushing is not advised for cardiac reasons.

Third-stage management

- Complex fluid shifts occur as the placenta is delivered and the uterus contracts
- High-risk patients are at highest risk of cardiac events in the first days post partum and require high-dependency care
- Drugs given routinely to prevent post-partum haemorrhage have significant haemodynamic side-effects
- Ergometrine should be avoided in most cases as it results in prolonged hypertension due to peripheral vasoconstriction. Also risk of coronary vasospasm
- Low-dose infusion of syntocinon is recommended, rather than a bolus, which can cause profound hypotension and bradycardia

- Misoprostol is usually safe
- Senior input required if post-partum haemorrhage severe, as benefits of ergometrine may outweigh risks.

Regional analgesia/anaesthesia

- Good choice for effective pain relief
- Used in most Caesarean sections but contraindicated if patient is anti-coagulated.

General anaesthesia

- Rarely indicated
- Risks include failed intubation, aspiration, haemodynamic instability, and with induction/ maintenance of anaesthetic
- General anaesthesia can result in death in patients with pulmonary hypertension
- Risk of systemic air embolus if the patient has right-to-left shunting
- Risk of neonatal respiratory depression and impaired bonding with baby.

23.6 Specific cardiac conditions

Valvular heart disease
Left-sided valvular heart disease in pregnancy

- Left-sided obstructive valve lesions are a significant risk factor for maternal morbidity and mortality. As systemic vascular resistance decreases the effective obstruction increases
- The foetus is at risk of death, growth restriction, low birth weight, and premature labour can occur
- Left-sided regurgitant lesions, in contrast, are generally well-tolerated in pregnancy due to the decrease in systemic vascular resistance.

Stenotic lesions
Mitral stenosis

- Usually rheumatic, increasingly common due to increased immigration
- Often presents for the first time in pregnancy
- Poorly tolerated in pregnancy. Increased functional obstruction due to the increased preload and tachycardia of pregnancy. Resultant raised left atrial pressure and reduced cardiac output
- High risk if mitral valve area is <2.0 cm^2 pre-pregnancy.

Clinical assessment:

- Presents with breathlessness, pulmonary oedema, or paroxysmal nocturnal dyspnoea, typically at 20–24 weeks. Tends to then stabilize and peak post partum
- May precipitate atrial fibrillation, which causes further decompensation
- Progression to pulmonary venous hypertension may also cause right heart failure.

Investigations:

- MVA is a more reliable parameter in assessing MS severity in pregnancy than the pressure gradient across the valve
- Assess valve area, valve morphology, and suitability for balloon valvuloplasty.

Treatment:

- Options to reduce heart rate and optimize cardiac output include oxygen, bed rest, beta-blockers, digoxin, and diuretics
- Consider anticoagulation if the left atrium is large, even if in sinus rhythm due to the increased risk of left atrial thrombus formation
- If in atrial fibrillation, thromboembolism prophylaxis with LMWH needed. Aim to restore sinus rhythm as soon as possible. Consider transoesophageal echo-guided DC cardioversion
- Balloon valvuloplasty should be considered, even if there is mitral regurgitation to relieve pulmonary oedema and allow progress of pregnancy. 95% success rate with little risk to the mother or the baby. Should be performed in centre with established experience.

Delivery:

- If mild, should be able to have a normal delivery
- If maternal situation critical and foetus viable, deliver and then treat mitral stenosis
- Preterm delivery is likely with resultant low birth weight baby unless stenosis is mild
- If moderate to severe, vaginal delivery with epidural analgesia is recommended, with careful balance of preload and afterload and the use of invasive monitoring
- Patients should be carefully monitored post partum.

Aortic stenosis

- Almost always due to bicuspid aortic valve disease
- In a patient who is asymptomatic and has lone aortic stenosis (AS), if resting ECG has no strain, good LV function with pre-pregnancy mean gradient <50 mmHg/peak gradient <80 mmHg, AVA >1.5 cm^2, normal exercise capacity and a normal exercise-tolerance test, pregnancy is likely to be well-tolerated
- Severe stenosis associated with increased maternal and foetal risk
- Aim to manage medically with oxygen, bed rest, and BBs to reduce heart rate and cardiac output
- Monitor gradient. Increases throughout pregnancy
- Signs of decompensation include worsening dyspnoea, decreasing gradient, and/or tachycardia
- If decompensating, admit for bed rest; consider beta blockade and balloon valvotomy if still symptomatic in spite of this and foetus not yet viable
- Advise against pregnancy or advise termination (if already pregnant) if any adverse features present.

Delivery:

- If well at term should be able to have a normal delivery
- If the maternal situation is critical and the foetus is viable, deliver the baby and treat aortic stenosis afterwards
- If the mother deteriorates, interventions include balloon valvotomy (usually a bridging/palliative procedure with a risk of severe aortic regurgitation), surgical valvotomy, or prosthetic valve replacement
- Vaginal delivery with slow incremental low-dose epidural analgesia recommended to avoid vasodilatation and rapid fluid shifts associated with Caesarean section
- May need invasive monitoring depending on the severity of lesion.

Regurgitant lesions

Mitral regurgitation

- Usually well tolerated, even if severe
- Aim to treat medically with nitrates and hydralazine *not* ACE inhibitors if decompensating
- Consider valve repair/replacement if heart failure develops but aim to deliver baby first
- Caution with pre-pregnancy valve repair in case mechanical prosthesis required.

Aortic regurgitation

- As with mitral regurgitation, aim to manage medically.

Prosthetic valves

- Significant risk to both mother and baby
- Crucial to consider future pregnancies when selecting type of prosthetic valve in a woman of child-bearing age. Patient needs to be counselled regarding risks and benefits of each valve type with respect to pregnancy and anti-coagulation issues.

Bioprosthetic valves

- Low risk in pregnancy
- Less thrombogenic than mechanical valves
- Warfarin can be avoided, which significantly reduces maternal and foetal risk
- Degenerate more rapidly in young patients, requiring re-operation, usually within 10 years. Pregnancy itself is not thought to cause degeneration
- Mitral prostheses degenerate more rapidly than aortic.

Mechanical valves

- Problematic in pregnancy due to need for warfarin, which crosses the placenta
- Hypercoagulable state of pregnancy increases risk of valve thrombosis and thromboembolism as well as risks of bleeding from warfarin
- For the baby, risk of miscarriage, foetal loss, haemorrhage, and foetal embryopathy
- Risks increased with older types of valve and those in mitral position.

Management of anti-coagulation for prosthetic valves in pregnancy

- Difficult
- Heparin, as a substitute for warfarin, does not cross the placenta and so is safe for the baby. However risk of valve thrombosis high.

Unfractionated heparin

- Superseded by LMWH due to the risk of valve thrombosis and heparin-induced thrombocytopenia (HIT) and osteoporosis
- Need to do periodic anti-factor Xa assay to guide therapy. APTT response to heparin often decreased due to decreased Factor VIII and fibrinogen
- May need a TDS regime or even an i.v. infusion to achieve this.

Low molecular weight heparin

- Does not cross the placenta
- Lower incidence of HIT
- Longer half-life thus harder to reverse effect
- Multiple reports of valve thromboses in literature despite careful monitoring
- Need meticulous anti-factor Xa monitoring and addition of aspirin
- Careful management around labour. Induction often required to facilitate this.

Warfarin
Causes four separate problems in the foetus:

- Warfarin embryopathy. Characterized by skeletal abnormalities and low birth weight. Risk directly related to the dose of warfarin taken
- Central nervous system effects: spasticity and optic atrophy. Risk throughout pregnancy
- Foetal haemorrhage
- Foetal loss.

Options for anticoagulation
The following options must be discussed with the parents by an experienced multidisciplinary team, preferably pre-pregnancy. It is important that the mother is made aware of the risks of each option for her and the foetus. The woman is at most risk around the time of changing therapies.

- Warfarin throughout: most risk to foetus, least risk to mother (reasonable to consider this option if warfarin dose <5 mg)
- Heparin–warfarin sandwich: i.e. heparin for weeks 6 to 12, when the risk of embryopathy is high, warfarin from week 12–36/38, heparin prior to and peri-delivery. Some risk to mother and foetus
- Heparin throughout: least risk to foetus, most risk to mother
- Aspirin: 150 mg aspirin may be used as an adjunct in second and third trimester but there is no consensus for this.

Note that it takes three weeks to clear warfarin from the foetal liver and that regional anaesthesia cannot be used if the mother is on warfarin.
Note also that the new oral anticoagulants cross the placenta and are not yet routinely used in pregnancy. They are not advised for use in patients with mechanical valves.

Congenital heart disease
General principles:

- All patients with congenital heart disease require pre-pregnancy risk assessment and counselling
- Foetal echocardiography should be offered
- At the first visit, the anatomy and physiology of the heart should be assessed
- In complex congenital heard disease, prematurity and low birth weight infants are common
- Infant mortality is higher than normal due to prematurity and recurrence of cardiac defects (recurrence 4–10% depending on lesion, compared to 1% in general population unless single gene defect).

Atrial septal defect/ventricular septal defect/patent arterial duct
Unrepaired:

- Low risk if shunt small and pulmonary artery pressure normal
- If shunt is large, increase in cardiac output may precipitate an atrial arrhythmia or ventricular dysfunction
- For atrial septal defects care should be taken to reduce the risk of paradoxical thromboembolism, e.g. by using compression stockings post-partum and i.v. line filters. Consider aspirin +/− LMWH if immobile.

Repaired:

- Low risk if pulmonary artery pressure normal.

Repaired tetralogy of Fallot

- Unrepaired tetralogy of Fallot rare
- Low risk if good functional capacity and good right ventricular function, even if severe pulmonary regurgitation
- If severe pulmonary regurgitation and pulmonary valve replacement is indicated, this is best done pre-pregnancy
- Need regular reviews during pregnancy with assessment of right ventricular function and cardiac rhythm. Risks include the development of supraventricular arrhythmias and worsening ventricular function
- Vaginal delivery usually recommended
- Consider genetic counselling pre-pregnancy if DiGeorge syndrome suspected.

Ebstein's anomaly

- Rare
- Can present with right heart failure due to significant tricuspid regurgitation or right ventricular dysfunction, atrial arrhythmias, and cyanosis (as 50% may have an inter-atrial shunt)
- Usually well tolerated if right ventricle is a reasonable size with good function and fully saturated
- If cyanosed, increased risks to foetus
- Monitor during pregnancy for cyanosis, right heart failure, and arrhythmias.

Cyanotic heart disease

- In cyanosis one in three patients will have a cardiac event and one in three foetuses will be premature
- Clotting factors and platelet function are impaired, so increased risk of haemorrhage and thromboembolic disease
- Right-to-left shunting increases with decreased systemic vascular resistance so increased risk of paradoxical embolism and desaturation
- Increased foetal loss. High risk if oxygen saturation <90%
- Consider prolonged bed rest with oxygen
- Usually low birth weight and premature, so delivery by Caesarean section typical
- Meticulous haemostasis is required, with good hydration, avoiding vasodilatation, and using line filters
- Univentricular hearts and fontan operation: risk of pregnancy considered to be moderate to high, but highly variable
- Fontan circulation dependent on good venous return and low pulmonary artery pressures so avoid dehydration, supine position, and venous thrombosis
- Aim for a vaginal delivery with limited pushing and assisted delivery. Epidural useful to facilitate this
- All patients with a Fontan circulation should already be on warfarin so convert to clexane as soon as possible.

Pulmonary stenosis

- If severe may present with right heart failure, tricuspid regurgitation, or arrhythmias
- Aim to treat pre-pregnancy if severe, although no evidence that there is significant impact on maternal or foetal outcome
- Pregnancy normally well tolerated if right ventricular function preserved, even if pulmonary stenosis severe

- If mother develops symptoms during pregnancy, consider balloon valvuloplasty
- Aim for vaginal delivery.

Pulmonary arterial hypertension

- May be idiopathic or due to Eisenmenger syndrome
- 30–50% maternal mortality in pregnancy, with foetal loss rate also of same magnitude. Due to:
  - Decrease in systemic vascular resistance resulting in an increase in the right–to-left shunting in Eisenmenger syndrome, decreased pulmonary flow, and progression to low output cardiac failure
  - Failure of the right ventricle to cope with the additional haemodynamic strain and also presumed hormonal effects on pulmonary vasculature and vascular tone
  - Death due to pulmonary hypertensive crises or heart failure; higher risk with higher pulmonary arterial pressure
- If woman wishes to proceed with pregnancy, she should be managed in a centre with expertise in managing pulmonary hypertension and heart disease in pregnancy
- Management includes oxygen therapy, bed rest, prophylaxis against thromboembolism, and pulmonary vasodilators
- Most deaths occur in the first few days post partum. High-dependency care required for at least a week. Deterioration may be sudden.

Coarctation of the aorta

- Close monitoring of blood pressure crucial; BP should be measured in right arm as may be underestimated on the left
- BBs are used as first line treatment to reduce BP and risk of aortic dissection.

Native coarctation

- Unrepaired lesions predispose the mother to the risk of severe systemic hypertension, heart failure, stroke, and aortic dissection. Placental and thus foetal blood flow is also compromised due to lower body hypoperfusion. Collateral vessels are variably present. Significant risk of intra-uterine growth retardation and foetal death
- Treatment options are limited and termination of pregnancy should be strongly considered
- Trans-catheter stenting is usually the treatment of choice in the non-pregnant state but carries a high risk of rupture or dissection during pregnancy and for 6 months afterwards due the changes in the vascular media
- Surgical repair is associated with significant morbidity in the adult and cardiopulmonary bypass carries a high risk of foetal death
- Medical therapy with anti-hypertensives can be considered if there is good collateral flow on CMR scanning. Monitor with regular growth scanning of the foetus.

Repaired coarctation

- Relatively common
- Low risk if no aneurysm at repair site (should be excluded as high risk of rupture with pregnancy)
- Blood pressure must be carefully controlled to avoid aortic wall stress
- Vaginal delivery with regional analgesia recommended with limited pushing. Consider Caesarean section if aneurysm present
- Risk of hypertension, even if no re-coarctation
- Keep blood pressure <130/80 with BB.

Bicuspid aortic valve

- If aortopathy risk of dissection and increasing aortic dilatation formation (higher risk if co-existing coarctation)
- Treat as for 'aortopathies'.

Turner's syndrome

- Patients commonly have BAV and coarctation
- Usually subfertile but mosaics may become pregnant due to assisted fertility techniques
- At increased risk of dissection compared to other patients with bicuspid aortopathy and coarctation.

Ehlers-Danlos syndrome

- Vascular type (type IV) is rare and associated with vasculopathy, increased risk of large artery rupture, peri-/post-partum haemorrhage and uterine rupture
- Treat as high-risk aortopathy with elective Caesarean section, with cardiothoracic surgeon on stand-by.

Aortopathies

- Compliance of the aorta increases in pregnancy
- Oestrogen inhibits collagen and elastin deposition in aortic media, increasing the risk of dissection
- Half of all aortic dissections occurring in women under 40 years occur during pregnancy and half of these have aortopathy
- 20% have hypertension
- Most are type A
- Maternal mortality from aortic dissection is 15% and aortic dissection accounts for 20% of maternal deaths
- Foetal mortality 30%; worse for type B
- Risk of dissection is highest in third trimester or immediately post partum.

Marfan's syndrome

- Complications in pregnancy include aortic dilatation/aneurysm and dissection, aortic regurgitation, worsening mitral regurgitation due to mitral valve prolapse, early pregnancy loss, premature rupture of membranes, pelvic instability and back pain, post-partum haemorrhage, and poor foetal outcome
- If root already dilated, pregnancy will accelerate increase
- Patients with previous aortic root replacement also at risk.

Management in pregnancy:

- Pre-pregnancy counselling at specialist unit crucial. Pre-pregnancy root replacement should be considered if root >43 mm
- Meticulous BP control and 4-weekly aortic root imaging
- If aortic root >43 mm, very high risk
- Risk greater if family history of dissection
- BBs should be given to all patients. Monthly growth scans of foetus are required (risk of intrauterine growth restriction)

- If patient dissects:
  - Surgical emergency; proceed to urgent surgery and deliver foetus by caesarean section if viable
  - Meticulous BP control critical; use BBs and hydralazine
  - If the aorta dilates during pregnancy delivery should be expedited and aortic surgery undertaken.

Delivery:

- Aim for elective epidural with passive/assisted second stage if aorta not dilated. If dilated, Caesarean section with cardiac surgeon on stand-by
- Dissection most common peripartum or in early post-partum period.

Acquired heart disease

Maternal infective endocarditis

- 10% of maternal cardiac deaths
- Early discussion with cardiac surgeons recommended
- If surgery needed in third trimester, consider delivery of baby before proceeding.

Prophylaxis and prevention of IE during pregnancy:

- Professional consensus-based guidelines rather than based on robust scientific data
- Antibiotic prophylaxis no longer indicated for childbirth (class IIIC evidence)
- If infection occurs, e.g. chorioamnionitis, prompt treatment with antibiotics is recommended
- Prior to pregnancy ensure women understand risks of endocarditis, how to prevent it, its clinical presentation, and need for early assessment.

Maternal cardiac arrhythmias

General principles of arrhythmia management:

- Arrhythmias very common in pregnancy due to physiological changes
- Most are benign
- 95% of pregnant women shown to have supraventricular or ventricular extrasystoles on Holter monitoring
- Risk factors include congenital heart disease (especially if surgically repaired), any pre-existing acquired cardiac disease, or cardiac failure
- Give reassurance for benign or self-limiting arrhythmias and avoid drugs if possible, especially in the first trimester
- Treat only if arrhythmia is sustained, particularly troublesome, or is causing haemodynamic compromise to mother
- If patient is haemodynamically stable, aim to manage tachyarrhythmias medically due to the associated risks of sedation/anaesthetic required for a DC cardioversion.

Use of anti-arrhythmic drugs in pregnancy:

- Flecainide, lignocaine, digoxin, adenosine and cardio-selective BBs thought to be relatively safe, although limited data from human studies
- Amiodarone may be teratogenic and is associated with foetal hypothyroidism, intra-uterine growth restriction, and pre-term birth and thus its use is not recommended
- CCBs thought to be relatively safe but verapamil reported to cause foetal bradycardia, heart block, and hypotension.

Direct current cardioversion/defibrillation:

- Can be safely used at any stage of pregnancy if drugs ineffective
- Recommend foetal heart scan post-procedure and cardiotocography to check for transient foetal bradycardias. Obstetric/neonatal team must be present
- Patient should be intubated, because of increased risk of aspiration in pregnancy, and positioned in left lateral decubitus position.

Pacemakers/ICDs:

- Permanent pacemaker insertion is recommended for women presenting with symptomatic sick sinus syndrome or non-transient second degree Mobitz type II/third-degree block in pregnancy, ideally after the first trimester
- Pelvic shielding should be used to protect the foetus from radiation
- No increased risks associated with pacemakers or implantable defibrillators implanted prior to pregnancy
- Lower pacing rate of pacemakers needs to be increased in those implanted for sinus node disease to mirror the increased chronotropic state of pregnancy
- Women who have devices will need special precautions such as care with diathermy, access to programming (or a magnet in the case of an ICD if a programming is not available acutely). Abdominal systems implanted in childhood may have leads close to the uterus.

Labour, delivery and lactation:

- Normal vaginal delivery recommended
- Intravenous adenosine useful for paroxysmal supraventricular arrhythmias in labour due to its short half-life. Intravenous esmolol also useful
- All anti-arrhythmics are excreted in breast milk although the levels are generally low; amiodarone is an exception and should be avoided
- Experience limited for many drugs, thus use with caution.

Inappropriate sinus tachycardia
- Heart rate persistently above 100 bpm
- Usually resolves within one month post partum
- Can occur at any time in pregnancy
- May recur with subsequent pregnancies
- Responds to BBs.

Supraventricular tachyarrhythmias
- Common
- Known SVTs recur in a third of cases; consider catheter ablation pre-pregnancy
- Vagal manoeuvres should be tried first. Intravenous adenosine safe and effective. Flecainide can be used if adenosine fails
- Cardio-selective BBs useful in preventing paroxysmal SVTs, including sinus node re-entry tachycardias.

Atrial flutter
- Haemodynamically unstable; DC cardioversion
- Can rate control with BB and digoxin
- If haemodynamically stable, consider flecainide/propafenone combined with a small dose of a BB to restore sinus rhythm
- Need for continuing medication and anti-coagulation will depend on whether further episodes develop.

Atrial fibrillation
- Rare in pregnancy
- Associated with increased morbidity and mortality in pregnancy due to haemodynamic effects in those with pre-existing heart disease and the increased risk of thromboembolism, especially in third trimester
- If haemodynamically unstable, DC cardioversion
- Aim to cardiovert pharmacologically; consider flecainide/propafenone in combination with a BB
- LMWH should be used for anticoagulation and continued for 4 weeks after sinus rhythm has been achieved.

Ventricular arrhythmias
- VT can occur in structurally normal hearts but more commonly associated with underlying cardiac disease
- In symptomatic VT, urgent therapy needed to preserve maternal circulatory status and protect foetus; DC cardioversion
- Consider BBs, lignocaine, or mexiletine if haemodynamically stable.

Bradyarrhythmias
- Often seen in women with repaired congenital heart disease
- Transient first- and second-degree atrioventricular block and RBBB can be seen in normal hearts during pregnancy
- Complete heart block should always be taken seriously and pacing considered
- In repaired congenital heart disease patients with sinus node dysfunction, second- or third-degree heart block, pacemaker insertion prior to pregnancy should be considered. If this has not been done, the patient needs to be carefully monitored for bradyarrhythmias.

Myocardial infarction and ischaemic heart disease
- MI historically due to coronary dissection
- Risk in pregnancy 1 in 15–30,000 but increasing due to increasing ischaemic heart disease secondary to increasing obesity, smoking, and diabetes in mothers, as well as women choosing to have children later in life
- Maternal mortality 11%, foetal mortality 9%, mainly due to death of mother
- 10% of women presenting with acute MIs are <35 years of age
- Peak incidence in third trimester, in parous women aged >33 years.

Management:

- Emergency coronary angiography and primary angioplasty as per normal situations
- Minimize radiation by using an abdominal shield and (ideally) radial approach with shortened fluoroscopy times
- Little data on thrombolysis in humans but streptokinase (as used for massive pulmonary embolism) is associated with serious complications for both the mother and the baby, such as maternal haemorrhage and foetal loss
- ADP antagonists preclude the use of regional anaesthesia for delivery. If possible, strategies should be pursued which avoid this but saving the life of the mother is paramount and decisions made in the cardiac catheterization laboratory should be based on this premise
- ADP antagonists thought to be safe for mother and baby though evidence limited.

Drug management:

- GPIIb/IIIa inhibitors/ADP antagonists can be used in pregnancy if benefits outweigh risks. Limited data available
- Caution with i.v. nitrates (systemic hypotension and placental hypoperfusion)
- Aspirin and BBs should be used
- ACE inhibitors and statins are contraindicated. Spironolactone and loop diuretics are best avoided
- Delivery should be delayed until 2–3 weeks post MI if possible
- Best mode of delivery is vaginal with elective regional anaesthesia, passive second stage, and assisted delivery
- Future pregnancy risk determined by LVEF
- The risks to the baby of using drugs post partum for secondary prevention in CAD must be weighed up against the benefits of breast-feeding to both mother and child.

Stable coronary artery disease:

- Good prognosis if normal exercise tolerance prior to conception with no residual ischaemia
- Low-dose aspirin should be continued after the first trimester
- Statins, ADP antagonists, and ACE inhibitors should be stopped
- The development of angina may not indicate unstable coronary disease but rather a demand/supply mismatch in the myocardium due to flow-restricting lesions. Therefore, if the patient develops angina and the foetus is viable, delivery should be expedited. If not, symptom control with anti-anginals should be attempted
- Angina at rest, with or without a troponin rise, should be treated by PCI. Close communication between cardiologists with experience of heart disease in pregnancy and obstetricians is crucial
- Vaginal delivery best as for myocardial infarction.

Cardiopulmonary bypass in pregnancy
- High risk for both the mother but especially the baby
- Maternal risk of death 3–9%
- Foetal risk of death 20–30% due to tissue pulsatility of bypass, hypothermia, and foetal bradycardia
- Cardiotocography during surgery essential, with foetal scanning afterwards
- Best done in early second trimester.

Hypertension
- Affects 10% of all pregnant women
- Major cause of maternal and foetal morbidity and mortality, accounting for nearly 15% of maternal deaths
- Hypertension in pregnancy can be classified in to four subtypes:
  - Pre-existing or chronic hypertension
  - Gestational hypertension
  - Pre-eclampsia
  - Pre-eclampsia superimposed on chronic hypertension or gestational hypertension
- Generally managed by obstetricians, even if eclampsia. Cardiologists may get involved if there is cardiac decompensation, which is rare.

Management of hypertension in pregnancy:

- Severe hypertension (>160/110 mmHg) in pregnancy requires treatment
- Aim is to allow time for foetal maturation and a planned, safe delivery, often induced
- First-line agents for non-severe hypertension are methyldopa and labetalol, with nifedipine as third line
- First-line agents for severe hypertension are intravenous labetalol and hydralazine
- Oral nifedipine if no parenteral treatment
- In pre-eclampsia, complete resolution of hypertension and associated features usually seen by 6 weeks' post partum. A few cases may go on to develop chronic hypertension
- Post-partum hypertension can also occur.

Cardiomyopathies

- Most important are peripartum, dilated, and hypertrophic cardiomyopathy
- Peripartum cardiomyopathy defined as cardiac failure occurring in the last month of pregnancy and up to 5/12 post-partum in the absence of an identifiable cause/recognizable cardiac disease in association with left ventricular systolic dysfunction and an ejection fraction <45% or fractional shortening <30% on echocardiography
- Incidence approximately 1 in 5–10,000 pregnancies
- Risk factors include primigravidae, multiple pregnancy, hypertension (pre-existing, pre-eclampsia, or gestational hypertension), multiparity, increased maternal age, and black race
- May present with heart failure, arrhythmias, or systemic emboli due to the formation of intracardiac thrombus
- Aetiology unknown, although recent interest in prolactin playing a casual role
- Mortality rate high (in excess of 20%), with poor functional class a predictor of poor outcome
- Left ventricle returns to normal in 50% by around 6 weeks. If left ventricle is still abnormal at 12 months, mortality rate in next pregnancy is 20%
- Recurrence risk for future pregnancies 50%
- Risk to woman's health of undertaking future pregnancy predicted by left ventricular dimension/function but can be unpredictable. If left ventricle does not return to normal, future pregnancy not advised
- Risks to foetus of prematurity, low birth weight.

Management:

- Exclude other causes of heart failure and confirm by echocardiogram
- Manage with standard heart failure care but liaise with obstetricians/anaesthetists closely
- Risk: benefit of ACE inhibitors need to be considered
- Delivery usually needs to be expedited. Ventricular function may deteriorate with continued pregnancy
- Thromboembolic prophylaxis crucial due to high risk of embolic stroke
- IABP/VADs and cardiac transplant may need to be considered
- Bromocriptine has recently been shown to improve outcome.

Dilated cardiomypathy

- Often occult until the volume load of pregnancy
- Typically presents at 17 to 20 weeks

- Manage similarly to peripartum cardiomyopathy
- High risk of death if NYHA class ≥III, EF <20%, mitral regurgitation, right ventricular dysfunction, atrial fibrillation.

Hypertrophic cardiomyopathy

- Usually well tolerated in pregnancy if no symptoms pre-pregnancy and no severe outflow tract obstruction
- At risk of atrial arrhythmias, syncope and worsening dyspnoea (usually if past history of these), and pulmonary oedema. Often difficult to predict who will have problems, unless gross LVH
- If symptomatic pre-pregnancy, consider BBs, AADs, septal myomectomy and ICD implantation
- Manage VT as in the normal heart
- Avoid vasodilators that can worsen LVOT obstruction
- Caution with regional anaesthesia. Avoid hypotension and rapid fluid shifts. Care with diuretics but use if pulmonary oedema present.

23.7 Pharmacological treatment in pregnancy

- Evidence for drug treatment and safety in pregnancy based on case reports, observational studies, and clinical consensus, not from randomized clinical trials
- Therefore, need to check every drug for safety profile and pharmacokinetics before use in pregnancy and lactation
- Drugs may have unpredictable effects in pregnancy due to changes in gastric motility and drug absorption, changes in the volume of distribution and protein-binding, increased renal blood flow as well as transfer of the drug transplacentally, which depends on the lipo/hydrosolubility of the drug, its molecular weight, and the pH of maternal and foetal fluids
- Generally use drugs with a long safety record, at the lowest doses and for the shortest duration
- See Table 23.1 for safety profile of drugs that are used in pregnancy.

Table 23.1 Safety profile of cardiac drugs commonly used in pregnancy

Generally safe	Unsafe	Affect baby but used
Adenosine	Amiodarone	Beta blockers
Flecainide	ACE inhibitors	Furosemide
Lidocaine	Angiotensin II receptor antagonists	
Sotalol	Spironolactone	
Verapamil	Thiazides	
Digoxin	Warfarin	
Hydralazine	Statins	
Nitrates		
Aspirin		
Clopidogrel		
GPIIb/IIIa inhibitors and ADP antagonists		

23.8 Contraception

- Contraception needs to be discussed in all patients with congenital heart disease from puberty
- Progesterones including progesterone-based morning after pill are safe for all cardiac conditions
- Need to consider efficacy of agent, thrombotic risk, drug interactions, infective risks, and risk of bleeding/vagal stimulation with insertion of intra-uterine devices
- Sterilization should not be recommended as the most failsafe means of contraception. Hormonal contraceptives, such as Implanon and Mirena coil are more effective and do not involve a surgical procedure with its attendant risks
- Advice regarding termination and emergency contraception is also important. Termination of pregnancy should be attended by experienced anaesthetist.

Further reading

Baumgartner H, Bonhoeffer P, de Groot NMS, et al. ESC Guidelines for the management of grown-up congenital heart disease (new version 2010). Eur Heart J, 2010; 31: 2915–57.

Gatzoulis MA, Swan L, Therrien J, Pantely GA. Adult Congenital Heart Disease: A Practical Guide. Blackwell/BMJ Books, 2005.

Heart Disease and Pregnancy website. Available at: www.heartdiseaseandpregnancy.com

Hiratzka LF, Bakris GL, Beckman JA, et al. ACCF/AHA/AATS/ACR/ASA/SCA/SCAI/SIR/STS/SVM guidelines for the diagnosis and management of patients with thoracic aortic disease. Circulation, 2010; 121: 266–369.

Presbitero P, Boccuzzi GG, Groot CJ, Roos-Hesselink JW. Pregnancy and heart disease. In: Camm AJ, Lüscher TF, Serruys PW (eds). The European Society of Cardiology Textbook of Cardiovascular Medicine, 2nd edn. Oxford University Press, 2009.

Regitz-Zagrosek V, Lundqvist CB, Borghi C, et al. ESC guidelines on the management of cardiovascular diseases during pregnancy. Eur Heart J, 2011; 32: 3147–97.

Siu SC, Sermer M, Colman JM, et al. Prospective multicenter study of pregnancy outcomes in women with heart disease. Circulation, 2001; 104: 515–21.

Steer PJ, Gatzoulis MA, Baker P (eds). Heart Disease and Pregnancy. RCOG Press, 2006.

Thorne S. Pregnancy in Heart Disease. Heart, 2004; 90: 450–6.

Warnes CA, Williams RG, Bashore TM, et al. ACC/AHA 2008 guidelines for the management of adults with congenital heart disease. A report of the American College of Cardiology/American Heart Association Taskforce on Practice Guidelines. Circulation, 2008; 118: e714–833.

Radiation use and safety

24.1 Characteristics of X-rays

- X-ray is a type of electromagnetic radiation with wavelength of 10^{-8}–10^{-11} m (see Figure 24.1)
- Has a shorter wavelength than visible light and therefore higher frequency (30×10^{15} – 30×10^{18} Hz) as well as energy (>120 eV)
- Enables X-ray to ionize matter (by knocking off electrons from atoms) as distinct from non-ionizing radiation such as radiowaves, ultrasound, ultraviolet rays, and microwave radiation
- X-rays travel in straight lines and penetrate matter
- X-rays interact with matter in two ways:
  - Photoelectric effect
  - Compton effect.

Photoelectric effect

This is due to the absorption of a photon when it interacts with a bound electron.

- It occurs with lower X-ray energies and especially on interaction with matter with higher atomic number, such as bone or contrast media
- X-rays have differential absorption between different tissue types and density thereby producing image contrast.

Compton effect

This accounts for majority of interactions of X-rays and tissue.

- Occurs when a high-energy photon interacts with a free electron and is scattered as a 'weaker photon'
- It is independent of atomic number
- This scattering effect produces weaker radiation in different trajectories, which degrades image quality.

Decreasing wavelength in metres -->

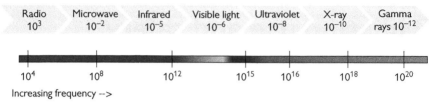

| Radio | Microwave | Infrared | Visible light | Ultraviolet | X-ray | Gamma |
| 10^3 | 10^{-2} | 10^{-5} | 10^{-6} | 10^{-8} | 10^{-10} | rays 10^{-12} |

10^4 10^8 10^{12} 10^{15} 10^{16} 10^{18} 10^{20}

Increasing frequency -->

Figure 24.1 Electromagnetic spectrum.

24.2 Radiation doses and monitoring

- The **absorbed dose** is the energy absorbed per unit mass (1 Gray (Gy) = 1 J/kg). Relates to deterministic effects (see Section 24.3)
- The **equivalent dose** is that absorbed dose weighted by a radiation quality factor (=1 for X-rays), which attempts to take into account the biological damage potential of different radiation (Sievert). Thus 1 Gy = 1 Sv = 1 J/kg
- **Effective dose** (Sievert) is the sum of all mean equivalent doses to organs multiplied by a tissue factor (takes into account the sensitivity of tissue or organ). Effective dose is used to extrapolate the effects of partial exposure and relate this to the risk of equivalent whole-body exposure (stochastic effects)
- **Dose–area product** (DAP) (Gy.cm²) is a function of entrance dose and field size (measured automatically within the tube). Estimates the energy delivered to the patient (procedural dose) to predict stochastic effects.

24.3 Adverse effects

- X-rays can ionize atoms and molecules and thus cause damage to DNA
- At a cellular level (due to free radicals) this leads to inflammatory response, cell repair, cell damage or death
- Blood cells are the most sensitive to ionizing radiation, whereas muscle, brain, and nerve cells are the most resistant, with epithelial, connective tissue, and bone cells having intermediate sensitivity.

There are two types of clinical effect:

- **Deterministic effects** (see Figures 24.2 and 24.3) are generally acute or sub-acute and due to cell death, leading to skin burns, cataracts, bone marrow suppression, or sterility
  - Deterministic effects are dose-related and occur above a threshold dose **(absorbed dose (Gy))**
- **Stochastic effects** are long-term effects and due to cell damage, causing cancer induction or hereditary effects
  - While the severity is not related to dose (therefore no threshold), the probability of effect or risk is dose-related
  - There is also a latent period for stochastic effects
  - Stochastic risk is predicted using the **effective dose**

Tissue effects	Fluoroscopy time (@0.05 Gy/min)	Cinetime (@0.3 Gy/min)	Threshold	Onset
• Early transient erythema	• 0.7 h	• 0.1 h	• 2 Gy	• 2–24 h
• Hair loss	• 1 h	• 0.2 h	• 3 Gy	• 3 weeks
• Main erythema	• 2 h	• 0.3 h	• 3–6 Gy	• 1–4 weeks
• Skin necrosis	• 6 h	• 1 h	• 12–18 Gy	• Early > 10 weeks
				• Delayed > 1 year

Figure 24.2 Deterministic effects of cardiology procedures.

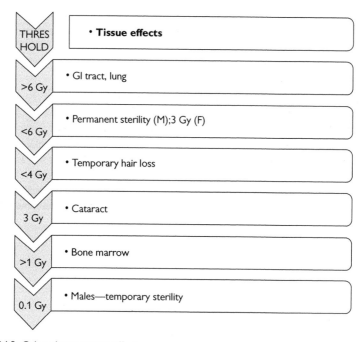

Figure 24.3 Other deterministic effects.

- The risk of causing a fatal cancer is approximately 1 in 20,000/mSv
- Angiography has a typical effective dose of 7 mSv and therefore cancer risk of 1 in 3000
- Percutaneous coronary intervention (PCI) has a typical effective dose of 15–20 mSv and cancer induction risk of approximately 1 in 1,000
- Due to the long latency period for stochastic effects and lack of comprehensive studies assessing stochastic effects of low-dose radiation procedures, this cancer induction risk is a rather simplistic extrapolation from nuclear explosion data
- The risk of cancer induction is also age-dependent, with children being twice as prone as adults
- The dose to the foetus from cardiology procedures is very low (<1 Gy) and although there is a minimal risk of adverse effects due to radiation, it is important to use shielding precautions in pregnant women to eliminate these risks.

24.4 X-ray components

- The X-ray generator tube (source), the patient, and the image receptor are the three essential components of imaging during cardiology procedures (see Figure 24.4)
- The source consists of a vacuum tube with a cathode emitting electrons, which are then accelerated towards an anode (metal of high atomic number, high melting point, and good heat transmission, such as tungsten) by applying a high voltage to the tube
- Potential difference between the cathode and anode is the energy gained by the electron (kV)
- The interaction of the electron with the tungsten atom releases energy, the majority in the form of heat and a small fraction in the form of X-ray radiation (1%)
- This method produces X-rays by two processes: *Bremsstrahlung* and X-ray fluorescence
- Heat produced during the process is dissipated by using a rotating anode and often also by active cooling via water-cooled heat exchangers
- The X-ray generator controls the quantity (number) and quality (spectrum of energy) of the X-rays produced
- Modern fluoroscopy systems utilise flat plate detector technology of image intensifier that converts this energy into an electrical signal viewable on a monitor.

24.5 Factors influencing radiation exposure

- Staff radiation doses are influenced by factors such as the complexity and duration of the procedure, patient dose, distance of the operator from the primary beam as well as from the patient, and use of personal protective equipment and shields
- No portion of the operator's body should be in the primary beam during imaging
- Thus the majority of the radiation dose received by the operator is due to scattered radiation from the patient.

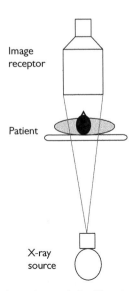

Image receptor

Patient

X-ray source

Figure 24.4 The three important determinants during X-ray imaging.

Distance

- Inverse square law (see Figure 24.5) expresses the relationship between the intensity of radiation and distance
- The number of X-rays travelling through a unit area, and thus the level of radiation, decreases with increase in distance such that the intensity of radiation is inversely proportional to the square of the distance from the source of radiation
- This is expressed by the equation:

$$I_A/I_B = (D_A/D_B)^2$$

where I = intensity of X-ray, D = distance, and A and B are points in space
- Thus, doubling the distance from the source of radiation decreases the intensity of radiation by a factor of four
- Conversely, halving the distance increases the intensity of radiation four-fold
- Important when adjusting table height: if the tube is too close to the patient they will receive a large skin dose
- Conversely it is important to minimize the source-to-image distance by ensuring the image intensifier is as close to the patient as possible; this reduces dose to the patient and scatter to staff
- Radiation exposure can be further reduced if the operator takes a step back during fluoroscopy or cineangiography.

Patient characteristics

- Raised BMI significantly impacts X-ray imaging
- As X-rays have to penetrate more body thickness, the quality of the imaging is often affected

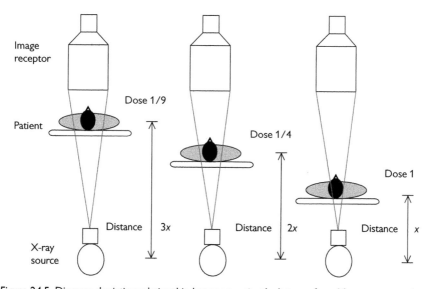

Figure 24.5 Diagram depicting relationship between patient's distance from X-ray source and dose delivered (inverse square law).

- Increased BMI also leads to more scatter radiation and thereby more radiation exposure to the operator
- Hyperexpanded chest (emphysema) can also be relevant, increasing the distance of the image intensifier.

Filtering and collimation

Filtering

- Filtering the X-rays preferentially removes lower energy photons, which would otherwise be absorbed by the patients skin (skin dose reduced) and do not contribute to the image
- As the X-ray beam is attenuated, scatter production reduces
- More scatter is emitted at beam entrance than beam exit
- A removable grid (consisting of alternate strips of an X-ray-absorbing material, such as lead, and a relatively non-absorbing interspace material, such as carbon or aluminium) can be attached to the image detector to absorb scatter radiation, thereby reducing contrast and improving image quality (see Figure 24.6)
- Additional 'wedge' filters should be moved into place during the procedure to optimize image quality and exposure e.g. 'bright' lung areas bordering the cardiac areas of interest are filtered.

Collimation

- Collimation ('coning in') is the process of elimination of the more divergent portion of an X-ray beam, thereby reducing the field size and scatter as well as improving image contrast (see Figure 24.7)
- Use of collimators or lead shields reduces the size of the X-ray field and thus leads to reduced radiation exposure to the patient as well as operator

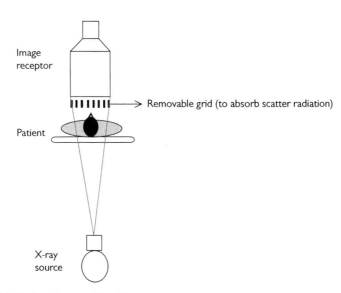

Figure 24.6 Placing of removable grid.

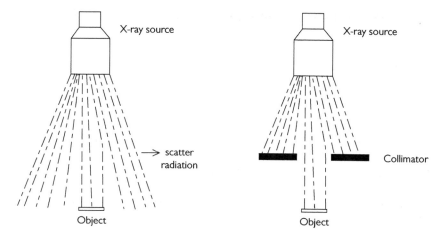

Figure 24.7 Collimation.

- Optimizing the imaging geometry by having a small focus and low magnification (by having the image intensifier close to the patient) reduces blurring and restricts X-ray intensity
- However, when very small fields of view or magnified views are used the radiation is increased and skin exposures can become quite high.

Fluoroscopy and cineangiography duration

- Procedures in the cardiac catheter laboratory produce radiation exposure during both fluoroscopy and cineangiography
- Fluoroscopy (or 'screening') is used to image catheter, balloon, stent, or lead placement and contributes to the majority of the X-ray operation time, whilst leading to less than half of the total radiation exposure to both staff as well as patients
- Cineangiography (or image 'acquisition'), however, contributes to nearly two-thirds of the radiation exposure despite accounting for less than 10% of total X-ray operation time
- Although it is important to limit total fluoroscopy time, the priority is to limit the number and duration of cineangiography acquisitions
- Fluoroscopic images can be stored ('fluoro-grab'/'last image hold') in preference to cineangiography in situations where the operator intends to document information for reference without the need for superior image quality.

Angulations and personal protection

- Scatter radiation is highest near the X-ray beam entry point on the patient, and radiation levels are lower on the image intensifier side than the X-ray tube side
- The highest scatter radiation is usually where the primary operator stands and at a distance of 1 m from the X-ray beam entrance area; the operator receives 0.1% of the patient's exposure
- When the X-ray tube is below the patient, radiation levels are highest beneath the table
- Left anterior oblique angles are the most dose-intensive to a right-sided operator
- Steep (left or right anterior) oblique projections (>60°) produce especially high doses due to the length of the beam path (also lateral projections)
- A variety of personal protective equipment is available to shield the operator from radiation: lead aprons, thyroid collars, eye protection, (ceiling suspended shields and lead-loaded glasses), lead shin pads, and lead glasses.

Regulation and dose references/monitoring

- The organ dose or effective dose cannot be measured directly on people and is calculated on a computer model
- The National Radiation Protection Board has carried out computer simulations of the passage of diagnostic X-rays through a patient's body (called Monte Carlo calculations) in order to calculate doses to the radiosensitive organs in the patient
- A variety of techniques, using thermoluminescence dosemeters, electronic dosemeters, and X-ray-sensitive films such as gafchromic film, have been used to measure skin dose
- The measured skin dose has been found to be on average a quarter less than the equipment readout
- If a procedure carries a high risk of skin injury, the patient should be counselled prior to the procedure
- If the skin dose is more than 3 Gy, they should be followed up for signs of skin injury
- The average patient doses in the UK from cardiology procedures are shown in Table 24.1
- Diagnostic reference levels (DRLs) are typical doses for an average patient and national DRLs are set at the third quartile of national data
- Local DRLs should be set for each standard radiologicial investigation and therapeutic procedure
- DRLs should be set lower than national DRLs and audited regularly
- National DRLs for coronary angiography are a DAP of 36 Gy cm^2 and fluoroscopy time of 5.6 min
- Recommended national reference doses are shown in Table 24.2
- Usual effective dose for Tc99m myocardial perfusion scan is 8 mSv, whereas the same using Thallium 201 is 28 mSv
- Multi-gated acquisition scan (MUGA; using Tc99m) delivers a dose of 6 mSv and PET scanning for myocardial imaging delivers an effective dose of 8 mSv
- Typical effective doses for CT angiography vary from 4 to 20 mSv
- Effective radiation doses of cardiology procedures are in the range of 1–25 mSv and this corresponds to fatal cancer risks of about 1 in 1000 (compared to the natural cancer incidence of 1 in 3)
- Complex cardiac intervention or repeated procedures can lead to acute skin damage because of higher than threshold doses (1–2 Gy).

Table 24.1 Average patient doses

Procedure	DAP (Gy cm^2)	Fluoroscopy time (min)
1. Coronary angiography	26	4.1
2. Permanent pacemaker	9	6.6
3. PTCA (1 stent)	43	12.2
4. PTCA (2 stents)	64	13.9
5. PTCA (3 stents)	98	18.3
6. Radiofrequency ablation	25	22.3

PTCA, percutaneous transluminal coronary angioplasty.

Reproduced from HPA-RPD-029, 'Doses to patients from radiographic and fluoroscopic X-ray imaging procedures in the UK', D. Hart, M. C. Hillier, B. F. Wall, copyright 2005 with permission from The Health Protection Agency.

Table 24.2 Recommended national reference doses for complete examinations on adult patients

Procedures	DAP (Gy cm2)	Fluoroscopy time (minutes)
Coronary angiography	29	4.5
PTCA(1 stent)	50	13
Pacemaker	11	8.2
Femoral angiography	36	5.5
Venography	7	2.2

PTCA, percutaneous transluminal coronary angioplasty.

Reproduced from HPA-RPD-029, 'Doses to patients from radiographic and fluoroscopic X-ray imaging procedures in the UK', D. Hart, M. C. Hillier, B. F. Wall, copyright 2005 with permission from The Health Protection Agency.

24.6 Regulations

The Ionising Radiations Regulations 1999

- IRR99 (see Further Reading section) is the instrument that forms the main legal requirements for the use and control of ionizing radiation in the United Kingdom
- Framework for ensuring that exposure to ionizing radiation due to work activities is kept as low as reasonably practicable (ALARP) and does not exceed specified dose limits
- Rules are framed for staff protection as well as protection of members of public
- These regulations also cover equipment aspects of patient protection
- A dose assessment must be carried out if suspected dose >6 mSv, 10% of any dose limit, or 1 mSv per annum
- The member of staff must be kept under close scrutiny if he or she receives statutory 30% of any dose limit
- The employer must also review work of pregnant staff to ensure dose to foetus during pregnancy likely to be <1 mSv
- The annual dose limits as per IRR99 are shown in Table 24.3.

Ionising Radiation Medical Exposure Regulations

IR(ME)R (see Further Reading section) was framed in 2000. It covers patient protection and defines the roles of duty-holders such as:

- Referrer (medical or dental practitioner or other registered health professional), who is responsible for providing appropriate medical data to the practitioner to justify the radiation exposure

Table 24.3 Annual dose limits per IRR99

Who	Effective dose (mSv/year)	Skin, extremities (mSv/year)	Eye (mSv/year)
Employees	20	500	150
Trainees	6	150	50
Others	1	50	15

Reproduced under Crown copyright from 'The Ionising Radiations Regulations 1999 (IRR99)'.

- Practitioner (medical or dental practitioner or other registered health professional), with adequate training to justify the procedure, ensure compliance with ALARP principle (see Section 24.7), as well as employer's procedures (justification is the process of taking into account the referral information, the total investigative or therapeutic benefits of the radiation exposure, as well as available alternatives in order to ultimately decide whether there is sufficient net benefit for the referred procedure)
- Operator: anyone trained and authorized to carry out the practical aspects of the radiation procedure; the operator should ensure procedure is justified, ask patient if pregnant, and ensure dose is kept as low as reasonably possible
- Employer: must provide a robust framework and regulations to ensure that the procedure is delivered safely and efficiently in according with established guidelines.

24.7 Tips to reduce dose of radiation

- Use the central principle: as low as reasonably achievable/practicable (ALARA/ALARP)
- Use low intensity fluoroscopy modes
- Ensure appropriate dim lighting of catheter lab for adequate viewing of images during procedure
- Keep X-ray beam-on time (time the pedal is depressed) to the minimum possible
- Use last-image hold (previous static image saved)/reduce time and number of acquisitions
- Minimize use of lateral or oblique views
- Increase distance of operator from the patient (by stepping back, using automated contrast injectors) and from the X-ray tube (especially when using lateral or oblique views)
- Vary angulations during lengthy procedures
- Reducing air gap between the patient and the flat plate detector or image intensifier: keep X-ray tube as far away from the patient as possible to reduce scatter and improve image contrast
- Use kV as high as possible (higher penetrative power) without comprising image contrast
- Minimize use of magnification
- Use collimation and removable grid (Figures 24.6 and 24.7)
- Use personal protective equipment.

Further reading

Department of Health. The Ionising Radiation (Medical Exposure) Regulations 2000 (together with notes on good practice, 23 April 2007).
Health and Safety Executive. The Ionising Radiations Regulations 1999.

Community cardiology

CONTENTS

25.1 Overview

Policies, strategies and guidelines for cardiac care in the community

These are set out by a series of national bodies.

- The Department of Health (DoH) sets National Service Frameworks (NSFs) for healthcare
- The NSF for CHD (2000) includes recommendations for the provision of community cardiac services including:
  - Community development strategies for reducing heart disease in the population
  - Increasing investment in the skills and equipment to diagnose CHD in community settings
  - Multidisciplinary support in the community for patients with heart failure
  - Community-based cardiac rehabilitation programmes
- The DoH builds on the NSF in the Cardiovascular Disease Outcome Strategy for England (2013) which set 10 key actions to improve care for patients with CVD including:
  - The new improvement body in the NHS Commissioning Board (CB), NHS Improving Quality (NHS IQ); set to develop and evaluate service models to manage CVD as a family of diseases. NHS IQ will develop a standardized template that can be used in hospitals and in the community to assess patients with cardiovascular problems
  - NHS IQ will work with Public Health England, Local Authorities, and the NHS to support the successful implementation of the NHS Health Check programme
  - The NHS CB will collaborate to develop new tools to help identify patients with CVD in primary care. NHS IQ and the Strategic Clinical Networks will provide support to GP practices that have low detection rates for CVD
  - The NHS CB will support primary care to provide good management of people with or at risk of CVD, including review of relevant QOF indicators and promotion of primary care liaison with local authorities, the third sector, and Public Health England
- The NHS Heart Improvement Programme (which is now incorporated into NHS IQ) focuses on a series of national priorities, including:
  - The diagnosis of AF in primary care
  - Cardiac rehabilitation services

- ■ Heart failure diagnosis and management (including community heart failure services)
- ■ Screening for CVD via the NHS Health Check
- The National Institute for Clinical Excellence (NICE) guidance includes:
  - ■ Community-based cardiac rehabilitation for patients post MI and in chronic heart failure patients
  - ■ No recommendation for the use of telemonitoring for patients with chronic heart failure as further research required.

Other relevant government strategies

- Saving Lives: Our Healthier Nation (DoH white paper, July 1999):
  - ■ Set targets for improving health and proposed the creation of an integrated strategy to reduce the burden of CHD through a contract for health
  - ■ Set target to reduce mortality from CHD, stroke, and related disorders by 40% in people aged under 75 by the year 2010
- Equity and Excellence—Liberating the NHS (DoH white paper, July 2010):
  - ■ Plan to establish an independent and accountable NHS Commissioning Board
  - ■ The board now acts to lead on the achievement of health outcomes, allocate and account for NHS resources, lead on quality improvement, and promote patient involvement and choice
  - ■ The board has an explicit duty to promote equality and tackle inequalities in access to healthcare
  - ■ PCT responsibilities for local health improvement transferred to local authorities, who employ a Director of Public Health jointly appointed with the Public Health Service
- Putting Prevention First (DoH, April 2008):
  - ■ Plan for the NHS to introduce a programme of vascular risk assessment and management for those aged between 40 and 74
  - ■ Implemented via the NHS Health Check programme.

25.2 Implementation of community cardiology

The interaction of different stakeholders

There are many different stakeholders who have an interest in the provision of community cardiology services:

- National government through the Department of Health
- Local Authorities
  - ■ Act to promote public health and commission care and support services.
- Clinical Commissioning Groups (CCGs)
  - ■ Budget holders, 'purchasers', have overall accountability for healthcare commissioning— local investment to achieve the greatest health gain and to reduce health inequalities, at the best value
- Health and Wellbeing Boards
  - ■ Ensure that services work together to respond to communities' needs and priorities; include local people and community organizations, and inform CCGs and local authorities when they commission services
- Local Healthwatch
  - ■ A voice for patients and communities; represented on Health and Wellbeing Boards. Report views and concerns to Healthwatch England to raise issues at a national level

- Acute care trusts: the 'providers'
- Directors of public health
- Private healthcare companies
- Patients and patient groups
- The voluntary sector.

Cardiac networks

Across England regional cardiac networks (or cardiac and stroke networks) have been set up and bring together representatives from the different stakeholder groups.

Cardiac networks aim to:

- Bring together clinicians, other professionals, patients, and managers from all organizations so that they can improve services for patients
- Set local standards and targets
- Provide integrated services between primary, secondary, and tertiary care
- Provide equity of services across a region
- Guide local commissioning of cardiac care services.

The role of community cardiology

The aim in all cases is to improve access to cardiac services and to improve the patient pathway through the healthcare system. All community services should have a clear and effective protocol for accessing support from specialist cardiologists in secondary or tertiary care when needed.

- Services may include:
    - Satellite clinics provided by Consultant Cardiologists in Community Hospitals
    - Community cardiology clinics provided by GPs with a special interest in cardiology
    - Community cardiology clinics provided by specialist nurses
    - Community based diagnostic services (may be NHS or private providers):
        - ECG
        - Echocardiography: British Society of Echocardiography (BSE) offers specialist accreditation in community echo
        - 24-h tapes/Holters/ambulatory BP monitoring
        - Increasing use of B-type natriuretic peptide (BNP) measurement in the diagnosis of heart failure
        - Telemedicine
            - Use of audiovisual technology for remote consultations
            - Electronic transfer of locally acquired diagnostic data for centrally based analysis and reporting
    - Specialist intermediate care services run by skilled multidisciplinary teams:
        - Cardiac rehabilitation programmes (see Chapter 18)
        - Arrhythmia/AF services
        - Secondary prevention/CHD services
        - Heart failure services
            - Outreach follow-up by specialist nurses of those admitted to hospital with heart failure
            - Heart failure clinics for investigation (ECG/echo/BNP) and/or follow up
            - Access to palliative care resources
            - Telehealth/remote monitoring, which provides home based monitoring of vital signs in patients with chronic disease, and aims to deliver prompt treatment and a reduction in hospital admissions.

Improving the patient's pathway

- As well as providing care closer to home, community cardiac services can improve access to diagnostic tests, reducing unnecessary referral to secondary care and therefore by helping to reduce overall waiting times
- Clear guidelines should be put in place by local cardiac networks and commissioners to ensure the correct referrals are made and to avoid the inappropriate use of these key resources
- The pathways in Figures 25.1 and 25.2 compare the traditional models of primary and secondary care with the potential resources and flexibility of an integrated community cardiology service.

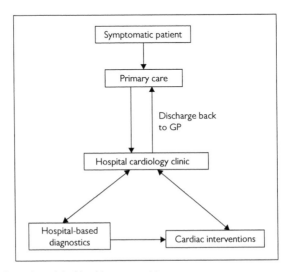

Figure 25.1 Traditional model of healthcare provision.

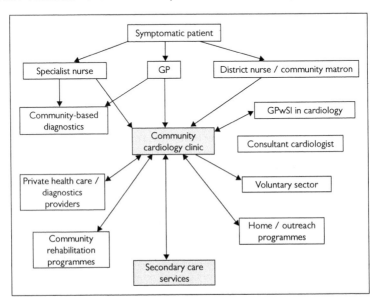

Figure 25.2 Integrated community cardiology services.

25.3 Screening programmes

NHS Health Checks

- Based on the 'Putting Prevention First' strategy set out by the DoH
- Potential to prevent 1600 heart attacks and strokes and save 650 lives per year
- Offered to all people between 40 and 74, recalling patients every 5 years
- Assesses risk of heart disease, stroke, kidney disease, and diabetes by looking at age, sex, family history, height, weight, BP, and cholesterol levels
- Enables calculation of an individual's risk:
  - Low-risk patients should receive lifestyle advice (physical activity, diet, smoking cessation)
  - High-risk patients are those with a 10-year absolute risk of a coronary event (non-fatal MI or death from CHD) of over 30%
  - High-risk patients should receive lifestyle advice as well as primary preventative medication for hypercholesterolaemia and BP control.

Atrial fibrillation

- Opportunistic screening of patients over 65 in primary care using a manual pulse check
- The appropriate treatment of atrial fibrillation could prevent approximately 4500 strokes per year.

Further reading

Department of Health website (includes access to DoH publications archive). Available at: www.dh.gov.uk

Department of Health papers

Saving Lives: Our Healthier Nation (DoH white paper, July 1999)
National Service Framework for Coronary Heart Disease (March 2000)
Cardiovascular Disease Outcomes Strategy (March 2013)
Equity and Excellence—Liberating the NHS (DoH white paper, July 2010)
Putting Prevention First (April 2008)

Other websites

Arrhythmia Alliance website. Available at: www.arrhythmiaalliance.org.uk
Association of Public Health Observatories website. Available at: www.apho.org.uk
British Association for Cardiac Rehabilitation website. Available at: www.bcs.com/bacr
British Cardiac Patients Association website. Available at: www.bcpa.co.uk
British Heart Foundation website. Available at: www.bhf.org.uk
British Society of Heart Failure website. Available at: www.bsh.org.uk
Cardiomyopathy Association website. Available at: www.cardiomyopathy.org
CRY (Cardiac Risk in the Young) website. Available at: www.c-r-y.org.uk
Grown Up Congenital Heart Patients Association website. Available at: www.guch.org.uk
National Heart Improvement Programme website. Available at: www.improvement.nhs.uk
National Institute for Clinical Excellence (NICE) website. Available at: www.nice.org.uk
Office of National Statistics website. Available at: www.statistics.gov.uk
Heart UK website. Available at: www.heartuk.org.uk

Pulmonary hypertension

CONTENTS

26.1 Overview

- The term pulmonary hypertension (PHT) is used when the mean pulmonary artery pressure is abnormally high
- It is also used to collectively describe a group of clinical conditions defined by elevated pulmonary artery pressures
- Just as for anaemia, the search for a diagnosis starts rather than stops once PHT is identified
- PH is classified according to five separate clinical groupings as agreed at the most recent World Symposium in 2013
- A systematic diagnostic approach is essential to define the cause(s) of PHT and its impact on functional ability
- Although there have been significant advances in the therapy of patients with pulmonary arterial hypertension (PAH) and chronic thromboembolic pulmonary hypertension (CTEPH), the evidence base for treatment of other forms of PHT is inadequate.

26.2 Haemodynamics

- PHT is defined as a mean pulmonary artery pressure (mPAP) ≥ 25 mmHg *at rest*, when derived invasively by right heart catheterization
- Values during exercise are currently excluded from this definition because there is no normal range
- It is helpful to localize the problem in the pulmonary circulation to either a *pre- or post-capillary* site
- Post-capillary haemodynamics are a consequence of left heart disease or pericardial disease
- Pre-capillary haemodynamics are caused by the other clinical classification groups
- To distinguish between pre- and post-capillary PHT requires left atrial pressure to be known
- This is most commonly assessed indirectly using the pulmonary wedge technique, with normal values defined as ≤ 15 mmHg.

26.3 Classification and epidemiology

Clinical diseases recognized to underlie PHT are grouped into five distinct groups according to shared features (see Table 26.1):

Table 26.1 Updated classification of pulmonary hypertension*

1. Pulmonary arterial hypertension
   1.1 Idiopathic PAH
   1.2 Heritable PAH
       1.2.1 BMPR2
       1.2.2 ALK-1, ENG, **SMAD9, CAV1, KCNK3**
       1.2.3 Unknown
   1.3 Drug and toxin induced
   1.4 Associated with:
       1.4.1 Connective tissue disease
       1.4.2 HIV infection
       1.4.3 Portal hypertension
       1.4.4 Congenital heart diseases
       1.4.5 Schistosomiasis
1'. Pulmonary veno-occlusive disease and/or pulmonary capillary hemangiomatosis
1''. Persistent pulmonary hypertension of the newborn (PPHN)
2. Pulmonary hypertension due to left heart disease
   2.1 Left ventricular systolic dysfunction
   2.2 Left ventricular diastolic dysfunction
   2.3 Valvular disease
   2.4 Congenital/acquired left heart inflow/outflow tract obstruction and congenital cardiomyopathies
3. Pulmonary hypertension due to lung diseases and/or hypoxia
   3.1 Chronic obstructive pulmonary disease
   3.2 Interstitial lung disease
   3.3 Other pulmonary diseases with mixed restrictive and obstructive pattern
   3.4 Sleep-disordered breathing
   3.5 Alveolar hypoventilation disorders
   3.6 Chronic exposure to high altitude
   3.7 Developmental lung diseases
4. Chronic thromboembolic pulmonary hypertension (CTEPH)
5. Pulmonary hypertension with unclear multifactorial mechanisms
   5.1 Hematologic disorders: **chronic hemolytic anemia**, myeloproliferative disorders, splenectomy
   5.2 Systemic disorders: sarcoidosis, pulmonary histiocytosis, lymphangioleiomyomatosis
   5.3 Metabolic disorders: glycogenstorage disease,Gaucher disease, thyroid disorders
   5.4 Others: tumoral obstruction, fibrosing mediastinitis, chronic renal failure, **segmental PH**

Note : *5th WSPH Nice 2013. Main modifications to the previous Dana Point classification are in bold.
BMPR = bone morphogenic protein receptor type II; CAVI = caveolin-1; ENG = endoglin;
HIV = human immunodeficiency virus; PAH = pulmonary arterial hypertension.
Reproduced from *The Journal of the American College of Cardiology*, Gérald Simonneau, Michael A. Gatzoulis, Ian Adatia *et al.*, 'Updated clinical classification of pulmonary hypertension', 62 (25), S43–S54, copyright 2013 with permission from Elsevier.

Group 1: PAH:

- Most widely studied form of PHT and is thought to occur in 15–50 persons per million
- The group comprises patients with no detectable cause (idiopathic PAH), heritable forms (formerly familial PAH), or those associated with other medical conditions.

Group 1: rare but important; pulmonary veno-occlusive disease and pulmonary capillary haemangiomatosis.

Group 2: including valve disease, LV systolic and diastolic dysfunction; left heart disease represents the most common cause of PH.

Group 3: PHT due to lung disease.

Group 4: PHT due to chronic thromboembolic disease:

- Occurs in 0.5–2% of patients suffering a pulmonary embolus
- Importantly, chronic thromboembolic disease can occur in the absence of a history of previous pulmonary embolus or deep vein thrombosis
- Chronic thromboembolic pulmonary hypertension (CTEPH) is more common in patients with pro-thrombotic conditions such as previous splenectomy, ventriculo-atrial shunt for hydrocephalus, myeloproliferative disorders and inflammatory bowel disease.

Group 5: A catch-all group for diseases whose pathophysiology is uncertain.

26.4 Features of disease

- The respective site of each disease for Groups 1–4 is shown in Figure 26.1
- The hallmark pathological features in Group 1 (PAH) are cell proliferation into the lumen of small pulmonary arteries leading to obstruction, plexiform lesions alongside medial hypertrophy, intimal hypertrophy, and in-situ thrombosis
- Lung biopsy is not used for diagnosis because of its high mortality in PHT patients
- These changes are associated with vasoconstriction (due to reduced production of NO and prostacyclin) at least in the early stage of the disease and cell proliferation
- PHT in Group 2 is driven passively by elevated left atrial pressures, although in some patients this is supplanted by pulmonary vascular remodelling and vasoconstriction
- In Group 3, hypoxic vasoconstriction is a key cause of PHT
- In parenchymal lung disease loss of lung tissue is associated with a loss of vessels
- In Group 4, thrombus becomes fibrosed, is incorporated into the elastic pulmonary artery wall, and obstructs blood flow.

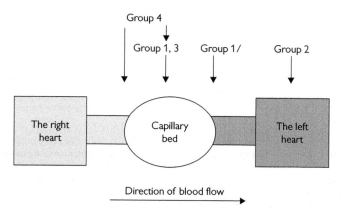

Figure 26.1 Five clinical groups of pulmonary hypertension according to the clinical classification.

26.5 General diagnostic points

- Delays in diagnosis are common
- PHT should always be considered as a differential diagnosis in patients with unexplained breathlessness, chest pain, or syncope
- This is particularly important in patients with diseases that are recognized to be risk factors for PHT, i.e. in those with a previous history of pulmonary embolism or diseases associated with PAH
- Investigations in PH are used to identify evidence of
  - Haemodynamic severity
  - Functional severity
  - Cause of PHT
- During this process, pointers to an underlying condition should be actively sought
- In the UK, a network of designated specialist centres has developed to manage the investigation and treatment of patients with various forms of PHT.

26.6 Bedside tests

See Figure 26.2.

- Blood tests include haematology, biochemistry (including liver function), thyroid function, hepatitis screen, autoantibodies, HIV testing, and, in patients with CTEPH, a thrombophilia screen

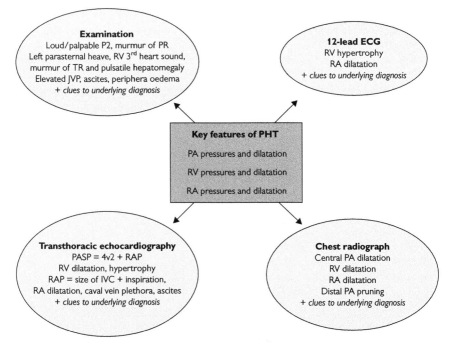

Figure 26.2 Bedside assessment of pulmonary hypertension (colour coded by key features, see Plate).

- The ECG may not show evidence of right ventricular hypertrophy or right atrial dilatation
- In IPAH the CXR is commonly abnormal
- Typical lung function findings in PAH are decreased lung diffusion capacity and sometimes mild restriction
- RV systolic pressure can be estimated using the Bernoulli equation (es. $RVSP = 4V^2$)
- When combined with estimated RA pressure (judged by dimension of IVC and response to inspiration), systolic PA pressure (PASP) can be estimated
- Mean PAP and PA end diastolic pressure can also be estimated by echocardiography
- A PASP of 40 mm Hg is 2 standard deviations above the normal mean
- RV function can be assessed using 2D echocardiography by a number of measurements, all of which have their own limitations
- Some, such as tricuspid annular plane systolic excursion (TAPSE), are load dependent
- Echocardiographic haemodynamic data are only estimates. Right heart catheterization is required to make a diagnosis
- LV diastolic dysfunction should be considered as the cause for PHT when left atrial dilatation and LVH are detected in older patients with AF, CAD, systemic hypertension, and diabetes
- Echocardiographic evaluation of diastolic function may be unreliable and cardiac catheterization may be needed to clinch the diagnosis.

26.7 Radiology

- A normal- or low-probability VQ scan excludes chronic thromboembolic PHT
- CT can delineate thromboembolic disease, interstitial lung disease, and pulmonary veno-occlusive disease (thickened interlobular septal walls, centrilobular ground-glass shadowing, mediastinal lymphadenopathy, pleural effusions)
- Abdominal USS is used to screen patients for portal hypertension.

26.8 Right heart catheterization

- Required data: PA pressure (systolic, mean, and diastolic), right atrial pressure, pulmonary artery wedge pressure, RV pressure, cardiac output and cardiac index
- A saturation run should also be performed to exclude shunts
- Transpulmonary gradient (TPG) is mean PAP less mean PWP, which is normally < 12 mmHg
- Diastolic pressure difference (DPD) is used to measure the pre-capillary remodelling, and is mean PAWP less pulmonary artery diastolic pressure. The normal range is 1–3 mmHg and a value ≥ 7 is abnormal
- In Group 2, a DPD ≥ 7 mmHg suggests superadded pulmonary vascular disease
- PVR = TPG divided by cardiac output
- PWP > 15 mmHg indicates Group 2, but care should be taken to ensure that an adequate recording has been obtained
- When in doubt, directly measure left ventricular end diastolic pressure by performing a left heart study
- In PAH a vasodilator challenge is used to identify the small minority of patients who will benefit from long-term calcium channel blockade
- This is commonly performed using inhaled nitric oxide
- This should not be performed in patients with imaging evidence of PVOD who may develop pulmonary oedema

- A positive challenge is defined by ↓mPAP ≥10 mmHg to ≤40 mmHg with ↑/normal cardiac output.

26.9 Identifying the sickest patients

- This is important in order to determine therapeutic needs. Patients may look remarkably well at rest. The following factors suggest severe disease in patients with PAH:
  - Clinical evidence of RV failure
  - Rapid progression of symptoms, syncope and breathless at rest (WHO functional class IV)
  - 6-min walk distance <380 m
  - Peak O_2 consumption < 12 ml/min/kg
  - High or rising BNP levels
  - Pericardial effusion or TAPSE less than 1.5 cm
  - RAP >10 mmHg, CI <2.1 l/min/m².

26.10 Treatments

General measures
- In patients with PAH, general measures and supportive therapies can be undertaken before referring to specialists
- Advice about exercise, i.e. avoid strenuous/heavy exertion but encourage regular gentle aerobic activity, should be given taking into account BP response to exercise (fall in BP on exercise indicates a high risk)
- PAH is a contraindication to pregnancy. Expert family planning is required. Note bosentan–oral contraceptive pill interaction, which reduces effectiveness of latter
- Influenza/pneumococcal vaccinations should be up to date
- Routine venesection is now avoided in PAH associated with congenital heart disease.

Supportive therapies
- These lack evidence from RCTs and attract class C grade of recommendation
- Warfarin (INR 2–3) is advised since patients with PAH can develop thrombus *in situ*
- Diuretics (inc. spironolactone) are useful in patients with overt right heart failure
- Oxygen is recommended in patients with group 3 to correct hypoxaemia.

Targeted medical therapies
- The majority of evidence available for treatment has been collected in PAH, mostly iPAH, FPAH, anorexogen-induced PAH, connective tissue disease, and CTEPH
- RCT data exists for individual subgroups, including CHD and HIV
- The treatment offered is dictated by functional class
- PAH-directed therapy may also be used in patients with CTEPH
- None are proven to benefit PH when due to left heart disease. CCBs are beneficial in a small fraction of PAH patients with positive vasodilator response (see section on 'Right Heart Catheterization') both at baseline and on reassessment 3–4 months later
- The following drugs described are used to treat PAH. Since they may cause clinical deterioration in patients who do not meet these criteria (i.e. Group1'), it is vital to have established the correct diagnosis before starting treatment
- Only Level 1-A drugs will be discussed here.

Prostacyclin pathway

- Address altered prostacyclin pathways in PAH
- Intravenous epoprostenol is the only treatment to improve survival in a randomized trial
- Used in patients in WHO-FC III who are deteriorating and WHO-FC IV
- Management of infusions is complex and requires a specialist centre to manage
- Short $t\frac{1}{2}$, so infused continuously, risking infusion interruption or infection
- Iloprost has longer $t_{\frac{1}{2}}$; in aerosol preparations
- Treprostinil is more stable; can be given s.c. Site pain may become problematic.

Endothelin pathway

- Endothelin 1 is a vasoconstrictor and promotes vascular smooth muscle proliferation
- Two receptors, ET_A and ET_B, are involved in its action
- Bosentan and macitentan block both
- Use in WHO FC-II/III
- Requires LFT and Hb monitoring given risk of raised hepatic aminotransferases and fall in Hb
- Also risk of foetal injury
- Ambrisentan inhibits ET_A; indicated in WHO-FC II/III. Requires LFT monitoring.

Nitric oxide pathway

- Nitric oxide (NO) has a central vasodilatory role and is augmented by sildenafil and tadalafil (phosphodiesterase-5 inhibitors) by inhibiting the degradation of cGMP (directly) and cAMP (indirectly)
- Riociguat is a soluble guanylate cyclase stimulator
- Sildenafil is indicated in WHO-FC II/III.

Summary of medical therapies
In patients with PAH, the treatment is indicated by functional class:

- WHO-FC II: ambrisentan, bosentan, sildenafil, macitentan, riociguat, tadalafil
- WHO-FC III: ambrisentan, bosentan, sildenafil, i.v. epoprostenol, iloprost inhaled, macitentan, riociguat, tadalafil, treprostinil s.c./inhaled
- WHO-FC IV: i.v. epoprostenol.

If response is inadequate, combination therapy will be considered from either of the other two groups.

Surgical therapy

- If poor prognostic features/refractory disease, list for lung transplantation
- Pulmonary endarterectomy is indicated in CTEPH at expert centres: all CTEPH patients should be referred
- Graded balloon atrial sepostomy is used rarely: indicated in refractory syncope and heart failure in selected patients.

Clinical genetics

27.1 Genetic concepts

Mendelian inheritance

- Mendelian inheritance: inheritance patterns caused by mutations in individual genes
- There are about 25,000 genes within the human genome. At least 4000 human diseases are caused by mutations in single genes.

Autosomal dominant inheritance

- All of the genes, excluding those on the sex chromosomes and the mitochondrial genes, are termed autosomal
- Autosomal genes occur in pairs. A condition caused by a mutation in one copy of a gene will follow dominant inheritance
- The offspring of an individual with an autosomal dominant condition has a 50:50 chance of inheriting the disease, causing mutation irrespective of gender (see Figure 27.1)
- For some conditions this may not always lead to the clinical features of the condition—the 'phenotype'. This is termed incomplete penetrance.

Autosomal recessive inheritance

- If mutations in both copies of an autosomal gene are required to cause a condition this is termed autosomal recessive inheritance
- Usually each parent has one mutation and is termed a 'carrier'
- There is a one in four chance of having an affected child irrespective of gender if both parents are carriers (see Figure 27.2)
- As a general rule:
    - carriers of recessive conditions do not display features of the condition
    - it is uncommon for those with mutations in both copies not to be affected, although there are exceptions such as the low penetrance in hereditary haemochromatosis.

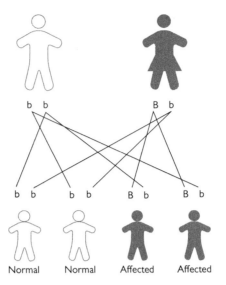

Figure 27.1 Autosomal dominant inheritance from an affected parent.

Reproduced from Discern Genetics, available at www.discern-genetics.org. Copyright University of Oxford 2005, with permission from the University of Oxford.

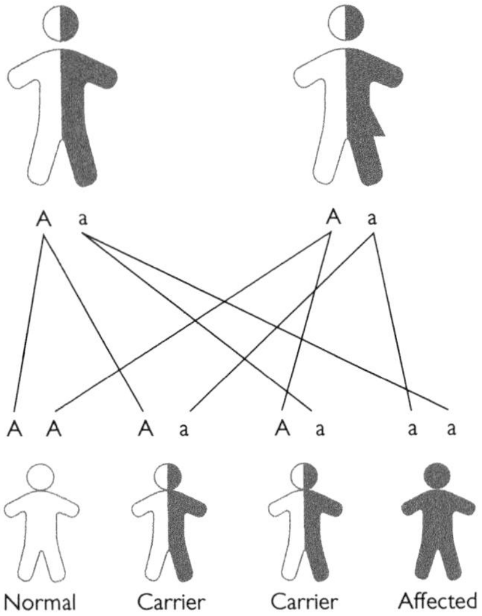

Figure 27.2 Autosomal recessive inheritance from two carrier parents.

Reproduced from Discern Genetics, available at www.discern-genetics.org. Copyright University of Oxford 2005, with permission from the University of Oxford.

X-linked recessive inheritance

- Apart from a small number of genes present on both the X and Y chromosomes—the pseudo-autosomal region—most of the genes on the X chromosome are present in two copies in females and one copy in males
- Most X-linked conditions may be 'carried' by females but only affect males: X-linked recessive inheritance

- The children of a carrier mother have a one in two chance of being affected if male or of being a carrier if female (see Figure 27.3)
- All daughters of an affected father will be carriers for that condition and all sons will be unaffected (see Figure 27.4)

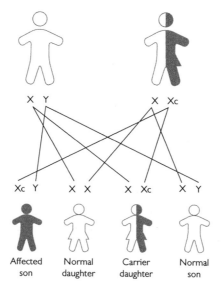

Figure 27.3 X-linked recessive inheritance from carrier female.

Reproduced from Discern Genetics, available at www.discern-genetics.org. Copyright University of Oxford 2005, with permission from the University of Oxford.

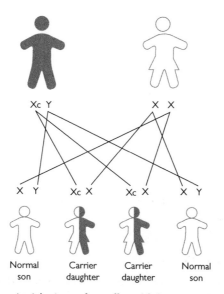

Figure 27.4 X-linked recessive inheritance from affected father.

Reproduced from Discern Genetics, available at www.discern-genetics.org. Copyright University of Oxford 2005, with permission from the University of Oxford.

- Rarely females may be affected by these conditions, most commonly where there is an abnormality or absence of the other X chromosome, i.e. Turner syndrome
- Some X-linked conditions may also give rise to the condition in females: X-linked dominant inheritance.

Non-Mendelian inheritance

Mitochondrial inheritance

- Disorders of the mitochondria are an uncommon but important cause of cardiac disease, most commonly cardiomyopathy and/or conduction disease, either as an isolated finding or as a part of multi-system disease
- Mitochondria have their own DNA, although the majority of genes essential for mitochondrial function are in the nuclear genome (these can cause 'mitochondrial' disease in a dominant, X-linked, or recessive manner)
- Mitochondria are only passed on to the resulting embryo from the ovum and not the sperm (see Figure 27.5)
- Therefore all children of a mother with a mitochondrial mutation may inherit it, whereas no children of a father with a mitochondrial mutation will inherit it
- Further complication comes from the fact that as there are tens to hundreds of mitochondria in each cell and frequently only a proportion of the mitochondria in a cell will have a particular mutation, 'heteroplasmy'. This level can vary in different cells, tissues, and organs affecting the phenotype

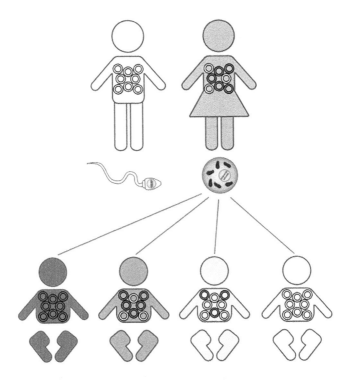

Figure 27.5 Mitochondrial inheritance.
Reproduced with kind permission of Clinical Tools Inc.

- A threshold level of the mutation must be surpassed to give rise to clinical features, this level being variable depending on the particular mutation, organ, and condition involved.

Multifactorial/polygenic inheritance

- This refers to the majority of medical disorders, where multiple genes, along with environmental factors, interact to give rise to the condition
- Between different conditions, and even different individuals with the same disorder, there are varying degrees of importance of the genetic component
- The role of an individual genetic factor is likely to be very small but together these factors have a cumulative effect. This either then leads to the condition, or acts to lower a threshold, which allows environmental pressures to cause it.

Mosaicism

- Not a mode of inheritance but an important concept is that all genetic changes, whether that be a mutation within a gene or a chromosomal abnormality, may be seen in only a proportion of cells of the body: 'mosaicism'
- This usually arises in an early mitotic division in the developing embryo
- In general those with a 'mosaic' alteration will have a milder clinical phenotype than those with the equivalent universal mutation.

Chromosomes

- The genetic material is organized within the cell nuclei as chromosomes
- These incorporate DNA and structural proteins (e.g. histones)
- Structural proteins facilitate efficient packaging of DNA and assist in the regulation of gene transcription (the copying of DNA into RNA) and replication (see Figure 27.6)
- The complement of chromosomes is referred to as the karyotype

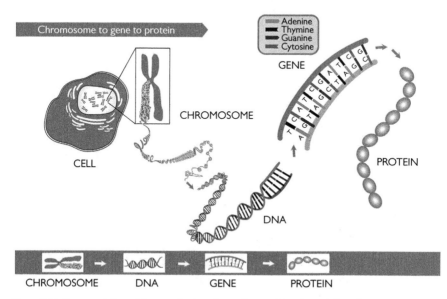

Figure 27.6 Representation of the organization of genetic material and translation of genes into proteins.
Illustration from *Genetic Counseling Aids* 5th Edition. Copyright Greenwood Genetic Center 2007. Reproduced with kind permission from Greenwood Genetic Centre.

- The usual chromosome number in humans is forty-six; twenty-three pairs numbered one to twenty-two and the sex chromosomes: XX in females (see Figure 27.7) and XY in males. Each chromosome has a two 'arms' from the centromere, the short arm (termed p) and the long arm (termed q)
- Testing of chromosomes in cardiology is most frequently performed in congenital heart disease, but may also be appropriate with other cardiac disease, particularly in the presence of other physical or developmental problems
- As well as standard karyotype analysis more specific chromosome tests may be appropriate, e.g. fluorescent in-situ hybridization (FISH) testing for specific disorders of chromosome imbalance, such as the 22q11.2 deletion
- Array comparative genomic hybridization (array CGH), allows analysis at a much higher resolution, permitting detection imbalance across the whole chromosome complement, and detecting both recurrent abnormalities (such as the 22q11.2 microdeletion) and also novel regions of chromosome imbalance
- Where you feel chromosome analysis—or other genetic testing—is indicated, referring to clinical genetics may be appropriate.

Genetic counselling and testing

- Genetic counselling is 'the process of helping people understand and adapt to the medical, psychological, and familial implications of the genetic contributions to disease'
- All patients who have or may have an inherited heart disease should have genetic counselling
- Key points to communicate about a potentially inherited heart conditions include:
  - The genetic origin (and certainty of this)
  - The likely mode of inheritance and therefore the probability of other family members and offspring being affected

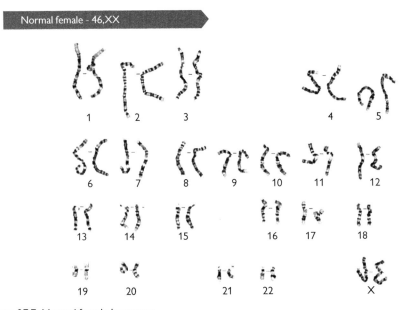

Figure 27.7 Normal female karyotype.

Illustration from *Genetic Counseling Aids* 5th Edition. Copyright Greenwood Genetic Center 2007. Reproduced with kind permission from Greenwood Genetic Centre.

- The clinical features of the disorder and its natural history
- Particular advice regarding pregnancy
- The role and benefits of cardiac screening for the family
- The availability and role of genetic testing
- Information oregarding appropriate patient associations and sources of reliable and understandable medical information

- Family screening, or 'cascade screening', is designed to identify those relatives who have the same disease as the patient identified as having a disorder: the 'proband'
- Screening of first-degree relatives of an affected individual is frequently indicated as an initial step in inherited heart diseases where dominant inheritance is likely. Immediate testing of more distant relatives is less commonly indicated
- The main aim of cascade screening is to identify those who would benefit from clinical screening, treatment, health and lifestyle advice, or discussion of reproductive options, and/or to clarify whether other family members may be affected
- The availability of a genetic 'predictive' test, i.e. a test for a disorder that a patient may have but does not have symptoms of, can help clarify some of these issues.

Drawing a pedigree
- Information on pedigree drawing, along with many other useful educational resources, can be found at the National Genetics Education and Development Centre website (see 'Further Reading')
- In summary when drawing a pedigree (see Figure 27.8)
    - Males are drawn as a square and females as a circle
    - It is easiest to start with the youngest generation and work back up generations on both sides
    - The person in whom a condition is first identified, 'proband', is marked with an arrow to the bottom left
    - Those affected are shaded in, and a key should be drawn
    - Where someone is deceased a line through the symbol is used
    - Siblings are traditionally drawn from eldest on the left to youngest on the right, and in couples the male is on the left and female on the right.

Interpreting a laboratory genetic test result
- DNA is extracted from an EDTA blood sample in the local regional genetics centre; specific tests may only be available in a small number of centres in the country (for a list of available tests refer to www.ukgtn.nhs.uk)
- Reports should be interpreted in collaboration between laboratory scientists, specialist cardiologists, and clinical geneticists
- Not all genetic mutations cause disease. They may be neutral changes, 'polymorphisms', or it may not be possible to determine whether an alteration is causing the condition, 'variant of unknown significance (VUS)' or 'unclassified variant'
- Where a definitely pathogenic mutation is identified the clinical diagnosis is confirmed and cascade screening is possible
- In the setting of a diagnostic test it is rare that absence of a mutation will change the clinical diagnosis. In a predictive test it is usually sufficient to reassure the patient they are not at increased risk of the condition being tested for and that screening is not required.

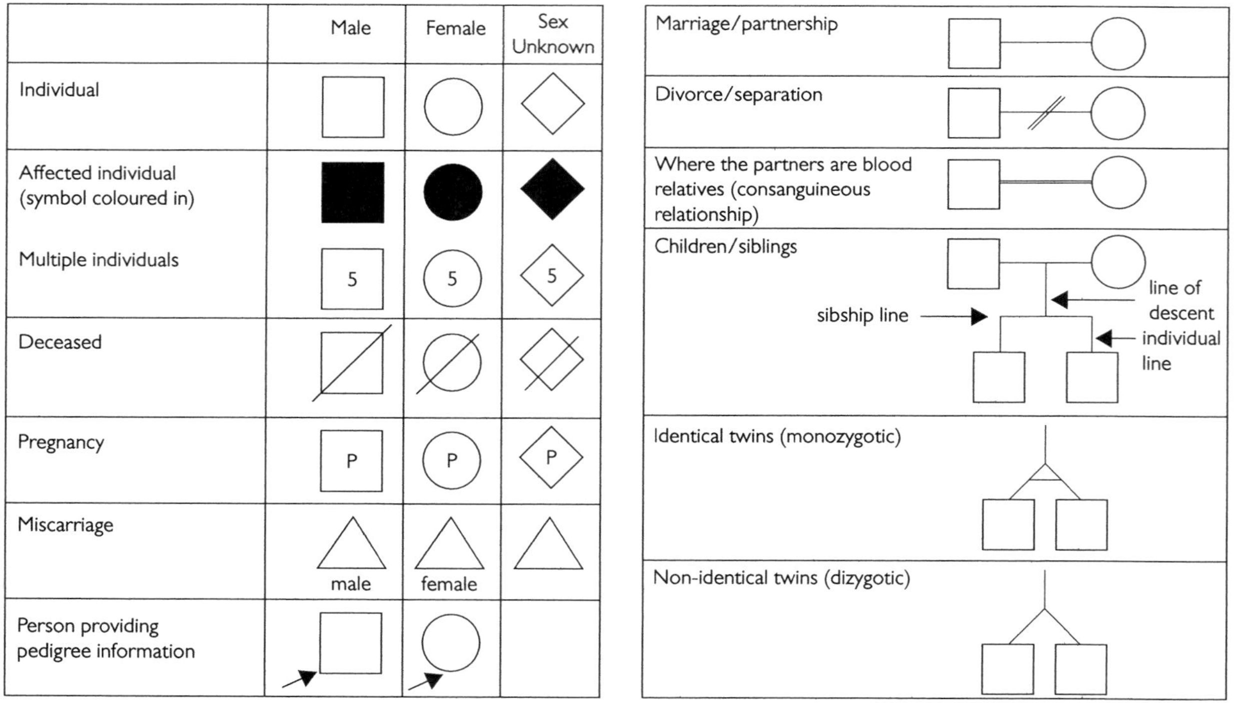

Figure 27.8 Examples of commonly used pedigree symbols and relationship lines.

Reproduced with permission of the National Genetics Education and Development Centre (http://www.geneticseducation.nhs.uk/), from 'Taking and Drawing a Family History'. Copyright 2008 NHS National Genetics Education and Development Centre.

27.2 Cardiomyopathies

- Mendelian patterns of inheritance common, most commonly autosomal dominant
- Inheritance pattern may be determined from the pedigree
- Genetic testing in cardiomyopathies has many potential issues:
  - Genetic heterogeneity, i.e. mutations in several different genes can all give the same phenotype
  - Proportion of genes are unrecognized, and some of those recognized may not be available as a clinical test
  - Large number of causative genes with a high rate of natural variability that can make interpretation difficult
  - Most cardiomyopathies are clinically variable despite there being the same underlying cause: 'variable expressivity'
  - A proportion of those with a causative genetic variant do not display clinical features: 'incomplete penetrance'. This is more common in younger individuals
  - Incomplete penetrance makes it very difficult to be completely confident on the basis of 'normal' clinical assessment
- Family cascade screening should be instituted following the diagnosis of cardiomyopathy unless an acquired cause is demonstrated
- Continued screening through adulthood is often advised. The age to which this is continued will usually be based on clinical judgement and patient wishes
- The age to commence clinical screening is also uncertain. Starting between 8 and 12 years old may be appropriate for most cardiomyopathies.

Hypertrophic cardiomyopathy

- Hypertrophic cardiomyopathy (HCM) affects approximately 1 in 500 people
- Most HCM is autosomal dominantly inherited. Autosomal recessive, X-linked, and mitochondrial inheritance are identified in a few patients
- The most common causative genes are those encoding proteins of the sarcomere (most commonly the thick and thin filament proteins but also less commonly the sarcomere-associated or Z-disc proteins); with mutations in β-myosin heavy chain (*MYH7*), and myosin binding-protein C (*MYBPC3*), accounting for up to a half of cases
- Due to the high probability of a genetic cause, testing should be considered in all patients
- LVH due to other reasons—'phenocopies'—need to be excluded, e.g. due to hypertension, aortic valve disease, or 'athlete's heart'
- A significant minority (around 5%) have two pathogenic mutations in sarcomere genes, and may have a more severe phenotype. Between a third and a half, depending on inclusion criteria, have no causative mutation identified
- At present, identification of a causative mutation does not alter clinical practice
- Mutations in some non-sarcomere genes are associated with differing prognoses and additional problems, e.g. mutations in *PRKAG2* give hypertrophy along with WPW syndrome, progressive conduction abnormalities, and myopathy in some
- Metabolic and syndromic causes of hypertrophy include: Fabry disease, Danon disease, Pompe disease, mitochondrial disorders, Freidreich's ataxia, *FHL1* mutations, and Noonan syndrome.

Dilated cardiomyopathy

- 20–50% of dilated cardiomyopathy (DCM) is shown to be familial on clinical screening. A causative mutation is identified in up to half of those with familial disease

- Unless there is a clear acquired cause of DCM, a three-generation family history should be taken and first-degree relatives should undergo full clinical screening including ECG and transthoracic echocardiogram
- Familial DCM is clinically and genetically heterogeneous. Along with mutations in some of the sarcomere genes, e.g. *MYH7* and *TNNT2*, mutations in many other genes can cause DCM
- Most familial DCM is inherited in an autosomal dominant manner. Autosomal recessive, X-linked, and mitochondrial inheritance are identified in a minority
- DCM is usually an isolated finding but may be a part of multi-system disease:
  - Muscular dystrophies that can cause DCM include Duchenne, Becker, and Emery-Dreifuss muscular dystrophies
  - There are also 'syndromes' incorporating DCM, such as Alström and Barth syndromes.

Arrhythmogenic right ventricular cardiomyopathy

- Arrhythmogenic right ventricular cardiomyopathy (ARVC) can be difficult to diagnose where a 'classical' picture is not present
- Clinical diagnosis is usually achieved through assessment of right ventricular function and morphology (via MRI), evidence of conduction abnormalities and/or arrhythmias, histopathology, and family history
- Usually an autosomal dominant trait with significant variability but recessive inheritance is also recognized
- ARVC can be best thought of as a disorder of the cell-to-cell junction. Genes identified are predominantly those encoding desmosomal proteins
- Limited genotype–phenotype correlations have been established in ARVC but again are not significant enough to alter management
- Cascade screening is important to identify relatives with sub-clinical disease
- Those without clinical disease do not require prophylactic treatment
- Treatment opinions differ: those with haemodynamically stable arrhythmias may benefit from BBs and/or class III anti-arrhythmics; in those with syncope, cardiovascular compromise, and/or a history of cardiac arrest ICD implantation may be advised.

Other cardiomyopathies

Left ventricular non-compaction

- Left ventricular non-compaction (LVNC) describes deep trabeculations in the left ventricular myocardium
- A degree of trabeculation is frequently seen in normal individuals, meaning diagnosis of LVNC as a pathological state may be difficult to establish
- There are several diagnostic criteria. For example, in the Jenni criteria a ratio of >2:1 of non-compacted endocardial layer to compacted epicardial layer in an adult is considered diagnostic
- Based on this definition LVNC is clinically and genetically heterogeneous
- The utility of genetic testing is limited; a minority are due to mutations in sarcomere genes
- Clinical screening of first-degree relatives is advised to allow management to limit disease-related complications, particularly embolic disease.

Restrictive cardiomyopathy (RCM)

- In restrictive cardiomyopathy (RCM) there is increased myocardial stiffness, with normal or reduced systolic and diastolic volumes, and normal ventricular wall thickness
- There are many causes of RCM: in western societies the most common is amyloidosis, with infective causes being the predominant cause in tropical countries

- Familial disease is seen in similar numbers as DCM; only a minority have an identified underlying cause
- Sarcomere gene mutations have been recognized, predominantly troponin I, but also troponin T, α-cardiac actin, and β-myosin heavy chain. Desmin has been recognized as causing RCM with myopathy and conduction disease
- Other genetic causes of RCM include haemochromatosis, pseudoxanthoma elasticum, hereditary amyloid, Fabry disease, and other storage disorders.

Peripartum cardiomyopathy

- Peripartum cardiomyopathy (PPCM) appears to be a distinct entity but resembles DCM
- Clinically the condition is variable, with very rapid progression in some but complete recovery of ventricular function in others
- Diagnosis is made on the basis of reduced EF, without other identified cause, starting towards the end of, or in the months following, pregnancy
- The cause of PPCM is unknown and, although familial disease is recognized, contributory genetic factors are yet to be identified
- In addition to standard heart failure/DCM management, bromocriptine may be beneficial and breast-feeding is advised against, both acting to reduce prolactin levels.

Metabolic

(Anderson-) Fabry disease

- Fabry disease is an X-linked disorder—deficiency of the lysosomal enzyme α-galactosidase A leads to accumulation of globotriaosylceramide (Gb3)
- Key features of Fabry disease are: angiokeratoma, neuropathy (sweating disturbance, acroparaesthesia/neuropathic pain, hearing impairment), ophthalmic abnormalities (corneal and lenticular opacities), renal impairment, and cardiovascular involvement
- Progressive LVH is seen in the majority of affected males, with right ventricular involvement also commonly seen, typically presenting in adulthood
- Conduction abnormalities are caused by infiltration of the conduction system and impaired autonomic control. There is also a high incidence of vascular disease
- Women with Fabry disease can get the full spectrum of features seen in males, although overall these are less common and often less severe
- Diagnosis is usually made in males by measurement of α-galactosidase A, although this is less sensitive in females. *GLA* gene testing can be useful in this situation and for cascade screening within a family
- Enzyme replacement therapy has improved morbidity and mortality in this condition.

Danon disease

- Danon disease is an X-linked disorder due to mutations in the gene encoding lysosome-associated membrane protein-2, *LAMP2*
- It is a rapidly progressive multisystem disorder incorporating: hypertrophic cardiomyopathy with progression to LV systolic dysfunction and enlarging cavity size, WPW syndrome, arrhythmias, learning difficulties, abnormal liver function tests, retinal pigment abnormalities, skeletal myopathy, and elevated creatine kinase. Death due to ventricular arrhythmia in adolescence is typical
- Females are less significantly affected than males, and more commonly may present as DCM.

Mitochondrial disorders

- Abnormalities of mitochondria have been found associated with a wide range of cardiac phenotypes, including HCM, DCM and conduction defects/arrhythmias

- Mitochondrial function is dependent on both genes in the mitochondria's own genome (mtDNA) and nuclear genes
- Most frequently affect the brain, eyes, endocrine organs, and skeletal muscle, along with the heart
- Outside certain distinct disorders genetic testing is complicated and should be undertaken with specialist neurological/clinical genetics input.

Muscular dystrophies

- Duchenne muscular dystrophy is an X-linked recessive disorder caused by the absence of dystrophin—sarcolemmal protein linking the cytoskeleton to the extracellular matrix
- Males present with delayed motor milestones, abnormal gait, and calf pseudohypertrophy. All require wheelchairs by the age of thirteen years
- The majority of boys develop dilated cardiomyopathy, with hypertrabeculation/ non-compaction in some
- At present therapeutic options are limited but there are several trials of drugs with the purpose of delaying disease progression. Early trials of 'gene therapy' are promising
- DCM treatment is as standard except that biventricular pacing is infrequently considered due to the progressive nature of this disorder
- Other mutations in the dystrophin gene cause Becker muscular dystrophy or, uncommonly, isolated dilated cardiomyopathy
- Males with Becker muscular dystrophy have later onset myopathy and ambulatory problems. DCM is a significant cause of morbidity and the main cause of mortality
- In both Duchenne and Becker muscular dystrophies, cardiac evaluation should be undertaken annually
- All isolated males with DCM, or those with a family history consistent with X-linked inheritance, should be assessed for evidence of generalized myopathy and have their serum creatine kinase measured
- Female carriers of dystrophin mutations can sometimes display evidence of left ventricular dilatation and/or DCM, although typically it has a fairly indolent course. Cardiac evaluation including echocardiography every 5 years from the age of 30 years is recommended
- Other muscular dystrophies may also be associated with cardiomyopathy, the next most common being Emery-Dreifuss muscular dystrophy (EDMD)
- EDMD is characterized by joint contractures, myopathy, and cardiac involvement (conduction defects, various arrhythmias, HCM or DCM). Creatine kinase is often moderately elevated, but may be normal. EDMD is usually inherited in a dominant or X-linked manner.

Syndromic cardiomyopathy

- 'Syndrome' just means an association of features and in this setting refers to genetic syndromes
- The presence of non-cardiac features may suggest a syndromic cause.

Noonan syndrome

- Noonan syndrome (NS) is characterized by short stature, facial dysmorphism (hypertelorism/ wide-spaced eyes with epicanthal folds and ptosis and low-set posteriorly rotated ears), unusual chest shape, and cardiac defects (see Figure 27.9); along with many other recognized features
- Cardiac defects include: pulmonary stenosis (50–60%), atrial septal defects (10%), ventricular septal defects (5%), and persistent ductus arteriosus (3%). HCM occurs in about 10%, typically in childhood or adolescence

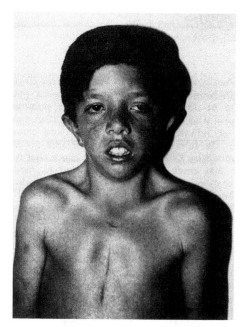

Figure 27.9 Appearance in Noonan syndrome.

Reproduced from 'Noonan syndrome', J. E. Allanson, *J. Med. Genet.* 24(1), 9–13, copyright 1987 with permission from BMJ Publishing Group Ltd.

- Abnormal ECGs, with broad QRS complexes, left axis deviation, and giant Q waves, are common
- NS is caused by mutations in the RAS/MAPK pathway; half are due to mutations in the *PTPN11* gene
- Other disorders of the RAS-MAPK pathway include LEOPARD syndrome, cardiofaciocutaneous syndrome and Costello syndrome (which all have some overlapping features with NS).

27.3 Rhythm disorders

Long-QT syndrome
- Long-QT syndrome (LQTS) is subdivided into at least twelve types on the basis of the underlying genetic cause. The majority are due to dominantly inherited mutations in *KCNQ1*, *KCNH2*, or *SCN5A*
- Types (see Table 27.1) are:
  - Romano-Ward syndrome: dominant, without other features
  - Jervell-Lange-Nielsen syndrome: recessive, with congenital sensorineural deafness
  - Andersen-Tawil syndrome: dominant, potassium-sensitive periodic paralysis, other arrhythmias, skeletal abnormalities, and facial dysmorphism
  - Timothy syndrome: dominant, multiple congenital abnormalities (syndactyly, teeth abnormalities, cardiac malformations), immune deficiency, infantile hypoglycaemia, learning difficulties, and autism
- LQTS is clinically highly variable and has incomplete penetrance

Table 27.1 Summary of LQTS types

Type	Syndrome	Gene	Characteristics and arrhythmia triggers	Prevalence
LQT1	RWS, JLNS	KCNQ1	Triggered by exercise, swimming and emotion	40–55%
LQT2	RWS	KCNH2	Triggered by sound or emotion	35–45%
LQT3	RWS	SCN5A	Triggered by sleep or emotion	2–8%
LQT4	RWS	ANK2	Triggered by exercise	<1%
LQT5	RWS, JLNS	KCNE1	Triggered by exercise and emotion	<1%
LQT6	RWS	KCNE2	Triggered by rest and exercise	<1%
LQT7	ATS	KCNJ2	Syndromic, triggered by rest and exercise, frequent ectopy	<1%
LQT8	TS	CACNA1C	Syndromic, severe early onset arrhythmias	<1%
LQT9	RWS	CAV3	Triggered by sleep and rest	<1%
LQT10	RWS	SCN4B	Triggered by exercise	<0.1%
LQT11	RWS	AKAP9	Triggered by exercise	<0.1%
LQT12	RWS	SNTA1	Triggered by rest	<0.1%

RWS, Romano Ward syndrome; JLNS, Jervell-Lange-Nielsen syndrome; ATS, Andersen-Tawil syndrome; TS, Timothy syndrome.

- LQTS is caused by 'loss of function' mutations in the repolarizing potassium channels, subunits, or interacting proteins (KCNQ1, KCNH2, KCNE1, KCNE2, KCNJ2, ANK2, CAV3, AKAP9, and SNTA1), 'gain of function' mutations in the depolarizing sodium or calcium channels (SCN5A and CACNA1C), or mutations in the interacting proteins (SCN4B)
- Different mutations within the same genes cause a variety of other arrhythmic phenotypes including Brugada syndrome, short-QT syndrome, CPVT, and familial AF
- Testing of the more common genes identifies mutations in about 70%
- Genetic testing is important in guiding treatment as BBs are effective in LQT1 and 2, but not 3.

Brugada syndrome

- Brugada syndrome (BrS) is clinically variable, with incomplete penetrance
- A family may exhibit a mixed phenotype along with other arrhythmic disorders
- Risk of sudden death can be assessed on the basis of several factors (male, spontaneous 'type 1' ST elevation pattern, syncope, previous ventricular arrhythmia or cardiac arrest)
- BrS is a genetically heterogeneous condition. The most common cause is dominantly inherited loss-of-function mutations in the SCN5A gene, accounting for 15–30% of cases.

Catecholaminergic polymorphic ventricular tachycardia

- Catecholaminergic polymorphic ventricular tachycardia (CPVT) should be considered in patients with syncopal episodes on exertion or emotion, and those with unexplained ventricular arrhythmia
- At-rest physical examination and ECG are usually normal
- Sinus bradycardia and prominent U-waves are seen

- An exercise stress test is useful in making the diagnosis in the context of a suspicious history. This may remain normal (particularly early childhood) and repeat testing may be required
- About half of those with CPVT have a dominantly inherited mutation in the cardiac ryanodine receptor gene (RyR2); these cause a reduction in calcium release from the sarcoplasmic reticulum (SR)
- A small percentage have recessively inherited mutations in the cardiac calsequestrin gene (CASQ2), which also leads to a reduction in calcium release from the SR
- There is still a significant risk of sudden death in those without symptoms
- BB therapy is commonly started in all patients and an ICD is appropriate in those with documented ventricular arrhythmia or syncope
- Avoidance of demanding sporting activities is recommended.

Short-QT syndrome

- Short-QT syndrome (SQTS) is characterized by a shortened QT interval with tall peaked T waves, a propensity to atrial fibrillation, and a risk of sudden death
- Although SQTS is a genetic condition, a shortened corrected QT interval can be caused by electrolyte imbalance and drug therapy
- Genetically, SQTS is caused by mutations in the same genes as those causing LQTS but with opposing consequences, i.e. mutations cause a gain in function of potassium channels or loss of function of sodium or calcium channels
- The standard treatment for SQTS is ICD implantation, although inappropriate shocks can be a problem.

Familial atrial fibrillation

- AF is very common but its presence in multiple family members or occurrence at an early age should raise the possibility of a genetic cause
- The underlying genetic factors identified to date are similar to those for other rhythm disorders, i.e. affecting cardiac potassium and sodium channels.

27.4 Vascular disorders

Marfan syndrome

- Diagnostic criteria for Marfan syndrome have recently been updated, placing more emphasis on aortic root dilatation and dissection, ophthalmic features, and molecular genetic results
- The Ghent criteria and revised criteria are summarized in Tables 27.2 and 27.3. In Table 27.2, Marfan syndrome is diagnosed with two major criteria and the involvement of a third system.

In Table 27.3, Marfan syndrome is diagnosed with aortic root dilatation and ectopia lentis, pathogenic FBN1 mutation, or system involvement (at least seven points; see table) or ectopia lentis with a fibrillin mutation known to cause Marfan syndrome. Other phenotypes can be diagnosed with other combinations of features.

- Marfan syndrome is caused by mutations in the fibrillin-1 gene (FBN1)
- Mutations in FBN-1 can also cause other overlapping phenotypes, such as the MASS phenotype (myopia, mitral valve prolapse, borderline non-progressive aortic root dilatation, skeletal findings and striae), familial mitral valve prolapse, familial thoracic aneurysm, and familial isolated ectopia lentis syndrome

Table 27.2 Ghent diagnostic criteria

System	Major criterion	System involvement
Skeletal	At least four of: • pectus carinatum • pectus excavatum requiring surgery • upper to lower segment ratio <0.86 *or* span to height ratio >1.05 • wrist *and* thumb signs • scoliosis >20° or spondylolisthesis • reduced elbow extension (<170°) • pes planus • protrusio acetabulae	Two major features or one major feature and two of: • pectus excavatum • joint hypermobility • high palate and dental crowding • characteristic facies
Ocular	Lens dislocation	Flat cornea Increased axial length of globe (myopia) Hypoplastic iris/ciliary muscle
Cardiovascular	Aortic root dilatation Dissection of the ascending aorta	Mitral valve prolapse Pulmonary artery dilatation under 40 Other aortic dilatation or dissection
Pulmonary	—	Spontaneous pneumothorax Apical blebs
Skin/integument	—	Striae atrophicae Recurrent or incisional hernia
Dura	Lumbosacral dural ectasia	—
Genetics	Confirmed diagnosis in a family member OR pathogenic fibrillin mutation identified	—

Reproduced by permission from Macmillan Publishers Ltd: *European Journal of Human Genetics*, 15, 724–733, John C S Dean, 'Marfan syndrome: clinical diagnosis and management', copyright 2007.

Table 27.3 Revised Ghent diagnostic criteria

Scoring of systemic features
Wrist and thumb sign (3 points for both, 1 point for one)
Pectus deformity (2 points for carinatum, 1 point for excavatum or asymmetry)
Hindfoot deformity (2 points, 1 point for pes planus)
Pneumothorax (2 points)
Dural ectasia (2 points)
Protrusio acetabuli (2 points)
Reduced upper to lower segment ratio and increased span to height ratio (1 point)
Scoliosis or thoracolumbar kyphosis (1 point)
Reduced elbow extension (1 point)
At least 3 of 5 facial features: dolichocephaly, enophthalmos, downslanting palpebral fissures, malar hypoplasia, retrognathia (1 point)
Striae (1 point)
Myopia >3 diopters (1 point)
Mitral valve prolapse (1 point)

Reproduced from 'The revised Ghent nosology for the Marfan syndrome', Bart L Loeys, Harry C Dietz, Alan C Braverman *et al., J. Med. Genet.*, 47, 476–485, copyright 2010 with permission from BMJ Publishing Group Ltd.

- Marfan syndrome should not be diagnosed unless diagnostic criteria are met, as the diagnosis can have significant implications. However, it is equally important that clinical follow-up and cascade screening are instituted where appropriate
- Marfan syndrome is frequently managed in a multidisciplinary clinic including cardiology, clinical genetics, and ophthalmology
- Other cardiac features seen in Marfan syndrome include mitral valve prolapse and regurgitation, left ventricular dilatation, and pulmonary artery dilatation
- Treatment has traditionally been with BBs and prophylactic surgery but there are currently promising trials of ARBs
- Surveillance should include annual echocardiograms, more frequent when close to surgical threshold (4.5 cm in women or 5 cm in men) or there is rapid change (>0.5 cm/year).

Other aortopathies

Familial aortic aneurysm

- Familial thoracic aortic aneurysm and dissection syndrome (FTAAD) is usually inherited in an autosomal dominant manner
- Isolated FTAAD is genetically heterogeneous, with mutations being identified in *FBN1*, *TGFβR-1* or 2 (Loeys-Dietz syndrome type 2), and *ACTA2*
- Congenital bicuspid valve is associated with a risk of aortic aneurysm and can be inherited in a dominant manner, often with reduced penetrance. A small number are due to mutations in *NOTCH1* but most are as yet unknown
- Aortic aneurysm with PDA can also be inherited in a dominant manner, commonly due to mutations in *MYH11*.

Loeys-Dietz syndrome

- Loeys-Dietz syndrome (LDS) can be categorized into type 1 and type 2 depending on the presence or absence of non-cardiac features, respectively
- Other features of LDS type 1 include hypertelorism, bifid uvula/cleft palate, and other congenital abnormalities
- Patients with LDS do not commonly have a marfanoid habitus and ectopia lentis is uncommon
- There may be widespread arterial tortuosity and aneurysm formation
- In LDS aortic dissection tends to occur at a younger age and at smaller aortic dimensions than Marfan syndrome and complications in pregnancy are common
- There is an increased risk of congenital heart disease in LDS, most commonly ASDs, PDAs, or valve disease
- LDS is caused by mutations in the transforming-growth factor beta receptor genes (TGFβR-1 and TGFβR-2).

Vascular Ehlers-Danlos syndrome

- Vascular Ehlers-Danlos syndrome (EDS), previously known as EDS IV, is caused by mutations in *COL3A1*
- It is characterized by vascular and tissue fragility; with translucent skin, easy bruising, dystrophic scarring, and gastrointestinal and uterine rupture being common in addition to aortic and other arterial rupture
- The kyphoscoliotic cardiac valvular subtype, and classical types of EDS are infrequently associated with aortic and other arterial rupture
- There is debate as to the benefit of vascular screening in EDS, as arterial rupture commonly occurs in normal-dimension vessels.

Table 27.4 Simon Broome Register diagnostic criteria for familial hypercholesterolaemia.

Definite familial hypercholesterolaemia		
<16 years Total cholesterol >6.7 mmol/l or LDL >4.0 mmol/l Adult Total cholesterol >7.5 mmol/l or LDL >4.9 mmol/l	plus	Tendon xanthomas in patient or first- or second-degree relative or Mutation in a recognized causative gene
Possible familial hypercholesterolaemia		
<16 years Total cholesterol >6.7 mmol/l or LDL >4.0 mmol/l Adult Total cholesterol >7.5 mmol/l or LDL >4.9 mmol/l	plus	Myocardial infarct at <50 in second-degree relative or <60 in first-degree relative or Total cholesterol in first- or second-degree relative as in lipid criteria

Reproduced from 'Risk of fatal coronary heart disease in familial hypercholesterolaemia', Scientific Steering Committee on behalf of the Simon Broome Register Group, BMJ 303 (6807), 893–6, copyright 1991 with permission from BMJ Publishing Group Ltd.

Familial hypercholesterolaemia (FH)

See the 2008 NICE guideline, in this chapter's 'Further Reading' section.

- Autosomal dominant FH is the most common monogenic cause of coronary heart disease
- It is estimated that FH is undiagnosed in 85% of those affected
- In men the risk coronary disease is >50% by the age of fifty if untreated
- Other clinical features include corneal arcus and tendon and skin xanthomata
- Diagnosis is usually made using the Simon Broome Register criteria (see Table 27.4)
- Where there is a definite family history of FH, screening using DNA diagnosis is the ideal. If this is not possible LDL level is used
- FH is most commonly due to mutations in the LDL receptor gene
- In the 2008 NICE guidelines some key priorities are stressed:
  - Family history of premature coronary disease should always be assessed
  - Children at risk of FH should be assessed by the age of 10 years
  - Generic CHD risk estimation tools should not be used
  - Cascade screening is recommended
  - Statin therapy should achieve a >50% reduction in LDL-C from baseline.

Pulmonary arterial hypertension

- Pulmonary arterial hypertension (PAH) will often have an identified cause (such as connective tissue disorders, HIV, congenital heart disease, portal hypertension, drugs, and toxins) but can be idiopathic and in a minority is heritable
- 70% of heritable PAH and 20% of idiopathic PAH are due to mutations in the bone morphogenetic protein receptor type 2 gene (BMPR2)
- There is reduced penetrance, with a lifetime risk of 10–20%, women being more commonly affected than men
- A small number are due to mutations in activin-like kinase-type 1 (ALK1) and endoglin (ENG), causing hereditary haemorrhagic telangiectasia
- Patients with BMPR2 mutations are less likely to benefit from treatment with CCBs.

27.5 Congenital heart disease syndromes

22q11.2 microdeletion syndrome

Also known as DiGeorge syndrome, velocardiofacial syndrome, and Shprintzen syndrome.

- 22q11.2 microdeletion syndrome is one of the most common causes of congenital heart disease
- This deletion includes the *TBX1* gene, which is predominantly reponsible for the cardiac and some other features
- The majority of individuals have cardiac malformations including tetralogy of Fallot, interrupted aortic arch, VSDs, truncus arteriosus, vascular ring, ASDs, hypoplastic left heart, or other left ventricular outflow abnormalities
- Other features can include facial dysmorphism (deficient alar nasi and broad nasal bridge giving a tubular appearance to the nose, micrognathia, almond-shpaed palpebral fissures; see Figure 27.10), short stature, cleft palate/velopharyngeal insufficiency, hypocalcaemia, learning difficulties (more commonly mild but can be severe), immune deficiency, hearing loss, and psychiatric illness. A very wide variety of problems have been associated with 22q11 microdeletion syndrome
- It is inherited in an autosomal dominant manner and is highly variable
- Detection of the microdeletion has traditionally been with FISH but diagnosis by array CGH is likely to become increasingly frequent
- If 22q11 microdeletion is diagnosed or suspected, liaison with clinical genetics is appropriate.

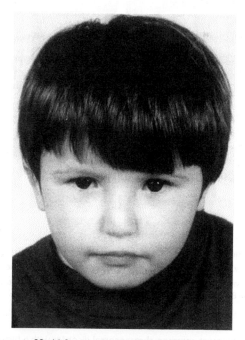

Figure 27.10 Appearance in 22q11.2 microdeletion syndrome.

Reproduced from 'Anal anomalies: an uncommon feature of velocardiofacial (Shprintzen) syndrome?', S. Worthington, A. Colley, K. Fagan et al., J. Med. Genet. 34(1), 79–82, Copyright 1997, with permission from BMJ Publishing Group Ltd.

Alagille syndrome

- Congenital heart defects are seen in the vast majority; these include pulmonary stenosis/ pulmonary artery stenosis, tetralogy of Fallot, ventricular septal defect, atrial septal defect, aortic stenosis and coarctation
- Other common features of Alagille syndrome are cholestasis, posterior embryotoxon of the eye, vertebral abnormalities, renal and pancreatic abnormalities, short stature, and typical facial features (prominent forehead, deep-set eyes with hypertelorism and upslanting palpebral fissures, straight nose with a bulbous tip, large ears, prominent chin; see Figure 27.11)
- The majority are due to heterozygous mutations in the *JAG1* gene.

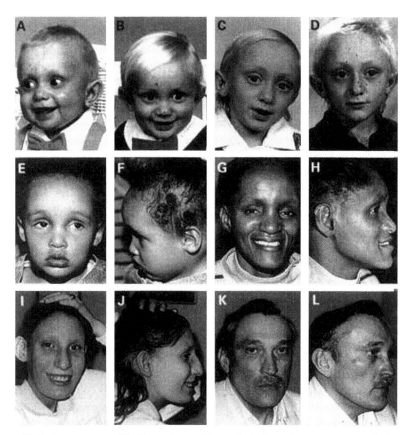

Figure 27.11 Appearance in Alagille syndrome. Photos A–D show the same patient at 1, 2, 4, and 6 years respectively. Photos E–H show an affected daughter and mother.

Reproduced from 'Alagille syndrome', I. D. Krantz, D. A. Piccoli, N. B. Spinner, *J Med Genet.*, 34(2), 152–7, Copyright 1997, with permission from BMJ Publishing Group Ltd.

Down syndrome

- Down syndrome is the most common chromosomal disorder with a birth incidence of about 1 in 1000 (with a significant maternal age effect)
- It is due to the addition of a whole chromosome 21 (trisomy 21)

- Congenital heart disease is common, particularly AVSDs or VSDs
- Other common features include: characteristic facial features, short stature, learning difficulties, single palmar crease, sandal gap, hypotonia, increased risk of leukaemia and dementia.

Turner syndrome

- Turner syndrome affects about 1 in 2000 female births and is usually due to only having a single X sex chromosome
- Left-sided outflow tract abnormalities are common: coarctation, BAV, aortic valve stenosis, and rarely hypoplastic left heart. Aortic root dilatation is common although the risk of dissection/rupture is not clear. In adult life CVD is more common
- Other features include: short stature, broad chest, lymphoedema/webbed neck, low-set ears, low hairline, gonadal dysfunction, thyroid abnormalities, increased risk of diabetes and autoimmune disease. Learning difficulties are usually mild and specific.

Williams syndrome

- Williams syndrome is caused by deletion of a region of chromosome 7
- This deletion includes the elastin gene, mutations in which can also cause the same range of cardiac defects
- Birth incidence is about 1 in 10,000
- Clinical features include: characteristic facial appearance (see Figure 27.12), short stature, hypercalcaemia and other endocrine abnormalities, learning difficulties, hearing loss, and GI abnormalities
- Supravalvular aortic stenosis is the most common cardiac defect; arterial narrowing at other sites, valve abnormalities, and septal defects also occur.

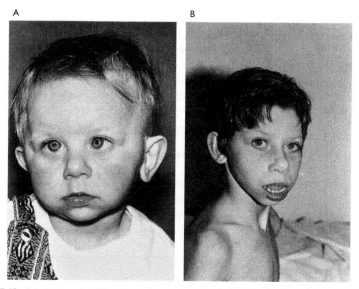

A   B

Figure 27.12 Appearance in Williams syndrome- same patient. (A) at 14 months and (B) at 17 years. Younger children typically have a broad forehead, periorbital fullness, flat nasal bridge, full cheeks and lips, a pointed chin, and wide mouth; older children and adults share some of these features but become coarser.

Heart–hand syndromes

- This term is used to refer to a group of disorders where limb abnormalities are associated with cardiac defects
- The prototype is Holt–Oram syndrome. This combines septal defects and/or AV node disease with abnormalities of the radial ray (ranging from subtle unilateral thumb hypoplasia to phocomelia)
- Usually due to dominant mutations in the *TBX5* gene.

27.6 Cardiac tumours

- Primary tumours of the heart are uncommon
- Most are sporadic. A few may be heritable, usually as part of a wider syndrome
- In children rhabdomyomas are the most common tumour type, whereas in adults myxomas are the most common
- The most common malignant tumours are sarcomas
- Cardiac rhabdomyomas are frequently associated with tuberous sclerosis.

Tuberous sclerosis

- Tuberous sclerosis (TS) is a dominantly inherited condition, which affects about 1 in 6000 people
- Non-cardiac features include central nervous system lesions, cutaneous lesions, renal features, and retinal hamartomas
- TS is caused by mutations or deletions at one of two chromosomal loci, *TSC1* or *TSC2*; these are frequently *de novo* (new mutations rather than inherited).

Gorlin syndrome

- Cardiac fibromas are the second most common cardiac tumour in the paediatric population
- Gorlin syndrome is characterized by basal cell carcinomas, jaw cysts, palmar/plantar pits, skeletal abnormalities, other tumours, ocular abnormalities, and characteristic facial features due to dominantly inherited mutations in the PTCH1 gene
- Cardiac fibromas occur in a small minority in this condition, although much more commonly than in the general population.

Carney complex

- Cardiac myxomas commonly present due to embolic symptoms. ECG abnormalities are common but non-specific
- Although most cardiac myxomas are sporadic a minority are due to Carney complex
- This is a rare dominantly inherited disorder characterized by atrial myxomas, non-cardiac tumours (including endocrine tumours), and pigmentary abnormalities due to dominantly inherited mutations in the *PRKAR1A* gene.

Further reading

DeMott K, Nherera L, Shaw EJ, *et al*. Clinical guidelines and evidence review for familial hypercholesterolaemia: the identification and management of adults and children with familial hypercholesterolaemia. National Collaborating Centre for Primary Care and Royal College of General Practitioners, 2008. Available at http://www.nice.org.uk/nicemedia/live/12048/41700/41700.pdf

Kumar D, Elliott P. *Principles and Practice of Clinical Cardiovascular Genetics*. Oxford University Press, 2010.

National Genetics Education and Development Centre website. Available at: http://www.geneticseducation.nhs.uk/media/16236/Family_History_Series.pdf

Nuclear cardiology

28.1 Overview

The term 'nuclear cardiology' encompasses three main types of scan:

1) Myocardial perfusion scintigraphy (MPS)
2) Radionuclide ventriculography (RNV)
3) Positron emission tomography (PET)

- MPS provides a functional and ischaemic assessment of the left ventricle and is sometimes known as 'thallium scan', 'MIBI scan' or 'Myoview™ scan' depending on the isotope in question
- RNV produces data on the left and sometimes right ventricular volumes and again this is sometimes known as a multi-gated acquisition (MUGA) scan
- FDG–PET (see Section 28.5) determines myocardial viability through the assessment of glucose metabolism
- RNV has been available since the 1970s
- Planar MPS started soon after, with single photon emission computed tomography (SPECT) in the 1980s and ECG gated SPECT in the 1990s
- Much of the impressive evidence base is from old studies with early technology
- Recent developments have allowed nuclear cardiology techniques to regain some of the ground that has passed over to alternative, and complementary, imaging techniques
- As a basic principle all these techniques use a camera designed to detect radioactive particles emitted from medical isotopes
- The practice of these investigations is closely governed by ionizing radiation regulations
- All practitioners of nuclear medicine must hold valid certification under the Ionising Radiation (Medical Exposure) Regulations 2000
- Consultants with responsibility for overseeing a nuclear cardiology service should hold an Administration of Radioactive Substances Advisory Committee certificate.

28.2 Radiation protection

- Lifetime risk of cancer is approximately 1:3 (30%)
- Annual UK background radiation exposure is 2.6 mSv
- A typical MPS study exposes the patient to between 6–14 mSv of ionizing radiation depending on the isotope used
- The long term carcinogenic effects of radiation are difficult to accurately determine, however the following examples are helpful:
  - For a stress-redistribution thallium-201 study the injected dose would be approximately 80 MBq, with an effective dose equivalent of 14 mSv. The lifetime risk of cancer would increase by 1:1429 (0.0007%) on a background lifetime cancer risk of 30%
  - For a one-day Tc-99m tetrofosmin study the injected dose would be approximately 1000 MBq with an effective dose equivalent of 8 mSv. The lifetime risk of cancer would increase by 1:2667 (0.0004%) on a background lifetime cancer risk of 30%
- Doctors and technologists performing the tests do not need to wear any protective clothing apart from everyday clinical gloves when handling the isotopes
- Badge monitoring is mandatory but rarely reveals excessive exposure during routine practice
- The isotopes are held under lead shielding
- Employees have a dose limit of 20 mSv/year.

28.3 Myocardial perfusion scintigraphy

- MPS is a robust and well validated technique for the diagnosis and assessment of CAD
- The technique uses rest and peak stress images to determine resting myocardial perfusion, inducible defects, and functional information which help to determine prognosis and guide therapeutic options
- Its use as an initial diagnostic tool for intermediate-risk patients has been cemented with its appearance in NICE 2010 guidance for the investigation of suspected coronary disease
- The NICE guidelines do not differentiate between MPS, DSE, or CMR
- MPS has a largest volume of evidence and is by far the most popular form of advanced ischaemia testing in the UK and the rest of the world
- Local expertise is crucial for a successful service
- Prior to NICE 2010, MPS also received a favourable assessment in 2003 (NICE technology appraisal 73)
- Typical evidence-based indications include:
  - Assessment of atypical chest pain
  - Identification of ischaemic territory and burden pre-revascularization
  - Assessment of symptoms post-revascularization
  - Assessment of the residual ischaemic burden post MI
  - Risk assessment before non-cardiac surgery, e.g. vascular and transplant surgery
  - Evidence of hibernating myocardium in LV systolic dysfunction
  - Identification of ACS in those presenting with acute chest pain.

MPS has also been validated in 'special' sub groups:

- Women
- Diabetics
- The elderly.

In all of these groups, MPS provides superior diagnostic and prognostic value over conventional risk factor variables and exercise test results.

Cameras and isotopes

- Technetium-99m (^{99m}Tc) and thallium-201 (^{201}Tl) continue to be the only used tracers for MPS
- Thallium is an older radioisotope the use of which has been in decline until recently
- Thallium redistributes freely between the blood pool and the myocardial cells via the Na$^+$/K$^+$ ATPase mechanism
- Technetium-99m is a more recent, but popular addition to nuclear cardiology
- The technetium is bound to either sestamibi or tetrofosmin before it is injected and it is then retained in intact cardiac myocytes
- These agents do not allow redistribution with the blood pool
- Thallium-201 has a half-life of 73 h
- The technetium-99m agents have a half-life of 6 h, which allows for up to two injections in one day
- Photons are emitted at characteristic energies, which are detected as scintillations on the NaI crystal within the heads of the gamma camera
- Thallium is cheaper but must be delivered ready to use to the hospital from the cyclotron
- Technetium isotopes can be reconstituted by hospital pharmacists from an onsite generator (delivered on a weekly basis)
- New scanners are reducing the time to image and the radiation dose
- Cadmium-zinc-telluride gamma cameras are revolutionizing MPS with scanning times as short as 2 min and with improved image quality
- This hardware solution coupled with innovative software (resolution recovery) has shifted MPS back into the spotlight
- Technetium-based isotopes have suffered from erratic supply lines in the last few years and these new developments are extremely important
- This technology also allows new tracers to be developed and older discarded tracers to be resurrected.

Principles of stress

- MPS acquires images in the resting state and at peak stress. The stressor may be:
  - Physical: treadmill, bicycle
  - Pharmacological: adenosine, dipyridamole, dobutamine
  - Other: pacing, mental (rarely used in clinical practice)
- Treadmill stress testing tends to follow the Bruce or modified Bruce protocols
- Bicycle stress involves starting at 25 W and increasing every 3 min by 25 W
- Both these physiological stressors also provide invaluable symptom, HR/BP, and ECG data, which cannot be so easily assessed with pharmacological stress
- Ideally physiological stress should be the default stressor for all patients attending a nuclear cardiology department
- The vasodilator stress agents are adenosine and dipyridamole
- Adenosine acts on A1 receptors causing coronary vasodilatation
- It has a very short half-life and is therefore given over a 6 min infusion, with the isotope injected during the infusion
- Dipyridamole reduces the uptake and inhibits breakdown of endogenous adenosine
- Peak hyperaemia is seen 2–3 min after a 4-min infusion of dipyridamole, at which point the isotope is injected

- With relatively reduced flow down a stenosed vessel and hyperaemia through normal arteries, areas of hypoperfusion are revealed
- Both agents can cause bronchospasm and are not used if significant bradycardia or second- and third-degree heart block are present
- They are also antagonized by caffeine and theophyllines, which must be avoided for at least 12 h prior to administration
- Newer A2a receptor angonists such as regadenoson are now in use
- These bolus agents are cardiac specific, with much lower rates of bronchospasm
- Dobutamine acts as a beta agonist, increasing both HR and coronary flow
- Isotope is injected at peak HR
- This agent should be used with caution in unstable coronary disease or after recent MI.

Stress protocols

- See Figure 28.1
- Thallium is injected at peak stress with imaging to be completed within 10–15 min of cessation of stress
- The redistribution acquisition is performed 4 h later, which allows the isotope to equilibrate with the blood pool, to provide a 'rest' scan
- If this redistribution scan identifies areas of hypoperfusion then a further image acquisition can be performed 24 h later to ensure that severe prolonged ischaemia is excluded
- Occasionally there is need for a re-injection of thallium to identify hibernating myocardium
- This occurs at 4 h post stress and is followed by immediate image acquisition
- Technetium protocols are simpler as there is no redistribution (or washout) of tracer with the blood pool
- Isotope is injected at peak stress and at rest

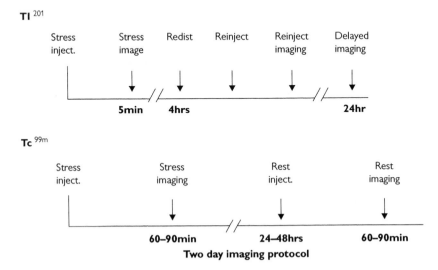

Figure 28.1 Typical scanning protocols.

- Protocols using peak-stress injections first are usually preferred, as a normal stress study precludes the need for the rest scan
- The best configuration is a 2-day protocol, which allows the activity from the first injection to have completely disappeared
- This protocol is not suitable for those patients travelling long distances, and therefore the one-day stress–rest protocol is also available
- The activity of the first injection is usually 2–3 times lower than the second injection, thus any residual activity from the first injection is 'drowned out' by the second one.

Image acquisition

- The patient is positioned under the gamma camera (see Figure 28.2), which usually has two heads
- The heads can image in a 'planar' (fixed) position or can rotate around the patient through 180° (SPECT)
- Planar acquisition has effectively been superseded by SPECT, which is now routinely ECG gated to provide regional and global LV functional assessment
- 3D reconstruction is also possible using gated SPECT
- Reconstructed SPECT images are displayed by convention in three orthogonal planes: short axis from apex to base, vertical long axis from septum to lateral wall, and horizontal long axis from inferior to anterior wall
- The stress images are placed in a row above the corresponding rest images. The count activity is shown with a continuous colour scale (see Figure 28.3).

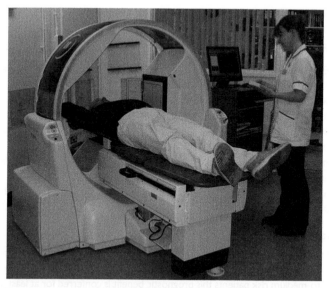

Figure 28.2 Typical dedicated cardiac gamma camera. It has a small footprint with no claustrophobia. Patient is able to lie flat and rest whilst image acquisition in process. Members of staff routinely sit in room to keep patient company and do not require lead shielding.

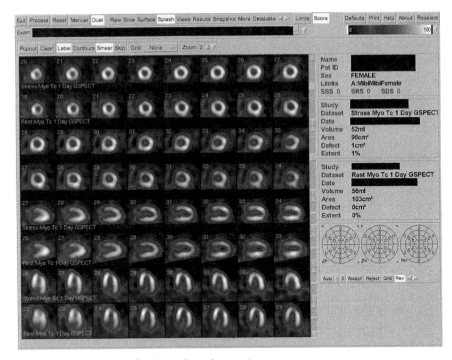

Figure 28.3 Normal study. See also colour plate section.

Image interpretation

See Figures 28.3, 28.4, and 28.5 for a normal study, diaphragmatic attenuation, and infarct/ischaemia.

- Gated SPECT allows detection of regional wall motion abnormalities and quantification of LV volumes
- Regional wall motion or thickening defects can be described in the same manner as for echocardiography (see Figures 28.4 and 28.5)
- Rest and stress scans are compared to identify areas of abnormal uptake, their extent, severity, and distribution, i.e. the total ischaemic burden
- Semi-quantitative scoring systems and measures are available, which have been validated. The most commonly used is the summed stress score
- The overall burden of ischaemia can be quantified by the proprietary software within most systems, presented as a percentage and risk stratified accordingly (see Table 28.1).

Clinical value

- A normal myocardial perfusion scan result confers an annual cardiovascular adverse event rate of less than 1% per annum for medium-to-high risk pre-test probabilities (see Figure 28.6)
- In the low-to-medium risk patients this prognostic benefit is conferred for at least 5 years
- A small defect is low risk, representing a MACE rate <3% per year
- Ischaemic defects greater than 10% of the myocardium are associated with a 4.8% cardiac death rate; >20% ischaemia is associated with a 6.7% cardiac death rate if treated medically (see Figure 28.7)

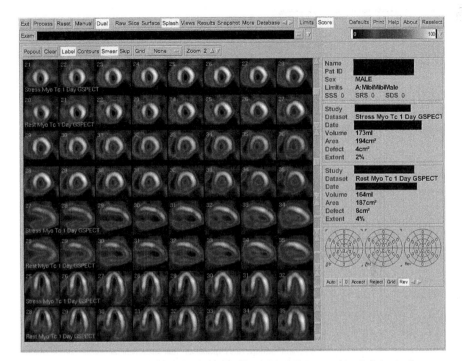

Figure 28.4 Diaphragmatic attentuation. Note uniform reduced counts along inferior wall, present both at rest and in stress. The gated study confirms normal wall thickening, which excludes a fixed inferior wall infarct. See also colour plate section.

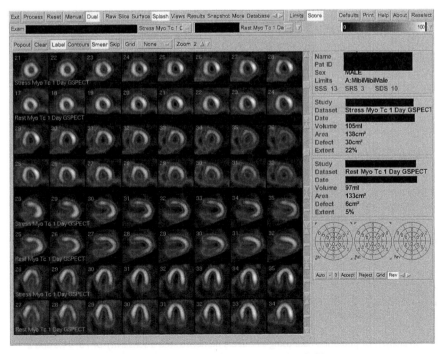

Figure 28.5 Abnormal study. There is evidence of a moderate sized inferior infarct with additional small volume of stress induced ischaemia in the anterior wall. See also colour plate section.

Table 28.1 Quantified burden of ischaemia.

Extent of ischaemia	Percentage of myocardium at risk	Myocardial segments at risk (out of 17)
Small	5–10	1–2
Medium	10–20	2–3
Large	>20	>/= 4

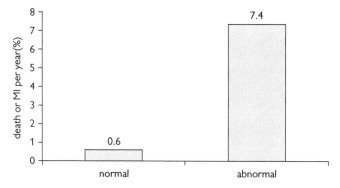

Figure 28.6 Cardiac event rates in 12,000 patients with normal or abnormal stress sestamibi scans.

Adapted from *J. Am. Coll. Cardiol.*, 32(1), Sherif Iskander, Ami E Iskandrian, 'Risk assessment using single-photon emission computed tomographic technetium-99m sestamibi imaging', 57–62, Copyright 1998 with permission from Elsevier.

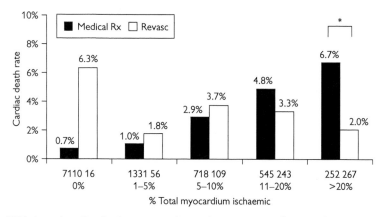

Figure 28.7 Annual cardiac death rate according to the percentage of myocardium with inducible hypoperfusion, stratified by management (10,627 patients followed for mean 2 years).

Adapted from Hachamovitch et al *Circ 2003*

Reproduced from 'Comparison of the short-term survival benefit associated with revascularization compared with medical therapy in patients with no prior coronary artery disease undergoing stress myocardial perfusion single photon emission computed tomography', Rory Hachamovitch, Sean W. Hayes, John D. Friedman *et al.*, *Circulation*, 107, 2900–6, copyright 2003 with permission of Wolters Kluwer Health.

- LV dilatation or drop in LVEF post stress is an adverse sign and provides incremental prognostic value over quantitative SPECT
- An LV ejection fraction of <45% confers a worse prognosis in the context of inducible defects, especially if the end systolic volume is >70 ml (cardiac death rate 7.9%/year) (see Figure 28.8)
- An analysis of published data using all tracers demonstrated a sensitivity of 73–94% and a specificity of around 90% for the detection of angiographically significant stenoses

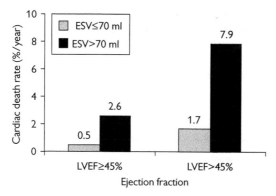

Figure 28.8 The prognostic value of combined LVEF and ESV after gated SPECT.
Reproduced from 'Incremental prognostic value of post-stress left ventricular ejection fraction and volume by gated myocardial perfusion single photon emission computed tomography', Tali Sharir, Guido Germano, Paul B. Kavanagh et al., *Circulation*, 100, 1035–1042, copyright 1999 with permission of Wolters Kluwer Health.

- A meta-analysis of pharmacological stress echocardiography reported a sensitivity of 85–86% with a specificity of 86–89%.

Limitations of myocardial perfusion scintigraphy

- Ionizing radiation is required (although doses are acceptable in most populations)
- MPS can struggle with ECG gating patients with uncontrolled AF; in these patients the LVEF may be inaccurate
- LBBB is a challenge with regards to interpretation
- Renal or hepatic dysfunction, claustrophobia, or metal implants are *not* a contraindication to the test.

Reporting of myocardial perfusion scintigraphy

Look at referral indication, PMH, and type/quality of stress.

- Assess quality of images (extra-cardiac activity, attenuation from diaphragm/breast)
- Defects at rest represent infarct; assess viability
- Assess peak-stress images; matched defects = infarct, mismatch = ischaemia
- Look at global and regional LV function.

Formulate report, giving diagnosis, estimate of prognosis, and answer to clinical question.

28.4 Equilibrium radionuclide ventriculography

- Equilibrium radionuclide ventriculography (ERNV) uses planar (fixed head) imaging to reproducibly measure the LVEF
- The blood pool is pre-treated with stannous pyrophosphate, which diffuses into red blood cells
- The blood pool is then labelled using technetium-99m, which binds to the stannous ions intra-cellularly
- Multiple gated cardiac cycles are acquired (up to 32 slices per cardiac cycle) and merged (hence alternative term 'multi-gated acquisition'), giving an accurate and reproducible assessment of overall LV function
- This procedure is therefore less suitable for patients with poorly controlled atrial fibrillation
- Clearly modern echocardiography is the first-line test for the assessment of LV function

- A modern refinement of RNV allows for ECG gated SPECT analysis of both LVEF and RVEF with again a high degree of accuracy and reproducibility
- Unlike all other techniques, RNV does not rely on endocardial border edge detection (c.f. MPS, TTE, CMR, and CT)
- This technique relies on accurately quantifying radiolabelled RBCs in their passage through the LV (and RV) cavity.

28.5 Positron emission tomography

- Positron emission tomography (PET) uses ^{18}F-deoxyglucose (FDG) to detect changes in glucose metabolism
- These changes are an indicator of myocardial viability
- This test is usually combined with an assessment of myocardial perfusion
- This usually requires cyclotron-produced NH_3, which limits its availability
- The recent introduction of rubidium-82 is likely to expand the use of PET myocardial perfusion throughout the world, but there are cost implications
- FDG–PET is considered the gold standard for the assessment of myocardial viability but use of specialist isotopes and co-incidence detection cameras limit its use to specialist centres.

28.6 Recent developments

- Specific A2a receptor agonists have demonstrated efficacy as pharmacological stress agents with good tolerability and fewer side effects than adenosine
- The recent introduction of cadmium zinc telluride (CZT) gamma cameras has revolutionized the acquisition time and image quality of myocardial perfusion scintigraphy studies. Typical imaging times are now only 2–3 min
- SPECT/CT and PET/CT hybrid imaging allows the addition of cardiac anatomy to perfusion and function; essentially a complete one-stop assessment for patients with suspected coronary artery disease
- The use of PET has expanded to include assessment of viability and inflammation, including infection (endocarditis and device related)
- Rubidium-82 and Flurpiridaz have shown promise as PET perfusion tracers, without the need for a cyclotron. Flurpiridaz F-18 tracer appears to increase sensitivity, have fewer artefacts and thus allow a lower radiation dose.

28.7 The future

Iodine-123-metaiodobenyzlguanidine

- Iodine-123-metaiodobenyzlguanidine (mIBG) is an isotope that acts as a false neurotransmitter to the sympathetic nervous system
- Its lack of cardiac uptake is a marker of adverse prognosis for sudden cardiac death and progression of heart failure in patients with LV systolic dysfunction
- MIBG has been available for many years for non-cardiac imaging but is likely to become an integral tool in the risk assessment of patients with heart failure.

Further reading

Abidov A, Bax JJ, Hayes SW, et al. Transient ischemic dilation ratio of the left ventricle is a significant predictor of future cardiac events in patients with otherwise normal myocardial perfusion SPECT. *J Am Coll Cardiol*, 2003; 42: 1818–25.

Hachamovitch R, Hayes SW, Friedman JD, Cohen I, Berman DS. Comparison of the short-term survival benefit associated with revascularization compared with medical therapy in patients with no prior coronary artery disease undergoing stress myocardial perfusion single photon emission computed tomography. *Circulation*, 2003; 107: 2900–7.

Haque WA, Schwartz RG, Fisher TJ, Watelet LM, Oakes D, Mackin M. Transient ischemic dilation provides incremental prognostic value to quantitative SPECT. *Circulation*, 1997; 96, 1–195.

Iskander S, Iskandrian A. Risk assessment using single-photon emission computed tomographic technetium-99m sestamibi imaging. *J Am Coll Cardiol*, 1998; 32: 57–62.

Jacobson AF, Senior R, Cerqueira MD, et al. Myocardial iodine-123 meta-iodobenzylguanidine imaging and cardiac events in heart failure: results of the prospective ADMIRE-HF (AdreView Myocardial Imaging for Risk Evaluation in Heart Failure) Study. *J Am Coll Cardiol*, 2010; 55: 2212–21.

Picano E, Molinaro S, Pasanisi E. The diagnostic accuracy of pharmacological stress echocardiography for the assessment of coronary artery disease: a meta-analysis. *J Cardiovasc Ultrasound*, 2008, 6: 30.

Sabharwal N, Loong CY, Kelion A. *Nuclear Cardiology.* Oxford Specialist Handbooks in Cardiology. Oxford University Press. Oxford 2008.

Sharir T, Germano G, Kavanagh PB, et al. Incremental prognostic value of post-stress left ventricular ejection fraction and volume by gated myocardial perfusion single photon emission computed tomography. *Circulation*, 1999; 100: 1035–1042.

Underwood SR, Anagnostopoulos C, Cerqueira M, et al. Myocardial perfusion scintigraphy: the evidence. *Eur J Nucl Med Mol Imaging*, 2004; 31: 261–291.

Magnetic resonance imaging

CONTENTS

29.1 Overview

Cardiac magnetic resonance scanning offers high spatial and temporal resolution imaging of the heart. A comprehensive examination gives detailed information regarding:

- Structure
- Function
- Myocardial perfusion
- Wall motion abnormalities
- Tissue characteristics
- Valvular abnormalities.

MRI can study the heart in any anatomical plane and is not limited by poor imaging windows. The examination can be tailored to the patient and specific pathology (see Table 29.1).

- Assessment of left and right ventricular function by CMR is highly accurate and reproducible, and is a regular component to most CMR examinations
- Blood flow can be measured with velocity-encoded imaging to assess intra-cardiac shunts and valvular abnormalities
- Topographical imaging is of vital importance in the assessment of congenital heart disease
- Gadolinium-based contrast agents are used for stress perfusion imaging, early and late gadolinium sequences, and angiography of the great vessels.

Table 29.1 Indications for cardiac MRI, sequence used, gadolinium, and stress agent

Indication	Sequence	Gadolinium (+/−)	Stress agent
Left and right ventricular function	SSFP: cine	−	−
Perfusion (ischaemia)	Gradient echo: stills	+	+ Adenosine/ dipyridamole
Inducible wall motion abnormalities (ischaemia)	SSFP: cine	−	+ dobutamine
Valvular abnormalities	Velocity-encoded imaging	−	−
Viability	Delayed contrast enhancement	+	−
Intra-cardiac thrombus	Early contrast	+	−
Oedema	T2-weighted	−	−
Fatty infiltration	T1-weighted	−	−
Infiltration (amyloid)	Variable inversion time	+	N/A
Pericardium assessment	Free-breathing	−	−

29.2 Basic physics

- Within a strong magnetic field protons (H$^+$ ions) line-up parallel to the field lines
- A radiofrequency pulse delivers energy to the protons, causing some to flip 180°
- As the protons flip back, radiofrequency energy is released, and is measured and post-processed to create an image.

29.3 Contraindications

The MRI scanner comprises a very large magnet with a power 30–60,000 times that of the Earth's magnetic field. There are three main areas of risk in the MRI environment (see Table 29.2):

- The static magnetic field
- The gradient fields
- The radiofrequency pulse.

Table 29.2 The risks and hazards of cardiac MRI

Areas of risk:	Risk	Hazard
Static magnetic field: helium-cooled superconducting magnet	1. Ferromagnetic material will accelerate towards the magnetic core 2. Interaction with medical implants	1. Projectile injury 2. Current induction and device malfunction
Gradient magnetic field	1. Noise >90 dB 2. Interaction with medical implants	1. Auditory damage 2. Current induction and devise malfunction
Radiofrequency pulse	Heating effect	Heating of implants

Reproduced from 'Non-invasive imaging: Contraindications to magnetic resonance imaging', T. Dill, *Heart* 94, 943–948, copyright 2008 with permission from BMJ Publishing Group Ltd.

Table 29.3 A short list of contraindications to cardiac MRI

Metal implants	Electromechanical implants
Cerebral aneurysm clips	Pacemakers/AICDs
Metallic foreign in body in the eye	Pacing wires
Ocular implants	Cochlear implants
Swan-Ganz catheters	Neurostimulators
Shrapnel, i.e. bullets	Programmable hydrocephalus shunts

There are validated screening questionnaires (see 'Further Reading') for patients, relatives, and staff who wish to enter the MRI environment. A list of contraindications is given in Table 29.3; this is not exhaustive and local protocols should be adhered to.

29.4 Patient selection and preparation

- Patients in atrial fibrillation or with ectopic activity can be challenging to scan, as the images are gated and rely on a regular R-R interval. Cine images suffer from artefacts leading to inaccuracies in volumetric assessment
- ECG attachment: these are gated scans and therefore a good trace is vital
- Head phones for protection and to communicate with the radiographer
- Cannula for gadolinium +/− stress agent
- Discuss breath-hold instructions (each scan is performed in expiration for 5–10 s)
- Patients lie supine head, first into the scanner, but prone, feet-first scanning is possible for those with claustrophobia.

29.5 Contrast agent

Gadolinium is an extra-cellular contrast agent.

- The risk of an allergic reaction is <1 per 10,000
- Nephrogenic systemic fibrosis is a rare condition characterized by widespread thickening of the skin and fibrosis of skeletal and visceral muscle
- It is associated with the use of gadolinium contrast in patients with advance renal impairment and is invariably fatal
- In our institution gadolinium-based contrast agents are not used in patients with a GFR of <30 ml/min or those receiving renal replacement therapy; it is used with caution in those with CKD stage 3.

29.6 Assessment of ventricular function

- Left ventricular systolic function is the most important prognostic marker in heart disease
- CMR is regarded as the gold standard for the assessment for left ventricular function in terms of accuracy and reproducibility
- Steady-state free-precession (SSFP) images are constructed in the short axis plane (see Figures 29.1 and 29.2).

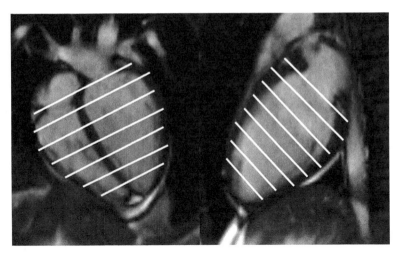

Figure 29.1 Assessment of left ventricular function. Short axis images are constructed from the two- and four-chambers views.

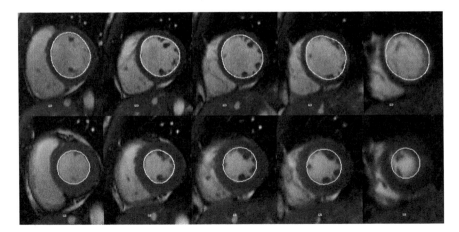

Figure 29.2 Diastolic data (top row) and systolic data (bottom row), demonstrating the measurement of left ventricular volumes and subsequently ejection fraction.

Measurements:
- Ejection fraction
- Stroke volume
- LV mass
- Diastolic wall thickness
- Systolic and diastolic volumes.

Clinical application:
- Drug intervention
- Device suitability
- Diagnosis
- Monitoring: pre-intervention for valvular lesions.

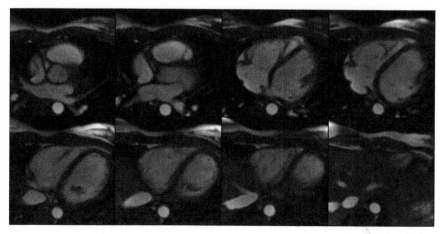

Figure 29.3 Axial images of the right ventricle used in the calculation of the RV ejection fraction.

Right ventricle

- Due to the non-uniform structure of the right ventricle, other imaging modalities, such as echocardiography, struggle to accurately assess its size and function
- SSFP CMR cine images in the axial plane (Figure 29.3) provide an accurate and reproducible assessment of the RV:
  - Ejection fraction
  - Stroke volume
  - Diastolic and systolic volumes
- CMR does not use ionizing radiation or contrast agent so is safe to use in the follow up and surveillance of grown-up congenital heart disease patients.

29.7 Assessment of viability

- Dysfunctional myocardium (which is not infarcted) has the potential for contractile recovery after revascularization and is therefore deemed viable tissue
- CMR delayed-contrast enhancement (late gadolinium enhancement; LGE) imaging is used to predict viability in patients referred for revascularization (Figure 29.4).

Gadolinium

- A paramagnetic contrast agent
- Diffuses rapidly through the capillary basement membrane into the extra-cellular space; it does not cross intact cellular membranes
- Collects in areas with an increased extracellular space, such as fibrosis or areas with infarcted cells, changing the paramagnetic properties and differentiating it from normal myocardium on the MRI scan.

Late gadolinium enhancement

- The extent of LGE predicts functional improvement after revascularization in heart failure
- Segments with no LGE have an 80% chance of functional recovery following revascularization

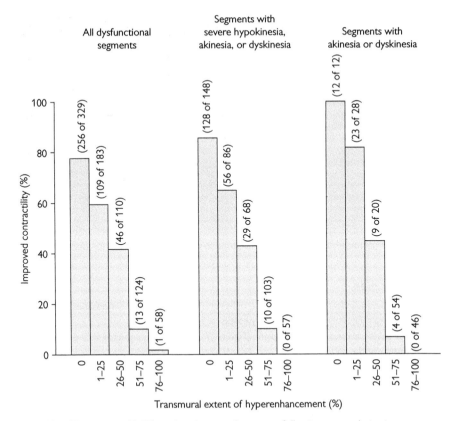

Figure 29.4 The extent of LGE predicts functional recovery following revascularization.

Reproduced from *N. Engl. J. Med.*, Raymond J. Kim, Edwin Wu, Allen Rafael, et al., 'The use of contrast-enhanced magnetic resonance imaging to identify reversible myocardial dysfunction', 343(20), 1445–53, Copyright 2000 Massachusetts Medical Society. Reproduced with permission from Massachusetts Medical Society.

- Segments with 75–100% LGE have a <10% chance of functional recovery
- The high spatial resolution of CMR enables quantification of the transmural extent of a myocardial infarction (Figure 29.5). CMR will detect sub-endocardial infarcts that are missed by SPECT imaging
- The revascularization of patients with viable myocardium has a significant effect on prognosis (Figure 29.6)
- Patients with viable myocardium who are revascularized have a significant reduction in annual mortality (79.6%) compared to those treated medically.

Thrombus

- Contrast-enhanced CMR can reliably identify thrombus in the left ventricle and LAA with the use of early and late gadolinium sequences
- In early images (2 min after injection of gadolinium) the thrombus appears black compared to the blood pool and other tissue that contains gadolinium
- On LGE imaging the thrombus does not contain gadolinium and therefore does not enhance (Figure 29.7).

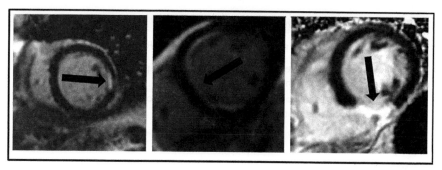

Figure 29.5 Different types of LGE in subendocardial and transmural infarction. Left, a small subendocardial lateral wall infarct; middle, a subendocardial anterior and septal infarct; right, a full-thickness inferior infarct.

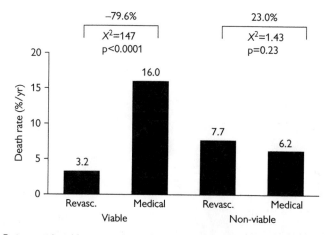

Figure 29.6 Patients with viable myocardium who are treated medically have a 16% annual mortality.

Reproduced from *J. Am. Coll. Cardiol.*, 39(7), Kevin C. Allman, Leslee J. Shaw, Rory Hachamovitch, *et al.*, 'Myocardial viability testing and impact of revascularization on prognosis in patients with coronary artery disease and left ventricular dysfunction: a meta-analysis', 1151–8, Copyright 2002 with permission from Elsevier.

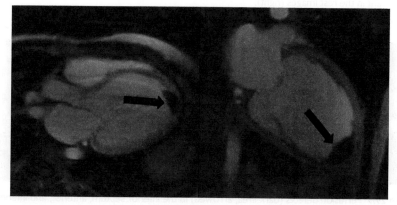

Figure 29.7 Early gadolinium enhancement demonstrating an apical thrombus in the three-chamber (left) and two-chamber (right) view.

29.8 Assessment of ischaemia

There are two methods to assess myocardial ischaemia with CMR:

- Adenosine or dipyridamole stress perfusion: studying the first-pass perfusion of gadolinium-based contrast agents
- Dobutamine stress CMR to look for regional wall motion abnormalities; similar to stress echocardiography and does not require gadolinium.

Stress perfusion CMR

Adenosine:

- Naturally occurring purine receptor agonist
- Induces hyperaemia by vasodilatation of the cardiac microcirculation
- T1 weighted images are taken during the first pass of gadolinium through the heart and myocardium; normally three images per heart beat in three slices
- Two sets of first-pass perfusion images are acquired for comparison, at stress and at rest (Figures 29.8 and 29.9).

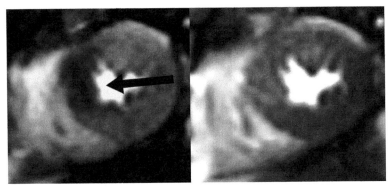

Figure 29.8 A mid septal perfusion defect during the stress scan. The arrowed dark area (left) not present in the rest images (right).

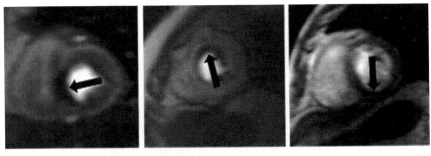

Figure 29.9 Perfusion defects (dark area, arrowed) in the inferior septum, anterior, and inferior segments (left to right).

Contraindications include:

- Asthma
- Concomitant use of dipyridamole
- High-degree atrioventricular block; risk of complete heart block requiring specialist intervention is low.

Diagnostic and prognostic accuracy

- Sensitivity: 89%
- Specificity: 80%
- The moderate specificity is due to dark rim artefact along the sub-endocardial surface (Figure 29.10) and microvascular disease
- Prognosis: the 3-year event rate for patients with a normal CMR perfusion study is 2.3% compared with 16.3% for a positive scan.

Dobutamine stress CMR

- Dobutamine is used to increase contractility and heart rate
- The study can be performed in patients with a contraindication to gadolinium as no contrast agent is necessary
- Diagnostic accuracy of echocardiography and CMR is equivalent in patients with good echocardiographic images
- In patients with moderate imaging windows CMR shows a clear advantage
- During a typical protocol, images are taken in a short and long axis view during incremental doses of dobutamine
- Atropine is used to augment the heart rate response to reach the target (85% of the maximal age-predicted heart rate).

Diagnostic and prognostic accuracy

- Sensitivity: 83–89%
- Specificity: 84–86%
- Prognosis: the 3-year event rate for patients without an inducible wall motion abnormality is 3.3% (18.8% for a positive scan)
- This event rate is comparable to those from stress echocardiography: around 1% per year.

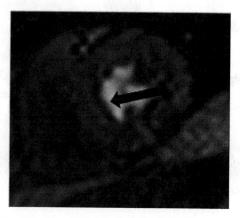

Figure 29.10 A dark rim artefact (arrow) on the endocardial surface.

29.9 Acute coronary syndromes

Myocarditis
- One in ten patients admitted with chest pain and a positive troponin blood test will have normal or unobstructed coronary arteries demonstrated at invasive coronary angiograph
- The differential diagnosis includes an ACS with recanalization of the artery, embolism, and myocarditis
- The LGE pattern is patchy, subepicardial,and in a non-coronary distribution, helping to differentiate between an inflammatory or ischaemic aetiology (Figure 29.11).

Microvascular obstruction
- During an MI, the ischaemic myocytes perish first followed by the endothelial cells
- In the centre of the infarcted region the myocytes and endothelial cells can undergo spontaneous necrosis resulting in occlusion of the intramyocardial capillary network with dying blood cells and debris (Figure 29.13)
- In this situation the infarcted area will not re-perfuse even with the restoration of epicardial blood flow; this phenomenon of no reflow or microvascular obstruction (MVO) is seen both clinically and experimentally.

MVO predicts (Figure 29.12):
- Left ventricle end-diastolic volume
- Left ventricle end-systolic volume
- Ejection fraction
- Survival.

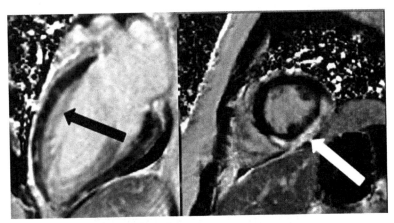

Figure 29.11 Mid-myocardial and subepicardial LGE in acute myocarditis.

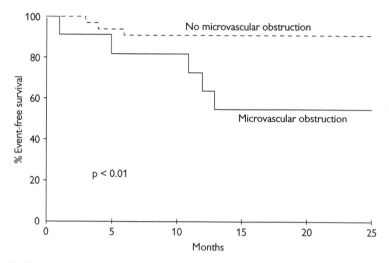

Figure 29.12 Microvascular obstruction observed at CMR, predicts long-term survival.

Reproduced from *J. Am. Coll. Cardiol.*, 32(6), Katherine C. Wu, Raymond J. Kim, David A. Bluemke *et al.*, 'Quantification and time course of microvascular obstruction by contrast-enhanced echocardiography and magnetic resonance imaging following acute myocardial infarction and reperfusion', 1756–64, copyright 1988, with permission of Elsevier.

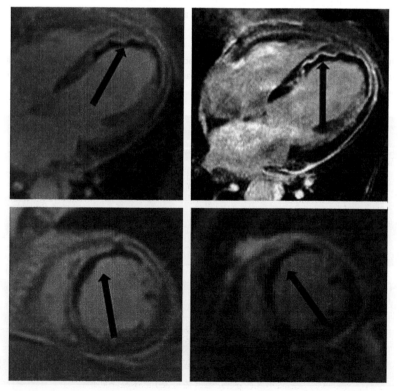

Figure 29.13 LGE images of the left ventricle demonstrating a large area of microvascular obstruction (arrows) of the anterior and antero-septal walls. Typically infarct at LGE imaging has a high signal (white), but the areas of MVO are dark due to the absence of gadolinium.

29.10 Assessment of heart valves and shunts

Velocity-encoded imaging

- Flow within the great vessels can be measured with velocity-encoded imaging and is used to calculate cardiac output, intracardiac shunts, and aortic or pulmonary regurgitation
- Rather than assigning a grey scale to each pixel to produce a topographical image, the MR scanner assigns a velocity to each pixel, the cross-sectional area of the vessel is measured and a flow (area × velocity) calculated (Figure 29.14).

Valves

- CMR is the gold standard for the assessment of the pulmonary valve and any consequences of a lesion
- Allows comprehensive examination of the right ventricular volume, ejection fraction, and mass
- For the assessment of left side valves, Doppler echocardiography is the imaging modality of choice for most lesions
- In patients with a poor echo window MRI can offer an alternative.

Aortic regurgitation:

- An accurate quantification of regurgitant volume and fraction is possible
- Cine images can clearly demonstrate a bicuspid aortic valve (Figure 29.15).

Mitral regurgitation:

- Quantification with through-plane velocity-encoded imaging across the mitral valve annulus, but this technique can result in inaccuracies because of movement of the annulus in and out of the sample volume

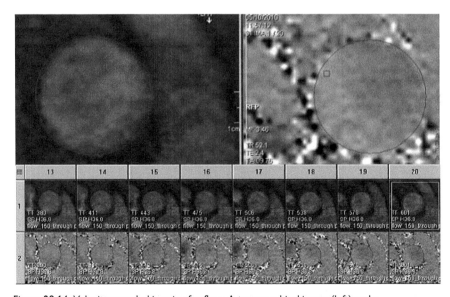

Figure 29.14 Velocity encoded imaging for flow. A topographical image (left) and a velocity-encoded image (right) are produced throughout the cardiac cycle (bottom two rows). Velocity × area = flow.

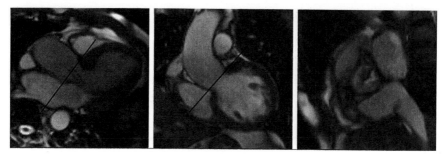

Figure 29.15 A bicuspid AV. Orthogonal views (left and middle) are used to construct a true short axis view through a bicuspid aortic valve (right).

- Measurement of the cardiac stroke volume in the aortic root with velocity-encoded imaging and measurement of the cardiac SV with cine imaging
- This method relies on a competent non-stenotic aortic valve and an accurate LV assessment and will be less accurate in the presence of arrhythmia.

Aortic stenosis:

- Stenotic valves lesions can be assessed with CMR
- The accuracy is reduced when assessing high velocities
- Velocity-encoded imaging should be used with caution in patients with moderate-to-severe aortic stenosis.

Mitral stenosis:

- Valves can also be assessed with cine imaging in the valvular plane and the valve area measured with planimetry. This method shows good agreement with echocardiography planimetry measurements.

29.11 Cardiomyopathies

Amyloidosis

- Suggestive anatomical patterns of infiltration and cardiac structural change
- Late gadolinium enhancement is present in 97% of biopsy-proven cardiac amyloidosis (non-coronary distribution: diffuse, with a subendocardial or subepicardial deposition; Figure 29.16). A coronary distribution of late gadolinium enhancement is demonstrated in Figure 29.17.

Hypertrophic cardiomyopathy

- In patients with poor echocardiographic windows or the apical variant of hypertrophic cardiomyopathy (HCM), MRI is a useful diagnostic test
- LGE can be used to assess areas of myocardial fibrosis in HCM
- The pattern of LGE is markedly different to IHD and varies between HCM patients
- The presence of fibrosis is associated with a greater likelihood of non-sustained VT compared to those with no fibrosis
- It is not clear whether the presence and extent of fibrosis as assessed with LGE is an independent risk factor for SCD (Figure 29.16).

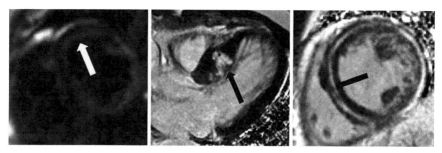

Figure 29.16 Differing cardiomyopathies. Left, amyloidosis with patchy LGE in the sub-endocardium; middle, LGE fibrosis in the septum of a patient with HCM; right, mid-myocardial ring of LGE seen in DCM.

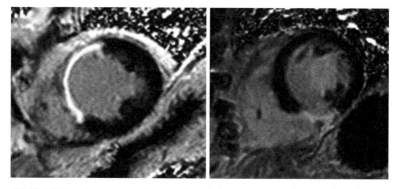

Figure 29.17 LGE imaging patterns due to ischaemic heart disease and myocardial infarction. Left, a full thickness septal infarction; right, a full thickness inferior myocardial infarction (white area arrowed).

Arrthymogenic right ventricular cardiomyopathy

- Arrthymogenic right ventricular cardiomyopathy (ARVC) is a disorder of the cardiac desmosomes leading to fibro-fatty replacement of the right ventricular myocardium
- In the initial stages of the disease structural changes may be absent, although there is still a risk of SCD
- There is a wide spectrum of disease severity and there are significant clinical challenges in the diagnosis and risk stratification of this condition
- CMR is the gold standard for the assessment of right ventricular size and function and offers the ideal modality for the diagnosis of ARVC
- Task force criteria are as follows:

Major criterion: regional wall motion abnormalities and one of:

- Increase in right ventricular end-diastolic volume($\geq$110 ml/m^2 for men or $\geq$100 ml/m^2 for women)
- Ejection fraction $\leq$40%.

Minor criterion: regional wall motion abnormalities and one of:

- increased RV end-diastolic volume (100–110 ml/m^2 for men or ≥90 ml/m^2 to <100 ml/m^2 for women)
- RVEF 40–45%.

Dilated cardiomyopathy

- CMR can help differentiate between an ischaemic and non-ischemic aetiology (Figure 29.16 and 29.17)
- CMR can also help in the risk stratification of patients with DCM
- Of those scanned in one series 59% have no LGE, 13% demonstrate a pattern of LGE consistent with IHD (possibly due to spontaneous coronary recannalization following an infarct) and 28% will have a mid-myocardial striae or patchy late enhancement
- Patients with a mid-myocardial ring of LGE are at increased risk of SCD or ventricular arrhythmias (Figure 29.16).

Iron overload and thalassaemia

- Thalassaemia is treated with repeat blood transfusions to prevent significant anaemia
- The body has no mechanism for the excretion of excess iron, so patients develop severe iron overload
- The commonest cause of death is heart failure secondary to cardiac siderosis
- CMR can identify patients with myocardial iron overload early in the course of the disease due to the effects of the haemosiderin deposits on the magnetic field
- Patients can be targeted with iron chelation therapies such as deferiprone, which has led to an improved prognosis.

29.12 Pericardial disease

- If the pericardium becomes thickened and stiff this leads to ventricular interdependence
- The filling of one side of the heart will have an effect on the other
- Inspiration leads to increasing filling of the right heart; as the total (left and right) cardiac volume is fixed due to the rigid pericardium this will lead to a reduction in left-sided filling
- This phenomenon can be demonstrated with Doppler echocardiography of the mitral and tricuspid flow patterns; transmitral filling of the left ventricle drops with inspiration
- CMR typically shows a 'flattening' of the septum during inspiration and this has been demonstrated in patients with a clinical suspicion of constrictive pericarditis (Figure 29.18)
- Measurements of pericardial thickening can be made with still CMR or computed tomography, which has a higher spatial resolution
- T1 and T2 weighted images can be acquired to differentiate fluid, inflammation, and fat
- 20% of patients with pericardial constriction confirmed at surgery will have a normal pericardial thickness at imaging
- The opposite is also true: a thickened inflamed pericardium may not have any haemodynamic sequel.

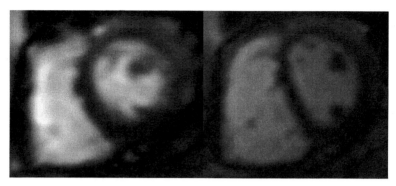

Figure 29.18 Stills from 'real time' cine images. The inter-ventricular septum flattens on inspiration (right) suggesting ventricular interdependence.

29.13 Great vessels

- MRI angiography is the imaging modality of choice for planned investigation of the aorta and great vessels
- In the unstable acute patient TTE/TOE or CT are superior due to the rapid imaging protocols
- CMR angiography can be used in the follow-up of:
  - Aortic aneurysms
  - Chronic aortic dissections
  - Aortic regurgitation
  - Intramural haematomas
  - Coarctation of the aorta before or after surgery
- Aortic stents can cause degeneration and artefact and are therefore followed up with CT
- As the scan can be acquired in any topographical plane the entire ascending aorta, arch, and descending aorta can be studied in a single image (candy cane; Figure 29.19)

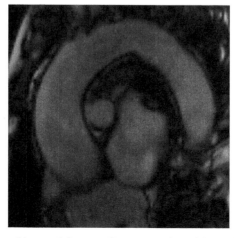

Figure 29.19 'Candy cane' image of the ascending aorta, arch, and descending aorta

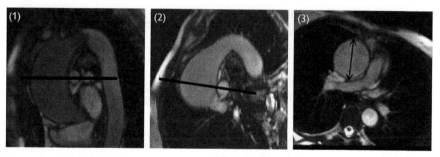

Figure 29.20 Orthogonal views of the aorta. Using orthogonal views (1,2) a true short axis view of the aorta (3) is constructed at the level of the main pulmonary artery.

- It is important to note that images are constructed in two orthogonal planes (Figure 29.20) rather than in axial slices to minimise inaccuracies.

Coarctation

The aorta can be visualized in any imaging plane and therefore a full assessment of aortic coarctation can be made:

- Collaterals and collateral flow
- Aortograms of the head and neck vessels
- Assessment of complications—local aneurysms
- Associated lesions (LVH and bicuspid aortic valves).

29.14 Congenital heart disease

- CMR is the imaging modality of choice for patients with complex congenital heart disease (Table 29.4)
- CMR offers high-resolution cine imaging for assessment of function, velocity-encoded images for assessment of flow and shunts, T1 and T2 weighted imaging for tissue characterization, and 3D reconstruction for overall assessment
- It is of particular use in the congenital population, who will need multiple examinations
- A sequential segmental approach is used to describe the anatomy.

29.15 Atria

- Identification of atrial isomerism: the left atrium is identified by the larger appendage and association with left-sided abdominal structures (stomach and spleen)
- Atrial septal defects can be identified with SSFP images though the intra-atrial septum in a perpendicular plane
- The shunt can be quantified using velocity-encoded images of the aorta and pulmonary trunk
- The consequences of the shunt can be assessed with a volume study of the right ventricle
- Associated abnormalities identified (anomalous pulmonary venous drainage).

Table 29.4 The ESC recommendations for CMR use.

Area	Condition
Left heart	Aortic regurgitation, Ross operation, Ao coarctation, Marfan's disease
Right heart	Ebstein, Fallot repair, pulmonary stenosis, pulmonary regurgitation, RV-PA conduits, major aortopulmonary collateral arteries
Shunts	Partial anomalous pulmonary venous drainage, patent ductus arteriosus, Eisenmenger's
Transposition of the great arteries	Mustard/Seening, arterial switch operation, Rastelli, congenitally corrected transposition of the great arteries
Fontan	Fontan operation
Coronary artery anomalies	

29.16 Ventricles

CMR volumetric studies are of particular use for the follow-up of patients after surgical palliation or correction of the underlying anomaly:

- Tetralogy of Fallot
- Transposition of the great arteries
- Univentricular hearts.

Right and left ventricular volumes can be measured sequentially with excellent reproducibility, allowing a confident assessment of volumes and guiding the timing of specific interventions such as pulmonary valve replacement.

29.17 Valves

Echocardiography is the gold standard for the assessment of left sided valves, particularly stenotic lesions.

- CMR is of great value in the assessment of pulmonary regurgitation which is often difficult to assess with echocardiography.

29.18 Cardiac masses

The primary investigations for the assessment of cardiac masses are the CXR and echocardiogram.

- Secondary tumours—metastatic disease—are significantly more common than primary tumours of the heart (ratio 40:1).

CMR assessment:
- Tumour site, size, and number
- Complications
- Tissue characterization (T1, T2, and first-pass perfusion)
- Invasion into myocardium and adjacent structures.

Primary tumours of the heart are more likely to be benign (70%):

- Myxomas (30%)
- Lipomas (10%)
- Papillary fibroelastomas (10%)
- Rhabdomyomas (7%)
- Lipomas typically bright on T1 weighted imaging, with a similar signal to subcutaneous fat
- Thrombus will remain dark on first-pass perfusion of gadolinium and early gadolinium enhancement scanning (see Section 29.7)
- Malignant tumours are typically well vascularized, demonstrating a strong signal on gadolinium first-pass perfusion
- For the diagnosis of a cardiac mass on CMR, the reporter must bear in mind all the imaging features available and not purely rely on tissue characterizations, as these are not specific for malignant or benign masses.

Common diagnostic pitfalls:

- Lipomatous hypertrophy of the intra atrial septum
- Thrombi
- Prominent crista terminalis
- Embryonic remnants of the right atrial (chiari formation or Eustachian valve).

Further reading

Allman KC, Shaw LJ, Hachamovitch R, Udelson JE. Myocardial viability testing and impact of revascularization on prognosis in patients with coronary artery disease and left ventricular dysfunction: a meta-analysis. *J Am Coll Cardiol* 2002; 39: 1151–8.

Dill T. Contraindications to magnetic resonance imaging: non-invasive imaging. *Heart* 2008; 94: 943–8.

Jahnke C, Nagel E, Gebker R, *et al.* Prognostic value of cardiac magnetic resonance stress tests: adenosine stress perfusion and dobutamine stress wall motion imaging. *Circulation* 2007; 115: 1769–76.

Kim RJ, Wu E, Rafael A, *et al.* The use of contrast-enhanced magnetic resonance imaging to identify reversible myocardial dysfunction. *N Engl J Med* 2000; 343: 1445–53.

McCrohon JA, Moon JC, Prasad SK, *et al.* Differentiation of heart failure related to dilated cardiomyopathy and coronary artery disease using gadolinium-enhanced cardiovascular magnetic resonance. *Circulation* 2003;108:54–9.

Nandalur KR, Dwamena BA, Choudhri AF, Nandalur MR, Carlos RC. Diagnostic performance of stress cardiac magnetic resonance imaging in the detection of coronary artery disease: a meta-analysis. *J Am Coll Cardiol* 2007; 50: 1343–53.

Shellock, F. Validated screening questionnaires for patients, relatives and staff who wish to enter the MRI environment. Available at: http://www.mrisafety.com/screening_form.asp

Wu KC, Kim RJ, Bluemke DA, *et al.* Quantification and time course of microvascular obstruction by contrast-enhanced echocardiography and magnetic resonance imaging following acute myocardial infarction and reperfusion. *J Am Coll Cardiol* 1998; 32: 1756–64.

Cardiac computed tomography

CONTENTS

30.1 Overview

- Multi-detector computed tomography (MDCT) offers high spatial resolution images of coronary vessels to demonstrate the presence or absence of coronary atheroma
- Scans can be performed in a single breath hold (with few contraindications) and without arterial vascular access
- Non-enhanced scanning (calcium scores) offers an additional risk assessment for coronary disease
- MDCT is useful in emergency investigation of patients with suspected acute aortic syndromes.

Calcium score exam

- Asymptomatic patients: Coronary atheroma calcifies over time and can be measured by cardiac CT. Patients with an intermediate risk of coronary events, as assessed by clinical risk scores, can be successfully re-classified with coronary artery calcification assessment (see Section 30.5)
- Symptomatic patients: for symptomatic patients with a low pre-test-like hood of coronary disease NICE recommend coronary artery calcification assessment as the initial investigation. For patients >50 years of age the sensitivity for the detection of obstructive coronary disease is 98%; but with a poor specificity.

30.2 Acquisition

Two main difficulties need to be overcome for the examination of coronary arteries:

- Continuous movement
- Relatively small size of the vessels.

MDCT scanners require:

- High temporal resolution (the shutter speed on a camera)
- High spatial resolution (ability to distinguish between two objects).

Temporal resolution (shutter speed of the CT scanner)

- Dictated by the rotational speed of the gantry
- Normally between 330–420 ms to complete a 360° rotation (2–3 times per second)
- Can be increased by acquiring data during half of the rotation (halving to ≈165 ms, or even a quarter of a rotation) and fusing the data from multiple cardiac cycles to make an image; can reduce temporal resolution to 80 ms
- Fusing of data to create a meaningful image requires a regular R–R interval (Figure 30.1)
- Another technique is to use a dual-source system—two X-ray tubes and detectors perpendicular to each other—which effectively uses data from a quarter of the gantry rotation.

Spatial resolution (ability to discriminate between two objects)

Dictated by:

- Size of the detectors (0.0625–0.5 mm)
- Beam width
- Geometry and collimation amongst other factors.

The number of detectors does not affect the spatial resolution of the image.
High resolution CT scanning is a relatively new technique.

- The focal spot of the scanner oscillates, increasing the number of sampling projections per rotation and increasing the resolution
- Holds particular promise in scanning patients with a high coronary calcium load and stents.

Patient selection and preparation

- Avoid caffeine and stimulants on the day (see Figure 30.2)
- BBs are routinely given i.v. (some centres give an oral dose on arrival in the department); aim for HR < 65 bpm

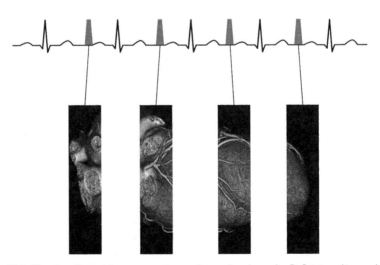

Figure 30.1 Data is collected from successive cardiac cycles. A regular R–R interval is needed to avoid movement artefact.

Patient preparation
1. Avoid caffeine
2. Advised not to drive
3. Pre-appointment beta-blocker
4. Cannulation
5. ECG attachment
6. IV metoprolol to a target heart rate of 60

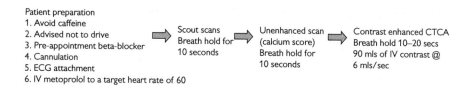

Scout scans
Breath hold for
10 seconds

Unenhanced scan
(calcium score)
Breath hold for
10 seconds

Contrast enhanced CTCA
Breath hold 10–20 secs
90 mls of IV contrast @
6 mls/sec

Figure 30.2 The typical scanning routine.

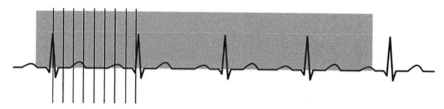

Figure 30.3 The R–R interval is divided into phases (%); images are usually reconstructed during diastole (70% of the R–R interval) and relative cardiac stasis.

- Patients with contra-indications to BBs can still be scanned with a retrospective acquisition but with a significant increase in radiation dose. In our experience pulse rate reduction with CCBs or ivabradine is not as effective at as β-blockade.

Patients with AF can be scanned if their heart rate is controlled, with a retrospective protocol and no dose modulation. Multiphase data is then used to evaluate each coronary segment individually (using orthogonal views); this process is laborious as automatic coronary analysis programmes are less effective.

30.3 Radiation dose

- Two algorithms for scanning: retrospective or prospective ECG gating
- Retrospective scanning: radiation (tube current) is one for the entire length of the scan (Figure 30.3)
- Images can be reconstructed at any point during the cardiac cycle; to reduce movement artefact normally reconstructed from diastole (relative cardiac stasis)
- Can be used with higher heart rates; enables functional and valve evaluation and in some cases can be used in patients with AF
- To reduce radiation exposure retrospective gating with dose modulation can be used; X-ray tube current is reduced during systole and increased during diastole (Figure 30.4)
- Images reconstructed at 70% of the R–R interval will retain image quality for analysis. Images reconstructed during the systolic phase may suffer from artefact.

Prospective gating

- During retrospective ECG gating the current is turned on throughout the scan
- As the coronary arteries are normally only analysed in a single phase (70%) the other phases are not reconstructed; unnecessary radiation burden to the patient (Figure 30.5)
- During prospective ECG gating radiation is turned on only during a preselected phase of the cardiac cycle (usually 70%)—dramatically reducing the radiation dose (with a saving of up to 83%)

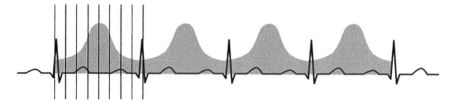

Figure 30.4 The X-ray tube current and therefore radiation dose is reduced during systole and increased in diastole.

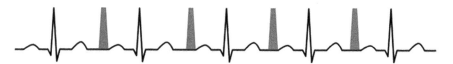

Figure 30.5 During prospective ECG gated acquisitions the X-ray tube current (gray line) is on for a fraction of a second during diastole.

- Multiphase data is not available and therefore assessment of left ventricular function, wall motion abnormalities, and valvular abnormalities is not possible
- Because temporal resolution is limited by the speed of gantry rotation, prospective gating can only be used with a regular HR < 65 bpm, but still remains feasible in >85% of computed tomography coronary angiography (CTCA) referrals with BB use
- Using dose-saving protocols and iterative reconstruction (image noise reduction technique allowing lower radiation) a median dose of 2.5 mSv is possible
- Prospective ECG gating should be the default mode.

Radiation dose calculation

- Most common method to calculate the radiation dose from cardiac CT is applying a conversion factor (or k factor) to the dose length product of the examination
- Most studies use a conversion factor of 0.014 mGy/cm
- There is increasing evidence that this significantly underestimates the effective dose; we recommend a k factor of 0.028 mGy/cm.

30.4 Image interrogation

Axial

Images are taken in the axial orientation and stacked together to produce a volume of data that can be scrolled through (Figures 30.6–30.10).

Multi-plane reconstruction

Images can be reconstructed along the length of the coronary artery to allow interrogation of all coronary segments (Figure 30.11).

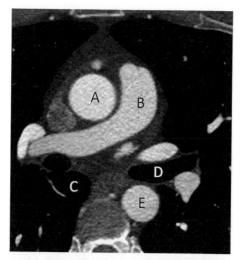

Figure 30.6 Axial images at the level of the pulmonary valve. A, ascending aorta; B, main pulmonary artery; C, right main bronchus; D, left main bronchus; E, descending aorta.

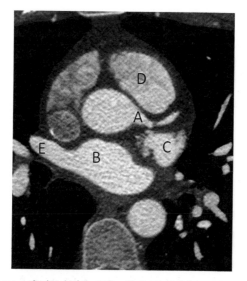

Figure 30.7 Axial images at the level of the left main stem. A, left main stem, B, left atrium; C, left atrial appendage; D, right ventricle; E, pulmonary vein.

3D volume rendered images

A 3D image of the whole scan volume can be constructed. This has limited utility in the assessment of the native coronary arteries but is of particular use for the detection of coronary bypass grafts (Figure 30.12).

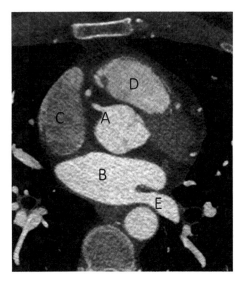

Figure 30.8 Axial images at the level of the aortic valve. A, ostium of RCA; B, left atrium; C, right atrium; D, right ventricle; E, pulmonary vein.

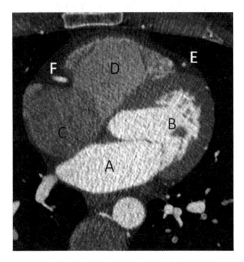

Figure 30.9 Axial images at the level of the mitral valve. A, left atrium; B, left ventricle; C, right atrium; D, right ventricle; E, left anterior descending artery; F, right coronary artery.

30.5 Coronary calcium scores

- This is a non-contrast-enhanced, prospectively gated acquisition with no limitations on HR
- The scan takes <10 s, with a radiation dose of <0.5 mSv
- One feature of atheromatous disease is the development of calcified plaque. This has been utilized in the risk stratification of asymptomatic patients

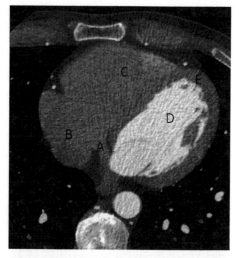

Figure 30.10 Axial images at the level of the coronary sinus. A, coronary sinus; B, right atrium; C, right ventricle; D, left ventricle; E, left anterior descending artery.

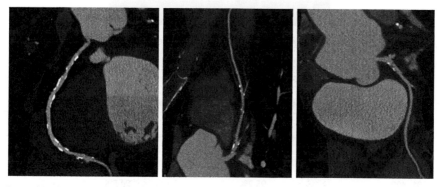

Figure 30.11 Multi plane reconstruction of (left) the right coronary artery, (middle) left anterior descending artery, and (right) circumflex artery.

- In a large prospective study coronary artery calcification (usually measured in 'Agatston' units) provided incremental additional information above traditional risk factors (Table 30.1)
- For symptomatic patients the negative predictive value (NPV) to rule out coronary disease is dependent on age and sex
- A typical history of angina, >45 years of age and a zero-CAC-score NPV for obstructive disease is 98%
- Studies including >7600 patients have shown a NPV of 96–100% in those with a CAC score of zero
- In younger patients and women (who have a higher prevalence of non- calcified atheroma) there may still be an element of doubt, necessitating the need for a full CT coronary angiogram
- With the marked reduction in radiation dose, some centres perform a full examination in patients suitable for low-dose scanning (prospective gating).

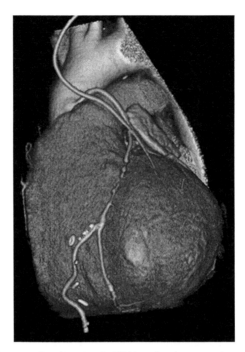

Figure 30.12 3D volume rendered image of a LIMA and saphenous vein graft at the top of the image and a gastroepiploic graft inferiorly.

Table 30.1 Incremental prognostic data from different levels of coronary artery calcification

Coronary artery calcium score	5-year survival	12-year survival
0–10	99.4%	99.4%
11–100	97.8%	97.8%
101–400	95.2%	94.5%
401–1000	90.4%	93.0%
>1000	81.8%	76.9%

Adapted from *J. Am. Coll. Cardiol.*, 49(18), Matthew J. Budoff, Leslee J. Shaw, Sandy T. Liu, *et al.*, 'Long-Term Prognosis Associated With Coronary Calcification: Observations From a Registry of 25,253 Patients', p. 1860–70, copyright 2007 with permission from Elsevier.

30.6 Accuracy and clinical application

Terminology and definitions

The accuracy of a test is usually expressed in terms of sensitivity, specificity, NPV and positive predictive value (PPV; Table 30.2).

One important consideration is the influence of the prevalence of a disease in a cohort on the NPV and PPV. If the disease prevalence is low this will improve the NPV of a rule-out test.

Table 30.2 Accuracy terminology for a diagnostic test

Sensitivity	Is the proportion of true positives that are correctly identified by the test
Specificity	Is the proportion of true negatives that are correctly identified by the test
PPV	Is the proportion of patients with a positive test result who are correctly diagnosed
NPV	Is the proposition of patients with a negative test result who are correctly diagnosed

Table 30.3 Accuracy of CTCA from clinical trials

Trial	Sensitivity	Specificity	PPV	NPV	Disease prevalence	No patients
Mowatt et al.	99%	89%	93%	100%	58%	1286
Meijboom et al.	99%	64%	86%	97%	68%	360
Miller et al.	85%	90%	91%	83%	56%	291
Budoff et al.	95%	83%	64%	99%	24%	230

Full citations given in 'Further Reading' section.

Coronary artery disease

Accuracy

NICE guidelines recommend a machine of 64-slices or greater. Table 30.3 lists the sensitivity, specificity, NPV, and PPV of a large meta-analysis and recent trials.

- Over a wide range of disease prevalence CTCA consistently demonstrates a high NPV, making it the investigation of choice to rule out CAD
- At higher levels of calcification the specificity of CTCA drops. For an Agatston score of >400 the specificity falls from 86% to 52%. Current UK NICE guidelines suggest the use of other investigations when there is a high calcium score.

Prognosis

Prognostic evidence available for cardiac CT:

- Annual event rate for obstructive CAD versus no atheroma: 8.8% vs 0.17%
- Un-obstructive coronary atheroma annual event rate of 1.41%
- Zero calcium score translates to an annual event rate of 0.4% in asymptomatic patients.

Valve assessment

Diagnosis

CT cannot offer functional assessment of valvular stenosis or insufficiency; anatomical information is available regarding valvular calcification and area via planimetry.

Aortic valve: stenosis

Calcification:

- Valvular calcification shows some correlation with the severity of aortic valve stenosis compared with echocardiography and catheterization
- Agatston score of >2200 is indicative of moderate to severe aortic valve stenosis and warrants further investigation.

Planimetry:

- Multiphase systolic data is necessary to study the valve during end-systole: increasing the radiation dose
- Aortic valve area correlates well with echo planimetry but underestimates stenosis when compared to Doppler
- CT is superior to TTE in identifying a bicuspid valve.

Regurgitation:

- To assess aortic regurgitation a regurgitant orifice area is measured
- This requires multiphase data in end diastole
- MDCT assessment correlates well with echocardiography for mild, moderate, and severe levels of regurgitation.

Mitral valve: stenosis

- Planimetry measurements of the mitral valve correlate well with echocardiography
- Morphological assessment of the aetiology can be made (rheumatic changes: thickened leaflets, commissure fusion, and shortening of the chordae).

Regurgitation:

- The regurgitant orifice area of the MV can be measured and CT can differentiate severe MR from mild or moderate disease
- The ability to differentiate mild from moderate MR is poor.

Aetiology and consequences

- As cardiac CT acquires a volume of data it is possible to assess the aetiology and sequelae of valve disease
- Chamber size, hypertrophy, wall thinning, aortic dilatation or coarctation can all be recognized at cardiac CT and add to the clinical picture.

Pre-operative and pre-electrophysiology procedures

- Invasive coronary angiography is recommended prior to valve surgery, but cardiac CT can be used to rule out significant coronary disease
- In TAVI assessment CT has the ability to assess the aortic annulus (which is often oval), the position of the coronary ostia, the angle of the aortic root, and illio-femoral access
- Topographical imaging of the cardiac chambers facilitates the planning of EP interventions. A 3D volume rendered image of the LA can be constructed to assess the pulmonary vein number and site.

Additional information regarding this is available to the electrophysiologist:

- Inter-atrial septum (PFO, ASD or lipomatous hypertrophy)

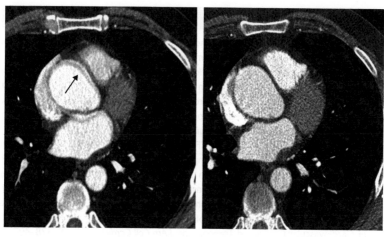

Figure 30.13 A non-gated examination (left), with a 'pseudo' dissection in the aortic root (arrow) not present in the subsequent ECG gated examination (right).

- SVC and IVC (anomalous pulmonary drainage)
- Left atrial appendage (thrombus).

Aortic assessment

- MDCT offers high spatial resolution imaging of the aorta and great vessels
- The speed of acquisition and good differentiation between the lumen and surrounding tissue makes it is the imaging modality of choice to acutely assess the aorta
- Acute aortic syndrome encompasses a range of processes including, complete dissection, intra-mural haematoma, incomplete dissection, and penetrating aortic ulcer
- The accuracy of aortic assessment is improved by ECG gating; movement artefact seen in the aortic root in non-gated scans can lead to false positive results (Figure 30.13).

30.7 Pericardial evaluation

- The high spatial resolution of CT enables an accurate measurement of pericardial thickness
- 4 mm is considered the cut off for diagnosis
- Calcification is easily recognized and the proximity of the coronary vessels to the calcification assessed.

30.8 Stress perfusion computed tomography

- CTCA has reduced sensitivity for the evaluation of coronary stenosis between 50–70%
- The functional assessment of lesions is not possible on a standard anatomical scan
- CT-MPI (myocardial perfusion imaging) is possible using adenosine/dipyridamole as a stress agent; studies are needed to evaluate the accuracy of CT MPI and the protocols developed to reduce the radiation dose to the patient.

Further reading

Budoff M, Shaw L, Liu S, et al. Long-term prognosis associated with coronary calcification: observations from a registry of 25,253 patients. J Am Coll Cardiol, 2007; 49: 1860–70.

Budoff MJ, Dowe D, Jollis J, et al. Diagnostic performance of 64-multidetector row coronary computed tomographic angiography for evaluation of coronary artery stenosis in individuals without known coronary artery disease: results from the prospective multicenter ACCURACY (Assessment by Coronary Computed Tomographic Angiography of Individuals Undergoing Invasive Coronary Angiography) trial. J Am Coll Cardiol, 2008; 52: 1724–32.

Greenland P, Bonow R, Brundage B, et al. ACCF/AHA 2007 clinical expert consensus document on coronary artery calcium scoring by computed tomography in global cardiovascular risk assessment and in evaluation of patients with chest pain: a report of the American College of Cardiology Foundation Clinical Expert Consensus Task Force (ACCF/AHA Writing Committee to Update the 2000 Expert Consensus Document on Electron Beam Computed Tomography) developed in collaboration with the Society of Atherosclerosis Imaging and Prevention and the Society of Cardiovascular Computed Tomography. J Am Coll Cardiol, 2007; 49: 378–402.

Meijboom WB, Meijs M, Schuijf J, et al. Diagnostic accuracy of 64-slice computed tomography coronary angiography: a prospective, multicenter, multivendor study. J Am Coll Cardiol, 2008; 52: 2135–44.

Miller JM, Rochitte C, Dewey M, et al. Diagnostic performance of coronary angiography by 64-row CT. N Engl J Med, 2008; 359: 2324–36.

Mowatt G, Cook JA, Hillis GS, et al. 64-slice computed tomography angiography in the diagnosis and assessment of coronary artery disease: systematic review and meta-analysis. Heart, 2008; 94: 1386–93.

Nicol E, Stirrup J, Kelion AD, Padley SPG. Oxford Specialist Handbooks in Cardiology: Cardiovascular Computed Tomography. Oxford University Press, 2011.

Skinner JS, Smeeth L, Kendall J, et al. NICE guidance. Chest pain of recent onset: assessment and diagnosis of recent onset chest pain or discomfort of suspected cardiac origin. Heart, 2010; 96: 974–8.

Heart rhythm

CONTENTS

31.1 Diagnostic testing in syncope

In patients >40 years old with a normal ECG and recurrent syncope, 50% will have an arrhythmia (usually asystole).

- Echocardiography is indicated where there is a suspicion of significant structural heart disease
- 24-h tapes have a low yield unless the patient's symptoms occur daily. Can be left on multiple days but requires labour-intensive analysis of continuous recording
- Automatic event recorders: Novacor's R test 'Evolution 3' can monitor for 8 days and only stores significant events. The number and type of events can be pre-programmed. The R test 'Evolution 4' is soon to become available and can monitor for 32 days
- The 'King of Hearts' monitor is a patient-activated monitor that can record 60 events or 5 min of data. In continuous use the battery lasts for 7 days and the memory can hold data for 128 days
- Implantable loop recorder is a small device implanted subcutaneously with two electrodes. Able to record a single-lead ECG. Battery life approximately 36 months. Can be activated manually by the patient or can be programmed to record significant brady- or tachycardia
- Head up tilt-table testing (HUT)—there are four main responses:
  - Mixed: HR >40 bpm without asystole >3 s; BP falls before heart rate
  - Cardioinhibitory:
    - Asystole for >3 s or HR <40 bpm; BP falls before HR
    - Asystole for >3 s or HR <40 bpm; BP falls after HR
  - Pure vasodepressor: HR does not fall >10%; BP falls to cause syncope
- Electrophysiology study is indicated if ventricular arrhythmias are suspected (VT-stim). In patients with reduced EF and syncope, the guidelines for ICD implantation will already be met.

31.2 Cardiac pacing

- The first pacemaker was implanted in 1958
- The indications for conventional pacing are to prevent bradycardia
- More recently cardiac resynchronization pacing has been used as a treatment for heart failure
- In patients with sinus node disease, atrial pacing can reduce the incidence of AF.

31.3 Indications

There are six main indications for pacing (for advanced indications see the ESC guidelines):

1. Sinus node disease
2. Acquired AV node disease
3. Chronic bifascicular and trifascicular block with symptoms
4. Conduction disturbances related to acute MI
5. Carotid sinus syndrome
6. Vasovagal syncope.

Temporary pacing

- The methods include transcutaneous, transvenous, epicardial, and oesophageal
- In the absence of fluoroscopy, balloon-tipped 'floating' wires can be used
- A relatively high rate of complications has been observed in case series including infection, local haematoma, arterial puncture, pneumothorax, haemothorax, and pericardial effusion/tamponade
- Softer balloon-tipped pacing wires have a lower incidence of cardiac perforation.

31.4 Permanent pacemakers

Pacemaker nomenclature

I   Chamber-paced: O (none), A (atrium), V (ventricle), D (dual), S (single)
II   Chamber-sensed: O (none), A (atrium), V (ventricle), D (dual), S (single)
III Response to sensing: O (none), T (triggered), I (inhibited), D (dual)
IV   Rate modulation: O (none), R (rate modulation)
V   Multisite pacing: O (none), A (atrium), V (ventricle), D (dual).

S only used by pacing companies.

Basic pacing concepts

Unipolar versus bipolar pacing

- See Figures 31.1 and 31.2
- Unipolar pacemakers have bigger signals and pacing spikes on the surface ECG
- They are more susceptible to electrical interference, i.e. myopotentials
- Bipolar pacemakers have smaller signals and the pacing spike can be difficult to see on the surface ECG
- Bipolar pacemakers are less susceptible to electrical interference.

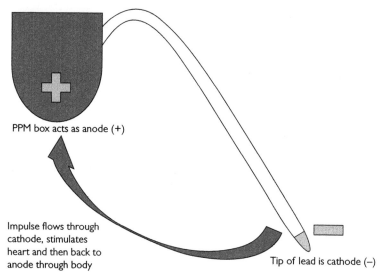

PPM box acts as anode (+)

Impulse flows through
cathode, stimulates
heart and then back to
anode through body

Tip of lead is cathode (–)

Figure 31.1 Example of unipolar pacing.

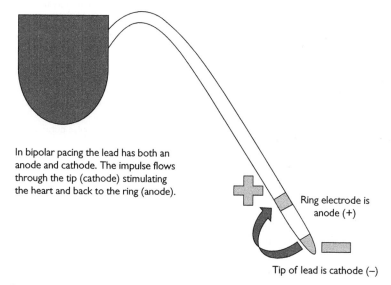

In bipolar pacing the lead has both an
anode and cathode. The impulse flows
through the tip (cathode) stimulating
the heart and back to the ring (anode).

Ring electrode is
anode (+)

Tip of lead is cathode (–)

Figure 31.2 Example of bipolar pacing.

Stimulation threshold

- Minimum amount of energy and duration required to reliably depolarize the myocardium
- There is an exponential relationship between the stimulus amplitude and
  pulse-duration–strength-duration curve (see Figure 31.3)
- At short pulse durations a small change is associated with a large change in threshold whereas
  at longer pulse durations there is only a small change in threshold

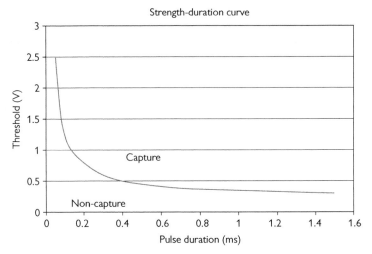

Figure 31.3 Strength–duration curve. Relationship between pulse duration and threshold. Measurements above the curve result in capture whereas below the line there is non-capture.

- Threshold can be affected by type of lead, distance between electrode and tissue, health of tissue in contact with the electrode, and AADs
- The relationship between threshold, pulse duration, lead impedance, and energy (battery longevity) is given by:

$$E = \frac{V^2}{R} \times PD$$

where E = energy, V = threshold, R = lead impedance, PD = pulse duration

- If V and PD are increased then the battery will run out faster. Higher lead impedance is beneficial for battery longevity
- Ventricular lead should have a threshold <1 V (unless active fixation, where higher thresholds are initially accepted and usually reduce over 24 h)
- The atrial lead threshold should be <1.5 V
- The safety margin for threshold programmed to the device is usually 2–3 times higher than implant threshold
- Some devices can recheck the threshold on a day-to-day basis and change the output each day, therefore adding extra safety, increasing battery longevity, and highlighting a problem sooner.

Lead impedance
- Impedance varies between manufacturers and is usually <1000 Ω but high impedance leads are now available to increase battery life
- Impedance can be thought of in simple terms as equal to resistance (R) and can be estimated by Ohm's law:

$V = IR$
where V = potential difference between poles (Volts), I = current, R = resistance

- However, in reality total pacing impedance is determined by a number of factors
- A very low impedance is usually is due to failure of the insulation (reduced resistance (R) due to current escape) and a high impedance occurs with lead fracture (increased resistance).

Sensing and sensitivity (terms can confuse)

Sensing:

- A pacemaker must be able to sense intrinsic cardiac activity and discriminate these from other forms of electrical interference, e.g. myopotentials, far-field cardiac events
- It senses the potential difference between the two electrodes, e.g. the two electrodes (distal tip and proximal ring) at the tip of the lead (bipolar)
- The ventricular lead should have R wave sensing of >5 mV and the atrial lead should have P wave sensing of >2 mV.

Sensitivity:

- The minimum amplitude of signal that the device is programmed to register as a sensed event (signals smaller in amplitude are ignored), e.g. a programmed sensitivity of 2 mV is more sensitive (higher sensitivity) than 5 mV (lower sensitivity)
- Smaller amplitude signals require a lower programmed value of sensitivity for detection (higher sensitivity)
- To increase sensitivity and treat undersensing, the value is lowered to sense smaller amplitude signals
- To treat oversensing, the sensitivity is decreased (i.e. the value is increased) to avoid sensing inappropriately.

Complications of pacemaker implantation

- Complications include infection (1%), bruising, lead displacement (2–4%), pneumothorax with subclavian vein approach (1–2%), haemothorax, cardiac perforation (<0.5%).

Optimal pacing mode

- In normal atrial activity, atrial-based pacing has been shown to be haemodynamically better than ventricular-based pacing and is associated with a lower incidence of AF and heart failure
- Isolated sinus node disease and no AV conduction disturbance—AAI(R)—as annual incidence of second- or third-degree AV block <1% (in modern practice most would implant a dual chamber system)
- Sinus node and AV conduction disturbance: DDD(R)
- Paroxysmal AT: DDI/DDD with mode switching
- Mode switching is the ability of the pacemaker to switch from one mode to another in response to initiation and termination of a paroxysmal AT; for example in sinus rhythm the pacemaker will operate in DDD mode but when an AT is sensed it will switch to VVI or DDI where there is no atrial tracking
- AV block or bi/trifascicular block: DDD(R)
- Permanent AF: VVI(R)
- Rate response (R) can be programmed in situations of chronotropic incompetence. This can be caused by IHD, heart failure or induced by drugs
- Chronotropic incompetence is failure to increase heart rate to 70–85% predicted and can be diagnosed by an exercise test. It can also be suspected by reviewing the pacemaker histograms
- Rate-adaptive sensors detect increased patient movement and respiratory rate. Some measure the QT interval, which decreases with exercise and increased sympathetic tone.

The closed loop system measures changes in cardiac contractility at the lead tip and requires a bipolar lead

- The trend now is for dual-chamber pacing with minimal ventricular pacing. Right ventricular apical pacing produces dyssynchrony (LBBB) and produces electrical remodelling of the ventricle. This may lead to LV dysfunction
- The DAVID trial showed an increase in death and hospitalization for heart failure in patients who had an ICD and DDD pacing at 70 bpm compared to those who had backup pacing at 40 bpm. Patients in the study who experienced >40% right ventricular pacing had a higher incidence of heart failure and death.

Magnet mode

- Placing a magnet over the generator converts the pacemaker to asynchronous mode (i.e. DOO, VOO) and the pacemaker will pace at a programmed rate without sensing or inhibition
- The rate varies according to company and battery life
- This can be useful to assess permanent pacemaker (PPM) function at the bedside, assess battery status if manufacturer parameters are known, and can also be used to treat oversensing if a programmer is not immediately available
- Placing a magnet over an ICD generator will inhibit shock therapy but not pacing function; it is useful treatment for inappropriate shocks.

Pacemaker syndrome

- Usually occurs in patients with intact sinus node and ventricular pacing alone (VVI, but can occur with DDI pacing)
- Most symptoms relate to loss of AV synchrony, loss of contribution from atrium to cardiac output and also VA conduction. Effectively, this can result in contraction of the atria when the mitral valve is closed
- Symptoms include SOB, chest pain, nausea, dizziness, fatigue, and chest fullness
- Hypotension can occur with ventricular pacing
- Management usually requires restoration of AV synchrony and consideration should be given to upgrading the system to DDD with the addition of an atrial lead.

Pacemaker-mediated tachycardia (PMT)

- PMT is re-entry arrhythmia in which the dual-chamber pacemaker acts as the anterograde limb of the tachycardia and the His-Purkinje-AV system as the retrograde pathway (see Figure 31.4)
- PMT is distinct from a pacemaker-facilitated tachycardia due to high rate ventricular pacing (dual chamber) whilst tracking an atrial arrhythmia
- Usually caused by a premature ventricular extrasystole leading to VA conduction. The sensed atrial beat leads to pacing in the ventricle and a re-entrant mechanism is set up. The maximum rate is limited by the pacemaker's programmed upper rate limit
- PVARP (post-ventricular atrial refractory period) can be extended to prevent PMT. Many pacemakers automatically extend the PVARP temporarily at the onset of a PMT
- A magnet can also be used to diagnose and treat PMT, as sensing is inhibited and asynchronous pacing takes place.

Pacemaker troubleshooting

Pacemaker malfunctions include the following:

- Failure to pace
- Failure to capture

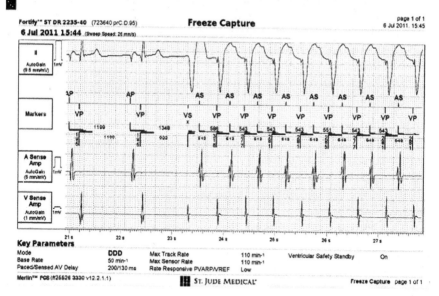

Figure 31.4 Example of pacemaker mediated tachycardia. A ventricular ectopic beat conducts retrogradely through the AV node producing a retrograde P wave, which is sensed. This is then followed by a paced beat and so on. The retrograde P wave can be seen in the T wave on the surface ECG.

Reproduced by kind permission of Richard Chambers of St Jude Medical Inc.

- Oversensing
- Undersensing.

Failure to pace
- Pacing does not occur despite an indication to pace
- Can be due to a battery at end of life, lead fracture, fractured lead insulation, oversensing, or cross-talk (atrial output is sensed by a ventricular lead in a dual-chamber pacer)
- If patient symptomatic or there is no underlying rhythm then the patient needs a temporary pacing wire
- CXR required to assess lead position, position of pin in header, and for lead fracture, which occurs most commonly at the clavicle or first rib
- Pacing check: battery life, lead impedances, and sensing parameters
- A very low impedance is usually is due to failure of the insulation and a high impedance occurs with lead fracture
- Will require lead reposition or new lead if fracture or insulation failure
- Cross-talk can be temporarily managed by magnet application and subsequently extension of the ventricular blanking period.

Failure to capture
- Loss of pacemaker capture occurs when there is appropriate output but no atrial or ventricular depolarization; may be seen as a pacing spike on ECG with no associated paced complex
- This may be intermittent or persistent
- Most problems occur at the pacemaker lead/tissue interface, e.g. lead dislodgment

- Increase in the pacing threshold occurs with
  - Lead maturation within a few weeks following lead placement
  - Fibrosis
  - Drug therapy (e.g. flecainide)
  - Electrolyte abnormalities
  - Myocardial infarction or ischaemia at the lead tip
- Mechanical problems that can cause failure to capture include
  - Fracture of the lead
  - Insulation breaks
  - Poor lead connection in header of PPM
- Requires pacemaker check and CXR
- Loss of capture requires a check of pacing threshold and lead impedance
- If the threshold is high then pacing outputs can be increased temporarily, and it is worth trying unipolar pacing
- Usually requires lead revision or replacement.

Oversensing

- Occurs when non-cardiac or cardiac electrical activity is sensed inappropriately and pacing is inhibited
- Sensing of this electrical activity can inhibit the ventricular output if sensed on the ventricular channel or can trigger a ventricular output if sensed on the atrial channel
- Unipolar systems are more susceptible
- Can be caused by muscular activity, electromagnetic interference (MRIs), fractured lead insulation, or oversensing of intrinsic P or T waves (see Figure 31.5)
- Diagnosis requires analysis of ECG and pacemaker interrogation

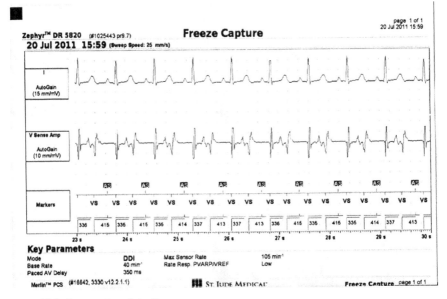

Figure 31.5 Oversensing of the T wave.

Reproduced by kind permission of Richard Chambers of St Jude Medical Inc.

- Treatment requires reducing the sensitivity to a level that avoids oversensing but still senses intrinsic cardiac depolarizations
- T wave oversensing can also be managed by increasing the ventricular refractory period
- Programming to an asynchronous mode or magnet application can be a temporary solution.

Undersensing

- Lack of sensing of intrinsic cardiac electrical activity (see Figure 31.6)
- An inadequate intracardiac signal can lead to undersensing. Usually more of a problem in the atrium
- At implant aim for P of >1.5 ms and R wave of >5 ms
- Undersensing can be as a result of lead dislodgement, lead insulation breaks, cardiac arrhythmias, electrolyte abnormalities, and infarction/ischaemia at lead/tissue interface
- Treated by programming an enhanced sensitivity (decrease sensing level)
- Functional undersensing can occur and is normal pacemaker function. For example, a PVC occurring in the programmed refractory period (blanking period) will not be sensed and pacing output will not be inhibited. This can be managed by shortening the refractory period.

Practical considerations

Driving

- For group 1 (cars/motorcycles) driving must cease for at least 1/52; driving may be permitted thereafter provided there is no other disqualifying condition
- For group 2 (LGV/PCV), disqualifies from driving for 6/52; (re)licensing may be permitted thereafter provided there is no other disqualifying condition.

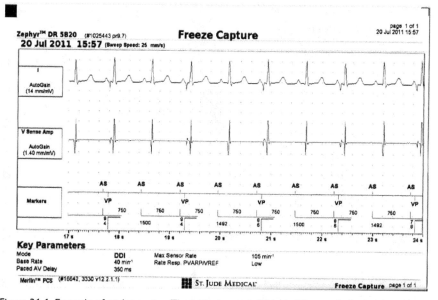

Figure 31.6 Example of undersensing. The intrinsic rate is 80 bpm. The pacemaker is delivering pacing spikes at the base rate of 40 bpm resulting in fusion and its not sensing the normal underlying ventricular rhythm. The markers show VP (V pace) at 40 bpm with no VS (V sense).
Reproduced by kind permission of Richard Chambers of St Jude Medical Inc.

Mobile phones

- Can affect pacemaker functioning if held in close proximity
- Patients are advised to hold the phone on the opposite side to the PPM and not to carry it in a pocket overlying the PPM.

Diathermy

- During surgery, diathermy use and power output should be kept to a minimum, using short bursts and keeping away from the device. However, diathermy is routinely used during pacemaker extractions as lead damage is less likely than with scalpels
- Bipolar diathermy is generally safe if it is not applied to the region of the PPM. PPM should be checked after the procedure
- A programmer or magnet should be kept close by to allow asynchronous pacing in case of PPM inhibition
- With unipolar diathermy the other electrode should be placed well away from the device so that it does not lie between electrodes, e.g. on the leg.

Defibrillation

- Defibrillation pads should be placed as far away from the device as possible to avoid damage and resetting of the device. The PPM should be checked afterwards to ensure normal function.

MRI

- The current advice is to avoid MRI
- Manufacturers are now producing MRI-safe pacemakers but the strength of magnet (measured in Teslas) needs to be checked before the patient has an MRI and the device may require specific programming (to fixed-output mode) prior to the scan.

Airport metal detectors

- Patients should always carry their PPM ID card
- The possibility of adverse events is low
- Patients are advised to walk quickly through gates or request a pat-down by security staff.

31.5 Implantable cardioverter defibrillators

Introduction and main trials

- The frequency of ICD implants is increasing; the majority of ICD implants in the UK are for secondary prevention of SCD
- Several landmark trials have established a role for ICDs in primary prevention
- The only effective prophylactic treatment to treat lethal ventricular arrhythmias is ICD therapy.

Careful counselling is recommended prior to implantation as the incidence of complications from ICDs is around 20% (including inappropriate shock therapy 2–4%) and there are lifestyle implications, e.g. driving.

Secondary prevention trials

AVID study: ICD versus AADs (amiodarone or sotalol):

- Trial featured survivors of cardiac arrest or poorly tolerated VT
- Significant decrease in mortality in the ICD group: RRR of 39±20%, 27±21%, and 31±21% at 1, 2, and 3 years respectively

- The benefit of an ICD was more marked in patients with an LVEF ≤35%.

CASH study: patients with prior cardiac arrest:

- Randomized to metoprolol, amiodarone, propafenone, or ICD implant
- 23% non-significant decrease in mortality in the ICD group compared to AADs. The propafenone arm was stopped early due to an increase in mortality.

Primary prevention trials

MADIT study: patients with coronary artery disease, LV systolic dysfunction with EF<35%, non-sustained ventricular tachycardia (NSVT) and inducible VT at EPS.

- Randomized to ICD versus conventional medical treatment (most commonly amiodarone)
- ICD use decreased mortality by 54% in patients with ischaemic cardiomyopathy.

MADIT II study: patients with previous MI and EF <30%: NSVT or EP testing was not required.

- Randomized ICD versus conventional medical therapy
- 31% reduced mortality in the ICD cohort after an average follow-up period of 20 months.

SCD HeFT study: patients with NYHA II/III heart failure and LVSD (EF<35%) irrespective of aetiology (ischaemic and non-ischaemic).

- Randomized to conventional medical therapy plus placebo versus amiodarone versus ICD
- Amiodarone equal to placebo in reducing mortality
- ICD implantation reduced mortality by 23%.

DEFINITE trial: patients with non-ischaemic cardiomyopathy and frequent ventricular ectopics or NSVT.

- Randomized to conventional medical therapy versus medical therapy plus ICD
- Significant reduction in SCD and a trend toward reduction of overall mortality rates.

NICE guidance

See Box 31.1. NICE guidance does not cover non-ischaemic cardiomyopathy, although in the SCD-HeFT study there was no difference in the mortality benefit seen between ischaemic or non-ischaemic cardiomyopathy.

Patients with DCM with frequent ventricular ectopics or a history of syncope are widely recognized to be at high risk of SCD and should be considered for ICD implantation (as per ESC and HRS guidelines).

Defibrillation threshold

- Defibrillation threshold (DFT) is the minimum amount of energy required to reliably defibrillate the heart. Most centres ensure there is a safety margin of 10 J below the maximum output of the device: the defibrillation safety margin (DSM)
- DSM testing may be omitted at implant and tested at a later date (e.g. non-anticoagulated AF). Some physicians do not perform DSM testing but it can be important on drugs that increase the threshold, such as amiodarone and flecainide
- Normokalaemia important
- Ventricular fibrillation can be induced by the device via (1) direct current shock, (2) shock on the T wave (overdrive pacing for 12 beats followed by a shock on the T wave), (3) burst pacing or stimulating the heart at 50 Hz

BOX 31.1 NICE GUIDANCE ON ICDS

Primary prevention

ICDs are recommended for people who have a heart condition with a high risk of sudden death that runs in the family:

1. LQTS
2. Hypertrophic cardiomyopathy
3. Brugada syndrome
4. Arrythmogenic right ventricular dysplasia
5. Congenital heart disease with corrective surgery.

Patients who have had a myocardial infarction

ICDs are recommended for people who have had an MI more than 4 weeks previously and have all of:

- LVEF that is less than 35%, and heart failure no worse than NYHA class 3
- NSVT on Holter monitoring
- inducible VT at electrophysiological testing.

ICDs are also recommended for people who have had an MI more than 4 weeks previously and have both:
- LVEF that is reduced to 30% and heart failure no worse than NYHA class 3
- QRS duration of 120 ms or longer.

Secondary prevention

ICDs are recommended for people who:

- Have survived a cardiac arrest due to either VT or VF
- Have VT that is sudden, unexpected and prolonged, and causes haemodynamic compromise
- Have VT that is prolonged that does not cause haemodynamic compromise and an LVEF reduced to less than 35%, and heart failure no worse than NYHA class 3.

National Institute for Health and Clinical Excellence (2006). Adapted from 'Implantable cardioverter defibrillators for arrhythmias: Review of Technology Appraisal 11' (TA95). London: NICE. Available from www.nice.org.uk. Reproduced with permission.

- The device is tested whilst the ventricular lead sensitivity is set to its highest setting; it can only detect ventricular fibrillation signals with a voltage greater than 1 mV. The test is performed in the worst-case scenario for the device, as the normal detection is set to >0.3 mV once the test is finished
- Once VF is induced most ICDs will rely on the programmed settings to detect the arrhythmia, diagnose it and deliver therapy. It is possible that defibrillation will not occur; it is important that the patient is connected to an external defibrillator so that rescue shocks can be delivered in this situation
- The device should be programmed to deliver backup right ventricular pacing after shock therapy as some patients may become bradycardic after shock therapy
- If a patient requires subsequent DSM testing, 5 min should be left to allow for full haemodynamic recovery.

Lack of appropriate defibrillation safety margin

- High DFT is any DFT within 10 J of the device's maximum delivered energy output
- Dual coil (SVC and RV shocking coils) rather than single coil leads (RV coil only) may help. Options include changing the shocking vector (dual coil) or polarity and, ultimately, moving the lead position (see Figure 31.7). Some AADs, including amiodarone, can increase the DFT dramatically. Sotalol can lower the DFT.

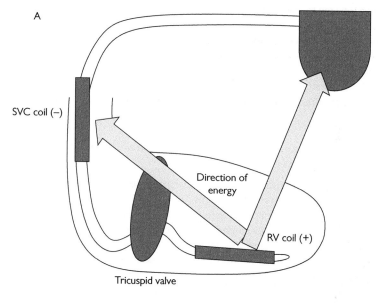

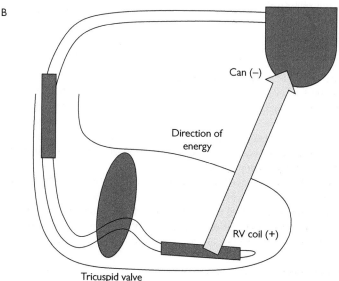

Figure 31.7 When a shock is delivered to the heart, energy travels from the positive pole to the negative pole. In defibrillation leads with two coils, the SVC coil can be turned on or off. The RV coil is positive and the SVC coil or can is negative. Changing the direction of energy across the heart can make defibrillation more effective. Polarity can be reversed so that the SVC coil or can becomes positive and the RV coil is negative. In a single coil ICD the circuit is between the RV coil and can.

Arrhythmia detection and therapy

- ICDs diagnose arrythmias by counting intervals on the intra-cardiac electrogram
- The rhythms recognized are normal sinus rhythm, VTs, and ventricular fibrillation. The device recognizes them from the cycle length or intervals (R–R interval) measured in milliseconds
- Cycle length = 60,000 ÷ rate (bpm), e.g NSR = 60–100 bpm = 1000–600 ms
- The ICD averages a number of cycle lengths to make a diagnosis. The number of cycle lengths required to make a diagnosis can be programmed by the operator but is usually around 12
- After a therapy has been delivered (antitachycardia pacing (ATP) or shock) the device then can 'redetect' to check the therapy was successful. The number of cycle lengths analysed now is less. If unsuccessful the device can deliver further therapy
- An ICD can offer bradycardia pacing, ATP, low and high output shocks
- The physician will program the device to have different detection zones (see Figure 31.8).

Programming

Aim is to detect dangerous sustained ventricular arrhythmias whilst avoiding inappropriate therapy or therapy for a non-sustained arrhythmia:

- Avoid shocking atrial arrhythmias or sinus tachycardia (young and active patients): SVT versus VT discrimination programming (see Figures 31.9 and 31.10)
- Atrial lead will aid discrimination of atrial arrhythmias (AV synchrony) but simultaneous paroxysmal atrial and ventricular arrhythmia are possible; very fast ventricular rates (>200–220 bpm) irrespective of origins are interpreted as ventricular arrhythmia for safety
- A single trial of ATP whilst or before charging to a shock, even in the VF zone (likely fast VT), can be effective and prevent shocks
- ATP delivered via both left and right ventricular leads (in CRT devices) is more effective than right ventricular ATP alone. ATP is delivered at a high voltage, typically 7.5 V to try to penetrate the VT circuit
- Long QT is prone to torsade de pointes and may not result in lack of consciousness. Torsade de pointes is often self-terminating and may be remarkably well tolerated. The detection interval is prolonged, with the aim that the patient does not receive unnecessary shock therapy. Atrial pacing at 80–90 bpm shortens the QT interval and prevents the occurrence of long–short intervals
- Secondary prevention: therapy can be tailored to the clinical VT. Often the device will be programmed empirically, according to the EMPIRIC study protocol, with three zones. A rate of >250 bpm is treated as VF and receives shock therapy, 201–250 receives one burst of ATP followed by full output shocks, and rates of 150–200 bpm receive three bursts of ATP followed by shock therapy
- Primary prevention patients may be programmed according to the PREPARE study. Rates above 250 bpm are treated with full output shocks, rates of 182–250 receive one sequence ATP followed by full output shocks, and those between 167 and 181 are recorded but do not receive therapy. The detection interval may be prolonged, e.g. 18 confirmed VT or VF out of 24 beats rather than a nominal 12 out of 16.

Device therapy

Pacing:

- All ICDs have pacing capabilities
- Backup bradycardia support; if no conduction issues anticipated left at a low base rate, e.g. 40 bpm with avoidance of atrial arrhythmia tracking, e.g. DDI

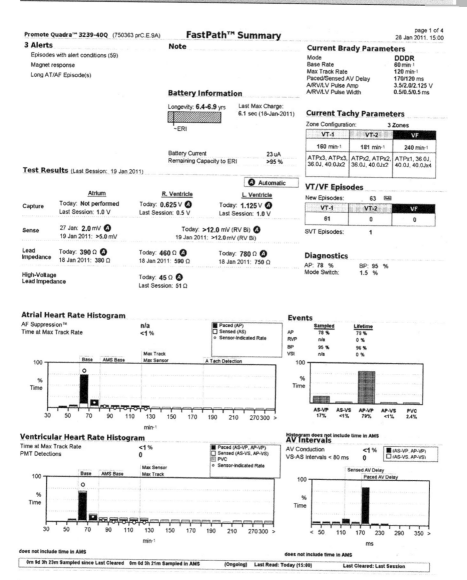

Figure 31.8 Typical summary page on interrogation of a St. Jude Medical CRT-D device. This particular patient has two VT zones and a VF zone.

Reproduced by kind permission of Richard Chambers of St Jude Medical Inc.

- Ventricular pacing prevents long pauses that occur after a shock; in some patients it is the post-shock pause rather than the primary arrhythmia that causes syncope.

Antitachycardia pacing:

- See Figure 31.11. ATP only works on monomorphic VT involving a re-entry circuit
- Pacing occurs at a rate faster than the VT (shorter cycle length)
- Burst pacing: sequence of paced beats at the same cycle length

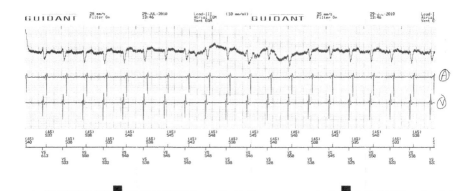

Figure 31.9 Supraventricular tachycardia. This patient was seen in the ICD clinic with this arrhythmia at a rate of approximately 110 bpm. There is VA conduction (A sense follows V sense). The rhythm was monitored, as it was below the programmed detection parameters for the VT-1 zone. This was terminated with i.v. adenosine.

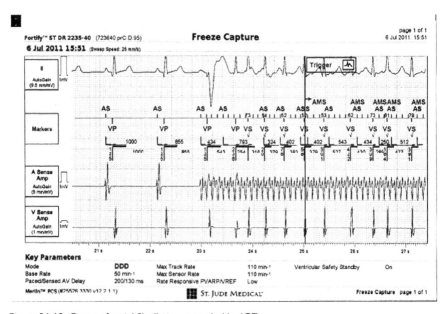

Figure 31.10 Onset of atrial fibrillation recorded by ICD.
Reproduced by kind permission of Richard Chambers of St Jude Medical Inc.

- Ramp pacing: burst of pacing with increasing pacing rate (decreasing cycle length)
- Scanning: changing the cycle length from one burst to the next, allowing a burst to be delivered and, if the VT persists, the next burst to be delivered at a faster rate.

Shock therapy

- See Figure 31.12. In a dual coil system the SVC coil can be programmed on or off; the electrical circuit is formed from the RV coil to both the SVC coil and the ICD can, or the ICD can alone
- The amount of energy an ICD is capable of delivering varies by make and model.

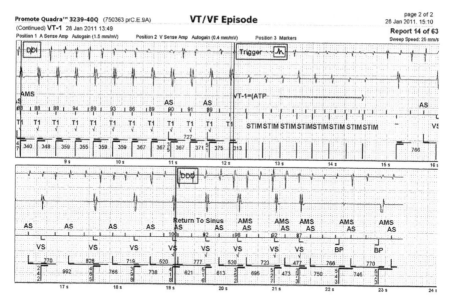

Figure 31.11 Antitachycardia pacing. A rhythm is detected in the VT-1 zone. All 12 intervals fall into this zone and so the device labels this 'VT' and initiates therapy. ATP is delivered and the device believes sinus rhythm is restored. Underlying rhythm is actually AF.

Reproduced by kind permission of Richard Chambers of St Jude Medical Inc.

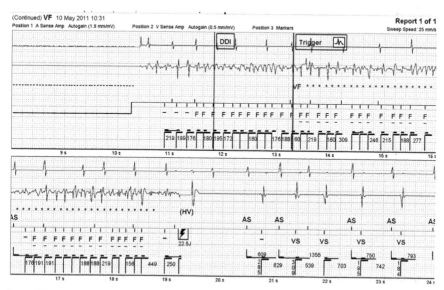

Figure 31.12 VF is detected by the device and so a shock is delivered at 22.5 J. Sinus rhythm is restored.

Reproduced by kind permission of Richard Chambers of St Jude Medical Inc.

SVT discrimination

- SVT discriminators are algorithms programmed into the VT zones. They cannot be programmed for the VF zone
- Different companies will have different algorithms based around the same themes
- Rate branch (only dual chamber ICDs): compares atrial to ventricular rate. If V < A or V = A the device assumes an atrial arrhythmia or sinus tachycardia respectively and inhibits therapy. If V > A the device assumes VT and delivers therapy
- Interval stability: this discriminator compares R–R interval stability. If R–R intervals are stable, the ICD diagnoses VT. If the R–R intervals are unstable (irregular) the device assumes AF and inhibits therapy
- Sudden onset: sinus tachycardia builds up gradually and VT starts suddenly
- Morphology discrimination: compares the patient's own sinus QRS complex to the QRS complexes during a tachycardia. If approximately 60% of the QRS complexes match then an SVT is diagnosed. If the device cannot match the current QRS complexes then VT is diagnosed
- These algorithms can be used alone or combined.

Driving (2011 DVLA advice)

See Chapter 8.

31.6 Cardiac resynchronization therapy

- Biventricular pacing was first described in 1994
- Randomized clinical trials evidence in atrial fibrillation is absent—cohort studies demonstrate a reduction in hospitalizations with cardiac resynchronization therapy (CRT) in this patient group
- See Box 31.2 for indications from the ESC guidelines.

Trials

- **COMPANION**: CRT-P and CRT-D in patients with NYHA class III/IV with EF <35% and a QRS >120 ms already on optimal medical therapy versus optimal medical therapy alone. CRT-P/D reduced hospitalizations, CRT-P reduced all-cause mortality by 24%, and CRT-D reduced all-cause mortality by 36%
- **CARE-HF**: CRT-P with NYHA class III/IV heart failure and EF <35%, QRS >120 ms on optimal medical therapy against medical therapy alone. RRR of 36% in all-cause mortality in the CRT-P group
- Recently **MADIT-CRT** and **REVERSE** have shown benefit in NYHA class II with reduced morbidity. 18% in REVERSE and 15% in MADIT-CRT were in NYHA I class at baseline, although most of these patients had been previously symptomatic. Improvement was primarily seen in patients with QRS ≥150 ms and/or typical LBBB
- In NYHA class II and III heart failure, CRT-D reduces the risk of death or hospitalization by 25% compared with ICD alone in the **RAFT** study. 80% of the patients were in NYHA class II.

At implant

- The threshold of the LV lead is usually higher than the RV lead. It will produce a RBBB morphology when tested; important to confirm a positive R wave in V1
- The position of the lead can affect the response; poor responses seen in the great cardiac vein or very apical positions.

BOX 31.2 INDICATIONS

Class I (level of evidence = A)

- CRT-P/CRT-D is recommended to reduce morbidity and mortality in patients with the following:
  - NYHA function class III/IV
  - LVEF ≤35%, QRS ≥120 ms, SR
  - Optimal medical therapy
  - Class IV patients should be ambulatory
- CRT preferentially by CRT-D is recommended to reduce morbidity or to prevent disease progression where:
  - NYHA function class II
  - LVEF ≤35%, QRS ≥150 ms, SR
  - optimal medical therapy
- In patients with a conventional indication for pacing, NYHA III/IV symptoms, an LVEF of ≤35%, and a QRS width of ≥120 ms, a CRT-P/CRT-D is indicated. RV pacing will induce dyssynchrony and chronic RV pacing in patients with LV dysfunction should be avoided.

CRT in patients with AF

Class IIa

- CRT-P/CRT-D should be considered to reduce morbidity where:
  - NYHA function class III/IV
  - LVEF ≤35%, QRS ≥130 ms
  - Pacemaker dependency induced by AV nodal ablation *(level of evidence=B)*
  - or slow ventricular rate and frequent ventricular pacing *(Level of evidence=C)*.

Adapted from 'The 2010 focused update of ESC guidelines on device therapy in heart failure', Kenneth Dickstein, Panos E. Vardas, Angelo Auricchio et al., *European Heart Journal* 31, 2677–2687, copyright 2010 with permission of Oxford University Press.

Non-responders

- The natural history of cardiac failure is to deterioration over time
- The majority of patients feel better but some do not notice an improvement. As a general rule one third feel a lot better, one third a little better and one third no better
- Young patients with LBBB who subsequently experience left ventricular deterioration (LBBB-induced cardiomyopathy) appear to respond particularly well to CRT and the EF may normalize 'super-responders'
- Lack of improvement may be due to the underlying condition, especially widespread MI or failure to receive biventricular pacing due to rapid atrial arrhythmias; it is important that the left ventricular lead is in an adequate vein and is functional
- In AF, consideration should be given to restoring sinus rhythm. If permanent AF, AV node ablation is effective to promote biventricular pacing
- Anodal stimulation: in a normal situation capture occurs at the cathode, but to improve pacing parameters CRT devices can be programmed to pace from LV tip (cathode) to RV ring (anode). Anodal stimulation occurs when the site of capture becomes the anode (RV lead) rather than the cathode (LV lead) and is an important cause of non-response. It can be difficult to detect unless considered, as the LV lead will appear to be capturing, but the ECG morphology of pacing will be exactly the same as RV pacing

- The AV interval can be altered to maximize LV filling whilst minimizing diastolic MR. The timings between the stimulation of the RV and LV lead can be altered, which may affect symptoms. The only trial looking at the effectiveness of AV optimization showed no benefit
- Some patients may require LV lead revision.

31.7 ICD troubleshooting

- Multiple appropriate shocks
- Shock therapy fails to cardiovert arrhythmia
- Inappropriate shocks
- Ventricular arrhythmias without therapy being delivered.

Multiple appropriate discharges

- May be due to incessant VT, acute ischaemia, electrolyte abnormalities, drug proarrhythmia, or non-compliance with anti-arrhythmics
- Acute treatment involves identifying the underlying cause
- If the problem relates to ineffective ATP then more aggressive ATP can be programmed (see Figure 31.13)
- BBs are important in acute setting to decrease sympathetic tone, which often drives incessant VT
- Intravenous amiodarone or i.v. lignocaine can be effective in an acute situation
- High rate pacing from the atrium (or ventricle) can be effective in preventing recurrence
- Ablation of VT may be required.

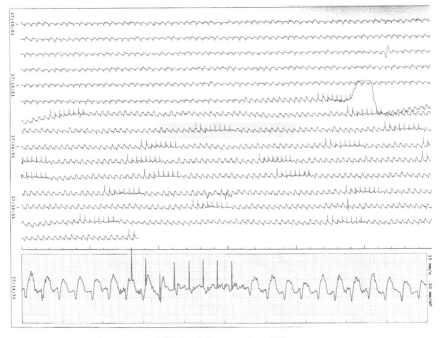

Figure 31.13 Several attempts at ATP that fail to terminate VT.
Reproduced by kind permission of Richard Chambers of St Jude Medical Inc.

Shock therapy fails to cardiovert arrhythmia

- The DFT should be re-evaluated
- The DFT can be increased by certain anti-arrhythmics (amiodarone, flecainide, phenytoin), infarction, cardiac surgery, hyperkalaemia, or lead movement
- Can be altered by changing shocking vector or by placing a subcutaneous patch or electrode array lead.

Inappropriate shocks

- In the situation of multiple inappropriate shocks the ICD should be deactivated, either with a magnet or programmer, and the patient should be placed on telemetry with external defibrillation pads placed
- Most commonly caused by atrial arrhythmias
- The atrial arrhythmias should be treated in the conventional manner and SVT discriminators programmed on the ICD
- Ablation of the arrhythmia or AV node can be useful
- Other causes for inappropriate therapy are oversensing of T waves ('double counting') and lead fracture (see Figure 31.14).

Ventricular arrhythmias without therapy being delivered

- The most common cause for this scenario occurs when the tachyarrhythmia rate is less than the VT rate programmed on the device
- Slow VT can occur spontaneously or the VT may be slowed by antiarrhythmic medication
- Can be treated by external DCCV, internal DCCV, or ATP using the device
- The VT zones can be changed. VT ablation can be used or withdrawal of antiarrhythmic medications may be helpful
- May also be due to magnet application, therapies not reprogrammed after being switched off, or no VT zone programmed at implant in a patient who has previously only had VF.

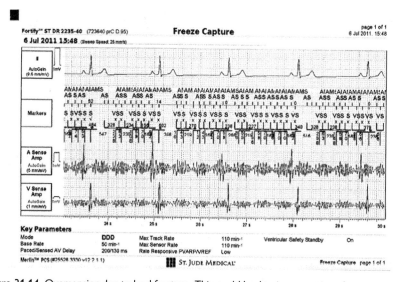

Figure 31.14 Oversensing due to lead fracture. This could lead to inappropriate therapy.
Reproduced by kind permission of Richard Chambers of St Jude Medical Inc.

31.8 Arrhythmia mechanisms

There are three main mechanisms for arrhythmias:

- Re-entry
- Automaticity
- Triggered activity.

Cardiac action potential

See Figure 31.15.

- Phase 0, depolarization: upon reaching the threshold membrane potential rapid sodium channels open and positive sodium ions enter cell
- Phase 1–3, repolarization
- Phase 1: starts with rapid outward potassium current; this results in a fast early repolarization
- Phase 2 (plateau phase) due to opening of calcium channels: Inward sodium and calcium currents balance the outward potassium currents. The cell is refractory to any stimulus in this phase
- Phase 3 due to opening of 'delayed rectifier' outward potassium channels: outward currents exceed inward currents
- Phase 4, resting phase: no net movement of ions; the cell is fully excitable.

Re-entry

- Most common mechanism for arrhythmias (AVNRT, AVRT, atrial flutter, VT)
- Requires two pathways with different electrophysiological properties (conduction and refractoriness); one pathway conducts quicker and has a longer refractory period and the other conducts slower but has a shorter refractory period
- Each involved pathway of the circuit must be capable of conducting an impulse in an anterograde and retrograde direction
- Initiated by a premature impulse.

Automaticity

- Not common (automatic ATs, automatic junctional tachycardia, automatic VT)
- Automaticity is the heart's ability to spontaneously generate electricity

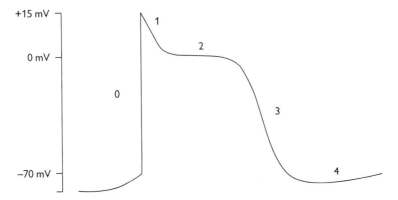

Figure 31.15 A typical ventricular action potential.

- Abnormal acceleration of phase 4 of the action potential produces an early depolarization
- Often have metabolic causes e.g. ischaemia, hypoxia, hypokalaemia, hypomagnesaemia, high sympathetic tone.

Triggered activity

- Produced by abnormal fluxes of positive ions into cardiac cells producing an afterdepolarization during late phase 3 or early phase 4
- If the afterdepolarizations are large enough they can cause another action potential to be generated
- Can cause digitalis toxic arrhythmias, torsade de pointes, and some VTs that respond to CCBs.

31.9 Therapeutics of anti-arrhythmic drugs

See Box 31.3.

Class IA anti-arrhythmics

- Block rapid sodium channels and potassium channels, prolonging action potential and slowing refractoriness. Act in both atria and ventricles and therefore can be used to treat both atrial and ventricular arrhythmias
- All class IA drugs are pro-arrhythmic. Quinidine can cause significant GI upset. Procainamide can cause agranulocytosis and disopyramide has significant anticholinergic side effects.

Class IB anti-arrhythmics

- Decrease duration of action potential and therefore reduce refractory periods. Have little effect in the atria and are therefore only useful for ventricular arrhythmias
- Low potential for causing pro-arrhythmia

BOX 31.3 VAUGHAN-WILLIAMS CLASSIFICATION

Class I: sodium-channel blockers:

- IA: prolong duration of action potential. Quinidine, procainamide, disopyramide
- IB: shorten duration of action potential. Lidocaine, mexiletine, tocainamide, phenytoin
- IC: no effect on duration of action potential. Flecainide, encainide, propafenone, moricizine.

Class II: beta-blockers.

Class III: potassium-channel blockers:

- prolong duration of action potential: amiodarone, bretylium, sotalol, ibutilide.

Class IV: calcium-channel blockers.

Amiodarone has properties from all four classes.

Modified with permission from Vaughn Williams EM. A classification of antiarrhythmic action as reassessed after a decade of new drugs. *J Clin Pharmacol*, 1984; 24: 129–47. ©1984 by Sage Publications Inc.

- Lidocaine can only be given i.v. because of first-pass metabolism
- Class IB agents mainly cause neurological and GI side-effects
- Gingival hyperplasia is common with phenytoin.

Class IC anti-arrhythmics

- Have a pronounced effect on the rapid sodium channels and significantly reduce conduction velocity. Do not significantly affect action potential duration
- Effective for both atrial and ventricular arrhythmias
- Class IC agents should not be given to patients with IHD or LVSD. The Cardiac Arrhythmia Suppression Trial (CAST) showed increased mortality in patients receiving flecainide or encainide following MI
- Torsade de pointes is very rarely seen with Class IC agents. Pro-arrhythmia is due to re-entrant VT.

Class II anti-arrhythmics (beta-blockers)

- BBs work by blunting the arryhthmogenic action of catecholamines
- Sympathetic innervation is greatest in the SA and AV nodes. This is where BBs have the greatest effect
- Phase 4 depolarization is blunted, automaticity is decreased, and HR is slowed
- In the AV node, BBs produce a marked slowing in conduction and a prolongation in refractory periods
- BBs reduce ischaemia and therefore arrhythmias. They reduce incidences of VF and can prevent formation of re-entrant arrhythmias
- BBs can be used to treat atrial or ventricular arrhythmias, especially when related to catecholamines or ischaemia
- BBs are useful in preventing arrhythmias in congenital LQTS
- Side effects of BBs include fatigue, bronchospasm, erectile dysfunction, unawareness of hypoglycaemia and Raynaud's phenomenon.

Class III anti-arrhythmics

- Increase the duration of the action potential, usually by blocking potassium channels, and increase refractory periods
- Used for atrial and ventricular arrhythmias
- Amiodarone is effective for reducing episodes of VT and ventricular fibrillation. It is also moderately effective in maintaining sinus rhythm in AF/flutter
- Amiodarone's use is limited by side effects. GI side effects are common. Elevation of liver enzymes is also common but is usually transient, although there are reports of hepatitis/cirrhosis. Thyroid problems are common. Photosensitivity occurs in approximately 20% of patients. Some patients can develop a blue-grey discolouration of the skin. Reversible corneal deposits occur in almost all patients. Pulmonary complications are the most dangerous side effects of amiodarone and include amiodarone-induced pneumonitis and pulmonary fibrosis
- Sotalol produces prolongation of the action potential in both the atria and ventricles. It has a class II action as well
- Sotalol produces a dose-related prolongation of the QT interval
- The risk of torsade de pointes is higher with sotalol than with amiodarone and class IA agents.

Class IV anti-arrhythmics

- Calcium channel blockers inhibit the calcium channel responsible for depolarization in the SA and AV node
- They reduce automaticity, slow conduction, and increase the refractory period in the SA and AV node
- CCBs can suppress early or delayed afterdepolarizations
- CCBs can be used for atrial tachyarrhythmias. Verapamil is very good at terminating narrow complex tachycardias
- CCBs are not good for terminating typical re-entrant VT. However, verapamil can be used to terminate ventricular arrhythmias in structurally normal hearts, e.g. RVOT VT and fascicular VT
- Verapamil and diltiazem are negative inotropes and can produce bradycardia and hypotension. Verapamil can cause constipation.

Further reading

Brignole M. Diagnosis and treatment of syncope. *Heart,* 2007; 93: 130–6.

Brignole M, Menozzi C, Bartoletti A, *et al.* A new management of syncope. Prospective systematic guideline-based evaluation of patients referred urgently to general hospitals. *Eur Heart J,* 2006; 27: 78–82.

Camm AJ, Luscher TF, Serruys PW (eds). *The European Society of Cardiology Textbook of Cardiovascular Medicine,* 2nd edn. Oxford University Press, 2009.

Dickstein K, Vardas PE, Auricchio A, *et al.* 2010 focused update of ESC guidelines on device therapy in heart failure. *Eur Heart J,* 2010; 31: 2677–87.

Ellenbogen KA, Wood MA. *Cardiac Pacing and ICDs,* 5th edn. Blackwell, 2008.

Fogoros RN. *Antiarrhythmic drugs. A Practical Guide.* 2nd edn. Blackwell, 2007.

Kenny, T. *The Nuts and Bolts of ICD Therapy.* Blackwell, 2005.

Kenny T. *The Nuts and Bolts of Cardiac Resynchronization Therapy.* Blackwell, 2007.

Moya A, Sutton R, Ammirati A, *et al.* Guidelines for the diagnosis and management of syncope (version 2009). *Eur Heart J,* 2009; 30: 2631–71.

Vardas PE, Auricchio A, Blanc JJ, *et al.* ESC Guidelines for cardiac pacing and cardiac resynchronization therapy. *Eur Heart J,* 2007; 28: 2256–95.

Invasive and interventional cardiology

CONTENTS

32.1 Invasive coronary angiography

Access

Radial

- This is rapidly becoming the preferred route in the UK (BCIS audit figures)
- Once the learning curve is climbed the obvious advantages outweigh the disadvantages (see Table 32.1)
- The recent RIVAL trial has shown significantly fewer vascular complications for the radial route and better outcomes in the STEMI patient subgroup among those procedures performed by radial experts
- The hand usually benefits from a dual blood supply from the radial and ulnar arteries (Figure 32.1)
- Testing for this clinically is advocated, usually via the *Allen's test* pre-procedure: both arteries are compressed and the patient clenches and releases their hand into a fist. The hand will blanch. In a positive Allen's test the colour returns to normal after release of the ulnar artery, thus confirming dual supply. This may also be performed using pulse oximetry plethysmography.

Strategies to minimize radial spasm include:

- Adequate local anaesthetic
- Use of smaller 5F sheaths and catheters
- Administration of a 'radial cocktail', often of nitrate and verapamil.

Routine administration of heparin is advised to minimize radial artery thrombosis and occlusion in the ensuing weeks.

Femoral

- The femoral route may be used for a variety of reasons:
  - Failed radial approach
  - Absent radial pulse
  - Possible IABP requirement
  - Procedure mandating 8F sheath (eg. 2-stent bifurcation, rotablation)
  - Complex graft anatomy

Table 32.1 Advantages and disadvantages of the radial approach

Advantages	Disadvantages
Earlier ambulation	Operator learning curve
Fewer vascular complications	Vessel spasm
Safer in anticoagulated patients	Vasovagal reactions
	Too small for >7F sheaths or IABP use
	Anatomical abnormality, eg. radial loop/subclavian tortuousity

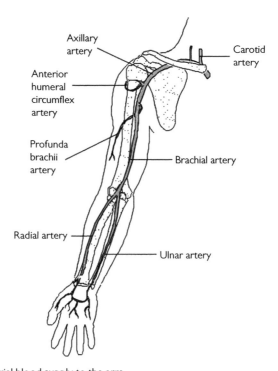

Figure 32.1 Arterial blood supply to the arm.
© EMIS, from http://www.patient.co.uk/diagram/Arteries-Of-The-Arm.htm, with permission.

- Artery is palpated and punctured two fingers-breadth below the inguinal ligament (see Figure 32.2)
- Punctures above the ligament risk subsequent inability to adequately apply compression post-removal and increase the risk of a retroperitoneal bleed. The greater calibre of the femoral artery means that use of vasodilators and heparin is not routinely mandated.

Coronary anatomy

- Invasive coronary angiography remains the gold standard test for imaging the coronary arteries, if done properly
- Acquisition is of a 2D image, and multiple views are necessary to image every section of each artery in orthogonal plains

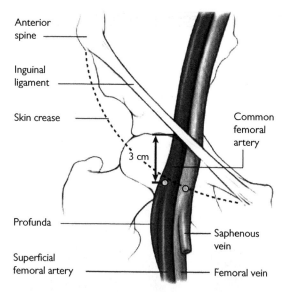

Figure 32.2 Relevant anatomy to femoral artery and vein puncture.

This figure was published in *Braunwald's Heart Disease* Vol 1, eds. Douglas P. Zipes, Peter Libby, Robert O. Bonow, Eugene Braunwald, Copyright 2005 with permission of Elsevier.

- Each angiogram will require the operator to adapt the next manoeuvre or view throughout the procedure to gain all the information required
- Expertise in this process will come with experience but the foundations of good coronary angiography are a sound knowledge and understanding of anatomy (normal and abnormal).

Normal aortic root anatomy
- Normally the coronary ostia arise from the sinus above the respective aortic cusps
- The ostia are best profiled and engaged in an LAO view (see Figure 32.3).

Normal coronary course and nomenclature
The right coronary artery
See Figure 32.4.

- The right coronary artery (RCA) arises anteriorly from the right aortic sinus and descends in the right atrioventricular groove
- The proximal portion (1) gives rise to the conus and sinus node branches
- The middle third (2) extends to the acute margin (the sharp angle between the sternocostal and diaphragmatic surfaces of the heart) at which point the distal third (3) continues on the inferior surface
- In 70% of cases it bifurcates at the interventricular groove and gives rise to the posterior descending artery (PDA; 4), thus conferring dominance (supplying the inferior septum and notably the posteromedial papillary muscle) and a posterior left ventricular branch (pLV; 16).

a

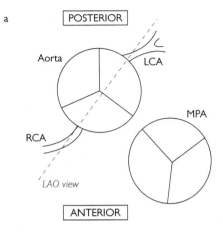

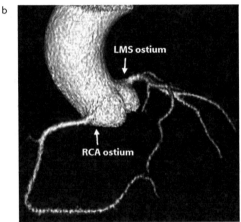

Figure 32.3 Coronary ostia anatomy. (a) Diagrammatic cross-sectional view of LAO projection and (b) 3D computed tomography reconstruction representing this view for optimal ostial profiling and engagement. LAO, left anterior oblique; MPA, main pulmonary artery; RCA, right coronary artery, LCA, left coronary artery.

Part (b) reproduced from 'Multidetector row computed tomography: imaging congenital coronary artery anomalies in adults', N. E. Manghat, G. J. Morgan-Hughes, A. J. Marshall, et al., Heart, 91, 1515–1522, copyright 2005 with permission from BMJ Publishing Group Ltd.

The left coronary system
See Figure 32.5.

- The left coronary system arises posteriorly as the left main stem (LMS; 5) from the left aortic sinus and branches behind the main pulmonary artery (MPA) into the left anterior descending (LAD; 6–8) and circumflex arteries (Cx; 11–15)
- Occasionally there is also an intermediate branch (17)
- The proximal LAD (6) runs up to the origin of the first septal branch
- Branching diagonals (9,10) serve the lateral LV wall
- The Cx descends in the left atrioventricular groove (11,13) and gives off posterior obtuse marginal (OM) branches (12,14) and, in 10% of cases, the PDA, and is thus dominant
- In approximately 20% of cases there is co-dominance with the RCA.

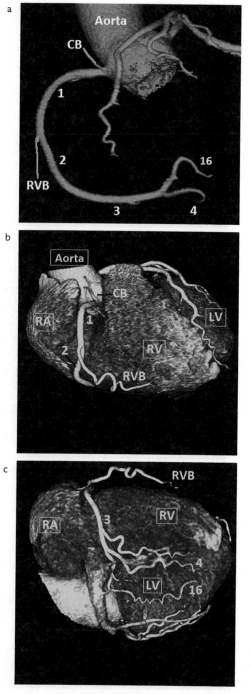

Figure 32.4 3D rendered CT image of the coronary tree demonstrating the right coronary artery (a) and 3D reconstruction in AP view (b) and inferior view (c), showing AHA-defined segments and arterial course. See text. CB, conus branch; RVB, right ventricular branch.

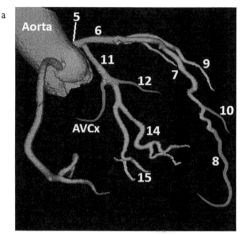

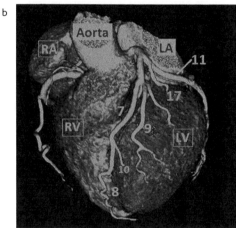

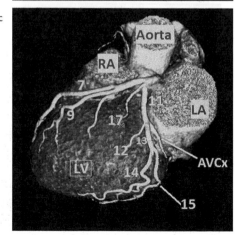

Figure 32.5 3D rendered CT image of the coronary tree. showing the left coronary system (a) and a 3D CT image in LAO cranial view (b) and posterior view (c), showing AHA-defined segments and arterial course. See text. AVCx, atrioventricular circumflex branch.

Common native vessel variations
- The LMS may be absent, with either a 'shotgun' origin to the LAD and LCx arteries, or these arteries may be separate entirely; the former may be obvious from dye reflux but the latter should be actively sought, with a sinus injection if suspected
- In approximately 10% cases the RCA may have a high and/or anterior origin, which can be difficult to intubate.

Vein grafts
See Figure 32.6.

- This 3D cardiac CT AP reconstruction demonstrates the usual origins and courses of saphenous vein coronary bypass grafts (SVG)
- The graft to the RCA usually arises from the lateral aortic wall (above the native RCA) with a vertical course and is hence best engaged in the LAO or AP views
- Grafts to the LAD and Cx arteries usually arise anteriorly and traverse the MPA as shown. Their engagement is often aided by an RAO view.

Coronary anomalies
Coronary artery arising from wrong sinus
- RCA arising from LC sinus, aberrant course
- LCA arising from RC sinus, aberrant course.

Branch of coronary arising from wrong sinus
- LCx arising from RC sinus, aberrant course
- LAD arising from RC sinus, aberrant course.

Single coronary artery
- Arising from LC sinus, aberrant RCA
- Arising from RC sinus, aberrant LCA.

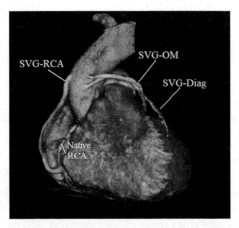

Figure 32.6 3D computed tomography reconstruction in AP view showing common anatomy of bypass grafts. SVG, saphenous vein graft.

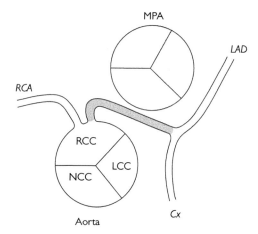

Figure 32.7 Diagrammatic representation of anomalous LCA (shaded) arising from right coronary cusp (RCC) with inter-arterial course. MPA, main pulmonary artery.

The course of the proximal aberrant artery is critical: is it interarterial, i.e. between aorta and main pulmonary artery (see Figure 32.7) and subject to compression with possible ischaemia and dysrhythmias (sudden death)? In the presence of symptoms, ischaemia testing is sought and treatment is surgical reimplantation.

Anomalous coronary artery arising from pulmonary artery

- Whilst very rare as a group, anomalous left coronary artery arising from pulmonary artery is by far the most common form (90%)
- Most present with infarction, sudden death, or heart failure and untreated 1-year mortality is 90%
- Management is surgical reimplantation into the aorta.

Angiography: catheter selection

Left coronary artery

- See Figure 32.8a
- A Judkins left catheter (JL4) is usually employed to engage the left coronary ostium
- The primary (distal) curve engages and the secondary curve stabilizes on the opposite aortic wall
- The number refers to the distance between the two curves. Hence a JL5/JL6 catheter may be required if the aorta is dilated
- If access is via the right radial artery, the steeper angle of approach usually mandates using a shorter JL3.5.

Right coronary artery

- See Figure 32.8b
- A Judkins right catheter (JR4) is usually employed for both femoral and radial approaches
- It requires steady clockwise rotation
- Femorally, a William's catheter is a commonly used alternative (AR1 radially)
- Larger roots may require a JR5/6 or an Amplatzer right (AR) catheter.

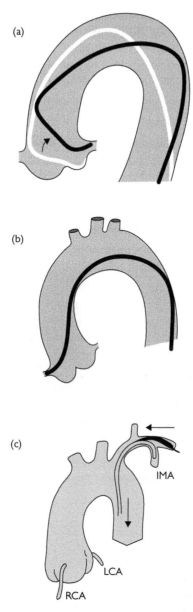

Figure 32.8 Catheter engagement. (a) left coronary artery engagement, (b) right coronary artery engagement, (c) internal mammary artery engagement.

This figure was published in *Braunwald's Heart Disease* Vol 1, eds. Douglas P. Zipes, Peter Libby, Robert O. Bonow, Eugene Braunwald, Copyright 2005 with permission of Elsevier.

Internal mammary artery

- See Figure 32.8c
- Pass internal mammary artery (IMA) catheter over wire into ascending aorta
- Withdraw J-wire into catheter
- Rotate catheter anticlockwise until pointing up

- Pull back until it engages the left subclavian artery ('3rd click')
- Pass J-wire beyond left IMA ostium, then catheter
- Dragging back usually engages the left IMA with some rotational adjustment
- A similar technique will engage the right IMA, after manoeuvring the catheter via the innominate artery ('1st click') to the right subclavian artery.

Vein grafts

Right-sided vein grafts are best engaged in LAO or AP view (see Figure 32.9a).

- JR4 will often click into ostium upon dragging up from RCA engagement
- Beware, if downward ostium; a JR4 catheter may point into roof and graft will only appear as stump
- MPA catheter usually better (or right coronary bypass (RCB) catheter)
- If reach needed use Amplatzer left (AL) catheter.

RAO view is often helpful to locate left-sided vein grafts (Figure 32.9b).

- Rotate JR4 to point towards sternal wires (anteriorly)

A

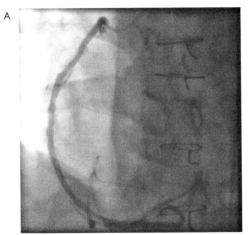

B

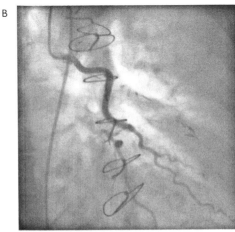

Figure 32.9 Vein graft engagement. (a) Right-sided vein graft engagement, (b) Left-sided vein graft engagement.

- Slide slowly up and down aorta until catches (may need rotational adjustment)
- If reach is needed use AR2/AL1/LCB.

General points for graft cases:

- If vein grafts are difficult to find or there is no operation note, an aortogram may prove useful
- Right femoral artery approach is often the default for angiography of graft patients
- With practice, the left radial is an excellent approach for left IMA and vein graft cases
- Indeed, intubation of the former is usually made easier.

Angiography: Views

- There are several standard views of left and right coronary systems
- Good angiography is not simply a matter of acquiring each of them in every patient
- One 2D acquisition is useless without the other complementary views
- Each angiogram is a dynamic process of image selection
- Some will not need all views and some will need further modified views
- The diagrams can therefore only be a guide
- They show the position of the C-arm during acquisition, juxtaposed with the corresponding angiographic image and a diagrammatic representation showing the specific anatomy best shown in that view (shaded).

Right coronary artery

See Figure 32.10.

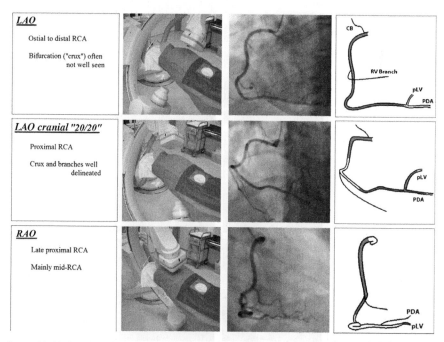

Figure 32.10 Standard RCA angiographic views and angiograms. Left-hand boxes show coronary anatomy best highlighted in each view, represented diagrammatically by shaded area in right-hand boxes. CB, conus branch; RV, right ventricular branch; pLV, posterior left ventricular branch; PDA, posterior descending artery.

Left coronary artery

See Figure 32.11.

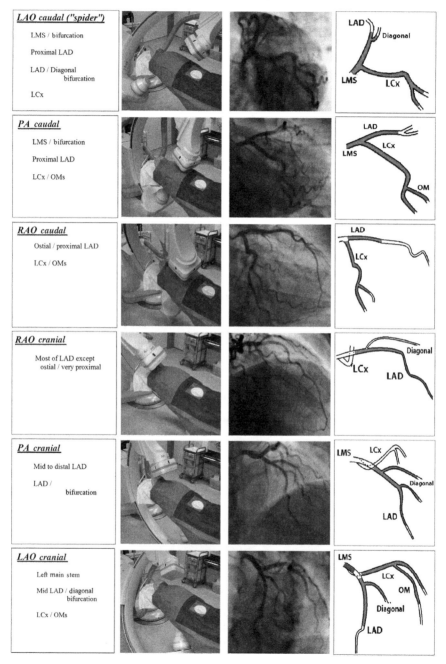

Figure 32.11 Standard LCA angiographic views and angiograms. Left-hand boxes show coronary anatomy best highlighted in each view, represented diagrammatically by shaded area in right boxes.

Left ventriculography

- A pigtail catheter is advanced down onto the aortic valve (with the introducer wire pulled back into the catheter) so that is curls up slightly
- It may pass straight through. If not, with some rotation upon slow withdrawal, it will often prolapse through
- Advancing the wire within the catheter may encourage prolapse, or the valve can be crossed with the wire J-tip prior to advancing the catheter
- Further strategies include using a soft-tipped straight wire via either a pigtail or AL1 catheter (particularly in aortic stenosis) to direct a course through the valve
- After measuring an end-diastolic pressure, a pump is used to give about 35 ml of contrast into the LV over 3 s, to assess function and regional wall motion as Figure 32.12 illustrates
- The pigtail should then be withdrawn whilst recording, to measure the pullback gradient across the aortic valve

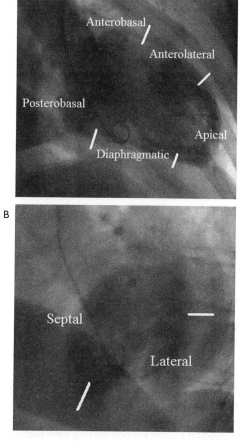

Figure 32.12 Left ventricular angiography in the RAO (a) and LAO (b) views showing profiled LV territories.

- It should be noted this is a peak-to-peak gradient (approximates to the mean echo gradient); similar readings may be made invasively using a pressure wire if the valve is difficult to cross
- These data may be useful to corroborate echocardiographic findings if the latter are not clear-cut.

32.2 Coronary intervention

Indications
- When treating the signs and symptoms of heart failure, *viability or ischaemia* should be demonstrated prior to revascularization
- The critical point is that *every other indication requires the demonstration of ischaemia*
- This is inherent in the diagnosis of an ACS, but angina requires investigation in the form of treadmill testing, stress imaging, or pressure wire evaluation.

Stable angina
Prognostic:
- >50% LMS or proximal LAD
- 2VD/3VD with impaired LV
- Single remaining vessel with >50% stenosis
- *All the above with positive ischaemia testing*
- Proven large area of ischaemia (>10% LV).

Symptoms:
- >50% stenosis with limiting angina despite optimal medical therapy
- Dyspnoea/CHF and >10% LV ischaemia/viability from >50% stenotic artery.

NSTE-ACS
- High risk; within 24 h
- Recurrent symptoms; within 72 h
- Inducible ischaemia; within 72 h.

STEMI
- <12 h pain, persistent STE/new LBBB: <2 h of first medical contact
- >12 h since pain, persistent STE/new LBBB, and ongoing pain: ASAP
- Pain >12 h but <24 h, persistent STE/new LBBB: ASAP
- Post-fibrinolysis, successful: <24 h
- Post-fibrinolysis, failed: ASAP.

Congestive heart failure
- If anatomy is suitable *and* in the presence of viable myocardium.

Limitations
- BCIS audit figures show that PCI rates have doubled in the UK in the last decade. This is a reflection of both an expanding service and advancing techniques
- Patient factors or angiographic anatomy may not be optimal for PCI, for example:
  - Patient factors (need for heparin and possibly long-term platelet inhibition): recent history of stroke, gastrointestinal haemorrhage, or impending non-cardiac surgery

■ Angiographic aspects: complex multivessel disease (MVD) which may include left main stem lesion

- Often both PCI and CABG are valid methods of revascularization. The ratio of revascularization through PCI versus CABG has risen in the UK from 1.3 to 3.24
- Almost all trials comparing these revascularization methods show no long-term difference in mortality nor repeat MI, but do show significantly *higher rates of repeat revascularization* in the PCI group
- Guidelines dictate that good modern practice involves the discussion of treatment options with both the patient and a 'heart team': a multidisciplinary meeting involving interventional cardiologists, cardiothoracic surgeons, and general cardiologists during which the patient and their imaging are presented and a consensus sought.

There are many risk stratification tools available. Some of the more common are discussed in the next subsections.

The EuroSCORE
- Initially validated to predict surgical mortality
- 17 simple questions regarding patient, cardiac and operative factors
- Independent predictor of MACE in studies for both PCI and CABG.

SYNTAX score
- Based purely on angiographic factors
- Independent predictor of MACE in PCI but not CABG
- Derived from the Syntax trial.

The SYNTAX trial
- Scored the angiogram according to complexity
- Randomized patients to either PCI (drug-eluting stents) or CABG
- Low scores: no significant difference in outcomes out to 3 years
- Higher scores:
    ■ Significantly higher MACE rates in PCI
    ■ Driven mainly by need for repeat revascularization.

The Society of Thoracic Surgeons (STS) score
- Validated in surgical patients only
- It is extensive and includes operative, demographic, patient, and haemodynamic factors.

32.3 Percutaneous coronary intervention in practice

- Stents were used in over 92% of all coronary angioplasty procedures in the UK in 2009
- NICE guidance now advocates their use routinely
- Improvement in outcomes has been achieved through a mixture of major advances in pharmacology, stent technology, advanced diagnostic techniques, and other therapeutic techniques.

Pharmacology

Three main drug groups are to be considered when undertaking any coronary intervention.

Antiplatelet agents
- The importance of aspirin in the treatment of CAD is well documented
- The first use of dual antiplatelets (DAPT) with clopidogrel conferred acceptable outcomes with stent use and their subsequent universal uptake
- There are now a newer generation of antiplatelet drugs, prasugrel and ticagrelor
- Interest in these drugs has grown since the recognition of clopidogrel non-responsiveness (associated with stent thrombosis) and with it platelet function testing, which aims to tailor therapy for specific high-risk patients
- Current recommendations for PCI are:
  - Aspirin 75 mg o.d. (300 mg preload); lifelong
  - Clopidogrel 75 mg o.d. (600 mg preload):
    - ACS or drug-eluting stent (DES): 1 year
    - Elective bare metal stent (BMS): 1 month
  - depending upon approval, clopidogrel may be replaced by
    - Prasugrel 10 mg o.d. (60 mg preload)
    - Ticagrelor 90 mg b.d. (180 mg preload).

Anticoagulants
- **Unfractionated heparin** has indirect anti-thrombin activity through its potentiating action on antithrombin III and is essential in preventing clot formation during coronary instrumentation. Dose is weight adjusted and its activity can be monitored in the lab using the activated clotting time (ACT)
- **Bivalirudin** has direct anti-thrombin activity and in trials is associated with comparable outcomes and less major bleeding in stable and ACS patients than with heparin and GIIb/IIIa inhibitors. Its effect does not require testing
- **LMWH** and fondaparinux target *anti-factor Xa activity* and also do not require monitoring, but recent evidence does not support their use in early ACS intervention or primary PCI.

Glycoprotein IIb/IIIa inhibitors
- Glycoprotein IIb/IIIa is found on the platelet surface and and binds fibrinogen or von Willebrand factor to induce platelet aggregation
- Early trials demonstrated a clear reduction in acute ischaemic events in patients undergoing PCI who received glycoprotein IIb/IIIa inhibitors (GPIs), such as abciximab or tirofiban
- They can be used 'upstream' in the initial treatment of high-risk patients as well as an adjunct for PCI
- Current recommendations for use include:
  - Stable patients (bail-out only)
  - High-risk ACS patients (high TIMI score, diabetic)
  - ACS patients who
    - Received no antiplatelet pretreatment
    - Were already on DAPT
  - Early presenting, high-risk STEMI patients.

Stent technology
'Plain old balloon angioplasty' (POBA, 1977)
- 'Plain old balloon angioplasty' pioneered by Andreas Gruntzig. Limited by complications such as vessel dissection, closure, and restenosis.

Stents (1987)

- In 1987, Palmaz and Schatz described the first balloon-expandable stent. Early human implantations were often complicated by acute stent thrombosis.

The European Benestent Trial 1994

Showed stent restenosis rates of 22% compared with 32% for POBA. Significant improvements were made with the realization of the importance of high-pressure balloon inflation. Then came an appreciation of the pathogenesis of restenosis.

- The vessel reaction to injury, which involves elastic recoil (hours), mural thrombus formation, neointimal proliferation and extracellular matrix formation, and arterial geometric changes (months)
- Ballooning causes endothelial damage and loss, so exposing the arterial wall, resulting in accumulation of platelets, macrophages, and polymorphonuclear neutrophils, and also damage to underlying smooth muscle cells
- These cells all release cytokines, which increase matrix metalloproteinase, which in turn leads to the migration and proliferation of the extracellular matrix and smooth muscle layer associated with intimal thickening
- It is the similarities between this process and tumour growth that gave rise to the notion of the local delivery of immunosuppressant drugs on stents to block the cell's mitotic cycle and therefore intimal hyperplasia.

Drug-eluting stents

- The first drug-eluting stent (DES) was implanted in man as part of the RAVEL trial. This, along with the SIRIUS trials, compared the Cypher™ (Johnson and Johnson) sirolimus-eluting stent to its bare-metal counterpart. The drug was impregnated into a polymer, which coated the stent, aiming to give a more sustained and uniform release. One-year major adverse cardiovascular event (MACE) rate dropped from 28.8% to 5.8% with target-lesion revascularization dropping from 20% to 4.9%
- Boston Scientific developed the paclitaxel-eluting Taxus™ stent and published a series of TAXUS trials giving similar results. They also gave confirmation of the particular benefit to diabetic patients, with reductions in restenosis rates by 81%, 1-year TLR by 65% and 1-year MACE by 44%
- Long-term follow-up in almost all trials continue to show better MACE rates with DESs driven by target lesion revascularization. There has been no consistent benefit of one particular drug over another
- NICE guidelines advise DESs for lesions <3 mm in diameter and >15 mm in length
- DESs now account for over 70% of all stents used in the UK.

Developing stent technology

- Newer generation stents have been developed, using newer drugs and incorporating thinner struts, and aiming to further improve upon the restenosis rates
- A small increase in the late and very late stent thrombosis rates associated with drug-eluting versus bare metal stents is associated with the nonerodable polymer and the current generation of stents therefore boast biodegradable polymers, effectively leaving a bare metal stent at 6 months. Early results have been favourable
- In 2011, research into the next-generation entirely bioabsorbable stents continues with RCTs in humans.

Advanced diagnostic techniques

Pressure wire assessment

- Increasingly, patients reach the lab prior to any ischaemia testing
- In this context measuring the fractional flow reserve (FFR) is a useful, well validated, on-the-spot physiological test to determine the significance of an angiographically indeterminate lesion
- 8775 cases were performed in the UK in 2009 (62% increase over 2008 figures).

Definition:

- FFR is the maximal blood flow in the presence of a stenosis divided by the theoretical maximal flow in the absence of the stenosis. It assumes resistance from vascular bed to be minimal and constant during maximal hyperaemia (see Figure 32.13).

In the lab:

- Heparin and intracoronary nitrates
- The pressure wire itself is the same calibre as a normal guide wire pressure transducer at the proximal end of a 3-cm radio-opaque tip equalized (synchronized) with simultaneous aortic pressure just out of the catheter in the coronary ostium

At maximum vasodilation

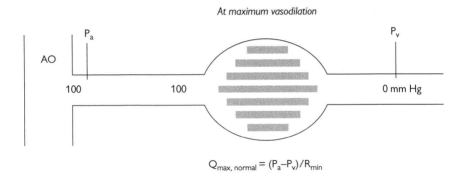

$$Q_{max, normal} = (P_a - P_v)/R_{min}$$

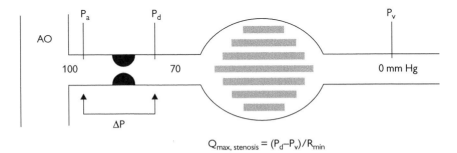

$$Q_{max, stenosis} = (P_d - P_v)/R_{min}$$

Figure 32.13 Diagrammatic representation of the measurement of fractional flow reserve. P_a, mean aortic pressure; P_d, mean distal coronary pressure; P_v, mean central venous pressure; AO, aorta; $Q_{max, normal}$, maximal achievable myocardial flow in normal coronary artery; $Q_{max, stenosis}$, maximal achievable myocardial flow in the presence of a stenosis; R_{min}, minimal resistance of the myocardial vascular bed.

- Wire passed across the lesion
- Adenosine, ideally via intravenous infusion (at 140 mg/kg/min) or as an intracoronary bolus
- Hyperaemia: BP drop/heart block/symptoms
- *FFR <0.75 indicates a significant lesion*
- There is a grey zone and the generally accepted cut off is <0.8
- Distal lesions, microvascular disease, and collaterals may confound the results
- Independent of BP, rate, and contractility.

Evidence:

- The DEFER study investigated the effect of stenting non-significant lesions. Not only did it show it was safe to leave lesions with an FFR >0.75, it also showed a higher MI and CABG rate in those patients stented with FFRs >0.75
- The FAME trial used FFR to guide revascularization in MVD. The primary end-point of death, MI, and TVR were significantly lower in the FFR group as compared to the angiographically guided group
- Furthermore, registry data shows that repeat FFR measurements immediately post-stenting are associated with subsequent event rates as shown in Table 32.2.

Intravascular ultrasound
- Intravascular ultrasound (IVUS) was initially a research tool but is now an everyday diagnostic technique giving histological information on vessel wall, luminal size, plaque morphology, and stent placement
- 3857 studies were performed in the UK in 2009 (up by 38% on 2008)
- Studies show excellent correlation with FFR measurements.

In the lab:

- Heparin and intracoronary nitrates
- Transducer mounted on a small (2.6F) monorail catheter
- Passed along standard guide wire into the coronary beyond lesion
- Pullback device produces a cross-sectional ultrasound map.

Main indications:

- Assessment of angiographically ambiguous lesions
- Estimation of functional stenosis
- Accurate vessel sizing pre-intervention
- Ensuring optimal stent deployment
- Left main/bifurcation intervention
- Investigation of stent failure
- Recognition of dissection and thrombus.

Table 32.2 Subsequent events rates and FFR

FFR	Subsequent event rate (%)
<0.8	29.3
0.8–0.9	20.9
0.9–0.95	6.2
>0.95	4.9

Optical coherence tomography

- Optical coherence tomography (OCT) uses infrared light to gain near-histological cross-sectional coronary imaging
- 10 times the resolution of IVUS
- Limited by penetration depth and the need for flush during acquisition
- Hence is not useful in larger vessels or for ostial lesions.

Other therapeutic techniques

Rotational atherectomy (rotablation)

- Circumferential ('napkin-ring') or significant (270°) calcification clearly diagnosed by IVUS can result in an undilateable lesion
- If high pressure inflations and 'cutting balloons' do not cause the lesion to yield, rotablation may be considered
- 1.25- to 2.5-mm diamond burrs are loaded over a guide wire and using an external driving device, rotated at 150,000 rpm in an attempt to fragment calcific plaque into small particles (<10 µm), which wash downstream into the venous system and are removed by the reticuloendothelial system
- Should be performed by experienced operators only.

Thrombectomy

- The most common device is the Export™ catheter, a monorail system using vacuum syringes to suck out thrombus. Backed up by evidence for improved outcomes in the TAPAS trial, which looked at its use prior to stenting in STEMI.

Intraaortic balloon pump counterpulsation

- Intraaortic balloon pump (IABP) inserted via the femoral artery and positioned in the descending aorta, just distal to the left subclavian artery
- Helium is rapidly shuttled into the balloon during diastole and out during systole, triggered by the ECG or arterial pressure trace
- This has several important haemodynamic effects as shown in Figure 32.14
- American and European guidelines favour the use of IABP in the setting of acute infarction, where cardiogenic shock cannot be quickly reversed, as a stabilizing measure prior to revascularization
- It is a class 1 indication based on trials showing improved mortality
- Generally accepted criteria are listed in Table 32.3.

Complications

Consent

- An understanding of the procedure and its possible complications is essential in order to gain informed consent (see Table 32.4)
- Complication rates are approximate in the UK and centre-specific data should be provided if possible
- Clearly these will vary according to patient-specific factors.

Coronary

Dissection

- This may be catheter-induced or post-dilation or stent deployment
- Early appreciation is essential to avert vessel closure
- Management: coverage with stent if possible to seal the flap.

A

Systole: deflation
Decreased afterload
• Decreases cardiac work
• Decreases myocardial oxygen consumption
• Increases cardiac output

Diastole: inflation
Augmentation of diastolic pressure
• Increases coronary perfusion

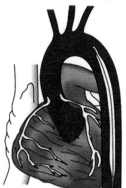

B

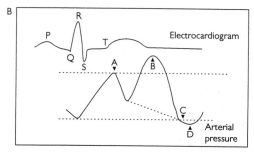

A = Unassisted systolic pressure
B = Diastolic augmentation
C = Unassisted aortic end diastolic pressure
D = Reduced aortic end diastolic pressure

Figure 32.14 Sequence of IABP inflation and haemodynamic effects. (a) the timing of IABP inflation relative to the ECG, (b) the augmented effect upon diastolic pressure.

Reproduced from 'Percutaneous coronary intervention: cardiogenic shock', John Ducas, Ever D Grech, *British Medical Journal*, 26, 1450, copyright 2003 with permission from BMJ Publishing Group Ltd.

Table 32.3 Indications and contraindications to IABP use

Indications	Contraindications
Cardiogenic shock	Severe PVD
Mechanical complication of MI (MR/VSD)	Severe thrombocytopaenia
Refractory ischaemia	Active haemorrhage
Support in high-risk PCI	Porcelain aorta
Bridge to CABG/transplant	Moderate-to-severe AR
Refractory ventricular arrhythmias	
Severe MR	

Reproduced from 'Cardiovascular hemodynamics for the clinician', ed. George Stouffer, copyright 2008 with permission from John Wiley and Sons.

Table 32.4 Complications and approximate incidences for consent purposes.

Complication	Treatment	Diagnostic	PCI
Vascular access damage[a]	Blood transfusion/surgical repair	<0.1%	Variable
Abnormal heart rhythm	DCCV/drugs	<0.2%	—
Reduced kidney function	Usually observation	Rare	Rare
Contrast reaction	Usually observation	<0.1%	<0.1%
Coronary damage	Stent or emergency CABG	<0.2%	1%[b]
Stroke	Specialist care	<0.2%	<1%
Death	—	<0.1%	<1%

[a]Radial, much higher if femoral access and/or complex PCI, up to 10% [b]MI approx 1%, emergency CABG <0.1%.

No reflow
- Seen after ballooning or stent deployment
- Occurs in the presence of a patent coronary lumen and is a reflection of microvascular obstruction, which may be appreciated by abnormal myocardial blush
- Associated with thrombotic lesions
- Management: difficult; may involve local injection via an over-the-wire balloon of nitrates, adenosine, verapamil, or GIIb/IIIa drugs.

Coronary perforation/rupture
- Perforation is associated with aggressive guide wire technique, as may be necessary in chronic total occlusions (where stiff and hydrophilic wires are used), and rupture with oversized balloons and coronary instrumentation such as rotablation
- The latter is usually obvious upon image acquisition in the lab, but a wire perforation may not become apparent until the patient returns to the ward where the accumulating pericardial blood becomes clinically evident
- Management: often emergency pericardial drainage with or without blood transfusion
- In the lab, deliberate prolonged vessel balloon occlusion and covered stents may be used to treat
- The aim is for supportive therapy until adjunctive pharmacotherapy given in the lab has worn off
- Heparin reversal is usually resisted and surgical repair may be necessary.

Stent embolization
- Rare, but dislodging from the delivery system may occur at the guide catheter tip or whilst traversing through struts of another stent in a bifurcation procedure
- Management :retrieval using partially inflated balloons or snare devices
- Embolization into the wider circulation does not often cause problems.

In-stent restenosis
- The incidence and pathology of in-stent restenosis (ISR) have already been described in the subsection on stents
- The patient will often represent some months later with recurrent angina: 'clinical restenosis'
- Management: usually through an IVUS-guided investigation
- If underexpansion is present, balloon optimization may be sufficient
- If it is in a BMS, a DES may be used to cover. There is also some evidence for the use of drug-coated balloons
- Aggressive ISR in DES, particularly in the setting of MVD will usually require referral for CABG.

Stent thrombosis

- Early stent thrombosis (ST) occurs within 30 days and is often due to stent underdeployment, particularly in bifurcation procedures, and clopidogrel hyporesponsiveness
- Late ST can occur years later and is associated with delayed endothelialization
- The most common cause is thought to be premature discontinuation of DAPT (30% of cases)
- Other associations include renal failure, bifurcation procedures, and diabetes
- Clearly the issue of clopidogrel resistance is of relevance
- Outcome: 60% suffer acute MI and mortality is 15%
- ST and DESs: concerns were raised through reporting services in 2004 with regards to the safety of DESs relating to ST
- The diagnosis was classified as definite, probable, or possible and the reports resulted in a sharp decline in the use of DESs worldwide in 2006
- These concerns have not been subsequently backed up upon review
- Meta-analyses including the SIRIUS, RAVEL, and TAXUS trials have suggested rates of between 0.6 and 1.0% out to 1 year and found no difference between BMS and DES
- There is data that suggest however that Taxus™ stents are associated with a slightly increased incidence of late ST
- DES uptake has now recovered to pre-2006 levels
- The optimal duration of DAPT remains unresolved, but the ongoing DAPT study will aim to assess the benefit beyond 1 year.

Vascular

Retroperitoneal haemorrhage

- Usually related to femoral puncture but may be spontaneous as a result of adjunctive pharmacology
- Presentation may simply be with unexplained hypotension, and high index of suspicion is required
- Hence any such presentation post-angiography should be aggressively investigated, usually via CT scan
- Management: supportive, and may require reversal of anticoagulation, although surgical repair is rarely indicated.

Haematoma

Associations:

- Femoral punctures
  - Long procedures
  - Large sheath (IABP use)
  - Anticoagulation
  - Removal technique
  - Patient factors (HPT, obesity, PVD)
- The sheath can usually be removed in the lab if no heparin was given, otherwise after 4 h or once ACT <150 s
- Manual pressure for between 5–10 min by an experienced member of staff is necessary on sheath removal followed by a few hours of recumbency

- Management:
  - Manual pressure
  - May be aided by clamping devices such as the Femostop™
- Vascular closure devices used to facilitate ambulation but have not been proven to reduce complications
- The Angioseal™ device uses an intralumenal anchor to sandwich the arterotomy with a collagen plug, which completely dissolves over 90 days
- Suture-based devices such as the Perclose™ aim to attain surgical closure without impinging upon the lumen.

Pseudoaneurysm

- This is common after femoral punctures and will present as a tender pulsatile swelling over the arterotomy site with an audible bruit
- Blood collects in a tear between the adventitia and media and is diagnosed with Doppler ultrasound
- Some may spontaneously resolve but the risk is of expansion, local impingement, and rupture and distal embolization
- Hence if flow persists into the pseudoaneurysm it will need treating
- Management: Doppler-guided compression (with success rates of only 30–62% on anticoagulation), ultrasound-guided thrombin injection (success rates of 90–100% and rare complications), or, particularly for larger pseudoaneurysms, surgical repair.

Limb ischaemia

- Occurrence is rare
- More associated with femoral route (e.g. closure device lifting plaque in diseased artery) and IABP use
- Compartment syndrome via radial route is very rare. Surgical intervention is often necessary.

Contrast-related

Anaphylaxis

- May not be obvious but should always be considered with unexplained tachycardia and hypotension and a rash should be sought
- Management: depending upon severity, is with intravenous steroids, chlopheniramine, fluids, and intramuscular adrenaline.

Contrast-induced nephropathy

- There is no everyday diagnostic test available to diagnose contrast-induced nephropathy (CIN) but it is usually manifest as deteriorating renal function 48–72 h post exposure, although this may of course occur for other reasons
- Management: there is no clinical evidence to show improved clinical outcomes using N-acetylcysteine, sodium bicarbonate, or iso-osmolar contrast
- Prehydration is essential in patients with reduced eGFR (<60 ml/min).

32.4 Cardiac haemodynamics

Measurements

Right and left heart pressure measurements provide important information in the assessment and diagnosis of many cardiac conditions. It is essential that it is done properly and an appreciation is needed of the normal pressures and waveforms (Table 32.5 and Figure 32.14).

Table 32.5 Normal chamber haemodynamic pressures

Chamber	Peak-systolic	End-diastolic	Mean
RA	—	—	2–8
RV	17–32	2–8	—
MPA	17–32	4–13	9–19
PCWP	—	—	2–12
LV	90–140	5–12	—
Aorta	—	—	70–105

Reproduced from 'Cardiovascular hemodynamics for the clinician', ed. George Stouffer, copyright 2008 with permission from John Wiley and Sons.

- Usually via simultaneous use of femoral arterial and venous punctures
- Alternatively, radial artery and antecubital vein sheaths
- A calibrated, flushed MPA (or Swann-Ganz) catheter is passed up the IVC into the RA and directed across the tricuspid valve (can be very arrhythmogenic, particularly in RV)
- It is carefully manipulated into the MPA (which may need the J-wire) and can cause transient heart block as it crosses the RVOT
- Then into one of the main branch pulmonary arteries whilst watching the pressure trace until 'wedging' occurs (see Figure 32.15). This pulmonary capillary wedge pressure (PCWP) is taken to equate to left atrial pressure
- A pigtail catheter is then passed into LV and simultaneous LVEDP/PCWP readings can be taken (for gradient of MS)
- On pulling back, recordings of the MPA are made and a recorded pullback across the pulmonary valve will reveal any gradient
- Simultaneous right and left ventricular pressures trace can be recorded (for changes of constriction) before withdrawing to right atrium and vena cava
- The pigtail can then be withdrawn across the aortic valve to assess gradient
- If cardiac output and shunt calculations are necessary, O_2 saturation samples should be taken in each chamber from branch pulmonary arteries back to high, mid and low right atrium, inferior and superior vena cava during pullback run and also from the aorta.

The Wiggers diagram (Figure 32.15) shows the temporal relationship of the ECG and chamber pressures. When attempting to 'wedge' the right heart catheter, angiographic screening beyond entry to the bronchial artery branch is not often helpful. One should look for the change in pressure wave from that of the pulmonary artery to the classic wedge appearance of left atrial pressure characterized by the A wave (atrial contraction, absent in AF), C wave (ventricular contraction, with subsequent retrograde movement of mitral apparatus) and V wave (peak atrial filling just prior to mitral valve opening).

Cardiac output

Cardiac output (CO) is often measured in the catheter lab using the Fick principle. The formula is:

$$CO(l/min) = \frac{O_2 \text{ consumption}}{A-V\,O_2\text{difference}} = \frac{130 \times BSA}{1.36 \times Hb \times 10 \times (SaO_2 - SvO_2)}.$$

Standard oxygen consumption is 130 mls/min; BSA, body surface area (m^2); 1.36 mm oxygen is held per gram of haemoglobin; Hb, g/dl haemoglobin (multiplied by 10 to convert to litres), and SaO_2/SvO_2 is expressed as a fraction.

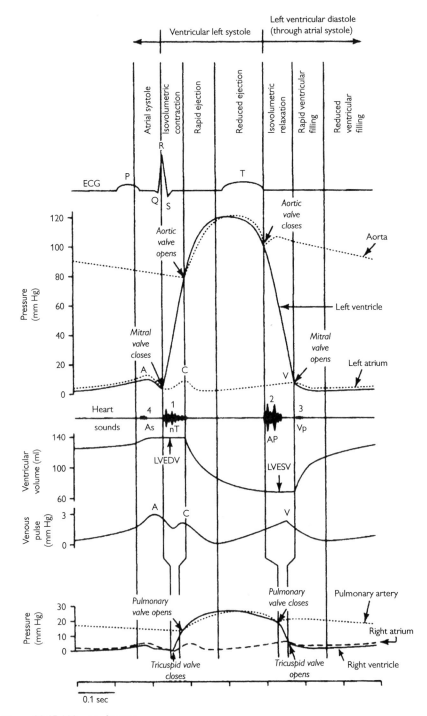

Figure 32.15 Wiggers diagram.
Reproduced from 'Cardiovascular hemodynamics for the Clinician', Alison Keenon, Eron D. Crouch, James E. Faber, et al., Wiley-Blackwell, copyright 2008 with permission from John Wiley and Sons.

Thermodilution to calculate cardiac output:
- 10 ml of cold saline is injected into the RA of a catheter with multiple ports and temperature is simultaneously measured in the MPA
- The area under the thermodilution curve is inversely proportional to cardiac output, which is calculated by a computer
- There are, of course, sources of error in both methods.

Cardiac index (CI) compares CO between patients of different size and and is obtained by dividing CO by the BSA. It is normally between 2.5 and 4.0 l/min.

Hence from this data it is possible to derive the stroke volume and the systemic and pulmonary vascular resistance (SVR, PVR).

Stroke volume

$$CO = SV \times HR \quad \text{hence } SV = \frac{CO}{HR}$$

Systemic and pulmonary vascular resistance

$$SVR \ (dynes/sec/cm^5) = \frac{MAP - CAP}{CO} \times 80 \quad Normal = 800 - 1200$$

$$PVR \ (dynes/sec/cm^5) = \frac{Mean\,PAP - PCWP \times 80}{CO} \quad Normal = 40 - 150$$

- Wood units are sometimes used and do not multiply by the factor of 80
- PVR is important in transplant assessments as it quantifies the afterload the transplanted RV will need to overcome
- Ideally it should be less than 3 Wood units.

Shunts

The ratio of pulmonary (Q_p) to systemic (Q_s) blood flow aims to quantify a shunt:

$$\frac{Q_p}{Q_s} = \frac{Arterial\,sat - Mixed\,venous\,sat}{Pulm\,vein\,sat - Pulm\,artery\,sat} = \frac{SAO_2 - MVO_2}{PVO_2 - PAO_2}.$$

- The mixed venous saturation should be taken from the chamber preceding the shunt
- So for a VSD, the RA should be used
- For an ASD, the IVC and SVC according to the formula: $((3 \times SVC) + IVC) \div 4$
- Generally speaking Q_p/Q_s ratios of 1–1.5 are observed, 1.5–2.0 suggest closure should be considered, and >2.0 indicate closure unless there is a clear contraindication
- An example calculation is given in Figure 32.16.

$$\frac{Q_p}{Q_s} = \frac{98 - 67}{98 - 83} = \frac{31}{15} = 2.06$$

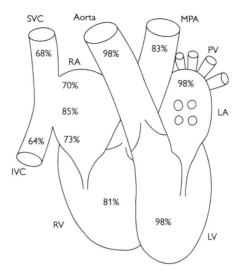

Figure 32.16 Diagrammatic representation of results of saturation run during left and right heart catheterization.

Valvular assessments

Aortic stenosis

- It should be remembered that echocardiographic-derived data will not correlate with pullback gradients in the lab
- In Figure 32.17, the peak-to-peak gradient from pullback is shown by the dotted arrow, the peak instantaneous gradient from echocardiography by the solid arrow, and the shaded area is the mean pressure gradient

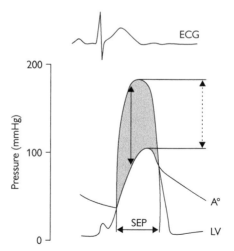

Figure 32.17 Comparison of invasive and echocardiograph-derived haemodynamics in a patient with AS. SEP, systolic ejection period.

Reproduced from 'Aortic stenosis and non-cardiac surgery', Jane Brown and Nicholas J Morgan-Hughes, *Contin. Educ. Anaesth. Crit. Care Pain* 5(1), 1–4, copyright 2005 with permission of Oxford University Press.

- It is possible to calculate aortic valve area in the lab using:

$$\text{Gorlin Formula}: \frac{CO/(SEP \times HR)}{44.3 \times \sqrt{(\text{mean pressure gradient})}}$$

$$\text{Hakki Formula}: \frac{CO}{\sqrt{(\text{peak-to-peak pressure gradient})}}$$

- There are sources of error, including the presence of significant AR and LV impairment.

Mitral stenosis
- Characteristic findings are:
  - Increased LA pressure
  - Persistent diastolic LA/LV gradient
  - Increased right heart pressures
  - Prominent A wave on atrial tracings
  - Decreased slope of y-descent on LA trace (slowed LV filling)
- The mean pressure gradient and the mitral valve area quantify severity of the lesion (see Table 32.6)
- The latter may be calculated in the lab using the Gorlin formula (see Figure 32.18):

$$\frac{CO / (DFP \times HR)}{37.7 \times \sqrt{(\text{mean pressure gradient})}}.$$

Mitral regurgitation
- Characteristic findings are:
  - Increased right heart pressures
  - Prominent V waves on PCWP trace (not sensitive/specific)
  - Bifid systolic PA peak (a reflected V wave)
  - Raised LVEDP, SV, lowered CO
- These will be most marked in acute MR in the context of a normal sized, hyperdynamic LV (see Figure 32.19)
- As chronic MR decompensates with dilating LV and reducing LV function, right heart pressures will elevate but V waves may not be prominent.

Other conditions

Pulmonary hypertension
- Many cardiac conditions can cause pulmonary hypertension but in the absence of a raised PCWP, other conditions must be considered, as in Table 32.7.

Table 32.6 Parameters of severity of mitral stenosis

Severity of MS	Mean gradient	MVA
Mild	0–5 mmHg	>1.5 cm^2
Moderate	5–10 mmHg	1–1.5 cm^2
Severe	>10 mmHg	<1 cm^2

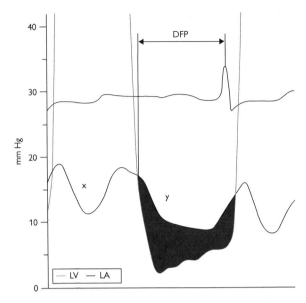

Figure 32.18 Simultaneous LV and PCW pressures in a patient with mitral stenosis. Shaded area is the transmitral gradient. (DFP, diastolic filling period).

This figure was published in *Braunwald's Heart Disease* Vol 1, eds. Douglas P. Zipes, Peter Libby, Robert O. Bonow, Eugene Braunwald, Copyright 2005 with permission of Elsevier.

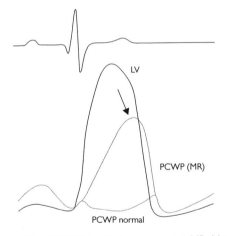

Figure 32.19 Simultaneous LV and PCWP tracing in acute severe MR. Note prominent V wave during systole (arrow).

Table 32.7 Causes of pulmonary hypertension and normal left atrial pressures

Parenchymal lung disease (cor pulmonale)	Primary pulmonary hypertension
Chronic thromboembolic disease	Collagen vascular disease
Congenital heart shunts	Sarcoidosis
Obstructive sleep apnoea	Toxins/drugs
Collagen vascular disease	HIV

Reproduced from 'Cardiovascular hemodynamics for the clinician', ed. George Stouffer, copyright 2008 with permission from John Wiley and Sons.

Restrictive cardiomyopathy/constrictive pericarditis

- Both conditions usually present with insidious predominant right-sided heart failure and are difficult to distinguish clinically, using echo or haemodynamic data (see Table 32.8 and Figure 32.20)
- Of note, radiation therapy can cause both conditions.

Table 32.8 Causes of contrictive pericarditis and restrictive cardiomyopathy and distinguishing haemodynamic findings.

	Constrictive pericarditis	Restrictive cardiomyopathy
Causes	Post-pericarditis	Amyloidosis/carcinoid
	Post-cardiac surgery	Haemochromatosis/sarcoid
	Radiation therapy	Metabolic storage diseases
	Tuberculosis	Metastasis/radiation
LV systolic function	May be normal	May be reduced
PA systolic pressure	Usually <50 mmHg	May be >50 mmHg
RV/LV systolic pressure	Discordant	Concordant
RVEDP/LVEDP separation	<5 mmHg[a]	>5 mmHg
RVEDP/RV systolic pressure	>1/3	<1/3
Kussmaul's sign	Present[b]	Absent

[a]Hypovolaemia may cause equalization of diastolic pressures in a normal heart and false negative results if constrictive pericarditis is present, hence intravenous fluid challenge during procedure is essential. [b]i.e. RA pressure does not decrease with inspiration.

Reproduced from 'Cardiovascular hemodynamics for the clinician', ed. George Stouffer, copyright 2008 with permission from John Wiley and Sons.

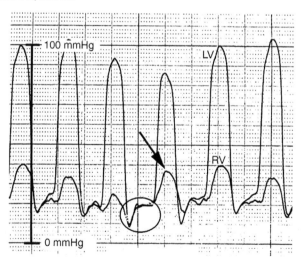

Figure 32.20 Ventricular pressure tracings with respiration in constrictive pericarditis showing ventricular discordance where peak RV pressure rises and peak LV pressure drops during inspiration (arrow) and equalization of RV and LV EDP, the 'square root' or 'dip and plateau' sign (circled).

Reproduced from 'Constrictive pericarditis in the modern era: a diagnostic dilemma', R. A. Nishimura, Heart, 86(6), 619–623, copyright 2001 with permission from BMJ Publishing Group Ltd.

Acknowledgements

My thanks to Dr Nathan Manghat for his assistance with the CT images.

Further reading

Guidelines

NICE Guidance TA71: Coronary artery stents, October 2003.
NICE Guidance TA152: Drug-eluting stents, July 2008.
NICE Guidance TA182: Prasugrel for the treatment of acute coronary syndromes with percutaneous coronary intervention, October 2009.
NICE Guidance CG94: Unstable angina and NSTEMI, March 2010.
Wijns W, Kolh P, Danchin N, *et al*. Joint ESC/EACTS guidelines on myocardial revascularisation. *Eur Heart J*, 2010; 31: 2051–555.

Text

Camm AJ, Lüscher TF, Serruys P (eds). *The European Society of Cardiology Textbook of Cardiovascular Medicine*. Oxford University Press, 2009.
Ludman PF. BCIS audit returns—adult interventional procedures, Jan 2009–Dec 2009. BCIS, 2010.
Norrell M, Perrins J, Meier B, Lincoff AM. *Essential Interventional Cardiology*. Saunders Elsevier, 2008.
Stouffer GA. *Cardiovascular Haemodynamics for the Clinician*. Blackwell Futura, 2008.
Zipes DP, Libby P, Bonow RO, Braunwald E. *Braunwald's Heart Disease: A Textbook of Cardiovascular Medicine*. Saunders Elsevier, 2004.

Index